BARBARA & STEPHANIE KEATING

Blood Sisters

VINTAGE BOOKS
London

Published by Vintage 2006

8 10 9

Copyright © Barbara & Stephanie Keating 2005

Barbara & Stephanie Keating have asserted their rights
under the Copyright, Designs and Patents Act, 1988 to be
identified as the authors of this work

First published in Great Britain in 2005
by Harvill Secker

John Masefield: 'Sonnet'. Quoted with permission
from the Society of Authors as the Literary Representative
of the Estate of John Masefield

Vintage
Random House, 20 Vauxhall Bridge Road,
London SW1V 2SA

www.vintage-books.co.uk

Addresses for companies within The Random House Group Limited
can be found at: www.randomhouse.co.uk/offices.htm

The Random House Group Limited Reg. No. 954009

A CIP catalogue record for this book
is available from the British Library

ISBN 9780099485148

The Random House Group Limited supports The Forest
Stewardship Council (FSC), the leading international forest
certification organisation. All our titles that are printed on
Greenpeace approved FSC certified paper carry the FSC logo.
Our paper procurement policy can be found at

Printed in the UK by CPI Bookmarque, Croydon, CR0 4TD

FOR THE KANISAS

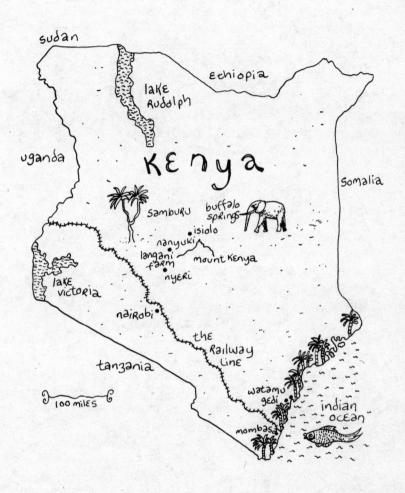

sudan

ethiopia

lake
Ruddlph

KENYA

uganda

Somalia

SAMBURU

buffalo
springs

isiolo

nanyuki

langani
farm

mount Kenya

lake
victoria

nyeri

nairobi

the
Railway
Line

tanzania

100 miles

watamu
gedi

indian
ocean

mombasa

Prologue

He had been running for more than two hours, his breath heaving in and out now, in ragged gasps. His body was drenched in sweat. It ran in rivulets down his greased torso, through the crusting of dried blood, sliding under the beaded wrist and arm ornaments, the copper leg bracelets and the leather loincloth which was all he wore. All around him, the bush rustled with the sound of creatures hunting for food. The African night reverberated with the heavy cough of a lion calling to his mate and the manic cackle of a hyena behind him on the plains. In the distance there was a rumble of buffalo, moving between their grazing grounds and the winding course of the river. The warrior heard none of these. He was only aware of his own breath, the saw and rasp of it, in and out, and the screaming that still echoed in his head.

There should have been only one at the killing ground, one man to scream, to beg, to plead for mercy. But he had remained silent to the last. Only his eyes spoke his contempt for his executioner, until the warrior could face their judgment no longer and his bloodied knife scoured out their condemnation for ever. He had not expected that there would be so much blood, or that the ripe, sweet smell would stay all this time in his nostrils. His body seemed to reek of it as he ran. Every predator in the bush must be able to smell him. Like the hyena. It had come for the blood, hunching and shuffling through the bush with its rank breath, and its matted, spotty coat. Drawn by the smell of death, and the promise of flesh and bone to tear.

He should have let it kill the woman. He had not counted on her appearance and she had no defence. In that one second, when he saw her eyes widen with recognition, the hyena had made its rush. He had flung the spear, seen it find its mark, watched the creature topple. Then the woman was falling too, and when the screaming began he knew what she had seen. He could see it too, no matter which way he turned his head. The body of the man was staked out on the ground, arms and legs spread wide, genitals sliced away and stuffed into the silent agony of his mouth, belly ripped open so that his entrails spilled on to the earth, sightless eye sockets turned in darkness to the moon. The warrior still saw that vision, still heard the screaming, long after he had escaped the place of sacrifice. He had left the spear in the hyena's neck and slipped into the surrounding bush, covering the marks of his passing in the way of his people, knowing that the trackers would soon be searching for him, casting all around the ridge for signs of the direction in which he had gone.

In those first moments he had been filled with a savage euphoria, had felt himself invincible. He had completed his quest, had carried out his oath. He could feel the power of the bhang that he had taken prior to the ritual, still coursing through his body, flashing scenes of colour and mystery before his eyes. He was beyond pain as he drew the air down into the fiery passage of his throat. It filled his chest with seared oxygen, whistling out again through his clenched teeth in a shower of foaming spittle. His heart was pounding, muffling the sounds he left behind him so that they were a distant buzz in the back of his consciousness. He came to an area of dense bush and thorn, and ran along its edge, veering away after a few minutes to climb on to a rocky outcrop where his footprints would be lost to anyone following. Then he retraced his path slowly, stepping in his own tracks until he came to another section of the scrub. He crouched and slid into the thicket, mindless of the thorns that tore at him. The drug gave him an altered vision, as though he was looking down into some far-off scene from a great height, and he could see himself moving under the bushes, undulating like a serpent, until he emerged on the other side of the dense undergrowth. His skin was ripped, and blood welled up to mingle with the blood of his victim, which already covered his body. He did not try to clean it away.

He had proved himself, slain the enemy. The great god Kirinyaga would be appeased. The spirits of his ancestors would be placated; his father's spirit would be placated. He straightened, turned and vanished into the forest, avoiding the animal trails until he reached a clearing far from the ridge. There he stopped, satisfied that he had covered his tracks sufficiently. His hands shook as he unfastened a small pouch from the leather thong around his waist, tapped some of its dark powder on to his palm, and inhaled it deeply into both nostrils. There was another rush of adrenalin to his system so that he shook with the power and the strength of it, and then he began to run again, loping through the night and out of the forest, along the edge of the plain, making for his other sanctuary. Twice more, he stopped to give himself another burst of energy from the contents of the leather pouch. But then it was all gone, and he still had a great distance to cover before he reached his destination.

The screaming had begun again in his head, and flashes of remembrance were confusing his vision, causing him to stumble on the rough terrain. The smell of the dead man's blood invaded his lungs, so that he felt he was inhaling his victim's death with every breath. Now he began to see shapes in the shadows around him. Hyenas. Running behind him. Tracking him. He thought he could smell them too, but it might be the scent of the animal he had speared, or the odour of the victim's sacrificial blood turned rancid by the heat of his own body. For a moment he thought he saw a fire flickering some distance ahead of him. In his imagination, figures moved in the red light, and his nostrils were filled with the stench of burning flesh. He swerved away, not wanting to see who might have built the fire, or what would be burning there. The image faded.

The darkness was beginning to dissipate, and in the limbo world between night and dawn, when all was grey and misted, he was no longer sure what was real and what was not. He feared that inadvertently he had entered the spirit world, that he would not be able to find his way back. He should not have killed the hyena. It had been coming to devour the spirit of the man, and he had prevented it from its task. Hyena and dead man wandering the spirit path, looking for him. They could smell the blood on him. He felt a surge of panic and tried to run faster. A branch whipped across his face and he felt his headdress fall, but he resisted the urge to stop and retrieve it. He was a true warrior now, whether or not he wore the plumed and beaded headdress.

He could hear a new scream, over the first one, and he knew it was coming from his own lips as he saw the fire again. This time it was right in front of him. This time it was real. There was a man standing beside it, holding up the panga with which he was skinning a bushbuck. The warrior saw the blade gleaming in the firelight. He stopped, panting. No one must be allowed to see him, to know he had passed this way. The man had stepped back, staring at him in alarm. A hunter. He had been chopping brushwood, making a fire to protect himself from the wild animals, but now he was facing a more dangerous enemy. A short spear lay on the ground beside him. Terrified, he bent to pick it up as the warrior sprang at him, snarling, his knife making the first slash.

In the distance, the pack of hyenas yipped and chuckled, and called out the news to one another. There was blood. Soon there would be feasting. As first light broke over the landscape they moved in, and the air was filled with the sound of their growling and squabbling, with the snapping of jaws and the crunching of bone as they buried their muzzles in the fresh carcass.

Chapter 1

Kenya, July 1957

The school bell rang, but the girl stayed where she was, halfway down the drive. Sooner or later she would be missed. In trouble again. But maybe the car would turn in through the gates before they realised she wasn't there, and then everything would be all right. She had been watching for it all morning from the classroom window, until she was reprimanded. After study she had slipped away down the avenue, stationing herself out of sight of the school buildings. It was a bright afternoon, with high clouds riding in a washed-blue sky after yesterday's downpour. Perhaps the rain and the muddy roads had made the going slow.

Sarah Mackay fixed her gaze on the band of murram road, the red soil still damp. Around her the boundary of blue gum trees rocked and shivered in conversation with the wind. She loved these high, silver-barked sentinels of the plateau, growing up here at 7,000 feet above sea level. At night they whispered and sighed to her as she lay in her narrow dormitory bed, imagining herself at the coast, at home in Mombasa, almost five hundred miles away.

The playing fields were deserted following the summons of the bell. A curious sense of abandonment engulfed her, as though the world had whirled away without her and she would never catch up with it again. She might survive for centuries in a time warp, waiting for a car that would never come. She had inherited her father's stocky form and dishevelled appearance, and whatever she did with them her clothes always looked crumpled. Sarah began to sing, trying to keep unease at bay. She was a sturdy girl with a round face and hazel eyes, small for her thirteen years. Singing helped to push worry or loneliness away until she could no longer feel them, and she knew that she was a natural singer. Sometimes she sang songs that other people knew, but often she composed secret words and melodies just for herself. It was like flying, never knowing if you were going to swoop or soar on the next phrase, or land on one of those long, satisfying notes that you recognised as the perfect ending. But this particular song, Sarah realised, was refusing to resolve itself. She paused to imitate the call of a golden oriole, perched in the wattle tree at the edge of the drive. His responding whistle pleased her, but he refused to prolong their chat and disappeared in search of insects. She liked to talk to animals. Smiling to herself, she made several grunting noises in an imaginary conversation with a warthog.

The sun was sinking, creating a soft chill that carried the scent of wood fires being lit for the night. Sarah was beginning to feel hungry. The road beyond the school stretched away, across miles of wheat and open fields to the dark band of trees on the edge of the escarpment. When she was out riding, she liked to lean down from the saddle and gather handfuls of seeds and berries. Later she would thread a wire through them and make a bracelet or a choker. They were in demand, these pieces of jewellery she crafted, and she was working on a birthday present for her best friend. She liked Camilla Broughton-Smith, even though she was so organised, always top of their class and very popular. Her father was important and popular too. Perhaps these things ran in families. They had started boarding school together, and on that first evening Sarah had wept inconsolably for hours, after her parents' car disappeared down the long drive. During the days that followed, her loneliness had increased. The other girls had made fun of her homesickness, of the dip in the hem of her uniform and the new school shoes that were too shiny. Camilla had come to her rescue, scornfully disposing of would-be bullies, offering to help with homework and to share her impressive weekend wardrobe. Camilla's pen never leaked, never smudged her fingers or her school shirt. Her exercise books were neat and so was her cupboard. She casually dismissed problems that made other people cry. The teachers sometimes said that the girl was unnaturally hard for her age, that her veneer would crack one day, with disastrous consequences. Sarah wished that she had been given the same tough shell.

She glanced up at the darkening sky. There would be deep trouble if they had to send someone out to look for her after tea. It could be nearly as bad as when she had found a grass snake and let it loose in the classroom. It was Hannah van der Beer who had given her away, looking over at Sarah, covering her wide, laughing mouth with her hand as Sister Evangelis shrieked and leapt up from her chair. Hannah, with her thick, flax-coloured hair, her loud voice and flat accent. Sarah secretly envied the overbearing manner of the Afrikaans girl. She made you feel inadequate, a weakling. Boers, her mother said they were, people of Dutch origin from South Africa. They had come at the turn of the century, trekking in their covered wagons to reach the highlands of Kenya and carve their farms out of the bushland.

Sarah's thoughts scattered as she saw the distant plume of dust behind an approaching car. Excitement burgeoned into whooping happiness, as the vehicle came into view, moving like a comet before its attendant dust tail. Yes! A grey Mercedes, slowing down now, turning in at the bottom of the drive. Her face was alight, eyes shining, arms outstretched in greeting as she ran to meet her mother. She had counted the hours it would take to drive up from Nairobi, where Betty Mackay would have spent last night. The school was halfway between their home at the coast and the capital of Uganda where her father, Raphael, was at a medical conference. Sarah had been given permission to stay at the Country Club with her mother for two nights, and to come in to school in the morning, like a day pupil. Just like Hannah van der Beer.

'Mummy! Mummy!' She was shouting out her welcome. The car had stopped. The door opened, and a figure stepped out. Sarah halted, confused. This was not her mother.

'Mummy?' The sun was in her eyes. She couldn't make out who this person was. The reply came in a voice tinged with the broad vowels of South Africa.

'I'm afraid I'm the wrong person for you, my dear. I'm Hannah van der Beer's mother. Do you know if she's around? I'm late collecting her.'

Sarah saw with embarrassment that Hannah was already approaching the car. A car exactly like the Mackays', only this one had a different number plate, and a dent on the front wing. Had the Boer girl been there while she was singing those mindless tunes, and making childish animal noises? Sarah's colour turned to scarlet. How would she ever live this down? She began to mumble, trying to prevent distress from turning to tears.

'I'm sorry. My mother's coming today. From the coast. From home. She has the same sort of car. I thought she was you. I mean, I thought you were her . . .'

7

Humiliation made her unable to look up at either Mrs van der Beer or her daughter. Sarah hurried up the drive towards the school buildings. In the quadrangle, she leaned against the wall, a study in misery. Hannah would tell everyone what had happened and the whole class would laugh at her. She knew it for sure. But Rule One of survival was never to let anyone know they could hurt you. Someone was standing beside her, speaking.

'Did you hear me? I've been looking for you everywhere,' Camilla Broughton-Smith said again. 'Where have you been?'

'I was waiting on the drive.' Sarah tried to swim out of her suffocating gloom.

'Well, your mother rang. The car windscreen was cracked by a stone. She's having it fixed in Nakuru, and she'll be here by lunchtime tomorrow. Oh, come on – it's not the end of the world, for heaven's sake!'

Sarah summoned a watery smile. It would be impossible to put into words her feeling of dejection when she didn't really understand it. She had made a fool of herself and tomorrow Hannah van der Beer would be feasting on her peculiarities. Maybe she should tell everyone about her humiliating mistake and try to laugh it off. In desperation she stared at Camilla and then she shrugged.

'Thanks for the message. Better start on my homework.'

The grey Mercedes passed through the convent gates. Hannah van der Beer watched the playing fields and blue gum trees slide past the window in coloured stills of light and sky. She thought of Sarah Mackay who could sing and dance in front of people, who was good at drawing, who could mimic any animal she liked and make beautiful things with her hands.

'And here am I, a big, brash, Afrikaans farm girl in size six shoes,' Hannah thought. 'I know they all call me a *yaapie* behind my back. No one ever thinks of me as Italian, like Ma.'

Carlotta van der Beer came from an Italian family in Johannesburg, but her husband was an Afrikaner who had always called her Lottie. Hannah turned to glance at her mother's straight profile, at her dark hair twisted into a knot, at the tanned, roughened fingers curled on the steering wheel. Sarah Mackay's mother was blonde and pretty. She wore lovely dresses and had smooth hands that did no housework.

'Who was that girl?' Lottie said

'Someone in my class.'

'Does she come from far away?'

'Mombasa. They have a house by the sea,' Hannah said. They could walk out of their garden on to a white beach with palm trees. The van der Beers had been to the coast on family holidays, and Hannah had never wanted to come home.

'That's far.' Lottie's tone was thoughtful. 'It must be hard to be so far away from home. Wouldn't it be nice to ask her out for lunch some weekend?'

'What? Ask her to the farm, you mean? To have lunch with us at home?' Hannah was a day pupil. An outsider really. Sarah was a boarder whose parents were English, or Irish maybe – from Europe, anyway. Different. The Afrikaans farmers did not mix much with the British colonial types or the English farming community. And her brother might tease Sarah and try some stupid horseplay, although he'd be impressed by her bird and animal imitations. Sarah had a brother of her own, though, so it would probably be all right. But if she found the farm too rough and ready she would tell everyone in their class, and Hannah would be more of an outsider than ever. She sighed. It was a difficult decision.

'Well?' Lottie was surprised at her daughter's long silence. 'What do you think?'

'We could ask, I suppose. But I don't know if she'd come.'

Three weeks went by as Hannah searched for the right circumstances in which to proffer her invitation. Sarah Mackay, for some reason, barely spoke to her and even seemed to be avoiding her. In truth, although Hannah had been at the school for two years, none of the boarders was her close friend. They always seemed to be part of a world that the daughter of third-generation Afrikaans farmers could not share. Her peers came from families whose roots were in faraway places like London or Dublin, or somewhere called 'the Home Counties'. They all came from country houses or city residences to which they would return someday. Late one afternoon Hannah finally came across Sarah alone in the art room, finishing a charcoal drawing.

'That's good, Sarah. I wish I could draw like that.'

'It's not coming out right.' Sarah was frowning, bending forward over the paper. Her cheek was smudged with charcoal and her hands were impatient as she used her fingertips to try and achieve better shading.

'Do you like doing landscapes? Out on the veld, I mean, with trees and animals like we have on our farm?'

'Not really.' Sarah did not even look up. 'I'm trying to concentrate on portraits for now. As you can see.'

Hannah recognised the snub, felt herself dismissed. She would have to find some other occasion to bring up the invitation. Sometimes she wondered why she had been sent to the convent at all. All the other Afrikaans farmers' daughters went to Kikoma School that had both girls and boys, and was not religious in any way. Hannah remembered the argument she had overheard as she had sat in her favourite window seat, concealed behind the heavy curtains in the sitting room.

'This is different, Jan.' Lottie's voice had been firm. 'You had your way over Piet's education. He went to Kikoma and he's done well. He's tough and bright, and very independent. But Hannah's not like that, in spite of appearances. And I'm not an Afrikaner like you. I want our daughter to mix with different kinds of people, to see beyond the blinkered vision of your gloomy Dutch Reformers.'

'Piet's not blinkered. Or gloomy.'

'He spends all his spare time with you and me.' Lottie brushed aside the words with impatience. 'You have to remember Piet was an only child for five years, until Hannah came along. He had all our attention, and we're more broad-minded than most of our neighbours.'

'So, we can make sure Hannah grows up broad-minded too. Without spending our life's savings on that school.'

'No, Janni. For Hannah the convent is the best choice. The nuns turn out girls with a refinement she won't get in Kikoma. Everyone calls that place a *heifer boma*, and I'm afraid it's true.'

'Better not let your friend Katja van Rensburg hear you saying that about her daughters.' Jan was laughing. His wife was beautiful when she was annoyed. Her olive skin became rosy, and the spirit of her Italian blood flashed in her eyes as she gestured to emphasise her point. 'It's a boarding school, Lottie. Surely you don't want Hannah to live there, with her home only ten miles down the road?'

'No, of course I don't. But they take day girls as well. There are about twenty from the town who—'

'They're the daughters of Britishers – district commissioners and doctors, and all those other business people and English farmers. I know you have friends among the wives, yes. But our family is different.' Jan sucked on his pipe. 'She'll find it hard to fit in at the convent. Everyone needs to belong somewhere. Especially at that age. Hannah's not going to spend the rest of her life with Britishers, or with your family in Johannesburg. She's an Afrikaner and I want her to be proud of that.'

'She should be comfortable on either side of her heritage, Janni, and be free to take advantage of that in later life, wherever she ends up.' Lottie leaned over his chair and kissed his forehead. 'I want her to go to the convent, I really do. I want you to put her name down right now, and come with me for an interview with the Mother Superior. That's it, as far as I'm concerned.'

'Where's the money going to come from?' Jan said. 'It's very expensive, the convent. We'd have to use some of what we have put away. And if there's a drought, or rinderpest among the cattle, or we need a new tractor, what happens then?'

'Our daughter is more important than a new tractor,' Lottie said. 'We can't deprive her of the best schooling because we're afraid of something that might never happen on the farm.'

Jan decided to retreat and save time. 'You can make the arrangements yourself. I'm not going to be interviewed by any Mother Superior. And that's it from my side.'

Two years later, Hannah felt her father might have been right. She didn't belong in the convent and she still had no close friends. But she excelled in sport, and on the afternoon of the inter-school hockey championships it was Hannah's turn to shine as she scored four of the five goals for her team, making them top of the league. She was the star of the day. At the end of the match she was flushed from exertion and triumph. When Sarah Mackay came over to congratulate her she felt a sudden upsurge of courage, and she blurted out the lines she had practised so many times in her head.

'Good teamwork, Sarah. Oh, here's my mother. She wants to know if you'd like to come to lunch with us one weekend.' As she spoke the words in a rush, she saw Camilla Broughton-Smith appear. 'You too, Camilla.'

Hannah could not believe what she was saying, but there was a better chance that they would come if she asked the two of them.

'Me too, what? Congratulations by the way, you played brilliantly.

That shocked the *heifers* out of their grubby little socks.' Camilla draped a pale arm around Sarah's shoulders.

'My mother would like you both to come to lunch with us. Next weekend. Well, any weekend. If you want to, I mean.'

Hannah's courage evaporated quickly and she began to feel the pain of embarrassment. She should never have started this at all. Sarah Mackay was staring at her open-mouthed.

'What a heavenly idea!' Camilla prodded her friend. 'Of course we'd love to come. Wouldn't we, Sarah? I've never been to a farm around here. Have you got cows and sheep? What about horses?'

'Ma, this is Sarah Mackay.' Hannah felt she had no option but to plough on. 'Remember, you met her before? And Camilla Broughton-Smith. They'd both like to come to lunch. As you suggested.'

'Good. I'll arrange it right now with Sister Evangelis.' Lottie smiled at her daughter. 'What about next weekend, if that's all right with you girls? We can have a *braai* if the weather's good. And Piet will be at home. Bring bathing suits if you like. There's a swimming hole, but I warn you, the water is cold.'

Langani Farm had been van der Beer property since 1906 when the family had first arrived in Kenya. They had brought their wagons with them on the boat, all the way from South Africa. In the cluster of shacks that would one day become the city of Nairobi, they had purchased a span of untrained oxen and a few basic supplies before setting out for the highland forests, fighting their way upwards with their heavy furniture and belongings, wheezing in the thinning air, trudging through miles of slippery mud that sucked them back and down at every step. Sometimes they hacked their way through thick vegetation, sometimes they shivered through bitter cold and fog and mist, to reach the new, promised land and their allocated acres. For years they had struggled with the raw earth, wresting new crops from the reluctant soil, suffering the heartbreak of dying animals, of rust in the ears of their wheat, of suffocating drought and drenching rain and locusts that swarmed over the ripening crops, leaving their harvest a vanished dream. But perseverance was the corner stone of the Afrikaners. Slowly, and with characteristic intransigence, they tamed and moulded their surroundings.

Her first sight of Lottie's garden at Langani Farm never faded from Sarah's mind. The house was long and low, built from local stone with thick walls and tall chimneys. A sloping roof of corrugated iron was supported by stone columns camouflaged by tangled bands of honeysuckle and bougainvillea. The deep verandah overlooked a velvet lawn and bright, curving flower beds, but beyond the lovingly tended trees and shrubs lay open plains, speckled with thorn trees and shared by herds of zebra, giraffe, gazelle, elephant and buffalo. A clipped hedge was all that separated the garden from the wilderness, a fragile rampart against the encroaching bush and marauding wildlife. Beyond the flat plains the distant snow peaks of Mount Kenya rose, glittering, into the dome of the sky.

On that first visit to the farm Jan van der Beer made a barbecue lunch outside under the trees, and then Lottie drove them down to the river. The water was indeed icy, rushing headlong from the melting snow peaks of the mountain. Sarah shrieked as she jumped recklessly from the bank, into the shock of a pool beneath the waterfall. Hannah was laughing from the safe retreat of the bank while Sarah fought for breath, splashing hard to thaw her freezing limbs.

'You were warned, but you weren't listening,' Hannah called out.

'Well, don't just stand there laughing like a baboon. Get into the water if you think it's such a huge joke. You too, Camilla. You can't just lie there in the grass, trying to look like a film star.'

Hannah was scrambling down the river bank when they heard another voice.

'Come on, you pathetic little women! Get in there or I'll help you in and it won't be gradual.'

Piet van der Beer, tall and gangling, appeared on the bank and stripped off a khaki shirt, boots and socks. There was a shout as he leapt into the air, caught his knees up close to his chest and cannoned into the water. Seconds later he surfaced beside Sarah, shaking the water from his skin, smoothing his blond hair with tanned fingers, grinning at her through eyelashes spiked with drops of water. Her chilled body felt warm. For the first time in her life she was aware of her small breasts beneath the plain school swimsuit, of her slightly pudgy arms and legs. He squinted through the sunlight, and then he winked at her. Laughed out loud, with his head thrown back in the hot sunshine. It was a moment of revelation that changed her life for ever.

Chapter 2

Kenya, November 1962

The low, rhythmic croaking of bullfrogs halted abruptly at the sound of Sarah's footfall, starting up again when she stood still to breathe in the cold, highland air. The African sun had begun its slide down the horizon and she leaned against the verandah post to watch its majestic, red-gold retreat into the earth. There was a chugging sound from the generator, a slow crescendo that brought with it the glow of lamps inside the house. Darkness always came so swiftly, with its sprinkling of early stars. Night jasmine and the scent of woodsmoke masked the daytime smell of dust and gum trees. Beyond the protection of Lottie's garden, she heard the high bark of a zebra. Voices and laughter drifted out into the beginnings of the night to blend with the whirr and rasp of crickets and tree frogs. From the servants' quarters came the faint, tinny sound of a radio playing African music. She turned back into the bedroom, realising that she would be the last one to appear for dinner.

She had come in from the ride charged with excitement. They had all started out in the early afternoon, ambling through a grove of jacaranda trees where the lavender-blue flowers had fallen to cover the ground in a drifting carpet that shifted and swirled beneath the horses' hooves. Beyond the trees, the brittle grass trembled in a white heat haze. They sat for a while on the edge of the plain, waiting for their eyes to become accustomed to the glare. Then Piet beckoned and they rode out into the blazing afternoon, skirting the boundaries of the tribal reservation.

Dotted across the hillside were the *shambas* of the farm workers. Their allotments were terraced and planted with maize, the heads of the corn cobs ungainly on their disjointed stalks, broad leaves falling, spiky and bleached, away from feathery tops. Every *boma* had a flock of goats and a clutch of scrawny chickens chucking and scratching in the dry, packed-earth clearing around the huts. Women sat on the ground outside, wrapped in bright *kanga* cloth, pounding the corn to make *posho*, the staple diet. Naked toddlers played and rolled in the dust. Dogs with curled tails opened an eye to the afternoon glare and growled half-heartedly. The sing-song of women's voices carried on the heat-laden air.

'You hardly ever hear the babies crying,' Sarah said. 'Unless they're sick or something.'

'Look at them,' Piet gestured with his riding crop. 'The *totos* are either strapped to their mothers' backs, or tucked up in front with their mouths next to the titties and the milk supply. There's no need to cry. It's all on draught, whenever they want it.' He laughed out loud, noticing Sarah's discomfiture over his choice of words. 'Is that not a suitable description for you sheltered convent ladies? No offence, but when you live on a farm the feeding of young, whether they're on two legs or four, is a natural part of the process.'

He spurred his horse forward and they burst out on to the scrubby plain at a wild, uncontained gallop. Red anthills spiralled out of the grass, and a herd of Thompson's gazelles flicked nervous tails at the sound of the horses and skittered away across the veld, vanishing into the visible tremor of heat. A male ostrich emerged from the tall grass and ran in front of them, his black plumes glistening in the sun. He was so close that Sarah could see the bird's eyelashes and the stubble on his pale neck before he peeled away into a dense thicket. She rode fast and level with Piet, keeping up with him effortlessly, exhilarated by the sound of the hooves and the smell of the red earth and the wild grasses. They left Hannah and Camilla trailing and raced across the plain, finally coming to a halt in a swirl of dust at the edge of a copse. Piet leaned forward and took the reins of Sarah's horse. He pushed his hat back and looked at her, breathless and smiling in the afternoon sun. His admiration was evident.

'Good going, girl. Not like my sister, or Lady Camilla. They're asleep on those horses of theirs. You're a fine rider, that's for sure.'

'We always ride with Hannah when we're here at weekends.' Sarah was unable to disguise the pleasure his remark had given her. 'It's more fun with you, though. When the syce comes with us we aren't supposed to take off in a gallop like that. And your father won't let us ride out on our own.'

'Pa's responsible when you're out of the nuns' clutches. He can't leave you racing around the *bundu* on your own. Anyway, Kipchoge's a great man to ride out with.'

'Yes. But it's better without him, all the same.' Sarah glanced sideways at him, hoping to catch his eye and see him smile again.

'We've been riding together since we were *totos* on the farm. His father was Pa's first stable hand. He used to ride and train horses for Lord Delamere, but he was always getting drunk after the races. When he was finally sacked, he came home to sit round and watch his wives work on his *shamba*. Now he rules the stables like the despot he is, but it's mostly Kipchoge, as his oldest son, who takes care of the horses.'

'And does he think he's going to have a stable of his own horses right after Independence?' Sarah asked. 'Apparently the new politicians are telling people they can have everything the white people own, as soon as the British leave.'

'I don't think Kipchoge has a very high opinion of politicians. Most of them are Kikuyu and he's a Nandi, so there's already ingrained tribal suspicion there. In my opinion there are going to be more problems among the tribes here than between the different races. But the transfer of power and ownership from white to black will be slow. Kipchoge and I grew up together and he's more like my brother. Our generation will work together, black and white, to make a new country.'

'What does your father think about that idea?' Sarah's comment was sly.

'Pa has old-fashioned ideas, but his heart is good,' Piet said, smiling. 'He's always known Africans who had no education, no interest in farming as we would define it. I think he's secretly optimistic though, for all his gloomy predictions.' He turned in the saddle and waved an arm. 'Here's the rest of our little posse. We can ride tomorrow if you like. Just the two of us, early in the morning before my sister and Lady Camilla get up. Let's head down to the river and water the horses.'

Piet led the way through thorn trees hung with the round, swinging nests of weaver birds. Sarah rode beside him in a trance of happiness, taking in the golden, sun-curled hairs on his forearm, listening to the broad cadences of his Afrikaans voice, finding each sentence quite beautiful in its mingling with the low whinnying of the horses, the creak of saddle leather and the saw of grasshoppers. They dismounted beneath a canopy of thorn trees, and Piet took a package from his saddlebag and a knife from a sheath attached to his belt.

'We can drink from the river. It comes straight down from Mount

Kenya, as clear and clean as you can get. And I brought some biltong that Pa and I dried and cut.'

They splashed their faces, gulping handfuls of the icy water. The horses drank deeply, snorting with contentment, and then turned to graze along the river bank. Piet lay in the shade, his arms behind his head. Sarah and Hannah sat cross-legged beside him. Camilla leaned her back against a tree trunk and stretched out long legs to full advantage.

'It's extra salty, this,' she said, making a face as she chewed on the dark, stringy meat.

'What would you know about biltong, Lady Camilla? You don't chew that at parties in Government House, I'll bet.'

'No, we don't. And if she saw me eating this stuff, my mother would haul me off to a doctor to check for worms and then to an emergency session with the dentist.' Camilla looked at him through a fall of blonde hair. 'While you've been away learning useless theories at college, we've had Hannah for our cross-cultural lessons. She brings us biltong at school. Part of our regular care package, along with your mother's treacle tart. And don't call me Lady Camilla.'

Piet sat back into the shadows, observing his sister and her friends. They were so unlike in their appearances, so different in their backgrounds.

'It always seems strange to me, the friendship between the three of you,' he said. 'You're like sisters in a way, but you're poles apart. I listen to you talking and it's like a kind of code, almost as though one knows what the others are thinking, or going to do, before it happens.'

'That's not even the half of it,' Camilla said. A clutter of memories made her laugh out loud. They had shared detentions and prize-givings, finished each other's homework, survived falls from horses and whacks from hockey sticks, and religious classes and exam nerves and school dances. Awful boyfriends, too, callow and spotty or slicked up and pressing for an advantage that they could brag about in some locker room. 'You've missed all kinds of fun, Piet, being away in South Africa. And you even passed up Sarah's invitation to join us all at the coast last year. Too busy playing rugby or something equally riveting. Bad choice.'

'I'd like to see South Africa,' Sarah said.

'It's beautiful. But I don't like the way they treat the Africans and the Coloureds. It's a police state, and there'll be bloodshed eventually,' Piet said with regret. 'Unfortunately, the Afrikaners will be mostly to blame for it. We're lucky to be here in Kenya, in spite of Pa's misgivings about *Uhuru*. And it's home, heh?'

'Imagine all this being your home. God, what a heritage,' Sarah's voice was reverential.

'Our great-grandparents dug this whole farm out of the wilderness.' Piet gestured at a dense wall of bush and tangled trees on the far side of the river. 'They lived in huts made from mud and thatch, until they could use the ox wagons to drag oak up here, and big cedar logs, to build their houses. Then their sons and grandsons took over, and worked like slaves to make what we have now. I'll be next, and there's so much I want to do here.'

'Like what?' Sarah was surprised. 'It seems perfect already. But I suppose that's because your dad is always out there working away at it.'

'A farm never stays in the same condition from one day to another. But apart from working with Pa to keep the livestock going, and the wheat, I want to turn part of it into a conservation area for game. He thinks it's a good idea.'

'You mean, like a national park?' Sarah stared at him. 'How would you do it? You can't fence it in, can you?'

'No. It would be too expensive at first. But we'd put a stop to the shooting or hunting of any animals in that area, even for food. I'd like to set aside part of the northern plain and the forest on the west side of the farm, just for the game. There's plenty in that area — leopard, buffalo, elephant, plains game. Even bongo, though they are the most shy of all the forest creatures and you hardly ever see them. I'll train some of our labour as game scouts and rangers. And I plan to build a lookout, somewhere to stay overnight and watch animals. Like Treetops, but very small. I wouldn't want mobs of people up here, ruining the place.'

'I'm going to have a clinic,' Hannah said. 'Not like Ma's dispensary for the labour and their *totos*. Mine will be for animals that are hurt or orphaned, like small buck or bush pigs that have lost their mothers, or a lame zebra. Remember the newborn giraffe that was abandoned, Piet? I'm going to start a place and look after them.'

'What noble schemes. I'll drop in to admire your dedication when I'm famous. Of course no matter where I go, I'll always have a home here. At the coast, I think.' Camilla waved an elegant hand. 'At Kilifi or Watamu

– right on the sea. Everyone in Europe will think it so exotic, and they'll beg for invitations. You can all come down for my scandalous house parties. Piet, you'll be the glamorous rancher. All the American ladies will fall madly in love with you and try and get into your tent on safari, when their filthy rich old husbands are soaked in gin and fast asleep.'

'And what will make you so famous?' Piet was chewing on a stalk of grass, smiling at the picture she had drawn.

'Drama school first. Then I'll be discovered overnight by a brilliant impresario who'll make me a star of stage and screen, with my name in lights. I'll come back to Kenya on location and make a film. Like Grace Kelly in *Mogambo*. And you'll take me and the other stars to watch the animals, from your treetop thing.'

'What about you, Sarah?' Piet leaned across and tickled her with a piece of coarse grass. 'No, let me guess. Either the nuns will lock you up in the cloisters, or you'll be a doctor like your father. That's it! A missionary doctor in some remote place, surrounded by grateful natives who've been taught to say their prayers.'

'I don't know why you should think of me as the missionary type.' Sarah was stung by his vision of her, so far from the picture of decadent glamour and success that he had accepted for Camilla. 'Anyway, my brother's studying medicine. Two doctors in the family are enough. If I pass my exams, I'm going to study zoology. At Dublin University. Then I'll come back here to do research. On the migratory animals in the Mara and the Serengeti maybe, or the bongo in your forest that no one ever sees. Or warthogs. I love warthogs.'

'You'll be the terrors of the country, the three of you. Like a pride of lionesses,' Piet said. 'Sisters in spirit if not in blood.'

'But we could be blood sisters.' Sarah leaned forward. 'Give me your knife, Piet, and we'll each make a cut on our hands and draw some blood. Then we'll mix it and make a promise to stick together always, to support one another through thick and thin. No matter what. We'll be sisters in blood, in the traditional way of the Kikuyu or the Maasai.'

'I'm not having any part in this.' Piet shook his head. 'It's a weird idea for a bunch of convent ladies. Only warriors do that kind of thing. And if Pa hears about this—'

'I can't imagine who would tell him,' Camilla said sweetly.

'I don't know, Sarah. That's something tribal that the *watu* do. It's a

19

spooky idea.' Hannah's face was troubled and she looked across at Camilla, anticipating her support.

'Oh God. You're always so dramatic, Sarah. And fey. That's the curse of being Irish, you know.' Camilla sat up straight and held out her hand, palm up. 'I think it's a great idea. One of your better fancies. Let's do it.'

Sarah got to her feet. 'I'll make a fire from some twigs. Come on, Piet, you rinse off your knife and then we'll put the blade into the flame to sterilise it. I'll make the cuts, if Camilla and Hannah are too squeamish. I'm not a doctor's daughter for nothing.' She glanced over her shoulder at him. 'Your knife is really sharp. If you don't give it to me I'll use my blunt old penknife, and I'll be hacking great lumps out of our hands. Then your parents really will have something to say.'

Sarah cleared a space on the ground. She was about to search for kindling when Camilla appeared beside her with a handful of dry sticks. Hannah sat still, her expression solemn, and Camilla looked at her, silent but with eyebrows raised.

'All right. I'll do it. We'll make our promise together.' Hannah turned to address her brother. 'And don't even think of walking off into the long grass, Piet. Because you're going to be our solemn witness. Give me your lighter.'

The twigs were soon crackling and a thin spiral of smoke rose from the heart of the woodpile. Sarah took Piet's knife and held it over the flames. Then she stood up and held it out so that the blade glittered in the afternoon light.

'I'll go first.'

She saw Piet step forward in protest, but she deliberately ignored him as she made a quick incision on the mound at the base of her thumb.

'Me now.' Camilla did not flinch or avert her eyes as Sarah made the cut.

Hannah held out her hand, watching in silence as the scarlet drops welled in her palm.

'Come over here, Piet, so we have a witness as we press our hands together and make the blood mingle,' Sarah ordered. 'By the way, Camilla's blood isn't blue. I hope that doesn't come as a shock to anyone.'

'We should make our promise now,' Camilla said. 'Something that always binds us, no matter how far we may travel from this day and place.'

'I promise never to forget, always to stay true to our friendship. Always to be there for my sisters.' Sarah's eyes were very bright as she spoke and her face was grave.

Piet looked at Hannah and saw that there were tears in her eyes as she repeated the words. But Camilla was smiling as she pressed her palm into the hands of her friends and made her own promise.

The ride back to the farm was a silent progress. In the stables Sarah leaned against Chuma, the chestnut gelding. She closed her eyes, seeing in her mind the ritual they had just performed, remembering Piet's expression, the crinkles that appeared around his eyes and the curved line of his mouth when he laughed. When he had handed her down from the saddle, her skin had prickled and she had shivered as he held her lightly for a moment to steady her. His wrists were very strong, and he wore a bracelet woven from the hair of an elephant's tail. To bring him luck and protection, he said. She could smell his skin and see the band of sweat on his forehead, just below the brim of his leather hat. Her sense of him was so unnerving that she had not been able to thank him as he helped her undo the horse's saddle and bridle.

'See you at dinner, kid. I'm off to catch up with Pa.' He gave her hair a little tug and then he was gone, to put away the tack.

In the guest bedroom she found Camilla varnishing her nails.

'Where on earth have you been? I've already had a bath and washed my hair. That was a wild ceremony this afternoon,' Camilla said.

'God, you're almost ready for dinner.' Sarah ignored the reference to their promise, not wanting to make light of the event. 'How do you always manage to be painting your nails or putting cream on your legs when I'm rubbing down horses or—'

'I intend to dedicate my life to the pursuit of glamour.' Camilla's tone was sly. 'Lucky devil, that Piet, with his great life plan already underway. Is that why you're late? Stayed on with the golden boy for a little private *je ne sais quoi*?'

'What rubbish,' Sarah's face was burning, and she was trembling slightly as she turned away to hunt for her hairbrush and sponge bag. 'What should I wear? What are you wearing?'

Camilla had already chosen a skirt and sweater that her mother had bought for her in Italy, and some high-heeled shoes. She slipped into her clothes, smoothed some sort of glow on to her cheeks and ran a lipstick across her mouth, making it full and shiny.

'I'm going to chat to Hannah,' she said. 'You can borrow my blue shirt if you like. The colour suits you. Don't worry – you'll look great. But you're going to have to find a way to stop your face turning puce like that. It's a dead giveaway. See you later.'

Sarah headed for the bathroom. The rainwater was soft and slightly smoky. She had seen the kitchen *toto* earlier, heaping logs on to the fire below the huge drum that held and heated the water for the house. Pink from the shower, she peered into the mirror. The generator had not yet started up and she was nervous about applying make-up in the dim light. It was something she had not done very often, and she wished Camilla was there to help. She tried some foundation, blending it inexpertly until she thought it hid the sunburn on her nose. Was it necessary to add colour to her cheeks? Sarah was doubtful, but it might give her face shadow and shape. She got the mascara right and was gratified to see that her hazel eyes looked larger and almost gold in colour. Camilla had left a pile of clothes on her bed and Sarah picked out the blue silk blouse. Should she be wearing someone else's shirt? Hannah would certainly know it wasn't hers. If she realised that her brother was the reason behind all this unusual effort she'd never let up, and Camilla could be pretty merciless too.

'To hell with them all,' Sarah said aloud. 'I've had to suffer their boyfriend crises for long enough. Now it's my turn.'

As she walked out on to the verandah, she felt reasonably satisfied that she looked sophisticated. When the generator brought the lights on she ran back inside for a last check, wondering whether Camilla would notice if she borrowed a dab of perfume. Something sultry and seductive, unlike her own fresh-smelling cologne. As she pressed the light switch she caught a glimpse of herself in the mirror. Her face looked as though she had covered it in war paint. All she needed now were a few feathers . . . She rushed into the bathroom and grabbed her flannel, muttering a prayer of thanks that she had seen herself in time. When the rouge was all gone she was left with skin that looked shiny and blotched. She groaned and started again, this time with only a light smear of the foundation, a little mascara and a hint of lipstick. At last she stepped on to the path between the guest cottage and the main house.

When Sarah came into the sitting room, Jan van der Beer was already in his favourite chair beside the open stone fireplace, a tankard of beer in his hand. There was a leopard skin draped across the back of his chair, and his three Rhodesian ridgeback dogs lay at his feet. He was a big man with a florid face, shrewd and weathered. His body was powerful and muscular and his arms and legs bulged out of his clothes, with his broad chest straining against the buttons on his shirt. He glanced up at Sarah with affection and nodded his head without speaking.

'What would you like to drink, my dear?' Lottie smiled and rang the bell for the houseboy. 'We have some sherry from the Cape. Or a shandy perhaps?'

'I'll try the sherry, please.'

On previous weekends at the farm the girls had been offered home-made lemonade or ginger beer, and during the past year an occasional glass of cold lager. But tonight Lottie had brought sherry and wine from the cellar, and the best of everything from her kitchen garden. This would be their last visit before they left school and began new lives in distant places. Sarah had sampled sherry before and had not enjoyed it particularly, but she had no idea what else to choose. Her mother liked a Spanish sherry that was dry and pale, woody in flavour. But this South African variety glowed dark in the glass, and was sweet. Potent too. Sarah sipped and felt it go immediately to her head. She glanced self-consciously around. Hannah sat on a stool beside her father's chair, her strong legs folded beneath her, blonde hair tied in a single plait that she had pulled down over one shoulder. Her wide face glowed with health.

'You look good, Sarah! Different. I wonder what the rest of the company's going to say?'

'I thought you'd drowned in the shower. I was just coming to look for you.' Camilla glanced up from the sofa, allowing her face to catch the light and to display a delicate ear and the lustre of unblemished skin. Her hair fell in a gleaming pageboy and she had draped her sweater across her shoulders, tying the sleeves in a knot between her breasts. She held her glass with a hand that seemed to float in the air.

'Sit down and pay no attention to these two.' Lottie's expression was kind. But knowing too, Sarah realised. 'Hannah's right – you look fine. In fact, you all look lovely tonight, each in your own way. Like perfect new blooms in my garden. Flowers made of light, as the poem says.'

'You're very romantic tonight,' Jan said. 'These girls will all get carried away with your Italian notions, Carlotta, and then they won't be able to concentrate on their final exams. Better steer them back to reality for now, I'd say.'

'There's no harm spending a few minutes in the clouds, while we're waiting for Piet. But it won't be for long because I know my son, and he's definitely experiencing hunger pangs by now. He doesn't usually take this much time to get cleaned up for dinner.'

'He doesn't usually have three young ladies surrounding him at the dinner table.' Jan raised his tankard of beer to his daughter and her friends. 'That must have had something to do with his turning down the rugby weekend in Nanyuki.'

'Evening, Ma. Everyone.'

Piet had changed into freshly pressed khaki slacks and a green shirt open at the neck. To Sarah he looked like a burnished god, standing there in the flickering light of the fire. He swallowed a draught of beer. She saw the froth cling to his lip and felt an immediate yearning to reach up and smooth it away with her finger. Taste it perhaps. A maddening flush of embarrassment crept up towards her face and her neck felt hot. He was watching her with a smile. Could he read her mind, see the ridiculous thoughts churning around in there? He wiped away the beer slowly with the back of his hand. Sarah took a gulp of sherry and began to choke. He came to stand behind her, patting her hard on the back.

'Sorry. It went down the wrong way!'

She was gasping, spluttering, her eyes were streaming. The mascara she had so carefully put on her lashes must be running down her cheeks. She fought to control her breathing, digging in her pocket for a handkerchief. God, what a mess – what a stupid, clumsy impression she had made. She began to protest.

'Hey! I'm not dying, you know!'

The incident turned to laughter as everyone surrounded her, offering advice and consolation. Piet's hand was resting on her shoulder and the sympathetic pressure of his fingers burned into her skin. The gong sounded for dinner and she rose shakily to her feet.

Lottie had lit candles and in the centre of the long table there was a bowl of scarlet blossoms from the Nandi flame tree. They sat with heads bowed as Jan said grace and then the door to the kitchen opened and Mwangi the houseboy, dressed in a white *kanzu*, carried in a large tureen of soup.

'Where did that old rogue come from?' Jan asked, when Mwangi had

24

retreated back to the kitchen. 'I thought you said he was going off to his *shamba* for a few days.'

'He told me he was going to see his brother who was on the brink of death and would soon have to be buried,' Lottie said, her dark eyes sparkling with amusement. 'He wanted an advance on his salary and a week's leave. Oh, and his bus fare there and back. When I asked him his brother's name he said it was Kariuki. He had forgotten that he'd taken leave to bury poor old Kariuki last year. So I told him he could have half of what he was asking for, five days off with no pay, and I would dock the loan from his salary at the end of this month. That was yesterday, and it seems the brother has experienced a miraculous resurrection.'

'You'd think the old fool would have stopped playing that game by now,' Jan said. 'He's been hanging around here for more than twenty years, and he still thinks we're a bunch of *domkops*. He was more likely going to pay for a new wife. What's in this soup that's so good?'

'Fresh peas from my vegetable garden, and sprigs of mint. My contribution to dinner. And Janni caught the trout.' Lottie regarded her husband with affection. 'The major share comes from Piet, though. Do you girls like game meat?'

'I adore venison. And guinea fowl,' Camilla said. 'When we're home on leave my father always goes shooting on a friend's estate in Scotland.'

'Well, tonight we have a leg of young impala. Piet bagged it. He's a good hunter, my boy.' Jan looked at his son with unguarded pride. 'And Lottie makes the best gravy. There's nothing like a home-grown dinner, heh?' He turned to Camilla. 'Does your father shoot here?'

'He hasn't had any time lately. There always seem to be dozens of politicians and officials and reporters wanting to see him. Mother's been complaining that they never get a weekend to themselves. There are so many late-night meetings and last-minute changes of plan.'

'Well, he's certainly in the news enough, for better or worse.' Jan's face was grim. Lottie gave him a warning look, and rang the bell for the first course to be cleared away.

'So. You girls are going to be well occupied for the next few weeks.' Jan changed the subject. 'Lottie tells me we won't be seeing you again until all your exams are over, and your school days are behind you at last.'

'No more weekends out.' Camilla was now picking delicately at her trout. 'They say your school days are the best days of your life. But perhaps there are some things that will be as good or even better.'

'Of course there are!' Lottie was surprised at the girl's sadness. She was too young to be anything but optimistic, full of enthusiasm for the life ahead. 'With your background you have so many opportunities, my dear. There'll be no stopping you, Camilla. I wish I'd had your freedom when I left school.'

'Just as well you didn't.' Jan had risen to carve, and now he handed plates filled with roasted meat and rich gravy to Mwangi for serving. 'Better that I came along and took you under my wing. You've got enough crazy ideas as it is.'

'It's just that I wonder if I'll ever get back here again.' Camilla did not seem to have noticed Jan's attempt at humour and her response was directed at Lottie. The glass of wine she was drinking too quickly loosened her tongue. 'Once we leave school it will all be so far away. Out of reach for me, at any rate. I don't know how I can be sure of coming back. You've been here for generations. You'll always be here. And Sarah's parents are staying on after Independence. But my father could be posted to the other side of the world next year.'

'My dad has always warned us that we don't really belong in Kenya, that we're here for just a few privileged years.' Sarah was shocked at the sight of Camilla, forlorn and close to tears. 'But he's been asked to stay on, and he's delighted. And even though my brother's in medical school in Ireland, I wouldn't be surprised if he returned too. So maybe we do belong here after all. I'm certainly coming back to work in Kenya. You could too, Camilla, if you wanted to. Don't you have any idea where your father will be sent next?'

'Sometimes people like Father spend a year or two in the Foreign Office in London after an appointment like this,' Camilla said.

'I wouldn't complain about being in London.' Hannah's voice was dreamy. 'All the theatres and concerts, the museums and shops. And afterwards you might be going off to live in an exotic place you've never even heard of.'

'Father will probably be made a governor or a high commissioner one day, and he'll be sent to some far-flung colony. Meantime, Mother will love London if we do wind up back there. She'll be in her element at Ascot and Henley and organising bridge lunches.' Camilla sounded scornful.

'If you go to London, I'm coming to visit you,' Hannah said. 'And after that they'll have a time of it, trying to figure out how to keep me down on the farm.'

'My daughter will travel, yes. But she'll always want to come back here,' Jan said. 'We can all be sure of that.'

'You know, this is the place where I've been the happiest and had the best days of my entire life.' Camilla's voice was shaky. 'Nothing will ever be like Langani and the times we've spent here, where I'm part of the family.'

There was an awkward silence. Lottie had often wondered why Camilla's parents had never appeared at any school events, in all the years their daughter had been there. And although the three girls had enjoyed holidays at the farm, and in the rambling Mackay house at the coast, they had never been asked to stay in the residence provided for the Broughton-Smiths in Nairobi. Camilla was vague whenever she was questioned about her family.

'It's different being an only child,' she'd say. 'My parents aren't set up for looking after children. Father is always so busy with the Governor and all his official stuff. But he writes me wonderful letters, and I keep them all. As for Mother – she's a nervous person. Highly strung, Daddy says. She could never drive up here on her own like your mother does, Sarah. And she has so much to do in Nairobi, what with all the parties and charity things.'

As the friendship between them had grown, both Hannah and Sarah had learned not to ask questions about Camilla's family situation. She was plainly embarrassed by her inability to repay their hospitality, and the only occasion on which she had tried had been less than successful. George Broughton-Smith was accompanying the Governor on a tour of the highlands and he arranged for his daughter and her two friends to have lunch with him in the nearby town of Nanyuki.

He had done his best to make conversation with the three girls, but it had been a stiff occasion. The meal was punctuated by bursts of chatter and forced laughter, followed by awkward silences that seemed to stretch and amplify the sounds of their eating. After lunch George gave them each twenty shillings pocket money and took them into town where they searched for something to buy in the Indian *dukas* while he read a newspaper in a local café. The drive back to school in a magnificent Bentley was the only part of the day they remembered with any pleasure.

'Well, like it or not, Lady Camilla, I'll be dropping in on you. In jolly old England,' Piet said.

'You're going to England?' Hannah stared at her brother.

'Not England exactly. But Pa is thinking I could do a year at the agricultural college in Aberdeen.' He was grinning, enjoying the surprise in his sister's face. 'It's expensive for us right now, though, so I might go to work on a farm in Scotland instead. On an estate with some relations of the Mackenzies from Mau Narok, and—'

Hannah turned towards her mother and saw that Lottie's face was glowing with satisfaction. So Ma had known too, had probably been instrumental in this decision. They'd all known except her. She felt resentful.

'It was only decided a couple of days ago, Han. And it is on condition that Pa can get someone to help out while I'm away.' Piet thought it wise to change the subject. 'Will you ride with us in the morning, Ma? I thought we'd go out before breakfast and see if we could find the family of cheetahs I saw last week.'

Sarah felt a shaft of disappointment. He had said they would ride out together – just the two of them. She had been so thrilled, had anticipated a perfect opportunity to spend time alone with Piet, to have his full attention, and not to share a single precious moment with anyone else.

'I'm busy in the morning. Your father and I are going to a meeting at the Murrays' farm,' Lottie said. 'We may not be back in time for lunch, but I'll be here to drive you girls to school in the evening.'

'Nobody can keep up with the government's intentions these days.' Jan frowned and helped himself to another spoonful of Lottie's new potatoes. 'One minute they're talking about protection for us minorities when Independence comes, and the next we're hearing rumours about having our land confiscated. We could be forced out – our farms bought by some compulsory scheme that would result in Langani being split up and given in small parcels to the kaffirs.' He grunted in disgust. 'No one will be able to farm economically on ten-acre lots. We can barely make it pay on the land we have now. And if our labour is anything to go by they'll let the wheat rot, and replace it with maize that doesn't grow well at this altitude, and they'll finish up broke and starving. It's a bad plan, I tell you, and it will get worse. We're going to discuss what we can do for ourselves in the event that the government lets us down.'

'We're not going to talk about this over dinner, Jan.' Lottie tried to head off her husband's gloomy predictions. 'And you should stop using the word "kaffir". It's not acceptable any more.'

'Lottie, we're going to have problems and we should all recognise it.' This time Jan was not going to be silenced. 'No one was attacked here at Langani during the Mau Mau years, and most of our labour didn't get involved in oath taking. But we won't get through the next two or three years without some trouble. Especially if the Britishers continue their plan to sell us down the river and walk away.'

'I disagree,' Lottie said calmly. 'I don't think Independence is going to change everything so much. Our *watu* are happy enough. No one on Langani is complaining.'

'It's not so long since I fought, side by side with our British neighbours, during the emergency years,' Jan said. 'They needed us Afrikaners then, but they've conveniently forgotten that now.'

'We have to put those times behind us,' Lottie said, her face tight. 'We can't live in the past, Jani. And Kenya's future can be bright for all of us.'

Jan shook his head, silent and remembering. He had seen his brother die in a forest ambush on the Aberdare Mountains, during the Mau Mau uprising. Their unit had hidden for months in the freezing damp of the forests, short of food, faces blackened, bodies rancid as they tracked the terrorist gangs. They had crept on cold, black nights through the undergrowth, in pursuit of Kikuyu oath takers who threatened the farms of white families with destruction and fear and savage murders. Many of his British and Afrikaans neighbours had left then, gone to Rhodesia or South Africa, or back to England.

'The Englishers don't care what happens to us,' Jan said doggedly. 'We were always outsiders among them. Most Afrikaners trekked further north and west, up to the Usain Gishu plateau, where they formed their own community. Very few of us came to farm around here, where the land belongs mostly to the British. They never mixed with us from the beginning, and they won't think twice about us when the Kikuyu try to take away our land.'

'I think you're exaggerating,' Lottie said. 'They're fair-minded, for the most part. And we're good farmers. Everyone around here will agree with that. I know it.'

'Our kaffirs have housing, food, medicine, and education, yes,' he said to his wife. 'But deep down they believe that we are on their land, Lottie. Even though there wasn't anyone here when we first came, and nothing grew but thorns. Now they can see the potential of the land. After we've done all the hard work, they bloody want it for themselves.'

'We have title documents from the British, showing this farm has been ours since 1906. No one can question that.' Piet leaned forward, rapping the table sharply with the back of his spoon. 'I'm going to become a Kenya citizen after Independence, and then I'll be just the same as Kipchoge or Mwangi or Kamau. With the same rights.'

'Never be fool enough to think of yourself as one of them, Piet. Those are dangerous dreams.'

'You're wrong, Pa. I have true friends among our Africans. Kipchoge is like – well, we belong to a new generation. We respect each other and we're going to do things together, but on an equal footing. In the spirit of *Harambee*, as Kenyatta says. I'm coming at this from a new viewpoint.'

'There are hotheads around, man, who have no love for us, whatever we may do. Look at that madman Odinga. His speeches are loaded with hatred for us white farmers. If he gets into power he'll destroy any form of democratic government the Britishers leave behind.' Jan shook a finger at his son. 'They talk about African nationalism, but it's just another name for communism. Look around you. See how many of our neighbours are selling up. Putting their belongings on the backs of trucks and heading south.'

'Janni, some of the farmers who are leaving have big debts,' Lottie said. 'Their farms are in danger of being bankrupt, and *Uhuru* is just a face-saving excuse for them to pack up and go.'

'And how are we different from them?' Jan demanded. 'Didn't you read the letter from the bank?'

'What letter?' Piet was shocked. 'Are we in some kind of trouble with the bank?'

'Janni! Our situation is completely different.' Lottie was clearly agitated as she caught the look of fear on Hannah's face. 'We're doing fine, and we'll continue to run our farm like before. Besides, the British would never allow—'

'The Englishers are about to wash their hands of the whole country,' Jan interrupted, his face red with anger. 'Ditch their responsibilities, and sweep any future problems under the carpet. Just like the Belgians left their people in the Congo, and allowed murder and rape and seizure of their land. Odinga could walk in here one morning and seize Langani, and parcel it out among his friends – there wouldn't be a thing we could do to stop him! We must prepare for a fight if we're going to survive this.'

'That couldn't happen, Pa, surely.' Hannah was close to tears. 'There'll still be British people here to see that things stay peaceful, plus there are some good Africans in politics. I've heard you say so yourself.'

'It won't be like Pa imagines, kid.' Piet's shoulders were hunched and tense. 'The British Colonial Office will support farmers who want to stay on, keep their land. Your father goes to all those government conferences in London, doesn't he, Camilla? And they're talking about repatriation money for the white farmers who do decide to leave.'

'Not all white farmers, Piet,' Jan warned. 'Only the ones who are British.'

'So. Our family has had British passports since we arrived here.' Piet leaned back, satisfied that he had made the final point of the discussion.

'And how do you think we came by them, heh? They gave those first Afrikaners their British passports and their land because they were collaborators during the Boer War, boy. Against our own Boer people. Did you know that? No, I can see that you didn't. The men that brought their families up here sixty years ago were mostly escaping. Because they had been informers. The British passports were the pay-off for betraying their countrymen. If they'd stayed down south they would have been hung up in the trees.'

'That's not true.' Piet was incredulous.

'It is true, although no one in the Afrikaans community ever cares to admit it. And the Britishers will never consider us as their own, no matter what they agreed to, or why. They won't give us the time of day when *Uhuru* comes.' Jan made no attempt to hide his scepticism.

'I'm sure that's not right.' Camilla's face was very pale. 'My father is working on this question of land settlement and citizenship. He'll make sure that everyone is treated fairly.'

'We're Boers, my dear. The British have no love for us, and they don't care if we stay or go, no matter what's written in our passports. And where would they repatriate us to? Holland, or the UK? We could never go there. South Africa? They won't pay for us to resettle in an apartheid country. They'll turn their backs on us, and good riddance they'll say!'

'I've never heard you talk like this before, Pa.' Hannah's voice was edged with fear.

'And this is not the time to begin.' Lottie was furious. 'I'm going to ring the bell and we'll get Mwangi to bring the next course.'

'I'm sure these things will never happen to you.' Camilla's distress had heightened her colour and she half rose from her seat. 'My father works directly for the Minister of State in charge of the colonies. I'm sure his office is aware of all these problems. They'd never treat anyone the way you're suggesting.'

'It looks like you'll follow your father into some diplomatic post, young lady,' Jan said with heavy sarcasm.

'Don't get upset.' Piet was leaning towards Camilla, his hand stretched out to urge her back into her chair. 'I've grown up with all the young Kikuyu and Maasai and Nandis in this area. They even made me their blood brother a couple of years ago. Just like – well, I'm a brother to them. I've fished with them, hunted with them, eaten with them since I was a *toto* myself. I tell you, it's not like Pa's generation. We younger people have a different relationship with—'

'You can't trust any of these munts. They don't think the way we do. They don't have the same loyalties. I've warned you about this before, Piet. You're a damn fool, son, if you believe otherwise. It'll lead to nothing but disaster.'

'This talk will stop right now!' Lottie brought her fist down on the table, making the glass and china clatter. 'Piet, you can pour everyone some wine. Janni, we're going to raise our glasses now, to our wonderful son and daughter and their friends. And to a bright, joyful future for all of us.'

Jan was silent, regretting that he had been so sharp with Camilla. She was only a child, eighteen years old like his own daughter. Lottie was right. He should never have started in on this subject. They toasted one another, but Hannah had tears in her eyes, and Sarah found that the lump in her throat made it difficult to swallow. As they put their glasses down Camilla felt Piet's hand find hers under the table and squeeze her fingers. After dinner they sat around the log fire and played charades. Jan's clumsy attempts at acting were received with hoots of laughter. Sarah won effortlessly, and then kept the whole company convulsed with a series of mimes and animal noises. At last Jan rose and put his arm around her.

'Enough, you crazy young miss! It's time for bed. I have to go out and look at some grazing early tomorrow, since Piet has abandoned work in favour of pretty women. And I'm going to the meeting at the Murray farm after that. Goodnight to all you young people.'

'The lights will go off in about half an hour, girls.' Lottie embraced them, touching Camilla's cheek with tenderness. 'Don't stay up all night talking.'

In Hannah's room the kaross that covered the blankets had been folded away on top of a trunk at the foot of her bed. She loved the soft fur and the supple feel of the animal skins that her father had cured and smoothed for her when she was small. Lottie had offered her a variety of new quilts since then, but Hannah stubbornly held on to her kaross. She sat down and patted the bed for Sarah to join her, while Camilla draped herself across the window seat overlooking the garden. The moon was full and the night sky seemed to offer a still, remote beauty that could not be marred by misunderstanding or greed or violence.

'I can't get over Pa tonight,' Hannah said. 'But maybe he's just sad that this place won't be the centre of the world for us now.'

'It's all right. I touched a raw spot with all that silly stuff about not being able to return here.' Camilla seemed to have recovered her poise.

'Well, it's true. We've had such happy times over the last five years, and it's scary to think that Langani won't be just a half-hour down the road, waiting for us at the weekend,' Sarah said. 'At least it will still be the centre of the world for you, Hannah. You and Piet will carry on the farm one day. He'll start his game reserve and his viewing lodge and—'

'I know it's home, and I love it. But sometimes it feels so far from everything.'

'Far from what, for God's sake?' Sarah said.

'From other people. From whatever's new in the world. It's fine for you. You come to visit for a short while. But if you had to live here all the time with just your parents—'

'And Piet. You can't really complain about having him around, can you? I wouldn't mind having a big brother like that.' Camilla turned away from the moon-washed garden.

'I used to think I'd have a ball when all his friends came visiting.' Hannah rolled her eyes. 'But all they do is drink beer and talk about farming and politics and rugby, and the girls they've met in Nairobi or Nanyuki. They don't even notice me.'

'My brother's friends have never thought of me as a human being either. But one day someone will see you – really see you – and that will be it,' Sarah said.

'I'm too big. Big and heavy like Pa's oxen. I don't know why I couldn't have been small and neat and dark like Ma instead. Maybe they should have sent me to the *heifer boma* after all!'

'You're tall, not big. You've got thick, blonde hair that's beautiful, and you run like the wind. When I run, I get scarlet in the face and I'm ashamed to let anyone see me until I look normal again. Plus you play good tennis and ride really well. You looked so stately today on your horse.'

'Stately? That's not very attractive.'

'We can't all look like Camilla,' said Sarah. 'It's unfair that she has a perfect figure, large blue eyes and no spots on her skin. She even has a brain.'

Camilla said nothing. She seemed to be peering at something beyond the window, and she leaned forward and tapped lightly on the glass. Then she turned, put her feet back on to the floor and smiled at them.

'Are you coming to bed?' Sarah asked.

'Not for a few moments. You go on. I'll see you in a while.'

Sarah walked out into the night. The mountain air flowed cool around her and she heard a dry cough in the distance, just beyond the boundary of the garden. Leopard! If Piet had been with her they might have gone in search of it, using the powerful lamp he kept for watching game at night.

The moon cast a bright band of light into the bedroom and there was no need for the hurricane lamp or a candle. She cleaned her teeth in the icy water and climbed into bed. Tomorrow was hours away. Her body felt fiery and tingling and impatient. How would she wait until tomorrow before seeing him again, how would she ever sleep? But the afternoon's ride, the sherry and the wine combined to send her drifting downwards almost immediately.

She was not sure what woke her. The sound of a low voice and something like stifled laughter found their way into her consciousness. Alert and puzzled, she sat up and looked over at Camilla's bed. It was empty. Sarah pushed her feet into her slippers and went to the window. The verandah was bathed in moonlight, cold and white. Shadows in sharp relief hoarded the night's secrets. At the edge of the darkness Camilla was leaning against the wooden railing. Then she moved into the light with a low, soft laugh, murmuring words that Sarah could not hear. The cold air set the gum trees whispering and blew the folds of Sarah's nightdress against her body, making her shiver. Then Piet stepped out of the shadows and caught Camilla in his arms. Sarah could see her eyes shining in the moonlight. She watched as Piet's hand came up and touched the place where Camilla's breasts curved beneath her sweater, saw her lean back and laugh up at him.

Sarah stood frozen in the dark, struck by a pain so fierce that she felt as though she had been stabbed. She forced herself away from the window, but even though she closed her eyes and pulled the blankets over her head, she could not banish the image of Piet's fingers on Camilla's face as he bent to kiss her mouth.

Chapter 3

Kenya, December 1962

They stood close together on the station platform in the fog of early morning, laughing and crying, hugging the nuns and teachers whom they had never once embraced during all their years in school classrooms, promising to keep in touch, to write letters, to visit one another soon. Hannah had come to the station to say goodbye and she stood beside Camilla, making bad jokes, hiding self-conscious sadness. Sarah moved away, unable to mask her tears. Part of her life was already over and she felt dislocated, heading into an empty space without guidelines or familiar faces. The Indian stationmaster appeared on the platform. His breath vaporised in the frosty air as he broke up farewells and directed the chattering, tearful girls into the carriages. He slammed doors, shouted orders at the train driver, the engineers and the sleeping-car attendants. The girls hung out of the windows, waving and calling out their very last goodbyes as the train pulled out of the highland station, trailing a mournful whistle as it carried them away from their childhood years.

As they shunted into Nairobi in the late afternoon, groups of parents were standing on the platform, faces beaming with anticipation. There were shouts of welcome as children and their luggage were deposited on to the platform. Porters wheeled school trunks away to waiting cars. Sarah tried to guess which of the crowd was Marina Broughton-Smith.

'Saidi, *jambo*. Our luggage is over there.' Camilla addressed a young man in a chauffeur's uniform. 'This is my friend Memsahib Sarah who has come to stay with us.'

'Where are your parents?' Sarah knew instinctively that she should not have asked, but the words came out before she had time to consider their implications.

'God knows. They're busy, I suppose. We'll get to them all too soon.'

Saidi drove them through the broad streets of the city to the residential area of Muthaiga, where tree-lined avenues bordered acres of manicured lawns and flower beds. There was a cold formality about the Broughton-Smith house that was immediately disturbing, and the silence unnerved Sarah as she stepped across the threshold. She felt that it was a place without a soul, an impressive pile of stone bearing no resemblance to home as she knew it. There was no sign of Camilla's parents as she followed the houseboy upstairs to the guest wing. Her room had a canopied bed, a velvet sofa and matching armchair, and her own bathroom. It was impressive and too large, and it felt lonely. She thought it must look like an expensive hotel suite, although she had never seen one. Outside, a huge expanse of lawn was framed by shrubs and a rose garden. When she opened the window the air was cool, and sweet with the scent of flowers.

In all their school years no one had ever been asked to stay with Camilla, and Sarah had accepted the invitation with both alacrity and curiosity. But the sight of Piet and Camilla in the moonlight had almost severed their friendship. The following morning's ride had been agony as she tried to behave cheerfully, to talk casually to Piet, as though nothing was the matter. All through the long, ruined day she struggled to conceal her pain and hostility. Back at school she had nursed her sense of betrayal, as she waited for Camilla to bring up the incident and offer some explanation. But none had been forthcoming. Camilla seemed not to have noticed her distant manner, and although there were moments when her anger boiled, Sarah was unwilling to confront her outright. She tried telling herself that Piet had never thought of her except as another kid sister. But this only served to exacerbate her jealousy. Then exams began and she blocked out everything else, spending every spare moment with her books, until one evening she was unable to find her biology notes.

'I borrowed them yesterday,' Camilla said. 'I knew you wouldn't mind.'

It was the pin taken out of the grenade and Sarah's anger exploded. 'I do bloody mind,' she shouted. 'You seem to think you can take anything you want and never bother to ask, because you're posing as my friend. But you're not my friend, never mind my sister, and when we get out of here I don't want to see you again. Ever.'

37

Camilla's expression was one of utter bewilderment and she opened her mouth to protest, but Sarah was in full spate and all her pent-up misery poured out. Camilla tried to apologise, promising that she had not initiated the incident, infuriating Sarah even further.

'I don't care who bloody started it,' she said furiously. 'You knew how I felt about Piet. Now stay away from me. I just want to finish my exams and go home.'

Camilla sat down, white and shocked, with no sign of her usual composure. 'You're coming to Nairobi,' she said. 'You're coming to stay with me. It's all arranged.'

She began to weep, suddenly and uncontrollably, and Sarah turned in astonishment. She had never seen Camilla cry. No one had. Her body shook and she bent forward, her face hidden in her hands, pleading between the sobbing.

'Please, Sarah. Please. You must come with me. I can't go home alone. You can't turn your back on me, Sarah, please. I need you to come to Nairobi. You and Hannah are all I have, and now that school is finishing we have to stay together. We have to. We promised.'

It was the promise that had changed Sarah's resolve, and brought her to Nairobi after all. On the evening of her arrival she met Marina Broughton-Smith for the first time, and saw instantly the source of Camilla's beauty. Mother and daughter had the same oval face framed by ash-blonde hair, the same blue eyes and smooth skin, the straight nose and perfectly shaped mouth. She's pure Botticelli, Sarah thought, but sad. Marina's hands seemed to be in constant motion, fluttering everywhere, lightly touching crystal vases and leather-bound books, resting for a fleeting moment on her pale hair, fingering the pearls around her neck. Her presence seemed to permeate the room and spread a rippling uncertainty around her. Her voice was light and slightly breathless and she smiled a great deal, but there was something in her eyes that spoke of a fragile soul.

'I do hope you'll enjoy your few days in Nairobi, my dear. It's lovely that Camilla has brought a friend to stay. It's Sally Mackay, isn't it?' Marina leaned forward and Sarah was reminded of photos of the Queen as she bent to accept a bouquet. 'We have Scottish friends called Mackay, in Blairgowrie. Perhaps you're related to them? We go there for the shooting, you know. At least we did before George got us stranded out here all the year round.'

'Sarah – I'm called Sarah. We're not related to that family. My parents are Irish. Not from Scotland at all, although maybe years back—'

'Oh. I see. Irish. How interesting. So full of charm and lovely words, the Irish.' Marina's smile brightened and reached her eyes. She seemed, for some inexplicable reason, to be relieved. 'We do have some Irish friends. Racing people in County Kildare. Perhaps your parents know the O'Dwyers' stud farm? It's a marvellous estate.'

'My mother came from Sligo originally, and my father's from County Monaghan.' Sarah watched the subtle dimming of interest in Marina's face as the likelihood of common ground faded. 'I don't think they were ever involved with breeding horses. But perhaps they did have—'

'Sarah's father is a doctor,' Camilla said. 'He deals with people rather than horses, Mother. You wouldn't be terribly interested in that.'

Marina's smile faded altogether and there was a sudden glittering in her eyes. Sarah looked away, embarrassed by the barbed remark, aware that Camilla had hurt her mother. Marina turned, like a wounded animal, drawing her shoulders forward.

'County Monaghan. Ghastly little towns on that troublesome border. So grey and dreary. I drove through Sligo once, though, and that was rather wild and quaint, with Yeats and so on – quite lovely.' She touched Sarah's arm fleetingly, clearly anxious to be gone. 'Well, I must rush, my dears. I have to be at the club by seven. Saidi can drop you at the cinema later, if you like.'

Sarah was intrigued by the routine of the house as the week progressed. Most days there was no sign of Marina until she appeared in the sitting room at about six, exquisitely dressed for a cocktail party or a dinner, with a drink in her hand. She would sip from her glass and smoke several cigarettes, leafing through a magazine or a book while she waited for her husband. When George arrived he would kiss her lightly, enquiring about her day with a curious, old-fashioned formality that Sarah had experienced only in the pages of period novels. But with Camilla he was different, and there was a real bond of affection between them. At the breakfast table he hugged his daughter with enthusiasm and was obviously interested in her questions and opinions, and her plans for the day. He was a large, handsome man, a little too heavy but dressed in beautifully tailored suits that hid any excess weight. His hair was thick and wavy, and almost white, but his tanned face was without lines, as though someone had ironed them away and left his skin as it had been when he was a child. He wore a heavy signet ring with a coat of arms engraved on it. Sarah was fascinated by his smooth hands, and his fingernails which were shaped into neat, polished ovals. She thought they might have been manicured. When Camilla looked at him her face was soft and unguarded, and she liked to place her arm through his and hold his hand as she talked to him.

The Broughton-Smiths rarely spent an evening at home, however, and as soon as George had changed into evening clothes he left with his wife to attend whatever social event was on their calendar. At breakfast there was never any sign of Marina. But long after she had gone to bed at night, Sarah would hear her light steps as she retired, followed much later by the sound of George, climbing the stairs with a tread that sounded heavy, even weary.

'They're certainly busy, your parents,' Sarah remarked on the second night of her stay. 'When do you talk to them about what you're going to do now? Or about anything?'

'They've signed me up for an art-history course in Florence. You know that. One of those places where young ladies go if they haven't got anything else to do. And then I'm booked on a dreary course in London, with typing and shorthand, and deportment and make-up lessons. It's for well-bred girls who want to be a secretary for a minute and a half, before getting married. Awful. After that I can apply for one of the drama schools, once I've got a safety net of some kind in place.'

Sarah was taken aback. 'Why don't you go to university and join a drama group? There are always talent scouts at college productions.'

'I don't want to spend another three or four years doing more exams and learning things I don't need to know.' Camilla's face was calm, but Sarah saw that her hands were tightly clasped and her body tense. 'They keep saying I can't expect to make it on the stage, just because I've been in plays at school and here in Nairobi. Not that they've ever come to see me, except for once when it was a charity thing and Mother was involved in organising it.'

'Well, I suppose with their schedules . . .' Sarah trailed off.

'Don't bother inventing excuses for them. They ignore my ambitions, hoping I'll become discouraged or forget about them. But I won't. I'm going to be a brilliant actress, and that's all I want.'

'Maybe, if you discuss it again, now that school's over, you can get them to see that applying for drama school right away isn't such a bad idea.'

'They see what they want to see, and I'm not going to waste any more time arguing with them. Daddy's disappointed that I don't want to try for the diplomatic service, and Mother is only interested in my eventual marriage prospects. They've offered a compromise I can live with. And then I can get on with my life.'

'But they're your parents. Maybe they haven't understood how much this acting career means, how serious you are.'

'Oh, come on, Sarah. They're not going to pay any attention to what I want. Now, let's get out of this morgue and have some fun.'

They spent their morning at Muthaiga Club, lazing beside the pool. Sarah lay out in the full sun, drawing the heat into her, glad to be out of the silent, oppressive house. Camilla wore a large hat and sat under an umbrella. Waiters came and went with cold drinks and meals and little pink and white pieces of paper that she signed. A stream of friends and acquaintances came to exchange Nairobi gossip, to organise tennis games, and to discuss invitations they had all received to the same parties and dances. Sarah felt left out, intimidated by the talk of the week's social events among the main players in Nairobi's party scene. Camilla drank large, frosted glasses of Pimm's at lunchtime, and when they were ready to leave Sarah was concerned to see that she was unsteady on her feet.

'Hey, are you tipsy?'

'Probably. But I can sleep it off this afternoon. In time for inspection hour, before they go out for the evening.'

The driver was always available to take them into the centre of Nairobi where Camilla seemed to spend much of her time. They would find a pavement table in the Thorn Tree Café, where they ordered iced coffee topped with ice cream. Camilla knew everyone, and she appeared to be interested in all aspects of their lives, enquiring about children and grandchildren, siblings and lovers, golf handicaps and bridge scores.

'How do you remember all these people's friends and relations, and their various peccadillos?' Sarah asked.

'Everyone has a story, you know. Even some dreary old man with yellow teeth and a frayed bush jacket will have something amazing to tell.

I've learned by watching Father. He does it all the time in his job, and he's very good at it. And it means I've always got someone to talk to.'

The words were such a stark admission of loneliness that Sarah turned away to hide an unwelcome feeling of pity. The idea that these passers-by were a substitute family for Camilla flashed into her mind, but she dismissed the thought as being foolish and far-fetched.

'But you never tell them anything about yourself,' she said as Camilla lit another cigarette.

'They all know my glamorous parents, and they think I'm bound to be just like them.' Camilla was watching the safari cars being loaded with tin trunks, expensive leather suitcases, and wooden boxes containing guns and ammunition. 'Look at those mountains of luggage – what are they going to do with it all, in the middle of nowhere?' she said.

'God, I'd love to be rich and going off to my own tented camp. White hunter, craggy looks, big rifle, lions roaring in the night.'

'Primitive and sweaty. But I can see you right there in the thick of it. When Piet starts up his game reserve you can go with him.' Camilla saw the flicker of pain as Sarah looked away. 'Oh, for heaven's sake, Sarah. I've said I'm sorry dozens of times.'

Sarah hesitated, wanting to comment but reluctant to let the misery re-surface during her Nairobi stay. She sat there in silence, watching as Camilla projected a dazzling smile at someone, looking up through the beat of long eyelashes.

'Anthony. Are you off on safari?'

'I'm going out with one of the Ker and Downey hunters as a back-up. Four clients, with three shooting. One looks a little shaky this morning. I think he sank a bottle of Scotch last night in the Long Bar. We'll be gone for about a month. Coming with me?'

'God, no. I have no interest in sharing some swampy safari camp with a bunch of strangers.'

'I'm not a stranger. There's room in my tent.'

'Don't be ridiculous, Anthony.' Camilla was laughing. 'This is my friend Sarah Mackay. Anthony Chapman.'

He sat down with them and ordered Tusker beers all round. Sarah was instantly taken with his straightforward manner and the way he looked at her, his gaze direct. His brown eyes were hooded and an aquiline nose made him seem a little aloof, but his smile emphasised a sensuous mouth.

He had reddish hair that was rather too long and curled over his shirt collar at the back, and his face and hands were tanned and peppered with freckles. He sat absolutely still while he was listening, like an animal in the wild, using his every instinct to absorb and understand the sounds and implications of his surroundings. But his laugh was uninhibited and she plied him with questions about his life in the bush, listening with rapt attention as he described the days in camp.

'I've been on safari,' Sarah said, 'but only in our family car, and just a few days at a time. We stayed at self-catering *bandas* in Tsavo and Amboseli and I never wanted to come home. The shooting part seems sad, though. Cruel, too. I'm surprised you can do it, if you really care about the game.'

'Hunting is carefully controlled, you know. You can't go out into the bush and just bang away at anything that moves. It's not random killing.'

'But it's killing, all the same.' Sarah did not wish to antagonise him, but the subject was relevant to her own plans for the future. 'You do shoot elephant, and lion and buffalo and leopard. In fact, you can polish off anything you like as a decoration for your library wall, can't you?'

'It's not like that.' He stubbed out a cigarette, impatient at her ignorance. 'You have to apply for a licence to shoot each individual trophy, whether it's a buffalo, a kudu or a leopard. Most clients want to obtain at least two of the big five, it's true, but they don't always succeed.'

'The odds are stacked against the animals, though. They're virtually helpless, up against men armed with powerful rifles and fast cars, and a desire to kill,' Sarah said.

'We don't shoot from fast cars. Not even from slow cars. There are regulations about distance from the vehicle, from the animal itself, and so on.' Far from being upset, Anthony was now enjoying the exchange. 'You have to be out there on your feet. Every step you take makes a sound or a signal which a buffalo or a lion, hiding in thick bush, can hear long before you get close. And apart from our trophy licences, we only shoot for the pot. To feed the camp.'

'You're killing off animals, for all that,' she said stubbornly.

'So is your butcher,' he retorted, smiling at her.

'I seem to recall Sarah tucking into a leg of impala recently,' Camilla said with relish. 'She was full of admiration for the person who shot the poor innocent beast and brought it to the table.'

Sarah's face began inevitably to redden.

'Your halo is slipping it seems.' Anthony raised his eyebrows. 'We have a population that's expanding too fast, Sarah, and there's a huge increase in the demand for land needed to grow food. Blind preservation of all game can't work.'

'I know all that. We have friends who farm, and they sometimes have to shoot a leopard that has killed livestock, or get rid of a buffalo that has trampled the labourers' *shambas*. I do understand the need for balance. But that's not the same as killing for fun.'

'It's a thin line to tread, I suppose. But the money for hunting permits pays for rangers to patrol the reserves and the parks. In theory, anyway.'

'Goes to buy another Mercedes or a new wife for some politician, more like,' Camilla said brightly.

'You can't afford to be completely cynical around here,' Anthony said. 'Some of the money reaches its intended target, and that's better than none. And the professional hunters are pretty good game rangers themselves. They're the first to report illegal activity to the Game Department and they often prevent poaching of rhino and elephant.'

'So you're saying that the means – like taking pot shots at magnificent old tuskers, for example – justifies the end.' Sarah was unconvinced.

'Once again, in theory, yes.' Anthony pushed his leather hat back from his face and drained his glass. His eyes were no longer laughing. 'There's plenty of political jiggery pokery going on, it's true. After Independence it will probably get worse if corruption becomes a serious issue, and that is more than likely. God knows what will happen then.'

'What a gloomy scenario,' Sarah said. 'I hope there'll still be people like you around, to go on making the case for wildlife survival.'

'You seem extremely interested in the whole question.'

'She is,' Camilla said. 'She's the crusader sort, like you. She's planning to study zoology, and when she has her degree she's going to come back here and work in conservation. Do her bit towards saving the country.'

'Good girl. Maybe we'll find ourselves working together one day. I have a friend who plans to start up a private game reserve on his farm. He's going to build a small lodge, where people can see game in a place that's not overrun by noisy tourists in groups. I'd like to put some money into the scheme myself, when I have a few bob available.'

'Where would that be?' Sarah leaned forward, disbelieving.

'A place called Langani Farm. It's going to be organised by a mate of mine from way back. Piet van der Beer. Actually, he comes from up near where you girls were incarcerated.' He listened to their exclamations, surprised at the coincidence. 'Well, he's got a fine plan there, although it won't be easy to find the money for it. But Piet's a good man and if anyone can pull it off, he can.' Anthony turned his attention to Camilla. 'So, what's the latest?'

'Same as before.' She shrugged. 'The parents are still adamant that my chosen career is too bohemian, whatever that means. I don't think either of them has ever set eyes on anything bohemian. So I've agreed to obtain some worthy qualification before starting drama school. Let's not talk about it. Just rest assured I'll be beautiful, brilliant and famous sometime soon.'

'Well, you're most of those already.' His eyes narrowed as he lightly touched her wrist, and Sarah saw tell-tale goose bumps appear on Camilla's bare arm. 'I'm off to join my clients. Good to meet you, Sarah. Behave yourself, Camilla. I have my spies, so I'll be keeping an eye on you from afar. Maybe you'll come with me to the Christmas Eve thing at Muthaiga? My clients will probably want to come into town for a couple of days around then.'

'Maybe.' The obvious pleasure in her smile belied the nonchalant reply. 'What a surprise that you know about Piet's great scheme.'

'Us good guys have to stick together. Salaams to you both.'

Sarah watched him stride away, his limbs absurdly long, his movement loping and graceful. When he was out of earshot, she turned back to Camilla.

'You have an admirer.'

'He's just a bush baby.' Camilla's eyes followed him as he climbed into his Land Rover and drove away. 'Looks particularly good on a horse, I must say. I've seen him playing polo. But better suited to a rattling four-wheel drive full of dust, in the middle of nowhere.'

'He's much more than that. Intelligent. Passionate about what he's doing. Plus he's nice looking.'

'Too skinny and gingery. There are plenty more where he comes from.'

'Oh come on, Camilla. I think your heart was fluttering there.'

'I'm not going to be derailed by a Kenya cowboy. I have plans that he doesn't fit into at all. Now, let's go back to Muthaiga and swim. It's much too hot here.'

'Darling.' Marina was in the sitting room when they arrived back at the house in the late afternoon. 'We're going out for dinner, but Daddy's home early. He'll be down in a minute. Let's all have a drink together.'

'Brace yourself,' Camilla muttered in an undertone. 'This will be "Happy Families" like you've never known it.'

George Broughton-Smith mixed their drinks. The noise of ice clinking into glasses was amplified by the silence in the room and Sarah thought of the sitting room at Langani, with everyone talking and laughing and happily exchanging views. She wondered how long Camilla had lived in this desolate atmosphere and whether her parents had always been so remote.

'What's the news from Nairobi's café society?' George said, looking fondly at his daughter.

'The same. We met Anthony Chapman. He was on about conservation and money for the national parks. His usual hobby horse.'

'We need young men like that around here. Especially now.'

'He thinks there'll be more poaching and corruption after Independence,' Camilla said.

'Sadly, I agree. I'd like to say otherwise, but there are already signs of it on a fairly grand scale.'

'It can't all be bad.'

'Of course not. But it's common for politicians, newly in power, to have their heads turned by bribes and by access to larger amounts of money than they ever imagined possible.'

'Let's not have politics with our drinks, George. There are all kinds of things going on that would be much more amusing for the girls.' Marina's pale fingers alighted fleetingly on Camilla's arm. 'I was wondering if you'd both like to come to Limuru for lunch tomorrow? Would that be fun?'

'We've organised for Saidi to take us to Nairobi National Park in the morning, and we thought we'd take a picnic. We might stumble across a lion, or even a rhino.'

'Oh dear,' Marina said, her expression childlike with disappointment. 'I invited Chantal Dubois from the French Embassy to join us. She's going to bring her daughter who's your age. I'm sure Sarah would like her too.'

'Sarah's more interested in wildlife, and in people like Anthony Chapman,' Camilla said. 'Or the van der Beers.' Camilla turned to her father. 'Daddy, how will the British government compensate farmers whose land is given to Africans after *Uhuru*?'

The uniformed houseboy arrived, bearing a tray of elaborate canapés. Sarah felt an overwhelming hunger, a need to escape the tension surrounding her. She heaped several of the tiny offerings on to a plate, only to find that no one else was eating. She stared down at them in embarrassment.

'Why on earth would you be interested in farm compensation?' George Broughton-Smith looked at his daughter in surprise. 'Your mother won't be pleased if you start expressing an interest in things political.'

Camilla turned her attention to the plate of canapés.

'You met my friend Hannah once, Daddy. She and Sarah and I are like sisters after all this time. Her family owns the farm where Sarah and I spent all our exeat weekends. It's my favourite place in the world – the place where I've always been really happy.'

Sarah saw pain in Marina's face, and she searched frantically for some way in which she might take hold of the conversation and direct it elsewhere. But Camilla had her father's attention, and she was determined to make the most of it.

'They want to stay on after Independence and become Kenya citizens. But they're worried that they'll be forced to sell up for a pittance, or be made to give their farm over for some resettlement scheme.'

'I don't think you need to take on the worries of the Kenya farming community, darling.' Marina said. 'They've had plenty of good years. I'm sure the ones who know what they're doing have been able to put away considerable amounts of money. Most of them have numbered bank accounts overseas. We don't need to pass the hat round for them.' She closed her eyes as if to stem any further reference to farming and politics.

'That's a notion widely bandied about, my dear, but it's far from the truth,' George said. 'Some of these farmers are going to be in dire straits when independence comes.'

'They'll go and farm in England. Or somewhere rough and unpleasant, like Australia.'

'You don't understand the problem, Mother. These are third-generation Afrikaners. Their lives are here, in Kenya. They have nowhere else to call home.'

'Boers. How extraordinary. I've heard they wear black clothes and hats, and still drive around in horse-drawn carts. Rather like those strange people in Pennsylvania who live in barns with no electricity. Would anyone care for another drink? Sally?'

'It's Sarah, not Sally,' Camilla said angrily. 'And we're not talking about strange Americans. We're talking about the van der Beers – my second family.'

'Nothing more to drink, thank you.' Now that someone had finally addressed her, Sarah rushed into the conversation. 'These are terrific people. A wonderful family, totally dedicated, and their son hopes to take over their farm some day. They have miles of wheat and a big herd of cattle. Camilla and I have had great times there.'

'Really? I can't imagine Camilla as a milkmaid, although she assures us she can play any role.' Marina smiled and lifted her wine glass with a trembling hand.

'Jan van der Beer taught us trout fishing at Langani, and we've been out walking in the bush, learning to track animals and identify birds. We've ridden across the plains among the zebra and gazelle,' Sarah said. 'It's an extraordinary place, and it would be tragic to see all that broken up and taken away from them.'

'I never cared much for farms.' Marina's face had stiffened. 'Flies everywhere when you have livestock.' She looked straight past Sarah and addressed her husband. 'George, I think you should ring for the car, darling.'

'These farmers have two years after Independence to decide whether they want to become Kenya citizens.' George ignored his wife's request. 'It's risky, of course, and some will be bought out by the British government, it's true. Then their land will be parcelled out in co-operative schemes, to the local people.'

'Yes, but Jan and Lottie don't want to sell,' Camilla said. 'And they don't believe they would get a fair price anyway.'

'There are disagreements about the amount of compensation being offered,' George conceded. 'And there are plenty of people who are angry about the large areas being marked out for compulsory purchase and redistribution – more than a million acres, in fact. Personally, I don't believe those huge farms can be split into smallholdings and remain viable. But it will be the beginning of a new class of native landowners. That in itself may prevent violence in the future.'

'But Hannah's family are Boers, Daddy. What will happen to them?'

'It's a tricky one. Some of them may go back to South Africa, or Rhodesia perhaps. Others will apply for Kenya citizenship. But their applications might not be looked on very favourably. The Afrikaans farmers haven't endeared themselves to either the British or the African communities over the years. They've never made any real attempt at integration. Rather like the Asians, although neither would relish the comparison.'

'But could you look into the van der Beers' situation? Find out if their property is likely to be subject to a government purchase offer? Maybe you could even meet Jan and talk to him, Daddy.' Camilla was pleading. 'He's been so good to Sarah and me. Lottie is our second mother. Maybe you could ask them here next time they come to Nairobi.'

'We can't possibly find time to entertain your farming acquaintances, Camilla.' Marina's eyes were glassy bright. 'Your father is far too heavily committed as it is. I'm sure there are official avenues, darling, and I don't think we need to become involved.'

'Mother, the van der Beers made my time at school into something wonderful. They treated Sarah and me like daughters. I was at home every time I went to the farm. Part of the family. A family you wouldn't even be able to imagine.'

Marina blinked and put one hand up to her face, as though she had been slapped. 'Your family is here, Camilla, and we have our own traditions.'

'We're both grateful to the van der Beers for all their hospitality and kindness to you,' George said. 'I'll try to look into the situation of the farms in his area. In the meantime we should be off, Marina.'

Sarah felt limp with relief when they left the house. She longed for the whole visit to be over, to reach the normality of her own home. The girls had dinner and then took themselves back to the drawing room for a ferocious game of Scrabble that made Sarah laugh again.

'A typically jolly evening at the Broughton-Smiths.' There was resignation in Camilla's voice. 'Mother lives in a fantasy world that poor Daddy can't seem to penetrate at all. Maybe it's just as well. If she had to face real life she might disintegrate altogether.'

'You don't seem to be able to talk to each other very well,' Sarah said cautiously.

'There's one thing I've promised myself.' Camilla stood up abruptly and Sarah saw that her hands were curled into tight fists. 'I swear I'll never be like them. Never. I'll go to any lengths to be different. Come on, let's go to bed.'

They were putting away the Scrabble board when they heard the front door opening.

There was a murmur of voices in the hall. 'Keep quiet,' Camilla whispered. 'Otherwise we'll be trapped in another skirmish.'

'I'm going to have a brandy,' George was saying. 'Do you want to join me?'

'Perhaps. If you'll stop lecturing me.'

They moved into the study, leaving the door open so that there was no way for Camilla and Sarah to reach the staircase without being seen.

'I'm not lecturing you, Marina. Our daughter's friends are very important to her, and that's something you haven't quite grasped.' George's tone was placatory. 'I think you should be less disparaging about the van der Beers. You were perfectly willing to let them take up all Camilla's weekends and half-term breaks over the years.'

'I couldn't have driven that distance on those awful, muddy roads. My migraines—'

'Saidi would have driven you up there.'

'To stay in that dreary club, and talk to thick-necked farmers and their frumpy wives with their tight perms?'

'You could have tried talking to your daughter.'

'Camilla should never have been sent to a school with people like—'

'Oh, for God's sake, Marina! The world is full of genuine, normal people that you can't even recognise.'

'Genuine and normal like you, I suppose.' The words came out like drops of acid. 'I've seen enough of the world from your viewpoint, George, and I've decided I'm safer within walls of my own construction.'

'But you never think of Camilla. Never. We only have one child, Marina, and—'

'I was hardly likely to have any more children, George. You saw to that. And I tried with Camilla. In the beginning I tried so hard.' Marina was crying. 'I never wanted her out of my sight. But you criticised me for that too.'

'You smothered her. She was an obsession, not a child. You never allowed her to play with other children. It was almost as though the rest of the world had some ghastly infectious disease. Camilla might as well have been in an isolation ward.'

Sarah put her hands over her ears and looked imploringly at Camilla. But there was no way out now. If they made for the stairs it would be clear that they had been eavesdropping. Camilla shook her head. Her eyes were dull with misery, and she lifted her shoulders in a helpless apology.

'I was terrified something would happen to her.' Marina's voice was pleading, and they heard the click of her lighter and the intake of her breath.

'And then you abandoned her. You went out every day and left her with the nanny. Because of your new friend, no doubt.'

'Don't ever mention him to me.' Marina's voice rose. 'Don't ever speak his name, or raise this subject. Do you hear me? Do you, George?'

'Oh God,' George said wearily. 'There's no point in going over all this. I've given you a choice. I think that would be better for you. God knows, almost anything might be better than this.'

'A separation? So that I can live alone in some stultifying village in Sussex, and join the local Women's League, while you travel around the world and do as you wish? Oh, I don't think so, George. You'll have to do better than that.'

'I can't afford a house in Belgravia or Knightsbridge, Marina, with the kind of entourage you have in mind. You have to get that clear. In the meantime your indiscretions are becoming a little too obvious, and too frequent.'

'There're a great deal more acceptable than your sordid affairs. I'm the one keeping your career together, after all, and you're in no position to comment on—'

'We've been through all this before, goddamnit.' George was trying to control his anger, but his voice rose. 'You know we can't have a scandal, and I'm not willing to step down right now. This is a pivotal time in my career.'

'And that's why I'm trapped here, in this godforsaken continent. I'm dying here, George.' She was almost screaming at him. 'I'm dying in the prison you've made for me. You promised you'd only do one tour and we've been here for six interminable, bloody years. Away from anything and anyone civilised. No, don't touch me! Don't!'

Camilla sank down on the sofa and buried her head in her hands. Sarah remained standing, close to the door, mute and appalled.

'We'll be posted after Independence. There's no doubt about that,' George said. 'But for the time being, don't ruin this bond Camilla has with her friends. That school was good for her. And we owe a debt to the van der Beers.'

'She should have gone to Cheltenham, like I did. Instead you chose a bourgeois little convent in the middle of Africa. What is she going to do next year, in Europe, where she doesn't know anyone in the right set? And look at her friends, for heaven's sake.'

'What's wrong with them?'

'We've just had a week of that plain little girl whose father is some provincial doctor. A nobody. I can only thank God we haven't had the farm girl foisted on us as well. At least Camilla had more sense than to ask me if she could come to stay. And now you're being asked to rescue a Boer who probably can't speak recognisable English, and has never read a book in his life. It just won't do, George.'

'Christ Almighty, Marina, there can't be anyone else alive as bigoted as you are.'

'I certainly don't have sufficiently liberal ideas for your preferred lifestyle. You're never prepared to admit how sickening your—'

'Shut UP.' George's words came through gritted teeth and there was a crash as he slammed a table. 'Shut up, or leave me once and for all, so that we can stop torturing each other. I'm doing all I can, and I can't take any more of this tonight. I'm going to bed.'

'No. No, George. Please don't walk away.' Hysteria rose to the surface in Marina's voice. 'You're an expert at walking away. You never try to resolve our—'

'There's no solution, Marina. Will you never understand that? God damn you, you unforgiving bitch, you'll never understand or give me a moment's peace, never live for anything but revenge.' He sounded close to tears and for a moment there was a desperate silence. 'You'd better look at tomorrow's diary and decide what you want to attend.'

Marina turned on her heel and left the room. George slumped into an armchair and sat for a few moments, undecided. Then he rose to his feet and walked across the hall, calling up the stairs.

'Marina? Marina, I'm sorry. I'm coming up now. Just need to find my glasses.'

As he turned back towards the study a movement caught his eye and he changed direction, only to come face to face with his daughter and Sarah, frozen to the spot.

'Oh God! There's just no end to this.' He pushed his hand up through his hair, his face sad and defeated. 'Camilla, darling, I'm so sorry. I didn't know. I just didn't – God, what a bloody disaster!'

Chapter 4

Kenya, December 1962

They drove through a grove of coconut and cashew trees on to the road leading to the ferry. It was little more than a dirt track along the cliffs, emerging close to the boat ramp. Sarah could see the ferry, making its lumbering way across the shipping channel that separated the island of Mombasa from the mainland and the blinding glare of the wide, south coast beaches. She eyed her brother as he inspected himself in the driving mirror, smoothing his wiry hair. The ferry pulled in, clanking and swaying on the tide, slowly disgorging cars, bicycles and foot passengers. Poor Tim. He hadn't a chance with Camilla.

In the airport building they sat on benches under the dusty blades of a wooden ceiling fan. When the aircraft finally landed, Sarah watched her brother take in every detail of Camilla's cool appearance as she stepped down on to the tarmac – her crisp khaki slacks, the woven leather belt around her narrow waist, the soft cream shirt. Her feet looked delicate in leather sandals and her toenails were painted scarlet. Sarah was aware of her own creased blouse, and her canvas shoes frayed from walking on the reef. Her hair was frizzy from drying in the wind, and her sunburnt nose was peeling.

Tim hovered over Camilla, taking her bag, opening the car door, asking whether she was comfortable, his hand resting for a second on her bare arm. Just like Piet. Sarah buried the thought, avoiding regrets that might derail this last, shared holiday before they were dispatched to far-flung places of learning. She climbed into the car, taking her usual back seat to Camilla. The sun was sinking behind the coconut palms as they drove across the island, and the pink dusk was spiced with the scents of cooking fires and tropical vegetation. Shopkeepers were lighting up their *dukas* with kerosene lamps or dangling, naked bulbs, and music came from tinny radios, sending a pulse of drumbeats into the warm evening. Camilla leaned back in her seat, welcoming the heat, the smell of seaweed, and the sound of rushing waves.

The deckhands sang as they clanked the ferry chains to lower the ramps. The Mackays' house stood on the headland overlooking the shipping channel and the entrance to Mombasa harbour. It was built from coral blocks, and topped by a tiled roof. The central, two-storey section had long windows shaded by dark, oiled shutters, and carved Arab doors with bronze hinges and studs. On either side were the bedroom wings, with deep verandahs overlooking the garden where Betty Mackay fought the pitiless sun to maintain a semblance of lawn. The property was bounded by a coral wall built by the Arabs centuries before, and covered now in a riot of purple and orange bougainvillea. The evening was filled with the perfume of flowers. Betty was on the steps to welcome them, with Raphael's stocky form in the doorway behind her. His face was beaming as he greeted Camilla.

'Drinks at seven,' Betty announced. 'Raphael is threatening to open a bottle of champagne in honour of you girls.'

Oleanders and frangipani flowers gave off a heady fragrance, and crickets sounded their scratchy songs outside the guest-room window. The rush of surf over the reef below the house heralded a full tide. Camilla tossed her travel clothes into the washing basket. She showered, humming to herself, feeling the softness in the coastal air, the sensation of slowing down, the enveloping warmth of her welcome.

The sitting room looked out on the ocean through a tracery of flame trees. Doors and windows were all open, and a breeze stirred the night air. An old ceiling fan whirred and rattled. In place of coffee tables there were wooden chests from Zanzibar, brass studs gleaming. The red, waxed floors shone from daily polishing. Sarah had loved this ritual from childhood. She would sit on the stairs and watch Moti, the houseboy, with two coconut husks strapped to his feet. He always sang as he poured the Cardinal Red polish on to the floor, moving his feet in a jerky dance, sliding and buffing and altering the tempo of his tune as he covered the shining surface. The great expanse of floor was broken up by Persian carpets that Raphael Mackay had bought over the years off the dhows in the old port. He was often called to treat the sailors from the Persian Gulf, and he enjoyed sitting cross-legged on the decks, dispensing advice and medicines, drinking syrupy coffee and haggling over the price of any rug that had taken his fancy. Two large clay jars stood on a carved Arab sideboard. Betty had filled them with bare acacia branches with frangipani flowers planted on to the thorns. There was a Mozart piano concerto on the gramophone.

Camilla arrived barefoot, drifting in to the room in a sarong with a sleeveless top. She had tied her hair back on to the nape of her neck and fastened gold Indian earrings into her ears. Sarah joined the company a few minutes later, her blouse twisted into a knot below her breasts.

'I like the knot thing.' Tim gave a gentle whistle.

'Come along, everyone.' Raphael was handing out champagne cocktails. 'Time to wish success to these young ladies, as they start a new phase of their lives. To Sarah and Camilla! May all your hopes and dreams be realised.'

'And Hannah, too,' Betty said. 'The van der Beers will be here tomorrow evening for dinner. They're down at Diani Beach.'

'We've booked a table for us all at Mombasa Club, on New Year's Eve.' Betty said. 'The last year as a colony. What are your parents planning for New Year, Camilla?'

'Actually, they're going to be down here, at the coast,' Camilla said. 'They're staying with friends at Nyali Beach.'

'Good gracious!' Betty exclaimed. 'We must invite them for dinner with Jan and Lottie tomorrow. That would be grand.'

'Then Jan could talk to Camilla's father, about the situation at Langani.' Sarah was delighted.

'Sarah,' Raphael frowned a warning. 'Talking shop is probably not what the poor man has in mind. He is on holiday, after all.'

'But it's such a perfect opportunity. I'm sure your father wouldn't mind. Would he, Camilla?' There was no response and Sarah tried again. 'Camilla?'

Camilla's face had the closed look that she wore in her parents' company. 'Sounds like fun, all of us together.' The words were light, but her hands were clasped in her lap, and Sarah could see that her knuckles were white with pressure. 'I'll find their phone number after dinner.'

'I met your father some weeks back, Camilla.' Raphael broke the silence that enveloped them. 'It was at a conference. We needed money for the new children's wing at the hospital and he was very helpful. It would be delightful to have all of us parents here. Maybe we could prevail on them to join us for New Year's Eve as well.'

After dinner they moved out to the verandah for coffee. The night was still and breathless.

'I think we'll leave you, children.' Betty had tired of swatting the tiny bugs that kept landing on her arms and face, and in her hair. 'Raphael had another bout of malaria last month and we've been taking it very easy. This is the first time he's been up to having drinks and a real dinner. Sleep well, all of you.'

'I'm really concerned about that girl,' she said to her husband as she lay down beside him and put her head on his shoulder. 'There's something terribly wrong there. Sarah said the house was a desperate place to stay. Apparently the father was pleasant enough, but the mother was very difficult. Maybe we shouldn't have them to dinner at all.'

'Of course we should,' said Raphael, folding her in his arms. 'It would look strange if we knew the Broughton-Smiths were at the coast, and never bothered to contact them.'

'I don't know, Raphael. It's odd that Camilla didn't mention before that they were here.'

'I still think you should telephone them first thing. It's very short notice, but at least you will have made an effort. You'll like George Broughton-Smith. If his wife is a bit tricky she's not the first unhappy memsahib we've come across. And our Ghanaian guest is remarkable. It'll be a grand mix.'

'That's another thing. Do you think I should tell the staff there's going to be——?'

'We've had plenty of non-Europeans for dinner before. *Uhuru* will be upon us within months, and then the whole country will be sitting down to meals together every day.'

Betty spent the next morning preparing for her dinner party. To her surprise, the Broughton-Smiths had accepted her invitation, and she felt a vague apprehension as she polished crystal and silver, raided the garden for flowers, and set the table with her best china. The house was quiet and the ritual of preparation calmed her. Tim had taken the girls to join the van der Beers at their rented beach house, and they would not be back until late afternoon. When she cast her eye over the table for a final inspection, Betty saw with pride that she had done a fine job.

At seven-thirty the sitting room glowed in the candlelight. There was dance music on the gramophone, and the houseboys were dressed in starched white kanzus and scarlet cummerbunds. In Sarah's mind her father and brother had been transformed into divinely handsome beings in their white dinner jackets and black bow ties, while her mother resembled some creature from one of the fashion magazines that came each month from England on the mail boats.

'You look very lovely.' Raphael had not yet come to terms with the fact that his daughter was no longer a schoolgirl. Time had snatched away her childhood, and he had not seen the chubby little girl vanishing, had not spent enough hours with her, watching her grow into this young woman with the polished skin and womanly shape and shining eyes. He handed her a glass of sherry, his face gentle with love. 'I'm very proud of you.'

Camilla had taken charge of Sarah, turning her wilful mop into wings of hair that swept back from her face, and blending colour and shadow on to her cheeks and eyelids. Her halter-neck dress was pale green and swirled around her as she moved.

'Here, use these earrings – I'm not wearing jewellery tonight.' Camilla had tugged and pulled and adjusted until she was satisfied. 'That's perfect. Wait till Piet arrives, my girl – we may have to tie him to a chair.'

In the mirror Sarah could see a small pulse thumping at the base of her throat. She had felt transformed until her face and neck reddened in anticipation, blotching her skin and ruining her Cinderella illusion.

'Where's Camilla?' Raphael asked his daughter.

'She helped me to get ready first, so she's a few minutes late.'

'Jaysus!' Tim's exclamation made them all turn.

Camilla's black dress was strapless, pulled in at the waist by a wide belt and a spray of flowers. Her skirt clung to the shape of her legs, and she had fastened more flowers behind one pearly ear. Sarah watched her brother, awed and openly admiring. There would be no support from Tim this evening. He would hardly be able to take care of himself. She winked at him, slowly closing one shadowed eyelid, smiling in exaggerated conspiracy as they heard the sound of the first car on the gravel.

'Well, here we go.' Betty touched her necklace and then clasped her husband's hand briefly as he turned towards the front door.

'Betty, my dear – this is Dr Winston Hayford from Ghana.' Raphael propelled his guest into the sitting room. 'He's been on a fellowship in London for the past year, and now he's here for the conference.'

'Dr Hayford. I'm delighted you were able to join us,' Betty said.

'And I am very glad to see that Raphael has recovered from his malaria,' he replied.

Sarah was fascinated by the sight of the tall black man. His voluminous robes were printed with a geometric pattern of bright yellow and green, brown and scarlet, and he wore an embroidered cap on his large head. The horn-rimmed glasses on his wide nose looked ordinary and out of place. He spoke perfect English with an accent that must have been the product of an expensive overseas schooling, or hours of listening to the BBC World Service. Sarah had never seen an African like this before, so imposing and handsome. As she shook hands with him she saw Moti emerging from the kitchen with the first tray of hors d'oeuvres. He stopped, open-mouthed, and stared at the big Ghanaian, before wheeling round and heading with unaccustomed speed back through the door from which he had come. Raphael poured a whisky and soda for his guest and left the group as the second car drew up. Betty looked around for the tray of canapés, but there was no sign of the houseboy. She sighed and called out to Moti before going out to welcome the Broughton-Smiths.

'George has probably told you that we've run into each other before.' Raphael was ushering Marina towards the sitting room. 'But we've been looking forward to meeting you. Our daughters have already turned us all into some kind of extended family. We're so happy you were able to join us.'

Camilla put down her glass and crossed the room to hug her father and kiss her mother lightly on the cheek. Betty sighed with relief. Raphael completed the introductions and mixed drinks.

'How do you do.' Marina's voice was light, her smile brilliant as she greeted the big African. She held her glass in one hand and smoothed the chiffon stole over her shoulders with the other, then took Dr Hayford's outstretched palm. 'What a magnificent costume. I've never seen anything quite like it. Is it something ceremonial you wear in your village? For special occasions, perhaps?'

George Broughton-Smith stepped forward in haste. Betty drew in her breath. She placed a hand on the Ghanaian's wrist and found herself clasping a heavy, gold watch strap.

'As a matter of fact, I've never lived in a village.' His response to Marina was amused. 'I was born in the city of Accra and I spent my early childhood there. So these are my town clothes. But you're quite right, this particular robe is for special occasions.'

'Hot and dusty and crowded, I believe. But I think there's much more to your life story than running about in Accra.' Marina was gazing at him, her mouth curving upwards, openly flirting with him.

'Ah yes. I was packed off to boarding school in England, and then on to London for my medical studies.'

'How perfectly wonderful. You must tell me about your hat too. The embroidery is so intricate. One could never find anything like that here on the east coast. Or at home. Come and sit beside me here on the sofa, Dr Hayford.' Marina took his arm. 'I want to hear all about your life. Not the gory medical part, of course, but your real life. Do you have a wife? Several perhaps, causing you concern and quarrelling over their status? And dozens of children, I imagine?'

'Oh God!' Camilla turned away, muttering to Sarah. 'She's probably had a few drinks.'

In the kitchen Betty found her staff unsmiling and fidgeting, eyes downcast.

'Is something the matter? Where's the tray with the—'

'Memsahib, we cannot serve the food.' Moti moved from one large foot to another, acutely uncomfortable.

'What's wrong with the food?' Betty's heart was hammering.

'Memsahib, the food is good.' The cook scratched his greying head. 'But we cannot serve this black man. It is not right.'

'What kind of *shauri* is this?' Betty felt panic rising. 'This man comes from another part of Africa, far away He is an important chief, a doctor just like Bwana Mackay.'

'He is a black man, memsahib. Our friends and families will laugh at us if we serve him.'

'That's ridiculous! Dr Hayford is our guest, just like the other guests here.' Betty glared at the old cook who had served her reliably for fifteen years, but he refused to meet her eye. 'Very well, Johannes. Is the meat in the oven? Good. We'll speak about this in the morning. You can all go to your quarters. Memsahib Sarah and I will look after the dinner.'

Betty turned on her heel and left the kitchen. Behind her she heard them murmuring uneasily and then the back door closed. Headlights swept the garden and the steps to the front door.

'Merciful God!' Betty murmured. 'I had a premonition that this evening would be some kind of nightmare. Sarah, a moment please?'

'What's wrong?'

'The staff won't serve Dr Hayford and I've sent them all to their quarters. Don't stand there gawping, dear. We'll have to organise the dinner ourselves. Can you get Tim to help, and Camilla too? Start with the canapés – they're long overdue. As soon as your father has introduced the van der Beers, I'll disappear to the kitchen. Thank God everything is just about ready.'

Raphael was already leading the Afrikaans family into the sitting room. Jan van der Beer was trying to disguise his astonishment at the sight of Dr Hayford. It was Lottie who took over, chatting easily, describing her small medical clinic for their staff. Hannah stood beside her mother, self-conscious in her evening gown, bemused by the unusual guest. Her blonde hair was neatly coiled into a chignon. Lottie had given her a necklace of seed pearls to wear, and she had a gold bangle that had been her Christmas present. Relief flooded through her when she saw Sarah beckoning.

'Crisis in the kitchen. Take this tray and offer it round. Camilla, you light all the candles while I help Mum to get the soup in place. And Tim can seat everyone when we're ready.'

'My dear, you must have spent all day in the kitchen.' Marina's smile flashed its way around the table and came to rest on Betty's harassed face.

'My cook was suddenly taken ill, I'm afraid.'

'And you stepped bravely into the breach.' Marina's eyebrows were raised in discreet surprise. 'I'm so impressed. I couldn't possibly cook and serve an entire dinner party without house staff. George – could you imagine me slaving away all day in the kitchen like that?'

'No, my dear. It's beyond my wildest imaginings.'

'It's just a matter of getting it to the table.' Betty was smiling desperately. She should never have placed Marina next to Jan van der Beer. So far, they had apparently found nothing to say to one another. At least the conversation between the other guests was animated, and there was laughter around the table.

'So you're the stalwart farmer.' Marina suddenly turned her attention to her left, as the soup was served. 'You look the part exactly – so rugged and tanned. I rather enjoyed farms when I was a child. As one does. But once I grew up I found them too messy, and one always had to wear heavy rain jackets and wellingtons. Even so, one ended up covered in mud. And the smell! One can't avoid that smell.' She put her hand on Jan's muscled arm and squeezed gently, leaning closer to him. 'All that time out of doors obviously keeps you very fit, though. So much more attractive than the pale, desk-bound people who are my usual dinner partners.'

'It's a good life. You just need determination.' Jan was unsure whether her comments were genuine or meant in some way to make fun of him. He would never understand these Englishers and their hidden codes.

'Your wife tells me your family has farmed here for several generations, Mr van der Beer?' Winston Hayford said. 'Will you stay on, now that the country is to become independent?'

'Langani is our home and our land,' Jan said deliberately. 'There was no one there when we came, and we've put almost three decades of hard work into it. I run a good farm and I look after my Kaf – my labour, very well. So we deserve to stay, and we will. Yes.'

'I believe there's a place here for people with faith and vision, and goodwill. I hope so,' George said. 'The Secretary of State is attempting a tricky balancing act, but I think we can provide a fair arrangement for most interests. We won't be able to please everyone, though.'

'You must find yourself in an increasingly difficult position, George.' The Ghanaian doctor smiled and Betty caught the glitter of gold teeth. 'Surely Her Majesty's government cannot expect to sort out the emotive issue of land, before Independence? And Kenya has the additional problem of the Indian population and their vast commercial enterprise. They seem to be much less popular than the white man.'

'I'm taking a break from the politics of Independence this week,' George said. 'It becomes a little wearisome from time to time. Right now I'm more interested in finishing a couple of thrillers, and spending a few days deep-sea fishing.'

'Now, this is a red wine from Spain – a Rioja.' Raphael's tone was overly jolly. 'Very palatable. Tim, perhaps you'll pour while I carve the meat.'

'But this time next year, it will all be over for you, sir.' Piet could not let the subject drop.

Lottie looked up, surprised. Sarah heard the determination in his voice and choked a little on her food. He seemed to her so brave, his face passionate in the candlelight, as he addressed the older men. Her heart was thumping and she put down her knife and fork to still her hands.

'I've no idea where I might be this time next year, young man.' George was visibly irritated.

'You'll be in some other embassy, sir. But we will still be here, trying to hold on to our land and to build a new country under the rules you left behind.'

'Piet, this isn't the time for a discussion about farming after Independence.' Lottie stared hard at her son and then turned to her husband for support. But Jan sat back in his chair, his expression proud as he regarded Piet.

'It's all right, Lottie,' George said. 'It's the younger generation, like your son, who have the responsibility of continuing here, if they can leave the old prejudices behind and see themselves as Kenyans first, regardless of their origins or colour.'

'But the priority is surely the future of indigenous Kenyans?' Dr Hayford said. 'Their politicians have made promises they cannot deliver. There are tribal loyalties that will not be easily resolved. In Ghana we have already discovered these pitfalls, and we are far from resolving them.'

'Kenyatta is doing a great deal to bring all the players together,' George said. 'His spirit of *Harambee* is not just a catchphrase – he seems able to make people believe in the possibility of integration. He's a remarkable man, and I think he'll prove a great statesman.'

'But he's a Kikuyu,' Raphael said. 'How will the other tribes, with their own scores to settle, fit into this process of sharing out parcels of land?'

'They are unlikely to behave like British gentlemen.' Dr Hayford's tone was sceptical. 'Many Africans will be too proud, too short-sighted, to accept advice on running small farms. New foreigners will come and tell them what to do, in place of the experts they already know.'

'Africans are already taking over key jobs in government, and in the commercial sector at every level,' Raphael pointed out. 'And there's the buyout scheme. Up to a million acres of land previously owned by the

European farming community – which will be divided up as small holdings for African farmers.'

'A crazy scheme that will destroy some of the most fertile land in the country,' Jan said. He felt the pressure of Lottie's foot under the table, but he was unable to contain himself. 'And we Afrikaners are caught, like the Asians, in a no man's land between the departing British and the natives. The only difference is that the Indians can go back to India, or to England with their new British passports if they wish.'

'I'm sure that ludicrous idea will be abandoned.' Marina's voice rose above the murmurs around the table. 'Thousands of Indians into Britain? It's out of the question. The country is too small, and it's far too cold. There wouldn't be any suitable work, and they'll simply hunker down and breed like rabbits. Next thing, we'll be overrun with—'

'I don't think you have an informed attitude on this subject, Marina.' Her husband was acutely embarrassed. 'It's a complex question that I certainly wouldn't want to explore this evening.'

'I don't see why you should try to silence me, George. I'm just as entitled to my opinion as anyone else. An honest exchange of views is so stimulating. Don't you think so, Dr Hayford?'

'Indeed I do, madam. I'm finding you most enlightening. And much more honest than anyone else I have met recently. Very refreshing.' He was smiling at Marina with open amusement.

There was a hiatus before a rush of small talk filled the void. Betty placed the dessert on the table and sank into her chair. Thank God, the dinner was almost over. She felt limp with exhaustion, as though she had been through an endurance test, or run a marathon. At least the food had arrived on the table piping hot and truly commendable. Now she was grateful for the distraction as her guests offered compliments on a vanilla mousse that was covered in crisp threads of spun toffee. Perhaps she could relax at last, and the conversation would settle at a manageable level. There would be coffee in the sitting room in a few moments, and the men would go to Raphael's study for brandy and cigars. What in the world had they always talked about before this political upheaval, she wondered. And would things ever be the same again? As Raphael rose to pour dessert wine into their glasses, Camilla suddenly spoke out. Her eyes were hard and bright. Just like her mother's, Betty thought.

'You said you'd look into the question of Langani Farm, though,

Daddy. You promised you'd see what could be done to help Jan and Lottie to stay on there.'

'I can't arrange special favours, Camilla.'

'But you promised,' she persisted, ignoring George's discomfort. 'So what have you managed to do, Daddy darling?'

Dr Hayford was leaning forward with a smile on the corner of his wide lips, intrigued by the predicament of the British diplomat.

'I think I'll discuss that with Jan and Lottie at some later date, if you don't mind, my dear.' George turned to address Jan directly. 'I gather you'll be down here for a few more days?'

'We will, yes. And if you have the time, I'd be glad to have a talk.'

Jan was more than willing to shelve the matter for the present. The atmosphere had become tense. He wondered where the Ghanaian doctor fitted into all this. It was difficult to understand why Raphael had invited a kaffir to dinner – even a well-educated one. The man was charming, but they were all the same, no matter where they'd been to school or what they were wearing. He could not envisage ever having a black man at his own dinner table.

They rose after the meal and the women made their way to Betty's dressing room beside the main bedroom. She could hear the men in the study, their voices cheerful and companionable.

'I think we've had enough talk about our uncharted future for one evening.' Betty stood at the open window and took several deep breaths to compose herself, but the air seemed heavy and dull and she felt no better when she turned back into the room. 'It seems that the old rule of no politics, sex, or religion at the dinner table is good advice.'

'Sex and religion might have been a better choice on this occasion. But it was a delicious dinner and one we won't forget.' Lottie put an arm around her hostess.

'Very original of you to have that extraordinary man from Nigeria.' Marina touched her already immaculate coiffure.

'Ghana, Mother. He was from Ghana.'

'Well, it's the same thing, darling, no matter what the outside trappings seem to be. I've never sat next to a black person at a dinner table before, not even in Nairobi. I had a perfectly lovely time. He's so open-minded and intelligent. It's quite astonishing to think he's a Fellow of the Royal College, and now he's been offered a consultant appointment in London.'

Marina's face was animated. 'I hope he didn't find our ideas too much removed from his own. He seems quite concerned about the development of this unfortunate place, when we leave.'

'Most of us support the idea of partnership, although that may be hard for you to understand.' Lottie could not disguise her antagonism. '*Harambee*, as the Mzee calls it.'

'You're quite right – it's totally beyond me. And I can't imagine why anyone would trust that dreadful old man,' Marina said. 'Until recently Kenyatta was just another terrorist we'd locked up. Now, suddenly, he's a celebrity, in full fancy dress with his ridiculous fly whisk and beaded hat, and that straggling beard. I hope you're not placing any great faith in *him*, my dear.'

'We might as well place our faith in him, since the British government seems quite willing to sell the farmers down the river, as far as we can see.' Lottie scraped back the stool in front of the dressing table and rose to her feet, no longer making any attempt to hide her anger.

'Ma, let's not go on with this. Not tonight. It's the beginning of our holiday. In a couple of days we'll be celebrating a new year, and I'm sure it will bring us all good fortune if we wish for it enough.' Hannah felt close to tears. She had never before been surrounded by currents like these, hostile and disruptive, carrying her parents and friends in uncharted directions.

'Let's go and join the men.' Betty opened the door on to the verandah and stood aside to let Marina Broughton-Smith past. The woman was insufferable. One came across people like that in books and films, but it was unbelievable that they actually existed. Betty wondered what could have happened to make her that way. It was impossible to imagine anyone being born with so much prejudice.

In the sitting room, the women stood in uneasy silence, no ripple of conversation breaking the chilly surface. Fishing seemed to be the neutral topic of conversation between the men, and Dr Hayford was describing the painted fishing boats of Ghana. Raphael thought he might lighten the atmosphere with a little music, and chose a record.

'Oh, how lovely – I adore Nat King Cole.' Marina turned to Dr Hayford. 'Only black singers have that sound that feels like warm treacle being poured over one. Would you like to dance with me, Winston?'

Lottie fixed a stern eye on Jan who had made an involuntary, hissing noise. Betty's hand flew up to her pearls and she was at a loss for suitable words until her husband held out his hand.

'And you, my dear. Will you come and dance with me? I know this is a favourite of yours.'

Bright headlights beamed through the long windows and Winston Hayford smiled regretfully. 'Ah. My car is here.' He lifted his embroidered cap from a small table and handed it to Marina. 'I'd like to offer you a small gift, madam. I hope it will remind you of this evening, and perhaps bring you to an understanding of my country and my continent one day.'

'How terribly kind.' She looked up at him, smiling a little and placing her hand over his. 'I shall look forward to your helping me, on that issue. If you are still here over New Year, perhaps you can join our celebrations? Dinner and dancing?'

'Ah – not this time, I fear.' His smile was wry. 'I think that day has not yet arrived. However, I hope we will dine and dance together on a future occasion. Under other circumstances, and a different flag perhaps. I will look forward to it. Goodnight to you all.'

Betty accompanied him to the door. 'We've never met Marina Broughton-Smith before. She seems a little unpredictable.'

'My dear lady, you and Raphael have been wonderful hosts. I thoroughly enjoyed my evening.' He paused, weighing his next words. 'Sometimes, when a beautiful woman carries a great deal of unhappiness with her, it adds to her mystique. One can only hope that she will find harmony one day. In the meantime she is only succeeding in hurting herself.' He smiled. 'Don't chastise your staff too much, Betty. Or your guests. Adjustment takes patience.'

'Interesting man. A wonderful example of the best that can happen, when our two cultures meet and learn from one another.' George Broughton-Smith sipped his brandy. 'I'd be happy to see more like him on the political benches in Nairobi.'

'In years to come, perhaps. After all, West Africans are very different people. More sophisticated and cultured.' Raphael had been unnerved by the political conversation in the Ghanaian's presence. Here in Kenya any subject with racial connotations was now a minefield, if there were Africans present. 'It's easy to believe that everything is in better order where he comes from, but corruption is a gigantic problem in West Africa.

In any case, he has abandoned his country and accepted an appointment in London for the next couple of years.'

'I think it's time we left, George, darling.' Marina had risen and was gliding towards the hall. 'Camilla, why don't you join us tomorrow night? We're going to celebrate New Year with our friends from the High Commission. I know you like Robert Harper, the PC's son. He'll be there, I'm sure.'

'I'm staying here, Mother. With my own friends.'

'Camilla, your mother deserves rather more—' George was looking at his daughter with something like despair.

'Oh, I expect we'll see her soon. Won't we Camilla, darling?' Marina's face had become white and strained. 'Unless you plan to spend all your time with your various surrogate parents.'

'We should make our way back to the beach house.' Lottie suddenly realised that this woman's twisted expression was a sign of jealousy. Jealousy, and anguish too. For a moment she was sorry for Marina. She signalled to her family, anxious to distance herself from the Broughton-Smiths and the fraught atmosphere that surrounded them. 'Betty and Raphael, thank you for a fine dinner. We'll see you tomorrow night.'

'Camilla?' George spoke her name urgently, pausing on the front steps.

'Don't worry, George, darling,' Marina said. 'Your little girl will be knocking on your door all too soon, pressing you for a discussion on her cause of the moment. For all the good it may do.' She turned to Jan. 'I'm sure you realise that my husband cannot afford to make representations on behalf of people with reputations like yours.'

'What does that mean, Mother?' Camilla stepped forward.

'That's enough, Marina. It's time we were leaving.' Her husband addressed her with barely concealed fury. He turned to hug his daughter briefly. 'We'll discuss this another time, Camilla.'

'Why don't you dispense with all these false hopes, George?' Marina ignored his warning. 'Tell them the truth.'

'What truth is that?' Piet was beside Sarah and she reached for his hand, but he moved away from her.

'Marina, we're leaving. Now.' George took her arm in an attempt to lead her down the steps and away from the group.

'I don't care to see you blamed for not humouring Camilla's naive little whim,' Marina said, removing her husband's hand and standing her ground, so that they were all trapped on the steps. 'These powerful new politicians aren't going to forget what happened during the bad old days. I've seen the blacklist that was in your study, George. You left the file open. Mr van der Beer knows very well what I'm talking about. He knows he can't stay on his farm after Independence. No matter what you do for him.'

'People like you don't know anything about the Mau Mau years,' Lottie said, shaking with anger. 'You weren't even in the country. You don't understand the hardship there was, the fear and the danger that we lived with.'

'Stop, Lottie,' Jan said. 'We have nothing to say to this woman.'

Marina ignored the interruption and addressed her daughter. 'There's no place for the white criminal class in the new Kenya, Camilla. I'm afraid you haven't selected very suitable surrogate parents, darling. You haven't made a good choice at all.'

Piet and Hannah were staring at their father. But Jan turned his back on them and strode away, hands deep in his pockets, shoulders hunched, head down. His family followed without a word. The Mackays waited in horrified silence as George took a firm hold of Marina's elbow and steered her to their car where she sat, staring ahead. Doors slammed and tyres crackled on the driveway. Then they were all gone, the headlights picking out the canopy of palm trees. Camilla was left standing alone in the beam of light that streamed out from the hallway. She looked at the frozen expressions that surrounded her, and then walked along the verandah to her bedroom.

Unable to contemplate sleep, Sarah followed. She tapped on Camilla's door, but there was no response, so she climbed the circular staircase that led to the roof terrace, a wide, tiled area overlooking the shipping channel. Vessels passed so close that you could make out every detail on deck, and she had often stood there with her parents, watching friends who were leaving Mombasa, their figures shrinking into sticklike silhouettes as they stood on the starboard side and waved. A slight noise made her turn round to see Tim appearing at the top of the stairs. He came to stand beside her.

'Couldn't sleep?' he asked.

'No. I can't stop wondering what she meant. I think Lottie knew, though. She brought up the subject of the Mau Mau right away, so maybe it's about that. I know Jan's brother was killed during the emergency. Up in the Aberdare forest.'

'That was a particularly savage time,' Tim said. 'People sometimes do desperate things when they're fighting for their lives, or their families, or to protect their property. The Mau Mau didn't kill that many Europeans, but those they did died in pretty barbaric circumstances. And many innocent Africans were terrorised. Forced to go through the sickening oathing ceremonies, or be maimed or killed. The Kikuyu massacred hundreds of their own people who wouldn't join them.'

'Langani was never attacked directly, although Jan left home for a while.

'Most of the farmers joined the King's African Rifles or the Special Forces, and went into the forests to hunt down the gangs. They covered themselves with animal grease and blackened their faces, and wore wigs. Pseudo gangs, they were called. They lived in mortal danger and semi-starvation for months on end, tracking down terrorist cells and wiping them out. I'm sure some of those chaps did go a little mad. God knows what Jan might have seen or done during those years.' Tim lit a cigarette.

'Give me one, please.'

'Smoking? Since when?'

'Everyone at school smoked occasionally. I just need one right now.' She dragged on the cigarette. 'I can't fathom why Marina would talk about the van der Beers like that. Why should she care what Jan might or might not have done, years ago? What's the point in hurting them? And Piet – did you see his face?'

'I think she's desperately jealous because Camilla is happier with people like us. Oh, God knows. She's a miserable, twisted bitch.'

'Poor Camilla,' Sarah's face was full of compassion.

'Camilla's a tough nut.' Tim said. 'She'll survive. It's Hannah who could be really affected. She's far more vulnerable. She's the one who needs your friendship most.'

Sarah looked at her brother in surprise. 'I thought you had the hots for Camilla.'

'Oh, I do. But she'd gobble me up and spit me out before I could take a breath. She's for – well, for lusting after. Not for fulfilment. But Hannah, now she's an Earth Mother type – much more promising.'

'Shall I tell her you said that?' Sarah had begun to chuckle. 'You're quite a wise old thing, it seems. And here was I thinking you were just my idiot brother.'

'Get thee to thy chambers, girl. We can't solve Africa's problems tonight. Hopefully our expedition tomorrow will make up for any unpleasantness. If Hannah and Piet are still planning to join us.'

In the guest room Camilla heard their muffled laughter and whispered goodnights as they passed her window. When silence enveloped her once more, she lay in her bed, watching the night shadows shift and sway. She was still awake when the first pink slivers of dawn touched the flat calm of the early-morning sea.

Chapter 5

Kenya, December 1962

The sun was high when they set off in Tim's ancient car, driving fast through the spiky lines of the sisal plantations until the tarmac gave way to a rutted, sandy surface.

'I feel rather mean, not spending New Year's Eve with our parents,' Sarah said. 'It's going to be full of nostalgia. But I agree with Tim and Piet – we should be looking to the future, not dwelling on the past.'

'Talking of the past, I'm sorry about Mother last night,' Camilla's face was calm, but her voice sounded unsteady.

'Forget it. Most parents have some things they don't want to discuss,' Piet said. 'Pa wouldn't say a word when we got back to the beach house, and Ma told us never to bring up last night's incident again.'

'But maybe it's something we ought to know about,' Hannah said.

'No. We should respect his wish. It sounds like he had a run in with the British government, and it's been recorded somewhere. But he's not the only farmer who's been in that position. Anyway, our friendship isn't based on our parents' lives – it's our own thing.'

'I suppose you're right,' Hannah said, doubtfully. 'They're a different generation and we can't spend our time thinking about what they did or didn't do.'

She was prevented from saying more as the car hit the dirt road with a spine-juddering leap. They opened the windows and sang at the tops of their voices. Further mention of the previous evening was, by tacit agreement, taboo. At Mida Creek they skirted the tidal mudflats, bright with birds and ringed by the mangrove trees that flourished in the brown water. There was a slight breeze and the air smelled of salt as they turned off the main road to reach the ruined city of Gedi.

'We can wander around first, and then have our picnic at the Sultan's

Palace,' said Tim. 'And when we've had enough of ghosts and ruins, we'll head down to the beach at Watamu. That sound OK?'

'Just as long as we're out of here by nightfall,' Sarah said

'Ah yes. A haunted city isn't the place for our Sarah after dark!' Camilla was teasing as Tim turned down the narrow track. 'I hear there are ghosts all over the place.'

'It's strange that it never appeared on the old Arab charts,' Tim said. 'A thriving city, but their closest neighbours were completely unaware of it. And no one knows to this day whether they were killed off by malaria, or hostile tribes, or if they just abandoned the place. Watch out for snakes and *siafu*, by the way – you don't want to walk into a line of those ants.'

'Lovely. It sounds so welcoming that I'm wondering why we're here.' Camilla was the first to step out of the car. The air was heavy with humidity, and carried the scent of decaying leaves from the jungle in which the ruins lay hidden. 'God, it's spooky. Even in the middle of the day.'

A wave of heat and silence enveloped them, broken only by the ticking of hot metal as the car engine cooled, and by the scream and chatter of monkeys in the branches overhead. The old city loomed out of the encroaching forest, sinister, mottled with mystery and rampant vegetation. Through the tangled undergrowth they saw the flash of sunbirds hovering over the bushes that had fastened themselves to the deserted buildings. It seemed like an invasion to enter this other world, and they walked slowly and in silence until they came to the area surrounding the former palace. The bare arms of the baobabs loomed over the forgotten dwellings, and the roots of lesser trees seemed to have grasped the ancient walls in a stranglehold, squeezing the last vestiges of life out of the crumbling stones.

The buildings peered through the greenery like silent watchers, their coral walls and carved tracery looking out as a woman in purdah might watch the world from behind her veil, revealing only tantalising glimpses of her hidden presence. Three pillar tombs stood sentinel, close to the remains of the Great Mosque and the Sultan's Palace whose windows gaped open, sightless and unresisting.

'Man, what a place!' Piet gave a long whistle, staring through overgrown avenues that disappeared into a wall of impenetrable foliage. 'I feel like an interloper. Like we have no right to disturb its dreaming.'

'My goodness, Piet!' Camilla looked up into his face, smiling. 'I didn't know you had the soul of a romantic. You're as bad as Sarah with her mystical pronouncements.'

'You could discover all kinds of things about me, Camilla, if you wanted to. If you took the time.'

'It's too hot to go any further. Let's open the picnic box and have a cold drink, and something to eat.' Sarah's voice sounded strained, even to her own ears.

They sat down in the grassy shade of the Sultan's Palace. There was cold chicken and salad, fresh bread rolls, neat twists of paper filled with salt and pepper, and ice-cold beer from the cool box, with lemonade to make shandy.

'Beer never tasted so good.' Hannah leaned against the old stones, eyes closed, and took a long draught from her glass. 'I hope the Sultan isn't watching too closely. He wouldn't be pleased to see women with their heads uncovered, legs and arms on display, and drinking alcohol in his rooms. Can't you feel him stirring in his grave?'

'I'd say we'd have been chased off already if he was that unhappy.' Tim was attacking his beer and chicken drumstick with enthusiasm.

'Chased off by whom?' Camilla said.

'The people who lived here used to bury a clay jar in the doorway of the house, with a written spell inside to attract a powerful spirit. Then a djinn would take up residence in the jar and protect the house from enemies.' Tim smiled. 'If the Sultan's djinn was angry with you, he'd have hurled you out already, or made you choke on your lunch maybe.'

'Or sent a mamba to strike you down with its venom,' said Piet. 'Like that one!'

He leapt to his feet, pointing into a dark corner. Hannah screamed as a mottled green snake slithered across the ground in front of them, its body iridescent in the patches of sunlight.

Piet gave a whoop of laughter. 'Silly! Don't you recognise a harmless grass snake when you see one? Some tracker you've turned out to be!'

Camilla looked at him severely. 'Don't tease your sister like that. You gave me the fright of my life too.'

'Sorry.' Piet still had the light of mischief in his eyes. He turned to Sarah, who was looking out at the ruined monuments and tombs, dappled by trees and flowering lianas.

'You're very quiet. What are you thinking?'

'John Masefield's poem,' she said dreamily 'I can't remember the name of it, but he could have written it about this place.

> 'Like bones the ruins of the cities stand,
> Like skeletons and skulls with ribs and eyes
> Strewn in the saltness of the desert sand,
> Carved with the unread record of King's lies.
> Once they were strong with soldiers, loud with voices,
> The markets clattered as the carts drove through,
> Where now the jackal in the moon rejoices
> And the still asp draws death along the dew.'

There was a long silence when she had finished reciting. Hannah shivered slightly.

'I wonder what really drove them away. Why they would have left all this.' It was Camilla who broke the spell.

'Perhaps, in the end, life became too fraught with hardship and danger, and they simply gave up,' Tim said.

'Leaving everything they had worked for and struggled to create, to be swallowed up by the forest and crumble away into nothing.' Piet's voice was full of sadness. 'That's been the story of Africa, hasn't it? People with no idea how to use the land drove out the previous tribes. Until we came, no one really cared about the soil.' He jumped up, ramming his fists into his pockets. 'But I won't allow a bunch of greedy politicians to steal our farm, or drive us out. Man, I don't care if they're Africans or British, black or white or bright green. No one is going to take away my right to remain here, in the country where I was born.' He stopped, embarrassed by the astonishment his outburst had caused. 'I think I'll go for a walk,' he muttered, and strode off, touching the crumbling lintel of the carved doorway as he stepped through it, in a gesture of homage and regret.

'Piet!' Camilla rose in a fluid movement. 'Wait for me. I'll come with you, if you're going to explore.'

Hannah, looking up, saw the expression on Sarah's face. 'No, Camilla. He needs a few moments on his own.'

'Well, I'm going for a stroll.' Sarah cursed herself for trotting out the stupid quotation that had sparked Piet's outburst. What had she been thinking of? Trying to impress him with her literary knowledge, because Camilla had said he had the soul of a romantic. 'I'm going to take a few photographs. Just to disprove the myth that film comes up blank when you try and develop pictures of Gedi.'

She picked up her camera and set off along one of the forest paths, taking care not to go in the same direction as Piet. At first she felt uneasy, but after a while she began to mimic the bird calls and enjoy their reactions. She wandered to the limits of the empty houses, the forest growing denser as she walked. At last she came to an open space where the ruins of two buildings stood side by side, with a great stone well in front of them.

She stopped, feeling a prickling sensation on the back of her neck, as though she were being watched. There was a curious smell in the glade, sweetish and sickly, and she could hear a buzzing noise. Wary now, for she had gone a considerable distance from the picnic site without thinking, she moved forward cautiously. On the far side of the well the ground had been cleared, and she could see a black mound that heaved and swayed as she approached. She drew nearer and the smell caught her throat, making her retch. A moving carpet of flies, bloated and lumbering, rose into the air around her, revealing the thing on which they had been feeding. She screamed.

It was a young goat, pegged out on the ground, its belly slit from end to end, entrails glistening, blood seeping into the depression in the ground where it had been laid. In horror, she realised that it was still alive. Desperate, shuddering breaths jerked its body and she saw that its eyes were turning milky as life ebbed away. Staring at it, Sarah felt the world go dark around her. Then she was standing in another place, and the bleeding, quivering creature on the ground was a man, lying helpless and groaning, his face looking away from her as he struggled to stem the gush of blood from his wounds. A panga had slashed again and again across his body, slicing through his chest and arms and legs, ripping his belly apart. She screamed in horror as the torn, bloody remains of his head turned to her in supplication, and she saw that where his eyes should have been there were only empty sockets. She gagged, turned and tried to flee, but her legs were giving way, and she could hear people running towards her, hands grabbing at her as she struggled to escape. Then she became aware of Piet's voice, and Tim holding her as she collapsed on to her knees and was violently sick.

'It's all right, old girl. All over now. Not a pretty sight to come across.' Tim was supporting her head as she tried to say something about the goat.

'It was pretty horrible.' Piet was kneeling beside her. 'I've put the poor thing out of its misery.'

'I don't know if you should have done that,' Tim said, glancing over his shoulder. 'This forest is a sacred site, you know. It's often used for ritual sacrifices and stuff. That's what this is all about, probably. Part of an exorcism, or some such ceremony. An evil spirit is transferred from a person into a goat, and then the animal is sacrificed – slit open to drain the spirit's power into sacred ground. The animal has to be alive for the blood to flow.'

'Ugh! It's so barbaric!' Camilla was staring, white-faced, at the grisly remains. She backed away as the flies rose again. 'No wonder you were screaming your lungs out, Sarah. I would have fainted dead away.'

'You shouldn't go wandering into the *bundu* on your own like that.' Tim studied his sister's pale face and the fear still in her eyes. 'There are elephant around here, you know, and the odd buffalo who wouldn't hesitate to protect his territory.'

'I think we should make a move.' Piet held out a hand to help her up. 'The people who did this are quite likely to come back. You didn't see anyone on the path, did you? Or hear anything?'

Sarah remembered the uneasy sensation she had experienced of being watched. But that was probably her own overwrought imagination. She shook her head. 'No. Nobody,' she said.

'Let's be off, then.' Tim took out a large handkerchief and wiped her face and hands. 'Feeling better?'

'I'm fine,' she said, keeping her gaze away from the dead animal. 'Sorry about the almighty fuss. I can't think what came over me.'

She shuddered, trying not to dwell on the horrible transference from sacrificial beast into man for those few terrifying seconds. Chiding herself for her foolishness, she walked slowly back to the car, with Hannah's firm, guiding hand on her arm. She heaved a sigh of relief as they drove away.

'You know, they say that the headlights of motorists who visit Gedi at night will suddenly fail for no reason. Leaving you sitting alone out there, in the dark.' She tried a laugh.

'The Sultan's djinn on the trail, no doubt,' Tim picked up on her attempt to lighten the atmosphere.

Hannah stirred in the back seat. 'Let's say goodbye to the subject of Gedi. I've had enough of those old ghosts that are lurking everywhere,' she said.

'What about some snorkelling at Watamu?' Tim said. 'Before we get our tents organised.'

'Sounds divine,' Camilla said. 'And then we'll head for the Turtle Club and dance until we've worn the soles of our feet away. Speed up, Tim. I'm ready for tropical seas and food and starlight.'

When Sarah woke again the car had come to a stop. In front of her, bands of turquoise and cobalt water shimmered under a cloudless sky. The wind whispered in the casuarina trees and the tide was high. Within moments, they were in the lagoon, diving down into the cool of the ocean, washing away dust and fatigue and uneasy dreams. Shoals of small fish swam beside them, their dazzling colours like jewels in the clear water. Further from the shore they found the first of the coral gardens. An hour passed and then two, as they drifted in the silent beauty of another world, free from notions of envy and destruction, or voices raised in anger. At last they signalled to one another and swam back to the shallow water on the edge of the beach.

'Magical, it is. There's nothing more beautiful in the world,' Tim said as he surfaced, his face a crinkle of smiles as he shook the water from his wiry hair. 'It's a fantasy place, filled with blessed silence and weightlessness and peace.'

Hannah lay back in the water, trailing her fingers in the lap of the waves, tracing lines on sand ripples. He is so like Sarah, she thought. They are both constantly moved and swayed by the blur and beauty and frailty of passing humanity. She had loved being in the blue-green sea with Tim Mackay, swimming, diving down alongside him to reach the coral beds, moving effortlessly with the current. 'I'd rather be weightless under the water than floating in space,' she said.

'Where's your sense of adventure, Sis?' Piet rolled over on to his stomach, closer to Camilla.

'Firmly rooted on this earth. In this sand. On our farm. But maybe I'll go to the moon on my holidays, when I'm an old lady. If the Americans or the Russians really do get there in the meantime.'

'You might have to rethink all that, if Pa decides to leave Langani,' Piet said, and Hannah's exclamation made everyone look at her.

'Well, I'm staying. And so are you.' Hannah delivered her words with a ferocity that surprised her brother. 'You said it yourself. This is our home and our country. We're staying.'

'Oh come on, you two!' Sarah dug anxious fingers into the sand. 'We'll all be here after Independence. One way or another we'll be back from whatever we're doing. I know we'll all end up here – even you, Camilla. This country will never let us go.'

'She's off again.' Camilla raised herself on one elbow. 'But I suppose we can be grateful for one of her more cheerful predictions. She's right, though. I can't imagine not ever coming back here. No matter what I do, it's always going to be a part of me, this country.'

'Well, I'm more interested in the immediate future.' Tim stood up and reached for his clothes. 'We've had the best of the sun and we have to rig up the tents. After that it will be time for a cold beer and a shower. And then food and dancing.'

The Turtle Club was packed with up-country families who had come down to the coast on holiday. The place vibrated with noise and laughter, and the gurgle and clink of glasses being poured and raised. Tim counted out the contents of all their purses and wallets and ordered fresh lobsters and cold white wine. Friends came over and invited them to make up part of a larger group, but they deliberately avoided the general mêlée. They were halfway through dinner when Camilla felt two hands covering her eyes, and heard Piet's exclamation.

'Anthony! Man, it's good to see you. How come you're not out in the *bundu*?'

'Clients took a break in Nairobi, just as I expected. So I drove down here. I knew I'd be sure to bump into some *rafikis*.' Anthony Chapman was talking to Piet, but his eyes were fixed on Camilla. 'Can I join this exclusive little group?' He sat down and ordered more wine. 'And here's the future zoologist, surrounded by strange specimens ripe for study. Or would you rather come and dance with me, Sarah?'

She nodded and smiled, but as she turned towards the dance floor she saw Piet sliding an arm around Camilla's waist, leaning across to whisper something in her ear. Sarah's stomach cramped and she tried in vain to concentrate on what Anthony was saying, as he led her into the heart of the crowd and their table was lost from view. When they returned to their small group, Piet stood up and held out his hand to Camilla, but Anthony reached her first and spun her away. For a moment Piet hesitated. Then he pulled Sarah on to the floor where he began to move in a series of wild gyrations, twisting and reeling and turning, laughing and hooting, so that she started to feel dizzy and extremely hot. Then the music slowed and he drew her close to him. She leaned against him, painfully aware of the fact that a trickle of sweat was running down her face from her hairline, willing herself to calm down, to take in a few breaths of the cool sea air. She wanted to drift away with him, out on to the beach where there was no music other than the unceasing sea. But as the melody ended he grinned down at her, touched her cheek and brought her back to the table where she found herself swooping between euphoria and regret. As midnight approached, there was champagne on every table. Toasts were already being made as the music stopped.

'I've seen in many a New Year here, with my *rafikis*, and I've never been tempted to make or encourage speeches.' The owner of the Turtle Club had jumped on to a table on the edge of the verandah. 'But tonight is different for all of us. Tonight is the last New Year's Eve under the good old British, and this time next year we'll be living in an independent Kenya, under a different flag. So tonight we'll raise our glasses to all that has gone before. We'll drink to those who made this wonderful country what it is, and to those who have the courage to stay on and work towards a bright future. Many of you are in this room tonight.' He raised his glass, standing above the crowd, and looked around at the hopeful faces before making his toast. 'To the great country that has guided us all to this moment in our history. God Save the Queen, God bless Kenya, and all of us.'

A lone voice began to sing the first words of the national anthem, and after the first tentative notes the crowd joined in, until the swell of the music rose up through the palm thatched roof and out over the ocean. People crossed the room to embrace each other with optimism or regret, to offer words of hope, to proclaim a determination to stay or a resolution to move on to new and unknown lives. Streamers flew through the air as the countdown to midnight began. Whistles blew, the chanting grew louder and louder, and circles of dancers formed on the floor, jostling and laughing as midnight struck and the band played 'Auld Lang Syne'.

It was Piet who beckoned them away from the heaving crowd and out on to the beach. They walked along the edge of the water, distancing themselves from the lights and the music, until there was nothing to be heard or seen except the soft splash of waves, and a ribbon of moonlight stretching and flickering all the way to the horizon. Anthony took off his shirt and slacks and plunged into the sea. Piet followed him, flinging his clothes on the sand and soon they were all floating in the water, ringed by the glitter of phosphorescence and reflected starlight.

'So what are your plans for tomorrow? Are you all staying on a few days?' Anthony said.

'No. We're driving back to Mombasa in the morning. For us it's home to Langani in a couple of days,' Piet said. 'Tim goes back to his medical studies in Ireland next week, taking Sarah off to Dublin.'

'What about you, Camilla?' Anthony put his hands around her ankles, and pulled her towards him in the water. 'You don't have to leave right away, do you?'

'We're all leaving together,' Piet's response was sharp. 'Camilla's staying with the Mackays.'

'Lucky Mackays,' Anthony said lightly.

'Let's not go back at all.' Hannah's words were apprehensive. 'Let's make our lives together, starting right here and now. We'll open a simple bar and some thatched cottages to rent. The country will keep us captive, as Sarah says. But away from quarrels, and fears about the new government, and all the changes that are looming.'

'No.' Sarah was definite. 'It isn't time. We should plan to return here, though. We'll come back, no matter what, during the year that the three of us turn twenty-one. And we'll stay at Piet's new lodge, maybe go on safari together, and spend some time down here at the coast.'

'I'll subscribe to that idea,' Anthony said. 'And if Piet is going to entertain you at his lodge, then I'll organise the safari part.' He looked at Camilla. 'You said you'd come on safari with me, when you're rich and famous. Remember?'

'It's getting chilly in this water,' Piet said. 'Come with me, Lady Camilla. I'll fix up a lantern for your tent. Make sure you don't set the place on fire.'

There was a brief silence. Then Camilla laughed.

'I'll make do with the moonlight. I just need my beauty sleep, even if it's in a space barely large enough for a sardine.'

'You can dream about the opulent tents, with chandeliers and silk carpets and bathrooms, that I'm going to create for your great reunion safari,' Anthony said.

'I agree it's time for bed,' Tim made an attempt to defuse the growing tension. 'Piet, we should go and sort out water and lanterns for the tents. You girls can follow us up in a few minutes. Where are you staying, Anthony?'

'I'm down the road – bunking with some friends who have a house. Happy New Year, everyone. I'll see you around. Soon, I hope.' Anthony walked away down the beach, heading towards the distant light and noise of the Turtle Club.

'What a wonderful night this has been,' Sarah said. 'It's hard to let it go, not knowing where we'll all be even in a few days' time.'

'Let's make a promise,' Hannah said. 'A solemn promise like before. That we'll come back here together, when we turn twenty-one.'

'I'll promise.' Camilla held out both hands. 'We'll all promise. Won't we?'

They knelt in a circle on the sand, surrounded by the ripple and swirl of the dark, star-spattered ocean and embraced one another, laughing at the brightness of the future, and the achievements they would relate to one another in the heady days of their reunion.

Chapter 6

London, November 1964

Camilla awoke to a shrill chorus of birds. Not the whistle of robin chats or the low crooning of doves that heralded each Kenya morning. Here the birds you could see were mainly crows, black and raucous, shrieking at the leaden sky from their perches on telephone wires and bare trees. In Italy there had been sunshine, and a glorious extravagance of landscape and architecture. Her father had been posted to the embassy in Rome for a year and she spent a great deal of time with him, exploring the ancient streets and monuments of Italian cities, walking in the Tuscan hills, gliding through the canals of Venice. At his insistence she had taken the art-history course in Florence and had enjoyed it. But now they were all back in London, and she counted the days to the completion of the obligatory secretarial course, and longed for the freedom to live another kind of life.

At least they were close to the park. Everyone told her how fortunate she was to live a stone's throw away from its grassy spaces and rain-washed trees, and Camilla walked there every day. Her mother proclaimed frequently on the perfect location of their flat, although she was rarely to be found there. Marina's diary was largely taken up with lunches, bridge parties or the organisation of charity events. Camilla found that she was happy with her own company, and she could not envisage any close friendships that might compare to the bond she shared with Sarah and Hannah. Letter writing did not come easily to her, but she sent regular postcards with breezy messages on the back, and gifts from each new place that she visited. She did not think her friends would understand the sense of isolation she felt in London, her inability to belong to any of the groups of people her mother approved of, and she detested Marina's obsession with London's social hierarchy.

Her father had returned to the Africa Desk in the Foreign Office, and he still regularly travelled between London and Nairobi. When he was not abroad he seemed to be caught up in late-night meetings at Whitehall. He remained a key player in complex negotiations between the British and Kenyan governments, as they drew up the new constitution that would turn Kenya into a republic. Camilla had heard him on the telephone, discussing the contentious problem of the Asian community and their right to live in Britain. In Parliament, Enoch Powell was strident in his opposition to unrestricted immigration, and the press was full of emotional rhetoric on the subject. Many white farmers in Kenya still ridiculed the land redistribution scheme, claiming that vast tracts of the country's most fertile territory would be destroyed by ignorance and mismanagement. There were angry accusations that the British government, in its haste to hand over the former colony, had abandoned the very people who had made the country prosperous. When Camilla had brought up the subject of the van der Beers, her father's reaction was brusque.

'They chose to join the exodus to Rhodesia, my dear, so that their son could start afresh. Now it's up to your young friend to make a go of it.'

'They'd never have left, if it hadn't been for Mother's outburst,' Camilla said. 'And you've never explained what that was all about.'

'You know I can't discuss sensitive information.'

'So sensitive that she had access to it?'

'Jan van der Beer made an unselfish choice for his son's sake. As a result Piet should do well, if he keeps his head and works hard,' George said. 'It was probably best that it worked out this way.'

'How can you say that? They hate Rhodesia. And it can't be a good place to start again, with Ian Smith, and all the confusion and bitterness about Independence and votes for Africans. You needn't look so surprised, Daddy. I read everything I can about it, because of Hannah being down there in all that mess.'

'The most Important thing to remember, my dear, is that young people like Piet have a perfectly good chance of succeeding. Jomo Kenyatta has given strong assurances that there's room for everyone to work together.'

'I wish I'd been there, at the *Uhuru* ceremonies,' Camilla said. 'Seen it all happening.'

'It was an emotional event. The Mzee in all his tribal finery, and the Duke of Edinburgh and the Governor with their swords and plumes.'

George smiled over his reminiscences. 'Kenyatta and Prince Philip were driven to the ceremony through a series of side roads, to avoid being held up by the crowds. But the plan backfired, because their car got stuck in the mud, and they were half an hour late! I saw former Mau Mau leaders at one function, wearing some sort of military-style uniform, with long matted hair hanging down their backs. And there they were, standing around on the Government House lawns, with the politicians and embassy people all dressed up to the nines. The so-called Mau Mau generals shook hands with all kinds of high-ranking foreigners and their wives, as though they'd been at it for years. But they didn't get a royal handshake. Kenyatta himself tactfully headed them off, and avoided any diplomatic gaffes. Wise old bird, he is. It was generally a happy occasion, and very moving. Astonishing really, the enormous goodwill that carried it through.'

'I wish we'd stayed in Kenya,' Camilla said. 'It was the only place I ever thought of as home. It's where my real friends are. I'd love to be planning Christmas holidays at the coast, or going up to Langani. Has it changed?'

'Not yet. I think most people who had the guts and the faith to stay on will be happy with their decision, in the long term. And young Piet has as good an opportunity as anyone.'

'That still doesn't excuse what Mother did.'

'There were a number of people with access to the file your mother found on my desk. Anyone could have brought the case to light. It's not a straightforward matter. Even at the time the lines were blurred.'

'What matter?' Camilla demanded, but George shook his head.

'Tell me, how is Hannah getting on? What is she doing?' It was clear that he would not be drawn any further into a discussion about Jan.

'I haven't heard from her for a while. My fault. I'm not good at letter writing.'

'You should make the effort,' George said. 'She must be especially anxious to keep in touch with you and Sarah, after all the changes in her life.'

'What could I say to her?' Camilla said, angry and defensive. 'It was my mother who caused the upheaval that landed Hannah in some Rhodesian dorp that she hates. It was dear Marina who destroyed their future at Langani. What can I say that will make any difference now?'

'It wasn't your fault, my dear,' he said. 'You shouldn't use the misplaced idea of guilt as an excuse not to stay in touch. Those two girls have been like sisters to you over the years. No one can afford to throw away friendship like that. And I'm sure the van der Beers feel nothing but affection for you.'

'You don't know that at all,' said Camilla. 'You can't even begin to understand what this move has done to them. And you obviously don't understand what I feel about it either.'

'Your mother made an unfortunate mistake that night.' George's expression was bleak. 'She was jealous and unhappy, and—'

'An unfortunate mistake?' Camilla's frustration exploded into the room. 'I don't know why you always have to protect her. Why can't you see Mother as she really is? Why don't you get a divorce, Daddy?' She saw her father recoil, stepping back to distance himself from her, but she could not stop. 'You're not happy together, and she's angry and bitter all the time. She'd be better off on her own, and then you could get on with—'

'Camilla, that is a matter for your mother and me, and no one else.' George turned abruptly, his face stony. He reached for his car keys and opened the front door to let in the sullen London morning. Then he hesitated and swung round to embrace his daughter, making an attempt at a smile. 'I won't be back until very late, and tomorrow is going to be a bugger of a day. But we'll do something together at the weekend.'

They had not discussed the thorny issue of the van der Beers since that day. Camilla did not want to argue with her father, and she avoided any subject that might spoil the precious hours they spent together. She thought about him now, as she peered through the speckle and splash of rain on the window panes. The damp air had crept into her bedroom during the night, and she shivered as she pulled down the sash window, blocking out the noise and fumes of the morning traffic. Her head ached from the cocktails and the number of cigarettes she had smoked at last night's party, and she had no idea what time she had got home. She wondered if George had gone to the office. It was Saturday, but he often worked at weekends. If he was still in the house, they might have some breakfast together, and that would make a good start to the day. But there was no sign of him in the drawing room. Disappointed, she made her way into the kitchen and put on the kettle. She pushed a slice of bread into the toaster with unnecessary force, and searched the fridge for butter and jam, and some milk. The kettle gave off a high-pitched whistle that drilled into her aching head. She snatched it up to pour boiling water over the tea leaves, and splashed some on her hand, swearing out loud in pain. Upstairs Marina was still asleep and would probably not rise until noon. Well, it didn't matter. The last thing Camilla wanted was a pointless exchange with her mother, on the social possibilities of the weekend.

All she needed to do now was to get through the last weeks of her course. She had mastered the tedium of shorthand and typing, and her French was fluent. There had been superficial lectures on English literature, on the history of art, on table settings and soufflé-making. She had sat through them all, almost in a trance. Her peers were largely concerned with obtaining invitations to the most desirable parties in London, and spending weekends in draughty mansions in the country where suitable marriage prospects could be advanced. Camilla had little in common with them, but she threw herself into all that London had to offer, disappointing and then enraging her mother in her choice of companions.

'You're going around with the most unsuitable people, Camilla.' Marina had looked her daughter up and down with distaste. 'And those clothes are quite dreadful. Vulgar and cheap, and badly made. You look like a shop girl.'

'Maybe that's what I'm aiming to be. You no longer have to be rich, or brought up in some upper-middle-class home, to be acceptable. A cockney barrow boy or a shop girl are just as likely to be the toast of the town as a duchess. And although they may not talk or dress the way you do, my friends are artists and writers and people with something fresh to say. The world is changing, Mother. We're a new generation with different values from yours, and we don't have to hide behind a wall of bigotry. You can't imagine how grateful I am for that.'

'Don't be ridiculous, Camilla. You belong in a certain level of society because you were fortunate enough to be born into it. You should be extremely grateful for that.'

'Your rules about class and money and possessions will soon be history, thank God.' Camilla applied a line of kohl around her eyes and pulled a knitted hat down over her hair. 'In the meantime I'm off to the cinema.'

'You're only harming yourself with this childish attitude.' Marina sighed. 'Your reputation is the only thing you have, Camilla, and once you lose it you'll never get it back. Your cockney barrow boys would be only too delighted to see people like us destroy ourselves. I can only hope you'll grow out of all this nonsense, if we can be patient for long enough.'

When she was not in class, Camilla spent her time at plays and films, where she could sit for hours studying the expressions and gestures of the actors in whose steps she hoped to follow. She gorged herself on art and music of every kind, soaking up the diversity of London's cultural offerings, trailing through museums, frequenting concert halls and cinemas. At night she danced in noisy clubs where she drank vodka and smoked, drifting through hazy hours of marijuana and strange, disconnected conversations in dingy basements. The city's manic energy and sense of change swept through her, filling her with defiance, drawing her into a vortex of activity that lasted round the clock. But even in the midst of a crowd, where she was often the centre of attention, she remained an observer, an outsider in a frenzied world that did not really move her.

She combed the new boutiques of Carnaby Street and the King's Road, returning home with thigh-high leather boots, short skirts and bell-bottom trousers, or Indian garments embroidered with beads and feathers. Battles ensued as she discarded the cashmere sweaters, pearls and silk scarves that Marina hoped her daughter would eventually wear for her engagement portrait in *Country Life*. At the Lucie Clayton School she learned to apply make-up professionally, and to move like a fashion model on the catwalk – a kind of swaying motion with hips protruding forward and a pout on her lips that came naturally. The school said she had a face and figure that was ideal for the camera. They said she could wind up on the cover of a glossy magazine.

At first Camilla resisted the idea, afraid that it would distract her from her goal of a life in the theatre. But finally she agreed to pose for a fashion photographer she had met in a nightclub. Ricky Lane had stared at her across the room and then approached her, holding out a drink decorated with a paper umbrella and a smoking volcano. She had seen his photographs and she liked his infectious smile and his cockney accent. He promised to show the results of their session to a leading model agency, and he was optimistic.

'Come on, darlin',' he said, grinning at her. 'You ain't going straight to stardom on the overnight express. With a face and a body like that, you can make a mint to tide you through the gaps. A few bob in your piggy bank will make all the difference on the way to fame. I might even be asking to borrow a quid or two.'

The practical side of her recognised that an acting career might bring periods without work. Resting, everyone called it. It would be better to fill in as a model, than to work in some grubby café as a waitress. She had already been recalled for a second audition at the drama school, and she was certain that she had made a good impression. An acceptance letter would come soon. In the meantime, modelling would be a useful sideline, and it wouldn't matter if she was not successful at it. She was nervous, however, when she arrived at Ricky Lane's studio. The room was cold and ugly and smelled of stale cigarettes. Her body felt wooden as she turned towards the glare of the lights and the camera. But as he called out to her from behind his tripod, she began to understand his requirements. He had loud music on the record player, and she immersed herself gradually in its rhythm, mouthing the words of the song as she turned and posed and smiled and pouted, moving her head so that her hair swung out in a halo around her face. She could tell that he was pleased as he came towards her with the camera, tilting it from side to side, clicking faster, his voice rising in excitement.

'Blimey! You're a natural. I knew it! I bloody knew it! We're going to do great things together, darlin' – mark my words. Now turn back to me. Away again. Take down that strap and look over your shoulder like you want to bring me on. Yeah – this is it, Princess Camilla. This is it!'

But several weeks went by after the session and she heard nothing from him. As Christmas approached, she was filled with a terrible loneliness and dejection that she could not overcome. She posted cards and presents to Hannah and Sarah, and wondered when she might see them again. If ever. On weekends she chose to spend her time alone, lying in bed with the curtains drawn, blocking out the dismal light that made her long for the wide, sunlit plains and warm seas of her childhood. She began to enjoy her own melancholy, sinking deeper into sadness and lethargy. Marina knocked on her bedroom door with proposals for a shopping spree or lunch. Her father suggested a weekend visit to Scotland or Paris. But nothing appealed to Camilla, and she was approaching despair when the phone call came from Sarah. Betty and Raphael Mackay were in Ireland on leave, and they had rented a house in the Wicklow Mountains. Would Camilla like to come for Christmas? Her stupor was replaced by a bubbling energy, and she rushed out to the travel agent, and to shop for more presents.

'But we're all going to the ball at the Dorchester. The table is arranged. And so is Scotland for New Year. Please don't do this, Camilla. It's utterly selfish, and it puts us in such an embarrassing situation at the last minute.' Marina tried persuasion, then fury, and finally tears. George retreated to his study. But Camilla held fast. She had bought her ticket to Dublin, and now she counted the days.

As the plane descended, she looked down over the network of emerald fields that surrounded Dublin's sprawl, enjoying the fluttering anticipation in her stomach. Even the sullen toss of grey waves and the slow spirals of chimney smoke pleased her, as the aircraft bumped down on to the runway. She was alive again, and surprised by the childlike excitement and pleasure that coursed through her. Sarah was at the arrivals gate, wrapped in a shapeless woollen coat and a long scarf, her hair blown into a frizz by the wet wind. Tim stood beside her, drawn and tired but grinning with unabashed delight, his wire-rimmed glasses slipping down his nose as he hugged Camilla, crushing the breath out of her slight body.

'Too skinny. Guinness and mashed potatoes every hour on the hour. That's doctor's orders for you, my girl.'

'You look perfectly dreadful yourself. I'd hate to be sick unto death and find you leaning over me like a veritable Grim Reaper.'

'It's called making the juniors work for their pennies. This will be my first weekend off for a hundred years, I think. Jaysus, what have you got in the suitcase? I should have done a weightlifting course.'

Camilla tucked her arm into Sarah's copious sleeve and squeezed. 'You've saved my life. Another day over there and I would have killed myself. And deprived the world of my budding genius.'

'There's nothing exciting going on here over Christmas. We're done with visiting the relatives scattered all over the country, thank God. So there's just ourselves and Tim's latest conquest.' Sarah lowered her voice as Tim heaved the luggage into the boot. 'A little blonde nursey, all scrubbed and rosy. She must be very warm and cuddly on a winter's night, though, because I don't know what else he—'

'I may be half blind with exhaustion, but I'm not deaf, Sarah. We do not need a preview of Deirdre.'

'I can see she's made a great impression on Sarah.' Camilla turned an enquiring gaze on Tim who was scarlet with annoyance. 'I thought you preferred the dark, dangerous type, Timmy darling. I hope you're not becoming a decent Catholic boy, looking for someone to share a semi with and produce a large brood.'

'Right now, I'm looking for a way of strangling my sister and disposing of her remains.'

Camilla awoke on the following morning light in spirit, all anxiety and resentment vanished. She was free and she was on holiday. It was like coming home, after a very long time, to the family and friends she valued most. Outside, the sky was impossibly blue and the fields glittered with frost. In the distance the sea rimmed the horizon with a thin band of silver. She spent the day with Betty and Sarah in the kitchen, preparing the turkey and stuffing, making brandy butter and mince pies. In the evening they sat by the fire, wrapping gifts and exchanging stories. After dinner everyone struggled into warm coats and thick, hand-knitted scarves, and made their way into the village where church bells were peeling out the call to midnight mass. In the small church Sarah's clear, pure voice sang the familiar hymns and carols that they had sung together at school, and Camilla tried to overcome the catch in her own throat and the threat of tears as she joined the canticles of joy and praise.

On Christmas Day they were grouped around the log fire when Tim arrived with his prize. Deirdre was a softly rounded, pretty girl with a tilted nose and large, china-blue eyes. It was plain that she was ill at ease and for the first hour she mainly listened to the conversation swirling around her. But after two unaccustomed glasses of sherry she was no longer reticent about offering her opinion, starting with a comment on Camilla's thin frame and the dangers of smoking. Sarah's skin and hair were a little dry, she said, and would benefit from a daily spoonful of cod liver oil. It was the treatment she used herself. And it would be grand if Tim gave up drinking and smoking so much, but all the young housemen were the same. Then she turned her attention to the older generation. Raphael was subjected to a treatise on the virtues of nursing and the tyranny of doctors on the wards. He had begun to look trapped when Camilla reached across the table and covered Tim's hand.

'Do you remember our Christmases in Kenya, Timmy?' Her voice was high and arch, her expression flirtatious. Betty looked up in alarm. The girl sounded just like her mother. 'It's so thrilling that we're together again, even though we don't have an African moon and palm trees. But we will, when we all go back. You said yesterday that you'd be going back, didn't you?'

'I said I'd have to finish my time at the hospital – just survive it, in fact.' Tim shifted in his chair, plainly uncomfortable. 'I can't think beyond that.'

'Of course you can't, poor darling.' Camilla pursed her mouth and made a soothing, caressing noise that could have been a kiss. 'Meantime, you're going to show me your fair city, and all those pubs with stout and oysters.'

'Tim's worn out. The next few days are the only ones he has to rest himself.' Deirdre glanced around, unsure of herself. 'I wonder if going back to Africa would be such a great idea for him. I've read about the problems they have over there, what with the dirt and the heat, and the ignorance. And there'll be less money for hospitals, now that these countries are ruling themselves.'

'But he doesn't care about any of that, do you, Timmy?' Camilla avoided his answering glare and turned her full attention to Deirdre. 'When you live in Africa you learn to ignore unavoidable things, like beggars or lepers pestering you in the markets, and naked warriors pursuing you with spears, or people spitting betel juice all over your best shoes. You stop noticing them, so that you can enjoy your own life. And Timmy's certainly able to enjoy life in Kenya. Isn't he, Sarah?'

'You're the one that knows.' Sarah could not look up for fear of catching her brother's eye. She felt disloyal and at the same time on the verge of laughter.

'They're pulling my leg,' said Tim desperately. 'They've been doing it for years. It's always a problem when they're together.'

Deirdre tried to smile. 'I'd say they need to learn some better jokes.'

'You can't have heard many of Timmy's awful jokes if you think that,' Camilla said sweetly. 'Hasn't he told you the one about the Catholic missionary who gets the gorilla pregnant, and—'

'Deirdre, have some more pudding, my dear, and pay no attention to these girls.' Even Raphael was embarrassed. 'Tim is right, they're merciless.'

'But have you ever considered living abroad, Deirdre?' Sarah had the scent now. 'I mean, it's true that we all want to be back in Kenya. More than anything.'

'I don't know that I'd want to deal with that kind of a place. There's plenty to be done in Ireland, and that's good enough for me.' Deirdre looked at Tim. 'Are you really thinking of going back?'

'I haven't time to consider it,' Tim said.

'When we were at school, I remember you saying that Kenya was a temporary place for people like us.' Camilla directed her next remark at Raphael. 'But it never lets go of you, does it? We're exiles here, really. Just waiting to go home.'

'I thought you were dedicated to treading the boards in England,' Tim said. 'You'll soon have to do your own training in some grimy provincial town. You'll be learning the ropes in Bognor Regis with a travelling repertory company, getting a feel for real life and for your craft, living in digs that smell of cabbage and disinfectant. Or have you abandoned the theatre?'

'Of course I haven't,' Camilla said. 'I have a place at drama school for next autumn. And you needn't be so disparaging, Timmy. I'm not afraid of getting my hands dirty. I may well choose to do rep. For a season or two, just for the experience. I'll send you tickets to my opening night, and book you a room in my digs. We can share the English seaside experience together.' She was pleased to see that Tim was finally laughing.

'Deirdre, tell us about your family down in Galway,' Betty said, trying to draw the girl out a little. 'I'd love to go to the Oyster Festival again.'

But Deirdre was curiously reticent about her home and family, and Raphael's kindly questions met with answers that were vague and told them nothing. Tim left the party soon after lunch, on the pretext of taking her for a walk in the fields. They reappeared briefly to say their goodbyes and then drove away into the dark evening, leaving the others drinking tea by the fire.

'That was a little cruel.' Raphael could not entirely disguise his amusement.

'Don't be such a hypocrite, dear. You know I have my doubts about her.' Betty put her arm around him. 'I don't think she's really his type.'

'She's too locked in for Tim.' Camilla yawned. 'Why don't you bring him to London at Easter, Sarah? We could try and get Piet to come down from Scotland, and then we'd all be together again. Timmy would love that.'

'Have you heard from Piet?' Sarah's voice was strained.

'No.' Camilla's mouth twitched and she looked away. 'Just a postcard. It was Hannah who wrote to say that he was in Scotland, now that there's a manager at Langani. It's strange to think of the farm without Jan and Lottie there. I still feel responsible, in some way.'

'Oh my dear, you weren't any part of what happened,' Betty exclaimed.

'Has Hannah written to you recently?' Sarah said.

Camilla nodded slowly. 'Yes. But I've neglected her, which was very wrong. I was feeling rather sorry for myself before Christmas. Stupid. It's a family trait.' She lifted her shoulders in a gesture of regret. 'I must be more vigilant about stamping it out. I'll make amends as soon as I get home.'

At the airport Betty Mackay hugged her, trying to fill the girl with the kind of warmth and love that would keep her heart from freezing. She had suggested, on their last night in Wicklow, that Camilla might like to finish her secretarial course in Ireland.

'You could share a flat with Sarah. There's plenty of opportunity in Dublin for talented young people. Maybe you could join the Abbey or the Gate Theatre, instead of studying for the theatre in London. Raphael has a cousin who is one of Ireland's leading actors and producers. You could start by talking to him.'

Camilla shook her head. 'You're all so kind to me. But I'm nearly at the end of my time in that boring place. Then I'll be at drama school and on my way.'

'Are you sure, my dear, that they are going to accept you?' Raphael asked. 'Because I could definitely organise an introduction for you, at the Abbey.'

'Thank you a million times. But yes, I'm sure. I've been called back for a second audition, and I'm taking private lessons with someone who's taught at RADA. He's certain that I'll be given a place.'

Camilla regretted the lie as soon as it was uttered, but she wanted to reassure them, to show them how strong her vocation and convictions were. Above all, she did not want anyone to feel sorry for her, to be aware of her insecurities. She hugged Betty. 'In the meantime, I might get some work as a model, through the photographer I told you about. So I'll stick it out in London for now.'

A month later she had her typing and shorthand certificates, and an imposing piece of paper confirming that she had graduated from Lucie

Clayton's Secretarial and Fashion School. She was looking at her diploma when the telephone rang.

'Hallo, darlin'. It's Ricky. I was on a shoot over Christmas and New Year. They're taking pictures on location more and more now, and I've been in Spain. Sunshine even on Christmas bloody Day, and plenty of the old vino – a gallon or more for five bob. Bloody pissed I was half the time.'

'Sounds thrilling.' She liked the upbeat timbre of his voice, the way it brought a smile to her heart and mind.

'Yeah, well. I showed your photos to a mate of mine. An agent. He'd like to see you. Friday at three if that's OK? I'll come with you. Make the introductions an' all.'

She knew at once that they would take her on, and within moments she was handed a slip of paper and told to report to a photographic studio the following afternoon. There was an advertising campaign for a shampoo, they said, and the company wanted a natural blonde and a new face. Camilla emerged from the interview with a contract, the guarantee of a sizeable cheque, and another interview for a clothes shoot the following week. Her face was alight as she floated along the street, propelled by a new sense of power. Finally, her looks might be of real use to her. Assignments like this would allow her to rent, or even buy, somewhere of her own, away from her mother's constant disapproval. By the end of the year she would be learning the skills of the stage, and in the meantime Sarah and Piet and Tim had decided to come to London for Easter. If she started looking now, she might have her own flat where they could all stay. She would show them the town, share her favourite places and discoveries with the friends she loved. The way ahead was clear at last and she was on top of the world.

Her first assignments resulted in a flurry of additional bookings, and a newspaper article claiming that she was the most beautiful new face on the London scene. From that day forward the telephone rang incessantly, she was always in demand. She flew to Paris and was photographed at the Eiffel Tower, at Versailles, on the Left Bank and at champagne receptions, and she was grateful that she was fluent in French. It was exhilarating and confusing and exhausting, and often lonely. By the time Sarah arrived in London for Easter, Camilla's face was on posters and billboards all over town, and in glossy magazines.

'My God, imagine opening a magazine and seeing your own face looking out at you!' Sarah said. 'What on earth does that feel like?'

'It feels like freedom. It's given me my own life.'

'But you must get a thrill out of it? What do your parents think?' Sarah wanted to provoke some kind of response that she herself would consider normal in the circumstances.

'It's just a temporary thing, until I start studying acting full-time.' Camilla lifted a bucket full of water out of the kitchen sink and opened a cupboard to pull out a string mop. 'Come on – we've got to do this floor.'

'No one would believe this,' Sarah said. 'You're famous, your face is everywhere, and you're washing floors.'

'It's not my chosen occupation, but my cleaner phoned to say she has a cold.' Camilla attacked the polished surface of the floor with grim resolve. 'Piet's arriving tomorrow afternoon, and your brother too. I can't have them staying in a slum.'

'I'll give you a hand.' Sarah looked around for something useful to do. Anything to distract her from the thought of Piet. She felt ill.

'You can't do housework,' Camilla said. 'You'll mess up your nails, so perfectly manicured this morning for the benefit of Mr van der Beer. Make us some coffee, and stop looking like a hen on a hot griddle.'

The flat was on the top floor of a white stucco building in Knightsbridge, and they had to walk up three flights of stairs to reach Camilla's door. Two long sash windows gave the living room its sense of airy space and height. A fitted kitchen was hidden behind folding doors, but they had barely used it since Sarah's arrival from Dublin. Below them was a rectangle of lawn which was lush and green and quiet, and the trees spread a leafy canopy just beneath the window sill. The rumble of buses on the nearby Brompton Road was muffled, and a more common sound was the luxurious growling of taxicabs as they halted in the square at the front of the building. Sarah compared it to the untidy flat that she shared with her brother, and concluded that only Camilla could have arrived at this glamorous, independent existence within such a brief time span. And she had done it alone. There was no question of the silver-spoon treatment from her parents, or help from influential friends. She had been catapulted straight into the centre of swinging London, and she seemed totally at home there. On the first night, they had sat up into the small hours, reminiscing, discussing Sarah's family and Hannah's life in Rhodesia, and the whereabouts of mutual friends from Kenya.

'How are your parents?' Sarah said eventually.

'The same. Daddy is away somewhere. Kenya maybe. He spends weeks at a time there, but he usually drops in as soon as he gets home. I don't see Mother much. Right now she's organising a charity ball for abandoned children. That's rich, isn't it? Fortunately she hates the stairs here. She rings occasionally to complain about my lifestyle. When she has nothing better to do.'

Sarah looked around at the expensive furniture and curtains, the silk lampshades and the rugs on the floor, and bookshelves filled with volumes in bright jackets. They bore Marina's unmistakable stamp. She must have cared enough to plan all this.

'Didn't she help you with this flat?'

'I started out with a sagging bed and some stuff that belonged to the last occupant. A bit shabby, but I didn't mind. It was my own. But after creating an awful fuss about my moving, and weeping for days, Mother turned up here to make peace. And a couple of days later a Peter Jones van arrived outside the door and delivered all this. Except for the books. Daddy dropped in with those and the record player.'

'Haven't they been here together? I mean, for dinner or something?'

Faced with a silent response that combined derision and bitterness, Sarah made no comment.

'Look,' Camilla said, 'you've never said a word about my family or lack of it. Not while we were at school and not since. I've always been grateful for that. No, don't interrupt.' She dug her fingers into Sarah's arm. 'The fact is, some people have parents that don't get on, and were probably never made to have children. But I've learned to look after myself. I like where I am. My final interview is in two weeks' time, and I'll be studying drama in the autumn. Before that there's the summer in Kenya, to celebrate all our twenty-first birthdays. So don't even think of feeling sorry for me.'

'I still pray it will turn out better with your parents some day.'

'Pray! Some good that does.' Camilla snorted and then caught the offended look on Sarah's face. 'Don't tell me you're still doing mass on Sundays and holy days, and all that?'

'Yes, I am.' Sarah was defensive. 'I can't throw that away, just because the nuns aren't behind me every minute. It's different for you. You were at a Catholic school, though you weren't brought up as a Catholic. But it's lodged in my psyche, for better or for worse.'

'I can't imagine why I would want to set foot in a church ever again. All that piousness and guilt, and furtive covering up of every feeling you have. It's just an excuse to repress your every natural instinct. And heaven forbid that sex should cross your mind, or you're damned for all eternity.'

'There are good things about religion.'

'Not for me. Catholics want every woman to be the Virgin Mary, long-suffering and sexless. And terrified of going straight to hell if they get run over by a bus and die after a heavy kissing session.'

'It's not all hellfire and brimstone,' Sarah insisted. 'There's love, and taking care of other people. Helping the not so fortunate along. Those things are good.'

'It's all I can do to help myself along,' Camilla snapped. 'I can barely keep my own head above water, never mind looking after the rest of humanity as well.'

'Well, I help out at this place in Dublin. It's a sort of refuge where drunks and homeless people can come and get a meal, and a night's sleep, somewhere secure. I like being part of that, making a contribution.'

'Don't tell me you've turned into a professional do-gooder! Soon you'll be wearing hair shirts and open sandals and weaving macramé pot hangers.' Camilla made exaggerated motions with her hands. 'You'll become a Jesus freak if you're not careful. You always had a tendency in that direction.'

Sarah laughed and turned away. Stupid to be hurt. Impossible to explain how alone she felt in the student halls of Dublin, where everyone had known one another since early childhood, where the corridors were endlessly long and dark, and the grimy windows offered no hint of the streaming sunlight she had once taken for granted. At St Joseph's Shelter she could immerse herself in lives a thousand times more alienated and desperate than her own. She could feel that she was making a difference in the cold, crowded world she now inhabited. Camilla seemed to be so much a part of glamorous, swinging London, and Sarah was ashamed to describe her own inability to mix with her peers in Ireland.

'So what are we going to do in the big city?' she asked, anxious to avoid any further revelations about her life in Dublin. 'I haven't much money to spend. But I've saved some, from working as a weekend waitress for the last three months.'

'I'll show you Carnaby Street where all these new boutiques are setting up. But I'm not going to let you spend money there,' Camilla was firm. 'It's fun to see, but it's already full of trippers gawping at the shops and at the famous people who like to be seen there. I can take you to fantastic places where I buy clothes and all kinds of other things at half the price, because I'm a model. Now go to sleep, so you'll be ready to splurge in the morning.'

After a late breakfast, they set off on their shopping expedition. Sarah found the crowded streets stimulating. Everywhere she looked there were flared trousers and short skirts, kohl-ringed eyes and geometric haircuts. Men wore jackets with velvet collars and high-heeled boots, and had long hair that hung over their ears and collars. Hippies and flower children stood on street corners, drifting along in diaphanous skirts and loose trousers, hung with beads and feathers. The cafés were serving strong coffee called espresso in tiny cups. Customers lolled on their chairs, staring into space with distant expressions and a curl of sweet-smelling smoke trickling from mouth and nose, or sitting bolt upright with knees bouncing and fingers snapping in an amphetamine-induced other world. Music blared out into the streets and the air seemed to pound with tumultuous energy.

'That was spectacular,' Sarah said, when they staggered back to the flat some hours later, with a mountain of carrier bags. 'I'd never have found any of this stuff without you. I wish you'd let me repay you for the haircut and the streaks, though. I've more than enough to—'

But Camilla brushed aside any protests and went to raid her wardrobe for additional accessories, including a pair of shoes from Charles Jourdan that she insisted were a poor fit.

'Stop twittering and take them. After some photo sessions the people don't want the clothes any more, and I can take my pick. I'm tired of all this stuff, and I don't use half of it. If you don't want it I'll give it away to the charlady for her ghastly daughter. Come on, Sarah. Get dressed. I've got tickets for a play.'

After the theatre they went to a nightclub in a dark cellar, where Sarah met people that Camilla called her friends, although she did not seem close to any of them. A photographer with a broad cockney accent flirted with her and tried to persuade her to smoke some marijuana, but Sarah was scared to try it. She sat beside him for a while, enjoying his conversation, watching his eyes narrow as he squinted at Camilla through the spiral of smoke that drifted constantly from his lips, openly infatuated with her. But his advances went unnoticed and after a while he left them. Later, Sarah saw him over at the bar, his arm draped around a young girl with green streaks in her hair and a very short dress. Someone called Jonathan Warburton joined their table for a while and ordered champagne. He was good-looking in a sullen way, and he smoked incessantly through a cigarette holder. His accent was very grand, and Sarah thought his velvet jacket and flowered shirt were quite beautiful, even though she had never seen a man wearing anything similar. She was excited by his attention and surprised when he sat down very close to her. After a time he put a hand on her thigh, while he entertained her with a pithy commentary on the people that eddied around them.

'Dance with me?' he asked, and she nodded, flattered. He held her tightly, pressing his body against hers, but she backed away in confusion when she felt desire rising in him and realised that he had intended her to know it. They had only been on the crowded floor for a few minutes when he bent to whisper into her ear, suggesting they leave and go to his flat. She refused him, smiling, and he became irritated and sulky, leaving her alone among the pulsating couples, and drifting away to try his luck elsewhere. There was no sign of Camilla, and Sarah sat alone for a while nursing a vodka, putting on the brakes because she did not want the alcohol to redden her skin. When Camilla finally returned to the table, she was trailing a young man wearing high-heeled cowboy boots and blue jeans.

'I'm Baxter,' he said smiling at Sarah. 'Camilla says you're from Dublin. Good place for photos and drinking. I hear you like your camera.'

'Yes. I take pictures in the city, but I'm not so great at the drinking. I haven't the stamina of my friends.' Sarah was glad to have found someone with whom she had a common interest. Her accustomed shyness evaporated with the remains of the vodka. 'I'm trying to build up a portfolio of portraits – faces in the pubs, old ladies on the Green with their bags of bread for the ducks, the flower sellers in Moore Street. If you know Dublin, you'll have seen them all. I'm studying zoology, and my camera will be very important later in my work. What kind of pictures do you take?'

She saw Camilla roll her eyes as Baxter threw back his head and roared with laughter.

'I take pictures of birds like your mate here, wearing all kinds of fancy frocks. Gives me the chance to spend all my time with beautiful women, and I even get paid for it. Sometimes I get them in the sack too. Can't beat that for a living.'

Sarah was scarlet with shame as she realised that she was talking to David Baxter whose fashion pictures had become a worldwide sensation. Dumb with embarrassment, she tried to think of something clever to say but nothing came to mind. Baxter did not seem to notice, any more than anyone else had noticed what she'd said or done since her arrival in London. He ordered champagne, and talked to Camilla about a trip to the country where he planned to photograph her in a field with some ruined buildings and wild horses. Noise and smoke rose all around them. More people arrived and stood three and four deep at the bar. Some couples were in full evening dress, while others sported leather jackets and jeans, and sweaters with rolled necks. After three hours Sarah's head ached, and she would have been happy to leave and walk back to the flat along the cool, wet pavements. But Camilla showed no sign of tiring. She twisted and spun with ceaseless energy, partnered on the dance floor by people that she knew, but seemingly happy to switch without notice and dance with complete strangers, or even alone.

It was two in the morning when they finally left the club and walked home through streets that were silent except for the sound of an occasional car as it splattered through the rain. Camilla recommended a nightcap that consisted of aspirins and several glasses of water, and Sarah fell into bed in a stupor from which she did not waken until almost noon. When she finally stumbled into the kitchen she found Camilla, dressed in a pair of frayed jeans and a blue voile shirt that clearly showed her breasts and the fact that she was not wearing anything underneath. She had wound a printed scarf around her head so that it resembled a turban and her face was smeared with white paste that she said was some kind of moisturising mask.

'Here's coffee, and there's fruit and yogurt and fresh bread. You'll have to stay in all afternoon,' she remarked with mischief in her eyes. 'I've got a photo session at three. So you'll be the solo welcoming committee for Piet.'

'No! Oh no, I can't!' Sarah said. Panic filled her, and her throat was dry with fright so that she choked on her mouthful of coffee. 'You can't leave me here to meet him. Alone.'

'Sounds like a dream opportunity.'

'No. I need to see him with other people around, so I can get used to him again. I can't meet him alone. I don't know what I could even say to him.'

'Don't say anything,' Camilla said. 'Just fling your arms around him, kiss him on the mouth and drag him down on to the sofa. That should do it.'

'Don't laugh at me. I need time, and some sympathy. I don't know what to do.'

'Oh, for God's sake, Sarah. You sound like you're still some fawning teenager in a convent. You're a fabulous, grown woman ready to seduce a grown man. Eve and Adam. Just do it.'

'I need time, and—'

'You've got time. You've got a whole Bank Holiday weekend with him. There's no point in wasting a moment of it. Just look alluring and beautiful. And gaze up at him like he's God.'

'But I'm not beautiful.'

'Yes, you are. The Irish weather has turned your complexion into something enviable, and you look great in your new finery. Besides, he's just a simple farmer – an escaped hayseed. Now let's roll up your hair and choose something for you to wear. Then all you have to do is sweat it out till he gets here.'

Camilla left the flat soon after lunch, munching on an apple and carrying a canvas tote bag full of hairbrushes, combs and cosmetics. In the square below Sarah heard her hail a taxi and listened to the finality of the door slamming as the cab revved up and purred away. Then there was silence and the faint ticking of an alarm clock to remind her that he would soon be here. She would not be able to disguise her excitement at seeing him. She could never master the art of nonchalance that Camilla did so well, and he would guess and find her foolish. Or worse, feel sorry for her.

Waiting for Piet to arrive, she sat by the open window and lit a cigarette. He had written a few times, brief notes about his experiences in the Scottish Highlands. The wild countryside was beautiful, he said, with the grandeur of the lochs and the craggy shores and brooding mountains.

But he could not fathom how people lived all their lives in the endless cycle of driving rain and mist, squelching through the mud in heavy boots and jackets, waiting for the next storm to blow in, grateful for a few hours of watery sunlight. They would have so much to talk about, Sarah thought. Her heartbeat was too fast and she felt breathless at the idea of seeing him face to face. She stubbed out the cigarette and jumped to her feet. What was she thinking of, smoking now, just before she might kiss him? She went into the bathroom to clean her teeth and had just put the toothbrush into her mouth when she heard the doorbell.

'Dear God,' she muttered, 'are you never on my side at all?' She rinsed her mouth hastily, splashing water on her face, inadvertently removing all the lipstick she had applied so carefully. 'I'm coming,' she called out as she flew across the sitting room and into the tiny hallway. Then she stopped, took a deep breath, and made the sign of the cross before flinging open the door.

'Sarah! It's so good to see you, my little Sarah! Man, you look great!' He hugged her and then stepped back to examine her in detail as she stood, mute with joy, looking up at him. She reached up to place her arms around his neck, but his gaze had shifted over her shoulder to search the area beyond her. She heard the disappointment in his voice, watched his smile fade.

'Where is she? I thought she'd be here. I even thought of asking her to meet me at the station, but then the train might have been late. Sarah, you know what I'm telling you, heh?'

'She had to go to a photo shoot. She's in all the smartest magazines. It's amazing.'

'Yes. She sent me a couple of pictures and I've seen her in the papers. I can't believe it – how she looks in the magazines and so. When will she be back?'

'Around six, I think.' Her voice was thick with frustration and jealousy, but she knew he would not even notice. 'Meanwhile, would you like tea or a cold beer? Or we could go out for a coffee somewhere.'

'No, let's stay here. There's so much to tell you. And I want to hear all your news, little sis.'

'I've told you most things in my letters,' she said, stung by the idea that Camilla had sent him photos. She had never forwarded any to Dublin, or mentioned that she had sent pictures to Piet.

'No, you haven't. I don't know a thing about your real life. Only your studies.' He grinned and squeezed her hand, and her heart thudded in her ears. 'How are your parents? And Tim?'

She made fresh coffee and sat down beside him on the sofa. 'You're so pale,' she said. 'I've never seen you without a tan. You look quite strange, as though you need to be put out on the grass with the laundry, to seep up the sunlight.'

'There's not much of that where I've been,' he said. 'Come on now, don't try to change the subject, girl. Tell me all your secrets. Have you got a boyfriend?'

She found herself telling him about Dublin, about the foggy air and the crowds, and the suffocating smell of wet clothes in smoky pubs. She tried to describe the emerald colour of the fields, the skies that were purple, and the flocks of crows rising off newly ploughed soil, and she spoke of voices singing Celtic love songs around turf fires, and men that played the fiddles and the spoons. But she did not speak about her loneliness and the ache in her bones for hot, yellow sunlight and the taste of salt in a cobalt sea.

'What about Hannah and your parents?' she asked him at last. 'It sounds bad down there, with all the talk of Rhodesian independence, and the government locking up black people who want to be politicians, and this man Ian Smith with his all-white party. It sounds bad, with worse to come.'

'It's rough down there, yes. And Pa doesn't like his cousin, or his job. He has no interest in tobacco farming, and there are security problems on the farm. He's often out on patrol, looking for *tsotsis*, and he hates that.'

'What are *tsotsis*?' Sarah asked.

'Thugs, I suppose, is the nearest English word for them. They've started attacking white farms and businesses, and organising ambushes on the roads. They've killed a number of people already.'

'You mean like the Mau Mau?'

'Similar, in some ways. They're after the white community. And there are problems on the Mozambique and Zambian borders, with insurgents coming in on raids, taking cattle and so. It's no life for Pa, working as a hired hand in a place like that, when he's always been on his own land. He's an angry man these days and Ma is taking the worst of it. It's rough,' he repeated. 'I keep hoping he'll change his mind and come home.'

'What about Hannah?' Sarah asked. 'She seems to hate it down there.'

'It's true, yes. But she's doing well in her business studies. And I know Ma hopes she'll go on to college in South Africa. Maybe get a scholarship for part of the fees.'

'I think she'd like to go home,' Sarah said. 'To Langani.'

'Ma's adamant that she should finish her education first. And I agree, it seems sensible. Plus, what would she do at Langani?' He shook his head. 'We have a few problems there, too. No, Hannah should stay down south for now.'

'What problems? Are you having trouble with your manager?'

'No. Not at all. Lars Olsen is a fine man and he works hard.' He was silent for a moment, and Sarah saw that he was trying to make a decision. Then he put down his coffee cup and looked her straight in the eye. 'After Pa left, I discovered that the farm was carrying a big debt. It took Lars and me a while to sort out a plan, and make a new agreement with the bank that would give us enough time. That's why I delayed going to Scotland. Langani is still borderline, but the bank has backed off for the time being, thanks to Lars.'

'And Jan never said anything?' Sarah found it difficult to believe what she had heard. 'Didn't he realise how things were?'

'Oh, he knew. Yes.' Piet was resigned. 'I can't decide if he didn't realise the extent of the problem, or if he just couldn't bring himself to admit that he'd allowed things to get into such a mess. He's not a great man for figures, but he would have to have been blind and deaf not to see what was happening. I don't know what he was thinking at all.'

'Have you discussed it with him?' Sarah asked.

'No.' Piet's face was bleak. 'I reckoned he had enough troubles down south. And I've never told Hannah either. So it would be hard to bring her back right now. Besides, they need her down there. Ma relies on her for company. I don't know what she would do without Han.'

He reached out to take Sarah's hand and she pressed his fingers, praying that he would understand how desperate she was to share his problems and his dreams. She leaned forward, hoping that this moment would finally bring them closer than they had ever been, and she was wondering if she could kiss him when they heard the sound of a key in the door. Piet leapt to his feet, bounding away from her.

'Thought I'd never get out of that draughty studio. Awful clothes, too. Not worth the rolls of film. Piet, you look like a ghost. Very strange in that city gear.' Camilla tossed down her bag and put her arms around his neck, kissing him square on the mouth. 'How long have you been here?'

He could not answer and Sarah realised that he was shy, overcome by Camilla's casual embrace. Dumbstruck in the presence of his dream, she thought bitterly. She bent to lift the coffee tray and there were tears of rage and despair in her eyes as she put the empty cups into the sink and made an effort to compose herself, before joining Camilla on the sofa.

'Scotland has been a great place to work,' Piet was saying. 'I've learned so much, seen plenty of new techniques, some great machinery we could do with at Langani, if we can ever scrape up the money. I spent a week in Edinburgh, too. It's a friendly city. I had good times in the pubs and I went to the theatre festival. But oh man, after all these months I'm so ready to go home.'

'You can't take the farm out of the boy, it seems,' Camilla said. 'Maybe when you get back you'll find that you miss everything you've done here.'

'There's no chance of that,' he said, smiling. 'I just want to get back into everything at the farm. Especially the idea of turning part of Langani into a game reserve. Just before I left I met an architect in Nairobi. He's drawn up plans for a small safari lodge, and Anthony Chapman has agreed to put some money into it. We're going to form a company to get the whole thing going. I'm starting on it the moment I get home.'

'You're a true jungle baby, Piet. Goodbye purple heather and single malt and bonny lochs, then. And never a backward glance.' Camilla lit a cigarette and blew smoke towards him.

'I just don't know how people can live in that climate. There's no bright colour to light up the land, and the sun never really warms the heart of you.'

'Well, Sarah and I have plans for the next few days that will warm you. Have a snooze while we wait for Timmy. He should be here in an hour or so. Then we'll find plenty of bright lights to cheer you.'

In the bedroom Camilla chose clothes for the evening, insisting on flared trousers and a tight-fitting top for Sarah. Then she chose a dress with a very short skirt for herself. It appeared to be made from some kind of shiny, plastic material, with a pattern of circular holes punched along the hemline.

'Well?' she asked, as she hunted for accessories.

'Well what?' Sarah made no attempt to disguise her disappointment.

'He's only here to see you. He doesn't give a damn about me, except as some kind of kid sister. And you know it.'

'He has a schoolboy crush on me, but he knows in his heart that it doesn't mean anything.'

'Promise me that you're really, really not interested in him. Tell me the truth, so I know for sure.' Sarah was pleading, on the verge of tears that she brushed away with the back of her hand. 'Oh shit! Now look at me.'

'I'm not interested in him. I never was. I'm not in love with him, or with anyone for that matter. And that's the truth,' Camilla said. 'I don't know if there could ever be a man I might really love. I've hardly been groomed for lifelong bonding. But if there is, it certainly won't be Piet van der Beer.'

Within an hour Tim had arrived from Dublin, embracing Camilla, slapping Piet on the back with enthusiasm. He dug in his battered suitcase for packages of smoked salmon, soda bread and Irish whiskey. In the pub around the corner they planned their evening. Piet leaned against the bar and regarded Sarah with new admiration.

'Man, you look beautiful,' he said. 'Your hair is all streaky like a lion's mane, and your eyes are so green and shining. Little Sarah – who would believe it?'

She put up her hand and placed her palm on the side of his face, and he smiled down at her with tenderness, so that she had to take her fingers away because they had begun to tremble. They ate in a French brasserie where Camilla was immediately shown to the best table. She waved the menu away and ordered for them all. Soon they were devouring oysters and white wine, and large sirloin steaks with perfect *pommes frites*. Blue cheese and red wine followed, and Piet put away half an apple tart with a glaze like golden glass. They drank double espresso coffee that made Sarah's head buzz as they smoked and talked without a break, filling in the time spent apart, reminiscing over their days at Langani and on the white powdery sand of the Kenya coast. At last they rose from the table, laughing and a little drunk.

'We've got to walk back from here,' Sarah said. 'I'm on overload, and if I don't get some exercise and fresh air I'll fall over.'

'I know just the place to work off dinner,' said Camilla. 'Let's go.'

The street was noisy and full of people spilling out of theatres and cinemas. Inside the nightclub the music thumped and boomed, and they danced like dervishes until exhaustion, heat and smoke overcame them and they escaped into the cold air to clear their heads.

'Where to now?' asked Camilla. 'What d'you fancy? I know a good spot for jazz. Quiet and more for the older night owls. You often see film and stage people there, with their latest conquests. Ideal for winding down.'

'I'm opting for home. I'm nearly dead, and there must be blisters on the soles of my feet.' Sarah was drooping. But she was a minority of one and they dragged her into a taxi, teasing her for her lack of stamina.

In the discreetly lit cellar they sat back on deep cushions while Camilla ordered drinks that she called swimming pools, served in wide-rimmed glasses filled with a mixture of gin, glittering blue curaçao and other unnamed and dangerous ingredients. The pianist played Gershwin and Cole Porter, and a singer delivered subtle songs of love and desire. Camilla moved closer to Tim. He turned towards her and hesitated, but then he placed an arm around her shoulders and lifted her drink, tipping her glass to her lips as she smiled and glanced sideways to flirt with him. Piet looked away. Sarah concentrated furiously on the piano player until Tim and Camilla rose and moved away from the table, towards the small dance floor in the adjoining room.

'Want to dance?' Piet asked. As she stood up Sarah wondered whether he really wanted to dance with her, or whether his idea was simply to follow Camilla and Tim. But she did not care to analyse his reasons as they moved towards the music.

Camilla had stopped to greet a couple at a corner table and Sarah passed her, following Piet through a low archway and on to the dance floor. She glanced around at the other couples. Some were in formal suits or evening dress, but there were also men in jeans and black polo-neck sweaters, and women wearing ropes of ethnic beads and gauzy skirts that swirled around their ankles. On the opposite edge of the small floor she saw a black man, moving with slow grace to the music. His back was turned to her, and he was holding his partner in an intimate embrace, so that only the jewelled fingers she had wound around his neck were visible. Their bodies were fused together in a sensuous, swaying motion and as they drifted towards her Sarah realised, with a shock, that she had seen him before. She looked away quickly, feeling it would be better not to show any sign of recognition. There were too many complicated associations and she did not want them to contaminate the pleasure of her own evening. But it was too late. Dr Winston Hayford had noticed her. He stiffened in surprise and summoned a smile of greeting with obvious effort, as Sarah stared at the perfect face and form of his companion. Camilla was making her way towards them, her expression at first reflecting surprise and then outrage.

'Darling,' said Marina in her low, breathless voice. 'How lovely to see you here. Not your usual type of place. You remember Dr Hayford?' The tall African held out his hand as Marina turned towards Sarah, bestowing a dazzling smile in her direction. 'Of course you and I met at your lovely house in Mombasa, and in Muthaiga. Are you living in London now?'

'No. I'm over from Dublin for the Easter break,' Sarah said, desperate to get through the minimum of polite words and be gone.

'And you must be the brother.' Marina turned her attention to Tim, reaching out to touch his arm and smiling at him. 'You're so alike. Weren't you studying medicine? You must get Camilla to bring you both to the flat. Come for dinner. Or a drink.'

Piet stood beside Sarah, rigid with antagonism. She tried to find his hand but fumbled in an empty space as Marina focused on him for a fleeting moment and then looked away.

'Mother. What a surprise.' Pure hostility propelled Camilla's greeting. 'I don't see Daddy around, but perhaps he wasn't invited this evening. It's so lovely to see you doing your bit for international harmony. Aren't you going to say hello to Piet? I'm sure you can't have forgotten Piet van der Beer.'

'Don't, Camilla, please.' Sarah's voice was low. Her throat was burning as though it was filled with fire, although she had begun to shiver. She moved towards Dr Hayford and looked at him, beseeching. 'Are you here for a medical conference?'

'No. I've been based in London for a while now.' His expression was polite, neutral, although she detected sympathy and regret behind his large spectacles. 'Marina, I think we should continue to Park Lane.'

'Good evening, Mrs Broughton-Smith.' Piet had stood his ground, and now he proffered his hand, forcing an acknowledgement.

But Marina made no attempt to respond, and Winston Hayford saw that she was determined to ignore the greeting. He grasped her elbow in an attempt to steer her towards the stairs, away from further confrontation. She glanced at him briefly and brushed his hand away.

'I thought you had broken off any association with this young man, Camilla,' she said. 'I thought we all understood that.'

'Well, Mother darling, you'll have to think again.' Anger reared up in Camilla's head, obliterating everything around her. 'Because Piet and I have decided to become engaged. We're going to get married.'

In the chasm of silence that followed, Marina spun on her heel and walked away from them, her high heels clicking on the polished floor, Dr Hayford following in her wake. Sarah watched mesmerised as they reached the top of the stairs and stepped out into the night, away from the joyous, carefree evening they had ruined. She turned back to her friends, her pulse hammering out her anxiety.

Piet was staring at Camilla, his face radiant. He reached out to take her in his arms.

'Camilla – I never dreamed you – I don't know what I can say, except that I'll always—'

'Piet, I'm sorry.' Camilla was looking at him, dazed. 'I'm really sorry. I don't know what made me say such a stupid thing.'

Tim turned to her in fury, spinning her round, spitting his words into her face.

'Don't you ever learn anything, you selfish little bitch? Do you realise what you've done tonight, playing your vicious games? You never think about anyone else, least of all your friends. Because we're not important, except to prop you up in your eternal war with your family. No one is really important in your bloody, screwed-up life. Except yourself.'

'No. Oh no. I'm so sorry, I really am.' Camilla leaned against a table in an attempt to steady her shaking body. 'I didn't mean to hurt anyone. I was just so shocked to see them, together like that. And Daddy – she always does something to ruin things when I'm happy, and I don't know how to deal with it. I never get it right. There's always a—'

'You're going to have to learn the hard way,' Tim took her thin shoulders and shook her. 'Because it will all come round in a backlash one of these days, and you'll pay a heavy price for using your friends in your sick, horrible schemes. You're going to wind up a sad, messed-up woman just like your mother, and you needn't come asking any of us for help.'

'I only wanted to shock her. To punish her for what she's doing to Daddy.' Camilla made no attempt to brush away the tears that had begun to slip down her face. 'For what she's done to him and to me, all these years. I wanted to pay her for the way she's treated each of us here. That's all I meant to do. Please, please try to understand.'

Piet stood like a stone pillar, his face white, his mouth set in a thin, twitching line. Then he took Camilla's hand.

'Come on, Lady Camilla,' he said. 'We should go home now. We should all go home and get ourselves together.'

But Sarah could not find it in herself to walk with them. Tim called out her name as she rushed away from the group and found the ladies' room. She locked the door. Then she slid to the floor, leaning against the tiled wall of the stall and sobbing, before she vomited all her foolish dreams into the cold, white bowl.

Chapter 7

Rhodesia, April 1965

Hannah slammed the screen door and went out to sit on the steps of the porch. In the midday heat, dust devils whirled desiccated leaves into the air with a dry rustling, then died into hot silence. In front of the verandah was a small patch of ground from which Lottie was trying to coax the beginnings of a garden, planting bougainvillea and portulacca and periwinkles, to bring a little colour to the drab face of the bungalow. Beyond that was the tobacco, miles of tall green stalks, their broad leaves rattling and swishing rumours through their ranks as the wind curled around them. High above her in the brassy sky a kestrel sailed the up-currents, watching for unwary prey below. It had already plummeted down once, grasping a mouse in its talons, carrying it off to some barren place to be devoured.

Just like me, Hannah thought. Poor, helpless mouse, hoisted from its home without warning, and swallowed up. How could Pa have done this? Taken them here to this godforsaken place, without asking her, ignoring her frantic pleading to be allowed to stay with Piet. He had been like a stone during those last days at home, standing in the office or the living room at Langani, staring out of the windows, not speaking. Pouring yet another whisky from the bottle, drinking it down in great swallows, as though he was not even tasting it. How could Ma have let him do this to them? It had broken her mother's heart. Hannah knew that. She remembered the day they were leaving, how sick she had felt, caught between impotent rage and misery. How she had gone out at sunrise to walk in the garden, to look at the mountain, to touch the wood of the verandah rail and feel its rough, kindly roundness, to absorb every memory of the childhood that was being torn from her. And then she had seen Lottie, kneeling in the flower bed, stroking the plants with trembling fingers, whispering something to them that Hannah could not hear, tears coursing down her cheeks unchecked. She had crept away, unable to watch her mother's grief. And when the time came to leave, she had looked into her father's eyes, making one last desperate appeal, and seen only a sick despair. Then she had turned in panic and run away from the car, tried to hide in her old room, so that Piet had come and pulled her from her bed.

'You must be brave,' he had said. 'It's just as hard for them – harder maybe. They need you to help them do it.'

And she had wanted to scream at him, to say that it was fine for him. He was staying. He did not have to say goodbye to everything he had always loved. He did not have to go away with Pa and Ma, who were clearly in a pit of misery themselves. Why was she the one who had to uproot herself and go with them?

She still could not understand why they had to come to this dreadful place. She hated it! Hated it for herself, and for what it was doing to her parents. And she loathed the feeling of envy and resentment that stifled her whenever she heard from the others. Sarah wrote often – long, newsy ramblings about university life in Dublin. And Piet sent pithy, 'little sisterish' notes that drove her mad with fury and longing. Worst of all was Camilla, who sent breezy postcards that told her nothing at all, except to illustrate a life of excitement and sophistication.

I'm going to die out here, Hannah said to herself. I'll dry up, like those skeleton leaves. The wind will carry me off, and I'll be forgotten. Or worse still, I'll grow old and fat, like that cow Mrs van Riebeck, and then it will take a crane to carry me anywhere, never mind the wind. I'll end up smelling of sweat, doused in April Violets cologne, heaving around in a shapeless cotton shift with a dreadful flowered apron tied across my sagging bosom. Man, what a horrible thought! And they'll pair me off with someone like that cretin Billy Kovaks who sniffs all the time. Imagine having to kiss him! All blubbery wet lips and dead fish hands prodding me everywhere. She shivered violently at the thought, then smiled. Well, it would be something to write about to Sarah. 'These are my waking nightmares. Aren't they gross?' What really was gross, though, was that they were all she had to offer. A frightening dream of the future that offered no future. And on the other side of the world, her friends and her brother were discovering what it was to live. Not fair, just not fair.

Pa was drinking again. She could smell the sourness of his breath, and his eyes were dull and bloodshot. Today he had shouted at Lottie, before leaving on another patrol with his cousin. At Langani he had never shouted at his family. How could Ma put up with it now? Hannah hated to see her mother's face, pinched with pain, her eyes so sad and so understanding at the same time. But it was no good being kind and understanding – how could she not see that? It just made him more angry, encouraged him to wallow in self-pity. He should pull himself together, stop hiding away in this wretched hole where the work was nothing like what he had done at home. It wasn't even his farm. His cousin, Kobus van der Beer, treated him like a servant. Her pa was overseer on a tobacco plantation, a hired hand taking orders from an ox of a man who was mean and rude, and hadn't anything but straw between his ears. Pa should be back on his own land, raising his cattle and his wheat. When they had talked about it, Jan had said his name was on a list because he had fought against the Mau Mau. That the kaffirs would remember. He said Langani could have been confiscated after *Uhuru* if he had stayed on. Now the subject was forbidden and the possibility of a return to Kenya was no longer mentioned.

But anything would be better than this place where Jan spent increasing amounts of his time out in the bush, hunting down gangs of black guerrilla fighters hungry for their share of the white man's land. The talk on all the farms centred on the growing number of dangerous thugs hired by black nationalists to terrorise the white community, and to destroy oil and power lines coming into Rhodesia. Everyone said it was vital to resist a sell-out of white power, and to deal swiftly and harshly with any show of violence from the tribes. Ian Smith would keep them on the right road, they agreed. He had already banned the black political parties and exiled their leaders, and he promised to crush any movement towards majority black rule. The result was a constant state of tension in the country, and the formation of private patrols like the one that Kobus van der Beer had organised. Hannah hated to see them ride out with guns, and that closed-down expression on their faces. Sometimes he and Pa were gone for days. When Jan came back he smelled horrible. His eyes were red-rimmed and he had obviously been drinking heavily. And Ma was miserable in the run-down house with the leaking roof, and the sagging verandah where termites chewed relentlessly at the foundations. They should all go home. Take their chances.

Everything had been ruined on that terrible night in Mombasa, when Camilla's mother had made her accusation and destroyed the family. Jan's face had gone hard as stone when she spoke. Then it had sort of crumbled, and the fight had gone out of him. He had shrivelled before Hannah's eyes, become an old man. But Pa wasn't old. He was her pa, a giant who could do anything, take on any difficulty and triumph over it. This sullen hulk who left the house with a gun in his hand, and returned to fill his belly with whisky, who sat in the half-dark and shouted at her mother, this wasn't her pa. When he was not working in the fields, or out on patrol, he drank and drank. He had a haunted look now, as though ghosts walked with him, whispering words of judgment and retribution in his ear, and he shouted at Lottie just to silence them and keep them at bay. Today Hannah had tried once more to talk to her mother, to make her see that she must get him to bring them home.

'If this black list is something to do with the emergency, why can't we talk about it?' she had asked. 'Plenty of people fought the Mau Mau. The British brought in soldiers from England to fight them. That woman is a spiteful bitch. She was jealous of us, that's all! Pa should go back to Langani and forget what she said, or take it up with the government. Something. Anything. He hates this place, Ma. We all do. You should be in your garden at home, not in this *shenzi*, no-hoper of a place. Look at this house – soon it will collapse around us. It leaks. It's mean and rotting. We can't get rid of the cockroaches. I'm sick of being stuck out here in the *bundu* every weekend with nothing to do. And he's so angry all the time. Ma, are you listening to me?'

Lottie had risen then, gripped her daughter, and shaken her none too gently.

'You listen to me, my girl. The truth is unpalatable at times, but you have to accept it. It's no good fooling yourself. Things happen – people sometimes make decisions that they bitterly regret. Your pa did something at a time when everyone was a little crazy, when your uncle had been murdered, hacked to pieces in front of poor Katja and the children. He wasn't the only one, and he has tried to make amends, although it hasn't been easy.'

'But what did he do that was so terrible? What?'

'You don't need to know the details, Hannah.' Lottie sounded tired, defeated. 'But if there was a blacklist in George Broughton-Smith's file, then it was a serious threat to Langani. It would have affected the decision about whether we could keep the farm or not. Black politicians don't like to remember that their own people were killed by the Mau Mau. Far more of their own, in fact. There were very few white people murdered. But they don't want to think about what one Kikuyu did to another, how they massacred their brothers and cousins who wouldn't take the oath, how they raped and tortured and killed their own women if they refused to bring food into the forests for the gangs hiding up there. They only remember what a white man did to a black man.'

'So she was talking about the Mau Mau, then,' Hannah said.

'Yes. She was. So we can't just forget what she said, Hannah, and go on as if it never happened. Your father left Langani so that Piet could keep the farm and make a life there for himself, like the generations before him. It means everything to him. Pa knew that and he gave up his own future there, to protect your brother.'

'Piet's future? That's all you two ever think about! Piet's future! Piet goes to college in South Africa, Piet goes to Scotland to further his studies, Piet stays in Langani. Pa gives up everything to keep the farm safe for Piet! Don't get me wrong, Ma, I love Piet and I'm glad he got all those chances. But what about me? Do you and Pa never think about my future? You've put a farm manager you hardly know on Langani while Piet's away, and you've given up your home to come down to this – this shit hole!'

'Hannah!'

'No. Let me finish. You've paid for Piet to go to Scotland, and Pa is doing a crummy job down here that he hates. He's being exploited, used as cheap labour, and sent out into the bush to fight for a lost cause, for a place that isn't his. There's no chance of things ever being any better for him, as long as he stays here. And there's nothing left in the treasure chest for me. Is there? Is there, Ma? No money for me to go to a university in South Africa, to go anywhere or do anything! All I get is a stupid business course in a second-rate secretarial college in the back of nowhere. I'm living out here in the middle of tobacco fields with the rats and the cockroaches, and no future. No future, do you hear me? I never wanted to leave Kenya. You knew that, but you wouldn't let me stay in Nairobi and do my course there. Then at least I could have gone home to Langani in my time off, once Piet went back. I could have helped out, worked there. Why couldn't I have stayed?'

'Hannah, Hannah, we've been over this already. We couldn't leave you on your own in Kenya. You were too young, and there wasn't enough—'

'Exactly. There wasn't enough money to provide for me, because it was all being ploughed into bloody Piet's bloody future!'

'Hannah! Watch your mouth! That's enough now. Pa and I were trying to do what was best.'

'Oh yes? And is this what's best for me? To stay here and watch Pa drinking himself to death and making life hell for both of us? We have to put up with his temper and his self-pity because of something he did years ago, that has come back to haunt him. Is that it? Well, you shouldn't let him do that – you shouldn't let him treat you like he does. If he can't pull himself together, you should leave, and so should I. We should both go now – today!'

Lottie had reached out a hand in sympathy to her daughter, and winced as Hannah pulled away.

'My poor little girl,' she said softly. 'You are so young. You still see everything only in black and white. As you grow older you will know that nothing is so clear cut.'

Hannah had felt all her rage and frustration exploding in her head. Her eyes and her throat hurt with the effort of containing it. She was afraid of what else she might say if she stayed.

'You keep your blinkers on, Ma, if you like. But I'm sick of this place, sick of everything. I'm going out.'

Lottie had not followed her, and she was glad. She was ashamed now of her outburst, but she had been pushed into it, she thought resentfully. Jan had always been her hero, strong and capable. Telling her what was right. But that woman had said her father was a criminal, a violent man, and no one would tell her what he had done. So, if Marina was right, how could Ma stay with him? How could she sleep in his bed, sit at the same table with him? Hannah had tried to convince herself that Camilla's mother had been lying for her own malicious purposes, but the moment she had looked into her father's face, she had known in her heart of hearts that he had done something very bad. And she was afraid. Afraid of him, afraid for him, and for them all. What was this going to do to them in the end? And now there was all that awful stuff she had said to her mother about Piet. Ach man, she really loved her brother. Why could she not get rid of this corrosive jealousy and be glad for him?

She wished that Sarah was here. Sarah would have brightened up the gloom – she could always make people laugh. God, how she missed her friends, wondered what they were doing, longed to be with them. Sarah's last letter had been full of outrageous comments about her lecturers and her fellow students, and complaints about the Irish weather, and how lucky Hannah was to be out in the veld with the tropical sun beating down on her back, eating mangos and smelling the dust and the wildlife of Africa on the morning wind. Nobody had ever even heard of a mango or a pawpaw in Dublin. Such ignorance! Sarah had said she was going to London at Easter to meet up with Camilla, who was consorting with the nobility and famous people, who was famous herself with her picture in magazines and newspapers. And they hoped to catch up with Piet too, if he could get down to the swinging city from Scotland. Sarah was going to visit Carnaby Street and the nightclubs where groups like the Rolling Stones had started.

Hannah smiled in spite of herself. Sarah's spiky handwriting fled along the pages of her letters as if her pen had trouble keeping up with her jostling ideas. Piet was such a fool, hankering after Camilla when he could have Sarah with the raising of an eyebrow, or a crook of his little finger. Why didn't things ever work out in some simple, uncomplicated way? She wondered if Tim would ever write to her. Sarah said he'd enquired after her several times, and she had told him if he wanted to know how Hannah was, he should ask her himself. Except he was a doctor now, working round the clock, so he probably wouldn't have the energy to write. Plus he was going out with a nurse from the hospital, but Camilla had made short work of her, whatever that meant. Camilla, of course, was far too taken up with her new life to write letters. For a time she'd sent postcards, with pictures of all the exotic places she was visiting, but the messages on the back were vague and brief. Then silence.

The old antipathy roiled up again, as she thought of the Broughton-Smiths. They did say like father like son. Who was Camilla like? Her father was a decent enough sort, but the mother was an evil bitch! If Camilla hadn't come to the farm with Sarah, all those years ago, this might never have happened. No, that wasn't fair. Whatever Pa had done would have come out sooner or later, no matter what. She just wished it hadn't been her friend's mother who had caused them so much pain. And George Broughton-Smith had done nothing to help them, even though he was back in London in a powerful job. He was still working with the Kenya government, Sarah said. Would he be in a position to help Piet, if there was a future showdown on land acquisition? Would he turn a blind eye while the new government seized their farm and parcelled it out to the natives?

Her thoughts constantly returned to Langani and what was happening there now. Before he left, Pa had taken on a young Norwegian manager. The man seemed to be doing well on his own since Piet went to Scotland. According to reports. But then he would say everything was fine, wouldn't he? No one could tell, from this distance, if he was managing well or running the whole operation into the ground. There'd be no way of knowing if he was lining his own pockets while the owners were away. People did that. She had nightmares about Langani, its gates hanging crooked, the house crumbling, the farm machinery rusting in the yards, the cattle wasted by disease, and Lottie's beautiful garden choked with weeds.

'Stop! Stop it – that's bloody stupid!' Hannah muttered to herself. Things couldn't go to ruin like that so fast. Someone would write, old friends or neighbours, and warn them if there were problems. But Hannah wanted to be there to see for herself. Suddenly, she wanted it more than anything in the world. It was her farm too, as well as Piet's. She had ideas – maybe not a degree in agriculture like her brother, but other skills that would be of value. She had discovered that she was good at her business studies. She had an excellent head for figures and organisation, her teachers said. They were impressed with her work. Piet wanted to develop a game reserve, bring tourists in. She could help with that. He could run the farm, and maybe the Norwegian would stay on to help. And she could manage the tourist side of things. Yes, that was it! What she must do now was persuade Piet to take her on, to understand that she wasn't just his nuisance little sister, but a partner who could make a useful contribution to the farm. He'd have to see that. It was her heritage as well. She was sure that her brother cared enough for her to accept that he should give her a chance. A part to play.

The persistent worm of envy was murmuring again. 'If you'd been a brother instead of a sister, you wouldn't have to fight like this to be recognised.' A part of her acknowledged that this was true, but now she felt that Piet would understand. He'd be back from Scotland next month, full of new ideas and plans, and he would surely have too much to do. This was a perfect time to make her appeal. He would back her if she could show him she was serious.

In all her letters to him since she had come south, she had railed against the tobacco farm, the business course, everything. She had felt guilty about complaining so much, but it was a way of letting off steam. His answers had been typically blunt, pointing out that naturally it was a drag, but it was only for a couple of years, and Pa and Ma needed her. She had to put up with it, was what he was saying, more or less. It had compounded her anger and her sense of injustice. All very well for him to be pontificating from his lofty position in Scotland. He wasn't stuck in this miserable dump. She remembered how she had felt constrained in Langani as a teenager, far away from Nairobi and all the excitement she believed she was missing. Man, if she could only get home now, back to the farm, there would be no more complaints.

The kestrel was in the sky again, hovering, watching, ready to plummet down on to its next target. Hannah stood up. She would not be the mouse, the powerless prey. She would be the hunter – go after what she wanted, watch, wait for her opportunity, then swoop in and carry off her prize. She would stick it out, get qualified, and prove to Piet that she wasn't a self-indulgent whiner. She would show him, she would show them all.

Two months went by, and she studied with a new determination. In the evenings she helped Lottie in the house and tried not to allow Pa's moods to get to her when he was at home. It was hard. Her father had always been interested in everything she did, quizzing her about her studies or her sports achievements. Now he never asked her anything. She felt sometimes that he could not bear to look at her, for fear of what he might find in her eyes. Often when she came back from the college and walked into the room, he would get up and shuffle off to his bedroom or out on to the verandah, staying there till the meal was ready. She wished there was something she could say or do to tell him that she loved him, but she was not sure any more if she did. How could you love someone whose actions had put in jeopardy the happiness of your whole family?

Lottie had started sewing. She had always been a fine needlewoman, and now she took in orders from neighbours to try and eke out their income. She also made jams and sold them in the market on Saturdays, and baked pastries and cakes for a local café. These days she looked tired all the time, but she still flashed her bright smile for the customers who bought produce from her stall. Back home, though, the smile was strained. Hannah felt increasingly ashamed as she watched her mother taking on all these extra tasks, while her pa sat over the kitchen table with his beer or whisky, whenever he was there. He went out in the mornings to check the crop and the tobacco sheds, returning at lunchtime red-faced and sweating, reaching for another bottle, cursing the kaffirs who toiled in the fields. At Langani he had always treated his workers well. Here he was belligerent and unreasonable, and the men did not meet his eye as he shouted his orders. When he was out on patrol, Hannah felt guilt at her relief in his absence, and a dull fear for his safety. Once, he had been shot at, and the truck he used was still punctured by bullet holes.

She asked Lottie if she could take a job as a waitress in the local café and when she saw the spark of gratitude in her mother's eyes she felt ashamed, because her offer was not as generous as it sounded. She wanted more than anything to be out of the house. And she was embarrassed at seeing her mother behind the market stall in her apron, smiling with determination as she served thickset farmers and their wives and well-dressed ladies from town, taking cheek from kids younger than Hannah herself. But Lottie touched her daughter's cheek gently.

'No job for now, my dear. I want you to concentrate on your studies, Hannah, and I don't want anything to distract you. First, get your diploma. Then I have a plan for you.' She bent down to a drawer in the bottom of the dresser and took out an old box.

'Pa doesn't know about this. If he did—' she hesitated. 'Well, you know where it would go. Everything I've earned from the sewing and the things I make, I've put away for you. When your course is finished, I'm going to send you to university in Johannesburg. Any subject you want. You can stay with my brother while you're there. It will take a while to get the money together, but it will come. Just be patient a little longer.'

Lottie pushed her hair back from her face with a tired gesture, and in the light filtering into the room Hannah saw lines on her mother's face that had never been there before. Her eyes blurred with tears. She wanted to scream at Lottie, to tell her that she couldn't stand being the reason for her own mother's drudgery. She didn't care about university in Johannesburg. What she wanted was for things to be as they were, and no amount of hard-earned money was going to make it better here. She looked at the scratched lid of the tin box that held her mother's dreams for her and turned away, sick with guilt.

Three weeks later, Lottie was at the market when Hannah heard the post arrive. She ran to the box, and lifted out the letter with the Kenya postmark. Piet! Piet was home! She ripped open the envelope and started to read.

Dear Ma, Pa and Hannah,

I got back yesterday, and it's so good to be home. Lars has kept things running very well, and the farm looks great. We sold five bullocks and got a fair price for them and the wheat is looking good for this year. Lars is a sound man. I'd like him to stay on if possible, at least till I can get the game reserve and the lodge up and running. I could do with the help, and he seems to like it here. I can't really run everything on my own, and I do think we need to go ahead with the lodge now. It will boost our income and help the farm over this present bad patch. I saw Anthony Chapman in Nairobi on the way home, and he's going to come up soon, to take a look at the land I want to set aside for the game reserve. He's willing to put up some of the cash for construction. There are other hunters and private safari operators who have assured us they will use the place for their clients.

The garden looks OK, but not up to your standard of perfection, Ma. I think it misses you. Kamau and Mwangi and all the staff miss you as well. And so do I. Thanks for the letters that were waiting for me – it was good to see your handwriting on the envelopes and to know that you are doing fine.

Pa, how's it going with the tobacco crop? At least you should have plenty of labour out there. We've had a bit of trouble with poachers taking plains game for meat, and the Maasai have been sneaking their cattle and goats into our grazing, cutting the fences to get in. Lars and I are going to talk with the headman early next week. Apart from the poachers, Lars has managed very well and we were lucky to find him. He sends you his greetings and will soon post you his monthly report. Don't worry about things up here. We'll pull through somehow.

Hannah, I hear from Ma that you're really hunkering down to your course now, and doing well. Keep it up. Maybe you can come up for a holiday in a while. In the meantime, be good and help out in every way you can.

I saw Sarah and Tim, and Camilla too, in London at Easter. We spent the weekend together and we had a few experiences that I'll tell you about some day. I don't know if the idea of you all being here for Han's 21st summer will work out now. Things have changed so much for everyone.

Got to go. Will be in touch again soon. This is just to let you know I'm home. I have a lot of new ideas – I'll describe some of them in my next letter. I can't wait to get started!

Love to you all.
Piet

Hannah felt tears burning behind her eyes. He had plans. He couldn't wait to get started. And this Lars was going to be asked to stay on. She couldn't bear the idea that she would have no part in it. She would be trapped here in this awful place where she would rot, homesick and lonely in her desolate prison. For a moment, she hated Lars with an unreasonable intensity. Then she carried Piet's letter into the kitchen. Jan was sitting at the table. He had come in from a patrol early in the morning and he was still wearing his dust-covered clothes. In front of him was an untouched plate of cold meat and cheese that Lottie had prepared before she went out. His eyes looked burned in their sockets and he had not shaved. He reached for a bottle of whisky and sloshed a measure into a glass. His hands were shaking a little as he poured.

'There's a letter from Piet. Do you want to see it?' Hannah saw him look up, but he did not answer. 'I said there's a letter from Piet—'

'Show it to your mother when she comes in.' Jan's voice sounded hoarse. 'Where's she gone anyway?'

'To deliver the sewing to Mrs Kruger. She's making chair covers for her, remember?' Hannah's answer was clipped and surly. 'Not that you really care where any of us are,' she added in an undertone.

'What did you say?' Jan's head came up, and he winced at the sudden movement.

'I said, "Not that you care". That's what I said.' She spoke very clearly, glaring down at him.

Jan half rose from the chair, his face flushed. 'And what's that supposed to mean, heh?' He sank down again, heavily, and reached for the bottle. Hannah leaned forward and jerked it from his hand.

'It means that you don't care about anything any more, except turning yourself into a sodden mess with this stuff! Look at yourself, Pa. Just look at yourself. Ma is working every hour of the day every day of the week to keep this family together. And all you do is come back from work and lie around drunk, and give her abuse. You're destroying your life, and ours as well! You won't even have this lousy job for long if you go on like you are now. And then what do we do?' She took the bottle to the sink, and started to pour the contents away.

'Give me that!' Jan had surged to his feet in fury. 'Give me that now!'

He towered over her, his great hands gripping her arm as he swung her towards him. A wave of stale alcohol from his breath engulfed her and she turned her face from him, struggling to free herself from his grasp.

'What's the matter?' he roared at her. 'Can't look at your pa any more, is that it? You don't want to think about how he crawled around the forests for weeks at a time on his belly, so you and your ma and Piet could sleep safe in your beds, heh? I did it for you, you hear? I did it for all of you, yes. But no one wants to think about that now.' His eyes filled with tears, and he shook her roughly.

'You did what for us?' Hannah shouted back. 'Tell me what you did that was so noble, that cost us our future at Langani? Why won't anybody tell me?'

'You know nothing! You've been sheltered all your life, protected, given everything. You didn't see your uncle after they finished with him, with his belly split open and his throat slit, and his organs stuffed into his mouth. It's what they would have done to me and to you, and your mother and your brother!'

'Well, now it's all destroyed anyway. You've destroyed it. You've destroyed all of us.' Hannah lifted the bottle in fury, and smashed it on the edge of the sink.

'Damn you, girl!' Jan reached for the jagged remains, cutting himself on the broken glass. He looked down at the gash dripping on to the floor and then raised his bloodied hand and struck her with full force on the side of her face. She staggered and fell against the sink, slithering to the floor. The red handprint pulsed through the mist of rage and despair that possessed him. Hannah was trying to stand, her eyes glazed in shock. Her hand came up to the livid mark on her cheek, and she took it away and looked at it dumbly. Jan sank to his knees beside her, weeping.

'Hannah! Ach, God, my little Hannah, I'm sorry! I don't know what came over me! Hannah, I'm sorry. Come here, let me help you. Ach, I'm so sorry, my little girl—'

Hannah left him there on the floor and walked from the kitchen, down to her bedroom where she locked herself in. Then she sat down on the bed, and stared at the wall. She started to shake. In some distant place, she could hear her pa hammering on the door, pleading with her to let him in, begging for forgiveness. He would stop drinking, he said. He would never raise his hand to her again. He wept and implored as she sat in the suffocating little bedroom, mute and disbelieving, until she heard him go back down the passage. He was mumbling to himself, and after a few moments there was the crunch and clink of his attempts to clear up the broken glass. Later still, she heard the screen door creak open and shut, and then silence.

She stood up, opened the door quietly, and went into the bathroom. Even after she had washed her face, it seemed the print of his hand still flared out at her in her reflection in the mirror. The back of her head where she had struck the sink throbbed painfully. She went to the cupboard, took out a suitcase and packed a few clothes. In the kitchen, she opened the bottom drawer of the dresser, and removed Lottie's tin box. Inside was a bundle of notes, tied in a rubber band. She counted it out carefully, put it into her purse and left the house, closing the screen door behind her.

The bus to Salisbury crawled down the escarpment, and Hannah stared out the window without seeing anything. At the airport she bought a ticket to Nairobi and sat waiting for her flight to be announced, terrified that her name would suddenly be called out on the loudspeakers, that Lottie would guess where she had gone, that she would not be able to escape. She tried to focus her thoughts on the garden at Langani, painstakingly remembering every flower and bush and tree, dwelling on their colour and shape, their place in the landscape. She would not look yet at the house. To look at the house would be to remember people, and she did not want to remember anyone. When the plane took off at last, she refused the meal service, closed her eyes and slept.

At Embakasi Airport she realised she did not have much money left.

There were taxis outside the terminal, but she decided to take a bus. The driver and passengers stared at her with open curiosity. White memsahibs did not travel on buses, and certainly not alone. She spoke in Swahili as she paid her fare and enjoyed the broad smiles of approval that were her reward. A small *toto* came to sit beside her, looking up into her face with glowing eyes. He reached out tentatively and touched her, and she took his small hand in hers. Then she adjusted her sunglasses against the glare and stared out the window. The bus swayed and jolted with its cargo of tightly packed humanity. More passengers clung to the windows and doors as the driver stopped to pick up additional fares on the way in to the city.

At the Norfolk Hotel, she went to the reception desk and asked to make a reverse charge call. Standing in the small, panelled phone booth, on the edge of exhaustion, she heard the insistent burr of the phone at Langani. A foreign voice answered, and despair took two steps closer.

'Lars Olsen? Is that you, Lars? I want to speak to Piet. Is he there? What did you say?' Her voice was edgy with impatience and weariness. 'It's Hannah, his sister. Can you get him please, it's urgent.'

The seconds seemed to crawl by. Then the familiar voice.

'Han? Where are you? Ma has been going frantic with worry. Where are you, for Chrissake?'

Hannah stood clutching the telephone. The enormity of what she had done struck her fully for the first time, and her courage disintegrated

'Piet? I'm in the Norfolk.' She began to sob. 'Can you come and get me, Piet? I just want to come home.'

Chapter 8

London, May 1965

Camilla had walked away from her second audition sure that in the autumn she would be at drama school. In the evening she had gone out with Ricky Lane to celebrate, and she could barely remember their return to her flat. They had collapsed with laughter on the landing as she stabbed the key repeatedly towards the lock. Then she had firmly closed the door on his entreaties and fallen on to her bed fully dressed, to sleep for ten hours. Three days later she returned from a long day's fashion shoot to find the letter. She read it twice, a wave of despair crashing over her as she sat alone on the sofa. Tears of humiliation slid down her face and she poured herself a shot of neat vodka with ice, tormented by the rejection and by her own arrogance. She had been so sure of herself, and now she was paying the price of her conceit.

She could not telephone Sarah because she was afraid. The telephone stood on the polished table, black and accusing. After Easter she had received a stiff note of thanks from Dublin. Since then there had been no communication between them. Neither Sarah nor Tim had understood her reaction to Marina on that dreadful night. Camilla knew that her treatment of Piet had been unforgivable, and she bitterly regretted the thoughtless words she had hurled into the constant battleground between herself and her mother. But she felt that Sarah might have tried to understand. Each time she thought of that evening, Camilla remembered her mother's pale, jewelled fingers clasped around the black man's neck, saw his strength and ownership in the way his arms held her close to him as they danced their slow, sensuous dance, flaunting their desire and their intimacy. She could not accept their reckless display, and she knew that the consequences of such a public affair could be dire for a Foreign Office diplomat. Camilla feared for her father, and despised Marina for her total want of discretion. Still, she should never have used Piet to extract revenge, by making a shocking declaration of her own. Now she was paying the price for her betrayal and conceit. Camilla gagged a little as the vodka burned its way down her throat. The letter of rejection lay face up in front of her. She crumpled it up, opened it again, and finally tore it into tiny shreds. Then she threw her glittering stage career into the waste-paper basket and poured another drink.

For two days she saw no one, cancelling her photo sessions and infuriating her agent, Tom Bartlett, by taking her telephone off the hook. The doorbell rang on the first afternoon, but she made no attempt to leave her bed where she lay face down, pulling a pillow over her head to block out all contact with an intruding world. After an eternity of persistent ringing and knocking, she heard the footsteps going down the stairs, and the sound of a car door being slammed in the street below. On the third morning she crawled out of bed and made her way to the kitchen, rummaging in the cupboard for coffee and rinsing a stained mug that was lying in the sink. The porter had pushed the morning's scattering of letters under the door. Camilla bent to pick them up without enthusiasm, and was surprised to recognise her father's neat handwriting on one of the envelopes. He had been trying to telephone her, he said, but there seemed to be a problem with her phone. He assumed she was away on a fashion shoot. There was something he wanted to discuss with her. She shuddered at the thought of the explanation she would have to make about her drama school rejection, put his letter aside, and pulled on jeans and a sweater.

Her random choice of a bus took her to an area of London she had never been in before, and she walked aimlessly under a heavy sky. It was the first time she had failed at anything, or been refused something she passionately wanted. The first time she had been obliged to assess her own worth and true ability. In the dismal streets, with their cracked window panes and overflowing dustbins, she encountered faces that were slack with defeat, imprinted with the knowledge that their early dreams had been gobbled up in their daily fight for survival. Sitting on a bench beside a huddled old woman, Camilla recognised that her parents had tried to protect her, to guide her towards a life that would keep her safe. Even her mother had made an effort to reach out through the cocoon in which she chose to live, and to suggest some kind of secure framework. She found a public phone box and dialled her father's number. The sound of George's voice raised her spirits for the first time since the letter. They made a date for dinner at his club. In the bath she tried to form the sentences that would explain her exaggerated optimism about drama school. Her eyes looked flat with misery and shame as she applied her make-up. She lifted her shoulders with resignation, acknowledging that she had made a fool of herself and that there was no way out but to admit it. He would be the first one to know and she could, at least, practise her first lines of humility on a sympathetic audience.

'I'm so sorry. I know how disappointed you must be.' George reached for his daughter's hand across the table. 'But you can apply to other schools, you know. I think your worst mistake was setting your sights on one place only.'

But Camilla shook her head, looking down at her plate to hide unshed tears, grateful that he had not questioned her too closely, or chided her for her misplaced confidence.

'Everybody goes through this sort of thing.' He looked at her gravely. 'If you still plan to pursue an acting career I'm afraid you've got to learn to love rejection. What does this tutor you told me about have to say? The one who was so certain you'd get in.'

'I made him up,' she said, sick with shame.

George nodded. 'That was foolish,' he said. 'But it doesn't matter now. Let me introduce you to a friend of mine who's involved in the running of the Royal Court Theatre. He's a sympathetic young man with a great many contacts, and I think you'd like him. If you don't want to apply to another drama school maybe you could start out working backstage, and go on from there. There are plenty of outstanding actors who've come up that way. They start out with small parts and as understudies, until a suitable role comes up. And then they're on their way.'

'I don't know, Daddy. Right now I haven't the heart to think about it. But I do have some good photo bookings coming up. As many as I would like, in fact. I'm lucky enough to have one of the best agents in London – his name's Tom Bartlett. I have a shoot in Scotland next week with Ricky Lane. We're doing clothes for *Queen* – first time my photo will be in their pages, and maybe on the cover. And there's talk of going to Paris again in June, and to New York in the autumn.' Camilla raised her eyebrows in mock surprise. 'I'm getting to be quite famous, you know. People recognise me in restaurants and give me the best tables. Strangers even come up to me in the street these days. It can be a bore, actually.'

'But it's not what you want to do, ultimately. You mustn't be tempted to give up on your acting ambitions, just because of one rejection.'

'I'm not giving up. I'll get there in the end.'

'I'm glad to hear you say that, darling. Stick with it, even if it's tough, and I'll be so proud of you. What are your immediate plans?'

'I hope I can go to Kenya for August and early September. It's something we promised each other – Hannah, Sarah and I. We said we'd go back to celebrate our twenty-first birthdays, and our newly discovered wisdom.' She tilted her head and smiled at her father, but her mouth was lopsided and sad. 'That's supposing they still want me to come.'

'Why wouldn't they, for heaven's sake?' George was surprised.

But Camilla could not tell him that she had seen Marina and her black lover, blatantly fawning over one another in one of London's best-known night spots, while he was away in Kenya or working to the point of exhaustion in Whitehall. The risk of hurting her father, the one steady element in her life, the person that she loved and trusted, was too great. Nor could she confess what she had subsequently done to Piet and Sarah. Her mind shied away from the memory and she forced her attention back to the moment.

'So what did you want to discuss with me?' she asked.

'I'm making a major change in my own life,' George said. He hesitated, poured them some wine and lit a cigar. There was a long silence and she waited, puzzled. 'I'm leaving the Foreign Office,' he said, at last. 'I've resigned.'

'What?' Camilla was incredulous. 'But you love your job, Daddy. It's your life. They must be about to make you a governor or a high commissioner or something, surely? Why on earth would you leave now?' He did not answer immediately and she saw that he was formulating his reply. 'No, don't tell me,' she said. 'This is about Mother. I know it is. She's persuaded you to do this. It's about money, isn't it?'

She stared at him hard, her eyes demanding an answer, her instinct telling her that she was right. His gaze wavered, and then she could clearly see Marina in the nightclub. Marina, creating a scandal that had forced his resignation. But she did not dare to ask any further questions, because she could not be sure that he knew about Winston Hayford.

'This is nothing to do with your mother.' George was looking at her directly now. 'I've accepted an interesting job in the private sector. Something with more scope.'

'More scope than changing the face of the world? I don't believe you.'

'It's a challenging position.' He was quietly insistent. 'I'm going to run an international fund for wildlife and the environment. It's a job that will take me all over the world. But I've been given special responsibility for East Africa, because of the years I've spent there. These new governments have very little money for national parks and conservation, and they have a crisis, particularly in Kenya. There are huge numbers of elephants being slaughtered by bandits coming across the Somali border, and by ivory hunters in other areas. And the rhino population has been butchered to the point where they'll become extinct if something isn't done.'

'But money like that simply disappears into greedy pockets, because of corruption. You've often said so yourself.'

'I'm going to control a fund that can be administered properly, where money goes directly to a supervised project and not into the national kitty. I'm very keen on the whole thing.' He tried to draw some sign of enthusiasm out of his daughter, but she did not respond. 'The foundation has a flat in Nairobi that I can use when I'm there.'

'So you and Mother are finally going to live apart? Separate officially?' Now that the moment had possibly arrived, Camilla felt a strange apprehension as she waited for his reply. It would be a logical decision, and she wondered if a divorce was the real reason behind this change in her father's life. It would spell the end of their small family, flawed though it might be. She was surprised to discover a deep sadness at the realisation that they had reached this point.

'No. We're not going to make any changes.' George was not looking at her.

Camilla sighed. She would never understand why he stayed with her mother, why they could not reach some amicable settlement and go their different ways. At least one of them would then have a chance at happiness. 'When do you start your new appointment?' she asked.

'In a couple of months. July, in fact.'

'You must have been thinking about this for a while, but you never said a word. Not to me anyway. It's all so sudden.' Now she was sullen and hurt, although she could not explain why. 'How much time will you spend in Kenya?'

'I hope it will be about half and half, by the end of this year. I'm flying out to Nairobi next week for talks with the Ministry of Tourism and the national parks. Then on to Tanzania and Uganda for more of the same. And there are other projects in Asia – tigers and pandas, and forests that are being hacked down with no thought for the future of the resident wildlife.'

'And where will Mother be, while all this is going on? I'm sure she has no intention of wandering through the world's jungles with you.'

'She may join me for some of the time.'

'You know she won't.'

'I think she'll be happy to stay here in London for the main part. She's looking for a house in the country. Something small, for weekends.'

'I knew it! This is about her. Now she'll get what she always wanted – a flat here and house parties in the country at weekends, for her smart chums from London. This new job will finance her social dreams, even though you've had to give up doing what you love.'

'Life isn't that simple, Camilla.'

'It is for her.'

She was still bitter as they parted in Pall Mall and she watched him walk away, his shoulders hunched down against the wind. She did not want to spend the rest of the evening alone contemplating her parents' strange lives, and she hailed a taxi and made her way to Ricky Lane's studio. It was late, but she was sure he would be there.

'Where the hell've you been, darlin'? If you miss another session, without giving me any notice or any reason, I'll be out looking for other talent. And there's plenty of it around.' He lit a cigarette. 'You look bloody awful.'

'I had a bad week.'

'They don't give a toss what kind of week you've had at Mary Quant or *Tatler*. And neither do I. I just want to earn my living.'

'I'm sorry.'

'Yeah, I'm sure you are. You toffs are all the same at the end of the day. You don't give a fuck about anyone. You think your posh family connections will pull you through every time you screw up and can't be bothered to get out of bed in the morning. You're spoiled rotten, all of you.'

'I'm not like that, Ricky.'

'What are you like, then?' He sauntered towards her, tossing his cigarette aside and pulling her into his arms. 'Come on then, darlin', show us what you're really like.'

His mouth was surprisingly soft as he kissed her, and she inhaled the smell of tobacco and whisky on his breath. She felt his hands working up her back underneath her shirt and sliding round to touch her breasts and she pushed him away.

'Get off me, you fool!' She was laughing but a little shaky. 'We've been through all this before. Some photographers might wind up on top of all their girls, but I'm not going down that road. Not with you or anyone.'

'Not unless they're a lord, or a banker or something.'

'Oh come on, Ricky! Don't give me any shit about it being a class thing. You know I don't think that way.'

'I sometimes wonder if you think at all, if ideas can sprout and grow in that icebox you call a head.'

'You're supposed to be a photographer, not a psychologist,' she said, ruffling his hair. 'What day are we going to Scotland? It's bound to be cold and wet, so you should bring wellies and a Barbour jacket like those toffs you're always talking about. And you'd better behave, or I'll put a few lead pellets into your backside. I've been shooting in Scotland before, and not with cameras. Come on – let's go somewhere for a drink and some dancing.'

It was cold on the moors, and raining. Ricky was evil-tempered, frustrated by the weather and the light. Camilla consoled herself with large plates of porridge and cream in the mornings, and after the first disastrous day on the moors she sat down at the bar of the hotel and ordered single malts for both of them.

'Look,' she said, 'I know the light is grey. And it's probably going to rain the whole time we're here. So why don't we take advantage of this dismal weather? Make a feature of it.'

'Very funny,' Ricky said, downing his drink in one gulp. 'What have you got in mind then, darlin'? Shoot the whole bloody thing under an umbrella, or what?'

'Yes,' she said. 'Something like that. For example, with some of the sweaters I could get them soaking wet, so they really stick to me – so you can see there's nothing underneath, I mean. The wool will take on the shape of me, nipples and all. Jumpers will suddenly be oozing sex. The colours are really bright, so they'll look brilliant against a grey sky and all those miles of misty fields. I can put masses of oil in my hair and plaster it into a slick shape against my face, as though I've been standing out in the rain for hours. Waiting for someone who's never going to turn up. We'll have huge kohl eyes, maybe allow the black to run down my cheeks. And impossible eyelashes with very bright lips. The flat light will show it all up brilliantly. A sort of "girl abandoned" theme. Lost in the rain. Bare feet even. The clothes will tell a whole story.'

'You'll catch your bloody death of cold,' Ricky said, but he was laughing like a maniac, rubbing his hands together. 'It's bloody brilliant. That's what it is.'

'Just as well one of us has brains. Get ready to pay my medical bills,' Camilla said. 'And in the meantime you can buy me another drink.'

Driving back to London after the shoot Camilla was tired, positive that she would never rid herself of the damp that had permeated her entire body as she posed in the rain, barefoot and shivering in empty fields, on horseback and at the village bus stop, with the bright clothes making their bold statement. When Ricky dropped her outside her flat, she ran up the stairs, anticipating an hour in a steaming bath. She was surprised to find a note from Anthony Chapman among her piles of mail, and she telephoned him immediately.

'What on earth are you doing here?' she asked

'Big sales trip. I've been phoning you non-stop, for the last forty-eight hours. Where were you, Camilla? I'm leaving in three days for New York. What about coming to my slide presentation tonight? One of my clients in Cadogan Square is laying on an evening for a few chums who might like to go on safari. You could help me chat them up.'

She was surprised at how much she wanted to see him. In Nairobi he had taken her to charity balls and rugby matches, and she had watched him play polo or joined him for tennis at Muthaiga Club. In between safaris they had occasionally met for dinner and he had kissed her on several occasions. But she had refused his attempts at further advances. Her future lay in London and there was no room in it for Anthony Chapman, hunter and safari guide. Now she was overcome with nostalgia for the smell of the dust and the sound of the first rain falling on scorched earth, the tussle between humanity and wildlife, the incomparable majesty of endless plains, the glare of snow on mountain peaks and the dazzle of blue ocean. In the smart London drawing room, she was pleased when Anthony's hosts and their guests recognised her and were impressed by his choice of companion. As his slide photographs flashed across the screen she sat a little apart from the other guests and allowed the power and essence of Africa to reclaim her. Over dinner she enjoyed talking to his potential clients. Some had travelled with him before, while others were contemplating their first safari experience, and she used all her charm and powers of persuasion to help him sell his vision of the land he loved.

'Nice work,' he whispered into her ear, as the evening drew to a close. 'Between us we've really got them going. Two of the couples will definitely sign up. How about dinner tomorrow evening?'

When she woke the next morning, the world seemed changed. The day dragged and she whiled away the last hours making an extra effort with her appearance. Anthony arrived early, bringing flowers and chocolates from Fortnum & Mason. He could not hide his admiration for her exquisite beauty. He was wearing a suit that was definitely old-fashioned. His shoes were polished but slightly scuffed, and they looked as though he had trudged through the bush in them once too often. In the crowded restaurant that Camilla selected he looked slightly out of place, but he was amused by the fact that everyone recognised her. She was delighted to find that he was unfazed and completely at ease in the glossy surroundings.

'I don't suppose you'll be back in Kenya any time soon, now that you've arrived in the halls of fame. Just as you predicted.' His eyes crinkled at the corners as she protested. 'Not that I'm surprised. You were made for all this razzmatazz. But maybe one day you'll need a break, and then you'll be tempted by the idea of a few weeks in the *bundu*.'

'I don't know why everyone makes sweeping assertions about how I feel, or what I want to do,' she said. 'As a matter of fact I plan to be in Kenya in August. To join Sarah, and hopefully Hannah, and celebrate the year of our big birthdays. We promised, that night in the sea at Watamu. Remember?'

'I remember the sea. But I've filed away the rest of the evening with the other occasions when you gave me the brush-off, one more time.' He was grinning at her. 'Is this reunion at the coast? Am I invited?'

'Probably and possibly, in that order. We'll be at Langani too, so we can see the beginnings of Piet's game reserve and the lodge. Your lodge too, I gather. He mentioned it at Easter when he was here. Has he started building?'

'Any minute now. It should be well advanced by July, and you'll love it. He found this terrifically talented architect. A mad Polish chap called Szustak who drinks like a fish, and writes dubious poetry in his spare time. But he's a superb designer. It's totally different from all the existing safari lodges – much smaller of course, and unique in its use of local materials. The buildings will be set into the side of a kopje, with the existing rocks forming part of the walls. There are great views across the plain, all the way to the mountain. Piet's creating a permanent waterhole and a salt lick, to bring in elephant and buffalo, and even rhino. There's nothing like it anywhere. He's a fantastic guy, Piet, and he's doing something extraordinary up there.'

'That's quite an accolade.'

'He deserves it. I'm proud to be a part of it, and I think the whole project is going to set an example for other private landowners to do their bit for the wildlife.'

'My father's switched careers, you know,' Camilla said. 'He's joined a fund that provides money for national parks and the environment. He's going to be in Kenya a great deal, I think.'

'Yes, I'd heard,' Anthony said. 'Conservation people in Nairobi are optimistic. It's an organisation with plenty of money, and he already knows the country so well. Kenya's crawling with two-year wonders these days, and although they're well meaning they haven't a clue how to cope with local problems. We need experienced hands like George. What about your mother?'

'She'll visit sometimes, but she's happy to be based here. I can't wait to go back, though.' She looked at him across the table, enjoying the lack of artifice in him and the open, natural rhythm of their conversation. In his company she could be herself. There was no hidden agenda, no need to impress or deceive. 'Maybe you'll come up to Langani while we're all there,' she suggested. 'You can join Piet and show us the lodge, since it's your project too.'

He nodded, evidently pleased with the idea. 'I have a gap between safaris, in late August. How about camping with me somewhere, for a few days?'

'All of us? Just like we dreamed it up, that night at Watamu?' She deliberately steered him into extending his invitation.

'Why not?' He could not find a way back to his original intention. 'I could set up a camp, maybe in the north, and perhaps Piet can get away. I'll provide the tents and the staff, and everyone can chip in a little towards food and drink and fuel. What do you say?'

'I say we're going dancing now, and I'll work like a maniac for two months, and then we'll come camping with you.'

In the packed nightclub they were given a table immediately and she sat close to him in the dim light, talking to him easily, admitting her disappointment over the drama-school rejection.

'I see that you're famous and successful. But you've got to really care about what you're doing to make life seem right.' He reached for her hand. 'So, if this modelling is a second-best situation, then you'll have to find a way back to where you really want to go. I can't imagine having to compromise on what I do. I have to be out in the bush, taking people on safari, sitting around the fire with my *watu*, doing my bit towards saving what we've got in East Africa.'

'You're lucky to be in that position.' Her voice was sad. 'In the autumn I'll probably try to join a theatre company, and start by working backstage. Make my way up via that route. Daddy knows someone who might give me a try. Or I'll just reapply for drama school next year.'

'Are you happy, Camilla?'

'What on earth does that mean?' She tried to laugh off the question, but it had unnerved her. The pressure of his hand was making small shivers dart through her, and she looked away.

'If you can't answer straight, then maybe you should take a look at your life,' he said. 'Decide what you want most and set out to reach it. Now, get me on to that dance floor to work off that huge dinner.'

Camilla slid into his arms with a sense of belonging and he held her with firm, light hands. They danced without speaking. In the taxi he put his arm around her, and she leaned back against him with her eyes closed. When they reached the door of her flat he placed the key in the lock with unhesitating precision and led her towards the bedroom.

'I don't know, Anthony,' she whispered. 'I haven't thought of this—'

'We've both thought of this for as long as I can remember,' he said.

He kissed her slowly, waiting for her lips to part so that he could taste her. She sighed and lay back on the bed as he slowly took off her clothes. He was murmuring in her ear, laughing a little as he slid the long boots from her legs and ran his hands up her thighs, listening to the soft sounds she was making. When he drew back from her to unfasten his belt and his trousers she sat up and gently pushed him away.

'There's something I have to tell you,' she said.

'You don't have to tell me anything. I want you, Camilla, and you know this is the right moment for us.' He pulled her back to him with a groan of longing. 'You know we both want this. We don't need to play games.'

'No. Wait, Anthony.'

He looked at her, puzzled and sensing a shift between them, unable to understand the hidden thing she was trying to express. Then he placed his hands beneath her and drew her towards him, kissing her again and again, feeling her resistance as he pressed harder in his urgent desire for her, halting when she gave a little cry of pain.

'What is it?' he asked, leaning away from her, stroking her face, kissing her eyelids. 'Am I hurting you?'

She shook her head, pulling him down with abandon, moving beneath him until she was swept away into a soaring, jubilant intensity. When they lay back afterwards he kissed her again, caressing the moist skin of her breasts, then reaching down to touch the secret part of her that he had discovered.

'Camilla? Have I hurt you?' He raised himself up on to his elbow, looking at his fingers, and then he searched her expression, disbelieving. 'Oh God, Camilla, was this—?'

'I was trying to tell you, but I didn't know how to say it. I thought you might laugh at me. All those awful jokes about being a virgin . . .'

'Oh God, come here. Come close to me and let me kiss you very, very slowly and tell you how beautiful you are.'

He gathered her in to him, surprised at the humility he felt, and the sense of tenderness. She stared at him, her face luminous. Beyond her the moon seemed to be tumbling in through the window, shining its light into the sad corners of her mind, freeing her from all that had ever hurt or damaged her in the past. He led her gently to the bathroom and filled the bath, holding her close to him, stroking her, murmuring in her ear, kissing her face and her hands. When she stepped into the bath he joined her in the steaming water. She lay back, silent and dreamlike, as he sponged her body and dried her, wrapping her in a thick towelling robe and carrying her into the bedroom. Then she turned her face back to his shoulder and slept. When she woke at dawn he was still beside her. She studied his sleeping face, sunburned and already mapped with small lines. It seemed to her that his eyelashes were ridiculously long and she marvelled at the reddish lights in his hair and at his lean, beautiful body. She bent over him and blew softly into his ear, placing her hand on his stomach and stroking him awake so that he would make love to her again.

The morning came, sun-washed and warm. They wandered the city together, rowing a boat on the Serpentine, lying on the grass in Hyde Park, holding one another as the clouds drifted high above them across a powder-blue sky. In the evening they stopped at the corner grocery shop to choose the makings of a simple dinner, and then they ran laughing up the stairs to close the door on the world outside. They ate slowly and sipped their wine. He watched her every movement, saw her face light up with contentment as she reached out to touch him, as they smiled at one another through the candlelight. In the bedroom he undressed her with tenderness and lay down with her on the bed, looking at her body, pale and glimmering in the shadows cast by the moonlight. They made love with heightened senses, finding new places to explore, until they were sated and exhausted. Then he held her tight and safe, and they watched the moon and the milling stars through the rectangle of sky beyond the window frame.

After he had gone in the morning she sat on the couch, barely breathing, aware that she would never feel or know anything more precious or extraordinary than this, and that no one could ever take it away from her. In a few weeks she would see him in Nairobi. It seemed like an eternity. She floated across the living room, touching his empty glass, sitting for a moment and hugging the cushion he had leaned against earlier. In the hall she looked at herself in the mirror and saw the new softness in her face and the pure, shining joy in her eyes. Then she picked up the telephone to tell Sarah that a miracle had happened, and that nothing would ever be the same again.

Sarah was short with her, however, and Camilla thought that the memory of the nightclub at Easter would never cease to taint their friendship. But it transpired that there was a crisis with Raphael's health, and there was no chance for Camilla to explain the events that had transformed her. For the remainder of the day she stayed at home, not wanting to put on her everyday street clothes and close the chapter of her lovemaking, unwilling to relinquish the lingering sensation of his touch on her skin, or the intensity of the way she felt about him. It was late when the telephone broke the spell and she picked it up without enthusiasm.

'Darling, would you have lunch with me tomorrow?' Marina's light voice sounded anxious.

'I don't know, Mother. I've got an appointment in the afternoon, and I—'

'We can be quick. I haven't seen you for weeks and there's some thrilling news. Look, I'm meeting someone at eleven. In Harley Street. Perhaps you could join me at the Mirabelle after that. About half past twelve? Please, Camilla.'

Camilla's heart sank. Who was Marina meeting in Harley Street? Her black doctor friend, perhaps. She sighed. 'Join you and who else? I don't feel like being on parade.'

'No. It's just the two of us.'

Marina was already sipping a gin and tonic when Camilla arrived. She raised a slender hand to call the waiter. 'You look wonderful,' she said to her daughter. 'There's something different about you. What is it?'

'Let's order, Mother. I haven't got much time.'

'Have you spoken to your father lately?'

Camilla shook her head, silent now, and wary.

'He's going to love this new job. So varied. And he's not hampered by the old fuddy-duddies in the Foreign Office and all those preening, diplomatic types.'

'I thought he loved his old job.'

'They never really appreciated him, you know. And this is such a challenge. I think it will make a huge change in our lives.' Marina's smile was wistful. 'I wanted to tell you that we've bought something in the country. I'd love you to come and see it.'

'You're moving out of London?'

'Of course not, darling.' Marina gave a impatient flick of her fingers. 'But I've always wanted a little place for weekends. When things get too hectic here. I found this wonderful cottage in Burford. It's seventeenth century and rather small. Only two bedrooms and a tiny garden, and it needs doing up. I thought you might like to come down on Friday and see it.'

'Not this weekend. I'm going to Deauville. Clothes for a new French designer – they're taking the photographs on the beach and at the race course.' Camilla saw her mother's eyes begin to glitter with tears. 'Oh please, Mother, don't make a scene.'

'Don't be hurtful, darling. I'm just a little disappointed. Now let's look at the menu and you can tell me all your other news. I hope you're eating enough.'

'You've lost a few pounds yourself.'

'Yes, but I'm doing something about it,' Marina replied. 'Just be careful, darling. Your sort of work sometimes demands things of your body that may not be good for you. Are you sure you want to go on with this modelling thing?'

Camilla looked up, surprised. She was accustomed to Marina's devious methods of unveiling her real agenda for the day, and she had no doubt that there was something hidden in her mother's remarks. But she could not guess what it might be.

'I'm happy with what I'm doing, Mother. I'm planning to go to Kenya in the summer, you know. So I don't want to start anything new before then.'

Camilla braced herself for objections, but there were none. Marina nodded and then turned the conversation to the redecoration of the cottage, and the organisation of yet another charity ball that was occupying her time.

'Would you think of joining our table?' she asked. 'Your father will be back. We could go as a family. He'd love that, you know. And so would I. You can bring a guest, if you like. Maybe there's a secret someone responsible for making you look so beautiful.'

'Maybe it's one of my cockney barrow boys, Mother.' Camilla was smiling. 'I might disgrace you, if I came to your ball with someone like that.'

'Oh, darling.' Marina gave a breathless little laugh. 'I'll reserve two tickets for you.'

They finished their coffee, and Camilla noticed that her mother's hands were shaking as she replaced her cup. Too many cocktails last night, she thought. But she's very calm today. Almost sweet. She sighed. It wouldn't last.

'Would you come home with me, to the flat?' Marina was reluctant to end their meal. 'I'd like to show you some photographs of the cottage. It's really adorable.'

'I'm going straight to Tom Bartlett's office from here.' Camilla looked at her watch. 'I'm a little late, actually.'

'Of course. How silly of me to have forgotten. I'm sure the doorman can get us a couple of taxis. I'm rather tired, all of a sudden. Not quite steady on my feet for some reason. It's been a busy week, and some things didn't go as well as I had hoped. You do look exceptionally lovely today, darling, I must say.'

Marina paid the bill and rose to her feet. She took her daughter's hand, some silent request hanging in the air between them. Camilla suppressed the temptation to mention Anthony's visit, to say his name out loud. Her mother would not approve of her having an affair with a Kenya cowboy.

'We must do this more often, darling,' Marina said, as the taxi rolled up. 'I do hope I'll see something of you once in a while. I know you're busy now, but perhaps we could meet for lunch once more before you go off to Kenya. Or dinner. Even a drink at the flat. Anything you like. You're very precious to me, you know.'

The taxi growled away and Camilla was left standing alone in the street, surrounded by a hint of her mother's scent in the air, and disturbed by a feeling of uncertainty. There was something about Marina that she could not define, something that seemed almost like fear. For a moment she wished she had said something about Anthony, but it was too late now. She did not see her mother again before she boarded the plane for her flight to Nairobi.

Chapter 9

Dublin, May 1965

Sarah closed the door of the flat and pulled her woollen hat down on her head, battling the gusts of wind that tore at her as she made her way to the main road. She had decided to go into college, to see if the darkroom was free. There could be a good two hours of work on her enlargements if the bus came soon. The rain had been at it for days, falling out of the sky in a continuous deluge. Passing tyres threw showers of oil-slicked water on to the pavement, thrumming against her boots until she felt the damp seeping up through her whole body. The sly wind stole under her coat collar, pushing water down her neck and into her face, no matter which way she turned. She was sick of the interminable gloom. It wasn't like the monsoon in Kenya, when torrents of water plunged on to the parched earth for a few hours and then were gone, leaving steam rising into a shimmer of warm air. When it rained in Mombasa the children ran outside, shrieking with delight and splashing one another in the newly formed puddles. Pye-dogs lapped at the muddy water, and there was the rich scent of thirsty loam soaking up the promise of greenness to come. Here, people huddled in doorways or jostled in a sea of umbrellas, each in their private world of misery, trapped in the insistent drizzle that hung in a curtain from low clouds even when the heavy rain had stopped. She would never get used to this country. This was May. It was supposed to be spring turning into summer, for God's sake! Her bus pulled up in a watery squeal of brakes, as she thrust out her arm at the last minute to stop it.

She stood in the aisle, jammed in the heat and press of bodies huddled in overcoats, rain pooling beneath the spikes of furled umbrellas. Damp hair, damp wool, damp leather, stale feet, stale sweat all hemmed her in, circulating in the whirr of the heater, forming a mist on the windows that hid the world outside. This must be what cattle feel like, she thought, when they're herded on to the transport for the abattoir. Patient and enduring as they jerk and rattle towards their doom. If only there was a sliver of blue sky somewhere, even in the distance. She longed for the summer, for the end of lectures and tutorials and exams, and the crush in the library. Then she would leave it all behind for the light of an African morning, the sing-song voices of children passing on the road to school, the sound of the wind in the palm trees and the surf on the reef. She would be free, skimming over the lagoon in her dinghy, holding in the sail and shouting back to Raphael as they raced for the channel. Or they might take off on safari, driving into the *bundu*, with the sharp scent of acacia trees and red dust filling her nostrils.

She shifted her feet to balance better in the swaying bus and wondered again if she would ever feel at ease in Ireland. Her parents had always talked of 'going home' when they came back for holidays. But her home and her true friends were in Africa. A bleak chill settled on her spirits as she thought about the disastrous reunion in London. She had only written to Camilla once since then, a stilted thank-you note. The fuse of resentment still burned inside her when she thought of the scene in the nightclub. She could see Piet's face, bemused at first, with the blaze of hope suffusing his features as he reached for Camilla's hand, hardly daring to believe. And then the expression in his eyes when he realised the truth. He had laid himself wide open, no dissembling, no self-protection. The stupid ass! Could he not see what she was doing? They had all been pawns in a savage game Camilla had been playing. Perhaps that was all they had ever been. And then she had cast him off with a callousness that was unbelievable. Unless you considered that she was, after all, her mother's daughter.

Sarah had written to Hannah afterwards, but she had left out any mention of the nightclub. Another unpleasant incident involving the Broughton-Smiths. And this time it was their blood-sworn sister who had inflicted the pain. Hannah's reply had come by return, envious of Sarah's life in Ireland. She had mentioned Lottie's efforts to put by money for her own university fees, but it was plain that Hannah wanted to finish her business course as soon as possible, and go home to Langani. Her scribbled pages conveyed little about the reality of her life, and Sarah was struck by what had been left unsaid.

From Piet there had been no word. When they left the nightclub, Sarah had tried to comfort him, but he had been brusque almost to the point of rudeness. In the end, she had mumbled a few platitudes and left him nursing his humiliation. There was nothing she could have said to alleviate his misery. It was time to do what Tim had advised – and forget about the whole sorry affair, and find a life for herself in Dublin until she graduated. She thought about the plan that she had made with Camilla and Hannah to celebrate their twenty-first summer together. Life had been so simple when they had made that promise, so full of the belief that they were all invincible, inseparable. She shrugged, burying herself in her determination to survive the present. There were exams to cram for, and this abysmal weather to survive, before she could return to the world she loved. And in the meantime, photography had become her one pleasure. Her father had given her his single-lens reflex camera, a Leica, when she started college. It was a possession he treasured.

'It will be an asset later on, for your wildlife studies. Join the photographic society in college. Learn your craft,' Raphael had said, as he showed her the basics. 'I'll be expecting wonderful pictures as you get the hang of it.'

It had been the beginning of a new passion. Her first efforts had been mediocre. But gradually she had learned to use the light meter and the filters, to master the long, slow exposures that softened her images and made them part of her own way of seeing things. Now she was preparing a portfolio, hoping to do some freelance work for magazines. And there was the *Irish Times* competition coming up, which carried a substantial cash prize and the opportunity for the winners to exhibit their pictures.

The college darkroom was free when she got there, and she was relieved that there was no one else around to disturb her concentration. She liked the solitary process of developing and printing. It gave her space for her thoughts, and excused her from the awkward business of integrating with her fellow students. There must be something basically wrong with her, she thought, that she had been unable to adapt. She still felt like a foreigner after all this time, despite her roots. Strange how, in Africa, she had always identified herself as Irish, while in Ireland she felt like an alien. Ruth in the alien corn, except that she had found no Boaz in Dublin. Her Boaz was an Afrikaans farmer who lived thousands of miles away and looked on her as some kind of kid sister. Time and again now, she asked herself why she continued to cling to her impossible teenage dream. This torch bearing was ridiculous, and it was time she paid more attention to the young men in college who were friendly and interested. But the students of her own age seemed immature. Unformed somehow. And it wasn't just because of Piet. It was something in herself, some part of her that could not connect with Ireland, with college, with anything here. There were not many overseas students in Dublin. Among the Irish everyone seemed to know or be related to everyone else, while she remained an outsider. When she tried to describe her life in Africa, the immensity of the landscape, the tribal peoples and their customs, the wildlife on the plains, people listened for a short while and then their eyes glazed over and she realised that they had no conception of what she was talking about. They could not even begin to envisage the vastness of the Maasai Mara, the awesome experience of watching hundreds of thousands of wildebeest on their annual migration, the mystical feeling that stole over you as you watched the dawn light dancing on the Indian Ocean. Finally, she had stopped talking about it altogether. Except with Mike. Mike had been interested, had wanted to understand. Or so she'd thought. What a revelation that had turned out to be!

Sarah stood alone in the darkroom, absorbed by the ghostly images that emerged from the developing fluid like bodies drowned in a pool. Elation grew in her as the pictures materialised, gradually rising in clarity until she could see the spinning figures, the lined faces and gnarled hands, the curl of cigarette smoke hanging over eyes that had seen too much sorrow. These were good. Very good. She had been afraid to hope, but now she lifted each enlargement from the tray with the plastic tongs, rinsed it off and hung it up to dry, and knew that the photographs told a story. The men and women were sitting round a table in a shabby kitchen, on the margins of despair, propping one another up with bravado and cigarettes, smiling bravely into the lens, their fingers nicotine-stained as their lives were tainted by other dependencies. She had taken the pictures last week, in St Joseph's Shelter, the refuge for alcoholics and drug addicts on the Liffey, up near the railway station at Sarsfield Quay. Sarah had been working there as a volunteer since that first time last winter when she had gone to help at the soup kitchen. It was strange how one random, seemingly unimportant decision had given her life a sudden twist.

She had seen the poster on the college noticeboard one afternoon.

Volunteers wanted to help at a City Centre Dinner for the Homeless on Tuesday, 26 November

It was a day when she had been feeling exceptionally lost. She was sharing a flat with Tim, but as a houseman in a casualty unit he was seldom at home. When she did see him, he was so tired that he was incapable of being good company. Her dreams of shared student parties with new friends and Tim's colleagues from medical school had fizzled out, through a combination of her own crippling shyness and her brother's punishing hours. Looking at the college noticeboard, she decided that she should make a contribution to people less well off than herself, and perhaps she might make friends among the other volunteers at the same time.

Two nights later she arrived at the parish centre on Merchant's Quay. A Franciscan priest in a brown robe and open sandals steered her towards a young man laying tables in the hall.

'This is Sarah Mackay, Mike. Will you show her what to do?'

'Sure, Father Connolly.' The young man counted out another place setting before looking up.

'Can I help you with those?' Sarah asked. 'Or is there something else?'

His smile lit up a dark, rather serious face, making him less forbidding. He scanned her briefly, taking in the cut of her wool dress, the blue beaded necklace and pale suede boots she had inherited from Camilla.

'Well now—' He put down his pile of cutlery, then pointed to an empty table. 'I suppose you could—'

'Mike, have you not finished there yet?' A tall girl with her hair tied back in a red scarf was coming towards them, all efficiency and purpose. 'Leave those, will you? I told one of the others to take over the tables. I need you out at the door.'

'This is Sarah,' Mike said. 'She's new, just volunteered for tonight. Sarah – Cathy.'

'Hi.' Cathy's smile was perfunctory. 'They need someone in the kitchen. It's bedlam in there. Can you cook?'

Sarah felt panic rising. Cook? She had never needed to cook until she came to Dublin. Living in a flat with your brother had been a basic domestic training of sorts. But cook for a crowd?

'No. Not really. But I could serve at the tables, or talk to people—'

'I'm sure you can peel potatoes? Good. The kitchen's through that door.'

Peeling potatoes was not a skill Sarah had learned in Kenya either, but Cathy had already taken Mike's arm and led him away. At the kitchen door she hovered uncertainly until a stout, middle-aged woman called to her from the sink.

'Thanks for coming, love. Here's a bucket of spuds – just scrub them. Don't bother peeling. We'll boil them in their skins.' She looked Sarah over. 'Janey mackerel! You'd better try and find something to cover your dress – it's far too swish for this job. Sure, you're not out to a dance, you know!'

Sarah flushed. Stupid, stupid! She had put on her smartest clothes as a mark of respect for the diners she had expected to serve. But it looked more like she was showing off. Well, she would know the next time. She found a tea towel, wrapped it around her waist and set to work with the scrubber. The kitchen grew hot and steamy as the evening wore on and she sliced carrots, washed saucepans and scraped down the roasting tins and the gravy pans. Her cheeks glowed red and her carefully arranged hair rose in a frizzy halo above her forehead. She hauled vats of potatoes and vegetables from the cooker to the kitchen table and spooned them on to serving dishes. Then it was back to the sink and the greasy saucepans and platters.

Out in the hall the tables had filled up. Volunteers seated the guests, poured orange squash, and handed round plates of bread and butter with the soup. Once or twice Sarah got as far as the door of the kitchen to look in. Men and women of all ages huddled on the benches in threadbare garments, utensils grasped in roughened hands with dirty fingernails. There was a hunted look about some of them, a furtive hurrying as they spooned their soup and took bread to dip in it. She wondered what it was that had sent them out on to the streets to live in doorways, under cardboard boxes. Her earlier resentment at having been left with the worst job of the evening made her feel ashamed. Even her modest little flat was warm and dry, with hot and cold running water, scented soap, clean towels and sheets. Her days were a secure heaven compared to the desperate lives of these broken-down human beings who had gone without many a meal, and spent their days in fear of being beaten up or driven off pavements by busy shoppers or the police.

'If I did try to talk to any of them they'd probably resent my posh accent, and my grand clothes and privileged background, and they'd be right,' she said to herself. Then the cook summoned her once more, and she went back to her job at the sink.

It was after the pudding that the commotion started. Sarah heard the shouting as she struggled through another pile of sudsy plates. She followed the cook to the kitchen door and looked into the hall. Mike was in the middle of the room, remonstrating with a gaunt man in an old overcoat tied at the waist with string.

'I'm sorry John-Jo. You can't come in.' Mike's voice was firm and he had his hand on the man's arm. 'You know you're barred after last time.'

John-Jo tried to lunge past him, shouting unintelligibly, and pulling something from his pocket. People nearby moved out of the range of his flailing arms as Mike wrestled with him. The hall had become very quiet, everyone watching and waiting. Father Connolly came hurrying from his office.

'Now, John-Jo, you know the rules. No drink in here.' The priest took the bottle from him. 'Will we get you a good strong cup of tea? You're too late for much else. You should have come earlier if you wanted your dinner.' He placed his arm round the bony shoulder. 'Mike is right, you know. You were barred the last time. But if you sit down quietly we'll get you some tea, and you can warm yourself. Will you do that now?'

John-Jo spat on the floor and muttered something. The priest nodded and led him into the kitchen where he settled him at a table beside the back door. As he sank on to the chair the unwelcome guest looked up and saw Sarah watching him. His eyes were bloodshot but very blue, and bright with intelligence, although he looked ill and badly nourished. He held her gaze, unblinking. Embarrassed, she turned away.

'Is there any dinner left, Mary?' Father Connolly looked hopefully at the cook.

'There's a few potatoes and some carrots, Father, but the chicken's all gone.' She glared at John-Jo. 'I thought he wasn't getting in here any more. He's trouble, Father. A violent man. He did terrible damage the last time.'

'Ah now, he's not well, Mary. He looks a lot worse tonight than I've seen him in a long time.'

'You'd look as bad yourself, Father, if you drank the way he does!'

'Well, we'll give him whatever's left of the dinner, and a good hot mug of tea with some bread and butter. It's a bitter night outside.'

'I'll make up a plate, Father, but I'll not take it over to him. He has a tongue on him would flay a cat. Never satisfied with what you give him, and foul-mouthed into the bargain. I'll not stand for the kind of abuse he's doled out to me in the past.' Mary banged a pot on the counter for emphasis.

Sarah cleared her throat. 'I'll take it.'

The priest turned and noticed her with surprise. 'Is this where you were all evening? I thought maybe you'd gone home. Well, it'll be a kindness if you'll serve John-Jo. And don't mind what he says. Just give him his dinner and the tea, and Mike will see he doesn't bother you.'

Sarah organised a plate of food, and carried it over to the man. Mike stood nearby, keeping a wary eye on him. John-Jo was slumped over the table, his head in his hands. In the heat of the room his coat was steaming and a rancid smell rose from it. His knuckles were grazed and there was a scab on his scalp under the thinning patch of grey hair. She put the plate down in front of him.

'There's no chicken left, I'm afraid,' she said. 'But you might like this. And I'll get you some bread and butter to go with it, if you want.'

'Feckin' chicken. It's always feckin', stinkin' chicken. I hate feckin' chicken.' He was digging in one of the pockets of his overcoat. 'Here – can you cook this? I got it off a butcher down the street. Better than feckin' chicken any day.'

He held out a glistening piece of raw meat, covered in the furred contents of his pocket, and she saw a thick glob of juice sliding over his hand and dribbling down his long fingers. A wave of nausea assailed her at the smell of the meat and the man. For a horrible moment she thought she would faint. Mike turned away but Father Connolly had noticed her sudden pallor.

'Ah, come on now, John-Jo,' he said. 'You can't expect anyone—'

'No, it's all right,' Sarah found her voice. 'I'll be happy to cook it.' She took the bloody chunk from him, willing herself not to retch at the slimy feel of it. 'It'll only take a few minutes. Is it OK if I fry it? I'm not a great cook, but I could manage that for you.'

She fled to the sink and turned on the tap, rinsing carefully, removing the fluff and hair and other nameless horrors stuck to it. The fat around the edges had a shiny green look and she trimmed it off, afraid that it would poison him. He couldn't have had it for more than a few hours, or it would have been dried up. She shuddered as she dropped it into hot oil on the frying pan, and as it began to brown it didn't look so bad. The cook had moved away and was clattering her clean pans on to the shelves, muttering under her breath. Sarah warmed some leftover gravy and poured it over the meat. Then she took off her tea-towel apron, straightened her hair and brought John-Jo his dinner. The rest of the onlookers moved away as he set to work on his plate. Sarah found a stool and sat down opposite him. Through the door into the main hall she could see the priest and Mike showing people out, tidying away the long tables and chairs. The cook waved goodnight and called out her thanks. Then she was the only one left in the kitchen.

'Would you like some?' John-Jo was watching her with his vivid blue stare.

'Um – no thanks, John-Jo. No.'

'I'll bet these feckers didn't give you any dinner, did they? Go on – try a bit. It's good. You cooked it fine.'

He pushed a piece of meat towards her on the fork. Behind him she saw that Father Connolly and Mike had turned to watch her. Cathy raised her eyebrows and mimed being sick. Sarah felt an upsurge of determination.

'Thanks. A little bit, then. Just to taste. I had my dinner before I came out.' She steeled herself and put the meat into her mouth.

'Mmmm. Very good. And you're right – I did cook it well, although the gravy could have been hotter.' It was actually quite tasty. John-Jo suddenly beamed.

'Good on ye, girl. Ye're all right.' He shovelled up the rest of the dinner, gulped his tea down and then sat back with a sigh and closed his eyes.

Sarah got up quietly, took the empty plate to the sink and washed it. Then she stepped into the hall to see if there was anything else she should do, but the place was deserted. She heard the scrape of a chair behind her and glanced over her shoulder to see John-Jo getting up. He made his way unsteadily towards her and she felt a ripple of alarm. But he veered away past her, heading for an old piano that stood against one wall, and opened the lid. There was a rickety chair close by and he drew it up and sat down at the keyboard. Then he started fishing in his pockets again. Sarah wondered if he was going to produce another delicacy for cooking, or perhaps a bottle of forbidden alcohol. But it was only a crumpled packet of cigarettes and a box of matches. He lit up and squinted at her through the smoke.

'This is for you, girl. Because you dressed up nice, to give us our dinner. I like that. And you cooked me my meat and you weren't afraid to eat it with me. You're OK. You're OK, girl.'

And he began to play, his eyes closed and the cigarette hanging from his lips. The music poured from his fingers in a torrent of beauty. The old piano responded to his touch, its tinny tone transformed by his playing. With the last chord, he sat forward, his head bent over the keys, his foot resting on the pedal to let the notes reverberate into silence. Sarah realised she was crying. Crying for the beauty of the music and the talent of the player, for the ruin of his life, and for the perfection of the gift he had been given, and had given to her.

He looked up. And grinned.

'Ah, fuck it!' He stood up, slammed down the piano lid, and walked out of the hall.

'He was very well known in his day, you know.' Father Connolly was standing in the doorway. 'Till he let the drink destroy him. I think that's part of the anger he has in him – anger at what he's lost. What he threw away.'

'Where will he go now?'

'He goes to our shelter on Sarsfield Quay. When he's not barred for wrecking the place. Mary's right. He's very dangerous on a bad day.'

'Yes. Well, I'm glad I could help,' Sarah held out her hand. 'Goodnight, Father.'

'You did great tonight. I hope you'll come again. God bless you, my dear.'

'Thanks.'

'I'll get Mike to walk you to the bus stop. He's still here, and this is not the best area to be wandering around on your own late at night.'

Mike appeared, and Sarah was relieved that she would not have to negotiate the dark streets alone. They chatted as they walked. He was a final-year law student, he told her, but the long hours of study and his intense interest in his work had not left enough time for his girlfriend, and she had moved on. A year ago he had seen a poster asking for volunteers.

'I work at the shelter some nights, and do the soup run at weekends. Volunteer work, but it's very rewarding,' he said. 'It can be desperately sad, sometimes hilarious. It's made me aware of the amazing quality of human tenacity, even in despair. Maybe you'd like to come along with me one night?'

Sarah had joined his group the following week. She helped to prepare huge saucepans of soup, and sweet milky tea and piles of thick sandwiches, going out into the cold night to distribute them to people sleeping rough in car parks and derelict buildings and benches, or lying huddled under newspaper or cardboard boxes on the wet pavements. She signed on for night duty at the shelter on Mondays.

St Joseph's was a decaying Georgian wreck, a relic of past glory, with long sash windows that rattled in the wind. Inside, naked light bulbs hung from the crumbling plaster of ornate ceiling roses, and cast sinister shadows into unlit corners. The kitchen was the only warm place in the house. The big commercial gas rings and the oven gave off a comforting heat that the fires in the open grates never achieved – only a small area was ever warm in these huge, spartan rooms. Mostly people congregated in the kitchen, sitting almost on top of the fireplace, faces red with the heat of the glowing coals, backs still frozen from the draught that whistled under the door. In time Sarah came to love the procession of residents, lost people with sad histories and seamed faces that marked the failures of their lives. She began to feel a sense of purpose and fulfilment at last.

And she had a man in her life. She started to spend much of her spare time with Mike Daly. He was dynamic, intense, driven in everything he did, and he seemed to have a genuine passion for social justice, which she thought would make him a formidable lawyer. He seemed fascinated by her unusual background, and her reticence at talking about her life in Kenya slowly diminished as she got to know him. At least he tried to visualise what she described. She enjoyed the night-duty shifts they did together, and she began to tell him stories about her African childhood. She was flattered by his interest. He probed the lives of the 'Big Bwanas', as he called them, and the cultural diversities of the Africans and the white settlers. His own family were from Limerick, he said. His father owned a chemist shop and his mother was a teacher. He had decided to study law because there were so many people who could not help themselves, who had fallen on hard times, been forgotten or rejected by their families. They were the outcasts of society, and there was no safety net for them from the state. The politicians did little for them, apart from spouting about how much they cared.

For the first time since she had started college, Sarah felt she had found someone who genuinely understood her. As Mike plied her with questions, she became aware of how little she really knew about Kenya's indigenous people, despite growing up there. When he kissed her, a warm, pleasant sensation spread through her body, although there was no overpowering excitement. Perhaps that would grow as they became closer, she thought.

'I hear you've taken up with Mike Daly,' Tim observed, as she got ready to go out one evening. 'He's very busy making a name for himself in the far-left corner of politics.'

'He's interested in law, in defending the marginalised, not in politics.' She swung round to face him, sensing a criticism in his words. 'He's passionate about it, and that's no bad thing.'

'From what I've heard, he's a ranting leftist. I'm surprised you're tied up with him.' Her brother yawned and stretched out on the lumpy sofa.

'I'm not tied up with anyone,' she said defensively. She changed the subject. 'You look all in, by the way. You should eat, drink and go to bed. You're too long for that sofa and you'll wind up with a crick in your neck. Then you'll look like Quasimodo. As if you didn't look bad enough already! Here – I'll make you tea and toast.'

She put on the kettle and got out the bread.

'Been on duty thirty-six hours on the trot. I haven't the strength to go any further.' He swept a hand across his bleary eyes. 'Probably killed off half the patients in A & E. I can't remember what most of them were there for. So much for the zealous, caring young doctor. If it hadn't been for Deirdre this week, I'd be dead and buried.'

'Deirdre? I thought she was history.'

'What would make you think that?' Tim sat up, frowning.

'Well, I haven't seen her for months. Since Christmas, in fact. You certainly haven't brought her here.'

'Why would I want to bring her here? So that you can have another go at her?' Tim reached forward, scrabbling for his glasses. He put them on, focusing angrily on his sister as he spoke. 'It's no thanks to you, or your bitchy friend, that Deirdre is still speaking to me.'

'Oh come on, Tim. That was just a tease. I didn't think you and Deirdre were – well, serious, or anything.'

'You were so intent on making fun of her that you never stopped to consider how I would feel. You never thought to ask me about her.'

'It's just that she – well, I'm sure she's a good person. But—'

'Deirdre is a very good person. Genuine and straightforward. And she really cares for me.' He regarded his sister reproachfully. 'It's hard, you know, to come into a group of strangers, especially us colonials, and be at your best. You'd hope that the family would put you at ease, allow you to make friends. Instead, you and bloody Camilla made her feel like a bumpkin and a fool.'

Sarah stared at him with chagrin. It had never occurred to her that Tim had any deep feelings for Deirdre.

'It was only a bit of fun, Tim,' she protested.

'You should look for other ways to amuse yourself,' he said sourly. 'Or find more deserving targets for your spiteful little darts. Try being kind, even.'

Annoyance elbowed her remorse aside. Tim could be so pompous. They hadn't been that unpleasant to Deirdre. Not enough for all this fuss. The long hours in the hospital were making him peevish and unreasonable. He had never minded a bit of ragging before. She sidestepped her irritation and made an effort to be conciliatory.

'I'm sorry.' Sarah put a hand on her brother's shoulder. 'I am, honestly. I had no idea you liked her that much. Let's drop it. Start over again.'

'But it shouldn't matter how I feel about her, should it?' He would not let it go. 'She was a guest in our family and it was Christmas. She didn't go home because her mother's an alcoholic and she couldn't face another holiday, watching her fall down drunk at the end of lunch and piss in her pants.'

'Tim, I had no idea about any of this.' Sarah searched for some way to close this painful subject. 'Look, I've apologised. I had no right to upset her.' She handed him a plate of buttered toast and a cup of tea. 'Now get this down you and then go to bed for a few hours. I promise when you wake up tomorrow, you'll have a model sister filled with sweetness and charm.'

He drank his tea with his eyes half closed, and wolfed the toast, scattering crumbs down the front of his shirt. Before she left the flat, he was fast asleep.

At the shelter, still feeling guilty about Deirdre, she threw herself into work, cooking and stirring the pots of soup, scrubbing and cleaning. During the quiet of early morning she sat talking to Mike, enjoying the moments when he caressed her hair or her cheek. There was increasing passion in his kisses when he took her home later and asked if he could come in. But she used Tim as an excuse to refuse him. She realised it would only be a matter of time before he expected her to offer more, but she did not wish to confront that issue yet. It was ridiculous to feel disloyal to Piet, but he was still lodged in her heart, like an old habit hard to break. She would just have to take things a day at a time, weed him out slowly.

One evening late in March, Mike invited her to a party at the home of a member of the senate.

'Gerry McCall has asked me to dinner at his place. I'd like you to come,' he said.

Sarah was both pleased and nervous when he told her their host could be important to his career. So Tim had been right after all, she thought. Mike had political ambitions. She dressed with care, remembering all the things Camilla had told her she should do in order to make the most of her appearance. Mike's appreciative whistle told her she had got it right.

At the start of the evening, the guests discussed the situation in the North. Sarah was out of her depth, unable to make an intelligent contribution. But inevitably the conversation moved on to the British government and its dependencies in the far-flung colonies, and Mike described her background. All eyes were on her, and she had the uncomfortable feeling that this had been his agenda all along. He led her on, asking questions about her family and her lifestyle. At first she answered frankly. But gradually it became clear that his intention was to parade her in front of his socialist friends as his own personal specimen of the evils of colonial rule. She began to feel angry at their insularity, and the anti-British feeling among them.

'You had grown men doing all your housework, didn't you?' Mike prompted, and as an amusing aside added, 'they call them "boy", you know. No matter what age they are. Demeaning.'

'Did you not feel badly about exploiting people like that, having them living in cramped quarters behind your own grand house?' Tom Russell, a journalist, posed the question, watching her through a haze of cigar smoke. 'How many would there be to a room, would you say?'

'Each family would have two rooms and a—'

'A whole family in two rooms? Sounds a bit like the slave plantations in the southern states of America.'

'Ah, come on now. Give the girl a chance.' McCall broke in, and she cast him a grateful look. 'There's families living in conditions like that in Benburb Street, for God's sake. And who's doing anything about them? Half of them will be dead and gone before Mike here leaps to their assistance.'

There was laughter around the table, but Sarah was flustered.

'It isn't like that, really. You make it sound awful, shameful. But it isn't. Your African staff become part of your family. They're happy. They have good wages, education for their children, medical attention when they need it. And the quarters they live in are far better than the mud huts on their own land. They'd all be in one room there, with no running water or proper ventilation.' As soon as she said it she realised how patronising she sounded.

'Feudal. Isn't that it?' said Mike. 'It never fails to astonish me that the British can still get away with it. Now the colonies are all clamouring for Independence, but what kind of preparation have they received? They've never had a chance to be anything but dependent on their masters.'

She did not answer. How could she explain the dedication of her father in the hospital wards, her mother's constant care for the women and children who lived in their compound, or the pride their servants had in being part of their household. None of these people would understand the special relationship she was talking about. And now there were so many schools and colleges and training schemes where Africans could further their education. She had expected better of Mike, and she was puzzled and hurt by the way he had set her up.

'Keep the savages in their place, what what?' Another guest was doing a stupid impression of a British Army officer.

'Come on, Sarah,' Mike cut in, seeing her frown of annoyance. 'Is it really fair to keep your servants in a compound like cattle, and expect them to take orders from you day and night, to cook and clean for you, and watch you living in luxury? Well, in comparison to their lives, anyway. Is it right for them to be serving you a four-course dinner while they have to make do on their — what do you call that maize stuff?'

'*Posho*. It's the Kenya equivalent of the potatoes we eat.' She was ice cold with rage.

'Yes, *posho*. *Posho* and cheap meat. But of course they got the odd present and a bonus at Christmas, didn't they? What did you give them at Christmas, did you tell me? Didn't they all have to assemble in the hall on Christmas morning?'

'In the sitting room. Dad gave each family an envelope with money, and Mum gave them a present of food – special things they wouldn't normally be able to buy. Clothes for everyone too, and toys for the children.' Even as she listed them, the presents and the delight of their recipients seemed to fade, to become tawdry. 'It's the same thing you do here,' she said. 'Like the St Vincent de Paul or—'

'But people assisted by the St Vincent de Paul are desperate because they can't work, or they're old and forgotten and they need emergency help. They're not kept in a permanent state of servitude,' Tom Russell said.

'That's right,' Mike pounced, triumphant. 'A few shillings and a bit of gaudy cotton. The just rewards of their toil.'

Sarah felt fury rising in a scarlet rush to her cheeks. She felt like a bug under a microscope, wriggling in the glare of an enormous critical eye. Why could she not make them see?

'It was never a problem,' she said. 'It was the way life was.'

But her companions had lost interest in the subject and were moving on to local gossip and brandy. Mike just shrugged, and gave her that superior smile of his that always drove her mad when they had an argument. What did he know about it anyway? He'd probably never been further than Belfast, or maybe London, in his whole life. The remainder of the evening passed in agonising slow motion. When he dropped her home she stepped out of his car without a word. There had been a coolness between them after that, and she was relieved when he gave up his nights at the shelter to prepare for his final exams.

But his comments had stung, spreading into her mind like a slow poison, leaving her full of doubt and self-searching. She thought of her carefree childhood, untouched by the lives of the Africans whose country she had shared, unaware of how they really felt about their white bosses. She began to question her memory of things – the cheerful smiles of the staff who worked for her family, their apparent satisfaction with their lives, their pride in working for the *Bwana Daktari*, and the respect it gave them in their own community. Had that been real, or had she just taken it for granted that they were happy? She thought of Lona, the daughter of Walter, their cook. They were the same age, had played together in the gardens of the house, and in the servants' compound where Lona's mother had sat in the sun, wrapped in her bright *kanga* with a small baby tied against her ample breast as she prepared the *posho* for the evening meal. She always sang as she worked, her wide smile showing white teeth against an ebony face. She smelled different – Sarah had mentioned that to Betty once and asked the reason. It was probably the diet, her mother had said. She could almost smell the *posho* now, and the scent of the *kanga* cloth, the baby's milky aroma, the tang of hot skin in the sunshine. Lona had died of pneumonia when she was six. Her mother had gone to a witch doctor first, thinking the child had been struck down by a powerful curse. By the time Walter brought her to Raphael it was too late, and even the all-powerful *Bwana Daktari* couldn't save her. Walter and his wife had gone away soon after that, back to their home village near Lake Victoria. Sarah realised with shame that she didn't even know the wife's name, had never thought to ask, had never wondered what happened to them. They had gone, and were immediately forgotten. Was that because she had not seen them as real people, only as servants? Or was it merely her youth that had caused her to bury their memory without a qualm, until now?

Months later, standing under the red light of the darkroom, she made a promise to herself that she would not be so insensitive when she went back to Kenya. She would find a way, somehow, to make her own contribution to the country. Something to echo her parents' unceasing efforts at bringing improved health and education to the people they cared for. She examined her finished pictures critically. They had taught her so much, these battered souls whose faces stared back at her now. Her time at the shelter had been valuable and she saw that even Mike's hurtful behaviour had its positive side. It had forced her to think. But she had stopped going out with him. She no longer trusted him, feeling that he had used her. She sat back on the stool and waited for the prints to dry, reliving the night she had taken them.

There were only a few residents and workers sitting in the kitchen when she had arrived, but Sarah knew there would be an influx after the pubs closed. She was accustomed now to making sure that the residents did not bring in any alcohol, and adept at taking it off them when they did. If there was going to be trouble, that was when it usually started. The surrender of concealed whisky and gin often led to broken furniture, so that the chairs and tables in the downstairs rooms looked permanently battered. Her old friend John-Jo was one of the worst offenders. Sarah carried her mug of coffee to the table and took out her camera.

'So! What about these portraits?' she asked, smiling at the company.

'Mugshots! Jaysus, what would you want pictures of us for?'

That was Duncan, small and wiry with a bushy beard and terrible teeth. He was grinning at an old woman sitting beside him, her hair matted, eyes squinting against the evil-smelling smoke of a roll-up that was stuck to her lip. He gave Sarah a conspiratorial wink.

'Focus in on this beauty here, and me! Aren't we gorgeous?'

Soon they were all posing, gradually becoming less self-conscious, eventually forgetting that the camera was there at all. John-Jo arrived, miraculously sober, and opened the piano. Someone struck up a song. Sarah watched as the music softened their faces with nostalgia for better times, and she adjusted her camera, using fast film so that she would not need the flash. She wanted to capture these moments without the exploding light, and avoid reminding everyone that their lives and failures were being recorded. She turned her camera to focus on Joan, a thin, wild-eyed woman from Galway, with a tongue like a viper when she was riled, and Aggie, tiny and timid except if she'd put away a few pints and some whisky – then she could raise the roof with her curses, and fight like a demon.

Caught in the lens, they turned and stamped, the light capturing a moist eye, a gap-toothed smile, the flick of a greasy lock of hair, the rise of a shoulder, cocked heads and arms akimbo, following the music back down the paths to their youth. And as the dancers swung around the shabby room, the drab walls disappeared in the blur of their movement, so that the damp patches on the plaster were transformed into mysterious murals in their ballroom. Sarah moved among them, zooming in close. This was good. She knew that the atmosphere was soaking into her film. It made her feel almost divine – this ability to grasp these bright moments and preserve them. The images would remain, even after the house had gone silent except for the snoring from crumpled beds, or the sizzle of a late-night, sober-up supper. Even after reality had sent them all back to their private battles, this night of magic and release and camaraderie would still go on, printing and reprinting on glossy ten by eights, never to be forgotten. There was no trouble in St Joseph's that night. She had been impatient to develop these films, to see if the gold she thought she had was real. Now, as she examined them with rising excitement, she knew that she had a high-quality entry for the competition. And if her pictures made the exhibition, her friends at the shelter would have found a voice to speak for them. Satisfied that the prints were dry she slid them carefully into a folder, cleaned up the darkroom, and went home.

In the kitchen she washed up the frying pan and the greasy plate her brother had left in the sink. When she looked in on Tim he was lying across his bed, still in his working clothes, his shoes, glasses and white coat in a pile on the floor beside him. He looked so vulnerable like that, Sarah thought. So young. He hadn't mentioned the worthy Deirdre again. But what if he was madly in love with the girl and hadn't been able to confide in his sister? Sarah shuddered as she ran a hot bath and lay back in the tub, thinking. She was sure Deirdre was not the right girl for her brother. But at least he had someone, while she had simply made a fool of herself again.

There had been no word from Camilla. In London she had offered abject apologies, tried to salvage the remains of the weekend, taking them to the theatre, to a fashionable Italian trattoria, and a club where they had listened to the Rolling Stones and even met one of the band. But it was impossible to forget the débâcle with Marina. Tim had returned to Ireland a day early.

'She's trying to buy our approval, our forgiveness, and I can't take it,' he had said to Sarah. 'I'm off. See you in Dublin.'

'No, Tim. She's a mess, it's true, but she isn't calculating like that. Look at her background, for God's sake. What would we be like if we'd grown up in her circumstances?'

'You're too generous, Sarah. Too forgiving. Camilla's bad news. Maybe she can't help it but she's just like her mother, spreading unhappiness wherever she goes. Piet was a clown to fall for her in the first place. But he didn't deserve that. You should be careful or she'll grind you up too, and dump your ashes somewhere. And then she'll be full of regret all over again, after the damage is done. You don't need a so-called sister like that.'

How naive they had all been when they made their childish pact. Now they were far apart, divided by family circumstances and problems that seemed to dog all attempts to preserve their friendship. It had seemed so natural, so right, to have promised one another undying and unconditional love and loyalty. Sarah stepped out of the bath, rubbing the towel roughly over her pale skin, hating the pasty milk-bottle colour of it. She sat down at her small desk and filled in the entry forms for the competition, meticulously labelling the backs of the photographs before sliding them into a cardboard envelope. When she walked into the living room Tim was slumped on the sofa, looking at her with bloodshot eyes.

'I tried to wait up for you, but you're very late and I fell asleep. I didn't want to miss you.' He stared down at the worn carpet. 'There's some news from home. Mum rang while you were out.'

'Is everything all right?' Sarah felt a jolt of apprehension. Betty only called on birthdays and special occasions, or if there was something wrong. Tim did not answer immediately and she became aware of the gas fire, hissing a warning through the long silence.

'It is now. Or she thinks so, anyway,' Tim said. 'But they've had a bad scare. Dad had another serious bout of malaria. He was very sick, not responding to any drugs at all, and they thought – well, they thought it was all over. Mum was on the verge of phoning us two days ago, and arranging for us to fly out. In desperation they gave him huge doses of old-fashioned quinine, and he's come through. But he's been ordered to take some sick leave.'

'Can I phone now, and talk to them? See how things are?' Sarah sat down, trembling with shock.

'No. It's far too late. Mum's been spending all her time at the hospital and she'll be catching up on her sleep. She's been up with him day and night. Look, I'm sure he'll be OK now.' Tim stood up and put his arm around his sister. 'But there's a problem that they have to face, Sarah. They have to leave Mombasa. Choose somewhere else to live. Dad has been warned. He can't afford another bout of malaria. Ever again. He wouldn't make it the next time.'

'Leave the coast?' Sarah stared at him, incredulous. 'But where would they go, for God's sake? He'd never want to leave Mombasa. He's turned down all kinds of promotions and offers for years, just to stay there. It's our home.'

'They haven't really discussed it yet. He'll be too weak for a while to think anything through. But as I understand it, he has to move away from any malarial area. The doctors are adamant about that.'

Sarah sat down, tears forming in her eyes. 'Are you sure he's really through it? She's not keeping anything from us?'

'No. I don't think so.' Tim was rubbing his eyes. 'They may come back here while he's on sick leave. To recuperate, and maybe go to the Hospital for Tropical Diseases in London and the Ministry of Overseas Development to discuss possible postings. Then they'll be able to decide what their options are.'

'Oh God. Yes, of course. Options.' She was still numb with shock.

'The thing is, I don't think you'll be going to Kenya in the summer, Sarah. Because they won't be there. They may never be there again.' He saw her jaw tighten and the tears began to spill down her face as she tried to cope with the enormity of it. 'Sorry, kid. I know how you were looking forward to it.'

Not going to Kenya? Her spirits plummeted. It had been all that had kept her going, the promise of summer with Hannah and Piet, even Camilla. She could not believe that her dream would be snatched from her now. She tried, unsuccessfully, to banish her disappointment. Dad was ill. The important thing, the only thing, was that he should get better. She hugged her brother and put on her coat, stooping to pick up her umbrella.

'I'm going for a walk,' she said. 'It'll stop me brooding and I'd never get to sleep now, anyway. Don't wait up.'

In the street she tried to calm herself. It wasn't the end of the world. Her father was all right. But the idea that she might never see her home again! That was too painful to consider. And Piet. Her heart contracted and she attempted to focus on something else, to quell her mounting despair. She wanted to stand in the middle of the road and scream. She tried to imagine what she might do for the summer. She could enrol on a course to improve her photographic technique, expand her portfolio. It would be expensive, but she could get herself a part-time job to pay for it. The cold seeped into her mind, numbing her thoughts and driving her back indoors where she lay in bed, tearful and awake until the grey dawn crept into the sky.

When she spoke to her mother, Betty told her that they would be coming to Ireland as soon as Raphael was strong enough to travel. Sarah left the flat early to take her photographs to the post office. Looking at them once more before she sealed the envelope, she felt they were better than she had thought last night. There was a queue at the post office, but she waited her turn with patience and said one last whispered prayer before dropping the envelope into the box. She spent the remainder of the day in the library at the university, willing her drifting mind to return to the diagrams she had to memorise. Eventually she gave up the struggle and left, anxious to get back to the flat but afraid to open the door, in case there should be more unwelcome news awaiting her. As she put her bag on the table, the phone rang and she was sure that it was her mother again

'I've written you a letter and posted it,' Camilla said. 'I know it's long overdue, and you'll probably think it's a coward's way of dealing with what happened. So I just wanted to ring and tell you again that I'm sorry. Very sorry that I hurt you and Piet, and everyone.'

'You can't use other people for your own ends, Camilla, just because things go wrong in your life.' Sarah could not find it in herself to offer comfort or sympathy.

'I know that. I really do. I'll make it up to you somehow. And to Piet. I never seem to arrive at a point where I can handle Mother.' There was a long silence as Camilla waited for a response that did not come.

'Look, I'm waiting for a really important phone call, and I need to hang up quickly. Let's talk about it another time, Camilla.'

'Oh. Yes. But briefly, I still want to celebrate our birthdays in Kenya, as we promised.' There was some nuance in the words that Sarah could not recognise, a pleading perhaps and a sense of urgency. 'I'd like to go back this summer, if it's still all right with you. And Piet.'

Sarah felt anger begin to rise. This was the real reason Camilla had phoned – to make sure her holiday plans were still on.

'What Piet says or wants is nothing to do with me,' she said. 'In any case, I don't think I can go to—'

'Then, after the coast, we could all take a week and camp up north. Perhaps in Samburu,' Camilla interrupted. Her usual soft drawl had deserted her, and her voice was breathless with excitement. 'We could go on safari, with our own tented camp. We'd need a Land Rover and all kinds of stuff, but Piet and—'

'You've been in touch with Piet?' Sarah felt a roaring resentment threatening to choke her.

'No. Of course I haven't. But there's something I must tell you.'

'It will have to wait,' Sarah snapped. 'Right now I have more important issues to deal with. Dad has been very ill with malaria. He's still in hospital, and when he gets out they'll have to come over here to let him recover properly. So there won't be anywhere for us to stay at the coast.'

'Oh Sarah, that's terrible. What about your mother? How is she managing? God, is there anything I can do?'

'It looks like my trip is off, Camilla. I couldn't afford to go out on my own, if Dad and Mum aren't going to be there. So you're talking to the wrong person. Better get on to Piet and Hannah direct, and count me out.'

'But that's what I'm trying to tell you! Anthony Chapman has just been in London, and he's offered to set up a camp for us, at the end of August. I've worked out a good deal with him that I can easily afford, and that will be my contribution to our birthday celebration. I'm doing a shoot for *Vogue* this week, and I've been offered a big contract to advertise a new perfume. So I'm rather flush right now, and this is what I want to do. And I'd like to pay your airfare, Sarah. Please – I want to do this for you. For all of us. Please think about it. There is something else I have to tell you about too. It'll keep, though. I'd better get off the line, but I'll ring again in a day or two.'

When she hung up, Sarah sat down in an armchair. There had been something about Camilla's proposal, some missing element, but she didn't have time to work it out now. It was so tempting, the idea of going home after all, to the coast and to Langani and maybe even on safari. She had never dreamed that she might be able to stay in a private tented camp like Anthony's. She heard a sound and looked up.

'Who was that on the phone?' Tim was leaning against the door. 'I'm supposed to have the evening off, but I don't think it will last because they're short-staffed. Everyone seems to have the flu.'

'It was Camilla. She wanted to know if I was coming to Kenya in August. Apparently Anthony Chapman could take us camping in Samburu, to celebrate our birthdays. Camilla said she's just landed some big contract and she wants to pay for the whole thing. Even my fare to Nairobi.'

'Jesus. She never lets up, does she?' he said in disgust. 'Can't you see she's trying to buy your approval? It's pathetic, Sarah. How many times are you going to fall for this?'

'If there's one genuine thing in her life, it's her friendship with Hannah and me,' Sarah insisted. 'I'm not willing to turn my back on that. Not entirely, anyway. Why don't you come with us? You'd love the safari, and you've been working so hard.'

'Take Camilla's guilt money?' Tim gave a scornful laugh. 'Not a chance! Besides, Mum and Dad might need us here. Or are you so taken with your rich, spoiled friend and what she can buy you, that they're not important any more?'

'That's absolutely horrible!' Sarah was yelling. 'You know how much I care, how frantic with worry I've been. But this trip is more than two months away, and the thought of going home is all that's kept me sane this last year. Mum and Dad wouldn't mind if I went out, just for a few weeks. They might even be back there themselves, by then.'

'They won't. Can't you get that into your thick skull?' Tim thumped a fist into the sagging couch. 'You're a half-wit, Sarah. And Camilla is a calculating bitch. I can't believe you'd be dim enough to go back there on her terms. I can just see you making sheep's eyes at Piet van der Beer, while he ignores you and pants after her. Where's your bloody pride? Where's your common sense?'

'Common sense? What about your common sense, and the way dreary Deirdre seems to have got her hooks into you? She's turned you into a grumpy old badger. You have nothing in common with her at all.'

As soon as the words came out she regretted them, but she was smarting at his cruelty. She slammed the door of the flat and went back out into the street. The pain of his remarks dogged her footsteps as she tramped along the pavement. She found a bench and sat down, drawing her jacket around her. Tim's words churned in her mind, but she was determined not to be infected by his brutal analysis of her motives. She would talk it over with her mother during the next few days. She was tired of being a pawn in other people's lives, and she deserved this one chance to go back to the place she loved. With a sigh she walked back to the flat, resolved to give her parents all the support they required. But Camilla's proposal was still lodged in the forefront of her mind.

On the day after her parents' arrival in Dublin she read the announcement in the newspaper. Sarah Mackay had won five hundred pounds for her portraits of the residents in St Joseph's Shelter. The pictures were to be exhibited for sale in a smart gallery in Wicklow Street. When Mike Daly rang to congratulate her, she hung up on him. Then she booked rooms at a five-star hotel, and took her father and mother and her brother to Connemara for the weekend.

Chapter 10

Hannah ordered a shandy and turned her attention to Fred Patterson. He had been her tennis partner for the afternoon and they had won the mixed doubles. Now he wanted her to stay on for the Saturday-night party at the club. She had anticipated this, and before leaving Langani she had sneaked a bag with fresh clothes and shoes and perfume into the boot of the car. She knew Piet would not approve.

'You're spending too much time at the club,' he objected. 'The petrol is expensive, and so is the wear and tear on Ma's old car. We've got to keep it going for a while longer, Han. You can't use it like a private limousine. Plus there are all the chits you sign for food and drinks. You're carrying on like an Englisher memsahib with nothing to do except give the houseboys orders, and spend your time playing bridge or tennis. There's serious work for you here, at Langani.'

'I don't want to be in your office all day,' Hannah said angrily. 'I've spent the last two years cooped up in a miserable dump while you were here on the farm, or having a great time in Scotland, or fooling around in London with Sarah and Camilla. Now you're out somewhere all day, planning your lodge or driving the tractor or planting wheat with Lars. And I'm still shut away. It's not fair.'

Piet sighed. She was right. When Pa had gone south it was Hannah who had drawn the short straw. How could he deny her a little playtime now? But he was increasingly worried about her. Several friends had given him the nudge, remarking on his sister's enthusiasm for the wild parties thrown by the local rugby team. One part of him wanted her to enjoy a period where she had no responsibilities, while the protective side of him tried to keep her out of harm's way.

'Stop nagging,' Hannah had said this morning. 'I'm not a child. I'm old enough to think, and to look after myself. Lars goes to the club – I've seen him there, with girls swarming over him like locusts. How come you don't ask him what he's doing? Or is he spying on me?'

'Of course he's not spying on you, Han. That's ridiculous. He's a grown man and he can spend his wages and his spare time however he likes. But you're my little sister, and I want you to be safe. That's all.'

'You know everyone at the club,' Hannah pointed out, glaring at him. 'You've played tennis and rugby with them all for years. So what's the fuss, heh?'

And that was the problem, of course. Piet was only too familiar with the hungry bachelors of the area, released from their farms and from the nearby army barracks every weekend, out on the prowl for fresh young meat. Like his sister. If Lottie had been at Langani there would have been strict rules, and Hannah would have had the stern eye of her father to contend with. As things stood, she paid no heed to anyone. She had been home for almost two months, and was becoming more of a handful with every passing day. Piet had not explained to her the crisis that had hung over Langani since Jan's sudden departure. He was unwilling to seem critical of their father, and he had guessed that there had been a serious quarrel between Hannah and Jan. There was no point in widening the cracks in the crumbling edifice of the family. But Langani was still teetering on the brink of financial disaster, and he needed her help. There were frequent negotiations with the bank, and nothing left to fall back on if there were unforeseen problems with the next harvest. Lars had come up with ways of saving money, and his careful stewardship in Piet's absence had saved them from bankruptcy. He had trimmed down the labour, sold off surplus livestock and old equipment, and managed the land with imagination and dedication. He was careful and efficient, and more importantly he had become a good friend. Piet did not want to let him go. He would be even more essential when the lodge was operational.

'The lodge should bring in good money,' Lars agreed. 'It's not going to cost that much to build. This Viktor Szustak is a clever architect. If we follow his plan we can find most of the construction materials here on the farm – stone, thatch, the wood for building. And we have our own labour. We could even make the furniture here, in the workshop. But your father wants you to delay the whole project, until we have something in the bank to keep us going in a bad year.'

'Pa's not here,' Piet said decisively. 'He can't have a hand in running Langani from thousands of miles away. We have to make our own decisions as to how best to survive. The bank is backing the idea of the lodge, and Anthony's investment money has helped. Plus, the place could also give Hannah something constructive to do, instead of being a headache.'

'She's all right, your sister. It was tough down there, and she's broken out. She'll get back on the straight and narrow if you give her a little time.'

'Time is something we can't afford,' Piet said. 'Hannah has to pull her weight every day, if she wants to stay here.'

'Then you must tell her the truth.' Lars stood up. 'I'm going down to the dairy. There's some *shauri* down there about missing milk. I think someone is selling off a few gallons every day, or giving it away to friends and family. Maybe both.'

It was almost dark when Hannah telephoned from Nanyuki Club, and Piet's pent-up anger streaked down the line.

'You'll come home right now,' he said. 'You're not going to spend all night at the club, running up bills and putting yourself in a dicey position at another crazy party.'

'Ach, stop bellyaching, Piet. You're so boring these days, always stuck on the farm, talking about work and so.'

'I'm telling you to come home, Hannah. Now, this minute.' There was a click as she cut him off, and he stood staring at the phone in disbelief.

He snatched up the keys of the farm truck and headed for Nanyuki. Rain began to patter on the windscreen as he drove. Soon the road became a slippery morass and Piet could barely see his way as the old wipers scratched at the windscreen. He was drenched by the time he had run from the car park into the club. One of his rugby friends slapped him on the back and ordered him a tankard of beer. There was no sign of Hannah, but several rowdy groups were already drinking and dancing. The party was in full swing.

'Have you seen Hannah?' he asked Jamie Pincott, the rugby captain.

'I wouldn't go looking for your sister right now, old chap.' Jamie smiled knowingly.

'Got it,' Piet said, grinning back with effort. 'Who's her admirer tonight?'

'Fred Patterson. Same as last week and the week before. They have quite a thing going on there. How is everything at Langani? Haven't seen you around lately. All work and no play, and so on? You need to lighten up, old man. What about some tennis next week?'

Piet steeled himself to finish his beer until a pretty brunette claimed Jamie's attention, and Piet immediately left the bar in search of Hannah. There was no sign of her in the lounge or on the dance floor, and she was not at any of the tables in the dining area. The rain was pelting down as he made his way through the assortment of vehicles in the car park. He flashed his torch beam around in the downpour until he caught a movement, and then he heard her laugh. Hannah was in the back seat of Fred Patterson's car, giggling as he tugged at the zipper of her dress, his mouth clamped to hers. Neither of them noticed the beam of light. Piet flung open the car and pulled his sister out into the rain. He could hear her shouting at him, spewing out her rage and humiliation in a flow of words that he had never heard her use before, but he paid no attention. Fred Patterson scrambled awkwardly out of his station wagon and stood with a stupidly vacant expression, unprepared for the fist that landed just beneath his chin and toppled him back into the car.

'Hey – steady on, old man! I'm not doing anything she didn't—'

'You bloody well stay away from my sister,' Piet spat at him. 'She's in my charge, and you'll answer to me if I ever catch you fooling around with her again. Now get the hell out of my way and look somewhere else for your fun.'

Hannah was in shock as he grabbed her arm and led her to the farm truck. 'Get in,' he said, the words coming from between gritted teeth. He pushed her into the passenger seat. 'We're going home. Lars will pick up the car in the morning.'

'You're an ignorant bully, like Pa,' she yelled at him. 'You don't care about me, any of you – I'm just some baggage you have to protect because I belong to you. And that's all you know.' She began to sob, hiding her hands in her face, her wet hair plastered against her head.

Piet slammed the door and walked round to the driver's seat, already regretting his actions. They drove in silence with a storm directly overhead. Sheet lightning gave way to jagged forks that darted into the earth around them. The car slid and swung along the road and twice they found themselves stuck, so that Piet had to climb out and push as Hannah revved the engine and spun the wheels in an effort to escape the sucking, oozing mud. It was almost midnight when they reached the farm and stumbled into the sitting room where Lars was waiting beside the fire.

'Looks like I'd better retire from the family stuff,' he said, taking in Hannah's livid expression as she fled to the refuge of her room. 'Go easy, man, whatever it is.'

'She's gone to bed. Stay and have a drink with me, Lars. Get the glasses out, while I put on some dry clothes,' Piet said. When he returned he stood warming himself at the fire. 'I made a hash of it,' he confessed. 'Lost my head like an idiot. She was in the back of a car with Fred Patterson. I dragged her out and let him have it.'

'That'll improve the chance of your being flattened at the next rugby match,' Lars was smiling. 'If Hannah doesn't finish you off first.'

'I know. But she's my kid sister, for Chrissake, and I'm like her only parent right now.'

'She's not a kid any more,' Lars said mildly. 'She's a young woman with plenty of spirit. You've got to treat her as an adult with a good, sharp mind, instead of like a delinquent schoolgirl. And find another way of letting her know she's important to you.'

'You're right,' Piet said. 'I'll go and tell her I behaved stupidly. That I just want her to be safe.'

'I wouldn't do that tonight,' Lars said. 'Unless you want to jump into a boiling volcano and get yourself scorched.'

'Right again,' Piet agreed. 'Repairs first thing on tomorrow's agenda. Thanks, man.'

She was not at the breakfast table. Mwangi appeared with the news that Memsahib Hannah had gone out riding very early in the morning. It was almost noon before she came back.

'We have to talk,' he said, and put up both hands as she opened her mouth to object. 'I was an idiot last night, Han, and I'm sorry. I've been fussing over you like a mother hen, and I know it's stupid. I just don't want anything bad to happen to you, after all you've been through already. You know I'm an old-fashioned, *domkop* farmer. And Fred is going to be lying in wait for me at the next rugby match, so you'd better have bandages and splints ready afterwards.'

Hannah had begun to smile. 'We're lucky we didn't spend the night upside down in a ditch,' she said. 'Then we would have had to answer to Lars as well.'

'That would have been bad, yes,' Piet said, laughing. 'But there are things we need to discuss, Sis. I've kept them from you, but we should talk about them now, so we can decide together what's to be done.'

Hannah sat down beside him, and he opened the ledgers and files that detailed the farm accounts and began to go through them with her. Jan had left the farm in debt, and she saw that Lars had done what he could to keep the threat of bankruptcy at bay. Nonetheless, they were still on a thin line between survival and failure.

'I think we can make it,' Piet said. 'If we finish the lodge it will bring in another kind of income that can protect us during years when there's drought, or we have a problem with the wheat or the livestock. And it would give you a project to run, when the construction is finished. You could take care of the whole thing. People from all over the world will come here. Several of the hunters and the private safari companies are looking for places that aren't crowded with regular tourists. We'll only take ten people at a time. It will be a different experience for them, being on a real Kenya farm and a private game reserve, with a third-generation Kenya family.'

'If we're so short of cash and we owe the bank, how can we do it?' Hannah asked.

'We can build cheaply from materials right here on Langani, if we follow the plans Viktor drew up. And Anthony has put up some of the money.' He saw that her eyes were alight with interest for the first time since her return. 'The only thing is, Han, you'll have to run the office while the construction is going on..Later, there'll be the decoration of the place, staff to train, menus to plan and organise. That sounds like your territory.'

'It's just what I want,' she said, flinging her arms around him. 'I'm sorry, Piet. I've been a bloody nuisance since I came home. But this is something we can do together, and I love the whole idea. Now, take me through all these accounts files again.'

The running of the farm had changed from that morning, and Hannah had worked long hours each day, creating a new accounting system, filing and typing, ordering and checking incoming supplies. She did not enjoy the office, but she could look forward to a time when the lodge would be hers to run, and then she would be able to entertain guests from Europe and America. In the meantime, they had to survive.

Viktor Szustak came and went regularly, sometimes staying overnight at the farm. Hannah was mesmerised by his extravagant gestures and the thick Polish accent that was so exotic to her ears. He quoted writers and poets she had never heard of, drew her vivid sketches of how the interior of the lodge might look, and even made designs for the furniture. He flirted with her outrageously, making her laugh at his obvious manoeuvres. But she was flattered by his attention, and she always welcomed his visits.

They broke ground one morning early and celebrated with a picnic on the kopje where the viewing platform and the main lounge area would be situated. When the men disappeared to measure out the position and the size of the water pipes, Hannah was left standing alone. As the light began to soften and the clouds parted to reveal the summit of the mountain, she felt two strong arms suddenly grasp her around the waist. She turned, startled, and found herself looking up into Viktor's saturnine features. He made a grunting, animal noise and bent his head to kiss her, and Hannah felt excitement rushing through her limbs. But the sound of footsteps broke the connection between them.

'Ah – there you are, Viktor. Piet is waiting for you to make sure we have everything measured. If you're quite finished measuring here, that is.' Lars's expression was thunderous. 'The light is going, and I want to finalise the plumbing requirements today, so I can place an order for the pipes.' He looked at Hannah for a long, speculative moment. There was an odd expression in his eyes that she could not define, and she tilted her chin at him in defiance and walked away.

Viktor shrugged, his face full of amusement and mockery as he followed Lars outside.

'I hope Viktor isn't behaving like the menace his reputation suggests he is,' Piet said to his sister that evening.

'I like it when he's around,' Hannah replied. 'He's interesting and artistic and different, and he tells me about books and pictures and places I've never even heard of.'

'That may be.' Piet was frowning. 'But he's a terrible womaniser. Don't be taken in by anything he says, Han. He's fast at designing buildings, and even faster with his designs on women.'

'Piet.' Her answering gaze carried a warning.

'I know. You can take care of yourself. But watch out for this one.'

*

Piet formed a company and opened a bank account for the lodge, with Anthony Chapman as a shareholder. Lars managed most of the day-to-day workings of the farm, ploughing and planting the wheat, supervising the cattle and the dairy, looking after the machinery. But Piet was always on hand for their patrols and inspections, and they resolved logistical problems and labour disputes together. Their friendship deepened, and they began to take a little time off and to bring Hannah to occasional parties in Nanyuki, and even to the Outspan Hotel in Nyeri for an overnight visit and dinner.

'We need to look at hotel rooms and menus and laundry lists and service,' Piet said. 'And we deserve to have some fun while we're at it.'

Late one evening, during the month of June, Hannah pushed her chair away from the desk in her father's old office. She gathered up the sheaf of bills she had put to one side and rubbed her eyes. The paraffin lamp fizzed gently and gave off a faint, oily smell that she found oddly comforting – probably some throwback to her nursery days, she thought. The surrounding shadows held back from the glow of light, like a backstage cast waiting in the wings. Shadows of a time when the farm was her secure haven and her father had sat at this desk in this same pool of light, keeping other darknesses at bay. Resolutely, she discarded the memory. Pa was not going to help her now, and Piet was out at the kopje day after day, overseeing the building. Soon they would have to reschedule their bank loan, and there were parts of the farm that had begun to show signs of neglect. The wages and the bills for seed and animal feed still rolled in, and construction costs were eating into their meagre savings, in spite of Anthony Chapman's contribution.

Lars was a fine stockman. His family in Norway had a cattle farm, and he had spent many holidays in Kenya since his childhood, staying with an uncle who had a large coffee estate north of Nairobi. But he did not have experience of wheat, and he was still not familiar with all the problems that could arise from local pests or parasites in either the livestock or the fields. In spite of the fact that Hannah was now a serious member of the workforce, he was reluctant to take advice from her. Piet was the boss, the one with the degree in agriculture. And, more importantly, he was a man. Hannah suspected that in Lars's mind she was still the kid who had run away from her parents in Rhodesia, and now Piet was landed with the burden of taking care of her. She had tried to impress on him that she had grown up on the farm, knew the workings of the place through and through, that she could help outside as well as in a clerical role. But she had no diploma to prove any of this, and she was a mere girl.

Over the past weeks, she had worked almost exclusively in the office, and now she recognised that the house had begun to look shabby. She embarked on a cleaning and painting programme that had jolted the staff into a renewed attention to order. Lottie's garden was still there, but no one had planted new flowers and the neatly trimmed hedges were ragged. Hannah set to work with the gardener, weeding and planting and pruning until she was satisfied that the shape and form of the garden had been restored.

Piet had taken some of the more experienced farmhands to help with the construction of the lodge, but nothing had yet been done about training staff to cook and serve and clean. Hannah had reminded him that she needed time to train new workers, but he was unwilling to add the extra wages until the last moment. Finding the right people for the job was not going to be easy.

It had all seemed so simple, from the distance of the tobacco farm in Rhodesia. She would come home and work with Piet and they would create their own Utopia. She had not reckoned with the terrible sense of shame and remorse she still felt at having abandoned her mother in her headlong dash from Jan's fist. She had refused to speak to him since her return to Langani, and the pain of hearing Lottie's first words of relief on the phone, so brave but so desolate, had been more than she could bear. Hannah had hung up quickly and afterwards she had tried to write and explain. But she was determined not to go back, even for Lottie's sake, and the realisation of her own craven cowardice constantly made her feel guilty. She missed her mother with a gnawing grief, and deep down she yearned for Jan too. She wanted to recreate the father of her childhood, the powerful, all-seeing giant who had kept her universe safe and happy, not the sad drunk who was now a hired hand on his cousin's farm. No use dwelling on that, she thought. He's gone. We grow up. We move on. She rose, stacked her papers, and lifted the paraffin lamp. With a sigh she left the office to its ghosts, and stepped out on to the verandah.

Moths and night bugs swirled around the hissing globe as she walked to the sitting room. Two other lamps glowed by the armchairs, and the remains of the log fire rippled with red embers in the grate. Piet's dogs were nowhere to be seen, so he must still be up at the lodge where he had arranged to meet Anthony. She could see them in her mind, out somewhere under the stars, sitting by a fire they had made, drinking a companionable beer and making their plans. It would have been nice to join them. She had given up her visits to Nanyuki, except when they could be combined with farm business, and she felt lonely and isolated. Occasionally they had friends over for a meal at the weekends, but the talk was almost exclusively about farming and land distribution and politics. Lars had taken her to a party once, but she wondered if he was escorting her as a favour to Piet who was often in Nairobi now, trying to open some lines of communication with wildlife organisations and tour operators. He seemed to lead an active social life on those occasions, staying in Anthony's cottage at Karen, and going out on the town with Viktor whose activities were an endless source of Nairobi gossip.

Sarah had written about her new passion for photography, and her longing to come home to Kenya for the summer. Although Dublin sounded dreary, Hannah would have liked to sample the smoky pubs and the places where people played wild music on fiddles and danced all night. Camilla sent postcards of buildings in London or Rome or Paris, with brief, scrawled messages indicating that her life was full of glamour. At first Hannah had been glad of the cards, but lately she had begun to regard them as irritating and egotistical. They seemed an inadequate response to her own letters, and she felt sidelined by the obvious success of Camilla's career. Ach, come on, Hannah, she chided herself, you wanted to be at Langani and you're here. For now, you have to be satisfied with that. And you can't expect to have Piet sitting here with you every night, or letting you tag along wherever he goes.

He had taken her out to the site a few days ago and they had camped there overnight. In the late evening they sat side by side on the half-finished viewing platform, overlooking the waterhole he had created from a spring beneath the surrounding rocks. For several months he had been putting down salt to attract the animals. As darkness fell, the first shy bushbuck arrived. The male was dark and glowing, with twisted horns and a handsome band of white on his chest. In the lights that Piet had rigged from a small generator, they watched as the female followed, stepping cautiously towards the water, her reddish coat speckled with white, her eyes gleaming in the reflection of the lights. The next visitors were warthogs, trotting on to the scene in an orderly line, their tails sprouting straight up like bush aerials. Piet and Hannah ate their simple meal and, unable to tear themselves away from the scene, wrapped themselves in sweaters and blankets against the bone-chilling cold of the night. It was after midnight when the first elephants arrived. They sat enthralled in the starlight, as the great creatures flapped their ears and siphoned the water up through their trunks, looking like gargantuan ghosts. The younger members of the herd watched the adults and then put out their own trunks to take up the salt, shoving one another playfully. Two babies stayed safe between their mothers' front legs, peering out to learn from the more adventurous members of the family. When the buffalo appeared, snorting and shunting one another aside to roll in the mud, Piet put his arm around his sister's shoulders, whispering in her ear.

'It's phenomenal,' he said. 'The game is coming every night now. We mustn't ever forget how privileged we are, to have all of this for our own. We must keep it safe, Han, no matter how hard the going gets, no matter what the cost. It's our responsibility, our heritage, and our challenge to keep, for all the generations that come after us.'

'I know it,' she said quietly. 'And I want to help you every way I can.'

'You're a huge help,' he said. 'I could never find time to do this and be on the farm, and take care of the office work as well. Besides, it's not my strong suit, adding up all those numbers and paying bills and keeping the books straight.'

'We've sorted out the accounting mess Pa left behind, between the three of us,' Hannah said. 'We know exactly where we are now. So I'd really like to be out on the farm, for an hour or two each day. I know every square foot of it, and I don't want to be stuck in the office all the time, just because I've done a business course. Or sit at home in the afternoons, mending your bloody shorts. I want to play a real part here. I'm not just your little sister who ran away.'

Piet was silent and she could see that he was turning something over in his mind, considering something important that he wanted to say.

'What really happened down south, Han?' he asked at last. 'I know you're holding something back from me.'

She pressed her lips together and sat mute in the darkness.

'Do you think they'd ever come back?' he said. 'I mean, Pa was never officially accused of doing anything wrong, as far as I know. Ma told me he was involved in the death of some Mau Mau fighter captured by his unit. But so were thousands of others in the army and the police and the special units, both black and white. There was an amnesty at the end of the emergency, you know, and all that was put aside. I looked up the records of the King's African Rifles, one time when I was in Nairobi. But there's nothing bad about Pa in them. So why is he staying down there, with all those short-sighted farmers loyal to Ian Smith? They're under a government that no one outside of Rhodesia acknowledges, except for the South Africans with their apartheid brotherhood. And Pa has no real part in their quarrel. He should come home.'

'I don't want him back here,' Hannah said, her eyes blazing. 'I don't want to see him, ever again.'

'Hannah?' Piet turned to face her, shocked.

'He's a drunk. A useless, bloody, violent drunk. He hit me and that's why I left. He probably hits Ma too, and I hate him.' She beat her fist on the rock.

Piet did not speak for a while as he tried to absorb the awful shock of what she had told him. 'I'm sorry,' he said. 'I'm so sorry. And I'm not going to make excuses for him, no matter what problems he has. You're here now, Han, and we'll go on working together and looking after our land, you and me.'

Alone now in the sitting room, Hannah smiled at the memory of that night. Not much had changed and she was still buried in paperwork. She wondered suddenly if Lars was around. He would at least be someone to talk to. Any port in a storm. Mwangi materialised from the kitchen area, and gave her his wide smile.

'It's very late,' he said. 'Maybe you would like a hot drink?'

'Tea please, Mwangi. I'll have it here. And you should go to bed. Have you seen Bwana Lars?'

'He has gone out to check the lower fence. He said there were *nyati* coming up from the swamp. He said you would be very angry if they trampled your vegetables again.'

'He's right!' The buffalo were a menace when they got into the kitchen gardens, and Piet had had to shoot one a few weeks ago, after a patch of maize belonging to one of the *watu* had been destroyed.

Hannah sat down by the fire. She thought she could smell the aroma of her father's pipe tobacco still lingering in the upholstery, but perhaps it was her imagination. Jan had often sat here for a last smoke before he went to bed. She leaned forward and poked at the embers. She had brought the most urgent bills with her from the office, but maybe it would be better to wait till tomorrow and go through them with Piet. He'd be tired when he got in, and Anthony might be with him. Lars would probably appear too, and he always questioned her suggestions. Sometimes she wished she and Piet could have their home to themselves for a while, without the big Norwegian's constant presence. Hannah had wanted to move him into the old manager's cottage, a few hundred yards from the main house. But it needed fixing up, and all available money and labour were being ploughed into the lodge. Lars occupied one of the guest rooms, eating with them, looming up everywhere, filling every space with his large, gangling frame. No, she was being unfair. She knew very well that they could not manage without him, and she was grateful that he had driven out tonight to secure her vegetable garden from the marauding buffalo. He was a good man, with his deep, steady voice and droll pronouncements that made them laugh. There had been one evening lately when they had all felt low, and Piet had taken out the brandy after dinner. Lars had opened up then, and told them stories of his life in Norway. His descriptions of the eccentric and stubborn people who were his family and neighbours had helped them to forget their own troubles, and Hannah had been fascinated by the idea of living in a place where it was pitch dark, day and night, for several weeks of the year. He certainly looked the quintessential Viking, with his large, spare frame, and weathered features, and his slightly-too-long blond hair. But somehow she could not envisage him on a voyage of plunder. He seemed far too polite for rape and pillage. She preferred the undercurrent of danger that made a man that little more interesting.

Like Anthony. Hannah had always thought that there was something of the big cat about him – a fluidity of motion, an underlying power, a hint of calculation and even menace in the brown eyes that were always watching. Watching for she knew not what. And Viktor Szustak. He was truly wild, with his loud, crazy laugh and his hands flying and wheeling in the air as he spoke. He seemed to move like a whirlwind, even when he was not in a hurry, and his drawings were large and scrawling as he tried to explain an idea or a concept. But then he would produce a set of plans that contained every detail, thought out and marked on the page in meticulous lines and letters. She had no idea how he kept his hand steady enough to draw anything. He drank huge amounts of whisky and vodka and gin, encouraging her to try them all. Recently she had gagged and spluttered on some fire water he had brought from Nairobi, and she remembered Sarah choking on her sherry years ago. But Viktor knocked it all back, and sang and laughed his mad laugh, and then appeared next morning looking fresh and bright, armed with his pencils and his big drawing books, measuring everything to the last inch, incorporating the trees and rocks into plans that would make their lodge the most beautiful place in the world.

The sound of a vehicle brought her back to the present. Lars appeared in the doorway with his rifle still in his hand.

'Frightened an old *nyati* out of your vegetables,' he said. 'For the time being, anyway. He only managed to get a few cabbages.'

'Thanks, Lars,' she said. 'Do you want some tea? There's plenty in the pot.'

He sat down with a cup of tea, stirring it slowly, deep in thought. Then he looked up at her. 'I saw you down at the dairy the other day,' he said. 'Talking to the cows.'

'I always talk to the cows,' she said. 'I've been talking to them since the first day Pa took me in there, and taught me to say all their names. When I was about two, I suppose.'

'I think they like it,' he said. 'The sound of your voice. I can understand that. So I've been thinking that maybe you could take over the dairy. If you feel you have the time. You've been cooped up in the office for too long. It would be good to have you look after the dairy cattle. I seem to have my hands full with the wheat and the fencing and the *watu*, but I'd be around if you needed help. What do you say, Hannah?'

'You want me to take charge of the dairy?'

'Ja.'

'I'll do it,' she said, delighted. 'I'll start tomorrow.'

She was casting around for something else to say when Piet arrived with Anthony. The dogs were barking as they tumbled out of the Land Rover, and Hannah went out with a light heart to greet them. Anthony was standing in the headlights, his bush hat pushed back from his forehead, so that she could see the mark of the sun on his face below the band.

'Hannah! I haven't seen you for weeks.' He turned off the ignition and locked his vehicle. 'You look great. But of course I always knew you'd be a beauty.'

'Ach, such a flatterer.' She was laughing up at him and she flicked the coil of her blonde plait away from her face. 'Mwangi has made up a room for you. Have you eaten? I'll organise sandwiches and some beer, or a shot of whisky, maybe?'

Soon they were sitting around a tray by the fire. The room felt warm and welcoming now, and Hannah leaned forward, her face flushed with enjoyment. Anthony studied her as she handed round sandwiches and poured drinks. She was much thinner than when she had left for Rhodesia. Maybe it was just that she had grown up. She was lovely in a strong, earthy way, with her thick golden hair and her wide-set eyes, although there were undefined shadows in her gaze. He liked the shape of her chin, finding it both endearing and challenging, but there was something guarded in her that made him wonder what kind of hurt she might be hiding. Piet's kid sister had matured into a woman, and her comments on the development of the lodge were perceptive. He noticed that Lars was casting appreciative glances in her direction, although there were no smiles or secret looks in return.

'So what are your plans?' Anthony asked her. 'Will you stay at Langani, or go back down south for more studies?'

'I will never return to that place. Never.'

He was taken aback by the force of her reply. Piet was sitting very still in his seat, and there was a sudden tension in the air. Anthony sought to change the subject.

'I'm just back from a sales trip to England and the United States. I saw Camilla in London. Drop-dead stunning. And with plenty of guts, living in the thick of everything going on in that crazy city. Everyone knows her. Her picture is in every magazine and newspaper. It's amazing.'

'Piet and Sarah saw her at Easter,' Hannah said. 'Very reticent, my brother, on the subject of Camilla. He never did tell me much about that weekend.'

Anthony raised his eyebrows, but Piet had stood up and was stoking the fire, deliberately ignoring them.

'Anyway, we discussed a birthday safari,' Anthony said. 'I have a gap between bookings towards the end of August. There'd be the five of us, or six with Tim. I've suggested a camp in the Samburu or Shaba area where there are no tourists. I'm sure Lars could hold the fort here for a few days.'

'I have enough practice for that, yes.' Lars smiled his slow smile.

'I haven't heard a thing from Camilla, except for some postcards.' Hannah's evening was full of surprises.

'Well, she seemed sure that you'd all be here. We made an arrangement about the camping. She'll take care of food and wine and fuel for the cars, and I'll supply the tents and the staff. Plus the exceptional birthday present of myself, as your very own safari guide. Piet, if you bring a Land Rover and a trailer we won't need a lorry. I'm amazed you haven't heard from Camilla. I'd have thought she'd be on the phone to you right away.'

'It sounds like a dream,' Hannah said, but she saw her brother shrug and turn away. 'Is there something wrong, Piet?'

'Nothing wrong.' He came back to the small circle around the fire. 'Look, Han, you've all planned this get-together for your twenty-first, and it's a great idea. Anthony seems to have something organised with Camilla, and I can certainly throw in the Land Rover and trailer. But I don't think I can join you. There's too much going on here, and I want to have the construction finished by the end of November so we can open the lodge soon after Christmas.'

'But you *must* come with us!' Hannah was dismayed. 'Lars has already said he can manage.'

'Come on, old chap,' Anthony urged him. 'You can't leave me alone in the bush to survive those three sirens. God knows what might become of me.'

'We don't get much chance to do anything together, Piet, and it's my twenty-first.' Hannah was pleading. 'You're my only family here. I want you to be with us.'

'You should know when you're beaten, man,' Lars said. 'You'll only be gone a short while.'

Hannah threw him a look of gratitude and then turned back to her brother. He answered with a question of his own. 'Are you sure Camilla meant for me to come?'

'Of course she did.' Anthony looked at him in astonishment. 'She was hoping Tim Mackay might fly out too, if he can get away from the hospital.'

Piet nodded. 'So what are your dates again?'

'End of August and early September. College doesn't start again for Sarah until October. So, what about it?'

'I think it's OK, yes,' Piet said.

'It's settled then!' Hannah hugged her brother, her eyes shining with gratitude. 'Thanks, Piet – it's the best idea I've ever heard.'

'You ring Camilla or Sarah tomorrow, then.' Piet realised how much she deserved this. She was too young to have been through everything that had happened and she was working very hard. He owed her some pleasure. 'Tell them both we're looking forward to it. But don't spend half an hour gabbling on the phone. It's very expensive.'

When they finally stood up from the dying fire, Hannah reached up to kiss her brother and he rubbed his bristly chin against her cheek.

'Thanks again, Piet. You've no idea what this means to me.'

'You deserve it. You've been working like a slave, and you're not bad when all's said and done. For a girl, I mean.'

He laughed as she pummelled him on the chest, and he went to his room whistling. Hannah watched him go, filled with optimism for the months ahead. She was glad that he and Anthony were working together. The man was a mine of information and experience, and he knew everybody in the tourist industry both locally and overseas. He would be an ideal partner and he was an old friend. They would make it. It would be all right. And now there was the reunion in August and her birthday in September. There would be so many things to tell and share. In the garden she could hear the whistle and chirp of nightjars and tree frogs underpinning the distant whoo-wup call of hyenas, and the warning bark of a zebra moving away from a night predator.

At dawn she made her way to the dairy where Lars was waiting. They watched the cows being brought in and went round the stalls together, examining and discussing each one, talking to the herdsman and the dairy boys in charge of the milking, and Lars explained to them that she would be taking over responsibility for the dairy. Hannah's face was alight with pleasure as she made her rounds and she felt enormous pride at being given this vital role. When Anthony had driven away Hannah returned, with less reluctance than before, to her paperwork. She was frowning over an invoice that appeared excessive when Juma, the headman, appeared at the door.

'There is a man outside,' he said. 'He would like to see you.'

Hannah looked up from her paperwork. 'What man?'

'A young Kikuyu, Memsahib Hannah. He has a letter from the mission school at Kagumo.'

'Kagumo?' Hannah was surprised. 'He's come a long way, hasn't he? What does he want?'

'He wishes to see Bwana Piet,' Juma said.

'He's not here,' she said. 'He went to look at the bull that caught its leg in the fence last night. Tell the man to come back later.'

Juma disappeared from view, and Hannah heard the sound of voices on the steps outside. When he came back, he was holding a carefully folded letter.

'He asks that you read this,' he said. 'He is waiting.'

She took the note from his outstretched hand and read it quickly. It was written in a spidery, scholarly hand.

> *Kagumo School*
> *Kiganjo*
> *Central Province*

To Whom It May Concern

Simon Githiri came to us as an orphan when he was a small child. Since then he has been raised and educated at Kagumo Mission School. We believe him to be about twenty years of age. He is now looking for work. We have found him to be diligent, intelligent and honest, and keen to learn. He speaks English well, can read and write, and has passed his School Certificate and completed a basic bookkeeping course. He would be suitable for training in office work or some other clerical capacity. He would also be willing to do domestic or agricultural work should that be what is offered to him. He is a good filing clerk, and he has done some storekeeping work. During his school years he has spent time in our agricultural school, clearing and planting to pay his way.

I believe he would be a steady and useful worker if given the opportunity.

Father Carlo Caverde
Principal

Kagumo Mission was near the township of Nyeri, at the foot of the Aberdare mountain range. It was a sprawling complex run by Italian priests, and Hannah recalled with a smile that it had long been known as 'the Holy Roman Empire' by the Europeans in the area. The Consolata Fathers had a hospital, schools, an orphanage and an agricultural training facility. They had a reputation for turning out well-prepared students and workers. She made up her mind.

'Send him in, Juma, and I'll decide if he should wait for Bwana Piet or not.'

The young man was wiry and slender, of medium height, and with very black skin. He was dressed in clean, faded trousers and a checked cotton shirt and wore open sandals made from old car tyres. He stood respectfully at the door of the office, his eyes downcast after a quick appraisal of the person who was interviewing him. Hannah indicated his letter of reference from the Mission.

'Simon Githiri,' she said. 'I see from your chit that you were educated by the fathers at Kagumo?'

'Yes, madam. They have given me good schooling.' His voice was low-pitched, his English well pronounced.

'They think you could do an office job. I should have thought you would look for work in Nyeri. It's a busy town and there must be places there, needing staff. It's much closer to your home.'

'It is not my home, madam.' He looked up directly at her.

'You've travelled a long way,' Hannah said. 'Why come so far, to a farm? We don't have office work here. I'm not sure that we have any work, come to that.'

'It was told to me, by a man in Nanyuki this morning, that the bwana of Langani was making a safari business. It was told to me that there would be work with the safaris, or in the hotel that is being built. I would like to do such work. I would work very hard.'

He was articulate, Hannah thought, his words quiet but determined. He was also well informed. It always amazed her how the bush telegraph worked in this country. People seemed to glean information from the wind.

'How did you get here, Simon?'

'I walked,' he said.

'All the way from Nyeri? When did you start out?'

'Two days ago, madam.'

Forty miles in less than forty-eight hours. God knows where he had slept, but he was clean and he gave no sign of being hot or tired. He was certainly strong, and eager too. Hannah tapped her pen on the desk, an idea forming in her mind. She read the letter from Father Caverde again, and then got to her feet.

'Juma will take you round to the kitchen for something to eat. My brother will be back at lunchtime, but I don't know if there is any suitable work here. The safari business has not started yet and the hotel will be very small.'

Simon went away with Juma, and Hannah sat down to think. This might prove to be perfect timing. They had been talking, only yesterday, about looking for people to work at the lodge. Piet particularly wanted to train an African assistant. She waited with impatience for him to return, but when he came in with Lars he was preoccupied.

'We've got problems.' Piet rubbed his dust-caked face with a handkerchief.

'We went down with Kipchoge to look at the bull that got caught in the fencing,' Lars said. 'He's in a poor shape, and in a very bad temper. There's barbed wire wrapped around his leg and it's a mess. We've cleaned out the wound, but the infection may have spread.'

'He was trapped on the wire all night, and struggling,' Piet said. 'Unfortunately Juma didn't notice he was missing until late this morning. I've phoned for the vet to come out and have a look.'

'Worse than that, there's a whole section of that fence down,' Lars said. 'It has allowed buffalo into the far pasture. Piet and I think someone cut the wire.'

'It's been a bugger of a job trying to get it back up again,' Piet said, accepting a tankard of cold beer from Mwangi. 'It's taken us all morning, and it's still not a hundred per cent secure. It might be the Maasai, letting their cattle in for free grazing. But it could be poachers, using the bottom pastures as a way down to the river or the swamp. There's a herd of elephants down there, one or two with good ivory.'

'That's all we need,' Hannah said in frustration. 'We've had *watu* cleaning up and fencing those pastures for weeks. If the wires are cut and our cattle get out, and those scrawny Masai *ngombes* get in, our herds could be infected with foot-and-mouth and God knows what. Never mind the problems of elephant poachers.'

'That's true.' Lars nodded agreement.

'Juma should have spotted that the bull was missing last night,' Piet said wearily.

'No,' Hannah said, 'Juma can't be everywhere at once. He was helping you up at the lodge yesterday, until you came down with Anthony. We have a problem with labour, Piet. I've heard Lars talking to you about it recently, but you're not listening to him. Or to what I've been saying for a while. We need our experienced *watu* on the farm, and not out there on the building site. If all the old hands are working on the construction, then something will be left undone.'

'But I need to keep the place by the waterhole cleared and salted, if we're going to establish a permanent viewing area,' Piet protested. 'And I have to use existing farm labour for the building. We can't afford to bring in construction workers from outside. It's only temporary, until the lodge is finished.'

'I know, Piet. But soon we have to find staff that will work in the lodge. I need to start training them now.'

'You're right,' he agreed. 'I've been leaving it to the last possible moment, so we wouldn't have extra wages to pay. But I don't know where we'll find—'

'I think I might have one answer,' Hannah interrupted. 'I've got something you should look at.' She handed him Simon Githiri's letter from the mission. 'This boy is looking for work and he seems to be a cut above average.'

Piet scanned the letter. 'They have some good boys coming out of there,' he said. 'What did you think of him?'

'His English is impressive, and he's anxious to work. Someone we could train from scratch. He seems to have ambition, and a bit of *nguvu*. Talk to him yourself – I'll tell Kamau to bring him round.'

'All right.' Piet put the letter in his pocket. 'Lars, do you want to come and interview him?'

Piet sized up Simon Githiri and liked what he saw. The young Kikuyu looked at him steadily, submitting to the inspection without any sign of unease or embarrassment. He answered all the questions put to him, in both Swahili and English, explaining that he had learned some simple book-keeping and basic clerical training at the mission. During his spare time he had worked in the office at the college, to keep himself in funds and to pay for his continued education. The fathers had offered to let him stay on permanently.

'I would like to work in the safari business,' he said. 'I have seen the tourists in Nyeri. Once I have been with the laundry truck to Treetops, and I have heard about the National Parks from the safari drivers who stop in the town.'

'We're not running safaris from the farm,' Piet said. 'We're starting a small lodge for about ten people. It's not open yet, and it will take time before we have regular guests. You would not be travelling anywhere if you worked at Langani.'

'I understand, sir. But I would be happy to learn to take care of the *wazungu* visitors, and to tell them about my country.' He smiled, a little hesitantly. 'I could do fine work here.'

'How did you come to be in Kagumo?' Piet asked. 'My sister says you were not from that district.'

'I was taken there by a relative. My parents were dead and I was very small and sick. My family was too poor to keep me, and they thought that the fathers would give me food and clothes and medicine, and teach me to be clever. Then I would be able to get work and help my family. But after I was left at Kagumo, I did not see any of my relatives again. I have become strong, and I have learned many useful things, and I am ready to serve you as my family.'

Simon stopped. It had been a long speech, delivered in clear English. Piet could see sweat on his forehead from the effort of making it. He found himself admiring the boy's courage, and his honesty. He did not want to be considered just another orphan, raised by charity. This lad has an independent streak, Piet thought. He could turn out to be a valuable worker.

'Wait outside,' he said to the young man. He closed the door and looked at Lars.

'Good, heh? Plenty of *nguvu*, as Hannah said. I think we should give him a try.'

'He seems bright enough, ja. But you don't know anything about him, except for that piece of paper. You'd better call this priest first, and check him out. How do you know he hasn't made off with someone else's reference?'

'They all have to carry a *kipandi*, Lars, the same as those identity cards you have in Europe. It wouldn't be worth his while trying to pass off a letter belonging to someone else. I'm going to take him on, at a very small wage. Give him a chance. What's there to lose?'

He called Simon back into the room. 'I am willing to give you a trial, Simon, but you'll have to work very hard. You'll get your food and lodgings, but your wages will be low until I know whether I'm going to take you on permanently. After three months we will decide. And you will follow orders from me, or from whomever I tell you is in charge. Understand? Good. Now, have you got your *kipandi*?'

Simon produced his identity card, with his name and thumbprint on it.

'There you are, Lars. Simon Githiri, my new aide-de-camp.' Piet returned the card to Simon, and smiled at him. 'Off you go, then, Simon. Find Juma the headman, who brought you in here this morning. He should be over by the stores, and he will organise your quarters. You can report back to me after lunch – in one hour. Then we will go to the game lodge and look at what work is being done.'

'Thank you, sir.' Simon's smile was uninhibited, and he was still smiling as he passed Kamau who was standing out on the verandah. The old cook stood and watched the newcomer, pursing his lips and made a sucking noise of disapproval. This stranger might take the job he had wanted for his son David. It was not a good sign. He knocked on the office door and hovered at the entrance as Piet rose from his desk.

'What are you doing here, old man?' Piet asked him.

'Memsahib Hannah says the lunch will be ready in ten minutes.'

'Good. Did you see the boy who was here?'

'Yes, bwana.'

'I've offered him a job. I'm going to teach him how to work in the safari lodge. And you'll have to show him how to keep the storeroom, for the food and the drinks.' Piet picked up the keys of the office, but Kamau stood unmoving in front of him, his face grave. 'Is there something else you want?'

'Yes, bwana. I am again offering my son to be trained. To help you.'

'David is already working on the farm, old man. I can't afford to take him away from what he's doing, and he can't do an office job. This Simon has been to school for a long time. He knows about being a clerk, and he can do bookkeeping. David cannot do those things, but we will find something for him later. I think Memsahib Hannah has an idea for him.

Come on, Kamau, we've had this talk before, and it's an old *shauri* that we cannot resolve.'

'My son was born at Langani. He is like your family and you can trust him. He is not a stranger. You can teach him the things he would need to know.'

'Later, maybe, when the lodge is open. We'll talk about it again in a few weeks, I promise you. Now, *toroka* and tell Memsahib Hannah we're ready for lunch.' He watched as Kamau trudged away, stiff with displeasure, and then turned to Lars. 'That son of his is a good boy, but he hasn't had enough education to work in the office at the lodge. Hannah says he sometimes helps Kamau in the kitchen, and he's quite good. So maybe she can train him to cook. Meantime, I think I've got myself some potential with Simon. It will be interesting to see how he turns out.'

'He is eager,' Lars agreed. 'That was quite a speech, about the loss of his family.'

'A Kikuyu like that would feel the lack of a family unit. It would affect his marriage prospects and all sorts of things. He wouldn't have a right to clan lands, and there are other issues. I suppose he feels bad that his relatives didn't keep any contact with him. But they were probably so poor that they felt Kagumo was his best chance. You get a lot of orphans dumped on the missions and the charities like that. Their extended family has no resources to feed them or house them. As you saw from that letter, they don't really know how old he is. My guess is they might not even know his clan or tribal name. Anyway, the priests seem to think well of him. Now – where's lunch? We need to eat quickly before the vet arrives.' He raised his voice. 'Hannah, where are you? We're starving!'

In the afternoon Hannah was smiling to herself as she returned to Jan's old desk. Things were moving steadily towards a new order. Piet had come up with a good idea as they drank their coffee, and she was looking forward to telling Kamau that she would start training his son David as a cook. It was an important, face-saving gesture, and she would summon both father and son this evening, to give them the news. She bent to take a file out of the drawer and heard a knock on the door. Lars was standing on the verandah, his big frame blocking out the light, choosing his words with care.

'I'm going to Nanyuki this afternoon,' he said. 'I was thinking you might like to come with me. There's someone making good printed cloth, hand-dyed, that you could use for your curtains, maybe. At the lodge. It's being made by a Dutch girl who lives just outside town. I could take you there, and then we could go to the club for some tennis and a drink.'

She understood at once his offer of cooperation and encouragement, and she put away the files on her desk and picked up her wallet.

'Good idea,' she said, smiling up at him and putting her hand on his arm. 'Let's go shopping.'

Chapter 11

Kenya, August 1965

They lay in the sea, aimless and happy. Sarah closed her eyes against the yellow of a scorching sun and allowed a series of small, rippling waves to caress her, raising pleasurable goose bumps on her skin. It was their last day at the coast and she did not want it to end. She could hear the whisper of the wind in the casuarina trees that fringed the beach, and the soft clatter of the palm fronds surrounding the small cottage they had rented. Tomorrow they would fly to Nairobi where Piet would be waiting. They were going to spend the night at George Broughton-Smith's flat, and then they would go to Langani. She opened one eye and looked at Camilla's perfect form, floating a few yards away.

'Why can't I have collarbones that stick out, and cheekbones that make shadows and shapes on my face?' Sarah said. But she did not really care, because her skin was tanned and her hair had been streaked blonde by the sun, and the grey skies of Dublin were thousands of miles away. She had moved through the last two weeks in a current of euphoria.

'God, you're such a halfwit, Sarah.' Camilla turned in the water and swam slowly towards the shore, calling back over her shoulder. 'You'd better shape up for tomorrow when the great man comes down out of his tree house to collect us. I'm dying to be at Langani. And we'll see Hannah's Viking.'

'She says he's one of those men who thinks a woman should be gainfully occupied in the kitchen, with a batch of children squealing around her lap. Or mending his socks. Not running farms. I think she only tolerates him.'

Sarah was more than happy to be discussing someone else. It helped to quell the fluttering of anticipation and fear in her stomach. She would see Piet tomorrow, look for what was new in him and relish the things she remembered. He would speak to her in the soft, Afrikaans lilt that she loved, and she would make him tell her all his dreams. No matter what had gone before, it would be wonderful to spend time with him. Hannah knew everything now, so there were no more secrets. On their first night at the coast there had been a tension between them all, as they sat talking after dinner. Finally, Camilla had broached the subject of the weekend in London.

'I behaved terribly,' she said to Hannah. 'What I did to Piet was inexcusable. It was a spur-of-the-moment thing – a knee-jerk reaction. He got in the firing line between myself and my dear mother. I apologised to him. To everyone. And I only hope he's not still angry with me, though he has every right to be.'

Hannah took another sip of wine and when she answered, her tone was cool.

'You know Piet. He didn't say much, just gave me the bare bones of the story. I was the angry one, not him. He made excuses for you, and he's not the kind who bears a grudge. So we should forget the whole thing. Move on. We all do stupid things from time to time.' She finished her wine and stood up. 'The tide will be out tomorrow morning at ten. We could go snorkelling on the reef, if we get up reasonably early.'

Sarah had listened to the exchange in silence. Camilla had got off lightly, she thought, but yes, it was over now. Piet had grown out of his puppy love for Camilla, had been shocked into a different view of her. So there was hope, Sarah thought. And now Camilla was in love herself – amazingly and madly in love with Anthony Chapman. She had even slept with him, and her impatience to see him could barely be contained. He was on safari with clients, but he would join them at Langani. In the meantime, the days at the coast had been glorious. They walked miles along the beach each morning, slept through the heat of the afternoon, snorkelled in the coral gardens at the edge of the reef among shoals of tiny fish in impossibly vivid colours, skirting the drop where kingfish and barracuda and sharks patrolled the cobalt of a deeper sea. In the early morning they would sit on the low coral wall that bordered their beach house, and watch the fishermen guiding their long canoes through the mosaic of shallow water inside the reef, rolling up their canvas sails as they reached the beach, balancing the long masts on their shoulders, and spreading their nets out to dry across the white sand. Storks and gulls congregated on the edge of the water, squabbling over scraps of fish, and small boys sailed wooden replicas of their fathers' boats in the rock pools. Beneath the shade of the palm trees, the women prepared fires for the fish and cooked pots of bubbling rice that would provide their sustenance for the day.

At sundown, Sarah and Camilla sat out on the verandah, while Hannah worked in the kitchen. She had brought David, her trainee cook, down to the coast with her, and she was trying out recipes for future guests at the lodge.

'You're ideal guinea pigs,' she said. 'You can taste the food and give us some ideas about how it would look on a plate if we were serving it in some place in London or Dublin.'

They offered a critical analysis of each dish as it was served. Camilla found some passable wine in an Indian shop in the village, and stored it in the paraffin fridge. She paid a local boy to climb the surrounding palm trees and bring down green coconuts, full of their own sweet water to which she added gin or vodka for coastal cocktails. After dinner they sat on the beach and watched the moon rise pale and mystical out of the Indian Ocean.

They talked for hours of the circumstances that had forced them apart. Hannah told of her anguish about abandoning Lottie in a place where her father was no more than a hired hand. At last she admitted the unpalatable truth about her sudden departure from Rhodesia, and found comfort in her friends' support. Time would set balm to the wound, they assured her, and then she would be able to let forgiveness in. Sarah recounted the humiliation of her experience with Mike, her anxiety over her father's health, and the sad knowledge that her parents would never return to her childhood home in Mombasa. Camilla described her devastation at being rejected by drama school, and tried to explain her sense of isolation in London, despite her modelling successes. They retired to bed, sunburned and glowing, lulled into sleep by the swirling, rolling music of the sea on the distant reef. They were so close, so tuned in to one another, aware that they had withstood an assault that would have destroyed a weaker bond. But their friendship had been born again, rekindled and nourished by the peace of this place and the slow rhythm of their days in the sun. Nothing could break them apart now.

They were met by George Broughton-Smith at Nairobi Airport, and taken to his flat. There was hardly time to bathe and dress before Sarah heard the doorbell, followed by the sound of voices, and ice clinking in glasses. She tried to calm herself, standing in front of the bathroom mirror, clutching the edge of the basin and counting to ten. As she came into the sitting room she knew that Piet was saying something to her, but she could barely hear his voice for the thumping of her heart. When he leaned forward and kissed her cheek she felt tipsy before she had even lifted her drink. When Camilla appeared, there was a moment of awkwardness as she faced Piet across the room, but he gave no sign that he harboured any ill feeling. No one mentioned Marina, or Jan and Lottie and their self-imposed exile. But Raphael Mackay's health and his future were of genuine concern.

'There are other areas in Kenya that have minimal risk of malaria,' George said. 'I know your father always wanted to stay at the coast, but upcountry isn't such a bad place. It would be a great pity if he didn't return at all. He's done so much good here, and his experience is priceless.'

At the New Stanley Grill they ate Mombasa oysters and highland lamb, and took turns dancing with George who seemed totally at ease, more friendly and approachable than Sarah remembered. Perhaps it was because they were older, and he was comfortable with them now. Old friends and acquaintances stopped at their table, asked them to dance, plied them with compliments and wildly exaggerated stories of the bush and the scandals in the city. It was as if they had never been away. Sarah was light-headed with wine and laughter when Piet finally asked her for a dance. For a second or two she had a sense of déjà vu, a vision of him in London when Marina had ruined it all. But this time there was only the closeness of him, the sound of his breathing and the smell of his skin, and the feel of his fingers on her hand. Later, at the flat, when they had all said their goodnights, she heard him make up a bed on the sofa and her body felt strung out with longing for him as she tossed and turned, and finally tumbled into a restless sleep.

Camilla sat up late with her father, on the small balcony overlooking the city lights.

'So you like this job, Daddy? I mean, really like it?'

'I do, yes. It's already proving frustrating, the clash of conservation interests with the demand for more agricultural and grazing lands. Kenya politics are diabolical. There is international pressure to save the game, and local councils desperate to get their hands on funding, and crooked officials who want to siphon some off to buy themselves cars and wives. And we have a bunch of eager research scientists crawling all over every national park and game reserve, with a host of largely unproven theories as to what should be done. It's a powerful cocktail that can blow your head off, if you don't handle it carefully. But I like the challenge, yes. I'm hoping to spend more time here. I think your mother might even come out for a visit.'

'I saw her before I left. She was different, somehow. Calm, almost. I found her quite strange.'

'She likes the little cottage in Burford, and she's busy decorating,' George said. 'It's good for her. She probably told you that she hasn't been very well. Tired and anaemic. But she's been to a specialist and some medicine should take care of that. She goes down to the country whenever she wants. To be quiet on her own, or with a couple of friends. I wouldn't have been able to afford a second house in my old job. So that's one immediate advantage. It would be nice if you could go down there one weekend, Camilla.'

'Perhaps, when you're home the next time. We could go together.' Camilla wondered what kind of friends her mother invited to her Cotswold retreat. She did not want to refuse him outright.

'I'll tell her,' he said. 'I talk to her on the phone once or twice a week when I'm away.'

'Why, Daddy?'

'Why what?'

'Why do you phone her all the time? Go on looking after her like this, living with her?'

'We'll talk about it one day, darling, but not tonight,' he said. 'Let's turn in. We've had a terrific evening and I'm delighted to see you with your friends. They're fine young people.'

'No, wait. Sit for a moment or two longer. I have something to tell you. I've fallen in love, Daddy. Not with some suitably well-bred gent from Belgravia and Sussex, or a rich banker from the City. I've fallen in love with Anthony Chapman.' Camilla was suddenly self-conscious, and she tried to laugh off her discomfort. 'A bush baby from Nairobi. Mother doesn't know. She'd probably have a fit.'

'Oh my dear girl! No wonder you look so tremendously happy and beautiful. I knew there must be something, but stupidly I didn't guess. So where is your young man? I like him very much, by the way.'

'You know him?' Camilla was surprised.

'I've come across him on a couple of wildlife committees. He's a balanced and dedicated conservationist, without being sentimental. He has a good head on his shoulders and a great deal of courage. Not afraid of anything, and very determined. Was he down at the coast with you?'

'He's out on safari, but he's picking us up at Langani and then we'll travel north to the camp he's setting up for us in Samburu.' There was a kernel of regret that he had not yet telephoned her, or found some way of sending her a message in the two weeks since her arrival. True, he was in the bush, but when his camp moved from one area to another he always took his clients to a hotel or a lodge where communications were surely possible. She closed her mind to the sense of disappointment. 'I expect you'll see him at the end of our safari, if you're still here in Nairobi.' She reached up to kiss her father and to rumple his hair. 'Goodnight, Daddy. I love you.'

They set out early for Langani, driving past the fenced-in boundary of Nairobi National Park, where rhinos and lions now gazed at the silhouette of tall buildings that formed the city's broken skyline. Their route north took them up through the glassy green of terraced coffee plantations, and the steep red earth where the Kikuyu toiled in deep, fertile soil. Along the roadside wooden stalls were hung with bulging hands of green bananas, and piled with neat pyramids of mangos, oranges and tomatoes. They passed women laden with bundles of firewood, or balancing tin drums of water on their heads as they swayed along narrow paths that vanished into the tangle of vegetation. It was Sunday morning. People spilled out of the small mission churches, their songs of worship floating in through the open windows of the car. The Aberdares rose in a blue haze, above a framework of verdant forest and ragged banana trees shredded by the wind. A waterfall roared out of a narrow gap in the hillside to become a gently meandering river, curling through the valley below. Trays of coffee beans were drying in the morning sunshine, and the road was shaded by flame trees with scarlet blossoms, and trees of tumbling yellow cassia flowers. As they climbed higher the trees held out bare branches draped with veils of old man's beard, and the summit of Mount Kenya soared before them, glittering and magical in the distance.

When they drove through the gates of the farm they were suddenly silent, and as they stepped down from the car they embraced one another, tears blurring their first sight of the old stone house where a riot of honeysuckle still obscured the chimney. Camilla was struck once more by Lottie's lawn, and the tenuous boundary of the clipped hedge that separated the homestead and the garden from the expanse of untamed, open plains. She was the first to shake hands with Lars Olsen. In spite of his size and his air of calm authority, he seemed a little awkward among Hannah's friends, and he soon disappeared on the pretext of organising their bags.

'There's nothing that means more to me in the whole world than what we are looking at right now,' Camilla said, turning to Piet. 'Thank you for bringing us back to this. Thank you so very much.'

Dinner on that first night was subdued. The joy of homecoming was tempered by the absence of Jan and Lottie. So much had changed since they had last dined here together. They sat around the fireside late into the night, reluctant to retire with their memories and their loss, eager to recapture the simple, uncomplicated pleasure of the days at the coast.

'Bedtime. We're going out early in the morning,' Piet said at last. 'Lars and I are taking you to the lodge. It's almost finished, and Hannah is doing a fantastic job, making bedspreads and cushions and curtains for all the rooms. We're going to serve dinner up there for the first time. Sarah, I can't wait for you to see this.'

She was not sure if he had mentioned her deliberately, if his words had any special significance. But Sarah hugged them to herself.

'In fact,' he went on, 'I was going to ask you if you'd like to ride there with me – it's a full morning's trek, but we might see some game on the way. I've been considering horseback safaris up there, for people who'd be interested. Either of you other ladies like to make up the expedition?'

'I've been away for more than two weeks and I need to check the store-room and a pile of paperwork,' Hannah said, a shade too quickly. 'Camilla's going to help me. It will take us the whole morning.'

'Then Lars can bring you out in the afternoon, when he's finished his other work. I'll take Simon. He's still not that good on horseback, and it will be good practice for him. Kipchoge will come too, for tracking any game and looking after the horses when we get there. That all right with you, Sarah?'

'I'll bring my camera,' she said. They would spend the whole day together. There was nothing she could possibly want more.

In the room they had always shared Camilla remained awake, staring into the darkness and the pinpoints of starlight beyond the window panes. For the first time since she had left school she said a silent prayer, wishing for Sarah to be happy, and for Hannah to find her way through all the sorrow and change she had traversed with such courage. It was only a few hours now until Anthony arrived, and Camilla felt a tight pain and hammering excitement at the idea of touching him, kissing him, making love with him, and afterwards listening to his breathing as he slept. She lay without speaking to Sarah, because there was no need for words. They were back at Langani, and all that they had dreamed about in the years away seemed possible once more.

She knew now that her real home was not in any of the great cities of Europe. There was no need to be in London. Success had come to her easily and with dizzying speed, but she realised that it was hollow, that it had eaten away at her spirit. She had tasted the swinging cities and bright lights, seen what they had to offer, often through a trancelike haze of sweet-smelling smoke or the bottom of a cocktail glass. She was famous, flattered and pampered wherever she went. The allure of an acting career had faded with the advent of her easily won fame, and now she was ready to move on, away from it all. She had not yet worked out how she could stay here in Kenya, or what she might do, but there would be time for that when she saw Anthony. There would be time for everything that was really important. Meanwhile, she had better get a good night's sleep or she would look like shit in the morning.

When dawn filled the bedroom with saffron light they were already awake. On the edge of the horizon, the mountain stood proud and silent, dark in outline and then fading and retreating into a blue haze as the sun rose in the wide eternity of the African sky. Mwangi served them pawpaw and juicy limes, then fresh coffee and steaming bowls of porridge swimming in thick cream from Hannah's dairy.

'I tell you, those cows have produced more milk and better cream than ever before, since the day I took over,' Hannah said proudly. 'It's true, isn't it, Lars?'

'It's something she says to them.' Lars smiled ruefully. 'I think they don't speak Norwegian too well, and I'm not so great in Afrikaans. But I can chase the crowned cranes out of trampling the wheat, when they start their mating dance. And I certainly know the right words to scare off a buffalo. I can swear in Kikuyu and Maasai too, at those bastards that keep stealing our fencing wire.'

'Who's this Simon? Piet was going on about him last night.' Camilla helped herself to another bowl of porridge. 'I need this, by the way, to ward off the shock of getting up at this hour.'

'You'll need a size up in clothes, for your next shoot,' Sarah said.

'Who cares?' Camilla waved her spoon in the air. 'Bring on more cream and sugar, I say. And bacon and eggs and toast, and a cold beer before lunch. Oh, and afternoon tea, of course, with honey from your bees, Han. So, what about Simon?'

'He's a young Kikuyu I've taken on,' Piet said. 'He'll be good in the lodge when it opens. He'll look after the reception area. Under Hannah's eagle eye, of course. But he's coming on well.'

'Just don't get carried away over that boy, Piet,' Hannah warned him. 'You always see the best in people, but you need to look more carefully sometimes. You can't give an inch to any of them. These days especially. Look at old Kamau. He's been the cook at Langani for more than twenty-five years and he's one of the family. But he's still upset that you gave Simon the job he wanted for his son. Even though I'm training David to be a cook. Kamau can't get that into his head, and he's been sulking for weeks.'

'Aren't things different since Independence, though?' Sarah asked. 'I mean, Africans have a better chance to train for all kinds of jobs they never did before. They don't have to settle for being houseboys and *shamba* boys and ayahs all their lives. Now they have a chance to run businesses, or work as managers in the tourist industry, or own farms like Langani.' She looked around the table and was surprised to see Hannah fling down her napkin with obvious annoyance.

'That's the kind of thing you hear from two-year wonders who've just arrived here and haven't a clue how Africans think,' she said. 'The locals don't give a damn about farmland or protecting it. Look what happened to Piet earlier this year – he allowed some Maasai to bring a few of their cattle in to graze, during the drought. Next thing, they've got ten *rafikis* and thousands of their bony, diseased *ngombes* and sheep and goats all over our pasture. He had to fight like hell to get rid of them, and several of them threatened him. That's what Piet got for his kindness. That's what they know about farms and protecting the land.'

'But what would have happened to their livestock if they hadn't been allowed in here?' Sarah said. 'Wouldn't they have starved to death, and created another set of problems?'

'They've created a permanent problem, anyway,' Hannah retorted angrily. 'They're canny and they're greedy, the Maasai. They've got too many cattle for the amount of grazing available, and they're not prepared to give up one scrawny beast, to prevent the land from becoming a bloody dustbowl.'

'People have romantic visions of magnificent Maasai warriors with spears who kill a lion now and again, in order to prove their manhood,' Piet said. 'But there's not much understanding of the conflict that's brewing over the use of land. Tribal jealousies are causing big trouble. It's not just we whites who have to look at things differently – Africans have to do the same. And that will take a long time.'

'They wanted Independence and they've got it,' said Hannah dismissively. 'Now they have to find out that it hasn't changed things for them, in real terms.'

'We need to educate people in land management,' Piet said. 'Before *Uhuru*, the politicians promised everyone they'd have land and farms and houses and cars handed out to them right after Independence. And the ordinary *wananchi* believed that. But of course their lives are no better now than when the British were here, and there's resentment in many quarters as a result. So the new government is afraid to talk about respect for other people's property.'

'But whether we like it or not, it's their country now.'

'It's just as much my country,' Hannah said. 'I was born here and so was my father. We also have a right to decide how to manage our land.'

'Don't fall into the trap of oversimplification, Sarah,' Lars said. 'Hannah does great things here, bringing on young people like David, for example. Having huge herds of Maasai cattle breaking down fences and turning the grazing to dust doesn't help anyone.'

'Too bloody right,' Piet agreed, thumping the table. 'That's no way for this place to survive.'

'There's no single way to deal with change,' Lars said. 'Everyone is entitled to his own opinion, and we're not going to solve this problem over breakfast. We should ban all questions of politics for now, and finish our coffee.'

Hannah was grateful for his support, for the way he had praised her efforts. And she resented Sarah's comments. Neither of her friends could know how hard she had worked in the last three months, nor had she told them about the financial threat that still loomed over Langani's future. She looked across the table at Lars and smiled, realising how balanced he was. Sarah was already regretting her provocative remarks. She felt Hannah was beginning to sound hard, but maybe the break-up of her family was the root cause. She glanced up and saw Camilla watching her with an amused sympathy.

'I've always had a big mouth and two big feet, Han.' Sarah stood up and walked around the table to put her arms around her friend. 'I haven't a clue what I'm talking about, really. I'm sorry.'

'And I've become a bossy cow. I have to really fight to survive around here.'

'She's not so bossy,' Piet looked at Sarah. 'Hannah is the best. It can be lonely here and she works very hard. So don't take it to heart that she sometimes has to let off some steam.'

'Well, there's certainly nothing wrong with her dairy produce,' Camilla said, spreading a thick layer of butter on to her toast.

'I've never seen anyone so skinny eat so much breakfast. Hurry up, Camilla.' Hannah was embarrassed, anxious to put the incident behind her. 'I have plenty to do around here, and you're supposed to be helping me. Piet, the horses are ready, and Kipchoge's waiting.'

Apart from the two Africans trotting some way behind them, Sarah had Piet all to herself. Joy fizzed through her veins as he began to talk about all that he hoped to accomplish, describing not only the lodge but the details of his plan to turn part of the farm into a conservation area.

'I'm sorry I spoke out of turn at breakfast,' Sarah said. 'I believe you'll do something that's great for this country. You're an exceptional person, Piet, and your workers are lucky. But most Europeans still seem to think Africans are inferior and lazy, and not capable of managing a democratic country. I read that book by Jomo Kenyatta, *Facing Mount Kenya*. It made me realise that they had a tribal system in place here, and we just blundered in and changed it to suit ourselves. So why should Africans be expected to accept a set of laws totally alien to them, without rebelling?'

Piet reined in his horse and looked at Sarah sternly. 'Come on, Sarah.

I've read Kenyatta's book. Even Hannah has read it. But you're surely not telling me that the Mau Mau was justified? Those bastards tortured and murdered thousands in the most savage way. Most of them innocent Africans from their own tribe. You're not trying to tell me you feel sympathy for them? That they had the right to do that?'

'No. No, of course not!' Sarah was flustered. 'The Mau Mau was utterly barbaric, with the oath taking and the massacres. But I don't think there's any revolution in the world that didn't degenerate into blood-letting before it eventually became respectable. And Kenyatta has become an eminently respectable statesman in the same way. Hasn't he? He's a wily old bird.'

'And British-educated!' Piet flung back his head and laughed. 'Taught by the very men he came back and defied. But some Africans who were sent away, who attended the same kind of classes and lectures, have turned out to be rabble-rousers for the most part. They've come back here and used their education to make a power base for themselves, and they don't give a damn if they destabilise the country, or destroy relations between black and white. They're not interested in working together in a spirit of *Harambee*. There's no side that's all good or all bad in this.'

'You're right,' Sarah said. 'It's no different in Ireland, with this terrible situation between north and south.'

'I suppose. And when Kenyatta describes the perfect tribal kingdoms of bygone days, you can be bloody sure he's leaving out some uncomfortable truths, like the dishonesty and the murder and the graft. Man, there isn't any society free of it, unless you believe in the one where you wear a white dress and wings, and spend your days playing a harp.'

'I suppose I see things too perfect, and dream that they can actually be like that,' Sarah's smile was contrite. 'Is that such a bad thing?'

He covered her hand with his, looking at her with mock solemnity. 'I love your clean, wholesome vision, Sarah Mackay,' he said. 'You hold on to your ideals, girl, and your faith in the human race. You always see so much more than other people do.' He reached over to tuck a stray strand of her hair behind her ear. 'That's why I wanted you to be the first to visit my lodge. It's almost finished. Lars and I have been working on it like blacks. Sorry – like slaves. Is that better? Or worse?'

He was laughing, and she would have laughed with him but she could not breathe properly. His touch on her cheek and his eyes smiling into hers made her limbs feel like they were dissolving, and she could not trust her voice.

'So. First, you're going to tell me what you see.' He seemed not to have noticed her silence. 'You are my prophetess, Sarah. My personal seer. I know you love this place and you understand what I want it to be.'

Sarah reached for his hand and held it against her cheek, closing her eyes for a second, imagining herself sliding from her horse into his arms. She wondered how he could understand the feeling she had for this place without sensing the love that she had for him.

'Sarah? Are you all right?' He was relieved when her eyes snapped open to meet his concern. 'For a moment there I thought you were going to faint! Is it the sun?'

She could feel the tell tale red rising to her cheeks, and she gathered up her reins and forced herself to laugh. 'Of course not. I was doing my impression of a seer, looking into your future.'

'And what did you see?'

'That you were about to be beaten in a race to that kopje over there, Piet van der Beer.'

She spurred her horse to a mad gallop and sped away from him. He was shouting something after her, but her face still burned from his touch on her skin, and she could hear only the rush of wind and the crazy hammering of her heart. They waited at the kopje for Kipchoge and Simon to catch up with them, drinking from a water bottle that she took from her saddlebag.

'Here you are,' she said, smiling and holding it out towards Piet. She wanted him to drink first, so that she could hold the bottle to her own lips afterwards, covering the place from which he had drunk, tasting him in the water. She watched him take several long draughts and then wipe his mouth with the back of his hand. When he gave her back the bottle she let her fingers brush his hand, but he bent to adjust his stirrup, oblivious to her touch.

'Memsahib Sarah is very fine on the horse.' Simon had ridden up with Kipchoge.

'Memsahib Sarah is from a mad tribe called the Irish, Simon. These people are very wild when they are riding horses,' Piet said, grinning at her. 'Simon has only started riding since he came to work here. Kipchoge is teaching him. He's come on pretty damn well, don't you think?'

'I have been working hard on the riding of these horses.' The young Kikuyu smiled, his face lit with pleasure at Piet's compliment. 'But I am not yet able to go as you do. Perhaps if there was a lion behind me, I would not mind to go so fast.'

'You've done well,' Sarah said. She heard Kipchoge make a sound that was clearly not flattering and she turned in the saddle to see him spit and look away. 'Maybe I can show you how to sit more comfortably on your horse. That will also give you better control,' she said to Simon.

'Simon has a great deal of work to do,' Piet cut in crisply, and the young man immediately fell back a few paces to rejoin Kipchoge.

'Have I put my foot in it again?' Sarah asked.

'No, but you know how Kipchoge is. We've been together since we were *totos*. He can't understand why I've taken on this mission boy who knows nothing, and he's jealous. Simon has to prove himself, and I don't want to single him out for any special treatment. Otherwise it will take him even longer to be accepted around here.'

'And how does he feel about that?' Sarah asked.

Piet shrugged. 'I don't know. Like anyone else coming into a new job, where the rest of the people have known each other for a long time. He just needs to survive it for a while. That's all.'

An hour later, they reached a place where the land rose in a pile of giant boulders from the base of thorn scrub and the background curve of riverine forest. As they approached, Sarah could see that there were buildings tucked into the hillside, but they had been cleverly positioned to follow the natural contours of the terrain. They were open at the front, with deep verandahs, and the overhanging roofs were thatched. From the main building a viewing platform jutted out to overlook a waterhole, and the muddy ground was criss-crossed with animal trails and strewn salt, white against the red soil. The rooms were fashioned out of mud, and decorated around the doors and window frames with bands of earthy colours. In several places the boulders formed the walls of the rooms. The entire complex melted into the landscape, so that from a distance it was barely possible to make out the buildings at all. Sarah gazed at it, entranced.

'Piet! What a brilliant concept. Completely different from any of the main tourist places. Who designed it?'

'It was my idea. I wanted it to be natural. But I found a mad Polish architect called Viktor Szustak to help me. He fancies himself as a poet, drinks buckets of any available alcohol, and is an absolute genius with a pencil, a few sheets of paper and a ball of string. That's how he measured everything. I never saw him with a tape measure. I told him what I wanted, how it should feel. Then we came up here and camped for a few days, studying where the wind came from, how the sun hit the kopje at different times of the day, how the shadows fell, where it was coolest in the afternoons. He drew the whole thing out on the ground with a stick first, pegged out all the lines with his string and started building. He made drawings of how each area should look, wrapped around the rocks and the tree trunks. Beautiful pictures that could have been framed for an art show. Nothing technical about them at all, and our labour understood them at once. Even the wiring and the plumbing charts were simple and easy to grasp. No builders' diagrams, or jargon that only engineers and architects use. The *watu* love him. They all drank awful *pombe* together, while they were building. And cases of beer that Viktor brought in his car – that's probably why everything is so wobbly, heh? But he got them to work like demons, all day, seven days a week. There isn't a straight line anywhere. Look . . .'

Sarah took her camera from her saddlebag and began to walk around the complex with Piet, stopping to photograph the interiors. The main lounge area was built into the face of the rock, and the counter on the bar had been cut from a single tree trunk, so highly polished that she could see her face in it. On the adjacent viewing platform were comfortable armchairs, and Simon appeared with cushions covered in hand-printed fabrics with African designs. There was a pile of thick blankets in a woven basket, so that guests would be able to stay warm at night as they watched the animals coming to the water. The bedrooms were in six separate rondavels, structured in the same fashion as the main building, each one looking out over a different view. Large, roll-down mosquito screens hung from beams on the verandahs, as a protection against nocturnal bugs and insects, and also from the colony of rock hyraxes that Sarah could hear chattering all around her. She walked on ahead of Piet, photographing the outside of the buildings. Dappled blue guinea fowl strutted on the rocks below her, and lizards with bright orange heads and turquoise bodies sunned themselves on the hot ground. The waterhole was empty of game, except for a troop of baboons on the far side. They watched her for a few moments before resuming their activities of the day, chattering and swinging from the trees, grooming each other, pulling one another's tails. Then the place went silent, and for a moment Sarah felt something deeply sinister in the stillness. She shivered and looked around, as though some ominous presence might be lurking in the surrounding forest. But there was nothing to be seen. She shrugged the strange sensation away and turned her attention back to her camera.

Piet was thrilled by her questions, and her praise for the ingenuity of the design. Simon appeared with more cushions, and Piet encouraged him to answer some of her queries. Kipchoge stood under the trees below the viewing platform, his ebony skin blending into the shadows cast by the midday sun. At last they climbed the wooden steps that led back to the main viewing area with its deep verandah, and stood looking out over the plains.

'That's my most favourite place of all.' Piet pointed to a ridge above them, its craggy head rearing up on the horizon. 'We won't have time to go there today, but I'll take you soon. It's the place I always go to when I want to solve a problem, or when I'm particularly happy about something. Or just to dream. My wishing seat. I feel close to the heart of the land there.' He gave a shrug, as if to apologise for his flight of fancy. 'Anyway, it's the best spot for an all-round view of Langani.'

Sarah looked at the ridge, touched that Piet had shared this secret place with her, aware of his nearness as she leaned in to follow the direction of his arm. He looked down at her, smiling, then turned round.

'Simon, bring us a beer from the icebox, will you? Then you could put out the picnic. Come and sit here, Sarah, where it's cool. I don't want you getting too much sun.'

After lunch they lay back in the reclining chairs, sipping coffee in the shade provided by the thatch. Sarah was tired after the long ride and she closed her eyes, making no attempt to fight off the heavy sensation of sleep that had taken hold of her body. When she awoke, a family of warthogs had come to drink at the waterhole, and she could hear rustling in the trees that overhung the rocks on the far side. From the pool itself, a small stream trickled away down the hillside to lose itself in the dense bush further down. She saw that its course could be plotted by following the winding ribbon of green that marched beside its banks. Far in the distance, the sharp teeth of Kirinyaga snapped at the sky. She glanced across at Piet, and smiled. He was fast asleep, his head tilted to one side, his mouth a little open, hands relaxed and dangling over the arms of the chair. She was tempted to reach out and touch his fingers, smooth the crease lines on his forehead, run her fingers over the cleft of his chin and on to his mouth. Instead she rose quietly, took her camera and walked over to the edge of the platform to photograph the ridge that was Piet's special place. But a sudden chill settled on her, and she felt an inexplicable unease. It was like Gedi, she thought. That was what had bothered her earlier. A sense of brooding. Of being watched. Of course you're being watched, you idiot, she said to herself. There's a whole colony of birds and animals surrounding you, observing your every move. But the hair on the back of her neck began to prickle, and she was inexplicably afraid. All around her she could feel menace and she wanted to cry out, but she seemed to be frozen. Then a hand came down hard on her shoulder and she screamed and cowered low, clinging to the wooden railings of the balcony.

'Jesus, Sarah, what's the matter?' Piet leapt from his chair and ran to her side. She was trembling as he helped her up and led her back to the place where they had been sitting. 'What happened?'

'I don't know, Piet. I'm sorry. I was standing there, looking out, and suddenly . . .' She glanced at him, anxious. 'Did you put your hand on my shoulder? When I was over at the edge of the platform?'

'No.' Piet stared at her, puzzled. 'I was having a kip, and next thing I woke up to see you crouched down and yelling your head off. What happened?' He could see her distress. 'Come on now, little Sarah, you can't go spooking the animals like that. You'll undo all the hard work we had, coaxing them in here.'

'There's no one else here? Where are Kipchoge and Simon?'

'I don't know. Out at the back with the horses, I reckon. Probably gone for a kip themselves.'

'I thought – oh, never mind.' She smiled weakly, embarrassed by her behaviour, but unable to banish the terror she had felt when that hand had gripped her. Surely she could not have imagined it? But there was no one else on the platform. 'I must have been half asleep myself, in some kind of weird daydream. Stupid. I'm sorry.'

'Well, if it frightened you, it frightened the hell out of me too. I thought you were under attack from an army of buffalo, or God knows what. Let's get Simon up here to make some tea.'

'No, I'll make it. I can produce a pot of tea without too much trouble, I hope.'

She went into the kitchen, still shaken by her experience. Piet had called her his prophetess and his seer, and she was acting like a hysteric. 'Get a grip on yourself, Sarah Mackay. This thing you have for Piet is sending you insane. You're like some Victorian miss with an attack of the vapours.'

She came out with the tray and sat down again, glad that she had the wall of the main lounge at her back, so that no one could come up behind her.

'Better?' He was looking at her curiously as she poured the tea.

'Yes, thanks.'

'So. Do you really like the place? Apart from the spooks on the viewing platform, that is.' His tone was teasing.

'It's—' God! She must shake off the panic that had taken hold of her. This was Piet's dream. She wanted to be enthusiastic, encouraging. 'It's the most amazing place in the world. You've done a fantastic job creating it all. You can only succeed, you and Hannah. I know it.'

He hugged her from sheer exuberance. 'Ach, I am so excited about this. The animals are coming in regularly now. We've seen all kinds of buck, elephant, some big cats, plenty of buffalo, and more! Hannah has worked very hard, getting the furnishings ready and training up staff.' He was standing out on the platform again, shouting for Simon. Sarah could not bring herself to join him.

'Bwana?' Simon appeared from the door of the lounge, making her start.

'Where have you been? Memsahib Sarah had to make the tea. Did you not hear the commotion earlier, hear her calling out?'

Sarah cringed with embarrassment. Surely he wasn't going to tell Simon that she was seeing things, throwing fits around his new lodge?

'I have heard nothing, bwana. I went with Kipchoge to look at some buffalo tracks. There must have been many here last night.'

'Good. You'd better start putting the drinks tray together. Everyone else should be here soon.'

'I will get them ready. And the toasts.'

Sarah glanced at her watch. Five o'clock already. She didn't want time to go this fast. At school the weeks had crawled by and she had longed for the times when she could spend a weekend at Langani, or go home for the holidays. Now the days were racing past far too quickly. I must be getting old, she said to herself. I didn't think you felt like this until you were old.

'Piet?' She forced herself to walk out to where he was standing, and tentatively took his hand.

He looked down, smiling. 'What?'

'It's been a wonderful day. I really appreciate your letting me see the lodge first – that you valued my opinion.'

'What are you hoping to do when you finish at university?' He was very close, but his tone was more companionable than romantic. 'Remember how we used to tease you about ending up in a convent?'

She laughed, but there was an undercurrent of annoyance in her reply. 'That was only in your imagination. But what I want is to come back to Kenya, to work. I'd like to join a wildlife research project. And I want to use my camera too. Luckily, photography can be a useful tool in the kind of work I'm hoping for. And it's turned out to be something I'm good at.'

'Camilla told me about the competition you won. Did you bring any of the pictures with you?'

Camilla. Inevitable, she supposed. For all that he had said to Hannah, his old flame was here between them. Still, he could not be expected to exclude her from his thoughts indefinitely.

'I brought prints of my best pictures from the exhibition, for anyone that wants to see them.'

'Of course we want to see them. Why wouldn't we? Or are they indecent, arty-type pictures?' He leered at her.

'No, of course not,' she said, laughing. 'They're portraits of all my down-and-out friends, in the shelter for the homeless where I work in Dublin. I'll show you them tomorrow.'

'You know, if you want to do a research project after your degree, maybe you could find a way to do it at Langani. We'll have this lodge going soon, and you could make some cash on the side, helping us out. I know Hannah would love to have you. It's often hard for her here on her own. She'd love your company. Another female to back her up now and again. Kipchoge and I could help you track game, or interview local tribespeople. I can speak Maasai and Kikuyu, and Kipchoge is a Nandi. Anthony would give you a few pointers too. What about it?'

Sarah pressed her lips together in an attempt to prevent the shriek of delight that might otherwise have emerged into the soft calm of the evening. A joyous vision flashed across her mind of evenings at the farm, with Hannah sitting opposite her and Piet bending over her research notes and photographs. She threw her arms around his neck, and he laughed and swung her in the air, his arms around her waist. Then he bent, unexpectedly, and kissed her. It began sweetly, a light, brotherly embrace. But within seconds he was kissing her in earnest, running his hands through her hair and along her neck and behind her ears. She could taste his desire, and she pressed against him, a glorious sense of triumph rising in her as his lips moved to the hollow of her throat, his tongue flicking over her skin. He kissed her again, softly on her mouth. In some distant place she heard the sound of a heavy-duty vehicle, changing gear as it came up the track, and then Lars was calling out to them.

'Where are you, Piet? Kipchoge, *jambo*. Where is Bwana Piet?'

Piet stepped back, still holding her. He seemed dazed as he let go of her and he stared at her for a long moment, as though he was seeing her for the first time. She tried to regain some semblance of composure before anyone else appeared. Camilla would know at once. She had an eagle eye, and Sarah knew that she must look dishevelled at the very least. Her hair was tangled and her cheeks felt as though they might have turned puce. Oh shit! Shit! Glorious, fabulous, happy shit! Lars came through the lounge on to the viewing platform, in a couple of easy strides. Hannah followed, exclaiming at the furniture and cushions and rugs that Simon had put in place. Camilla drifted in behind her, trailing her fingers across the smooth stone and polished wood, murmuring compliments. Piet was clearly discomforted, greeting everyone much too heartily. He called Simon to pour drinks and they stood together on the viewing platform, glasses raised. Sarah hung back, unable to look anyone in the eye, least of all Piet. Camilla raised her eyebrows enquiringly. Then they were doing the tour of the lodge together, and all seemed as it had been before she had set out that morning.

But for Sarah the world had changed into a new place of pure exhilaration, and she stood looking out at the African evening in a trancelike state, as though the whole earth on which she stood had opened up to offer her, at last, her life's dream of love and fulfilment.

Chapter 12

Kenya, September 1965

'What a bunch of princesses,' Anthony said. 'I thought I'd escaped from Park Avenue ladies for a while, but you're almost worse. There are drinks in the back of the car if you're that thirsty, but we'll be stopping in a few minutes. I need to call in at Charia's *duka* to pick up a few last-minute supplies. Piet should be waiting for us there, and it's the last pit stop where you can take a pee without getting pounced on by lions as you squat behind the car.'

They had left Langani with the early-morning mist still hanging in the blue air. Two hours later they were peeling off sweaters and socks, and demanding cold drinks. Anthony pulled up at a squat building, with a rusted roof and peeling paint. Piet's Land Rover was parked outside, with the trailer behind it, covered by a canvas tarpaulin that was already layered with dust. There was an overpowering smell of paraffin and disinfectant within the dim interior of the shop. Camilla saw Anthony greet Mr Charia, the owner, and discreetly slip some money to the African who worked for him.

'Poor bugger,' he muttered to her, as Charia read the supplies list and clattered away on his abacus. 'I'm surprised he's still able to walk upright, after ten years with that canny old bastard. I don't know why he stays here, wearing rags instead of a *shuka* and a ton of beads. He can't be more than forty years old, and he's bent double from carrying sacks as heavy as he is. But he's always cheerful. Beats me.'

Camilla watched as the Samburu lugged containers of paraffin and flour and maize, out to Piet's vehicle. Sarah fled the glare of noon and leaned on the counter, drinking from a bottle of warm lemonade and making a face. Hannah remained outside, ensuring that the trailer was loaded properly and the canvas sides securely refastened.

'We're ready,' Anthony called out. 'Let's go.'

'Bwana, I would like a lift to Isiolo.' A young Samburu warrior had appeared out of nowhere. He stood slim and upright before them in his tribal finery, a scarlet robe tied in a knot over one shoulder. Rows of beaded collars and bracelets adorned his ears and neck, wrists and ankles, and his long hair was plaited with red mud and cow dung. He smiled, a flash of white in a burnished, beautiful face. The series of raised marks on his cheeks proclaimed his journey through circumcision to manhood. He had planted his spear into the ground and he stood leaning against it on one long leg, a creature of perfect grace and balance.

'No room. Sorry.' Piet shook his head and finished loading the trailer.

'Why did you turn him down?' Sarah asked.

'He may look wonderful, but he stinks of cow dung and sweat, and he's covered in flies Not the ideal travelling companion inside a car. And I can't have him on top of the trailer. It's dangerous going over these corrugations. Han, why don't you drive with me for the next leg?'

They climbed into the cars and turned towards the main road, leaving the warrior gazing at them, motionless and impassive. As they drove past him he moved suddenly, pulling his spear from the ground and raising his arm so that Camilla ducked in her seat and Sarah let out a small exclamation of alarm. Then he spat on the ground and turned away before vanishing in the swirl of red dust behind them. The car rattled and skidded over the rutted surface, and a hot wind blew through the windows, bringing with it a film of sand that coated their faces and stiffened their hair and clothing.

'You'd turn a few heads on the King's Road, if they saw you now.' Anthony watched as Camilla wiped a trickle of sweat from her face, leaving a trail of dust across her cheek. He laughed out loud. 'Only an hour till we reach the camp. Then you have the choice of a shower, or a swim with the crocodiles in the river. And believe me, you've never seen crocs like these.'

They stopped at the headquarters of the reserve to check in. Anthony drove slowly now, following a winding track that meandered through several miles of thick bush before opening out into areas of bleached grass and stands of doum palms. The game was sparse, most creatures having taken refuge in the shade to sleep away the ferocity of midday. Sarah's eyes were beginning to close, and she had the unwelcome sensation of being unable to control her nodding head when Anthony pulled up and pointed into the bushes at the side of the road.

'Gerenuk,' he said. '*Swala twiga*, it's called in Swahili – giraffe gazelle.'

They watched admiringly as the gerenuk turned its head to look at them, sounding a soft call of alarm, curious enough to remain stationary but poised for flight.

'Look at that long, delicate neck with the small head balanced so gracefully on the top. And the ears are very wide and white inside, with black markings like the veins in a leaf.' Anthony said in a low voice. 'Easy to identify with the neck and the handsome horns sweeping backwards. You only see gerenuks here in the north. They can survive for a long time without water, and they're able to reach higher into the trees for grazing, way above smaller gazelles and antelopes.'

Sarah lifted her camera and made a small sound of satisfaction as the gerenuk reared up, balancing its forelegs on a branch, nibbling with dainty precision on a mixture of thorns and young leaves. Behind them Piet and Hannah had also stopped to admire the animal's coppery coat and white belly. Camilla stole a sideways look at Anthony as he raised his binoculars, holding them with the same hands that had caressed her into a state of willing surrender. The memory of it made her breath catch in her throat. It seemed so long ago. She wanted to wind her fingers around his wrist, with its band of bracelets made from leather and copper and coloured beads. A nomad's bracelets, fitting for a man who lived most of his life in the bush, moving from place to place, with no permanence of the kind that she knew. She wondered what his house in Nairobi was like, and whether he had asked some past girlfriend to decorate it for him.

Anthony's mother had left Kenya two years ago, a woman marred for ever by the death of her husband, haunted by visions of his life's blood pumping into the thirsting soil on which he had been raised. The buffalo that had gored him, tore his body apart and tossed it contemptuously away, had been shot by his gun bearer while a wealthy Swiss client stood frozen with horror, unable even to raise his gun, sobbing and mortally afraid. But it had not prevented Herr Villespan from having the animal sent to a Nairobi taxidermist and then to Switzerland, where its head adorned a wall in his lakeside mansion and provided his dinner guests with riveting tales of sacrificial bravery. And it had not prevented Anthony Chapman from taking up his father's profession, with a sense of adventure and a love for the bush that Camilla realised she must learn to understand.

When he had arrived at Langani on the previous evening, he had kissed her on the cheek in the same way that he had greeted her friends. At dinner there was no mention of the time they had spent together in London, and soon afterwards everyone had opted for bed, in preparation for an early start in the morning. As they made their way out on to the verandah Anthony had pressed his hand into the small of her back and whispered into her ear: 'Tomorrow.'

Camilla had lain awake for hours, wondering what he felt about her. If anything. It was difficult to recall the time when she had scarcely noticed him, had rejected his laughing advances, and she could not fathom how her feelings had changed so suddenly and without warning. At the coast, when there had been no word from him, she had begun to wonder if she had read too much into their ardent encounter in London. But then she thought of the way he had held her and remembered the tenderness in his lovemaking, and her mind rejected the possibility that she had been a mere distraction. She wanted desperately to know for sure, and yet she was fearful of any immediate revelation of the truth. They must now be nearing the camp, and she would know the answer, perhaps all too soon.

They drove on, until a line of trees told them they were approaching the curve of the river. Anthony halted briefly to engage the four-wheel drive and then descended into the rushing water, stopping on the river bed to point out several half-submerged crocodiles of frightening proportions. Their scaly heads and glittering eyes were just visible above the water, as they waited for an unwary victim to pass their way. Camilla looked at them with revulsion and shivered as Anthony revved the engine and slid over the rocks, crawling up the steep slope of the opposite bank. He turned down a narrow trail to the left, brushing against rampant vegetation, with the screech of thorns scraping the chassis.

Their camp had been set up in a clearing above the river. The sleeping tents were pitched in a line beneath the mottled shade of the acacia trees, and the crew was lined up and waiting, faces alight with anticipation and welcome. Camilla stepped down from the Land Rover, stretching stiff limbs, and Sarah scrambled out of the back seat, dragging all her camera equipment. Piet and Hannah arrived moments later and Anthony led them all forward for formal introductions.

'This is Francis, our cook. Samson and Daniel will serve your drinks and meals. William is in charge of your tents and any laundry. Equally important are Musioka and Joseph who look after the vehicles, and collect the wood for cooking and hot water, and for our campfire at night. Now – tents. Sarah, I've put you and Hannah in together, with Piet next door. Camilla, you have your own quarters in the middle there. If you prefer some other combination, you can swap around as you like. Showers and loos are behind your sleeping tents. You can use the small shovel in the loo tent to cover up whatever's in the long drop. There are lanterns and torches in every tent, and outside under the fly leaf.'

'What about going to the loo in the middle of the night?' Sarah said, embarrassed by her question, but more afraid of the consequences of ignorance. 'I mean, there could be hyenas and lions wandering around. Couldn't there?'

'Just don't stroll around with a half-chewed impala leg in your fist. If you come across a lion you can give me a shout.' He grinned at her. 'It's OK, Sarah. We have a fire going and an askari on duty all night. Now – there are canvas basins and buckets of water on your verandahs, for washing hands and faces. We've left the back of your tents unzipped for now, so that you'll get the benefit of what breeze there is. At night you close the zippers, front and back. All the windows have mosquito screens on them, and you need only roll down the canvas flaps if we have a rain-storm. There are cold drinks in the mess tent, and Samson makes a mean Bloody Mary.'

After his introduction Anthony showed them to their tents, and then left them to settle in. Camilla sat down in a canvas chair, absorbing the heat and stillness of the hour, listening to the sounds of the bush. She had never travelled this far north before, into the arid beauty of the semi-desert. Hornbills hopped, ungainly and comical, in the trees around her. A group of starlings strutted at her feet, decked out in iridescent plumage, noisy, fractious and vain, reminding her of the people she all too often encountered and had to work with in London. Shading her tent, the acacia trees held out pale branches festooned with the haphazard nests of social weavers, and in the distance she could see a herd of zebra standing motionless in the shimmering heat. Below their camp, the Uaso Nyiro River flowed brown and sluggish and slow, through the thirsty land.

Sarah entered her tent with a sense of wonder. The floor was made from some kind of plastic sheeting, but it had been covered with a sisal rug.

Twin canvas beds had crisp white sheets and pillows, and hand-printed bedspreads. Blankets and towels were laid neatly on storage chests at the foot of each bed. The bedside table held lanterns and torches, and a selection of soaps and shampoos had been placed in a reed basket. A mirror was attached to the side of the tent, hanging above a wooden console that served as both a dressing table and a small desk. Thermos flasks of cold water and two glasses stood on the polished surface. A vase filled with wild flowers and grasses provided the final touch.

'Not bad, heh?' Hannah sat on the edge of her bed.

'It's so grand,' Sarah said in astonishment. 'I never expected anything like this. I don't think I can ever go home again.' She smiled. 'I suspect it's no accident that Camilla has a tent to herself.'

'There's a message in that, yes.' Hannah was rolling eyes that were full of amusement. 'But she should go carefully. All these hunters and safari people have a reputation, and when someone gets hurt they stand back and tell you that some woman literally threw herself at them and they couldn't turn her down on pain of death. Anthony's no different from the rest of them in that respect.'

'He seems a decent sort, and besides, Camilla can take care of herself,' Sarah said. 'She must have been through this a hundred times in London, the way she lives.'

'I don't know about that. But I do know about Anthony. He's totally committed when it comes to his love of this country, and he's passionate about keeping the parks and the game reserves intact. But when it comes to women, he's different. I've see the way Camilla looks at him, and I think it might be the first time she's really loved someone. So I hope he behaves decently.' Hannah turned suddenly and placed her arms around Sarah. 'And it's as well my *domkop* brother has come to his senses. I'm very pleased about that, yes.'

'Nothing has happened.' Sarah saw the expression of exaggerated disbelief on Hannah's face and moved away, embarrassed by the ever-present reddening of her skin. 'Well, not really. I mean, he kissed me. Once. Before you arrived at the lodge the other day.'

'Not really? Just once? Ha!' Hannah was crowing with delight. 'He knows in his heart now. I'm sure he does. It may take him a while to admit it, but he knows. And that's good, it's very good.'

In the gold of early evening they set out from camp in Anthony's vehicle. A picnic basket with tea and biscuits was in the back of the car. Behind the driver's seat, a fitted rack held a variety of reference books on animals and birds, trees and wild flowers. The roof hatches were open so that they could all stand up on the canvas-covered seats and enjoy an uninterrupted view. The land seemed endless, streaming away from them towards a range of purple hills in the north. Piet sat on the roof, his bare legs dangling down through the hatch. Sarah longed for him to stretch out a foot and nudge her deliberately, but his eyes and thoughts were focused on the far distance as he searched for elephant and buffalo, or the stealthy movement of a cat in the tawny grass. The only sounds around them were bird calls, and the gradual crescendo of insects and frogs as they started up their evening symphony. As they rounded a corner there was a crackling of twigs and branches and Anthony came to an immediate halt. Blocking the track was a young male elephant, engaged in scratching his rump against the bark of a tree. He made brief eye contact with the intruders and then continued with his satisfying task. They waited as he placed his trunk delicately in the sandy soil and siphoned up a mound of dust which he blew all over his back. Sarah's camera shutter clicked and clicked again. She bent down to pull another roll of film from her camera bag and dropped the entire holder on to the floor of the vehicle, scattering lenses and film. The elephant paused and looked directly at the small group, as if seeing them for the first time. His vast ears fanned out on either side of his head and he began to paw the ground with one leg, moving forward purposefully, creating puffs of dust with each measured step.

'Better give him some space,' Anthony said. 'He's decided we're in his way.' He turned on the engine and began to reverse down the road. The elephant followed, walking a little faster now, his trunk waving from side to side, ears flapping like giant paddle fans.

'He means to see us off properly.' Anthony remained calm and steady at the wheel. 'I'll have to keep backing away until I can find a place to turn. He's speeding up. Get down into the car. I may have to take a bumpy detour, and we're coming to a corner.'

Camilla dropped like a stone into the seat beside him, her heart pounding as the bulk of the animal filled the windscreen and the first angry sound of trumpeting rent the soft evening air, chilling her blood. Anthony drove faster, bouncing backwards, skidding in the sandy soil as the elephant gained on them. They could see every fold and crease of skin and the glinting of the small eyes as he swung his trunk from side to side, and then raised it high and screamed his anger at his unwanted audience. The huge body was so close that it was impossible to see even a patch of sky beyond the windscreen. They came to the corner and heard the tyres spin as they tried to grip the loose stones and pebbles on the surface. The car tipped to one side and Anthony bent forward over the wheel, gripping hard as if willing the vehicle to remain upright. Camilla closed her eyes, knowing that she was going to die with him, that they were all going to die together, trampled into a twisted mix of bodies and metal, and lives that could have been. When she looked again they had rounded the bend in the track and the car was facing in the opposite direction. There was no sign of the elephant. Everyone was laughing, with relief and with the awful thrill of the charge. Piet shook Sarah in disbelief.

'I can't believe you stayed up there and kept taking pictures. Sarah Mackay, you're a madwoman! Completely insane. But you have guts, I'll say that.'

'He wanted to see us off, out of his patch. The moment we turned the corner and were out of sight he lost interest in us.' Anthony was laughing too. '*Kali* buggers, these young males trying to prove their strength. Let's go and look for something more welcoming.'

The remainder of their drive was one of awed discovery. A pair of oryx stood in the grasslands to pose for them, displaying their painted faces and tall, straight horns. On one section of the road they stopped for a pair of reticulated giraffes, admiring the precise geometry and elegance of their markings, and their long, loping strides. Flocks of guinea fowl criss-crossed in front of them, their black and white feathers fluttering over a layer of blue underlay. A herd of buffalo lifted heavy heads and snorted with ill-tempered disdain as they passed, and several Grevy zebra trotted briskly off the track before turning to display the perfection of their striped flanks, and their large, rounded ears. The heat of the day slowly dissipated as the sun vanished behind the rugged hills, leaving in its place a sky flooded with scarlet light. The first star appeared above the silhouette of the palms, and a new moon hung suspended over the river.

In camp there were welcoming lights in the tents, and lanterns hung in the trees. Chairs had been placed around a fire, carefully positioned so that the leaping, flickering flames lit the inky night, while the smoke drifted away from the tents and towards the river. They took their seats and accepted drinks from Samson, stretching out their legs and leaning back to look up at the stars as the last light faded into an all-extinguishing darkness. The hot water in their shower tents smelled of woodsmoke, and Camilla closed her eyes as the dust of the day vanished in the welcome pressure of hot water. She smoothed back her wet hair and wrapped herself in a towel, feeling reborn and filled with a contentment she had never known before.

'How can you bear to be in Nairobi for more than a minute?' Sarah asked Anthony over dinner.

'The longer you spend out here, the harder it is to return to town, and the—' Anthony hesitated, at a loss for the right words.

'The irrelevant posturing of people in crowded cities and suburbs,' Camilla finished. 'At the risk of sounding pompous, I don't think I'm ever going back.'

'It's a mouthful, but it sounds about right for your natural habitat,' Anthony was laughing. 'Still, I've seen you in London, Camilla. In your watering holes and places for posh spaghetti and thimbles of espresso, and your favourite night spots. You have your hairdresser, and a place for some sort of fancy mudbaths, just like that jumbo we saw earlier. You'd be just as unhappy finding your way around here as he would looking for a number ten bus.'

'I never travel on buses. And I don't know about him, but you're definitely underestimating me,' retorted Camilla quickly. 'You may have to eat those words before too long.'

After dinner they returned to the fire and sat talking, replete and contented in one another's company. Early-morning tea was ordered for six, and Piet was the first to rise and bid everyone goodnight. Hannah and Sarah followed, and then Camilla stood up and bent to retrieve the light wrap she had draped over the back of her chair.

'I'll see you to your tent,' Anthony said. He took her arm and then stopped to look at her in the starlight. 'Camilla. Camilla, I've spent all of last night and today watching you, looking at your beautiful face, remembering every part of you and wanting you desperately. I can't wait any longer.'

She turned without a word and walked away, aware of his footsteps close behind her. When they entered her tent he put out the lantern and took her into his arms, kissing her mouth and her eyelids and whispering in her ears. He stood behind her and lifted her long hair from the back of her neck to breathe his desire into her. He undid her bush shirt to reveal her breasts, and slid his hands across her stomach and down her flanks so that she could barely stand and she made a small, strangled noise of protest and impatience. Then he laid her on the canvas bed, and she buried her face in his shoulder so that no one would hear the sounds she could not suppress. In the morning she opened her eyes to find him gone, and she wondered how he could have left her, slipped away from her in the night with the stealth of a leopard, without her sensing his departure.

'*Hodi. Chai. Na maji moto.*' She heard the sound of water splashing into the canvas basin outside, and the setting down of the tea tray on the small verandah table. 'I hope you have slept well, madam.'

'Thank you, Musioka,' she said. 'I slept better than ever before in my life, and I know it's going to be a wonderful day.'

They left the camp while the air was soft with dew, and the first signs of sunrise opened out the land in an infinite canvas of blonde grass and verdant bush and pale sky.

'Listen to the coucals,' Anthony said, stopping the car and turning off the engine. 'They sing in pairs like that. Look over there – on the top of that bush. They're rather plain old things, but you can see the joy of their love songs shaking their whole bodies.'

He glanced at Camilla and in that moment Hannah caught the fusion of excitement between them. She looked away and in the turn of her head caught her brother's expression. He sat silent and tense, gripping the edge of his canvas seat with whitened fingers. His jaw was tight and a muscle jumped in his cheek. She avoided catching his eye, not wanting him to realise that she had observed the last twinges of loss and jealousy in him.

'Come on, Anthony, man,' he said. 'Where are the cats? I've never been up here when I didn't see cats. You can find all these feathered things at home on my *shamba*.'

They moved forward again and within a few moments they had discovered a male kudu, his body covered in so much dust that it almost obscured the handsome striped coat. It was Sarah who glimpsed the movement of bushes being pushed aside by the magnificent horns, spiralling upwards from the nobility of his head. He regarded them for a moment with grave distrust before he turned and vanished, simply disappeared, into the surrounding thicket. As the sun climbed into the sky and the land began to absorb its insistent heat they turned back towards the camp for breakfast, taking a different route that led them through a dry watercourse.

'Lions,' Anthony said, pulling up without warning. 'A whole family. Look at the two lionesses, quite young. See how their fur is still spotted, with those pale rosettes. They're in great shape, beautiful specimens. And there's an older one, in the shade over there, with cubs. Four of them.'

The females lay on their sides, the black backs of their ears twitching. The cubs scrambled around them, stalking and rolling over one another, before turning their attention to a rotten tree stump, taking it in turns to scale the old trunk and to pounce on their siblings below. Camilla was leaning out of the window, laughing at their antics when they stopped their play and looked up, twitching in anticipation. She drew in her breath. A male lion was padding towards them, regal and deliberate. He halted and stared directly at her, and she was mesmerised by his power and his unmistakable sway over the lesser orders of creation. Sarah held her camera against the window frame, trying to steady her hands. Hannah froze on the roof.

'Get down into the vehicle,' Anthony whispered, 'and wind the windows halfway up. He's very close and we're between him and his family.'

They sat in the car, awed by the power and ripple of the lion's shoulders, by the huge paws moving with perfect harmony and purpose, bringing him closer and closer. Beneath Camilla's window he paused and twitched his tail, so that it made a knocking sound on the door. Her heart was thumping as he flattened himself low on the ground, ready to leap, possibly in through the roof hatch. Then she heard the sound of laughter and saw that Piet was pointing. The cubs had rushed forward and taken his tail, pulling and tugging at him. He rose again and cuffed them gently as he led them to a patch of shade where he flopped down like an oversized cat, blinking his golden eyes, and throwing back his head to yawn and display the true ferocity of his nature.

'Home,' Anthony said at last. 'I don't think we can beat that for today.'

In camp the scent and sizzle of frying bacon floated on the air. The breakfast table had been set up under the trees, and hopeful birds waited in the surrounding branches for any leavings.

'I've never been so hungry in my life,' Camilla said. 'I'm going to resemble an elephant by the end of the week.'

'They'll have to let out the seams of those crazy outfits you wear, or mould them around you. Or perhaps they'll make the magazine covers bigger to allow for your enlarged image,' said Anthony.

'I'm not sure I want to appear in any more magazines, or put on any more crazy clothes,' Camilla said.

Her voice was light, suggesting a throwaway line, but Sarah felt the shift in her mood and saw the immediate wariness in Anthony's eyes. Perhaps this was just a holiday romance from his viewpoint, then. And Piet. How would Piet react when their days together had run out? There was an awkward pause in the conversation.

'More coffee?' Anthony looked around the table. 'Right. There's hot water for showers and there are chairs under the trees above the river. Don't go down on to the flats. A client of mine was almost eaten when she foolishly strolled down there to rinse her coffee mug.'

'She *would* have been eaten, if you hadn't gone down there at risk to yourself and created a distraction,' Piet said. 'The girl was trapped. This croc had gone for her arm. In another minute he would have pulled her away. Anthony rushed down there and belted the beast over the head with a huge piece of firewood. He got into the water himself, and created a terrific ruckus, until it let her go. He saved that girl's life.'

'I don't want stories like that spread around, or I won't find any more young ladies brave enough to go on safari with me.' Anthony was plainly embarrassed. 'You're safe from this distance. But when it gets a little hotter you'll see some monster crocs for sure. There's a Bloody Mary around noon – and a reward for anyone who can spot more than twenty different species of birds in camp.' He rose from the table and strolled away in the direction of the crew tents and the camp kitchen.

Nothing more was said about the future, immediate or distant. On their sorties from the camp they came upon herds of lumbering elephant and buffalo, and diminutive gazelles whose tails were in constant swishing motion. Camilla remarked that they must surely be ready to fall off as they neared the end of their lives. Around the campfire in the evening they listened to Anthony's tales of the bush. At night they could hear the distant roaring of lions and the snorting and splashing of the hippos wallowing in the river. Hannah watched as Camilla grew more radiant with each day.

She saw that Piet was sometimes withdrawn, but on their drives he was always enthusiastic about the wildlife and birds that formed the basis of his future business. On the third morning he spotted a flash of gold in the distance, and Anthony turned the car towards the tiny speck of movement to discover a cheetah with a young cub, preparing to stalk a gazelle. But youth and inexperience saved the gazelle, and it bounded away in a series of gravity-defying leaps, leaving them sighing with a mixture of relief and disappointment.

In the heat of the day they sat by the river with binoculars, or read their books, or simply retired to the tents to sleep. Evening game drives usually ended on a bend of the river where they opened cold beers or a bottle of wine as they watched a line of elephants appear through the trees, and admired the fiery globe of the sun as it vanished behind the outline of the hills. At night, Anthony would lead Camilla from the embers of the camp-fire to their own private world. She loved to observe him as he organised their days and talked to his camp crew, sitting on an upturned storage box beside the cooking fire, as much at home and at ease with his men as he was with his friends, aware of their family histories, their strengths and weaknesses, the last time they had got drunk or rejoiced at the birth of a child.

Towards the end of their stay, in the swelter of the afternoon, Sarah placed a camp chair on the cliff above the river. She had only been there a short time when she heard the sound of bells, a metallic music that heralded the arrival of a herd of cattle, red-brown and white with wide, curving horns and large humps. They appeared through a haze of dust, stumbling and pushing one another down the bank to the edge of the muddy water, bringing with them a fall of pebbles and plants that had struggled to take root and hold the loose soil of the steep incline. Behind them the herdsman whistled and called and made clacking signals with a pair of sticks, guiding his livestock down towards the water. He came to a standstill and Sarah lifted her camera. In a flash he raised his spear and began to shout, spewing angry words she could not understand, and picking up a small rock that he clearly planned to aim in her direction. She stood up in time to see Anthony appear a few yards downstream, calling out and raising a hand in salute. There was a dialogue in which the Samburu spoke for several minutes, stabbing his spear into the ground for emphasis, his words punctuated occasionally by a series of monosyllables and soothing grunts from Anthony.

'You have to ask permission to take their photograph these days,' he said at last, strolling towards her.

'Sorry. I should have realised that. What shall I do now?'

'Nothing. I suspect he was on his way here anyway, to ask if we wanted to visit his *manyatta*. He sometimes arranges for the young warriors to dance for my guests, and afterwards the women try and sell their beaded paraphernalia and smelly gourds and blunt old spears. They charge us a few bob for the dancing, and they make some more out of the handicrafts, and everyone ends up happy.'

'Does it cost much? Would I be able to photograph them?'

'Ach, Sarah. It's just a put-on show for tourists.' Hannah had come up behind them. 'And I don't think they should be allowed to graze all those *ngombes* inside the reserve. They're either eating all the vegetation or trampling it. Just look at the bank there – it's crumbling into the river. A typical example of erosion.'

'You can't keep this reserve alive and forbid the local tribes their traditional watering holes.' Piet had arrived to discover the cause of the commotion. 'And the package tour's were now creating more dust and damage than any herd of Samburu cattle, by driving off the roads.'

'He's right,' Anthony said. 'You're going to have to think about this at Langani, if you want our game reserve to run smoothly.'

'That's one reason we need rangers,' Piet said. 'But I don't know about these dances for tourists. I agree with Hannah that they're fake, and it makes me a little uncomfortable.'

'Is the dancing the same as when they do it for themselves?' Sarah asked.

'It won't go on for three days, if that's what you mean. And they're not likely to fall down frothing at the mouth, or in an erotic trance,' Anthony said. 'An hour is all you get, but it's dancing the way they always do it. And you can take all the pictures you like.'

'Can you arrange it then? Please?'

'I'll lay it on for tomorrow afternoon,' Anthony said. 'I'm going to drive over to Samburu Lodge, by the way. I can use their radio telephone to check in with my office. Anyone want to come along and hobnob with the tourists?'

'I'll stay here,' Sarah said. 'Your camp staff said I could take some pictures of them.'

She walked away, but from the corner of her eye she saw Piet standing very still, looking after Anthony's car as it swept Camilla away from the camp. She sat down on her camp chair and swallowed the lump in her throat that was threatening to transform itself into tears.

'Ach, don't worry, Sarah,' Hannah said. 'He's adjusting and it's taking a little time. It's mostly his ego now. That's all. Look down there, in the river.'

They watched with reluctant fascination as an enormous crocodile emerged from the water on to a sand spit to lie motionless in the sun. His mouth was half open, revealing his menacing power and cruelty. Inside the cavern of his jaws a small bird hopped and pecked fearlessly at the serrated teeth.

'He must be twelve feet long,' Hannah shuddered. 'He looks like his scales are going to split open, he's so bloated. I can never believe how they have their teeth cleaned for them, and those little birds get their dinner at the same time. Isn't it a chilling sight, though?'

When the car returned some time later Sarah was engrossed in her book. She glanced up to see Camilla running towards her, shouting out something that she could not hear and she was confused and surprised as everyone gathered round her, embracing her, clapping her on the back, taking her hands and swinging her around in a circle as she finally realised what Camilla was saying.

'You've got your degree, Sarah! There was a message in Anthony's office when he got through to Nairobi. Tim phoned yesterday to say you'd got a first! And you've been offered a place to do your master's. Your father's fine too.'

'Congratulations, old thing,' Anthony's face expressed frank admiration. He clapped his hands loudly and called out an order. 'Bring out the drinks, Samson. We're celebrating the future of science here. How long will it take you to get a master's degree, Sarah?'

Sarah could only stare at them all in silence, dazed by the news, trying to focus on the full implication of what they were saying. Then, as Piet came forward to put his arms around her, she knew at once what she would do.

'I'm not going back to Dublin,' she said. 'I'm going to look for a job here. Maybe with the museum in Nairobi, or with some international fund that's doing research. I'll take anything on offer. Because I'm never going

227

back to that wet, dreary place. No matter what.' She picked up a glass from the tray that Samson held out. 'Here's to all of us and to our being together in Kenya, where we're meant to be. Cheers, everyone, and thanks for the news!'

'Your parents may not be thrilled by your plan,' Camilla remarked later.

'It might be wise to go back and study some more, in a year or two,' Sarah conceded. 'When I have some field experience and some real-life knowledge that isn't gleaned out of looking at something in a metal dish. There's got to be a slot for an eager research assistant who'll work for slave wages.'

'Actually, there might be someone right here,' Anthony said. 'There's a couple called Briggs based at Buffalo Springs, studying elephant. They're funded by some American university. I've met them many times and they're pretty good people. Would you like to meet them, Miss Graduate Mackay?'

'I'd love to. Even if they can't offer me anything, they'll know about other, similar projects.'

'Why don't you and I drive over there in the morning?' Anthony suggested. 'Piet can take Hannah and Camilla on a game drive, and we'll see if we can track down Dan Briggs.'

Buffalo Springs was a stretch of sandy plains and scrub country, bordering the southern bank of the Uaso Nyiro River. The Briggses' camp was located close to a series of pools and swamps fed by under-ground streams that originated on the icy slopes of Mount Kenya. The compound was surrounded by a high thorn fence like a traditional Samburu *manyatta,* and shaded by acacia trees and doum palms. A chain-link gate enclosed the entrance. Inside, there were several mud and wattle buildings with thatched roofs, neatly kept and surrounded by rows of whitewashed stones and a few straggling plants. It was Allie Briggs who came out to greet them. She was a diminutive Scotswoman in her early forties, her russet hair peppered with grey and cropped short, her face freckled and wind burned.

'Anthony. Good to see you. Are you camped near here?'

'Yes. But I'm on holiday. This is my friend Sarah Mackay.'

They shook hands and accepted Allie's offer of a cold beer. 'Dan's in Nairobi with the desk-bound powers that be. We're vying for more funds, as usual. I was clever enough to find an excuse not to go. You know how I hate the city.'

'Sarah has just got a zoology degree, from Dublin. She grew up here in Kenya, and she's wondering if there's any research work going.'

'We'd like to take on someone ourselves,' Allie said, 'but I don't know if our funds will stretch that far. It rather depends on how much success Dan has this week. Do you have a particular field you want to work in, Sarah? We're studying elephants here.'

Two hours later, Sarah felt that she had made a good impression. Allie had asked her a number of searching questions, and had seemed satisfied with her replies. But it was the photographs that had caught her attention. Anthony had persuaded Sarah to bring her Dublin portraits, and some of the pictures that she had taken during the two weeks at the coast.

'You have a great eye for detail,' Allie remarked. 'And a visual understanding of things that are African. That can be extremely useful for a researcher. I don't know if we have anything just now, but I'll certainly ask around. And Dan may have a few ideas when he gets back. Where can you be contacted?'

'We'll be in camp for a few more days,' Anthony said. 'And after that Sarah will be at Langani Farm.'

'Oh, yes. That's where you're involved in setting up this private conservation thing. I hope more land owners will follow suit. Might see you again, Sarah.' Allie was brisk and noncommittal, but there was warmth in her parting handshake. 'It's always good to have you drop in, Anthony.'

'She likes you,' he said as they drove away. 'She can be a real battleaxe, but she's a terrific person. Their work on the elephants has gained a great deal of respect in the last couple of years.'

Sarah nodded, afraid to hope that she might be considered as an assistant on the Briggs project. She could imagine nothing more inspiring than to study the elephants and to be directly involved in their long-term protection. Back in camp, Camilla and Hannah plied her with questions, but she was reluctant to admit to the germ of hope that had lodged itself in her heart. Their game drives took on a new significance for Sarah as she concentrated on the elephants they encountered. She watched their movements, questioning Anthony endlessly about their habits and social structures, taking photographs and writing notes. And each night she said a fervent prayer that tomorrow would bring a message or a radio call from Dan or Allie Briggs.

On the morning of Hannah's twenty-first they started out a little later than usual, taking a picnic breakfast with them. As the sun climbed into the wide sky and the earth began to crack in the rising heat, they came across a solitary male lion resting under a bush. He looked at the insignificant visitors to his territory, his sovereign eyes far-seeing and disdainful. Sarah leaned out of the window with her most powerful lens, so that his magnificent head filled the viewfinder.

'What a way to begin a year of your life,' she said. 'It's an omen, you know. A good omen for all of us.'

'It's already the best omen that we're starting this year together,' Hannah said. 'The way we mean to go on. The way we always meant to go on, no matter what.'

They drove slowly, accompanied occasionally by glossy zebra that looked as though they might burst through one of their black-and-white seams. Sometimes an escort of spurfowl raced ahead of them in the dust, and the flashing wings and music of doves and hornbills and weavers floated in the air. In a glade that provided an umbrella of branches Anthony spread out their picnic. A troupe of vervet monkeys watched from above them, eyeing the feast and chattering in anticipation. In the river a fish eagle sat on a dead tree stump, observing the faster flowing pools where his own breakfast might be lying, using his long, haunting cry to summon his mate. The day passed in unhurried conversation and affectionate reminiscences. When they regrouped around the campfire after their showers, there was no sign of Samson with his smiling recitation of cocktail offerings. But Anthony was waiting for them.

'We're going out for supper,' he announced, grinning at their surprise. 'Come on – into the car.'

They set out into the night, surprising a pair of jackals in search of their dinner, and swerving to avoid a nightjar dazzled by the headlights. Within minutes they came to the base of a small hill that overlooked the river. They climbed down from the Land Rover and Anthony led the way up, flashing his powerful torch and making deliberately loud, clattering noises as they climbed up towards the star-spattered sky. At the top of the kopje Samson and the staff awaited them. A table had been set out on the rocky platform and lanterns hung in the trees. They stood side by side on the edge of the world as man had first known it, filled with a sense of wonder and gratitude for all that they had been given. After dinner they lay back against the still-warm boulders, or on the rugs and cushions the camp staff had set down for them. Camilla leaned against Anthony and watched the moon rise through the tops of dark trees that trembled in the night air. He put his arms around her and rested his chin on her head, and she felt suspended and surrounded by the beauty of the moment.

'What are you doing here with me?' he whispered into her ear. 'What can you possibly want with a simple bushman?' But Camilla did not answer, unwilling to disturb the harmony.

Sarah placed herself close to Piet, hoping that their evening would not be tainted by his longing for a lost dream. When she stole a glance at him he was smiling into the darkness, perhaps at the sight of his sister silhouetted in the moonlight with all of her life and hopes and her young strength before her. At last Sarah sat up, marvelling at the speed with which the night had absorbed the searing heat of the afternoon. She could hear the cracking of branches as a herd of elephant made its way through the bush below them, and the moon had turned the brown river into a band of silver.

'It's getting a little chilly,' Anthony said, disengaging his hand from Camilla's curled fingers. 'Time to go home, I think.' As he held out his hand to help her up, they all heard the dry, grating sound and froze.

'Leopard,' Piet whispered. 'Very close.'

They sat in breathless silence until he came padding soundlessly up through the trees, his spotted coat gleaming in the moonlight, his movements filled with voluptuous grace and purpose. For a moment he stopped and gazed at them, eyes green and calculating, whiskers quivering in the ghost-white light. He was a creature of utter perfection, proudly aware of his extraordinary power and beauty. He stood before them, only yards away, so that they could hear his breathing and smell the musky scent of his body. The minutes stretched away into an uncounted silence. Sarah felt a jolt of alarm and distress as Anthony stretched a hand out towards his rifle. The leopard had seen the movement too, and turned his head. No one stirred. Then he flicked his long tail, took one final look at his audience, and walked on past them to disappear into the trees on the edge of the kopje.

'Jesus Christ! What an experience. What a magnificent animal – a big male, young and without a blemish on him. I've rarely seen such a fine leopard, and he was in no hurry to conceal himself. What luck – what incredible good fortune!' Anthony was jubilant. 'Best get out of here, though. He won't be happy if we hang around indefinitely. Piet, you go first, girls in the middle, and I'll bring up the rear.' He lifted his gun.

'You wouldn't shoot him?' Sarah had to ask the question.

'If it was you or him, which would you want me to choose?' he said, laughing.

In the tent Sarah undressed and climbed into bed. The image of the leopard was still intact in her mind as she fell asleep. In her dreams she felt his breath on her face and the touch of his soft fur on her skin before she noticed that tears were slipping from his eyes, and turning into a rushing waterfall behind which he finally vanished without a trace.

They searched for the leopard in the days that followed, but they never saw him again. On the last morning, light flooded the river as the sun burst into view, hot and yellow on the horizon. Camilla stared at the grazing plains game and envied them the calm order of their lives. Tomorrow Anthony would drive them to Langani and then he would be gone, back to Nairobi and the preparations for his next clients. An American couple with their recently divorced daughter who needed a consolation present, a starting point in her new, solitary life. Camilla hated the whole family, envied and feared the people who would take him away from her. The daughter was probably on the lookout for an affair, to salvage her damaged ego. Anthony had said nothing about the future, except for a vague reference to a marketing trip that would take him to the United States in November. Last night she had hoped he would ask her to go with him. She was sure she could charm any number of possible clients in New York and San Francisco, and Beverly Hills. But he had said nothing to reassure her, or to indicate that he envisioned a future they could share.

During the day she tried to retain her sense of hope, to ensure that he would always remember these last moments, and all their moments, when he was alone in his tent. She made love to him with a savage passion which surprised and then aroused him to a pitch he had never experienced before. Then she lay beside him in the burning afternoon, stroking his long body, massaging his shoulders and his head with probing, insistent fingers, licking and kissing away the small trickles of sweat that appeared on his temples as he looked at her, dazed and exhausted but insatiably hungry for her. She waited for him to draw her close, to tell her that he loved her. But he stared at her in silence for a while and then he turned away and slept.

As evening cooled the land and painted the sky with pastel shades, they gathered in the Samburu *manyatta* to watch the dancing. Chanting warriors rose high into the air with a leaping, gravity-defying motion, their bodies adorned with necklaces and bracelets that jumped and rattled as the sounds and movements became more hypnotic and trancelike and the voices deepened. Feet and spears hit the dust, heads and necks moved back and forth, cobra like, as their ochred hair whipped at polished, sculpted shoulders. Beside them the women clapped and swayed and sang in high, nasal voices. Sarah turned her lens again and again, backing away from them, closing in on faces and unseeing eyes absorbed in the rituals of their forebears, unaware and uncaring when it came to the identity of their audience. Afterwards the women beckoned them over to the area of the *manyatta* where they had set out beaded jewellery and trinkets for them to buy.

'There's some lovely work here,' Camilla said, peeling off another banknote, and handing it over.

'What on earth are you going to do with all that stuff?' Anthony asked. 'We'll need another trailer to carry it away. You're not going to wear it, surely?'

'These collars and bracelets could sell in London, just as successfully as all the Indian stuff that everyone is so crazy about. But it stinks of firewood and cow dung, and I don't know what else. Someone should teach them how to cure the hides properly, and put some decent clasps on the jewellery. They could support this whole *manyatta* on the proceeds, if these pieces were better finished.'

'Well, there's a mission for you.' Hannah linked Camilla's arm. 'You could do it from Nairobi, if you really don't want to go back to the bright lights and modelling and so. Can't you imagine her, Anthony, visiting the *manyattas*, teaching Masai and Samburu women to produce high-quality work for some fancy boutique in London? It would be a great business.'

'There's a *moran* here who wants some of your hair, Camilla.' Anthony showed no sign of having heard the question. He pointed at a young Samburu who was looking Camilla over with undisguised admiration. 'He'd like to offer a good price for you as a bride.'

'What about me,' Sarah asked. 'Don't I fit the bill?'

'You're not blonde,' said Anthony.

'It's certainly the best offer I've had all day. All week in fact,' Camilla said. She laughed, a shade too heartily, and then cursed herself for her crude attempt to send him such an obvious message.

'We're going back by way of Samburu Lodge,' Anthony said. 'Piet wants to contact Langani and see if he should stop for anything in Nanyuki, on the way back tomorrow. We can sit on the verandah and watch the tourists at play.'

At the hotel they were greeted by a cacophony of clattering plates, and the intrusive buzz of humans eating and drinking. Land Rovers arrived in convoys, drawing up at the entrance in each other's dust, disgorging small parties of chattering, sweating people in shiny safari suits.

'I couldn't do this,' Hannah said, 'but I'm glad I'm here to see it. Camilla and Anthony, this has been the greatest birthday gift anyone could dream about. And looking at this place, I know that the quiet and the calm of our little game lodge at Langani is going to be the best.'

As she spoke she could see Piet at the reception desk, talking into the phone, beginning to frown. When he rejoined them she registered the anxiety in his expression.

'Lars wasn't there, but I spoke to Simon. There was a problem – an incident actually – two nights ago. I thought perhaps I should drive down right away, but there's no point.'

'What kind of incident?' Hannah looked up, her fingers pressed against her cheek.

'I'll tell you the details in camp,' Piet said. 'Let's leave these noisy people to entertain the animals. Simon sounded sensible. What a find he's been, that boy. He said Lars is dealing with the problem, and there's nothing else to be done right now. The police have been round to investigate, but we all know that won't be much help these days.'

'The police? Don't tell me someone's stolen the fencing wire again?' Hannah said. 'What is it, Piet?'

'Let's get back to camp, heh?' Piet said to Anthony. 'We'll talk about it there, over a quiet drink.'

He refused to comment further until they had settled themselves around the fire. Then he pulled his chair up close to Hannah and swallowed some whisky before speaking.

'We lost five of your milk cows last night, Han. Someone cut their throats and left them lying in the field. It sounds to me like a grudge. It wasn't rustlers after stock, or somebody who wanted to sell the meat. I don't like it at all.'

'Not my cows!' Hannah cried out. 'Five of my cows! Which ones? I don't believe it!'

'We've always had a problem with fencing wire being cut and stolen, and bloody Maasai herds coming into our grazing. Or our own cattle being taken on a raid.' Piet was frowning. 'But why would anyone kill five cows and not even take the meat? This is very strange. And ugly.'

'Do you think it's someone we fired that's making trouble?' Hannah asked, as she tried to come to terms with the news and its implications. 'What happened to that herder that Lars sacked a few months ago? Maybe this is his way of getting back at us.'

'He was just an old drunk, Han. I can't believe he would come in and kill your cows for revenge. Whoever it was slit their throats, and cut them open all down their bellies. Then they were left to bleed away in the dirt. Not a pound of meat taken. Old Matui would never have done anything like that.'

'You can't make assumptions,' she said impatiently. 'You seem to think that they all changed as soon as they became independent. But it will take years before there's any change. If ever.'

'Surely there are successful African farmers now?' Sarah said.

'Have you seen the Kinangop lately?' Hannah demanded angrily. 'Have you seen how it looks now, that place that was so rich and fertile? It's a desert. Grey and dusty, with tracks that you can barely drive over, and fences that are falling down. The farmhouses have been looted, and the cedar and oak floors and panels and doors chopped up for firewood. Just like the trees that were planted as windbreaks to protect the crops. All you can see now are a few shrivelled maize stalks. And an occasional line of onions and carrots and cabbages lying in bags on the edge of the road, because somebody's bloody wheelbarrow has broken down and he can't get them out of there to a market.'

'Come now, Han, it's not all bad. They're clever, the Kikuyu. And ambitious. They'll get there.' Piet put out a hand to calm her, but angrily she shook him off.

'They say we took their land,' she said. 'But the Kikuyu only came here a few hundred years ago themselves. They didn't belong here originally. They were chased out of the area north of the Tana River, by Galla nomads. No one mentions that, of course, or the fact that they killed off the Gumba people who were there before them. The Kikuyu started the Mau Mau in order to get rid of white farmers. They killed a few of us, and murdered plenty more of their own tribe who wouldn't take their oaths. But historically they didn't have any more right to the land than we did.'

'It's true that tribal wars were just as violent as anything that has happened since colonial times,' Anthony said. 'And the British created a truce between most of the tribes, and a legal system to replace their skirmishes. But we did appear out of nowhere to take the best land for ourselves, while the indigenous population were shunted into reserves.'

'That's it!' Sarah exclaimed. 'We're supposed to know better, to be fair and democratic.'

'We do know better,' Hannah stood up, knocking over her camp chair. 'Think of people like your father and what they've given. We've brought schools and better houses, and medicine. And steady work so people can eat every day, and their *totos* won't die of malaria or starve. But now we only read about how evil we've always been. And now they send officials out from England to tell us what to do, and give our land away, and insist that our country must be run by people who seem to be on a rampage of personal greed.'

'It's a difficult time, Hannah,' Anthony said, taking her hand and drawing her back to the fire. 'We have a big task in front of us as the country changes and the political picture—'

'Oh, for God's sake, we're talking about my cows, not about some bloody political picture,' Hannah interrupted. 'What's the good of talking about the future of the country, if we allow people to kill our livestock and to ignore the property laws? Who will benefit then? And Sarah, you sound like one of those left-wing Britishers who thinks everything should be given on a plate to the Kikuyu, or the Kamba or the Maasai or anyone who's black, so they can bring the whole country back into the stone age where we found it.'

'And you sound just as bigoted as your father was on that last night we had dinner at Langani!' The words were out before Sarah could stop them. They were followed by a thunderous silence and then the sound of Hannah, crying quietly, her face in her hands.

Sarah rose and put her drink down carefully on the arm of her chair. 'I'm sorry, Han. I'm so, so sorry. About your lovely cows and about the stupid things I've said. Not once but twice. I have to listen better, learn to hear all sides of a problem before I can say anything about it. And I promise you, I'll never be this dumb again.' She squatted on the ground in front of Hannah's chair and took her hands. 'I'm with you, Hannah, all the way and in everything you do. I'm with you and Piet. Am I forgiven?'

'Ach, you're just my stupid sister,' Hannah said, wiping her tears away. 'But if you're going to start looking for a job around here I'd better take a hold of you, and show you what real life is like. And you'd better teach me some of your liberal ideas, before we all get thrown out of the country for not moving with the times. Right, Piet?'

'Right. And the third sister here looks like a waif and stray this evening.' He looked at Camilla with a smile. 'So I suggest Anthony takes out the best wine we have left, and we'll sit by the river and drink it, while we put the world to rights. And tomorrow we'll go home. Home to Langani.'

Chapter 13

Kenya, September 1965

The atmosphere at Langani was sombre, as Lars described the vicious nature of the massacre.

'It reminded me of the emergency, when things like this happened on white farms. It was as if Hannah's cattle were part of a ritual. If they'd been stolen, or slaughtered for meat, I would understand it. But they were disembowelled and left to die. It seems senseless to me.'

'And the police?' Piet said.

'As you would expect.' Lars was resigned. 'We had a local fellow up here with big boots and a notebook. His men were all over the fields, trampling any evidence that could have been at all useful. No experience or knowledge. Pitiful. But you could see that even they were shocked. Then Jeremy Hardy turned up. Lucky he's still around. He's a good policeman.'

'Have you questioned all the labour?' Hannah's face was blotchy from weeping.

'They were as shaken as I was,' Lars said. 'It must have happened around three or four in the morning. Juma said he had passed through that area about two-thirty, and there was nothing amiss. He found the cows at daybreak, and he was in a real state, crying and shouting and wringing his hands. I heard him wailing long before he got to the house. I don't think that could have been put on.'

'I'm going to spend this afternoon and tomorrow asking more questions,' Piet said. 'You've already increased the security at night, Lars? Good. Now all we can do is to keep digging for information. One of the *watu* must have seen something. I'm sure our old-timers are loyal, and they would have come forward already if they had anything to tell. But we've taken on a few new people lately, to finish the construction at the lodge. We should check them out. What about Kipchoge or Simon? Did either of them notice anything significant?'

'Simon said there were a couple of fellows hanging around the gate close to the Nanyuki road, the day before the cattle were killed,' Lars answered. 'They were looking for work. Kipchoge saw them talking to Simon, but he doesn't remember anything particular about them. I was in Nanyuki that morning, and by the time I got back and Simon told me about them, they were gone. Poor old Kamau and Mwangi were really shook up, when they saw the cows. And Kipchoge was scared as hell, too. All the *watu* were. Of course Kamau immediately said Simon should be questioned first, because he's only been here a short time. But Simon was more upset than anyone else. Terrified. It's a bad *shauri* all round.'

'Kamau has never forgiven me since I chose Simon for the best job at the lodge,' Hannah said. 'The old man wouldn't have anything to do with this, I know. But what about David?'

'You're training him as a chef,' Piet said. 'And their grumbles don't mean that much. I've had similar sulking from Kipchoge who knows perfectly well he couldn't do Simon's job. He only spent four years at school, and he never learned any proper English, but his nose is out of joint anyway. I've told him he's the best tracker and *syce* anyone could want. I've explained that he's going to take charge of the game rangers when we start training them. But he still feels he's been passed over. He's convinced it's better to be working in an office.'

'While you were away there were arguments about who was in charge of the stores, and the ordering of kitchen supplies, and the feed for the horses,' Lars said. 'All manner of little power struggles.'

'I've showed Kamau the certificates Simon brought, explained that he can do bookkeeping and typing and so, but it doesn't make any impression,' Hannah said, her voice tired. 'They're all like children at the end of the day. We'll always have to go on sorting out their squabbles.'

'I'm not going to worry about any of them right now,' Piet said. 'It's always the same when we take on someone new. Pa often had the same problem. They'll find a way of getting along eventually. Maybe this thing will even pull them together. So what about security?' Piet asked.

'I've taken on two more herders for the day time,' Lars said. 'Two chaps who were laid off when old man Griffiths sold most of his cattle. He says they're reliable fellows. And I've switched a couple of our old-timers on to the night patrol. Plus I've been driving around myself. A couple of times each night, at random hours.' He tapped his fingers on the table and hesitated for a moment. 'Did I do the right thing, in not tracking you down in Samburu and interrupting your safari? It seemed to me that there wasn't anything you could have done here.'

'You were right,' Piet said firmly. 'Hannah's birthday was special, and we all had a great time. It would have been senseless to spoil any part of it.'

'I suppose it was a one-off thing,' Lars said. 'But I came across a fire, over near the lodge last week. Another half-hour and it would have been a problem, because it was a windy day and it had been set very close to the viewing platform. At the time I thought some idiot had started it to cook his meat and *posho*, but there was no one around. Now I wonder if it was something else. Another mischief like the cows, only I disturbed the plan.'

'We can't start looking over our shoulders constantly, getting paranoid about every little thing,' Piet said. 'We're always finding small fires on the farm, for one reason or another. And you can't go driving around the place day and night, Lars. You need regular sleep like the rest of us. We have to organise a better security plan. Especially if we want good support for the lodge. We certainly can't afford any incidents around there. The only problem is the cost.'

'There's a new organisation in Nairobi with funds to help people like you,' Lars leaned forward. 'They're apparently interested in encouraging private wildlife reserves. A friend of mine in the Norwegian Aid office told me about it.'

'But these outfits are so slow, unless you know someone who can put in a word for you.' Piet was not optimistic. 'You have to wait until they send a so-called expert to look your place over. They show up six months later, ask you five thousand questions, and then disappear to deliberate. It can take a long time to get through the formalities. I could be in a home for old fogeys before I see a penny. Still, if they did decide it's a suitable project they might provide money for rangers, and fencing too.'

Camilla knew at once what the organisation was. But the disastrous results of her earlier plea to her father came to mind, and she said nothing. George Broughton-Smith had returned to London while they were on safari, but she resolved to raise the issue with him as soon as she arrived back. This time, he might be able to help.

'Let's not talk about our problems any more.' Hannah rose to her feet. 'Our holiday's almost over, and we have to make the most of our last two days. Tonight I'll organise a *braai* in the garden, and tomorrow we'll ride early, when the light is so good for Sarah's camera.'

'I'll have to leave in the morning, I'm afraid,' Anthony said. 'My camp crew has gone on to the Mara, to set up for the next clients. But I need to be in the office, to catch up with some paperwork before they arrive.'

'You can still ride with us, before you set off for Nairobi.' Hannah was smiling broadly for the first time since she had arrived home. 'Sarah, you can share my room, heh? And we'll leave the guest suite for Lady Camilla to use as she pleases.'

'I could do with a siesta,' Anthony said, although even he looked sheepish. 'That was a long, bumpy drive this morning, and I was up before dawn, striking camp.'

Lars watched as Anthony held out his hand to Camilla and they left the room. An odd combination, he thought. The beautiful, fragile girl did not look as though she could survive the lonely regimen of life in Nairobi, with her man constantly away on safari. But she had lived there during her childhood, so she must know the score. Maybe she was one of those frail-looking women that had an inner core of steel. You never could tell. He glanced at Hannah who was arranging the dinner with Kamau.

'I'm sorry you came home to such terrible news,' he said, when the cook had gone. 'Are you going to unpack right away, or would you like to go for a walk with me? There's things I've had the gardener do while you were away. You could see if I got it right for you.'

She hesitated, afraid she would break down and cry like a child if he talked to her with such kindness. The killing of the cattle had really distressed her, and her sadness was tinged with a new sensation that she now realised was fear. She had never been afraid in her own home before. The idea crept through her like a poison, slowly infiltrating her mind, settling like bile in her stomach so that she had a sour taste in her mouth. She needed something good to look at.

'I'd like to see the garden, yes. And the place where you buried my cows, if you have time to take me there. I'm grateful you made a special place for them. And it was right not to give the meat to anyone, Lars.'

In the guest room Anthony beckoned Camilla to the bed. She had positioned herself on the window seat, recalling childhood memories of

Lottie's garden and the sense of security she had always felt there. Beyond the border of carefully tended hedges and the rose bushes, the wild grasslands shone pale and gold and vast, all the way to the slopes of the proud mountain. Such a fragile boundary between man and rampant nature had to be constantly maintained, otherwise the lawns and flowers would be devoured by the voracious wilderness until there was no trace left of their man-made order and beauty. She watched Lars and Hannah on the edge of the lawn, and hoped that in time something might come of his obvious affection for her. And Sarah was so full of optimism, glowing with her plans to remain in Africa, to be close to Piet. Camilla thought of the moonlit night when she had foolishly allowed Piet to kiss her. It felt like a very long time ago, and they had followed such diverse paths since then. Now it was only her own future that remained uncertain. There was a hint of rain in the sky, and the jagged mountain peaks had disappeared into a band of thick cloud. She moved away from the window to lie down beside Anthony.

'The time has gone too fast,' she said. 'As if someone had stolen hours and hours of it, while we were sleeping.'

He did not answer, but he began to caress her, breathing softly into her ear, running his fingers down her spine, finding the secret parts of her that only he knew. She hovered over him like a butterfly, taking him inside her, dipping down towards him and then leaning away, touching him lightly, kissing his body everywhere. She was already burning with separation and loss, willing him with every movement to tell her that he loved her, that he wanted her to stay, that she should wait for him in Nairobi, at Langani, in London. Anywhere. But although he cried out with the intensity of their loving, he said no words that would bind them together for the future. Afterwards she remained silent, not wanting to cry, determined not to raise the fearful questions that overshadowded her thoughts. He was soon asleep, gingery eyelashes curling away from his cheek, eyebrows shaped like delicate wings, his nose aquiline like a statue she had seen in Florence. She watched him as he slept, his face trouble-free on the pillow, his mind oblivious to her needs.

When she rose and left him, Camilla looked in the bathroom mirror. Her lips were swollen from his kisses and her hair hung in a tangle around her face. She turned on the shower and stood beneath it for a long time, washing his scent and his essence from her body, trying to distance herself from the sorrow to come. Then she dressed and sat in a chair, leafing through an old magazine with articles about wheat and sheep breeding, until the vanishing sun and the chill in the air signalled the oncoming night.

'I thought you'd be beside me when I woke up.' His voice startled her. 'I've grown accustomed to it.' He stretched out a long arm to bring her close.

'Will you miss me, then?' She had resisted his invitation and remained in the chair. But in defiance of every good intention she had asked the unwelcome question.

'Of course I'll miss you.' His eyes were already different. Cagey.

'How much?' She put out her hands, holding them further apart with each gesture. 'This much? Or this much?' Her voice was unsteady and she knew he could hear her fear.

'You're not going all sentimental on me, are you?' He was wide awake, propped up on one elbow, a hint of alarm lurking in his smile. 'It's been the loveliest of times and we mustn't spoil it by crying, now that we have to go back to real life. Isn't that so?'

'What's real life?' Now that she had started, it was impossible to bury the questions.

'Real life? For me it's being out in the bush. The place I love the best, the place I always want to be when I'm somewhere else. It's where I'm comfortable in my skin.'

'I can understand that. I've been there with you. Learned something precious from you every day. I want to learn more.'

'Real life for you is the glamour of what you have become in London, Camilla, with all your beauty and talent. Real life in your case is the buzz of the big city and the places you showed me, where I'm a country bumpkin and you're the reigning princess. Fun for a day or so, travelling in the light you generate. But not for me on a regular basis.'

'And these last weeks?' She hated the tone of his voice, conciliatory, almost pleading. 'Was I just an amusement, then?'

'Of course not! I'm not that kind of man, carrying on with every girl that comes on safari. I'm not a tart,' he protested. 'I thought we were happy with what we've shared. That we'd found a place in our different lives, when our paths crossed at the perfect moment. I thought you felt that too.'

'I did. I do.'

'But now we have to go back to our normal routines,' he said. 'I could never live like you do, in a city, going happily from cocktail parties to dinners to smoky nightclubs, and all that kind of thing. I can only cope with Nairobi for maybe a week. Two at the most. After that, I start counting the hours until I'm out in the *bundu* again.'

'Maybe I've had my fill of city lights. Perhaps they were merely a step on the way to somewhere else – an illustration of what life shouldn't be. A phase.' Camilla's expression was wan.

'Everyone who goes on safari feels like that,' he said. 'They never want it to end. It's an extraordinary, once-in-a-lifetime experience for most people. They see and do things they've never dreamed of, think they're living on the edge of danger and excitement. But someone else has set it up, thought it out, is there to keep them safe and make sure they're comfortable. Someone else has made the dream into a reality for a short time. I've never come across a tourist who could put up with the real grind of it all.'

'I know about drudgery. And I'm not a tourist, Anthony.'

'You don't know what it's like these days. The phones that don't work and the post office that loses your mail. The corruption and the incompetence, the problems of getting a permit stamped. Petty theft, parts of cars and trucks going missing, supplies that were promised but mysteriously aren't there.'

'Creating dreams is hard work,' she said. 'I have to do it too, in a different way. People look at the pages in magazines, at the beautiful clothes and the exotic settings, and they want to be like the pictures they see. But they never know about the clothes van that's parked in a cold, windy yard where you're putting on summer dresses in sub-zero temperatures. They never have a clue that you've caught your death of cold, that you're wearing stuff that's made to fit with safety pins and clothes pegs hidden at the back. And they never have to sit sweating under hot lights in some cramped dressing room, with everyone swearing and yelling for a hairdryer or a stick of pancake make-up.'

He was unable to make a connection between their worlds. 'I can't imagine anyone like you, or any of my clients from New York or Texas or London, loading tents into trucks, or changing tyres punctured with camel thorns. I don't see you combing Nairobi for one of the camp staff who's got drunk the night before and hasn't turned up in time for departure. You have no idea—'

'I have every idea,' she said. 'Don't forget I spent most of my childhood here. I'm not some coddled, New York heiress. I'd like to stay on and find a job here. I'm terrific at selling things, especially dreams, and I speak fluent French and Italian, which is useful now that more people are going on safari. My life isn't just about dressing up in silly clothes, and being welcomed like royalty in the newest smart restaurant in London. I hope you don't see me like that, Anthony.'

There was a long silence. He had not wanted it to come to this, had not expected it. They had found passion and shared pleasures, but Camilla was talking about something deeper and more permanent. He found himself unprepared, poised for flight. She was sophisticated in her tastes, worldly, used to moving in circles where conversations swirled around him in patterns and meanings he could not comprehend.

'Camilla, I never meant to hurt you or make you sad,' he said at last. 'You're the most beautiful girl I've ever met, and I've been telling you that for years.' He reached across the bed and took her hand. 'You always said I was just another bush baby, and you're right. I don't know what you're doing here with me, really, except that these weeks just fell into place by luck. The whole safari has been a blast. And I hope we'll have more fun together, if you'll—'

'If I'll just run along back to Chelsea, and be famous and glamorous and busy until you drop by next time.' Camilla had spent all of her life masking her emotions, watching in silence as her parents perfected the stinging shorthand of their communications system. She was not prepared for the throbbing, choking sensation in her throat as she battled with her self-control. She stood up and ruffled his hair, dragging from within herself every last scrap of bravado. 'I'll be in New York this time next week, for the best photos ever taken. And then there won't be anyone who's anyone left that doesn't know who I am.'

'And am I bidden to join the rich and famous for your twenty-first? If I'm passing through London on my marketing trip?'

'Oh, absolutely. You can canvass the guests. Sell them safaris.' Her laugh was a little bitter.

He knew that he had hurt her. 'Camilla, I do have very special feelings for you. I'm just not ready to share my life, or change it. But I would never want to upset you.'

'Don't be so twitchy, Anthony.' She stepped away from him. 'There won't be time to mourn your passing when I hit London the day after tomorrow. But I'm not keen on a birthday party, because I'm sure Mother would want some ghastly thing with a cast of thousands that I would hate. I was thinking of going to Ireland and celebrating with Sarah, but now it looks as though she'll be back here. I might try and escape to a solitary desert island, or something. These last weeks have been my real birthday celebration – a heavenly time that's not over yet. So let's get ourselves all tarted up for Hannah's barbecue.'

She hated the palpable relief on his face, and for the first time she understood the abyss that divides a man and a woman who cannot share their dreams. She winced with the pain of it, fought the hot, pitiful sensation of tears behind her eyelids.

'Come back to bed.' His voice was just the way she loved to hear it. 'You're so beautiful. I want to hold you some more.'

'You're greedy and we're late. Luckily I've showered already. Hurry up and get dressed. I'm going on ahead of you.'

Outside on the lawn, Hannah was assailed by a terrible sense of déjà vu. Lottie's damask cloth was spread out on a trestle table, decorated with a bowl of scarlet flowers from the flame tree, and set with her best plates. Starched napkins stood in old family glasses and Hannah could feel the ghosts of her parents, waiting silently in their accustomed places. Visions of their last night at Langani swarmed in her head, with Jan full of pessimism and dire warnings and Lottie mute and withdrawn. Hannah sat on a garden chair, steeling herself. But the feeling of loss had struck her with such force that she felt it like a physical assault, and she pressed her hands to her stomach in an attempt to soothe herself. She looked up to see Mwangi. He scanned her face for a moment and then began to lift the table settings.

'Tonight is for the young people,' he said. 'We should not have the old ways. I will put other dishes out, Memsahib Hannah, and you will choose different flowers. We will remember the *mzees* on another occasion.'

He gathered up Lottie's table settings and took them into the house, returning with everyday pottery and checked napkins. Hannah wanted to put her arms around him, to tell him how vital a part he played in everything she most valued, to say that she loved him for his kindness and his understanding and his loyalty. But she was afraid that the words would be out of place, might even embarrass him, so she squeezed his hand, hoping he understood. Then she picked up her secateurs and cut a basket of dahlias and roses and carnations in vibrant, defiant colours. As she put the newly arranged vases on the table, she felt intensely grateful for the childhood that her parents had provided. She had always believed that her father was wise and powerful, that under his protection no harm could come to her. He had proved to be less than the hero her childish mind had made of him, but he was still her father. And Lottie's unconditional love had enveloped them all, encouraged them to believe that dreams could be realised. Hannah left the garden and went inside, knowing at that moment that she must talk to her parents. She would speak to her father, tell him that the past was over and done with, that he and Lottie should come home to Langani where they belonged because she loved and needed them. When the telephone rang, interrupting her thoughts, she knew instinctively that it was her mother.

'Happy birthday, my darling Hannah. I couldn't get you while you were on safari. I've wanted so much to talk to you. It must have been wonderful, with Piet and your friends. I want to hear all the details, and I hope you'll write them to me.' Lottie's voice was full of longing.

'I will write,' Hannah said. 'I'll write to you about my amazing birthday. And thank you for the bracelet. It was waiting for me when I got back this morning. I've never had anything with real gemstones before. Everyone admired them. And the dress, too. I love you, Ma.' She took a deep breath. 'Is Pa there? I'd like to talk to him too.'

'Oh Hannah, my dear. He'll be so glad to know that. He's not here.' There was a pause. 'He's out on a patrol. A couple of farms have been attacked here, and people have been killed. Things are rather tense, with Ian Smith banning all the black political parties. There'll be more trouble, I'm afraid. And Kobus is difficult, as usual.'

'I know, Ma.'

'Lars rang and told us about the cattle. I'm so sorry.'

'It was a very strange thing. Frightening, too. Ma, would you think about coming home now? You and Pa?'

'I don't know, my dear,' Lottie said. 'It's a little complicated. I'll talk to your father. I'll try. I'll do my best. Happy birthday, my beautiful daughter. I'll ring you again in a day or two, with a plan.'

'I think they're going to come home,' Hannah said to Piet a little later. 'And I'm so glad.'

'Han——?' He moved towards her, full of hope and relief that the breach in the family would be mended at last.

'Ma's going to phone again, soon. Tell us when they can come. She sounds so different – like her old self. Happy and light. It's good, heh?'

'Yes, it's good. Meantime, I want you to promise me that you won't worry about anything. We've had our problems at Langani lately, but we've been able to get through them and I think——'

'No talk of problems and *shauris* tonight,' Hannah said. 'We'll drink to their return and all the good times we're going to have together.'

They assembled in the garden, dressed in sweaters against the chill of the night. Lars had lit the barbecue earlier, and now he poured drinks and then folded himself into a canvas chair beside Sarah.

'I want to hear about the safari,' he said.

He was more at ease than before, Sarah thought. Perhaps that had something to do with the glance that had passed between himself and Hannah – the hint of a private message in his eyes, the brief pressure of his hand on her arm as he handed her a glass. Sarah wondered if there were things going on at Langani that she had only just noticed. They had almost finished dinner when Mwangi came out on the lawn.

'There is a radio call,' he said. 'Memsahib Briggs.'

Sarah raced into the house, breathless and apprehensive. Allie's voice was faint, but she repeated the message twice, leaving no room for doubt.

'They've offered me a job!' Sarah stood on the verandah and shouted out her news, her arms raised in a semaphore of triumphant delight, her face glowing with excitement as her friends crowded around her. 'Oh God! I've got a job at Buffalo Springs – a dream of a job. I can't believe it!'

There were congratulations and embraces. Wine was poured and they settled themselves inside, around the sitting-room fire.

'We have to toast in the right way,' Lars said. 'Not just by touching glasses. We must look into each other's eyes and wish the best. Like this.' He leaned forward, gazing steadily at Hannah until she laughed and turned away. She held out her glass to Sarah and then to Anthony, her eyes shining in the firelight.

Piet put a record on the gramophone and they threw themselves into the music. The floorboards in the old house groaned in protest, and the staff peered through the door to watch with astonishment and laughter as Camilla taught Lars how to twist, sending his big, awkward limbs into contortions, egging him on until his knees gave out and he fell back on to the sofa begging for mercy.

'Ma always loved dancing,' Hannah said. 'She would make Pa shuffle around, even though he had no sense of rhythm and two left feet. She always looked so graceful, but I think I'm more like him.'

'Dance with me?' Lars had recovered from his exertions.

Hannah stared at him and then stood up, smoothing her skirt. The music was slower now, and he drew her closer to him. Sarah thought they looked good together, and she saw Piet watching them with an odd expression that she could not identify. Late into the night they all danced, and laughed and talked of the past, and the times to come when they would be together again. When they eventually went to bed, each one carried with them the renewed bond of their friendship.

'I'm not blind, you know,' Sarah said as she and Hannah finally collapsed into bed. 'Tell me what's going on with Lars.'

'There's nothing to tell. No, really!' Hannah had registered the sceptical look on Sarah's face.

'He's in love with you. It's obvious from the way he watches you. I saw it myself,' Sarah said. 'I may be tipsy, but I saw it plain as a pike staff.'

'I have thought about him, but it's awkward.'

'Awkward? He's big, but he's not what you'd call awkward!'

'Not him, you idiot. The situation. Lars gets up my nose at times.' Hannah was smiling. 'He's always so damn certain of everything and he often treats me like a child when I want him to recognise that I'm serious and professional. He's more like Piet's twin than his friend or manager.'

'I think you're scared! Maybe you should try swooning away into his arms.'

'This has nothing to do with being scared. I want to take on more of the running of the farm, and the responsibility for the lodge. And any other thing between Lars and me might be awkward, like I said.'

'The farm is doing well, though?'

'We're keeping our heads above water. There's a good system now. Lars deals with the breeding cattle and the grazing land. He takes care of the tractors and the harvester and the generators – all the mechanical things. And he helps me if I have a problem in the dairy. Piet looks after the *watu* and the farm as a whole. He maintains the fencing and boundaries, and the protection of our wildlife. The wheat is his area too, and this year is extra busy because we planted a big area that's been under grass for a while. And of course the building of the lodge is Piet's baby, and the horses. The arrangement works well.'

'So?'

'If Lars and I had a romance and it didn't work out, that would change the balance on the farm. He might leave, and we can't afford to lose such a good manager. I could cause a big problem for Piet, by fooling around with Lars. So personal stuff has to wait until we can get out of debt, and make a proper living between the farm and the lodge. Then I'll think about Lars.'

'I suspect Lars has gone past all that,' Sarah said. 'From what I saw this evening. And if he's not afraid, then you shouldn't be either.'

'And I suspect we should go to sleep.' Hannah turned out her lantern. 'Because I was stupid enough to arrange an early-morning ride. I'm already regretting it.'

'Oh God. There's something terrible going on in my head.' The dawn light was pale as Sarah groped for her teacup, her eyes still closed, body groaning in protest with every movement. 'Didn't we only just get into bed? We can't go riding – I'll die in the saddle. How could I have put away that brandy, Han? Why didn't you stop me, for God's sake? You know I can't drink.'

As they walked across the dew-laden grass to the stables she gulped in the cold air, hoping for an instant cure. There had been rain during the night and silver drops of water fell from the leaves into the veiled blue of the morning. By unspoken agreement they rode slowly and in silence as the sun appeared, crimson and slow at first, then rising rapidly through the sky as though propelled by the golden ferocity of its own heat. A herd of impala skittered away, tails fluttering, sneezes of alarm peppering the air. The sky seemed wide and lonely above the whisper of long grass and the deep, dark band of forest that marked the river bank.

'Stop.' Anthony's voice was low.

In front of them a young cheetah emerged from the bleached

grasslands, heading for shade and water. The sun lit her spotted coat and golden eyes and she held her tail in a perfect arc just above the ground. As Sarah raised her camera to capture her streamlined elegance, she stood obligingly still for a moment. Then she moved on, dismissing them and vanishing into the bush. They rode on, talking quietly, listening to the snorting of the horses and the startled, cracked voices of francolins on the grassy verge. In the distance, a dust devil spun across the plains and Piet rose in his stirrups to point out a herd of elands making their way towards the dam.

'There's nowhere more beautiful in this entire world.' Sarah spoke for them all. 'How can anyone who's seen this want to be anywhere else? Imagine having to live every day in a red-brick semi, under dark skies and constant rain. And the slog of dragging your shopping bag up the stairs, and finding a place for your dripping coat and the umbrella that's blown inside out.'

'It's not all bad,' said Anthony. 'There's variety in a big city. Theatres and museums, and ancient buildings with perfect proportions, and the sense of civilisation and refinement and culture.'

'Where's the bloody refinement when some drunken old bowsie shoves you aside, on a pouring wet night, and grabs the last place on the bus?' Sarah demanded, her indignation so fresh that everyone began to laugh.

'No place is perfect,' Camilla said. 'I have lived in Florence and London for three years, and I know where I'd rather be. There's an edge to life here, a sense that you can do something extraordinary, or different, at any rate. If you have the courage.'

'That's it exactly,' Lars agreed. 'You can create anything you want in this country, if you have the determination.'

'And the patience,' Hannah added. 'Above all you need patience, because nothing ever happens the way you think it should. New politicians, shirty officials who want power and bribes, things that don't work any more and can't be fixed because no one's ordered spares.'

'That applies everywhere,' Camilla said. 'Try getting a plumber in London, or dealing with someone in the income tax department.'

'You're ignoring the real issue.' Anthony broke into the conversation. 'It's easy to make light of it, but this country is teetering on the edge of chaos. We're on a huge learning curve here, and this is the uphill stretch. Hannah's right – you need endless patience and things will get much worse before they get better. You see a romantic Kenya that doesn't really exist, Camilla, because you're not here all the time.'

His voice was tense and Sarah realised that there was another agenda here. He's afraid, she thought. Afraid she'll stay on. He doesn't want that. She felt a pang of compassion for Camilla and she saw her understanding mirrored in Hannah's eyes.

'Anyone for real riding?' Sarah touched the horse with her crop and he broke into a canter. Then she was away across the plain, the dust-spiked wind in her face and the sound of wings whirring as the guinea fowl rose in alarm in front of her. She could hear Piet laughing and calling out as he raced to catch her up, and she was filled with joy at the thought that she would have so much to share with him in the days to come.

'We'll open the lodge just after the new year,' Piet said as they ate breakfast back at the house. 'Anthony is bringing the first guests.'

'One of them is a journalist from a Chicago newspaper,' Anthony said. 'He's been out with me before and he wrote up his safari. The article brought me more business than I could handle.'

'I'm taking Simon up there tomorrow.' Hannah's face was animated. 'The place has been crawling with carpenters and plumbers for so long, with electrical wires lying all over the floors like spaghetti. I'm tired of building sites. I want to decide where we're going to put the furniture, and think about lamps and rugs, and all the good things that I've been collecting for months.'

'I wish we could stay on, to give you a hand,' Sarah said. 'But I'll be back in a few weeks, and then I'll help all I can. The Briggs can't pay much, but the job will be fantastic and the camp is only a few hours' drive from here.'

'I'd love to be able to say the same. But I'll be here in spirit.' Camilla's smile was too bright.

'Maybe you could come back for Christmas,' Hannah caught the loneliness in her eyes. 'Or for the opening of the lodge. As our visiting celebrity. I'll bet Anthony's clients would be impressed. Even the journalist. All the newspapers here would write it up.'

'I'm going to lose my clients unless I drag myself away right now and drive to Nairobi,' Anthony rose to his feet. 'Time to head back. My bags are already in the Land Rover, so I'm all set.'

'Right.' Piet stood up, and they all moved out on to the verandah. 'Lars and I have work to do. Ah, there you are Simon. I want you and David to clean out the dry goods store and make a list of anything running low.' He saw the hostile glance that passed between the two young men, and frowned. 'Just do it, heh? And don't leave any old sacks or *taka taka* lying around the stores. If there's one thing that makes me truly mad, it's litter on my property.'

Farewells were brief. Camilla was airy and dismissive.

'London in November, I hope. I'll miss you. I really will.' Anthony kissed her mouth and got into his Land Rover, and then he was gone in a flurry of dust and gravel. Pain splintered her heart.

'Come, Camilla,' Hannah said. 'Sarah's going with Piet to check on the mare that's lame. You can help me with some filing in the office, and then we'll go to the lodge with Simon. You can advise me about the furniture. The rest of them will join us later.'

Later, from the viewing platform, Camilla could see a herd of buffalo making their way across the open ground. She thought of Anthony and the way he could mimic the rumbling sound of an old bull. Tears threatened, and she squared her shoulders and went to see how she could be of help. Simon was constantly at Hannah's side, writing with precise, neat letters and figures in his notebook, drawing chalk outlines of furniture on to the stone floors.

'I have made a list of furniture for each room, Memsahib Hannah,' he said, in his careful English. 'While you were away I went to your office and prepared them on the typewriter.'

Hannah looked at him in surprise. She was annoyed that he should have gone into her office and used her machine without permission, but relieved that there was yet another routine task he could take off her hands.

'I can type fast,' Simon said, proudly. 'They taught me at the mission and I have passed an exam.' He hesitated, trying to gauge how best to obtain her approval. 'You have seen that I have also taken my exam in elementary bookkeeping. I would like to be a proper accountant. But this takes many years and much money.'

'Maybe when we get the lodge going, we can arrange for you to do a course. If you continue to do well, I'll ask Bwana Piet about it.'

'Thank you.' His face lit up with pleasure as he savoured the idea, but then his expression became downcast. 'But I do not know if I can do that.'

'Just keep working hard, Simon, and you'll be fine. In the meantime, let's measure this window.'

Looking around her, Camilla realised what an immense labour of love the whole construction had been. Piet had created a haven of light and tranquillity up here on the rocks, above the glorious expanse of the land and the great mountain that presided over it. They deserved to be happy here, Piet and Hannah and Sarah. And perhaps one day Jan and Lottie would come home again, filled with pride at the way their children had carried on the work begun by their forefathers so long ago. She wondered where Lars would fit into the picture, and she looked up at Hannah who was fastening a lampshade on to a base made from a dried-out gourd.

'I noticed last night that Lars really has a thing for you,' she said, and laughed as Hannah's face turned red. 'Oh my, Han. You have a strong resemblance to Sarah when your skin turns that subtle shade of beetroot.'

'Did she talk to you about that? About Lars?'

'No. I could see it for myself. So what do you think about him? If anything.'

'I do wonder sometimes what it might be like with him.' She looked across at Camilla with some embarrassment. 'Sarah said I was scared, and she's right. Stupid, heh? A big, strong farm girl like me, full of common sense. That's how it is though.'

'Being strong doesn't help when it comes to love,' Camilla said. 'The heart makes a fool of the head, time after time. Trust me. I know.'

'Maybe I like him just because there's no one else around,' Hannah said. 'I've been working so hard, and I haven't got money to go and splurge in Nanyuki or Nairobi, so I've become a bit of a hermit. Anyway, there are always girls ringing up, looking for him.'

'I'll bet they're no competition.'

'I'm not sure. And there's another thing.' Hannah paused to gather her thoughts. 'I've come to value my independence. I spent more than two years down south, always thinking about Pa and his problems, always worrying about Ma. Now I make my own rules, and I'm not responsible for anyone else's emotions or happiness. I don't want that to change again, and I'm afraid Lars would swallow me up. He reminds me of Piet. They're so alike.'

'I think you're making that up to protect yourself,' Camilla said, smiling. 'But you're not fooling me. Now give me that drawing and let me try and work out where this table is supposed to be placed, before the others arrive.'

The jewel of the evening star appeared, and the dusk swiftly surrendered all semblance of heat to the oncoming darkness. They were squinting in the dying light, trying to decipher Viktor Szustak's plans, when they saw the headlights bouncing up into the sky and across the rutted track.

Lars came out to the viewing platform with Piet but Sarah hung back, strangely reluctant to join them. It was Camilla who drew her into the circle on the balcony.

'So what do you think, on second viewing, Lady Camilla?' Piet asked, surveying his domain with unabashed pride.

'No one who comes here will ever forget it,' Camilla said. 'It's an extraordinary, powerful place that grabs at your emotions and draws you in. I think you should be hugely proud of the way you've constructed the buildings so they blend with the rocks and trees, and the rise of the land. It's beautiful.'

They sat watching the stars light up the bowl of the sky and listening to the sounds of the wind and the high drone of night insects. Only Sarah was silent, gazing down at the waterhole, her face troubled. Piet turned to her, questioning.

'Not like you to be so quiet.'

'I like to listen sometimes. You should be grateful.'

He laughed, and she wondered if he could possibly have forgotten kissing her here in this same place, such a short time ago. Since then she had waited patiently for him to take another step, watching for any small sign that he loved her. But although he had often chosen to sit beside her in camp, or on their game drives, he had made no further attempt to touch her or to turn their friendship into something deeper. She wanted desperately for him to say something. Anything that would confirm what she hoped was true. When they left the lodge, Piet held the door of his Land Rover open, and asked Sarah to come with him. As they bumped along the rough track, and he leaned across and placed a hand on her knee.

'I'm happy you'll be back quickly,' he said. 'There are so many things we have to talk about, you and I, when we're together again. When there's just the two of us.' He gestured up towards the ridge. 'We'll sit up there and talk. I hope we'll do that very soon.'

She felt light-headed with joy and he smiled at her undisguised happiness and squeezed her hand, before turning his attention back to the road.

'Where's Mwangi with the drinks? And where on earth are the dogs?' Piet was the last to join the group in the sitting room before dinner. 'They're always around looking for a snack before we eat.'

'Lars had to go over to the Murray farm,' Hannah said. 'Probably he took them.'

'He'd never take all of them,' Piet said. 'I think I should send Simon to look for them, or go myself.'

At that moment they heard heavy footsteps in the corridor leading to the kitchen. The door burst open and Hannah stared, aghast, at the five men standing in the sitting room. They all held pangas, the blades shining in the lamplight. Their faces were taut and angry, and they were shouting. Piet bent down, reaching for the knife he kept in the side of his boot. But two men leapt on him, overpowering him instantly, and within seconds he was lying helpless on the ground. Hannah watched in terror as one of them lifted his machete and cut the telephone lines. He squatted down beside her brother, and bound his hands and feet with the wire.

'Do not make noise,' he said. 'If you cry out we will kill you. Do not look at us. Get down on the floor. Keep your eyes away from us, or you will die. Take off your watches and bracelets and rings, and give them to us. With any money you have. And guns. We want guns. You, Mama, take off your jewellery.' The words were directed at Camilla as she slid from her chair, the gleam of the raised machete reflected on her face.

'We don't have guns here in the house. They're out in the storeroom.' Piet spoke through clenched teeth, his face pressed on to the floor by his attacker.

Camilla's hands trembled as she tried to take off her jewellery, but her fingers were awkward and stiff with terror. The atmosphere in the room was alive with menace.

'Faster, Mama, or we will cut them off.'

The man spoke in a low voice, but he had raised his panga. She cried out as she saw the savagery in his eyes and he brought the long knife down sideways across her forehead. The skin broke easily. Blood ran down her face into her eyes as she blindly held out her jewellery with shaking hands. Then he lifted his foot and kicked her so hard that she fell, spread eagled, on to the carpet.

'Get on the floor. All of you, get down.'

Hannah put up a hand to her mouth, trying to muffle a sob, and the man shouted at her in his native Kikuyu, screaming abuse. She could not understand all the words, but she felt his hatred, sensed his craving for violence as he moved towards her. She cowered down, covering her head with her arms and hands as he threw her down on to the floor beside Camilla and Sarah. They were shaking with fear as their hands were tied behind their backs, each one expecting the sharp sensation of the knife blade as the panga was raised against them.

They lay on the ground, side by side. Sarah could see the rage in Piet's face, the veins standing out on his forehead and neck. The leader of the gang picked up a Persian rug and hurled it across the room. It landed on top of them all, leaving them choking and coughing in a fog of dust and darkness. For a long time Sarah remained still, her head turned to one side, her eyes closed, listening to the sounds of destruction all around her. Books were swept from shelves, glass crashed on to the floor around them. In the bedrooms clothing and linen were grabbed in armfuls from wooden chests that had travelled long ago on swaying ox wagons, to this untamed place of hope and renewal. Time and again they heard footsteps, stamping up and down the steps of the verandah as the contents of the house were removed. When they heard the sound of a car door slamming, and voices raised in discussion, they prayed that the raid was over. But the men returned to the house yet again, to continue their plunder.

'Help me get free,' Piet whispered. 'They haven't tied your hands so tight, Hannah. Roll closer to me, and see if you can't undo this wire.'

'No. If they think you're trying to put up a fight they'll kill you, for sure. Stay still, Piet. Please, stay still. It's our only hope.' She pressed her face into her shoulder to muffle any sound, trying to still her panic-ridden limbs, to stop them from shaking.

'What happened to the staff?' Piet's muttered question was bewildered and furious. 'And the dogs. They must have got rid of the dogs.'

Beside him Sarah was rigid with fear, praying that they would not die, at the very moment when she had begun to hope again. She turned her head towards Camilla, prone and unmoving on the other side of her.

'Are you all right? What about your head?'

'It's bleeding,' Camilla whispered. 'Don't worry about it. Just pray for us all. Oh God, they're back. Don't let us die here, please.'

They heard the sound of footsteps in the room and then the rug was thrown back, leaving them blinking and exposed in the sudden light.

'Get up.' One of the men kicked Piet, turning him over on his back and then stooping down to drag him to his feet. 'You come with us, open the place with the guns. And money. You have a safe with money. Untie his legs.'

'No. No, he can give you the keys. Please, just take the keys,' Hannah implored, unable to control her weeping.

They ignored her desperate plea, and she listened as her brother was pushed, stumbling, out into the night. For a long time a heavy silence blanketed the room so that they could hear only their own frightened, shallow breathing.

'Oh God, no, please don't take him.' Sarah was rocking herself to and fro, her hands still tied behind her back, her head beating against the floorboards as the agonising fear spread through her body. 'Please bring him back safe, dear God. Don't take him away from us. Please, please, dear God, just let him be safe. Have mercy on us, I beg of You. And above all, let him somehow be safe.'

Beside her Camilla had begun to shiver, her body quivering with fear and shock as images of Piet, living and laughing and vibrant, flashed across her brain. She opened her mouth to pray for mercy, and tasted the blood that was still welling and trickling down her face and across her lips. Hannah was huddled on the floor, her elbows tucked in against her sides to keep her shaking form intact. Suddenly she made an exclamation, turning her head and trying to scramble to her feet.

'I hear a car,' she said tersely. 'It could be Lars.' The beam of headlights approaching gave them a flicker of hope, and they drew back together. 'It must be him. But we have to warn him, somehow. They could—'

Then they heard a shot.

'Oh God. If there's shooting we'll all be killed. Lars won't realise there's five of them here. Oh God, we're all going to die now, for sure.' Hannah was petrified, moaning in her despair.

From outside they heard further gun shots, followed by the sound of pounding feet and car engines revving. Doors slammed, gears crashed, and the noise of vehicles died away. For what seemed like an age there was a deathly stillness. Not an insect could be heard in the awful cavern of the night.

'Hannah?' Piet's breath was coming in painful gasps as he stumbled up the steps, pulling out his knife to cut each one of them free. They clung together briefly, weeping with relief and revulsion and shock. 'Lars is badly hurt. Come quickly, Han. Jesus, Camilla! Your face – I hadn't realised it was so bad. And you're still bleeding!'

'It's not important.' Camilla pushed his hand away.

'All right, then. Hannah, get hot water and look for clean cloths – sheets, towels, anything. We have to get Lars inside, fast. The staff were shut into the kitchen. Sarah, give them some brandy and so. They were tied up in there, with one of the gang standing outside with a panga. And I found Simon. He'd been clobbered and locked in the office. He has a big bump on his head, and some cuts where he broke a window trying to escape. The bastards have taken our cars, loaded up everything from the house. No sign of the dogs. I'm afraid they've been poisoned. The truck is still out by the store, so I'm going to send Simon over to the Murrays' place to get help. And to call Dr Markham from there.'

In the driveway Lars was slumped on the ground. His breathing was erratic and he tried to focus on Hannah and to form a word. She put her shaking fingers to his lips.

'Shhh. Don't say anything. You have to keep your energy stored up, heh? Piet's sending for help. They cut the phone lines, so it will be a while. Can you walk with me, if I help you?'

He nodded and Piet helped her to hoist him on to his feet. Lars grunted with pain, unable to maintain his balance. His shirt had been ripped by the bullet, and blood was seeping from beneath his right shoulder. Hannah prayed that it was not low enough to be a serious injury. They made their way up the steps with maddening slowness. In the sitting room Sarah had several large basins of hot water ready, and a pile of cloths.

'I'm going to send Mwangi and Kamau to check the rest of the place,' Piet said. 'And the labour lines, too. Where's Camilla?'

'In the bathroom,' Sarah answered. 'She's got a terrible gash across her forehead. I can't tell how deep it is, because it's still bleeding. It will need a good few stitches, I'd say. I told her to put some gauze and cotton wool on it and lie down. She was close to passing out.'

They worked quickly, laying Lars on the sofa, wedging cushions and towels around him. His face was ashen, and his lips had turned a bluish colour.

'Get scissors,' Hannah said. 'We'll have to cut off his shirt. We need to stop him losing blood. He needs something for shock and pain. Piet, the first-aid kit is in my bathroom. Unless they've stolen that as well.' She began to cut.

'He's shivering,' Piet said. 'Look, we have to keep him awake. He mustn't go into shock. There's an airstrip at the Murrays'. Maybe they can get lights and take him to Nairobi tonight.'

'Lars? Lars, open your eyes. Say something to me, heh? This will not be good, but you're a brave boy.' Hannah realised how foolish the words sounded, directed at a man whose face was beaded with sweat, and whose every breath was an intake of pain and nausea. She washed the area around the entry hole of the bullet, and made a tight wad from one of the towels, pressing it as hard as she could into the wound to stem the bleeding. He gave a cry, and Hannah bent to press her lips against his forehead. Then she bound his shoulder and chest tightly, making soothing noises as a mother would with a sick child.

The first-aid box was still in Hannah's bathroom and Sarah began a frantic search through its contents. 'Morphine – I suppose we need that. And sedatives.'

Camilla sat on a stool in front of the washbasin, trying to stop the blood trickling from her forehead. She pressed a band of gauze over the long gash, but her hands were shaking and she could not position it. She bent down suddenly and vomited into the bowl beside her.

'Lie down and don't move.' Sarah helped her into Hannah's bed. 'Here's a clean dressing. Hold it over the cut and keep up the pressure, so the bleeding will stop. And stay very quiet for the time being. There's nothing you can do out there. Piet and Hannah are looking after Lars. And Simon will be back soon with help. Just lie still.'

'Is Lars going to be all right?'

'I hope so. He's still losing blood and he's pretty much in shock. We can't tell what the damage is, but I'd say we need to get him to a hospital fast.' Sarah went to the sitting room with the medicine.

Camilla lay back on the bed, stroking the soft fur of Hannah's kaross, to drive away the fear that had her in a stranglehold and would not let go.

The cut was bad. She knew it would have to be stitched. It would leave a scar across her forehead. A scar that could ruin her face and maybe put paid to her modelling career. Plastic surgery. Did anyone do that in Nairobi, or would she have to fly straight back to London? But it wasn't important for now. What mattered was that they were alive. She tried to calm herself and to rest, but the reek of violence and blood filled her nostrils. She could still see the men bursting into the sitting room, and the flash of the blade as it hurtled towards her eyes. A helpless terror had invaded her when the first shot rang out and she had believed that Piet was dead, and she could not prevent her legs from shaking as she lay on the bed. But Piet was not dead, and she said a prayer of thanks for each one of them. For a time she tried to lie still, until her head was no longer spinning and she believed that the bleeding had stopped. Then she sat up slowly. It would be better to be with the others in the sitting room. She did not want to be alone here. She never wanted to be alone again for the rest of her life.

Chapter 14

Kenya, September 1965

Hannah felt helpless. A sense of outrage made her edgy and fretful. Her secure haven had been violated, despoiled by evil, for a reason she could not fathom. She missed the dogs that had always lain at her feet in the evening, thrusting their soft muzzles into her hand. They had been found at daybreak on the morning after the attack, near the gate that led from Lottie's garden on to the open plains. Their throats had been slit, although it was clear from the glazed eyes and obscenely protruding tongues that they had already been dying from poison. Piet had taken a shovel and buried them in grim silence. Then he had walked away to give the day's orders to his *watu*, while Hannah flung a few clothes into a suitcase. He had chartered a small aircraft to fly Lars to the Nairobi hosptial, and the three girls went with him. The farewells at Langani had been quick. Camilla was ashen-faced and trying to cope with a crushing headache, while Sarah was shocked and subdued. Hannah focused her thoughts on Lars and tried to banish her feelings about the assault on her home. But on the following evening, as they gathered in the courtyard at the Norfolk Hotel to say goodbye, Hannah had begun to cry, her anguish pouring out as if something inside her had given way and could not be shored up.

'I'm sorry,' she said, gulping for air, rubbing her hand over swollen eyes. 'But I'm so scared. I'm frightened to go home. I don't know how I'm going to manage to do it, and it's so stupid and cowardly. So bloody stupid.'

They had stood with their arms around one another, offering words of comfort and reassurance. They would all be together again soon. It was a promise. Hannah had straightened her shoulders and disappeared into the cottage they had shared, closing the door, so that she would not be there to see them drive away. She had spent several days in Nairobi, staying

262

close to Lars as he lay recovering from his surgery. Now she wished she was back in the hospital room, instead of here in her own sitting room where fear threatened to extinguish her love for her home.

The drive back to Langani had been tense. It had been a bright morning, the air dappled with small clouds racing across the sky. Piet had insisted on coming down to collect her and was deliberately cheerful, whistling through his teeth as they travelled north. But he watched his sister with growing concern as she sat, mute and wan, gazing out the window, making no comment on the landmarks she loved the best. At the farm, Hannah stepped down from the vehicle and greeted the staff. She was determined to be courageous, to stand shoulder to shoulder with Piet and to do whatever was needed to protect their heritage. Just as her great-grandparents and her grandparents and Jan and Lottie had fought for their home and their land. But she did not feel ready for the demands that would now be made of her. She clenched her hands and prayed that she would remain strong, that she would show only loyalty and valour.

In the office she sifted through letters of support from friends and neighbours, answering several of them and paying urgent bills. An account of the raid had been in the newspapers, and she read the clippings and filed them away. Then she unpacked and made her way to the sitting room where she found Piet waiting for her. She sat down and tried to make conversation with him, talking incessantly about the chores she would take care of on the following day, clutching her glass in tight fingers, trying to ignore the gun that lay on the table beside her armchair and the rifle standing up against the wall. The doors leading out on to the verandah were locked, and the accustomed sounds and scent of evening no longer drifted into the room. It was claustrophobic. Around her there were gaping spaces where Lottie's pictures and ornaments had stood, and they seemed to Hannah like empty eye sockets.

'The police will be back in the morning,' Piet said. 'Jeremy Hardy wants to go through everything with us. The staff have all been questioned now. He's still banking on the idea that it was someone with a grudge, or radical political ideas.'

'This can't be any of our regular *watu*,' Hannah protested. 'It has to be some madman, passing through. Everyone is afraid. I can feel it. Simon is terrified they'll come back for another round, and he's not the only one. I wouldn't be surprised if he leaves.'

He had been hit across the head as he tried to take a vehicle and go for help. For some time he had lain unconscious, locked into the office. But he had come around, and when the first shot was fired he had used a heavy paperweight to break the glass in the French windows leading out to the verandah. His hands were cut and bleeding and he had twisted his ankle as he ran to the vehicle. Since that treacherous night he had barely spoken a word, and his normally cheerful face was grey with apprehension.

'Han, I know this is hard,' Piet said, hunkering down beside his sister. He knew that she was trying to disguise her fear, but he had seen the way she jumped at the slightest noise, how her eyes darted back and forth from the door to the window in the sitting room, how she hung on to the arms of her chair and made sure that she was not sitting with her back to the kitchen entrance. 'Let's ring Ma now. It would be good to talk to her.'

'Look, I'm sorry. We have to get through this, and I'm making a fool of myself,' she said, ashamed of her weakness. 'Don't pay any attention to me. It's my first night home and I have to get used to the fact that a terrible thing happened, but it won't ever happen again. I have to find a way to put it out of my mind.' She stopped, realising that he was trying to tell her something. 'What did you say?'

'Han, I haven't spoken to Ma and Pa since the robbery. I tried twice while you were in Nairobi, but there was no reply from the house, and then I felt it could wait, this bad news. We should tell them now. And ask them if they have any plans to come home.'

She looked at him for a moment, and then she cried out with relief. He was near to tears himself, as he put his arms around her.

'Yes. It's what I want above everything else.' She found a handkerchief and wiped the last tears away. 'You dial, Piet. Let's do it now.'

'We're going to be fine, you know, Sis.' Piet's voice was reassuring. 'Just fine.'

She smiled at him gratefully, then put her hand up to her mouth. 'But what about Lars?'

'With the lodge about to open, we'll need him on the farm. I hope he'll agree to stay on.'

When they got through, it was Piet who spoke first, recounting the nightmare story of the raid, telling Lottie about Camilla's face and the shooting and Lars's injury, and all that had happened since.

'Thank God you and Hannah weren't hurt, or Sarah. But Camilla's face

– that poor, poor girl has had so many problems in her short life,' Lottie said. 'And Lars, who has done so much for us all. This is a bad time, Piet.'

'Ma? When are you coming?' Hannah had snatched the phone from her brother. 'I can't wait for you to be here.'

'Hannah, I can't come now.' Lottie could hear the desperation in her daughter's voice. 'Your father isn't well and I can't leave him.'

'You mean he's drunk.' Hannah felt the bitterness rise into her mouth.

'I'm sorry, Hannah. He's trying his best, but it's difficult here. Kobus needles Pa all the time, and makes things even worse. I can't leave your father for the moment. Maybe at Christmas time, and then Pa might be ready to come too.'

'But I need you here now. Aren't I important too? Or are you always going to make me pay, for running away and leaving you there with him? Please come home, Ma.'

'Oh Hannah,' Lotte's voice carried all her weariness. 'You have to understand. And for a little while, you'll have to cope on your own. It's the way things are sometimes.'

'But you don't know what it's like now, after the robbery. And we have no idea who they were and whether they'll come back.'

'I'll be there as soon as it's possible. It's hard for me too, and there are bad things happening in this country. I'm here on my own most of the time and the house is isolated. Believe me, I'd love to be at Langani.' There was a catch in her voice, almost like a sob. 'But I'll be thinking of you every day. You and Piet. I love you both.'

There was a click on the line and she was gone. Hannah stood staring at the phone, disappointment rising in her like gall. A worm of jealousy had lodged itself in her gut. She spun round abruptly and Piet put his arms around her once more, conscious of her despair. He wanted to say something comforting, but her expression made him hold back. For the rest of the afternoon and evening he stayed close to her, postponing anything that had to be done away from the house, accompanying her as she went to the dairy and the stables.

'Remember, I'm next door if you need anything during the night,' he said, as they finished a simple supper beside the fire. 'All you have to do is call out, Sis. Mwangi and Kipchoge are both sleeping in the house for now. I've fixed up temporary quarters for them beside the pantry. Plus there are two of Juma's sons on patrol outside.'

'It's wonderful that we're forced to turn our home into a state of siege,' Hannah said. She saw his expression and relented. 'I know. It's just until they find those bloody savages,' she said. 'But it's my first night home, and it's hard. I'll manage better tomorrow, when I've had some sleep. I think I'll go to bed now.'

'Han, take this.' He handed her a loaded revolver. 'It's for insurance. You might feel better having it by you. You can keep it under your pillow at night.'

She took the gun without a word and went to her bedroom, closing and locking the door behind her. But when she stood alone at last, she was overcome by an uncontrollable avalanche of emotion, and she collapsed on to her bed, buckling under the force of it. She longed for someone to lean on, to confide in, because she did not think she could hold out on her own. Her mind felt as though it had splintered into shards, exposing her cowardice and her fears. She dried her eyes and went to sit down in her favourite chair but within moments she stood up again, afraid of being so close to the window. Before turning out the light she searched frantically in the drawer of her bedside table for a torch and placed it under her pillow, next to the gun. All around her the sounds of night were changed, as every creak and shift of the old house became a threat. The generator sputtered and the lights dimmed so that she was surrounded by total darkness. At four o'clock in the morning she was still awake, her limbs aching with anxiety, her eyes dry and raw and burning in their sockets. She felt as though she was strung out on some instrument of torture that had stretched her mind and body to a state of unbearable exhaustion. And she was angry with herself. If she could not adjust, if she could not find the courage to go on, if she could not lie in the bed she had occupied for most of her twenty-one years, then they had won. She would not allow that, would not be defeated. At last she slept, mercifully free of dreams and visions, until the dawn crept in through a chink in the curtains and she awoke to find that the world was a place of astounding beauty.

Inspector Jeremy Hardy arrived shortly after breakfast, his ruddy face concerned as he took in Hannah's sunken eyes and the strain that was visible in her face.

'I'm afraid there's nothing new,' he said, accepting a cup of coffee. 'So far, it's an isolated incident. There are no reports of problems on any other farms. It doesn't look like anything political, is what I mean.'

'Maybe. But I know the Murrays and the Griffiths are worried, and the Krugers too. I'll make a bet that there will be more attacks, Jeremy, until you find these bastards and lock them up.' Hannah refused to consider what he was trying to tell her.

'I've discussed this with Piet, my dear, and he thinks my theory is right.'

'What theory?' Hannah demanded.

'Your cattle were killed in a very particular way. With hindsight, it looks as though someone may have tried to start a fire out beside the lodge. And now you've had this attack on the house. All directed at Langani. So you might have someone on your hands with a particular grudge.'

'But we've had no real *shauris* recently,' Hannah insisted. 'Except for a drunken old shepherd, and Piet paid him off with three months' salary because he was sorry for the old fool. We've seen him on the road several times, drunk as a lord and smiling his toothless smile. I can't believe he has it in for us, and he's not capable of killing cattle or dogs, or organising a raid on the house. It doesn't make any sense.' Hannah pressed her fingers to her eyes in a tired gesture

'You may be right,' Jeremy said, conscious of her distress. 'But you know what these fellows are like. One minute they're loyal retainers, and the next they think they've been cheated or short changed in some way, and they go crazy. They're as unpredictable as children.'

'Those bastards were strangers,' Piet said. 'And now they've made off with two of our guns as well as the pangas they had. So they'd better be found before they kill someone. We were lucky that Lars had gone out the other night, that he came back and surprised them. But he could have lost his life. They didn't hesitate to fire at him. And at me too. Man, you'd better speed up your enquiries. Put a few more people on this case and get some results.'

'What are you doing about your stolen guns?' Jeremy asked.

'I replaced them when I went down to collect Hannah in Nairobi. Ammunition too. It was an expensive exercise I could have done without.'

'We may be looking for one of the people you caught stealing your fence wire, or grazing their cattle on your land without permission,' Jeremy said. 'Whatever the reason, we're doing all we can. I promise you that. How is Lars coming on, by the way? We sent a bottle of Scotch. Thought that would be more useful than another bunch of flowers, if the nurses don't take it away from him.'

'He's doing well,' Hannah said. 'He'll be away for another couple of weeks, and then he'll have to take it easy for a while.'

'Good news. Maureen asked me to invite you and Piet for lunch and some tennis on Sunday. I want to take advantage of the fact that we're missing Lars and his vicious backhand. I'm thinking I might even win a set or two, while he's out of action.'

Hannah was grateful for his attempt to inject a normal topic of conversation into their dialogue. 'I don't know about this weekend,' she said. 'But soon, yes. That would be good.'

Anthony phoned. He had heard the news at a lodge where he had taken his clients for lunch and a swim.

'I could come up for a night, if you like,' he said. 'I can leave my guests here in the Mara and spend tomorrow night with you.'

'No. It's a great offer, but it's too far,' Hannah said. 'You'd be driving all day tomorrow on that terrible road, and then you'd have to be up at dawn next morning to go back. It's got to be nine or ten hours on the road. We're fine, but thanks for suggesting it.'

'Could you cope with an overnight guest?' Piet asked her, when she had been home for a week. 'Viktor would like to come up and look at all the furniture before we move it from the workshop up to the lodge. In case there are any refinements, as he puts it, to be carried out.'

Her spirits rose. Viktor could help her to forget her fears, fill her head with nonsense and new ideas and strange poetry that she could not understand. She looked forward to it, and when he arrived on the following evening she had discarded her jeans in favour of Italian wool slacks and a silk shirt that Camilla had given her. Piet looked at her in surprise as she came into the sitting room before dinner. She had pinned her hair up in a French twist, and she was wearing lipstick and something on her eyes that made them look very bright. Viktor sprang to his feet and kissed her hand, and she looked at him a little self-consciously. His raven-black hair curled over his shirt collar, and a cigar hung from his lips. His face was dominated by a large nose and heavy black eyebrows that made him look like some predatory bird. He drew hard on the cigar and smiled broadly. His mouth was fleshy and sensual, and there were deep lines down each side of it.

'You are beautiful,' he said to her, still holding her hand. 'Like a warrior queen. Burnished and strong and magnificent. Later, I will recite to you a poem that describes the way you are tonight. Now, tell me what you have been doing, while we have dinner.'

Hannah was surprised to find herself recounting the happenings on the farm, and describing her attempt to immerse herself in its workings and to put aside the traumatic experience they had undergone. She talked about her day with a new enthusiasm. Piet sat silent for the most part, glad to see his sister so animated, the shadows gone from her eyes. Viktor listened, spurring her on, expressing interest in everything she said. And she was flattered. He had called her beautiful, a warrior queen. He knew a poem that described her, he'd said. She was not just a shadow of her brother, a big Afrikaans farm girl who would make good breeding stock for the likes of Willie Kruger and his brother up in Eldoret. Here was a man who had been educated in Europe, a poet and an architect who was part of Nairobi society, and he was flirting with her. She began to respond to the messages in his black, flashing eyes.

'But you cannot always be working,' he said. 'You must take time to laugh a little, play sometimes, not always be so serious. And I will teach you to do this.'

'Not right now, you won't,' Hannah said, smiling. 'My eyes are scratchy, and it's time for bed.'

'I'll go along with that,' Piet said. 'We'll visit the workshop first thing in the morning, and take a look at the chairs and tables. Hope you have a good night.'

'The generator will stop in about twenty minutes, Viktor,' Hannah told him. 'So you need to light your lamp when you get to your room.'

'You are all the light I require. Your smile could light the whole of Langani, and then I would not need anything else.' He stood up and kissed her on her cheek. 'Goodnight. Thank you for your fine hospitality.'

In the morning they went to inspect the furniture Viktor had designed. He had an ability to describe what he wanted in the simplest terms, and to obtain the best from the craftsmen who worked for him, inspiring them with astute comments, correcting their mistakes with a mixture of tact and laughter and persuasion. Hannah was disappointed when he announced that he would not be staying for lunch.

'I have had a call from Nairobi,' he said. 'My great talent is needed there this afternoon, at a very dull meeting. But I will be back, if you tell me I am welcome.'

A letter arrived from Sarah. She had not yet told her parents that she planned to return to Kenya to work for the Briggses. But she knew that it could not be delayed much longer, and she was clearly nervous about their reaction. There was no news from Camilla. The issue of a permanent scar on her face would be her priority, Hannah realised, but she hoped it would not be too long before she asked George Broughton-Smith about help for Langani. She had been obliged to replace a number of household items that had been stolen during the raid. Now they were spending money on extra guards at night, and they needed more funding for fencing and additional game patrols to deter poachers. Piet was out on the farm or at the construction site during every daylight hour, and Hannah pored over the accounts, trying to figure out new ways to cut down on the cost of final supplies that she needed for the interior of the lodge. It was still difficult to sleep at night. Every small sound left her staring into the menacing darkness, where shadows stalked and threatened and curdled her blood. She was relieved when she finally drove down to Nairobi to collect Lars and bring him home.

'I'm feeling good,' he said, plainly delighted to be on his way back to the farm. Hannah hugged him as she helped him out of the car at Langani, and Piet arrived to clap his friend on the back and call for Mwangi to bring cold Tuskers.

In the afternoon, they drove up to the lodge and around the perimeter of the farm, pointing out areas of progress and problems that had arisen in Lars's absence. Later, Hannah came into the office to find him looking through the ledgers, catching up on orders and accounts.

'You saved our lives, Lars. I'll never forget that,' Hannah said.

He saw that there was something else she wanted to say, but she hesitated and then changed her mind, turning away from him and riffling through a stack of papers.

'What were you going to tell me?' he asked. She shook her head, but he was quietly insistent. 'Talk to me. It's important that you can talk to me.'

'Did you think you would die?' she asked, almost inaudibly. 'Were you afraid, Lars? I was so afraid, and now I can't seem to get back to where I was before. Sometimes I lie awake at night and I hear something outside – the nightwatchman, or a hyrax scuttling across the verandah, and I know it's something I've been listening to all my life. But I start to shake and shake, until I can't hold myself together any more and my teeth are chattering. I don't know what to do, and I don't want Piet to realise how frightened I am. How useless I've become.'

He reached out and stroked her straw-gold hair as if he were comforting a small child. 'It will fade, Hannah. It will all fade in time. I'm going to be here now, to help you when you're afraid. And maybe soon there will be Lottie too, and your father.'

'I wouldn't hold out much hope for them,' Hannah said. 'In the meantime our overdraft is back up to near the limit, what with having less milk to sell, and extra *watu*, and all the things we need to complete the lodge. Sometimes I can't see how we're going to do it.'

'We'll get past this, and we'll be stronger and closer than we ever were,' he said.

Looking at him, she felt a new confidence. In the past she had not thought of him as a sensitive man. He had been Lars, her brother's farm manager, a pain in the arse who had no time for her theories on farming, and who did not treat her opinions with the seriousness she thought they deserved. But in his absence she had realised how vital he was to the farm, more important than ever now that the lodge was close to completion. And the Lars of today had listened without criticising her, or making her fears seem trivial. He had been encouraging and consoling. He had talked like a true friend. She would have to be careful now, not to damage this new balance between them. And time would take care of the rest.

Viktor returned on the following weekend, bringing French wine and champagne from Nairobi, and a cool box full of fresh lobster that a grateful client had sent up from the coast that morning.

'I don't think Kamau knows much about lobsters,' Hannah said.

'Then we will prepare it together. I will go to the kitchen and assist him.'

Hannah was not sure what the old cook would make of this idea. But within minutes it was apparent that Kamau was delighted, and proud to show Viktor around his domain. Dinner was a frivolous affair and Lars watched as Hannah's face became flushed and her eyes began to sparkle, with the effects of the wine and the flattery. Jealousy crept into his head, permeating his every thought, making him dour and ungracious. Piet wondered how he had not noticed Lars's feeling for Hannah before. In the later part of the evening Viktor monopolised the conversation, quoting from the romantic poets and from his own compositions.

Looking for Hannah on the following morning, Lars realised that she had left early and gone to the lodge with Viktor. He cursed under his breath as he tried to decide whether he should join them. Perhaps Piet was up there, in which he would be keeping an eye on Hannah. Everyone knew the stories about Viktor's exploits in Nairobi and Nanyuki and at the coast, the lurid tales of womanising and wild drinking sprees. He was amusing and colourful, but he must not be allowed to add Hannah to his list of conquests. She was so defenceless, so vulnerable right now. It would be easy for her to be influenced or seduced by someone who had no connection with the farm and its problems, someone who came from another life that was fast-paced and glamorous and different from anything she had known. Lars tried to think of some way that he could warn her, indirectly and with the tact the situation required. But he was not a man of innuendo, or clever words that masked other words, and he did not know how he could reach her without making her angry. Without showing her how angry he was himself.

When Viktor appeared for the third weekend in a row Piet was no longer able to suppress his concern.

'Hannah, it's fine having Viktor here occasionally,' he said 'He's amusing and good company in small doses. But be careful. He has a reputation with women that's—'

'Don't be silly,' she interrupted. 'He's working on this new lodge in the Aberdares, and doing something else up near Samburu. This is an ideal place for him to stay, instead of going all the way back to Nairobi for the weekend. And he's keeping an eye on the last part of the building here too, without even charging you anything.'

'He's a terrific architect, I agree, and completely dedicated when it comes to his work. But don't get involved with him, Han. He's not a man to be trusted when it comes to the opposite sex.'

'Oh, for God's sake, Piet!' She slammed down the ledger she was carrying. 'I'm not involved with anyone. Viktor makes me laugh when he comes here, and that's a good thing. I'm struggling day and night to keep all the balls in the air, and I need some light relief. Besides, I'm not some innocent little flower that's never had any experience with a man.' She saw his shocked expression and smiled. 'Come on, Piet. This is the Swinging Sixties, even in Nanyuki. Girls don't wear chastity belts any more, and it isn't a crime to have a little fun. So let's stop talking about this and get on with running our farm.'

Piet sighed. His sister was headstrong and stubborn, and he had chosen the wrong method of warning her about Viktor. He would have to hope that the man would soon get tired of Hannah and the farm, and move on to other pastures before any harm was done. But it was not long before Viktor telephoned again.

'I am in Nanyuki,' he said to Hannah. 'I thought I would come and see how you are faring. I'm tired of builders and forests and hotel managers and deadlines. I need a change, if you'll have me.'

When his car roared into the driveway Hannah was surprised to see him open the back and start to pull out a large object wrapped in a piece of sacking. She called Mwangi to help to carry it inside, and then stood back as Viktor pulled off the covering. It was a sculpture, a bronze leopard crouching on a log, all stealth and grace and power.

'That's magnificent,' she said. 'What are you going to do with it?'

'It has been made by a friend of mine in Nairobi,' he said. 'I have brought it because you must buy it. For the lodge. It will make a perfect focal point on the large table in the centre of the main room. With all your books and flowers. It is just right.'

She agreed with him instantly, and when Piet and Lars came in from the workshops, she led them straight to the sitting room and showed them the piece.

'It's great,' Piet said. 'But we can't afford it. It's by a sculptor called Martin Voorman and his work is very expensive. Far too much money for us right now.'

'But I told Viktor we'd take it,' she protested. 'He's right about needing one really good piece of art in that big room. It will give the whole place a different look, lift it up. And I know our finances better than anyone. I want to keep it.'

'Out of the question.' Piet was adamant. 'I'm afraid he'll have to take it back to Nairobi. Or sell it to someone else.'

Hannah felt like a fool. 'I don't think you should override my decision,' she said. 'I'm the one who has bought everything for the lodge. I've made all the curtains and the cushions and the bedspreads, and I've scrounged around for old prints and pictures that don't cost anything. But I want this one thing that is strong and beautiful, and I'm going to have it. Don't you think it's magnificent, Lars?'

'It's a good piece, ja. But I think you should take into account what Piet is saying.'

'And I think this is my department, and I'm not going to have the two of you taking sides against me. I'm perfectly capable of deciding this, and I'm not going to change my mind.'

'That's childish, Hannah. It's an extravagance we can't afford.'

'I've already entered it in the accounts ledger,' she said. 'And I've given Viktor a cheque for it.'

'That was irresponsible. To say the least,' Piet said, furious.

'Irresponsible? How dare you call me that, when I've scrimped and saved and worked round the clock for your lodge. And now you're down on me for buying this one item. Well, I'm not sending it back, and I'm not going to have you make an idiot out of me by asking Viktor to return the cheque. So don't push me, either one of you, or you'll regret it.'

Piet's face was red with anger as he strode out of the office. Lars remained in the doorway, looking at her in silence.

'You needn't say another thing.' Hannah looked at him coldly. 'It's late and I'm going to get ready for dinner. Excuse me.'

She pushed past him and went to her room where she hunted out a sweater with a plunging neckline, and a very short skirt to wear with it. There were strained greetings when Viktor appeared for dinner, looking sleek and expensively attired. He was carrying a bottle of French perfume for Hannah and a poem he claimed to have written for her. Lars watched as she leaned back on the sofa, accepting the gift, allowing Viktor to kiss her cheek and to take hold of her hand for an unnecessarily long time. And then he ran his fingers along her arm so that she shivered a little and looked at him with an expression that was dazed. During dinner Piet could feel the charge in the air, the tension between them all, but Viktor did not seem to notice it. Lars refused coffee and disappeared into the office, closing the door against all that he did not wish to see or hear.

'Don't stay up too late, Hannah,' Piet said, leaving the room reluctantly half an hour later, unable to keep his eyes from closing. 'I have to go to

Nairobi tomorrow, remember? I'll be back in a couple of days, with the tractor spares and the sisal rugs you ordered. And you have a big programme here.'

'There's nothing that can't wait for a day,' she said defiantly. 'It's not often I'm up late and enjoying good company. And if I don't get up early in the morning for once, the farm isn't going to fall apart. We do have a manager, after all.'

When Mwangi had cleared away the coffee cups and retired, Viktor moved close to Hannah on the sofa. She did not make any sound when he reached out to trace the curve of her face, touching her eyebrows and the line of her mouth, making goose bumps on her skin. When he leaned over to kiss her she froze, unsure of what she wanted. Then she put her arms up around his neck and opened her mouth so that she could taste him as he kissed her again. His hands moved over her body, caressing her expertly, sending riffs of pleasure through her. She had never been touched like this before and she drew back, afraid of what she might do.

'Viktor.' It was hard to breathe. 'We can't do this here. No. What I'm saying is that I'm not sure what I feel right now. Viktor – listen to me.'

But he silenced her by standing up and pulling her up with him.

'I'm going to make love to you,' he said into her ear, and she felt as though a jolt of electricity had rushed through her veins. 'It is time to do something joyful. Come now. It is time.'

He took her by the hand and she followed him to the guest bedroom and closed the door. He kissed her again, and she wrapped herself around him as he carried her to the bed and laid her down. She was nervous but filled with desire for him. He unpinned her hair and ran his hands through it so that it fanned out on the pillow around her face. His fingers were impatient as he unbuttoned her blouse, and she began to take off the rest of her clothes herself, because she wanted him to see her naked. She was no longer shy or hesitant as he unfastened his own clothes and threw them on to the floor. She ran her hands over his chest and stomach and dragged him down on top of her. It was impossible not to cry out as he kissed her and moved with her, bringing her an intensity of pleasure that she had never known. They lay in the darkness when it was over, and he traced lines along her stomach and the soft skin of her inner thighs, and later he made love to her again. It was a gentler, slower experience this time, and Hannah felt as though she was drifting, languorous and beautiful, in blissful perfection. She wondered if her body could withstand what was happening or whether she might dissolve entirely, and never return to the limits of the ordinary world she had known before.

Dawn brought a red-gold sky that matched her elation. It was the most beautiful morning she could remember. Viktor was still asleep, and for a while she studied him. His hair was blacker than anything she had ever seen, and she liked how it fell over his forehead, and how his skin was olive-coloured beneath the tangle of sheets and blankets. She kissed him lightly, not wanting to wake him. Then she slipped out of the bed and left the room, stealing through the house to her own quarters, praying that the servants would not see her.

She waited for the sound of Piet's departure for Nairobi before going to breakfast. Mwangi told her that Bwana Lars had gone out early, and that he would not be back until the evening. Hannah ordered toast and coffee and found that she was starving, that everything tasted like nectar, and that she could not keep Viktor out of her mind. Her instinct told her to go to his room and take off her clothes so that he could touch her and they could start to make love again. But she knew that she must wait here for him so she sat in her chair, filled with impatience and wondering if he would look at her in the same way that he had regarded her last night. When she heard his footsteps she thought she was going to be ill. But he stood behind her chair and placed his hands on her shoulders and then lightly trailed his fingers across her shirt to caress her breasts. The muscles in her legs disintegrated into a jellylike substance, and she was thankful that she did not have to stand up. Mwangi came to take the breakfast order, and she did not know whether he was looking at her particularly closely, or whether it was her imagination.

They spent the day beside the river, taking a picnic and binoculars and fishing rods. The banks were alive with bird calls and they watched a troupe of colobus monkeys flying through the trees above them, trailing their black-and-white capes like wings. When Hannah heard the grating sound of a leopard in the distance she clung to Viktor with mock alarm, and he kissed her and slid his hand under the waistband of her jeans to reawaken her excitement. They made love, hidden in the trees along the river bank. Later he made her laugh as he tried to fish for trout, spending much of his time retrieving his fishing flies and untangling his line from logs and branches where they were firmly caught. Finally, he landed a plump rainbow trout almost by accident, and Hannah caught two.

Lars was sitting at the desk when she returned to the house. He looked up and she recognised the jealousy and the misery in his eyes, and regretted it. His hands were folded in front of him and he was outwardly calm, but she saw that his fingers were clasped tightly together and his nails were white with the pressure.

'How are things?' she asked, as casually as she could.

'Busy.'

'I told Kamau we'd have dinner around nine.'

'That's very late,' Lars said. 'We always eat around eight. I've had a pretty long day.'

'Viktor's gone for a sleep, and I haven't cleaned up yet.'

'Oh, we wouldn't want to interrupt Viktor if he's sleeping.' Lars was heavily sarcastic. 'Excuse me. I'm going to check on the generator. They had a problem earlier on. So I may not be all togged up in Italian linen and aftershave at the dinner table, but I hope I'll be invited to eat with you anyway.'

'Don't be such an idiot, Lars,' she said, irritated by his outburst. 'You're being childish because I've spent the day out with Viktor, and you don't like that and your dinner is delayed. You're too set in your ways, you and Piet. Like part of an old married couple stuck in their routine. But I've had a *lekker* day, let me tell you. It was fun and it was the first in a long time. And you're not going to pour cold water on it.'

At dinner he was taciturn, responding to Viktor in monosyllables, refusing to meet Hannah's eyes as she pointed out that she and Viktor had caught the trout that Mwangi was serving.

'It's beautiful along the river,' Viktor said. 'A place that Shakespeare would have dreamed about for his forest settings. Piet and I talked briefly about putting the lodge down there, you know, when he first came up with the idea. But the kopje had such a fine view, even though we had to pump water up there.'

'So you spent the day by the river?' Lars said, trying at last to take some part in the conversation.

'Yes. Wonderful out there,' Viktor replied. 'It's hard to tear yourself away. Hard to tear myself away from any part of Langani. But I'll be leaving first thing in the morning.'

'I thought you would be staying until Monday,' Hannah's stomach lurched with dismay.

'I must return to the city lights. To the real world of work and noise and aggravation. I must leave this wonderful place of fresh air and natural grandeur,' he said, waving his hand in the air. She hated his cheerful expression. 'I will go to Nairobi in the morning, otherwise I may be seduced into who knows what kind of madness.'

After dinner Lars mumbled an excuse and vanished into the night, but Viktor helped himself to brandy and lit a cigar. Hannah sat beside him, breathing in the expensive, pungent aroma, counting the moments until Mwangi came to bid them goodnight and she would have Viktor to herself. He touched her softly, setting up an immediate current of desire, making her smile at her own impatience and her lack of inhibition. When they were finally alone he lunged at her, laughing, and she flung herself into his arms, kissing him with greedy delight until he dragged her to her feet and led her away to the bedroom.

When he said goodbye it was as though there had never been anything between them. Lars stood beside her, morose and uncommunicative, as Viktor pecked her cheek and then drove away. Hannah turned and went up the steps of the verandah, trying unsuccessfully to conceal her sense of abandonment. He had not said when he might come back. He had not said anything. The morning was bright with sunlight and birdsong and the scent of flowers, but she did not notice any of them.

'I'm glad you have no distractions today,' Lars said. 'There are several letters here that are urgent.'

'They're no more urgent than they were a couple of days ago,' Hannah said. 'Cheer up, Lars, for God's sake. You look like thunder and you're making me nervous.'

'Maybe because I'm nervous on your behalf.'

'Look, Lars,' she said. 'We have to work together, and for months now I've sat here wrestling with the problems of the bank, and the cows, and the furnishings for the lodge and the staff sulking. And now I've bought myself a present of a bronze leopard and had some fun. I think you should be glad to see me feeling better. But instead you're angry, or maybe even jealous.'

He picked up on the word and went forward recklessly. 'Yes. I'm very jealous, if you must know. If you would like to know about me at all. I'm very jealous because I love you, Hannah. I'm in love with you and I've been waiting for a good moment to tell you, when we were somewhere with just the two of us together. I'm afraid of what that man is doing to you, with his wine and perfume and all the fancy things he can bring you from Nairobi. So I want you to tell me that he can't come here any more, at weekends, like it's a hotel. He can't take you away and—'

'I'm not going to tell him anything of the kind,' Hannah said, her temper rising. 'He's Piet's architect and he's Piet's friend, and he can come to Langani any time he likes. And I can look after myself perfectly well.'

'I love you, Hannah. Didn't you even hear me? I'm in love with you.' He was horribly aware that this was not the right time to tell her again.

'Oh Lars, I can't talk about that. I'm confused. I always feel like I'm the short side of a triangle with you and Piet, and neither one of you rates me as being really capable, or having a brain. You're a great person, Lars. You've kept the farm from going under. You've been kind to me, and you're my brother's best friend. But we're all too closely bound in another way, caught in the same old problems all day long.' She brushed her hand across her eyes, searching for something wise and balanced to say. 'I can't think about this now, or talk about it. I'm sorry.'

Dammit, she was thinking as she walked away from him. I didn't want to hurt him or make him unhappy. But she felt trapped by the idea of Lars. She had never had a chance to finish her education, to travel to Europe, to meet people outside the circle of her own family background. She thought of Sarah at university in Ireland, of Camilla's fame and her glamorous life in Europe, though that might now be over, and she was saddened by her own narrow limits. There was no money for her to go abroad, or even to spend a weekend in Nairobi. Everything had to be sacrificed for the farm, for Piet's lodge. And that was right. She did not dispute it. Langani was her home, the place that was dearest in her heart, the centre of her universe. But she longed for some contrast, for a taste of the exotic in her life, for something that would make her feel light-hearted and beautiful and free for just a little while. Like Viktor. Viktor who whispered in her ear, told her colourful stories, and drew pictures with words and with strokes of his pencil. Viktor who had kissed and caressed her and smiled his wicked smile. She thought of him now, tickling behind her ear and making lewd suggestions, and she threw her head back and laughed out loud as she went down to her dairy.

Chapter 15

London, September 1965

'What the fuck happened to your face?' Ricky Lane stared at Camilla, his mouth agape. He raised his hands to cover his eyes and dropped them again, groaning and deliberately theatrical. 'Don't you bloody realise we're supposed to be in bloody New York in six days' time, and you've turned up here all bandaged and bruised and looking like Countess bloody Dracula?'

'You could try "Good morning and welcome back",' Camilla said. 'I was involved in an armed robbery on the farm where I was staying in Kenya. Since you're kind enough to ask. We were all lucky to get away with our lives. This is just a scratch, compared to what might have been.'

'It's scratched you right off the front of the American glossies, mate, and me with you. Didn't I bloody warn you it was dangerous going to Africa? That you'd be better off coming to Ibiza with me. That you'd be better off doing anything rather than going out there, among all those bloody nignogs. You've ruined us both, for God's sake. Screwed the best chance of our lives. It's all the same to you, I'm sure, with your posh family and all. But this was the biggest fucking offer of my career, and you've fucking ruined it!'

She was shocked by his words and the rage in his eyes. Her gaze shifted to the unmade bed at the back of the studio, from which he had stumbled to answer the door. On his work table were the pictures that had won them the shoot in New York. Camilla looked at her image, at a photograph of a girl in a satin evening dress standing in a field of flowers, her shimmering hair blowing back off her face. An unblemished beauty.

'I can have my hair changed. Go geometric and ask Sassoon to cut a big fringe. With a generous amount of pancake no one will see the cut.'

'Oh, right.' His voice was heavy with sarcasm. 'No one will notice at all that your forehead is bandaged from one side to the other. As long as there isn't the slightest bloody breeze out there in Central Park, where we were going to shoot the clothes. And we'll get down on our bloody knees and pray that the air is as still as a stagnant pond when we're taking pictures on Fifth Avenue, with all them tall buildings funnelling the wind along the street. Maybe the punters reading American *Vogue* will think that thing across your head is a new kind of hairband. Maybe you'll start a whole new look, for Christ's sake.'

Camilla sat down in a chair. It was cold in the studio and the chill of early autumn had entered her bones, filling her with weariness. She had come directly from the airport to see him, knowing that he would be dismayed. But she had not expected the blunt cruelty of his reaction. They worked together regularly, and she had assumed they were friends. Now she saw that this was an illusion. She was part of his meal ticket, a tool to advance his own ambitions.

'I'm going to see Tom Bartlett later this morning,' she said. 'He's not our agent just for the good days. I'm sure he'll have a dozen dolly birds only too ready to take my place on this shoot. And there's no reason why you shouldn't carry on with the project. You weren't chosen as a minder for me, Ricky. You got this job because they like your work. If you don't believe that, you've got a problem that's nothing to do with me. Thanks for your sympathy and concern and the cup of coffee you haven't offered me. I'll phone you later, when I've talked to Tom.'

'Don't do me no bloody favours,' he said, sulky and petulant.

'And don't bother to call me ever again, Ricky, not for anything.'

He did not make any move to see her downstairs. Camilla retrieved her suitcase from the hall porter and lugged it out of the building. It was rush hour and it had started to rain. She stood for half an hour on the cold street before she could find a taxi, and she was close to tears of gratitude and exhaustion when the driver climbed out and helped with her bag. It was too early in the morning to appear at Tom Bartlett's office and she needed to go home and rest for a while. In the flat she made herself coffee and sat down on the sofa where Anthony had made love to her a million years ago, and where she was now sitting alone and incomplete and adrift without him. She smoked a cigarette and developed a pounding headache. As she swallowed two aspirins she wondered if it was the tobacco or the long gash on her head that was causing her such misery. When she lay down in the bedroom and tried to sleep, her mind raced like an overheated engine. Outside in the square a car backfired, and she bolted upright in a state of panic.

Sarah had flown as far as London with her, offering to stay on for a day or two, in spite of having problems of her own that needed to be resolved quickly. On the plane she had been quiet, but her hands shook noticeably when she picked up her book or her knife and fork, and she had woken with a start each time she tried to doze and to put the horrible images of the raid behind her. Camilla had refused the generous offer, but now that Sarah was not with her she felt cast off, left to navigate her way through the after-effects of terror and injury, with no map or guidelines that might lead her towards recovery. She picked up the telephone and dialled her father's number, only to hear the lonely sound of the instrument ringing in an empty space. When she replaced the receiver she fought the self-pity that threatened to bring on tears. Then she remembered the phial of tranquillisers that the doctor in Nanyuki had given her, and she rummaged in her vanity case. The yellow tablets looked comforting and she swallowed one with a glass of water. In the bedroom she sat down in front of her mirror and took a pair of sharp scissors from the drawer of the dressing table. It was surprisingly difficult to cut a fringe, but she tried to shape the hair so that it fell in a straight line, hiding the dressing on her forehead. By the time she had showered and put on a warm sweater and trousers she felt calm, ready to face the London morning in a reasonable frame of mind. She found a jacket and umbrella, and went out into the grey drizzle.

'Jesus, Camilla. Of course you can't go to New York, but there'll be another time. You're alive, and that's all that matters.' Tom Bartlett took his feet down off his desk and leaned forward, looking for a pencil and notepad in the pile of letters and sheets of photos that covered most of the surface. 'Here's the name of someone you should see right now. Edward Carradine. He's brilliant at his job. You should ring him and go today if it's possible. I'll phone him too, and explain how important it is.'

'Is he a plastic surgeon?' she said.

'The best. Everyone goes to him for a tuck here and there. Not at your age, usually. But he's bloody good, and he'll have your face back to normal in no time.' He rose and handed her a piece of paper with a scribbled telephone number.

Camilla smiled at him and put the paper into her pocket. 'Thanks. I didn't know you had such a soft heart,' she said.

'I'll bloody murder you if you let on,' he replied, grinning her. 'If you so much as hint that I have a charitable corpuscle in me, I'll arrange to print pictures of you with that bloody awful fringe.' He lifted a small camera and took a photo of her, and she found herself laughing in protest.

'Would you do me another good turn?' she said, still smiling.

'Need a few quid, do you, to get through all this?' He opened the drawer of his desk and took out his chequebook.

'No, it's not that at all,' she said, surprised and touched at his offer. 'It's just that I went to see Ricky Lane this morning. I feel bad about having let him down and I'm hoping he'll still be able to do New York.'

'Put the squeeze on you, did he?' Tom's eyes were shrewd. 'Little shit, he is. But a talented little shit. Yeah, I'll make sure he still goes, if it's important to you. Now go home and lie down. And make an appointment with Carradine. He'd better do a bloody fantastic job. He's used his magic blade on plenty of major names that wouldn't like to be named.'

'Will you phone Ricky now?' Camilla found herself shivering at the idea of a knife blade slicing across her face again.

'No, I damn well won't. Let him sweat it out until tomorrow. And get your fringe cut properly, for fuck's sake, before anyone sees you. It looks like some African rat got into your hair.'

When Camilla stepped out into the street again the rain had given way to feeble sunshine and she walked slowly, admiring the tawny trees, the first bare branches, and the coppery gold leaves fluttering and fragile in the late-September sky. She was alive, after all. They were all alive. In the flat she began to unpack her suitcase, putting away her safari clothes with reluctance, holding her pile of Samburu bangles and beaded collars up to her nose, inhaling the pungent scent of cattle and woodsmoke. The scent of Africa. When she had stored everything neatly away she lay back on the sofa and gathered a rug around her. Within moments her eyes had closed and she drifted gratefully into the first proper sleep she had experienced since the traumatic night of the raid.

A shrill ringing woke her, and she was catapulted into full awareness, powered by the now familiar ingredient of fear. Her hands were trembling as she reached for the phone.

'Darling? I've seen the papers. I've been ringing you since yesterday. When did you get back?'

'Mother.'

'I'd like to see you before you rush off to New York, Camilla. I'm so thankful you're safe.' Marina sounded on the brink of tears. 'The *Express* said it was a robbery, and someone was shot. I'm just so grateful it wasn't you.'

'I'm not going to New York, Mother. I have a cut on my face from the raid, and I have to get it seen to before I go back to work. Otherwise I'm fine.'

'Oh God. Oh my God, Camilla, are you all right? You must be in a state of shock. I've just got in from the cottage in Burford, but I'm coming over right now, darling. Right this minute.'

'No. No, Mother, please, I don't need—'

But the phone had already gone dead. Camilla made a mental resolution to remain aloof, calm, disconnected from the hysteria that was approaching like a hurricane in full force. She went into the bathroom, opened the mirrored cabinet above the basin and took another yellow pill. A magic little thing that would help her to stay unruffled, to survive Marina's visit. She wished she had been able to speak to her father, to confide her inability to shake off the whole, terrifying experience. She wanted desperately to hear his voice at least, and to have him comfort her when she confessed her aching disappointment over her love affair. It did not occur to her for a moment that she might talk about any of these feelings with her mother. In the mirror her face looked strained and she squared her shoulders and closed her eyes for a moment, searching for balance. When the doorbell rang she was ready. Marina was out of breath, her face very pale, small beads of moisture on her forehead and upper lip.

'Perhaps you could get me a glass of water, darling. Three flights of stairs is ridiculous.' She embraced her daughter briefly. 'I'll never understand why you stay in this flat. I could help you find something much more suitable, if you set aside a few days to—'

'Not now, Mother, please. I don't want to talk about flats right now.'

'Of course you don't. How silly of me.' Marina sat down and closed her eyes for a moment. 'I want to hear everything, and I want to see your forehead. Then we'll decide what to do. Why don't we have some coffee, and then you can tell me exactly what happened and how you feel now.'

With reluctance Camilla began to describe the nightmare at Langani. She could see no way out, although she feared that each word would bring out Marina's inevitable anger at the idea of a visit to the van der Beers' farm. She chose her words carefully, speaking slowly and pressing the palms of her hands together to keep them from trembling. A surprising sense of relief surged through her as she recounted the incident aloud for the first time. In describing those hideous hours she began to define within herself what she felt about them, and how she might come to terms with the churning, relentless tumult of shock and anxiety that had become a part of her. Sleep had proved impossible without the little pills. Each time she closed her eyes, she could see the man standing in front of her and the panga rushing towards her face. In the dark every small sound pierced her consciousness, bringing her to a state of fearful alert. Several times, as she described the ordeal to Marina, she put her hand up to her face, feeling again the warm trickle of blood that had blinded her and filled her with sickening panic. Perhaps this telling of the nightmare would be cathartic, and would free her of the awful visions that leapt into her mind whenever she closed her eyes.

'But what about your forehead?' Marina said. 'Would it not have been wiser to wait, and have it seen to here?'

'The doctor in Nanyuki said he'd have to stitch me right away, otherwise the cut would never close properly. He explained that it would all have to be taken care of again, in Nairobi or London or somewhere. He was very kind, and he gave me painkillers and tranquillisers.'

'Oh God, darling.' Marina was crying. 'You were so brave.'

'Everyone was. Sarah and I flew back on the same plane last night. She offered to stay, but I told her to go on to Ireland. I just wanted to sleep, you know. But it's hard, because I'm still so nervous.'

'And the men who attacked you?' Marina asked. 'Does anyone know who they were?'

'No, not yet. The investigation has only just started, so there was nothing to report when I left.' She stopped, drained from the telling of the story, frightened by the vivid images that had flashed through her mind as she was talking.

'The only thing that really matters is that you're safe.' Marina's hands were shaky as she put down her coffee cup. 'It could have been a terrible, unbearable tragedy for us all. Now, I know someone who will deal with this beautifully. His name is Edward Carradine. He's perfectly marvellous. He looks after some of my friends, actually. I've met him several times myself but that was in Nairobi, strangely enough. He goes abroad to these hopeless places several times a year, and operates free of charge in cases where there's someone who has been badly burned, or is the victim of an accident. Or some poor creature with a dreadful birth defect. He even brings people to London for treatment. Quite remarkable, really.'

'I have his number already.' Camilla produced the scrawled note from her pocket. 'Tom Bartlett gave it to me.'

'Your agent? When?'

'I went to see him this morning. To tell him I couldn't go to New York. He said Mr Carradine was the man for me.'

'I can't believe you've been trailing around London after such a traumatic experience and that impossible, overnight plane journey.' Marina sounded peeved. 'Tom Bartlett may be important in your work, but I'm sure you could have made your explanations on the telephone. Really, darling, your sense of priorities is simply not—'

'Don't, Mother. I can't cope with a lecture just now. I need some rest. But if you know this doctor maybe you could arrange the appointment for me. I'm too tired to explain the whole thing on the phone to some faceless, snotty receptionist. Where's Daddy, by the way? I rang, but there was no reply.'

'He's in Holland, talking to Prince Bernhard about lions or tigers, or something wild. It's an important meeting. He'll be back tomorrow or Saturday. I didn't tell him about the robbery when he telephoned this morning, because there didn't seem to be any point in his rushing back early. For the moment, I'm afraid you'll have to make do with me.' Marina's expression was sad. 'Let's turn down your bed so you can sleep for a while, and I'll make the appointment with Edward.'

'Was that where you'd been in Harley Street, just before I left for Nairobi?' Camilla asked. 'You're not going to have a facelift, are you? It's not necessary, and you're too young to even think about such a thing.'

'How sweet. No, I wasn't contemplating a facelift. Actually, I hadn't been feeling very well, so I went for a few tests.'

'What sort of tests?'

'I just wanted to see if I was anaemic, because I'd been rather tired. It's all under control now. And the cottage is an ideal place to rest. I adore all that fresh air and quiet.'

'That's new for you.'

'Perhaps I'm becoming mellow,' Marina seemed pleased with this idea. 'Or lazy even, in my old age.'

'I'd hardly describe forty-three as old age.'

'I suppose not. Once upon a time I thought forty was unimaginably ancient. Now I'll be delighted if I'm still around at fifty. Let's look at your forehead.'

In the bathroom Camilla peeled off the dressing to expose the ugly mark. The black stitches ran the whole way across her forehead at a slight angle, dipping down into a small hook on the right-hand side, above her eyebrow. Marina's horrified expression was reflected in the mirror, and suddenly Camilla was convinced that she would never work as a model again. She saw her future evaporate, leaving her washed-up and unwanted without the beauty she had always taken for granted. Her mouth twisted and tears blurred her vision.

'Let's put this neatly back in place,' Marina said, and Camilla allowed herself to be led back to the bedroom where her mother applied a new dressing.

'What on earth are all these beaded things on your bed?' Marina asked. 'They smell quite dreadful.'

'I bought them in a Samburu *manyatta*. I thought I'd try to design some clothes and use them as decoration. Jackets or skirts in suede, with beaded collars and sleeves, or hems. Traditional African beading with expert European finishing.' Camilla hesitated. 'I thought I could even open a small workshop in Kenya. At Langani, perhaps. I could do it with Hannah. I'm sure I could sell things like that to boutiques here and in Paris and I have ideal connections.'

'But you wouldn't think of returning to Kenya, Camilla.' Marina was appalled. 'Not after what has happened. It would be madness to go back there.'

'It was a terrible thing, Mother, and very frightening. But it was an isolated incident. There's just as much violent crime in the East End of London as there is in Nairobi.'

'Yes, but we don't go to the East End of London, Camilla.' Marina's eyes were wide with alarm, but she did not want an argument at this moment. She tried a conciliatory tone. 'Let's discuss this later, darling. What you need to do now is get some sleep, and then we'll go out for tea or an early supper. Depending on the time and how you feel.'

Marina bent over the bed and kissed her daughter, stroking her hair, an odd expression on her face. There was something unfamiliar about her, an unknown element that puzzled Camilla. But she was too tired to think about it so she lay back and closed her eyes, grateful that she was not alone. On the edge of sleep, she realised that Marina had not reprimanded her for visiting Langani, nor had there been any disparaging mention of Sarah, or even the van der Beers. As she sank into an uneasy sleep she felt relief for her mother's uncommon restraint. Marina was in the sitting room, reading a magazine, when Camilla woke up. They had dinner in a local restaurant and then returned to the flat.

'I'm going to sleep here,' Marina announced. 'You'll have to lend me some night things, but I'm staying here because I don't think you should be on your own.'

To avoid any discussion on the subject of Kenya, Camilla turned on the television and they sat on the sofa in companionable silence, sharing a pot of tea and watching the portly, authoritative figure of Richard Dimbleby putting the world to rights.

The painted doors of Harley Street, with their discreet brass plates, seemed forbidding in the mid-morning drizzle. Edward Carradine's waiting room was expensively furnished, formal, and much too hot. Camilla focused on the headlines of the day's newspapers, avoiding direct eye contact with a middle-aged couple who had looked at her when she entered the room, and then whispered to one another. She did not want to be recognised, remarked upon. This was the private part of her life, and they had no right to encroach on any aspect of it. It angered her, illogically, that the well-groomed woman should be sitting there with her husband, holding his hand, anticipating that some notion of eternal youth would soon become a reality. The man should still love her, Camilla thought, even if her face was lined and her chin had begun to sag a little. He was probably having an affair with his secretary, and had come with his wife to ease his conscience. A facelift would be unlikely to help. They looked sad, both of them, as if they knew the whole exercise was a charade. A clock on the mantelpiece ticked loudly, and Camilla felt it was carrying her away from the life in London that she had so carelessly accepted as her right. Her apprehension grew as the minutes passed, and then the door of the consulting room opened and a teenage boy stepped out. His face was hideously scarred, the skin blotched purple and red, and covered in welts that ran like ridges across one of his cheeks. His smile was a lopsided grimace.

'He's doing very well.' Edward Carradine's voice was soothing, a professional tone that he must have used a million times to instil confidence. He placed his arm around the woman, and shook her husband by the hand. 'Don't worry, Mrs Bryson. Your boy is going to be just fine. He's healing up nicely. No infection, and the swelling is going down.' He turned to the boy. 'I'll see you next month, James. And it's only a short while now before we start planning the final surgery. After that you'll be looking pretty good.'

Camilla felt shame and pity as she caught the mother's expression. She looked away quickly, not wanting to intrude on their moment of hope and gratitude. The doctor walked across the room and greeted Marina with affection, his hand resting on her shoulder.

'Marina. How are you? London becomes you. Camilla, I'm sorry we aren't meeting in better circumstances. I'm Edward Carradine, I'm going to do my best to repair the injury to your face. Would you like to come in?'

She lay on the high, stiff couch, holding her breath as he bent to examine her forehead. He did not make any comment as he looked at the long scar through a magnifying glass, lightly pressing the surrounding skin.

'Open your eyes now. Look at me. Follow my finger – look up, down, side to side.' He leaned in close to her and tilted her chin up so that her face was in the full beam of his lamp. Then he touched her hand and she felt a sense of shelter, an unspoken promise that made her feel safe in a simplistic way. 'Come and sit down with your mother and me. It's more comfortable for us to talk over there. Would you like tea or coffee?'

'This may sound ridiculous, heartless almost,' he said when they were settled, 'but you've been lucky. The panga must have been sharp, so the skin is not badly hacked about. Jagged, I mean.' He held a mirror up as he spoke. 'The wound is deep and quite long, but it's a relatively straight line running across your forehead, except for this little tail at the end here. You were indeed fortunate that it didn't dip down into your eyebrow and more importantly, of course, your eye. It's the only spot that requires very great precision on my part. The doctor in Kenya did a good job, and he was quite right to stitch you up immediately. The skin has begun to heal, without leaving a wide gap. That's vital for minimum scarring.'

'I will have a scar then?' Camilla's mouth was dry. 'How bad will it be? Can something be done to hide it altogether? Not right away, I suppose, but eventually.'

He began to explain to her the process of healing and concealing, the necessity to wait for the wound to close completely, to mature, before any surgery could be carried out. There would be a period of three or four weeks before the superficial crust disappeared. Camilla's stomach heaved as she heard the word 'crust' applied to the skin on her face. It was vital to see how the closed wound would look, and he asked to see any other marks she might have on her body, in order to gauge the healing ability of her skin. He would excise the scar when the time was right, he said, sewing the skin of her forehead together in a straight line and closing it with very fine sutures that would not show. It would be several months before the new line began to fade, but after the first few weeks she could use make-up to conceal it. His words were breaking up in her mind like the crackling and fading of radio waves in a far-off place, and she felt faint with despair as she tried to imagine herself disfigured for months, or maybe years. She looked down at the carpet, trying to conceal her fear, unable to consider herself from this new perspective.

'Your skin is young and elastic,' Carradine was saying. 'If you look after yourself while the incision heals and closes, then I'm sure we will have good results. You need to pay close attention to your skin care, but in your profession that's essential anyway. You'll need rest. Perhaps you should go down to the country with your mother. Take advantage of the fresh air. She told me on the phone that she has a perfect little cottage in the Cotswolds. Now, let's put a more discreet dressing on this.'

He stood up and from her place on the sofa Camilla noticed how tall he was. He moved with energy and purpose. His clothes looked Italian and expensive, and his shoes were handmade, tasselled and highly polished. When he had finished he came to sit in an armchair opposite her, holding out the mirror for her to use.

'The only real problem we have to consider is the tail of the scar which does not run with the natural lines of your forehead,' he said. 'For the straight part of the line there is a new treatment I've been using when an injury leaves a welt along the edges, where it's been stitched. It's a little like sandpapering away the raised section of the skin, like smoothing a beautiful sculpture. I'm not sure yet whether that would be right in your case. We'll have to wait a little while before making a decision.'

'How long?' Marina spoke for the first time.

'I think two or three months. In the meantime, Camilla, you must take every precaution with your skin. No direct, harsh sunlight, no smoking because it constricts the blood vessels and may affect healing. Very little alcohol for similar reasons. We need to discuss what sort of cosmetics you can or cannot use. And I must emphasise that you need plenty of rest. But I'm confident we'll have a very good result.'

'I'm a model. I have all kinds of commitments. I was due in New York this week for a magazine feature.' Camilla was beginning to lose her self-possession.

'Yes. Tom Bartlett telephoned me yesterday. Just before I heard from your mother.'

'Isn't there a make-up that will hide the scar while it's healing? Otherwise, what you're telling me is that I can't work at all for months. And that's impossible.'

'Darling, you have to think of your health now,' Marina said. 'You have to be patient if Edward is going to get the best results for you. It won't matter that you can't—'

'Of course it will matter!' The words ricocheted in the quiet of the room. 'My face is ruined and one photographer has already turfed me out of his studio. Don't tell me it doesn't matter. God Almighty, Mother, what do you think this is all about? Where am I supposed to go from here? My face is ruined, I can't work, I can't get dressed and go out like an ordinary human being because I look like nothing on earth. I can't sleep, I can't get rid of the dreams, the images, even the sound of their voices. And you sit there and tell me it doesn't matter.'

Camilla's brain was spiralling away from the polite, clinical discussion. Disaster had overtaken her with a stealth and speed that she could not grasp. Her success in the fashion world had been immediate, and she had become accustomed to being admired and fêted. But on this grim morning she realised that her career could now be at an end, that her fame and popularity were indeed transitory. The defences she had built around herself had been paper-thin, mere self-delusion. The man she loved was thousands of miles away and he did not know, and probably would not concern himself with what had happened to her. She wondered if she could get a prescription for more tranquillisers, but she did not want to ask with Marina listening. Never mind. Most of her friends could get their hands on anything. Hash, dope, uppers and downers. In the meantime she needed a drink and a cigarette, and above all she wanted to escape from this suffocating room.

'I'm sorry,' she said. 'It's been a shock, this whole thing. I suppose I'm more strung up than I imagined.'

'I wonder if I could recommend something to help you sleep? You know, it's not just your body that has been injured.' Carradine was solicitous and measured. He reached into his desk and took out a piece of paper on which he wrote a prescription. 'You have suffered a severe trauma, and it will take time before the scars in your memory begin to heal. I'd like to see you again in about ten days. Then I will take those stitches out, and we can discuss our plan of action. In the meantime, you should talk about what happened to you – to your mother, to your best friend, to your boyfriend. Whoever you trust and love a great deal. That will make the most difference.'

She left the consulting rooms like a sleepwalker, following Marina to the corner of the street, climbing into a taxi and slumping back in the seat with her eyes closed. They stopped at a chemist and picked up the prescription. At the flat Marina sat down with her daughter and took her hand.

'Darling, it's going to be all right. The time will go quicker than you think. Edward was so positive. He wouldn't give you an opinion that was false in any way.'

'I know. I'm sure he's just as wonderful as you say. And when I've thought it all over I'll be very glad that he's going to take care of me. I'm grateful for everything, Mother. I really am.'

'Would you like to do something relaxing this afternoon? Take your mind off all this and escape for a few hours? We could go to a film, somewhere comfortable like the Curzon.'

'No. I think I'd just like to read a book, have a long bath, go to bed early. And I'll be able to sleep with these pills, if your doctor friend is right. I've got to spend a night on my own, Mother. I need to do it and I'll be fine.' She was too weary to press the point further and relieved when Marina rose and kissed her.

'All right, darling. I'll let myself out. Bye.'

Camilla made her way into the bedroom before Marina could change her mind. She stood looking out of the window, overwhelmed by a presentiment of loss, knowing that she was not really ready to be alone. Marina had reached the front door when the telephone rang, and she turned back to answer it.

'It's Sarah Mackay,' she said as Camilla emerged from the bedroom. 'Here's the phone, darling, but don't talk for long. I'll see you tomorrow.'

Camilla described the doctor's appointment, and the slow process that lay ahead.

'What about your father?' Sarah asked. 'He'll help you through all this.'

'He's been away. Back tonight or tomorrow,' Camilla replied. 'But Mother has been here. Sensible and calm, and no recriminations for once. Not yet, anyway.'

'I'm so glad I've talked to you. Hannah tried earlier, but I suppose you were with the doctor. Lars is doing well and should be home in two weeks.' Sarah hesitated, wondering whether Marina might be within earshot. 'Would you like to come over here for a while? Mum and Dad would love to lavish care on you. Smother you, in fact.'

'I have to get my stitches out next week. Don't worry about me. Daddy should be here for the weekend, and I'll be fine.' Camilla hesitated. 'Is it hard to get the whole thing out of your head?'

'I'll never get it out of my head. I thought they'd killed Piet. Then I was so frightened for you and for Lars. And I keep thinking of Hannah, still on the farm, with these maniacs roaming around loose, her cattle dead, and the dogs poisoned, and Lars so badly hurt. They're under siege at Langani, and it's hard to think of anything else.'

'But you're still going back.'

'I'm going, yes. Would you?'

'If he asked me, I'd leave first thing in the morning. But he hasn't. Probably he's still out in the *bundu*. Maybe he hasn't even heard yet.'

'Hannah says he's in camp somewhere, as far as possible from human contact. He probably hasn't checked in anywhere yet, because the clients only arrived a couple of days ago. He likes to keep them in his private wilderness for as long as possible.'

'I'd be on the next plane if he wanted me,' Camilla's voice was breaking. She did not see Marina, frozen with horror, standing in the small entrance hall. 'And maybe that would be the best way of banishing the horror of it, and going on. Like getting up on a horse or a bicycle the minute you fall off. I have another idea, too. It's something I could do with Hannah. I'll tell you about it when I've thought it through properly. What's your news. How is Raphael? How did they take your decision to go back?'

'They hit the roof. But they had some dramatic news of their own. And so did Tim,' Sarah said.

'What's happened?' As she asked the question, Camilla heard a noise in the hall. 'Hold on. It sounds like there's someone at the door.'

'Look, I'll write tomorrow and tell you everything,' Sarah said. 'And I'll phone again next week. Are you sure you're – well, you know – that you can manage all this?'

'I'm fine. Talk to you soon.'

Camilla put the telephone down and went to the front door. She opened it and glanced along the corridor, but there was no one there and she wondered if she had begun to imagine things.

She slept late and could not remember her dreams, so that when she opened her eyes she felt light with relief. It was Friday and her father would surely be home tonight or tomorrow. There were eggs and bacon in the fridge, and she thought of Marina as she made herself breakfast. Outside she could hear the familiar screech of buses pulling up short on the Brompton Road, and the sound of sweeping as a gardener raked early-autumn leaves from the garden square below her window. She stirred cream into her coffee and leafed through a new copy of *Vogue*. But the sight of her own face, perfect and unblemished, ate into her resolve and diluted her new-found courage. She put the magazine aside and turned on the radio. Why did anyone listen to *The Archers* anyway? But the sound of the familiar country voices was comforting, and she wrapped her dressing gown around her and lay on the sofa, happy to be in her own secure space, in a place where she felt at ease once more. She had survived a night on her own, had begun the return to normal. She would take it slowly as Mr

Carradine had advised. After an hour she dressed and pulled a wool hat from Biba over her forehead. She was hunting for her keys when she heard the telephone.

'Camilla, are you all right?' She felt as though she was floating as she took in the sound of his voice. 'Jesus, I just heard this morning when I took my clients in to Keekorok Lodge for lunch. I wish I'd still been there with all of you, that I'd been able to help. Killed the bastards if possible. Tell me you're all right.'

'I am all right. I have a plastic surgeon who says I'm going to look like new. I'm so glad to hear from you.' Her heart was pounding, her blood racing through her and making her dizzy. She tried to remain coherent, waited for him to say that he would fly to London the moment his safari was finished.

'I've been in camp since you left. The manager here told me the news, and I managed to get Langani and talk to Hannah. Look, I'll be back in Nairobi in three weeks. Then we'll talk more.'

'Do you still plan to be here in November?' She needed reassurance so badly. 'I'd really like that – the best medicine I can imagine.'

'Well, I hope so. I haven't worked out exact dates, but I'll let you know when I can.'

'Oh. That's fine, then.' Her delight at the first sound of his voice was now polluted by doubt. 'Bye, then. Hugs and kisses.' She did her best to sound casual.

'Kiss for you too. Salaams.'

Camilla's eyes clouded with disappointment and fading hope. There was something evasive in his voice and she was afraid he would never change, never be hers. She decided to telephone Hannah and dialled the international operator. The number was engaged, but she kept trying, desperate for a connection. After two hours she got through.

'I'm really glad to hear from you,' Hannah's sigh of relief was clearly audible on the phone. 'We've been so worried. I phoned twice yesterday, but there was no answer.'

'How are you managing at Langani – how is it, being back there? Have the police come up with anything? What about Lars?'

But there was very little news from the farm and no progress with the investigation. Lars would be out of hospital soon, and he was planning to spend a few days on his uncle's coffee farm before returning to Langani.

Obviously Hannah missed him. Piet was working like a madman, and they really meant to open the lodge early in the new year. They were determined to go on, to fight their corner.

When Camilla hung up she felt isolated, caught in a web, trapped a million miles from where she wanted to be. Marina rang and tried to persuade her to come to Burford for the weekend. But Camilla wanted space, time to savour the too-brief moments of Anthony's voice on the line.

'Maybe next weekend, Mother,' she said. 'I'd like to stay here and just be quiet. I feel much better today, and that's what I'd like to do.'

Later in the afternoon she left the flat, walking quickly out of the square into the maelstrom of Knightsbridge traffic. At Vidal Sassoon she had her hair cut straight and precise across her forehead, with the back very short to emphasise the length of her neck and the shape of her head.

'Looks good. I've been telling you for months you should cut it, and now you can see I was right. I'm sorry it took such rotten bad luck to bring you round to doing it. Look here at the back.' Sassoon held up a mirror. 'It's like a golden cap, cut close like that. Even with the problem of your forehead you look beautiful this very moment. Like an elf, you are. Not like Veronica Lake or some forties film star any more, with the long hair. You're a new person.'

Camilla paid the bill and thought of asking if she could use the telephone, but the desk was busy and she decided to take a chance. It was almost dark, and if her father was at home they could spend the evening together. Otherwise she would go to a film. She was not ready to see anyone else. In the street outside her parents' flat she saw that George's ancient car was parked under a tree, and she was filled with pleasure and anticipation. He had probably been trying to telephone her since he got in from Amsterdam, and he must be worried. Marina would have left him a note. Her set of keys was at the bottom of her handbag, and she fished for them impatiently. There was no sign of anyone in the sitting room, but she could hear her father's voice. He must be on the telephone. She made her way along the hall and tapped lightly on the bedroom door that was slightly ajar. George Broughton-Smith turned in surprise. He was wearing a silk dressing gown that was hanging open. His suit had been flung over a chair and his shirt and underwear lay scattered across the carpet. His expression was startled and then stricken as he spun round to stare at his daughter. She looked at him for a moment, eyes questioning, locked on to his face as she attempted to read the message he was trying to convey. Then she glanced around the bedroom. Lying on her father's bed was a young man, blond and good-looking. His eyes were glued to her, flashing signals of alarm and regret as he reached for the sheet to cover his naked body.

Chapter 16

Dublin, September 1965

Raphael was at the airport to meet her, his face creasing with joy as Sarah came through the barrier.

'Thank God you're safely back,' he said, his arms tightly around her. 'I don't mind telling you that your mother and I have been in a state of shock, ever since you phoned from Nairobi. How's the young man who was shot? What about Camilla?'

'I think Lars is going to be fine,' Sarah said. 'But Camilla will have to see a plastic surgeon. We'll know in a day or two.' She put her arms around both her parents, glad to be safe in their company. 'So, what are we doing now?' she asked.

She looked at her mother. Betty's lips were pressed together, to prevent an outpouring of relief. They linked arms as they walked to the car.

'We have quite a surprise for you,' Raphael said. 'We've taken back Grandpa's house in Sligo. The tenants are gone, and we're going to use it ourselves. We moved in a week ago.'

'That sounds wonderful! I love that old place, and the beach and the dunes. But what will you do with it when you go back to Kenya?'

Betty stopped walking and turned to face her daughter. 'We're not going back, Sarah. Dad and I have decided to stay in Ireland. It's a shock, I know, but we'll explain it on the way down to Sligo.'

It was impossible to take it in. Sarah sat in the back of the car, the true implications of the news preventing her from sharing her parents' optimism. She thought of the house in Mombasa, of the palm trees, and the smell and the sound of the tropical sea, and she could not accept what they were trying to tell her.

'I don't get it,' she said, when they stopped for lunch at a country hotel. 'Why are you going to abandon everything in Kenya, where you're really needed? It's our home. The place you've always loved, we've all loved. And if you have to move upcountry, there's so much you could do, Dad. But instead you're going to fix up a crumbling pile in the back of beyond, in the rain and the cold, and take on the kind of work you haven't done for years!' The whole scheme seemed to her sudden and ill-conceived. She could not imagine her parents living in this miserable country from which she herself had only longed to escape.

'I always had it in the back of my mind to retire here. It's a bit earlier than I had planned, that's all.' Raphael stopped to tamp his pipe and there was a moment's hesitation before he began to speak again. 'Kenya's a different place now, and I can't live at the coast any more, because of the risk of malaria. Going back would mean starting all over again. Different surroundings, new hospital, new friends and colleagues, no sea or boat for the weekends. If I have to do that at my age, I'd be better off in Ireland.'

'Oh come on, Dad, you're talking like an old man! You've years to go, no matter what you decide to do, or where.'

'Yes, I have a good few years in me yet, I hope. But there's another aspect to this,' he said. 'Your brother has finished his time as a houseman, and he's willing to join me in Sligo. We're going to take over a practice from old Dr Macnamara who's retiring. Tim and I will work together. It's good timing, and it will be a help to me to have him as a partner.'

Sarah opened the back door of the car and slid into the seat, wrapping her jacket around her as though to ward off any further revelations. 'I knew there must be something else behind this,' she said. 'What we're talking about is setting Tim up. Isn't that what it's really all about?'

'No, it certainly is not about Tim,' Betty said defensively. 'In fact, he'd probably do better going to a big hospital in England, working towards a specialty. This way he'll have a ready-made practice, it's true. But he'll be there to give Dad a hand. Don't be jumping to wild conclusions, Sarah. Your father's health is the most important thing. If we stay on in Kenya for another five or ten years, it will be too late to make a major change before he has to retire altogether. This is a good time for him to make a new beginning. You've always loved the house, although you haven't been there since Grandpa died. I think you'll see immediately why it's the perfect place for us all. There's a huge amount to do, but we've already made some of the rooms comfortable, while the builders are at work.'

Sarah backed away from any further discussion on the last part of the journey. She did not want to spoil their reunion, and she felt guilty that she would soon be returning to Kenya, while her parents had been forced to leave that part of their lives behind.

The old house was several miles outside the town of Sligo, and overlooked Donegal Bay. A sweep of lawn led down to a long white strand and the dunes of Streedagh. Behind them loomed the massive bulk of Ben Bulben, flat-topped, with its summit jutting out towards the sea like the prow of a great ship. Betty had inherited the large, ramshackle house in Sligo when her father died. It was a fine Georgian building with extensive grounds and a stable yard, but inside it was damp and had been neglected over the years by uncaring tenants. Now it would become the base for a whole new life. Sarah was astounded by the suddenness of her parents' decision, and deeply hurt that they had not waited to discuss it with her. During the brief period that she had been away, Raphael had terminated his overseas contract on the grounds of ill health, accepted a golden handshake and made up his mind to go into general practice in Ireland. Or had his mind made up for him.

Sarah finally revealed her own plans four days after her arrival. She had spent a long day in Dublin discussing her future at the university, and putting her case to the dean for a delay in starting her masters degree. It had not been easy.

'I've found a job in Kenya,' she told her parents. 'I'll be working on an elephant research project, based up around Buffalo Springs. Dan and Allie Briggs are the people running the programme, and they're willing to take me on as an assistant. I can live in their camp, and they'll provide meals and transport, and a small salary. I'm going back to live there. In a few weeks.'

'You can't be serious!' Betty was aghast.

Raphael shifted his position on the sofa and cleared his throat noisily, a familiar sign that he was uncomfortable, or trying to avoid a confrontation. He concentrated furiously on filling his pipe, and remained silent.

'I'm deadly serious.' Sarah regarded her parents with defiance, her chin set aggressively. 'The raid was an isolated incident. It's not something that happens every day. There are more robberies around Dublin these day than there are in Kenya. In any case, I won't be living in Nairobi or Langani. I'll be out in the *bundu* studying elephants as a penniless research student. No one would want to attack me.' She did not admit that she was constantly reliving the images of that awful night at Langani. Even in Ireland, the dark was no longer a friendly place.

'I can't understand why you wouldn't finish your studies here first.' Betty stood up and began to pace, plainly agitated in the face of her daughter's determination. 'You did splendidly in your exams and you have an offer from the university that most students would eat their hats for. You'd be mad to turn this down, Sarah, with your ability. It's such a waste. It's not like you at all.'

'It's no stranger than your decision to stay on here. And I haven't said I'll never go back to college. I've just asked for a leave of absence for a year or so, to get some fieldwork under my belt. In fact, the dean was quite encouraging yesterday, once he had read the material I brought with me. A copy of the study Dan and Allie Briggs are doing.' She knew this was less than truthful. It had been a stormy meeting, and she had had to fight hard for acceptance of her decision to take time out when her studies were going so well.

'But surely you could do this kind of fieldwork during university holidays, rather than break up your studies for one opportunity. There'll be others like it, after you're qualified. Better ones, even.' Betty was finding it increasingly difficult to keep her temper.

'This isn't a childish whim. I've got the most amazing job offer from two well-respected scientists. They're funded by donations from a major American university, and a grant from *National Geographic*, and there's a chance of money from the Smithsonian Institute. They're up there with the Adamsons and Jane Goodall and Diane Fossey, and I can't think of anything more fantastic than being part of their elephant study. It's a chance in a million. For someone like me, who has no experience, it's the realisation of a dream.' She was using every argument she could muster, although she was fully aware that a further grant for the Briggses' study was not in the bag, and she could be without a job within a few months.

'But you haven't even got a work permit. And I'm sure you won't be able to live on the salary they're planning to pay you.' Betty adopted a more persuasive tone. 'I can see what a great opportunity it seems to be. But you must be practical as well, love.'

'What would I be earning if I was here in Dublin? Nothing at all. You'd still be supporting me. You know pay isn't the real issue, Mum. Anyway, I won't need money when I'm in the camp. I'll have a tent or something to sleep in, and all my food and transport. It's only if I go to Nairobi that I'll need to spend any cash, and I'm sure I'll be covered for some of that.'

'You have to think carefully about your security, Sarah. You've already had one bad experience.' Raphael was frowning. 'There's a problem in the northern area of Kenya where you'll be based, and it has nothing to do with one-off robberies. It's a more serious affair involving a war along the borders of Kenya and Somalia, and it won't be easily resolved. It's dangerous territory these days, the Northern Frontier District. A tent at Buffalo Springs will offer you precious little protection from heavily armed Somali bandits. Do these Briggs people have guards, or firearms of any kind?'

'I don't know, Dad. But firearms or the lack of them never influenced you, when you stayed on during the Mau Mau.'

'Oh, don't be so silly, Sarah. That was quite different,' Betty snapped. 'In those days we had the British Army and the police to protect us, and Kenya was a colony under British law. In any case the Mau Mau never really took hold in the coastal area. There's no comparison at all.'

'Would you not think of waiting one more year?' Raphael asked, but with resignation in his voice. 'It's a very short time in the scheme of things, and I think you might regret a hasty decision in years to come. I mean, in terms of your future career—'

'I know exactly how I want to manage my future career. Look, let's not have a row over this. Please. I'm going back to Kenya to start on this research project. They need someone now. If I wait a year, the job will have gone. Right now there aren't that many people like me around – familiar with Kenya, able to speak Swahili, and with a degree in zoology. Allie Briggs also said my photographic ability would be very useful, so that's great for me too. Imagine if I was lucky enough for *National Geographic* to notice my photographs. It's an outside chance, but it's there.'

Sarah walked over to her mother and hugged her. 'I love you, Mum. I don't want to do anything to upset you and Dad. But this is an opportunity I'll never have again. Please, say you're glad for me.'

'I still can't believe you went off and arranged all this without saying a word to us.' Betty glanced at her husband hoping for his support, but he was saying nothing. She began again, a hint of desperation in her voice. 'I know how difficult you found these last three years. But Dad and I will be in Ireland now. And there's the house here to get ready, and the surgery. It's a big commitment. I thought we'd all be in it together. I imagined you here with us, during your holidays. It's a great part of the world, wild and beautiful, and it will be our home as well as your father's new workplace.'

'I know it will. But I've got to go back,' Sarah insisted. 'Everything I ever wanted is there.'

'Sarah?' Betty looked her daughter straight in the eye. 'I hope this isn't about Piet van der Beer. You know, if a man wants you, he'll come looking for you himself. He won't be pleased if you throw yourself at him, no matter how much you love him. It will only put him off, and that's the plain truth.'

'I'm not going back because of him.' Sarah was almost shouting. 'It's been my dream to do conservation work in Kenya. It's not some hare-brained scheme I came up with overnight. I do admire Piet, yes. And Hannah's been my best friend for years. This is about a fantastic job offer. I don't think you're being fair.'

'We only want to be sure that your youth and your zeal don't make you drop everything you've worked for at university, in favour of one of your crusades,' Raphael said, trying to placate her. 'Devil's advocates, if you like, putting the opposition's case for your protection. You're a chronic optimist and a romantic, love, and one more year of study would give you a far better qualification. Then you'd go back to Kenya with the chance of a well-paid job and the long-term security of your master's degree.'

Since she was desperate for their blessing, if not their approval, Sarah could not afford to be critical of her parents' decision on their own future. She looked at her father, but found that she had to turn away. He was very thin and his skin was still yellowed from the effects of the anti-malarial drugs that had saved his life. She had never imagined that he would age one day, and become frail. It had to have been a painful decision to leave Africa, to come back to Ireland for good. She wished she had been there when they had made up their minds. There were plenty of districts in Kenya where he could have gone on working, whole regions that were virtually malaria-free, and many places desperately needing his experience. But Sarah saw the fear in her mother, her outright refusal to put Raphael at the least risk. For the first time in her life she was surprised to find that she felt protective rather than protected. It was different for

Tim. He was young and fit and he could start anywhere, change his mind, move on at a later date.

She turned her attention to the fire, poking through the logs. Was it wrong to walk away when they needed her most? But it was impossible to stay. She had found a means to return to her true home, to a country where she could give something worthwhile to the land and the people, where she could make a difference. If she was honest, then yes, there was truth in what her mother had said about Piet. She had ridden out across the plains with him, seen his wildlife reserve and the lodge taking shape. They had sat together on the rocks in the pink dusk, watching the elephants come down to drink at the river. With Piet she had come alive again and, yes, she was willing to place herself in his path, and simply hope. Piet was her mainspring. She wanted to be close to him, even if he couldn't or wouldn't love her. Raphael was giving her one of his shrewd, diagnostic looks and she reddened, as she always did, when he caught her out.

'Well, since we can't talk you out of this, my dear, we should be proud of the fact that we have a daughter with so much courage and imagination.' Raphael placed a comforting hand on her head, as he had done so often during her childhood. 'She's right, Betty love,' he said. 'We can't live her life for her, and we mustn't ask her to live ours. She'll be twenty-one in a couple of weeks, old enough to make her own decisions. And it's no bad thing to follow your dreams.'

Sarah stared at him in surprise and then flung her arms around him. Raphael's eyes were bright with affection and amusement as he turned to his wife. 'Ah, come now, Betty. Give the girl a hug too. You must admit she has enterprise, even if she is a bit impetuous.'

'She always could wind you round her little finger,' Betty said. 'I'm not convinced, but what do I know?' She folded Sarah in her arms. 'Just be careful. Don't take chances, please. This is not the same country you're going back to. It's a place of great change and turmoil, with the safety nets all gone. You had a terrible experience at Langani, and you were lucky that there wasn't any loss of life.'

'I'll be very careful, Mum, I promise you.' Her joy and eagerness were childlike, as opposition to her plan dissolved. 'I'm so, so happy. So thrilled. And I know this is right. Just wait till Tim hears—'

'That should be interesting, all right,' Raphael chuckled. 'And he may surprise you with some news of his own.'

Tim. Sarah felt a twitch of nerves as she prepared to share her news with him. She suspected that he would not be impressed, and she was right.

'You're a fool,' he said immediately. 'And selfish with it. Can't you see how hard it's going to be for them? Mum particularly. She needs all the help she can get, and I know she's been relying on the fact that you'd be here during your holidays, and at weekends now and again. And I worry about Dad – whether he'll be fit enough to take over a general practice, with the long hours, and night calls. Even though I'll be there to help him.'

'But he's recovered,' Sarah said. 'He told me he's fine now.'

Tim shook his head. 'The malaria took a terrible toll on his general health. Frequent bouts can cause strain on the heart. You must have noticed. He's breathless, he tires easily, and his blood pressure is high.'

'Dad has a heart problem?'

'I can't say that for certain. But I think you should have stayed on, to give them a hand, at least for the first year.'

'There will never be a right time to leave home, to begin living my own life,' she said sadly. 'If I stay for a year, it will be even harder to go. And I might never find another research job half as good as this.'

'But can you not see how much this move will change everything?' He pressed her. 'You'll have a home within reasonable distance of Dublin, and the place is beautiful, with the sea and that long strand. It's a magnificent spot.'

'You love Ireland, Tim,' she said. 'It's lucky that Dad's golden handshake made it possible for him to set up here, and it's wonderful that you'll be working together. But I've found what I want too, and I have to get on with it.' She reached out a hand, seeking his acceptance and understanding.

'You need your head examined!' He turned away and poured himself some tea, glancing back to offer her a cup. Her face was stricken with hurt and disappointment and he regretted his harsh words.

'Look, I'm sorry, Sarah. But this is pretty sudden. You go swanning off to Kenya for a holiday, and in no time you're back to tell us you're dropping out of college and going to live in the bush with people you don't even know. More to the point, you could have been killed last week. How do you expect me to react? You did brilliantly in your exams. We're so proud of you. You've had your photographs exhibited in a Dublin gallery, and they're splendid. You could build on that if you were here, make a good bit of money taking pictures for newspapers and magazines.'

'I can do that equally well in Kenya, too.'

'Ah, come on. It's not the pictures. I'm anxious for you to be safe. And you may think you've fooled Mum and Dad, but I can see how jumpy you are. You can't go through an experience like that, and not suffer from the repercussions. What happened at Langani is symptomatic of what Kenya has become. It's not the country it was during our childhood.'

'How the hell would you know how it is, or how it's going to be?' Sarah's patience was exhausted. 'You haven't set foot in Kenya for two years. And I wish Dad and Mum hadn't made all these decisions while I was away. I'll bet I could have persuaded them to go back. But it's turned out very handy for you, Tim. Dad comes over here ill, Mum's scared stiff, and suddenly they're moving to the middle of the Irish bogs, and you drop neatly into a job. They could have gone up to the Kenya highlands, and for years they would have enjoyed the same kind of life they've been used to.'

'What the hell are you saying?' Tim jumped up, knocking over the kitchen chair. 'You think I've taken advantage of Dad's illness in some way? Jaysus! You're a real monster, Sarah. I can't believe you'd think that. Get a hold of yourself, girl, before I turn around and walk out of here and never speak to you again.'

Anger yawed between them, creating a chasm that was difficult to bridge. Tim looked out of the window, stiff and fierce with indignation. Sarah sat down at the kitchen table and put her head in her hands. She was the first one to speak.

'I'm sorry. Of course that's not what I meant.' Her lips twisted in an attempt at a conciliatory smile. 'The words came out all wrong. I suppose I feel left out. You made so many important decisions while I was gone, and changed everything. And I thought you, of all people, would understand about my job. Finding the ideal thing, that you know was made for you.'

'I do. I would have liked——' Tim did not finish what he had been going to say. Instead, he came over to sit beside her, his anger gone. She looked at him intently.

'Do you really want to be in general practice, here, with Dad? You're not doing it to——'

'No. Of course not. And I don't grudge you your chance. I only want you to be happy and safe. You musn't be tempted to throw an important part of your life away on a pipe dream, or let yourself be hurt by—'

'Oh, for God's sake, Tim!' She ran her fingers through her mop of hair and thumped her fist on the table in frustration. 'I'm going back to Kenya because of the job. And I don't need another bloody lecture about Piet! Yes, I have very deep feelings for him that may or may not amount to anything. We don't necessarily get handed the easiest path to love or fulfilment. We have to take the opportunities that come around.'

'But your choice seems to have the cards stacked against you at every turn. Not only with regard to Piet.'

'Will you shut up about Piet? You've no business pronouncing on that subject.' He opened his mouth to protest, but she would not allow it. 'I wouldn't be raising objections if you asked the saintly Deirdre to come down here to join you.'

'As a matter of fact, I have asked her.' Tim glared at her. 'And if you hadn't been so totally wrapped up in your own bloody ambitions, I might have told you. Deirdre's a wonderful girl with a lot to offer. She's coming into the practice as our nurse. And as my fiancée.'

'Your what?' Sarah was incredulous. 'You've actually asked Deirdre to marry you?'

'I have. And she has accepted. And you needn't sound so surprised, for Chrissake. Now, it's your turn for congratulations.'

'Oh Tim!' Sarah looked at her brother, appalled by his choice, saddened because she had to search for something diplomatic to say. 'Look, don't jump down my throat if I say this, but do you really love her? Passionately, I mean? I know you admire her and she's a good person, but is that enough?' When he did not answer she moved closer to him. 'Dear God, there are so many changes in our lives. Everything is upside down. I love you, Tim. And Mum, and Dad. So if Deirdre is the one, then I'll love her too. And you'll be proud of what I'm going to do in Kenya, I promise you.'

She was crying, dreading being parted from her family, and fearful of the dangers and uncertainties that lay ahead.

'We'll be fine,' he said, putting his arms around her, passing her a clean handkerchief. 'And you'll see what a great person Deirdre is, when you get to know her. We have the same ideas, the same goals. I'm desperately fond of her.'

'She's a lucky girl, that's for sure,' Sarah said, but in her head there was still a reservation, a sense that her brother was making a mistake. He had talked of admiration, respect and fondness for Deirdre, but he had not said he loved her. 'I'm happy for you, Tim, I really am. And as for Piet, I've always loved him and that's something I can't alter. He may not feel the same way about me. Not yet. But that may change. When all's said and done, love is the only important thing, isn't it?'

'Now who's lecturing?' Tim said. But he was smiling, relieved that they could share their hopes no matter how different they might be.

On the same evening Sarah rang London. She was surprised when Marina answered the telephone. Camilla had obviously made peace with her mother, although she must be waiting anxiously for George to return from abroad. It was his love and support that she needed to see her through. There was no news from Camilla during the days that followed. When a week had passed Sarah picked up the phone and dialled London again, but no one picked up the receiver. She tried to banish a persistent sense of unease. A premonition.

'Try ringing the country place,' Betty suggested. 'I really feel for that poor girl. I'd like to see her here on Saturday evening, for your birthday celebration. She's part of the family, and she should be here. Keep trying, Sarah. Maybe you can persuade her.'

Marina answered the telephone in Burford, her voice cool. Camilla was away. She would not be in London or contactable for a while. She would pass on the message.

'Did you get her?' Betty asked. 'How is she?'

'I got Marina again,' Sarah replied, frowning. 'She said Camilla was away. Maybe she's gone somewhere with George, although Marina didn't mention him. I'm sure she'll ring when she gets back from wherever they are. Let's get back to work with all these pots of paint you have, littering up the place.'

Sarah's birthday dinner took place out on the dunes at Streedagh. She had not wanted an expensive dinner in a fancy restaurant, and she knew that every farthing counted in the setting up of her parents' new home and the surgery. Tim and Raphael built a bonfire, and they cooked wild salmon and baked potatoes in the embers. Several of the villagers from Grange joined them down on the beach, bringing fiddles, an accordion and a bauraun, and the music leapt up into the night sky with the flames and the notes of old songs. It was not until they returned to the house that Raphael brought out the gift-wrapped box, and they watched as Sarah opened it and took out the heavy body of the Hasselblad camera. She was so astounded by the magnitude of their gift that she could not speak, and she put her arms around each one of them in turn and hugged them with a fierce love and gratitude.

Two days later Deirdre came to join them. She had resigned from her nursing post in Dublin. In Sligo she worked tirelessly and with an efficiency that impressed them all. And she was kind. Her chief drawback was an irritating habit of dispensing unsolicited advice in her sing-song Cork accent. Sarah began to feel a grudging respect for her. She could see the bond of affection between Deirdre and Tim, but there was something lacking in their relationship. They were more like sister and brother, and Deirdre seemed reticent about setting a date for the wedding. Nevertheless, she was Tim's choice. Sarah was more concerned about her father, noticing how he would run out of steam without warning, his colour turning chalky and his breathing erratic. He assured her that he only needed rest. Betty was not so confident. Reluctantly, Sarah cabled Dan Briggs to ask for more time. She was relieved when the post office delivered the reply. It was kind and understanding, and gave her an extension, up to early November. She realised that she would be going back during the period of the short rains, when travel and work could be slow and difficult, but there was no alternative.

The budget for the house was tight, but they had all agreed on one extravagance and Raphael bought three horses. The house fronted on to the beach where Sarah could remember her childhood years, trekking out with Tim on their grandfather's ponies. It was he who had taught them to ride, the first time they came home on leave from Kenya. The low tide exposed a long sand spit, and it was an ideal place to learn, to rejoice in a first gallop down the long stretch of beach, shouting aloud with the excitement of it, the speed, the slap of the pony's hooves on the wet sand, the wind rush and the snorting, and the swish and jingle of leather and harness. It had always been a special place for Sarah and her brother.

'I'd love to ride after lunch,' she said to Tim, after several days wrestling with grit and plaster.

'That's a grand idea,' he said. 'You certainly deserve it. How about it,

Deirdre? It's time you learned to ride. We could do a gentle little excursion on the beach.'

He was standing behind her, and he put his arms around her waist and pulled her close to him, but she made a small exclamation and moved out of his embrace.

'You know I don't care for horses,' she said, her tone sharp. 'You'd best go with Sarah. I'd only slow you down.'

Tim turned away, but not before his sister registered his hurt expression. They rode out across the dunes towards the ruins of Mullaghmore Castle, where they cantered into the surf and let the salt spray fly in their faces. When they turned for home through the incoming tide, the sky was glowing red above Ben Bulben, and seals slid off the spar into the water ahead of them. Leading the horses up from the beach in the autumn sunshine, Sarah felt very close to her brother, and she prayed that he would be happy. The house was bathed in the mellow light of late afternoon, its classic proportions graceful in the surrounding landscape. A bank of hydrangeas in full bloom flanked the French windows, and the glass panes reflected the line of distant surf beyond the headland. It was ideal, she realised at last, for her parents at this time in their lives. And a perfect place for Tim and Deirdre to bring up children.

The weeks in Sligo sped away with a sense of achievement and progress that dulled her impatience to be in Kenya and to be close to Piet again. The days had hardly begun when they were over, and it was time to fall into bed. She was glad of the sheer physical exhaustion. It blunted the memories of the raid that would otherwise have invaded her sleep. They were always there, lurking in every strange sound or sudden movement, but she kept them buried lest her parents should see how badly she had been affected.

'I'd forgotten what a beautiful place it is,' she admitted to her brother, as they stood on the front steps, looking out across the water. 'I imagine you'll be very happy here. You and Dad will make the best team anyone could hope for.'

'It's a big responsibility,' he said. 'Sometimes I wonder, are we mad, or what?'

'Come on now, Dr Mackay. Let's have none of the doubting stuff. They'll be queuing from miles around to consult with you, and the practice will have a great nurse in Deirdre. You'll do just fine.'

A long letter arrived from Hannah. Things were running normally at the farm. Piet was working round the clock, since Lars had not yet returned to work. There was no progress in the police investigation. She hoped that Sarah would be there soon, and that they would all spend Christmas at Langani. Piet sent his love. Sarah had hoped for a few lines from him, but she could understand that he was short of time. He had never been much of a writer anyway. The post brought nothing from Camilla, and two phone calls and a letter had elicited no response. Sarah wondered if she was in trouble, if there was a problem with the scarring on her face.

In Sligo things were falling into place, and Sarah was suddenly impatient to be gone. It was time to move on. She decided to leave a few days early and spend some time with Camilla. The telephone rang and rang, and it was two days before Camilla answered.

'Camilla! It's Sarah. Where have you been? I've been worried sick about you. Didn't you get my letters?'

'I've been floating around. Seeing chums. You know.' Camilla sounded as if she had just woken up.

'No, I don't know. You can't just vanish like that and say nothing. Where were you, anyway? Did you go away with George?'

'George. Dear old George. No, I haven't been anywhere with him. Nowhere at all.' Camilla's voice was slurred.

'Camilla, you're not drunk are you?'

'Absolutely not. A few little pills. Washed down with vodka, and all is well. All is so, so well. Glad you caught me. I'm off to Ad Lib for the evening. It's a happening, you know. I'm comforting Tom for the night. His bird left him and I'm the back-up.'

'But what's happened about the doctor, and your face? Are you really all right? Is there something you haven't told me?'

'Not a thing. Just waiting to be reopened and put back together again. Toast of the town, my scar. Are you going back there?'

'What?' Sarah was nonplussed by the sudden change of subject.

'Kenya. Are you going?'

'Of course I'm going. In fact, I was wondering if I could stay with you on my way over.' There was silence on the line. Sarah tried again. 'Camilla, did you talk to your father about funds for Langani? Is there something Piet should do to speed things along, someone he could contact in Nairobi? Or London?'

'Daddy. Oh yes, I saw my darling daddy. He was in fine form, doing all kinds of amazing things. Surprised the hell out of me.' Camilla's laugh sounded hysterical and Sarah heard her take another sip of whatever she was drinking. 'Maybe I'll come.'

'What? Come where?'

'Back to Kenya. To Hannah and Piet, and Langani.'

A cold fear scraped its way into Sarah's consciousness. 'Have you heard from Anthony?' she asked.

'Anthony? That's part of my impossibly romantic past. All over. History. But there are other lovely young heroes, waiting in the wings. Almost as good as your beautiful Piet. Well, maybe not quite up to his standard.'

'But did you ask George about funds for Langani?'

'I will, when I see him next. When I see him, I definitely will.' Camilla's voice sounded thick and muffled. As if she was crying. Or she'd had too much to drink, or too many little uppers or downers.

'If I came over a couple of days early we could talk to George together,' Sarah persisted. 'Between the two of us, we could make a good case, don't you think? And we could have some fun in London before I vanish into the *bundu*.'

'Doorbell's ringing, Sarah. Must fly. Talk soon. Maybe I'll see you on the farm.'

'Camilla—?'

'Don't make me feel bad. I've got things to think about too, you know. All kinds of things that would surprise you. Bye for now.'

Sarah stood looking at the telephone in disbelief as the line went dead. Camilla did not want to see her. And her casual dismissal of support for Langani was hard to stomach. Surely she did not expect Piet and Hannah to welcome her back, when she had not bothered to discuss their case with her father. And how would Piet react if Camilla came to him, looking for consolation? Sarah felt ill at the thought.

On her last day in Sligo, she stood on the terrace inhaling the scent of the sea and listening to the wind whipping the short grass on the dunes into a swirl of trembling emerald, while the gulls wheeled and screeched and danced in the sky.

'Are you sure you have everything?' Betty asked. 'Paludrine – we don't want another malaria victim coming home sick. And the creams for insect bites, and that new stuff for stomach upsets.'

'It's all right, Mum. Don't fuss. I'm as loaded up as I could possibly be. Really.'

'Time to go. All ready?' Raphael had come out to join them.

She nodded, finding it hard to speak. Her bags were in the car. She was going away. Away from her family who had always loved and supported her, going to a future that seemed all at once hugely daunting.

'Joy and success and everything you hope for, love. That's what I pray for every day.' Betty drew her close and hugged her and they wept together. She pushed Sarah's unruly hair back from her forehead and kissed her. 'Take care of yourself, now. And remember, if things don't work out for any reason, if you're not happy, your home is here for you. We're always here. If you need us.'

'Thanks, Mum. I'll remember.' Sarah's words were choked. 'I love you. I love you all.'

She threw her arms around her brother's neck, tears streaming down her face. God, this was like the days of boarding school, the agonising farewells, the attempts to put on a brave show that always failed, trying to smile till your face ached. If only you could have everyone you loved in one place, always accessible. But she had made her choice. She had a whole new life and career in front of her. And Piet. In two days she would be seeing Piet. He had promised to pick her up at the airport, and she would begin her life beside him and let it take her wherever she was meant to go. Deirdre had come out to say goodbye, her pretty, earnest face alight with concern as she dished out last-minute homilies.

'I'll heed everything you've said,' Sarah assured her, and for once the advice did not grate on her and she embraced Deirdre with affection. 'Keep that brother of mine in order – he needs a firm hand.'

Tim made a pretence of glowering at her and then laughed.

She turned and ran down the steps, and got into the car beside her father. Waving as she sped away down the drive, her emotions were a jumble of pain, anxiety and excitement. But as she left Raphael at the departure gate in the airport, the agony was almost unbearable, grasping her by the throat so that she was barely able to breathe.

'Dad – are you *sure* you're all right?' He looked unsteady on his feet, and she noticed that his trousers were gathered and held up by a broad belt, in an effort to disguise the weight he had lost. Taking her suitcase out

313

of the car had cost him all his energy, and it was minutes before he could breathe normally. Sarah clung to him, suddenly fearful that she might never see him again. 'I can still change my mind. Come back with you. If you want—'

He pushed her firmly towards the gate. 'Don't be getting cold feet now, child,' he said. 'I'm looking forward to my new adventure, as you must look forward to yours. Don't even think of backing out. We'll see you again soon, my darling, and we'll write often. Go away now, and be happy. Go.'

She showed her boarding pass, and went into the departure area. Looking back, she could see her father standing there, waiting for a final glimpse of her, puffing hard on his pipe to hide his distress. With one last gesture of love she turned and walked away from him and was swallowed up in the crowd of passengers making for the plane.

Chapter 17

London, October 1965

Camilla was angry, unable to accept the lie in which she had been trapped, the bitter masquerade that was their futile marriage. They had been in a position to choose, while she had been given no options at all. It was impossible to fathom how or why they could have added a child to the torment of their existence together, and it crossed her mind that George might not be her father at all. She resented them for making her an unwitting victim of their unhappiness. It was plain that her father must have lived a secret life all through her childhood years, fearful of the possibility that his homosexuality would be discovered, that it would destroy his career, put him in prison even. Their shared secret had poisoned the home they inhabited, and allowed Marina's isolation and unhappiness to grow like a cancer, and to distort all their lives.

Camilla had left the awful scene in the bedroom and rushed out of the house. Behind her she heard her father calling her name. As she slammed the front door, the desperate, rasping sounds of his pain and regret entered her brain like bullets, ripping apart all the trust she had invested in him since her earliest memories. She flagged down a taxi, but when she was safely inside she had no idea where she wanted to go. In the anonymity of the cab she began to weep uncontrollably.

'Now don't go breaking your 'eart, a pretty girl like you. I bet it's over a man, eh? Well, he ain't worth it. They never are, my love. That's what I say, and you'll soon see that I'm right.' The cabbie regarded her with sympathy in his driving mirror. 'Where shall we go then, miss? You want me to take you on a tour of the town, or 'ave you got somewhere special you'd like to wind up?'

Camilla searched for a handkerchief. Unable to make a decision, she gave the address of her flat. There was nowhere else she could go, no one she could lean on. She had never needed close friends in London, never sought out anyone in whom she might confide. In her mind she had always been apart, different from the people with whom she worked and dined and danced. She enjoyed being aloof, disconnected, unaffected by the realities of other lives. They had no power, no sway over her emotions or aspirations, no insight into her private thoughts.

'I never have a bloody clue what you're thinking,' Tom had often complained to her. 'You say things that sound reasonable and I listen, but I don't know what's really going on in that beautiful head. There's no way to tell what you're actually feeling, if you're feeling anything at all. One of these days you're going to find out that you're human like the rest of us. That you have to connect, or you'll start withering away like a plant without any water.'

'Well, I certainly don't need any watering from you,' she had replied, lofty and confident, pushing him away as he tried to kiss her. She had seen him turn away, muttering about pride and falls from high places, and she had laughed at him.

And now she had no one to confide in. As she opened the door of her flat Camilla could hear the telephone ringing and she stopped on the threshold, afraid that it was her father. She turned on her heel and made her way back to Brompton Road. It was raining again and she put up her umbrella, not wanting her fringe to part and reveal her scar. She had no idea where to go. It was too early to drop into one of the bars or go to a club. The evening traffic pounded past her. She felt dislocated and unsafe in the midst of it, and she wanted to flee the noise of engines and brakes and horns, and return to the harmony of the African wilderness. As she stood on the pavement, hesitant and oblivious to the curious looks of passers-by, a car pulled up close to her.

'You look lost. Indecisive at any rate.' Edward Carradine wound down the window and looked at her enquiringly. 'It's very wet. Can I take you somewhere?'

'Yes. Yes, you can.'

He climbed out of the car in the rain and opened the door for her, settling her into the passenger seat.

'Where to?'

'Somewhere. Just like you said.' Camilla was already regretting the fact that she had accepted his offer. Now that she was in his car, she had no idea where she could ask him to take her. 'Where are you going?'

'To a film, I thought.' He was watching her out of the corner of his eye, noting her anxiety, the twitch at the corner of her mouth and the redness around her eyes. 'If you're not busy, maybe you'd like to join me.'

'Aren't there rules about going out with your patients, Mr Carradine?' There was the beginning of a smile in her.

'Not in the normal, social sense. Otherwise half my private life would be spent on my own. And my name is Edward.' He looked at her directly now. 'You've had a haircut and it looks very good. It would have been a great idea even without the reason behind it. Makes you look like an elf rather than a fairy queen. Gamine is the word, I suppose.'

'What film were you going to?' she asked.

'I was thinking of Jimmy Stewart in an aeroplane crash. Something called the *Flight of the Phoenix*. But if you'd rather go to—'

'Jimmy Stewart is fine. I love that flat, twangy voice.'

Afterwards they had dinner and Edward was full of charm, questioning her about the fashion world. In turn he told her about his visits to Kenya, and to Nigeria and India, describing with real compassion the ravaged bodies he had tried to repair. He watched her carefully as they talked, seeing her beautiful face light up when she laughed at his stories, observing an underlying sadness that she did not seem to recognise herself. When he asked after Marina she shrugged.

'In case you feel obliged to make any further polite conversation about my mother, I'll save you some time,' she said. 'You might as well know that I've never been particularly close to her.'

Later he mentioned her father. She stiffened and the hand that was holding her wine glass trembled so that she had to put it carefully down on the table. He was busy, she said flatly. Away most of the time. She had not seen him since her return from Kenya. He thought he could see a hint of tears in her eyes, and changed the subject. He refilled her wine glass several times and understood that she was drinking herself steadily out of whatever it was that haunted her.

'What about you – do you have a family?' she asked, as they ordered dessert.

'I was married once,' he said. 'But that was a long time ago. Would you like a coffee? And a sambuco perhaps?'

'Too cloying. But I'd love coffee.'

He drove her home and accompanied her up the stairs to her door.

'This is where I'm supposed to ask you in for a drink,' Camilla said, as she searched for her key.

'It's not obligatory.' He was smiling.

'But is it acceptable, as one of your patients?' She was teasing him, aware that he wanted to come in.

'I'd love a drink,' he said, himself reluctant to let her go.

In the living room he looked around at her books, at the paintings and prints and the stylish decor. It was a sophisticated room that offered no clue to her personality. He could not see any photographs of family or friends. He wondered if she kept these things in her bedroom, but something in him doubted it. Camilla returned with a tray and sat down opposite him, her face tranquil and childlike as she poured coffee and a snifter of brandy. When she looked up and smiled at him, holding out the small cup, he knew that he was falling in love with her. It was a ridiculous admission, and his reason told him that there could not be anything real in this facile, instant tumbling into another's orbit. He reminded himself that he had just turned forty-two, and that this must be some preposterous, mid-life crisis that had taken hold of him. She was hardly more than a child, for all her worldly mannerisms. Besides which, she was probably involved elsewhere.

'You're very quiet all of a sudden.' Camilla studied him with an expression that was slightly mocking. 'Are your thoughts deep? Worth investigating?'

He continued to look at her in silence, knowing for certain that he would try to make her love him, and that it might bring him pain and even ridicule. But he was willing to risk this, as long as he could find a way to bring her close. He had always chosen his work as his constant love, and he had paid a heavy price for it in the past. But there would be no mistakes this time. He smiled without answering her question, afraid that she would see in his eyes the insane thing he had discovered in his heart. When he left her shortly afterwards, he kissed her cheek briefly and reminded her not to smoke if she could possibly avoid it. He would see her in a few days in Harley Street. She closed the door and prepared herself for bed, but when she lay down, the flat blade of the panga and the hatred in her assailant's eyes returned to torture her once more. She made her way to the bathroom and took a sleeping pill to banish her fear.

*

The telephone woke her early in the morning, but she let it ring. She had not slept well and she felt anxious and on the brink of tears. When she opened a novel and attempted to read, the pages swam in front of her and she put it aside. The strident sound of the telephone unnerved her when it rang again. But she did not pick it up, afraid that it would be her father, or Tom Bartlett trying to tell her that all her bookings had been cancelled. The phial of tranquillisers was in the bathroom. She opened it and swallowed one with half a glass of water. Then she went back to bed and shut her eyes, imagining herself in the camp at Samburu. She tried to see Anthony's face but the image remained elusive as she struggled to bring him into focus, and she fell asleep imbued with a sense of loss. The telephone rang again, and Camilla turned over in bed and tried to escape the sound by holding a pillow over her head. But she had never taken the easy way out, and since she could not avoid the ugly facts of her family's life indefinitely she eventually reached out and picked up the receiver.

'Camilla.' George Broughton-Smith was subdued. 'I want to see you. I *need* to see you.'

The sound of his voice brought back the sordid scene in the bedroom. 'No.'

'There are things I have to say. It's best if I say them now, and then you can decide what you would like to do.'

'No. I can't see you or talk to you. Please, don't keep phoning me.'

She wanted to scream at him, to see him face to face and to beat against him with all her strength, for having destroyed their family in his pursuit of some perverted pleasure. Miserably, she remembered her promise to ask him about funds for Langani, but she could not imagine herself discussing anything with him. She got up slowly and went to the window. Below her, in the square, the world looked the same. There were autumn roses still blooming in the garden and a light wind blew coppery leaves across the lawn. A thrush was splashing in the birdbath, and a child played with her doll's pram while her mother read a magazine on the bench nearby. In the hall she heard the shuffle and clatter of envelopes as the porter pushed them through her letter box, and she went to pick up the morning newspaper. Her head ached and she felt wrung out after hearing the sound of her father's voice. She dressed and went out for breakfast, taking the paper with her, determined to overcome her dark mood. In the café on Brompton Road she ordered eggs and bacon and coffee, and sat back to leaf through the paper. There was not much to read, but on the second page a small headline caught her eye. A Kenyan politician, Johnson Kiberu, was leading a government delegation that had arrived in London to discuss funding for the country's tourism expansion plans. There would be meetings with the Foreign Office and the Ministry of Overseas Development. The visiting delegates were staying at the Savoy Hotel. A plan began to form in her mind as she finished her breakfast and returned to her flat. The day dragged, and no one called until the late afternoon when she picked up the telephone to hear Marina's voice.

'Darling, you missed a lovely weekend. You should have come with me. Would you like to have supper?'

'No. Thank you. I don't want to go anywhere tonight.'

'Are you all right, Camilla? You sound a little down.'

'I'm fine. Really.'

'Well, good, darling. I'll talk to you tomorrow.'

Half an hour later Marina rang the doorbell. 'I was worried about you,' she said. 'You didn't sound right. Is your head bothering you?'

'No. I'm going out soon, Mother. This isn't an ideal time for a visit.'

'Camilla, I need to sit down. I'd like a glass of water, and perhaps some coffee.' Marina's face was grey, and she was unsteady on her feet as she made her way to the sofa, taking out her cigarettes and lighter. 'I know something's wrong. If you won't discuss it with me, perhaps you'd like to talk to your father. He's back, although he'd gone to the office by the time I arrived in from Burford. Perhaps you've seen him already?'

'No.'

'Why don't I telephone him, and see if he can join us for dinner this evening.'

'Why didn't you leave him?' Camilla shouted, incapable now of holding back her anger.

Marina's eyes were wide with surprise. 'I can't imagine what you—?'

'I know what he is. I know he doesn't love you, that he's—'

'Camilla, darling, you're overwrought. It's shock, delayed reaction—'

'Stop it, Mother! Stop this horrible charade, for God's sake, because I know what he is! I know he fucks men!'

Marina stared at her daughter, her mouth trembling, and then the words

320

spilled out with the tears. 'Oh God. Oh God, we never wanted you to be a part of this. We never—'

'You've made my life a misery. I hate you, Mother. I hate you both for everything you've been hiding all these years. For the whole sham. You should have left him, taken me and left.'

'No. It wasn't as easy as that. Nothing is ever that simple. The fact is, I loved your father.' Marina looked up, her face smeared with mascara. 'I always loved him. I still do. I could never have walked away. It would have ruined his career as a diplomat, finished his chances of being given a top posting.'

'Is that why he married you? So that he wouldn't spoil his career chances?' A deadly calm had come over Camilla. She wanted to know it all, to have every repulsive aspect of their lives explained to her. 'You must have realised. How long has he been like this? Is he my father, even?'

'He tried.' Marina was weeping again. 'He tried so hard in the beginning. I never guessed, because he tried so hard. But then he just couldn't go on. I thought he was having an affair with some woman from his office. I accused him of that. We quarrelled and fought so often, because I was jealous and angry. But I couldn't leave him.'

'And the effect of this farce on your child – that didn't count for anything, did it? You decided that security and climbing the Foreign Office ladder were more important?'

'I wanted to be with him. I thought that maybe he could change. That we could make a life together. He said he wanted that too. He was a brilliant young man with a great future, and I wanted to be part of it.'

'Part of what? You're telling me he had no guts. That he was glad to hide behind your skirts. Use you to advance himself.'

'You know what they think of divorced career diplomats. So many wives stay on, work out a different way of living their lives, take a little love where they find it. And being . . . being the other thing is still judged as a crime.' Marina's voice was pleading. 'Your father isn't a criminal, Camilla. He's not the same as other men, well, most other men. But he's not a criminal. We couldn't have survived a public accusation. That would have ruined him. I had to stand by him. I had to go on as though he was my husband like every other husband. I found some letters one morning, when I was sorting out his suits, changing over from our winter to summer wardrobes. They were from a boy, a kind of prostitute, who wanted money. At first I couldn't believe what the letters were saying. And then he promised. He said it would never happen again, that he would put it all behind him. He cried, and he told me he loved me. That you and I were all that mattered in his life. Then we left for Nairobi. We got through it together, in spite of the cost.'

'The cost? What about the cost to me? Living through your rows and your scenes and your loathing of him.'

'I've never even disliked him. Only what his life forced us to become.'

'So he stayed because he owed you something. You bailed him out, and he's had to pay for that, and will be paying for ever.' Camilla felt only contempt for them both. 'And neither one of you gave a thought for me. About what your twisted lives would do to me.' She took hold of Marina's arm, pressing hard until she saw her mother wince with pain. 'Get out of my flat, Mother, and stay away from now on. Both of you. Just leave me alone. You've done enough harm to last me all the way to hell and back.'

'Camilla—'

'Here's your coat, Mother. Go now. Please.'

For an hour Camilla sat trancelike in the empty room, a trace of Marina's perfume still in the air. Dusk approached, filling the room with a chill, yellow light and the wind rose, whispering at the window ledge. At last she stood up and went to dress for the evening. She bathed and smoothed cream into her arms and legs, made up her face with all the professional knowledge and care she could summon. She brushed her fringe down over her forehead and sprayed it into place. Then she chose a dress that was tight across her breasts and had a hemline just above her knees. At the Savoy Hotel she smiled at the barman and ordered a vodka.

'Haven't seen you around for some weeks, Miss Broughton-Smith,' he said. 'Are you meeting your father? Do you want a table for dinner later on?'

'I don't need a table, thanks, James. Just a drink.'

'Camilla. Where have you been, darling? Love the hair.' Keith Short was a journalist and she had featured several times in his gossip column. 'What about dinner? I'm hanging around in case any of these visiting chappies from Africa goes on the rampage, or comes up with something colourful for my piece on Wednesday. There's a certain aristocratic English beauty, who fancies a little dark meat of an evening. I hear she might drop in. I've got a photographer here in the hopes that she becomes marvellously indiscreet.'

'What a lovely profession you've chosen, Mr Short,' she said, only half amused.

'And aren't you glad of it, my love, when I write you up in my little square of newsprint. What about dinner, then?'

'I'm booked up later on, thanks,' she said. 'You'll have to find ways of enlightening the public all by yourself.'

'I suppose I will. So tell me, where have you been hiding of late?'

'I was in Kenya for several weeks.'

'These blokes upstairs are from there – the ones I'm keeping an eye on.' Keith signalled for another drink. 'James here tells me they're having themselves a high old time.'

'They're all like that,' declared the barman. 'These visiting spivs are all the same, no matter where they come from. You'd never credit how much booze they put away. Rivers of the stuff. I thought those places in Africa were all broke. They always say they need money and they come over here to beg for help, else they'll starve. That's what you read in the papers. Well, all I can say, just between us, sir, is they could probably run a whole country on the amount they spend on limousines and suites and booze in this place alone. And expensive women. They have those shipped in, the minute they arrive.'

'Do they spend much time in the bar?' Camilla said.

'Nah. Everything is sent up to the suite. Phone never stops ringing. Been at it for a couple of days, this lot. James, a bottle of Glenfiddich for four six three. James, a magnum of Dom Perignon for four six three. James, could you take care of the Armagnac they want in four six three. The best, always the best, and I'll bet the bills go to Whitehall, so you and I can pay them out of our taxes.'

Camilla finished her drink and left the bar. When the door of the lift opened on the fourth floor she stood still, suddenly unsure. Then she stepped out and walked slowly along the carpeted corridor, looking at the discreet numbers on the bedroom doors. When she knocked there was only silence and she felt deeply agitated, so that she had to put up her hand and steady herself on the door frame.

'Good evening.' The man who opened the door was surprised. 'I wasn't expecting anyone until much later. Are you a friend of Fiona's?'

'I heard there was party, from a little bird we both know,' Camilla said, opening her eyes wide, tilting her head to one side and smiling. 'I've just come back from Kenya, actually, so I'd love to join you if I'm not gate-crashing.'

'Come in and have a drink.' Johnson Kiberu led the way to the large sofa. He was a tall man with fine features, and his skin was very black. There was an ice bucket with champagne on the table, and a silver tray of hors d'oeuvres. 'There is always room for another beautiful woman in my quarters.'

The jacket of his impeccable suit was hanging over a chair, and Camilla saw that his shirt was monogrammed. He wore gold cuff links and shoes that must have been custom-made to fit his broad feet. She found it easy to talk to him, and was not surprised when he remembered her father. He had a charming manner and she was not offended at his obvious attempts to flirt with her. He had come up through the usual political channels, along with the brilliant Tom Mboya who had been his friend. Now he travelled a great deal, often to conferences concerned with economic aid. He was pleased that she knew Kenya well, and it was not difficult for Camilla to steer the conversation to tourism and the country's game parks and reserves. His attention drifted, however, when she introduced the subject of Langani. As she talked about the new lodge and Piet's efforts to protect the wildlife on the farm, he leaned over and slid his hand along her thigh. She moved away from him a little, but he shifted his position and then pounced, kissing her clumsily on the corner of her mouth. She wriggled out of his grasp and pushed him away.

'I don't think we're ready for this so early in the evening,' she said with a little laugh. 'I want to talk to you more about Langani.'

'Is that why you are here?' He sat back and eyed her with a gaze that was shrewd. 'To talk about this place?'

'Yes, it is,' she admitted, judging it preferable to tell the truth.

'And what is it you want to say about Langani?' he asked, still close but not touching her now.

'They urgently need help,' she said. 'They need money for patrols to stop poaching, and to make the place secure for tourists. The owners have put all they have into building this game lodge and conservation area, but they need help from the government for security, and since you are involved in tourism and conservation—'

'Why have they not applied for it through the usual channels?' His hand was back on her knee.

'They have,' she said. 'But it's a slow process, and in the meantime they've had problems with cattle being killed, poachers after the elephants, and recently an armed robbery. All the things that are bad for tourism. So I thought you might be able to speed up their request. See that they get funds soon, or . . .'

'Perhaps I could do that, yes.' He was openly bored. His face and tone had changed and she recognised the shift in him, his growing desire, his determination to seduce her. It was not the first time she had looked pure lust in the face. She moved back from him and reached for her coat.

'I'm afraid I have to leave now,' she said. 'But I hope you'll remember Langani when you return to Nairobi. I'm sure Piet van der Beer would arrange to fly you up there, to have a look around.'

He lunged forward to take hold of her, and she felt one large hand groping, and then his mouth clamped down on hers. His other hand took hold of her head, and Camilla struggled, unable to breathe, feeling the pressure of his onslaught on her forehead as he tried to force his tongue into her mouth. She thumped at his chest, trying to push him away from her, squirming under his weight. He pulled at the buttons on the front of her dress, but she fought free and leapt up from the sofa. His arm shot out to pull her back and she jumped sideways and lost her balance, tumbling down and hitting her head on the arm of a chair as she fell. Her cry of alarm brought him to his senses and he reached out again, this time to help her up.

'I think we have both made a mistake,' he said. 'I apologise. I'm afraid I am more accustomed to young ladies coming up here for a different reason. You seem to have hurt your head. It's bleeding from underneath that bandage. Let me help you.'

She scrambled to her feet, picked up her coat and handbag and ran from the suite. In the safety of the lift she looked at herself in the mirror and saw a grotesque reflection that seemed only faintly familiar. Her dress was hanging open at the front and her lipstick was smudged across her cheek. The fringe that she had carefully set into place had been pushed aside, revealing the dressing on her forehead. A trickle of blood was making its way down her temple and she found a handkerchief and dabbed at it. As the doors slid open she found herself standing face to face with Short and his photographer. There was a second of blinding light and then she realised what was happening.

'Oh God. Please, don't use this, Keith,' she begged. 'Please. I've made a mistake – an awful misunderstanding.'

He stood aside in silence as she moved past him into the lobby. Camilla looked back at him in desperation, a question in her eyes, but he was smiling as he walked away towards the bar where he and his photographer could put the finishing touches to their story.

In the security of her flat she stripped off her clothes and ran a bath. Several of her stitches had broken, and the cut was bleeding and had already started to swell above her right eyebrow. It would probably have to be stitched again and she would definitely have bruising. She cleaned the red welt with cotton wool and warm water, and covered it with a fresh dressing. When she lay down and tried to sleep, she was transported back to Langani, with the panga hurtling towards her in the lamplight as she wrenched the rings and bangles off her hands. She opened her eyes again but her mind still held the jumble of violent images, and in the back of her brain she could hear the strange, desolate sound her father had made as she closed the door on the tryst with his lover. It was impossible to consider seeing him again, even though she had failed to find help for Langani from Johnson Kiberu. She felt as though her life had been smashed to pieces and swept away.

For all of the next day Camilla stayed in the flat, her forehead throbbing, her head hazy with pain and regret. The telephone jangled several times but she did not answer it. She knew that she should telephone Edward and arrange a date to have her stitches repaired, but a deep lethargy smothered her, making her body heavy and dull so that it was an effort to move. When finally she dressed and made herself something to eat, she sat at the table, unable to face the food she had prepared. The television told her nothing of importance and she paced the room for a time, before pouring a large amount of vodka into a glass full of ice. She felt the power of it in the back of her throat as she swallowed it in two desperate gulps, and she slopped a second measure into the tumbler. When the telephone intruded yet again she picked it up, her head swirling. Sarah's anxious voice sounded far away and Camilla choked on her response. She stumbled over words that would hide her loneliness and sense of separation. She did not want pity. When she put the receiver back on its cradle she had no clear idea what she had said. The tranquillisers were in the bathroom cabinet and she swallowed one. An hour later it was her mother's voice on the line and she hung up and went to bed.

In the morning she drank strong coffee and hunted for her cigarettes, but the packet was empty. Keith Short's weekly column would appear today, and she felt ill as she thought about the photograph and the snide remarks that would accompany it. She put on a pair of jeans and a sweater, pulled a hat low over her brow and headed for the newsagent. But the paper carried no mention of visiting politicians or their preferred entertainment, and Camilla stood on the grey pavement weak with gratitude and relief. The hall porter greeted her as she returned to the flat.

'Your post arrived, Miss. I was about to take it upstairs.'

'Thank you, Albert,' she said, taking the bundle he handed her. There was a brief note from Short and she opened and read it as she climbed the stairs. 'Chucked out the negative and killed the story. You owe me one,' he had written, in his untidy scrawl. Inside the flat Camilla sifted through the remainder of the letters and tore up an envelope addressed in her father's hand. The telephone rang, and she picked it up and immediately replaced it. Then she lifted it again and left it off the hook. Escape. She needed to escape, to go somewhere she could think, straighten out her head. She took a suitcase from the top of the bedroom cupboard and flung some clothes and toiletries into it. On her dressing table was a photograph of her parents and she slid it out of its silver frame and ripped it into tiny pieces. She was still trying to decide where she might go when the doorbell rang.

'You have to come with me, darling,' Marina said. 'I have a taxi downstairs, and I want you to come with me now, so that we can sit down together and talk.'

'You're the very last person I want to talk to. Please, Mother, let me be. Leave me alone. Please.'

'Camilla, I want you to give me a chance. I'm begging you to give me this one chance. It's important for both of us.'

'No. What's important is to put as much distance as possible between us. Between me and both of my parents. That's the only thing that I want to do right now.'

'I'd like you to come down to Burford with me.' Marina put out a tentative hand to touch Camilla's sleeve. 'Just the two of us. There are things I need to tell you.'

'Things I don't need to hear.'

'This is not about your father. This is about you and me. Because I'm sick. I'm very sick, Camilla, and I'm not going to get better. I know I've done everything wrong in my life, but perhaps I can still put some of it right. Even help you a little, although I'm not good at this kind of thing. But I want to try. If I'm going to die, then I want to get some things clear before I go. Do you understand? Do you hear me?' Marina's words were delivered steadily, and her face was composed.

'Is this some new trick?'

'I'll be waiting for you downstairs. In the taxi.' Marina did not look back. After a moment Camilla followed her downstairs to the waiting cab.

'Paddington Station,' Marina said.

They did not talk on the train as it sped past suburbs and factories, and out into the countryside where cattle grazed in orderly fields, unmoved by passing trains and passengers whose heads were brimming with confusion and anxiety. The house in Burford was small and Camilla was surprised by its atmosphere of tranquillity. Marina showed her to a bedroom at the top of a narrow staircase. The casement window looked out over a tiny back garden lit by the evening sunshine. The lawn was bordered by flagged paving stones and flowerpots. Beyond the garden wall, the fields dipped down to the furl of a river and then rose again towards a tree-lined ridge. A man in a duffel coat and wellingtons was chopping wood in his back garden. He picked up a branch and threw it for his dog, and Camilla smiled as she heard the excited barking. She lingered at the window, reluctant to go downstairs and begin any form of dialogue with Marina. Her suitcase lay unopened on the window seat and she postponed the confrontation by unpacking, putting everything away in a cupboard that smelled of lavender and had a shelf of neatly folded bed linen. When she had made up her bed there was no further excuse for delay.

To her surprise, her mother was sitting back on her heels in front of the stone fireplace, rolling newspaper into tight balls and building a nest of kindling on the top of it. Camilla stood and watched as Marina arranged several narrow logs in a strategic pyramid, and then set light to her creation. She was rewarded by an immediate blaze, and looked up at her daughter with obvious pride in the task she had accomplished.

'I've become rather good at fires,' she said. 'We have a nice old chap who chops the logs and leaves them in the shed, so there's always dry wood. Will you make some tea?'

The kitchen was homely with a pine table and an old dresser on which antique china had been arranged. The back door led to the walled garden that Camilla had looked down on from her bedroom. There was a small patio area, not visible from upstairs, with a trestle table and chairs.

'Perfect, isn't it?' Marina said. 'I love coming here. There's a fruit cake in that tin, if you're hungry. You'll never believe this, but I made it myself when I was here last weekend. I think it will still be all right. There's milk in the fridge, and you'll find everyday crockery in the cupboard above the sink.' Camilla made the tea and poured two cups.

'Let's take this in to the fire,' Marina said.

They sat down in silence, listening to the hiss and crackle of the firewood. There was nowhere to begin, nothing but uncertainty between them.

'Leukaemia is the ugly word,' Marina said at last. 'A malignant disease of the bone marrow and the blood. Nothing to be done. I feel like some character in an opera, wasting helplessly away. Except that I can't sing of course.'

'How long have you known about it?'

'Just over a month.'

'Does he know?'

'Yes, your father knows. He's been with me as much as he could since the doctor told us the news. It was after he came back from Nairobi the last time. Just after you saw him there. He told me how wonderful you looked, from being down at the coast.' The words were full of sadness.

Camilla could not find anything to say. She drank her tea, staring into the cup, unable to meet her mother's eyes.

'He said you were in love and glowing with it. And I wished that you'd told me about it,' Marina said. 'He's been so kind and attentive. Bringing me my breakfast in bed, taking me to dinner or to the theatre on good days. I've been coming down here most weekends, and he's cancelled most of his other plans to stay here too. But he had to go to the Netherlands last week. Prince Bernhard is a patron of his organisation, and you can't really turn down appointments with royalty.'

Camilla could not equate this calm acceptance of a death sentence with the fragile, often hysterical mother she knew. Now she understood too late that Marina's depressions had been the result of something beyond her control, that her social position had been the one reliable post to which she could hold fast, the only way in which her life could remain outwardly normal. There was no preparation, no training for the path she had chosen to follow, nowhere she could feel safe or seek help. Marriage had brought her loneliness and betrayal, and a sense of shame. She had feared for her husband, resented her dependence on him, and she had loved him through it all.

'I don't know what to say.' Camilla felt completely inadequate. 'Is there something I can do? How do you feel now – I mean, are you in pain?'

'I'm tired mainly, and breathless if I do too much. I get fevers, and my joints ache as though I have flu. I'm glad it's not the middle of summer when everyone is running around in short sleeves and no stockings. My skin looks frightful – bruises and some horrible spotty things, and a cut that won't heal. Not pretty at all.'

'Actually, you look more beautiful than you've ever looked.' The onset of tears was close. Camilla stood up quickly. 'Would you like to rest for a while, and I'll go into the village and do some food shopping? There doesn't seem to be much in the fridge.'

'I'd like you to tell me about being in love. About how happy you are.'

'I'm afraid that was short-lived. An affair. I suppose Daddy told you that it was Anthony Chapman I'd fallen for. But I got it wrong.'

'You don't love him after all?'

'I love him terribly. But he's only interested in the short-term, because anything else would make too many changes in his life. I made a classic mistake, like some half-witted girl in a trashy novel. You know – great white hunter, adventure in the bush, passionate encounters in tents, with moonlight over the plains and roaring lions. I fell for it all. I was painfully naive.'

'I'm so sorry, darling. Sorry you're hurt. Sorry for everything, and it's too late to make up for it all now. But I do love you, Camilla. I truly do and I always have, and that's the only important thing left.'

Tears slid down her face and she was unable to form any more words. Her hands gripped the arms of her chair, whitening her already pale knuckles. Camilla stared into the distance and they sat without speaking, frozen in an awkward tableau that was broken by the sound of the telephone.

'If that's my father, I don't want to talk to him. I don't want to see him. I'm going to do the shopping now, but I'll be back in a while.'

Camilla took her bag and left the house, walking away down the lane towards the High Street. Marina picked up the phone. It was Sarah Mackay on the line. Sarah who was going back to live in Kenya, in spite of all that had happened there. Sarah, who might persuade Camilla to go too, in search of her bushman, or to start up a business on that terrible farm. Marina felt a shiver of panic pass through her. Camilla must not go away now, when time was so short.

'Camilla's not here, my dear,' she said smoothly. 'She's gone away for a while. Until her next doctor's appointment. Yes, her face is healing well. Some surgery later on should prevent permanent scarring. No, I'm not sure where she went. Somewhere on the Continent, I think. If I hear from her, I'll let her know you telephoned. Goodbye, Sarah.'

She replaced the receiver and knew that she had done the right thing. When Camilla came back from the village they would talk about her love affair, try to find comfort in sharing the sadness. They would spend time together in London and here in the quiet of the countryside as the autumn passed. She would try to effect a reconciliation between her husband and her daughter, make plain to them how much she loved them both. No one would be allowed to threaten this last chance she had at happiness, during the final months of her life.

Chapter 18

Kenya, November 1965

The morning air was heavy, laden with moisture from clouds that bulged, sullen, grey and threatening, over the plains. Sarah scanned the throng for a glimpse of Piet, but there was no sign of him. She picked up her baggage, and walked out into the arrivals hall with a fluttering sensation in her stomach. A group of hunters and safari guides were waiting at the barrier, and she spotted Anthony in their midst, his bush hat pushed back off his face, his eyes searching the line of emerging passengers.

'Sarah!' He waved to her, above the noise and press of reunions that swelled around them like surf on a distant reef. Her spirits plummeted, and he saw her expression of chagrin before she was able to mask it. She smiled as he pushed his way through the crowds to take her hand. It was good to see him, but what had happened to Piet?

'Salaams. Welcome back. Piet asked me to do the honours. I'm a poor substitute, I know. Sorry. *Pole sana.*' He took her bags, and she followed him out of the building.

'Thanks for turning out so early in the morning. There's nothing wrong, is there?' Anxiety made it difficult for her to sound offhand.

'Trouble with poachers. Yesterday they managed to bring down a big old jumbo. They hacked out the tusks and left the carcass lying near the waterhole, right in front of the lodge. Terrible sight from the viewing platform. Piet started after them with a couple of trackers, but they had no luck. He had to leave Kipchoge still on the trail and drive down here, because he had a meeting with the Game Department this morning. He's going to be up to his ears all day.'

'That's desperate.' Sarah understood that these crises had to be dealt with, but the disappointment lingered. 'Have you been at Langani?'

'No. I've been here for a few days, between safaris. Piet telephoned me last night. What worries him most is that those bastards seem to know exactly where his patrol is going to be. It's almost as if they have an informer among the *watu*.'

'Surely that wouldn't be in the interests of his workers?' Sarah said. 'I mean, the safety of the game is a guarantee of jobs at Langani. So why would anyone tip off poachers?'

'Bribes, probably. A few shillings in the hand is more than enough incentive. They've had three or four incidents at Langani where poachers killed off zebra and impala, and even a young buffalo. It's bad enough when they kill for the meat, or for a few zebra skins they can sell as rugs. But when they start taking down elephant, it becomes really serious.'

'And Kipchoge couldn't track them down?'

'It's easy enough for them to get away, with all that thick forest around. These guys were really brazen, taking the elephant down so close to the lodge. He'd probably been at the waterhole and was on his way to some good feeding, poor old fellow. We can't afford to lose game like this, to organised gangs. The fact that they killed right below the viewing platform seems like a challenge. And they did it the day Piet's patrol was on the other side of the farm.'

'You don't think that was coincidence?'

'It's become a pattern. Piet decides on the route for his rangers, and the game is hit in another sector, or just after the patrol has passed. Can you imagine the reaction, if visitors were faced with a butchered elephant carcass right in front of them? Tourists won't risk visiting a place where armed poachers are hanging around.'

'There's still no progress on funding?' Sarah asked, as they made their way to the parking area. She climbed up into the front passenger seat, pleased to be back in a safari vehicle with its bird's-eye view.

'Piet's been back to all the key organisations. Last month, he put a proposal to several of the neighbouring farms. The idea was that they would share anti-poaching patrols. Create a game corridor through their land. Make costs more reasonable and extend the conservation area. Everyone keeps telling him it's a great plan, but no one actually wants to cough up.'

'It's so slow, this business of finance,' Sarah said. 'Allie Briggs says that some of these agencies even have a policy of holding up grants. By the time they're ready to write the cheque, the problem might have gone away. Or the applicants are in their graves.'

'She has a point there,' Anthony agreed. 'Anyhow, on a more cheerful note, you look very well, Sarah. I admire you for coming back, after what happened last time.'

'Well, as Hannah says, we can't let them beat us.' She gazed out the window. 'I spoke to Camilla on the phone about a week ago. She sounded . . . I don't know. Are you going to see her on your way to the States?'

'Not sure yet.' Anthony stared at the road ahead, plainly uncomfortable.

'Have you talked to her recently?' Sarah wanted to gauge his feelings, to understand where Camilla stood with him.

'No. I've been out on safari most of the time since you left.' Anthony sounded defensive. 'I did talk to her directly after the raid, you know. She said she had a good specialist. That everything would be fine. Tell me about Ireland.'

It was obvious that he did not want to discuss Camilla. Could she really have meant so little to him? Sarah wondered. A meaningless affair, unimportant in his scheme of things? They had seemed so passionately involved, so intensely aware of one another.

'I thought you were going to her twenty-first birthday,' she persisted. 'She seemed upset on the phone, but I couldn't get to the bottom of it. I hope she's all right.' As soon as she said the words, Sarah realised that she should have tried harder herself.

'I saw George in Nairobi last week,' Anthony said. 'He hadn't seen her lately. Hannah said she wrote several times and got no reply. If she doesn't want to stay in touch, there's not much anyone can do.'

Sarah did not feel she could push him any further. It was really none of her business. Looking at it logically, Camilla had spent very little time with him since their affair had begun. But logic had nothing to do with love, and they had been friends for years. Still smarting from her own rejection by Camilla, she abandoned the subject.

'What about the police investigations at Langani?'

'I think poor Hardy is embarrassed by his lack of progress. He's an efficient policeman and a good man and he doesn't like to see this kind of enquiry left unresolved, because it makes everybody jittery. Besides, he's been a family friend for years.'

'I thought perhaps Hannah was holding back for fear of scaring me. In case I'd change my mind and stay in Ireland.' Sarah kept her tone light but she felt cold whenever she thought of the robbery. She still woke up in the small hours, hearing the shots, convinced that Piet had been killed, seeing Camilla's face smeared with blood, overwhelmed by the same helpless panic that had taken hold as they fought to keep Lars from bleeding to death.

'The inspector still favours the theory that Piet is the victim of a vendetta,' Anthony said.

'That's a hideous idea. I mean, who, or why?'

'God only knows. Piet certainly doesn't have a clue. But there are good things to report too. The lodge is looking spectacular. We should have a good season coming up. Hannah has plenty of bookings.'

Weariness overcame Sarah and she dozed off. When they pulled up at the farm, Hannah was on the steps to welcome her. They walked down the verandah to the guest bedroom, talking about inconsequential things, circled by three young ridgeback dogs, tails waving at maximum speed, eyes full of curiosity.

'These are the new members of the family,' Hannah said, laughing. 'They're a menace – chewing everything in sight. But Jeremy has arranged for them to have basic police training. They go to school every morning. Just watch your shoes, or anything else you might think of leaving on the floor. Kamau has made a special "welcome home" lunch. So you're obliged to eat it, whether you're hungry or not.'

'Oh, here's Lars.' Sarah saw him walking across the lawn, and she went out to greet him with pleasure. He seemed fully recovered.

'Welcome back,' he said. 'I thought you might be delayed by muddy roads, but you and Anthony seem to have chased away the rain. Come and have a beer when you're ready.' He was looking at Hannah, who had not acknowledged him. She turned away without speaking. Sarah unpacked, wondering if there had been some disagreement between them about the farm. Hannah had said that she would not be sidelined. It was obviously an ongoing battle, or a skirmish at least. Sarah was smiling as she made her way to the sitting room. It felt good to be back there, but the gaps on the shelves, where Lottie's family treasures had been, made her shiver.

'Any news from Piet yet?' she asked, to mask her unease.

'Nothing. But he's not one to waste words, my brother, unless he has definite progress to report. You know that boy,' Hannah said. 'He'll drive straight back when he gets finished, unless the rain is too heavy. Honestly,

I've stopped hoping for any support from government departments, or big organisations. They don't want to know about us. Our problems are too small, we're the wrong colour, and we're bloody Afrikaners.'

'Anthony told me about the poachers.'

'Well, they don't confine themselves to Langani,' Hannah said, bitterly. 'Killing animals is rife all over the country. Jeremy has a vendetta theory, but I don't believe in it. We're good employers. Our *watu* know it. They're better off than a lot of labour on other farms. The conservation area is going to bring in tourists and generate more jobs. Why will no one help us?'

'Everything is bottle-necked,' Lars remarked. 'These new politicians and government officials are having a fine time throwing their weight around, enjoying their power and importance, blocking anything and everything. It's going to be like this for a while. Everyone is suffering the results.'

'Maybe,' Hannah said, turning her back on him. 'I still think we're worse off because they see us as Afrikaners – stupid and thick-skinned, like the oxen that carried us up here. We're still outsiders, just as we always were. Even though Piet and I were born here and we're Kenya citizens. There's no excuse for it.'

'Irish characters are looked at in the same way, you know,' Sarah said with sympathy. 'At least we can be considered stupid together.'

Hannah was not to be mollified. 'These days you can't be Afrikaans or Indian in this country. You have to be black, or British, or from the UN, otherwise you don't count. And certainly not if you're some *domkop yaapie*. It's the same "old-boy connections" that applied before *Uhuru*.'

'I think Lars is right,' Anthony said. 'It's wholesale bribery and corruption and everyone has to deal with it at some level. I have endless *shauris* with permits and licences. There's chaos in every department of the administration.'

'Allie Briggs told me they have the same problems at Buffalo Springs,' Sarah said. 'Poachers and cattle rustlers and Somali bandits all over the place, and no proper patrols to go after them. Plus politicians who look the other way for all sorts of reasons, but mostly for cash.'

'So. Am I getting paranoid from thinking about it too much?' Hannah's question was like a challenge. Then she sighed. 'It's probably true. Even Viktor says so. He's trying to see if any of his government contacts might be able to push things along. But it makes me mad to see how they give Piet the run-around.'

'Viktor's method of pushing things along is the last thing we need,' Lars said sharply. 'He's just lost a commission for a new government building. What kinds of contacts are those?'

'That was rigged.' Hannah was clearly angry. 'The project was given to an architect who paid a big bribe.'

'Piet will find a way.' Sarah tried to sound encouraging. 'Just when you're boiling with frustration, Langani Wildlife Reserve will be recognised by some big foundation, and you'll never look back.'

'I thought we had an ally in London trying to promote that idea,' Hannah said. 'But I haven't seen any evidence of that. You haven't heard from her, have you, Anthony?'

'Out in the *bundu* I don't hear from anybody,' he said. 'Looks like Mwangi is calling us. Good idea to have lunch outside on a day like this. How's the progress at the lodge, Lars?'

'They've put in the water pump and all the bathrooms are now working. We hope!' Lars said. 'We should take a run up there after lunch.'

'You should have a siesta, Sarah,' Anthony said. 'Otherwise you'll be falling asleep when the master of the house gets back. And that would never do.'

Sarah turned bright red, and Hannah was laughing as they went out on to the verandah and stood arm in arm, breathing in the afternoon air, revelling in the jagged beauty of Mount Kenya on the horizon.

'Kyrinyaga,' Sarah savoured the name. 'Now I feel I'm really home! But Anthony's right. I need my bed for an hour or so.'

At seven, Mwangi was padding round in his starched white *kanzu*, beaming and serving drinks as usual, but Sarah noticed a loaded rifle by the door. They were all seated around the fire, with the three dogs lounging on the rug beside them, when Lars appeared. Sarah glanced across the room. Hannah had stiffened in her chair, and now she leaned forward to engage Anthony in conversation, deliberately ignoring Lars. There was something going on here, Sarah thought. She would have to grill Hannah about it later.

Lars folded his big frame on to the sofa beside Sarah. 'So tell me, when do you start your research work?'

337

She turned to answer his question and the moment of tension passed. Dinner was nearly over when Piet appeared. Sarah noticed that he was thinner, that there were lines of strain around his eyes, a tightness that gave his mouth a little twist. But his smile and the timbre of his sing-song Afrikaans voice were unchanged. He walked around the table, and put his hands on her shoulders, kissing her briefly on the top of her head.

'Sarah. It's so good that you're back. Sorry I couldn't meet you. Did Anthony look after you all right?'

'Indeed he did.' She leaned back in her chair to look up at him, making no attempt to disguise her joy at seeing him. 'What about you? What progress in Nairobi?'

'Ach, it's always the same. They make sympathetic noises, but whether their promises will ever come to anything is doubtful. They have finally agreed to send a chap from the Game Department next week, for discussions on patrols. They've got no money, they say, and it means weeks of sending reports and letters that nobody reads. It all takes so bloody long, and in the meantime the poachers have free rein.'

'If the Game Department send someone up here looking around, that in itself might deter the poachers for a while,' Anthony said. 'That kind of news spreads fast.'

'Tired, Piet?' Hannah passed him the basket of bread.

'Not too bad. The rain held off and the road was easy. Simon drove on the way back. He's good behind the wheel now. Did you see Kipchoge?'

'He was still out on the trail when I was up at the lodge this evening,' Anthony said. 'He doesn't give up easily.'

'Will you drive up there with me tomorrow, Sarah? So much has been done since you left.' Piet rubbed his hands together, proud like a child that has completed a difficult task. 'When do you have to be in Buffalo Springs?'

'Allie Briggs is coming down to Nanyuki on Monday. She said she'd pick me up at the Silverbeck Hotel, if someone can give me a lift that far. So I've time to see everything. Tomorrow would be great.'

'Good,' Piet said. 'Hannah has done wonders, specially with training the staff. We'll have five-star service out there.'

'David has turned into an excellent cook,' Hannah said. 'You'll be impressed, Sarah.'

'That's right,' Piet agreed. 'He couldn't have run the office, but he has

338

real talent in the kitchen. Kamau is proud as an old peacock. It's good all round.'

'He's pretty good, that David. Heh, Mwangi?' Hannah looked up and touched the old man's sleeve. He smiled broadly, pleased at the talk of David's achievements, ready to report back to Kamau in the kitchen as soon as he had served the pudding.

'He will be the best *mpishi* in the region, memsahib. Maybe better than his father.' He cackled at the idea of Kamau being usurped. 'He is a good boy, *ndio*. The young ones will make the future with us. It is *Harambee*!'

They drifted to the sitting room for coffee, and soon afterwards Lars made his excuses and retired. Hannah, too, rose from her chair, smothering a yawn.

'You people have a nightcap. I have a very early start in the morning,' she said. She hesitated and then framed the next question carefully. 'Sarah, will you be all right – I mean, comfortable? On your own?' There was relief in her eyes as Sarah nodded, coupled with regret at the need to ask. 'Goodnight then, you nocturnal animals. I'll be pretty busy until noon, but I'll see you at lunchtime.'

'What time do you want to leave for the lodge, Piet?' Sarah looked at him, waiting for some hint that her return meant something special.

'We could start off early, take breakfast with us. The light will be beautiful for your camera. Simon will have the car ready around seven.' Piet went over to the drinks table. 'Anyone for a brandy now? I'm going to have one, to wash away the day in Nairobi. Anthony?'

'Not for me, thanks. I'm off first thing, back to all those city *shauris* I hate. I'll leave you night birds to it.' He grinned at Sarah as the give-away colouring rose in her cheeks, but she was determined to be bold.

'Night, Anthony. Thanks again for today,' she said. 'Yes, I'd love a brandy, Piet.'

There was a comfortable silence between them as they sat by the fire, looking up at one another from time to time, listening to the crackle and spit of the logs, and the small, contented groans and dream-twitching yips of the dogs stretched out on the rug.

'So tell me about your folks, and Tim.' Piet stirred in his chair and stretched out his long legs. 'I'll bet they were pretty surprised about your decision.'

'Surprised would be a mild word for it.' Sarah sighed as she recalled the heated discussions. 'They were full of dire warnings, and I had an awful row with Tim. He's like an old man since he got engaged to this nurse. Stuffy, cautious and dull.'

'He was always more sensible than the rest of us.' Piet smiled. 'Don't be hard on him. I'm sure he's just worried about you.'

'Dad was the most supportive,' Sarah said. 'I was amazed when he took my side, against Mum particularly. But then I felt so bad when I left him at the airport, and I saw how he hated me to go.'

'I expect he saw that there was no point trying to stop you once you got that look in your eye. Little Sarah.' Piet's voice had softened. 'Such a stubborn lady you are. I thought they taught you to be submissive in the convent. I'm glad you skipped those classes and you're here.'

'I knew it was right, although I wish it hadn't been such a stormy issue.' Sarah felt the thump of her heart beating very fast, and wondered if Piet could hear it too. 'And I am nervous about the job. I don't know a thing, and I could be useless at it. Plus I'm going to be stuck in a camp with two people who mightn't like me at all.'

'It will work out fine.' Piet was firm. 'You have a feel for the land and for the wildlife, and you know a lot more than you think. The rest you'll learn as you go along. They've done good work up there, the Briggses, and they're well respected. And you can come down here whenever you want.' His eyes were very bright in the firelight. 'I'm so glad you're back, Sarah, and I know Hannah feels the same. She needs your company, that's for sure. So, Langani is home now.' He stood up and reached for her hand, drawing her out of her chair. 'Let's take our drinks outside and count the stars. It's a clear night for a change.'

They stood on the verandah in a wash of starlight, and listened to the sounds of the bush. His hand caressed the hair on the back of her neck lightly, and she shivered.

'Are you cold?' he asked.

She shook her head and leaned against him, wanting to stay like this for ever. She was disappointed when he finished his brandy in one swallow and turned her round to face him.

'Better go to bed, girl, if we're setting out early tomorrow. I have so much to show you, so many things we must talk about. I'm going to take you up to my ridge, as I promised.' He bent and kissed her on the lips. She slid her arms around his waist, resting her head against him, their breath

340

mingling in the chilly air. She wanted to kiss him and taste him again, but she was afraid to move, to spoil the magic. His fingers moved along the line of her neck, traced the curve of her cheek. She felt weak.

'Sarah,' he murmured, 'what a beauty you've become. And so brave too, coming right back after what happened, carrying on with your dreams and your plans. My little Sarah. I only wish—' He stepped away from her, clearing his throat. 'I'm afraid you will have to lock the bedroom door. A sign of progress, heh? It's just a precaution. The nightwatchman is outside. Sleep well.' In a split second he was gone, whistling for the dogs and calling for Mwangi to lock up.

She made her way to her room, bemused and frustrated by the abrupt change in him. What was it he wished? she asked herself, running her fingers over her lips where he had kissed her, playing back every word he had said. She collapsed into bed, unable to think clearly beyond the fact that she was here with Piet, and that was all she wanted. The sinister giggle of a hyena stalked the edge of her dreams and the rain drummed on the roof later in the night, but she did not hear it. She woke to Mwangi's soft tap on the door.

'*Hodi*, Memsahib Sarah. *Chai*. I hope you have slept well.'

The sun was a flaming orange disc in a smoky sky. Pulling a thick sweater over her bush shirt, she ran out to the Land Rover to join Piet. Simon greeted her with solemn courtesy, and Kipchoge pressed her hand between both of his, welcoming her in Swahili and in his own tribal language. The bush was alive with the new day. Birds and monkeys swooped and called and leapt through the canopy of trees, showering drops of rain from the wet leaves on to the ground. Zebra and waterbuck scattered before them as they drove down the track, sliding and splashing through puddles, spattering the car with red mud. A lone giraffe gazed on them from his lofty perspective, reaching out with long, black lips and a rough tongue to nibble at the tops of the thorn trees. Kipchoge stood in the back of the car, his short spear resting lightly in his hand as he scanned the horizon for the movement of game in the distance. Far away to the west, they could see vultures hovering in the air.

'Might be a fresh kill over there,' Piet said. 'There's a pride of lions over that way. Let's go and see what they've got.'

They followed the lazy circling of the birds until they came across the carcass of a zebra, the skeleton picked perfectly clean, although Kipchoge pronounced that the kill had been made fresh during the night or very early that morning. The stomach and its contents of half-digested grasses had been neatly laid to one side where the vultures and then the smaller rodents and insects would tear and burrow until there was nothing left to see. No morsel would be wasted in the frenzy of feeding, and Sarah marvelled at how a living beast could be reduced to a pile of bare bones in such a short time. She wondered if the white colonists of Africa would one day suffer the same fate, their institutions and their monuments lying open and empty on the sun-bleached land where only wild things remained. Piet jumped down from the car and walked over to the zebra, lifting up the head with its still bright, open eyes, poignant in premature death. Simon and Kipchoge watched, impassive, from the car, but Sarah felt regret for the brief life of the animal. There was no place here for sentimentality, however, least of all in the work she had come to do. Piet walked back to the Land Rover and started the engine.

'Let's go,' he said. 'We may find the lions resting up after their feast. I suspect they're not too far away.'

They were lying in the shade of a thorn tree a few hundred yards up the track, replete and comatose. Three lionesses with their cubs and, nearby in the dappled shade, Sarah could just make out the dark mane of a fine male. The cubs stared at the car inquisitively, but none of the adults moved, except to yawn or flick a tail lazily against a fly. The air was heating up and loud with cicadas and the rustling of baboons in another tree. Away to the left, where the plains opened out, herds of zebra and gazelles grazed, seemingly unconcerned that one of their number had been lost, perhaps aware that the lions would not hunt again today.

The rooms at the lodge were fully furnished now, and Hannah had planted the approach with indigenous shrubs, softening any raw scars of recent construction. The buildings had almost vanished into the rocky outcrop on which they were set, as though they had grown with it out of the earth.

'We have a radio telephone hooked in to the farm,' Piet was saying. 'And round the back is the garage for the supply trucks and the game-viewing cars. I've taken on a mechanic who worked for several years at a Land Rover garage in Nairobi, so he knows his stuff. He'll look after the generator too, and do the odd jobs. Stores for food and fuel are hidden behind the rocks, over here. All the guests will see is the waterhole and the salt lick, and the game trails leading down to the plains. Now, come and see the lounge and dining area all finished.'

He led the way, bounding up the path like a puppy, so that Sarah found herself running to keep up with him.

'Hey, wait for me,' she called. 'No use giving me the grand tour at this speed.'

'Sorry. I get a bit carried away here.' He strode back to her, contrite but laughing. 'I want you to see everything before we go to the ridge. Do you think all those fancy Americans will like it?' He watched her intently. They had come to the viewing platform and he took her hand. 'Something spooked you last time. Remember? Do you still feel it? It's important to me what you think.'

'So many questions! Give me a chance to answer them one at a time!' Sarah remembered only too well the sensation she had experienced on the platform. But today it was peaceful, and she squeezed his hand and gazed down at the tranquil scene around the waterhole and the glade below. Nothing could mar Piet's sense of achievement now.

'It's wonderful,' she said. 'Magical. Your guests will love it, I'm sure they will. And what happened last time was a stupid thing. You know how Hannah's always teasing me for being weird. Fey, they call it in Ireland, where everyone seems to have a touch of it. That's all it was. Really. The place is extraordinary. I love that leopard sculpture on the big table.'

Piet sighed. 'That was expensive. Whatever way you look at it,' he said. Sarah looked at him questioningly, but he moved away from the bronze leopard. 'I'll tell you another time. It's Hannah's personal treasure.' He gestured around the room. 'You know, there were times when I thought I wouldn't be able to finish this. It was taking up so much time, draining so much money away from the farm.' He paused. 'I told you before that Pa left the accounts in a shambles, and we had problems the first year I was on my own. And just when the bank was beginning to ease up the pressure a little, we had bacterial blight in the wheat. Then the slaughter of those cows set us back again. Plus I've had to bring in extra *watu* for security, as well as for new jobs at the lodge. Sometimes I thought the whole project would have to be scrapped. I'm still not sure how I'm going to keep it all together. I only hope it pays from the beginning, or we'll be in trouble.'

'You mustn't give up,' Sarah said urgently. 'Funding will come

343

through in the end. Have faith in yourself, in what you've already achieved. You've built this amazing place, the first of its kind, and clients will come. I know it.'

'You have to be right. Ach, you're my good luck charm, Sarah. I feel it in my bones, yes. We'll have an *ngoma* here for the opening – a big feast and dancing. The *watu* will like that. You must be here for it.' Piet grasped her arm, triumphant and laughing. 'Now, would you like to ride? I've been keeping a few horses here over the last month, to get them used to the trails. It's good having them at the lodge, but we've had to bring in a nightwatchman to guard them.'

'Surely poachers wouldn't—'

'Not poachers.' Piet shook his head, and smiled. 'This time it's the big cats. They can smell horseflesh from miles away. It's a delicacy for lions and leopards, and they're only too pleased to come round for dinner.'

'So you're planning to take your guests out riding?' Sarah asked.

'With a guide. He'll have a rifle, just in case. I think it will be good. Shall we go?'

They set out slowly, skirting the herds. At first the animals skittered away, but after a while they just stood and watched, tails flicking, moist noses twitching. Simon rode beside them and Kipchoge ambled along at the rear, carrying an old gun that had belonged to Jan. A herd of zebra snorted, turned their fat rumps and trotted parallel to the horses. Sarah felt her mount pick up pace, jinking and prancing in the midst of these strange creatures, muscles rippling with the desire to run ahead of them. Piet signalled, and then they raced away, feeling the ground shake with the thunder of hundreds of hooves until they left the herd behind, and started up a gradual rise, picking their way along a rocky trail that led up the side of Piet's ridge. The path was steep, and soon they had to dismount, walking in single file, with the noise of loose stones dislodged by their horses' hooves and clattering down the escarpment into the bushes below. Finally, the way became too sheer, and Piet stopped.

'Simon and Kipchoge can tether the animals, and wait for us here. Come on, Sarah. Last scramble to the top. But it's worth the effort.'

He led the way up the scree, and they came out on to the summit of the ridge. His hands on her waist, he turned her slowly, so that Sarah saw the whole panorama before her. She stood, buffeted by the wind, looking around her in awe. Langani ranch stretched below them, laid out in glowing colour. She could see the long, low spread of the house, with its stables and outbuildings, Hannah's cattle sheds and the milking parlour. The dairy herds were like toys on the green pasture, and the wind was making a gold sway of the wheat fields. As she moved, the thatched houses of the labour came into view, and then Lottie's red-roofed school and dispensary. Directly below her, the buildings of the lodge emerged from the shadowy canopy of trees and the burnt sienna of the rocks that formed the kopje. In between was the curve of the river and the *bundu*, peppered with scrub and the rounded tops of acacia trees, and the red fingers of termite mounds. Everything looked perfect, like a model set out on a gigantic trestle for the admiration of the gods. Sarah spread her arms wide and Piet stood back to watch with tender amusement. She was flecked with mud from the ride, and laughing with exuberance as she turned round and round, shouting that it was the most wonderful place in the world. When she was too dizzy to turn any more, he caught her, and she leaned against him, trying to wipe the drying soil from around her eyes, and creating instead a pattern of red streaks across her face.

'You look like a rock hyrax with that mask you've made,' he said, taking a handkerchief from his pocket to wipe away the smears. Sarah held her breath as he bent forward, one hand in the small of her back, drawing her close to him while he dabbed at her cheek with the other.

'There.' He put the handkerchief into his pocket, without letting her go.

She stood still for a second, then put her arms around his neck, and raised her mouth for his kiss. He was the only man she had ever wanted. She loved him. He had brought her here to his special place and that had to mean something. He bent his head, and his lips found hers, and then he was pulling her tight against him, and her whole body was filled with delight. He kissed her again and again – on her mouth, her forehead, her eyes, her throat – until she was breathless. She touched the short bristle at the nape of his neck, let her fingers stray along the line of his jaw, and bury themselves in the warm strawy thatch of his hair, then move downwards again to trace his cheekbones and his wide strong neck. At last, they drew apart a little, and stood looking at one another, their fingers entwined.

'Come and sit down.' His voice was hoarse. He led her to a seat hollowed out of the rock, and they sat close together, looking out at the land below. He took her hand, kissed each of her fingers, and she rested her head against his chest.

'I read your poem,' he said quietly. 'You know, the Masefield poem you quoted in Gedi? It haunted me. I went home and looked it up. The first part of it is very pessimistic. But Langani is not going to be like those ruined cities. It's going to live. And prosper. With vision and determination. You have that vision, Sarah. You give me courage, and faith in myself. You're my inspiration. Like the last lines in the poem.

> '. . . let the spirit dive
> Deep in self's sea, until the deeps unlock
> The depths and sunken gold of being alive,
> Till, though our Many pass, a Something stands
> Aloft through Time that covers all with sands.'

He put both arms around her, and rested his chin on the top of her head. 'I'm an awful fool, Sarah. I was looking for my true soulmate, and I thought—'

'You don't need to say this, Piet.' She turned to put a finger to his lips. 'It would have been hard not to . . .'

'I do need to say it, though. I don't want any taboo subjects between us. I was crazy for her. Idiotic, when you come to think of it. The Afrikaans farm boy chasing the princess.' She made a sound of protest, but he smiled down at her. 'No fairy-tale endings there, heh? She got into my blood, and for a while I hoped she felt the same. Like a touch of malaria, the kind that keeps recurring when you think you're cured. And I ended up making an idiot of myself.'

'No!' Sarah said. 'She tried to make a fool out of you. She used you, hurt you, and I was so angry with her it nearly finished our friendship. You were so sweet to her when she came out on safari with us, considering what she did to you. It must have been hard. Seeing Anthony . . .'

She stopped, uncomfortable. She really did not want to talk about Camilla. Didn't want the shadow of her on Piet's ridge. And was it completely over? She was afraid to ask him. What if he was choosing her as the next best thing? Someone he knew was fond of him, who was a good friend to his sister. Sarah closed her eyes in panic. Felt his hand under her chin, lifting her face towards him.

'There are things we have to talk about, Sarah. There's something deep and wonderful growing between us. But I need time to sort out what's going on at Langani.'

Sarah wanted to say something comforting, but she did not want to interrupt his train of thought.

'I'm worried about Ma, too. Since they went to Rhodesia, Pa has gone to pieces and he's still drinking. I know Hannah told you why she left there. She begged Ma to come home after the raid, but Pa – well, I think he can't see a role for himself at Langani any more. And Ma won't leave him there alone.'

'Hannah must be very disappointed,' Sarah said.

'My sister is a great girl. So courageous. It's lonely for her, and since the robbery, she's found it tough. I haven't been much help. I'm out a lot, on the farm and at the lodge. And so is Lars. I thought for a while there was something going between them. He's a good man, my friend Lars. Steady. Dependable. But she was in a strange mood after the raid. Then Viktor Szustak – you remember, he's my architect – he's started coming up here regularly, staying at the house and fooling around with Hannah. Viktor is a menace, because this won't last and it can only mean a bad outcome for Hannah when he moves on. Lars is furious, and it's created a big problem.'

'That explains a lot,' Sarah said. 'I noticed the tension between them yesterday.'

'That's the understatement of the year. It's like living on the slopes of a volcano! Lars and Hannah can't even look at each other, let alone work together. If it gets much worse, I'm afraid he'll leave. And I have no idea how I would manage without him. I can't get rid of bloody Viktor until the lodge is completely finished, but I've warned him about hurting her.'

'And?'

'He just laughs and says she's splendid and he adores her. And Hannah tells me it's none of my damn business.'

'I can try talking to her, to find out how she really feels. Poor Lars. He does love her – I'm sure of that. The sad thing is, he's absolutely ideal for her, if only she wasn't so stupid.'

'I know.' Piet gave her a lopsided grin. 'It seems to run in the family. But this thing of Hannah's is not going anywhere. Viktor will never settle down on a farm. Or anywhere. And Hannah wouldn't want to leave Langani. At least I can't imagine it.' He paused, and his arms tightened

347

around her. 'Anyway, enough of my *shauris*. You're starting a new job next week. A new life. I'll come up to see you in Buffalo Springs if I can get away. But in any case, you'll spend Christmas at Langani with Hannah and me. And maybe Ma and Pa will be here too. Is that all right with you?'

She slid on to his lap, put her arms around his neck. This was going to be hard. She wanted to shout her love to the sky, but she realised she must go carefully. She mustn't rush him. It was enough, for now, to have these moments to hold in her heart. He kissed her again, holding her tight and then took her hand.

'Better get down to the horses. Kipchoge and Simon will have turned to stone.'

It had started to rain by the time they reached the lodge. Piet dismounted, and helped Sarah down, leaning in against her as he lifted her from the saddle, looking into her eyes. She put out a hand to trace his lips.

'There you are. How was the ride?' Hannah greeted them cheerfully. Sarah turned, startled, and busied herself with the stirrup leathers, her face hidden from Hannah's knowing gaze. Behind her on the steps David stood in his starched drill uniform, and white chef's apron. 'We have a tour de force prepared for lunch,' Hannah said. 'You just have time to freshen up before we start.'

'I know how those lions felt this morning,' said Sarah later, with a groan. 'I can't believe I ate that much. I won't be able to move for a week.'

'It's so good to see Piet so optimistic again,' Hannah said. 'Things have been bad lately. He was beginning to lose heart. We all were.'

'I know how desperately you still need financial help.'

'When did you last talk to her?' Hannah asked, her aggressive tone reflecting the change of subject.

'A few days ago. I was planning to stop in London, but she didn't want to see me.'

'She obviously never spoke to her father. I was so worried about her. I felt partly responsible for what happened, because she was here on our farm and she had organised our wonderful holiday with Anthony. She did so much, seemed so happy. So concerned about Langani. And after she left I kept thinking about how scared she must be, after being attacked. And maybe having her career ruined as well.'

'I think her face is going to be fine.'

'I can't keep ringing her,' Hannah said. 'It's very expensive. She never replied to my letter. So we have to face it. All her fine promises were hot air. Langani is an unhappy memory, and she wants to put it behind her. I don't think she cares about us at all.'

'I don't know, Han. She sounded so strange on the phone. She said she'd seen George. They hadn't discussed Langani, but she hoped they would. I thought you might have heard from her, because she mentioned coming back here.'

'I must admit, I did feel sorry for her with Anthony. That was rough.'

'I agree. I remember you saying he's great out in the bush, but pretty superficial when it comes to other people's feelings. He had his fling with Camilla, and then he dumped her. She was really devastated.'

'So now she knows how Piet felt, when she wiped the floor with him,' Hannah retorted.

'Hannah!'

'I'm sorry. That was a bitchy thing to say. I hope her face gets repaired, and she can continue along her path to fame and fortune. But I can't believe she never spoke to her father. As for Anthony, we're not responsible for his behaviour. I'm sure he didn't make any promises. You know what these hunter types are like. Hell, let's get off the subject of Camilla.'

'Yes, let's. So what about the farm?'

'Not too bad, now. The thing with the cattle made a big dent in our dairy figures. The herdsmen were spooked, and two of them disappeared as soon as they were paid at the end of the month. Piet and Lars haggled with the bank and bought some heifers at a good price, so we're slowly getting back to normal.' She hesitated. 'He's clever when it comes to negotiating, Lars.'

'You two don't seem to be on very good terms.'

'I told you before, he thinks he's always right, and he interferes in what's none of his business.' Hannah shifted irritably in her chair. 'I can't work with him at all. And it's only because I'm involved with someone else that he's being such a bore.'

'Who? Come on, Hannah, tell!'

'Viktor. God, Sarah, he is so amazing. So exciting, and exotic and romantic. And when he makes love to me, I feel beautiful. He keeps telling me he adores me and he only wants me to be happy.'

Hannah's eyes were luminous, her face glowing, her hands clasped together tightly as she talked about him. Sarah felt a tug of fear for her. This man had awakened a powerful emotion in her, making her vulnerable.

'Does he love you?' she asked. 'I know he's wonderful and exciting and everything, but, well, you saw what happened to Camilla.'

'Of course he does. He's not hollow like Anthony. I suppose you don't approve of me sleeping with him.'

'That's for you to decide, Han. I'd need to know that I had a commitment, and for me it's a religious thing too. But Viktor has a bit of a reputation, you know. Not that I don't think he's mad about you, but—'

'You sound just like Lars. And my brother.' She looked at Sarah suspiciously. 'Have they been talking to you? Persuading you to get me out of Viktor's clutches?'

'Of course they haven't,' Sarah said hastily. 'I hope Viktor will always make you happy. But I did think you and Lars might get together. You always seemed so right for each other.'

Hannah shook her head slowly. 'When I saw him lying there that night, with blood pouring out of him and his face like putty, I was terrified he was going to die. I thought I couldn't survive without him. And afterwards, in the hospital, it was good, holding him up, feeding him soup, seeing how grateful he was.' She stopped, awkwardly. 'I kissed him once or twice, in a sisterly sort of way. But when I came back here after the robbery, it was so awful. I was afraid. All the time. I kept hearing things, seeing figures in the bushes outside, or on the verandah. I could only sit down if I had a solid wall at my back. And at night, that was the worst. I didn't want to be alone, but I couldn't run to Piet like a baby, and ask if I could sleep with him. It was a waking nightmare. You saw what they did to the dogs.' Her eyes filled with tears. 'I couldn't think of anything but the smell of that carpet over us, and the sound of the shots, and thinking they'd killed Piet, and then Camilla's face and Lars bleeding and making stupid jokes to keep me from falling apart.'

'I wish I could have stayed.' Sarah reached out and took Hannah's hand. 'I know what the nightmares are like. If we could have been together.'

'In fact, I did go to Lars's room one night. Quite soon after he came back to the farm. I was so scared and I wanted someone to hold me. But Piet heard me tapping on Lars's bedroom door and he called out. So I went to the kitchen and made a hot drink, and then Lars appeared. He'd heard me too. He took me back to my room and tucked me into bed like I was a child, and went away. I cried myself to sleep. But if he'd stayed with me, well . . .' She shrugged. 'Then Viktor came along. My prince of darkness, that's what he calls himself. I can't even begin to describe how he makes me feel, Sarah. When I'm not with him, every bit of me is burning until I can see him again.'

'When will I meet him?'

'He's supervising a job at the coast this week. I count every hour that he's away, and every second of the time I have with him when he's here. Wild, heh? Me turning into a quivering jelly at the touch of a man!' She gave a little laugh, but when she spoke again, her voice was full of sadness. 'I really miss Ma, you know.'

'How are things going down there?' Sarah said. 'That was a big turning point, with Smith and his Unilateral Declaration of Independence.'

'I don't know. There's so much violence and killing. Pa has to go out on more and more patrols, and his cousin chooses him every time there's a skirmish in the area. Ma says the man is downright crazy. She sounds so hopeless when I talk to her. I still feel guilty about leaving her. But I couldn't have stayed, and I can't see them coming back for the time being.'

'So your time is all taken up with the farm. And Viktor.'

'That's about it. And Piet's just as bad as Lars – they're like brothers. Neither of them can bear the idea of my falling for Viktor. Or for anyone, in fact. Piet once punched a guy who was kissing me at the Nanyuki Club, you know. He's worse than the dominee from the Dutch Reform Church!'

They laughed out loud, scaring a couple of warthogs in search of a mud-bath.

'And talking of Piet?' Hannah said, her eyebrows raised in enquiry.

'You know as much as I do.' Sarah ran her fingers through her dusty mop of hair. She could not look Hannah in the eye.

'He is still such a mutt!' Hannah said. 'But he really does love you. I know it, and he knows it too, even if he hasn't said it to himself in so many words. Just give him time. He's so taken up with the farm and the lodge and all.'

'Do you think he's really over Camilla?' Sarah asked, deeply unsure. On the ridge he had kissed her. But he had not said that he loved her. Instead, she had been given a summary of his troubles.

'You and Piet are made for each other, Sarah. You're soulmates,' Hannah said. 'He values your judgment, tells you things he never discusses with anyone else. He knows you understand him, and he talks about you all the time when you're not here. I've seen the way he looks at you. Like today, when I barged in on your little moment.' She gave a wicked grin. 'Don't fret about my thick brother. He'll come round. And you'd better watch out when he does.'

The weekend flew past, hours and minutes devoured at a relentless speed over which Sarah had no control. She worked alongside Hannah at the dispensary, visited the dairy, counted bags of feed and fertiliser in the stores, hemmed curtains for the lodge and framed pictures with driftwood she picked up in the forest. In the early mornings she rode with Piet, and as the sun rose to blister the land they stopped under the shelter of a thorn tree and reached for one another, touching, exploring, caressing. Then he would be off to work with Lars. She and Hannah often heard the sound of their rifle practice.

On the last day of her stay, Sarah found the atmosphere between Lars and Hannah particularly brittle. Hannah had been edgy all day – Viktor had not phoned, and she did not know when he would return to Langani. When the call had come through in the afternoon it was Lars who had answered. He did not know where Hannah was, he told Viktor. Later there was a furious argument outside the office, and Lars stormed off and did not reappear until dinner.

'You'll be back for Christmas, Sarah, and for the opening of the lodge and the *ngoma* too,' Piet said, breaking the icy silence at the table. 'Maybe the Briggses would like to join us for that. It will be a fine thing for the labour, and the local elders, and the wives and *totos*.'

She was glad when the meal was over and Piet pulled back her chair and asked her if she would like her coffee outside.

'It's chilly,' he said. 'But not as bad as it is inside.'

'You're right,' she said, laughing. They were leaning on the railing of the verandah, their shoulders touching. 'You look a bit preoccupied. Because of what's going on in there?'

'No,' he said. He lit a cigarette, scanning the dark area in front of the house as he smoked. 'I had a phone call from Jeremy Hardy today, and he may be right about the incidents here all being linked. No one else round here has had problems like ours recently. And if there's more trouble on the way, I don't have enough security in place even now. More and more, I think Pa was right when he said we wouldn't get any support from the British organisations, because we're Afrikaners.' He punched his fist against the verandah post. 'And the new whites on loan to the government are almost worse than the old guard. Because they've never set foot in Africa before, but they're armed with manuals and ready-made prejudices and solutions that can't work here. And they won't listen to those they see as old-time whites.'

Piet took a final drag of his cigarette, then stamped it out angrily. He looked back into the sitting room, but it was empty. Hannah had gone early to bed, and Lars was in the office catching up on his paperwork.

'Do you remember the last time we had dancing here?' he said. 'When Camilla was teaching Lars how to do the twist. Remember that? So, what can have happened to her? She wouldn't have let us down. I think her father has chosen to ignore us, like all the rest of them. She knew how much we were depending on her, but she's caught between her father and us. Or she has a problem with that gash on her head. It's so awful to think of her being marked for life. I know you tried to talk to her before you left. Maybe she's out of work, or scared or depressed and you should have gone there. To see if she was all right. Poor Camilla, she—'

His words triggered in Sarah the nagging guilt she already carried. Insecurity and frustration erupted in helpless rage.

'Bloody Camilla! It's always been Camilla and what she's thinking or doing! No doubt she's in some nightclub in London right now, drinking champagne and draping herself around some horny photographer! When are you ever going to see that she doesn't give a damn about any of us? The only one she wanted was Anthony, and that's probably because he never got caught in her trap. Why can't you ever see past the end of your nose? I'm sick of hearing about Camilla and what she might or might not do! I've loved you since the first time I saw you. I'd have done anything for you. You were only too ready to declare your love for her, but you haven't said you love me. Even on the ridge, when you kissed me, you didn't say it. And you couldn't say it was over – this Camilla thing.' Through the humiliating tears that blurred her vision she could see Piet's astonished expression, but it only fuelled her anger. 'You can keep holding your flaming torch for Camilla, then. I never could compete with her. But I tell you this – what I had to offer you, if you had

353

wanted it, would never have let you down, or shamed you or used you. Never!'

She broke off, horrified at what she had said. But there was no taking it back. Piet was gaping at her, dumb with surprise.

'Oh shit!' Sarah spun away from him, shouting into the night. 'Shit and bugger and bollocks!' She heard him make a strangled sound and spun round, blazing with defiance. 'I'm sorry. I don't usually swear. The truth is I love you, Piet van der Beer. I love you, and I don't mind who hears me say it. But I'm no match for cool, blonde Lady Camilla. So I'll just bugger off to Buffalo Springs in the morning, and you can go back to being a stupid farm boy, as you said!'

She was about to flee to the refuge of her room when Lars emerged from the office, taking in Sarah's angry, tear-streaked face .

'Sorry to break in on your little chat,' he said. 'But Juma says there's some *shauri* down at the labour lines. A fight. I think we'd better go down there before things get out of hand.'

Piet left the verandah without a word, and Sarah heard the Land Rover crunching over the loose stones in the driveway, and saw the flicker of headlights in the trees. She thought of unburdening herself to Hannah. But the idea of confiding her foolishness to someone who was so gloriously in love was too painful. She walked rapidly to her bedroom and shut the door behind her. That was it, then. Whatever germ of feeling Piet had for her, she had killed it stone dead. She had gone after him like a harridan, betrayed Camilla in a fit of jealous rage, and made a complete ass of herself into the bargain. With a groan she sank on to her bed, and beat her fists against the pillow in fury at her own stupidity.

Chapter 19

Kenya, November 1965

There was no sign of Piet at the breakfast table. Sarah hoped that he was already out on the farm, and that she would not have to face him. She could not think of anything she might say that would mend the débâcle of the previous night. Lars and Hannah were sitting at opposite ends of the table.

'Fried eggs, with sausage and bacon, for Memsahib Sarah?' Mwangi said. He knew her favourites.

'Just coffee, Mwangi, thank you.' Sarah forced a smile. 'With some toast, maybe.'

'Are you all right, Sarah?' Hannah was looking at her now. 'You look pale. Tired, too.'

'You do look a little rough,' Lars agreed. 'But you should eat, you know – it will be a long ride up to Isiolo, especially if it starts raining again. I'm driving to Nanyuki to get supplies, by the way, so I can take you.'

'Thanks. And I'm fine. Really. I just didn't sleep too well. What happened on the labour lines last night?'

'I hope that didn't keep you awake,' Hannah said. 'It was nothing important. It's all been sorted out.'

'But there was a fight?'

'You know how they are,' Hannah shrugged. 'Full of superstition. Kamau and David found a dead chicken outside their quarters, with its head cut off and its entrails spread all over the ground. Some sort of spell, they thought. Kamau was really worked up about it.'

'When Piet and I arrived, everybody was shouting and making wild accusations,' Lars said. 'Probably fuelled by a few gallons of some illegal brew. David said Simon had put a curse on his father. Then a fight started.

Poor Simon denied everything. But he's the newcomer, so he was blamed. And David is jealous of him.'

'But I thought David was proud of being the cook,' Sarah said, puzzled.

'He is,' Lars said. 'But he and Kamau have never accepted Simon. They still think he got the plum job at the lodge, over the old-timers. Anyhow, Simon was apparently drinking in his hut with Kipchoge for most of the evening, so I don't see how he could have been responsible. He tried to convince David, but I think everyone was too drunk. They're still upset about what happened to the cattle, and David wanted a fight. By the time we arrived, Simon had a swollen eye, and he was pretty scared. God knows who killed the wretched bird, or why. It was a typical sacrificial thing. Piet thinks maybe David might have done it himself, to make trouble for Simon. It's anyone's guess. Anyway, it's all died down. For now.'

'Poor Simon,' said Sarah. But she was relieved that the whole incident had saved her from making an even worse fool of herself.

'I came out to look for you when Lars and Piet left, but you'd gone,' Hannah said.

'I needed an early night.' Sarah was hot with embarrassment. 'But I didn't sleep. All the changes – you know. And I'm never at my best first thing in the morning. You should remember what a grouse I was at school until the end of first class.'

She stirred her coffee, concentrating on the spoon circling in the black liquid, creating a murky whirlpool like the one she had been sucked into last night. The dining-room door opened and her heart sank as she saw Piet's reflection in the mirror above the sideboard. He was singing something under his breath. Sarah mumbled a greeting, and kept her head down. He looked as though he had not a care in the world, she thought. And maybe he hadn't, now that he had wiped her off his slate as a jealous hysteric. Decided to treat her behaviour with the contempt it surely deserved. He strolled past her to take his place at the table. Now Sarah could make out the words he was singing.

'*Shit, bugger and bollocks, the truth is there to see . . .*'

Her face flamed, and he sang the words a little louder, so that everyone could hear.

Hannah stared at him. 'Piet! Really! Can't you see you're embarrassing Sarah?'

'Am I?' Piet looked down at Sarah with a guileless grin. 'Ach yes. I'd forgotten. She wouldn't ever use words like that, not with her convent education, and so.'

Sarah stood up quickly. 'I'll get my stuff together. I'll be ready when you are, Lars.'

She fled, his singing echoing in her ears. In the safety of her room she cleaned her teeth with ferocity and put the last of her belongings into her suitcase. As she closed the bag, there was a sound behind her and she turned to see Piet leaning against the doorpost, watching her. She closed her eyes briefly, and launched into an apology, but he cut her short.

'I can't take you to Nanyuki today,' he said. 'There's a lot to do before the man from the Game Department arrives. Lars will drive you.'

'Thank you,' she said in a small voice.

'So, I have to go now,' Piet said.

'Yes. Of course. Well, goodbye. I . . .'

She stopped, conscious of the fact that she had ruined her friendship with the person who meant more to her than anyone else in the world. Then he strode across the room, and gripped her arm. She looked at him in alarm, but he was laughing as he pulled her towards him and kissed her.

'Aren't you the most surprising girl, Sarah Mackay? And mighty desirable too, in spite of your terrible language. I imagine you learned that from your brother. Or the nuns? No, I don't suppose it was the nuns, somehow. You'd want to be careful you don't shock your new employers!' He smiled down at her, brushed her hair away from her face and kissed her again. 'Good luck with the job. Call us on the radio when you get there. You'll be back soon, heh? And I'll be waiting.'

He was gone before she could catch her breath, leaving her utterly confused. Had he simply been making fun of her childish outburst? She could hear him as he walked away along the verandah, singing cheerfully.

'*Shit, bugger and bollocks, the truth is there for me . . .*'

'What was all that about in the dining room?' Hannah walked with her to the pick up where Lars was waiting.

'What?' Sarah tried to look vague, aware that she was hopeless at deception.

'Why is my brother so weird this morning? And that dreadful song was obviously aimed at you. What's going on?'

'It's a stupid joke. I'll explain it some other time, Han.' Sarah did not

357

know what to make of Piet and this was no time for confessions. Lars had started the truck.

Hannah made a face. 'All right – keep it to yourself if you want.'

'I'll tell you when I come back.' Sarah squeezed Hannah's hand. 'Thanks for everything. I'll be in touch as soon as I'm settled.'

Lars put the truck into gear, and they rolled off down the drive. Lars looked at her speculatively, and she wondered how much of her outburst he had heard the previous night. She longed to say something to him about Hannah, but she was afraid to interfere and possibly make their situation worse. The unspoken problems hung between them in the cab of the truck. As they pulled up at the Silverbeck, Sarah leaned over and took his hand in both of hers.

'You are such a wonderful man,' she said. 'And I know things are tough right now. But you can stick it out, just for a while. Piet depends on you – you're his right hand. And Hannah does love you, Lars, only not in that way. At least not right now. So, try and be patient. Don't give up on her. And take care of Piet for me, will you? I know how you feel, Lars, because I've been there. You're the best, strong like a rock. And no matter how you feel about things today, there's always hope. Always.'

She hugged him and then went round to the back of the truck to get her luggage. After a minute, Lars followed. He was mumbling something she could not hear in reply to her little speech, but as he lifted her bags down he was smiling. Allie Briggs's Land Rover, mud-splattered and piled high with provisions, was already parked in the shade of a large flame tree. Two Africans in khaki drill uniforms sat in the back. Sarah found her new employer in the foyer, and Lars introduced himself briefly, said his goodbyes and left. Allie shook Sarah's hand briskly.

'Good to see you again,' she said. 'I ordered a curry lunch for two. I hope that suits. Do you know this place at all?'

'No. I've never been—'

'The equator line supposedly runs through the bar over there—' Allie waved a hand. 'Apparently the rooms on one side of the equator line have bathwater that runs clockwise down the plughole, and the others have an anticlockwise gurgle. I suspect this is particularly true if you watch them late at night, after you've had a few jars,' she said, grinning. 'As soon as we've had lunch, we should be on the road.'

The Langani truck had disappeared. Sarah felt shy and gauche, and lonely for Lars. She wondered what she could say to this capable, knowledgeable woman on the journey north. In the dining room several people greeted Allie and she introduced her new researcher. Sarah started to relax a little. She was asking about the camp and the work when their conversation was interrupted by a shout. Bearing down on them from the direction of the bar was a tall, thin man in his late thirties. His skin was sallow and although it was only shortly after midday he had a five o'clock shadow around his mouth and chin. He was smoking a cigar, and he carried a drink in one hand, while the other was raised in an exaggerated salute.

'Allie! What are you doing away from your elephants and your fine husband?'

His voice was loud, and heavily accented. He arrived at the table, banged his glass down, and gave Allie a bone-crunching hug from which she extricated herself, laughing.

'Viktor. I might ask why you're propping up the bar in this flyblown hole, when you should be out doing an honest day's work.'

Viktor. This must be Piet's architect. And Hannah's lover. The man was every bit as flamboyant as their descriptions. He was staring at Sarah through a haze of smoke, with eyes that were almost black. She thought that he would be a fantastic subject for a photographic portrait. He gestured towards her.

'And who is this splendid creature, Allie? Introduce me now, if you please.'

'This is Sarah Mackay. Our new researcher. A Celt like me, but Irish. She's joining us today – we're heading back to the camp. Sarah, this is—'

'You're Viktor Szustak.' Sarah put out her hand. 'Langani Lodge. I've just come from there, and I have to tell you that it's the most beautiful place I've ever seen. I'm delighted to meet you.'

'Well, well,' he said. 'An admirer. And such a pretty one! It is a good day for me.'

He bent to kiss her hand. She was conscious of his lips, lingering, warm on her knuckles, and she felt the magnetic sexual energy that emanated from him. She could see why Piet was apprehensive about his sister's love affair with the man. There was a feral sense about him. He straightened, and looked at her.

'And how do you know Langani and my lodge?'

'The van der Beers are old friends,' she answered. 'Hannah and I were at school together. I've spent a lot of time at the farm over the years.'

'Wonderful people. I'm on my way there now, to see how the work is going.' He had made no reference to his relationship with Hannah, Sarah noticed, although he must guess that she knew about it. 'What a pity you will not be there,' he went on. 'But we will meet again soon. Allie, you must bring this protégé of yours to Nairobi the next time you crave the city lights.'

'Don't hold your breath,' Allie said. 'I avoid Nairobi like the plague. Too much noise and seething humanity. That's the trouble with old fossils like Dan and me. We've lost the art of social chit-chat, if we ever had it. Why don't you come up to Buffalo Springs instead? Dan will be delighted to have you sink a few jars with him.'

It was a long speech for Allie, and Sarah saw that she was flirting with him a little. Viktor was clearly a favoured friend. He had put out his cigar and now he took Allie's two hands in his, turning them over to kiss the insides of her wrists. Then he turned his attention back to Sarah.

'I can see I will be forced to journey into the wilderness, if I am to improve my acquaintance with Miss Mackay.' He raised his black eyebrows and gave her a wide smile. Then he downed the remains of his drink in one long swallow, and signalled the waiter for a refill.

'What will you ladies have? Do you think they have good champagne here? No. It will not be of sufficient quality, or properly chilled. Pimm's. What about a Pimm's? Goes well with the curry, and it will put mettle in your driving, Allie.' He nodded at Sarah. 'You have not yet driven with this woman. It will be a testing time for your courage.'

'What rubbish, Viktor,' Allie exclaimed. 'But I'd love a Pimm's. Do you want to join us for lunch?'

Viktor drew up another chair and sat down with them. There was nothing wrong with his appetite, Sarah noticed, as he worked his way through two enormous helpings of curry, washed down with considerable quantities of gin. She marvelled at how much he could eat and drink, and remain as thin as he was and apparently unaffected by the alcohol. She sipped her drink warily, afraid that too much of it in the middle of the day would make her drunk or ill, or even both. She enjoyed Viktor's questioning, and found herself telling him and Allie about her Kenya childhood, the college years in Dublin, and her yearning to get back to

Africa. She had never been able to talk freely with strangers and she was surprised at herself. Allie seemed content to take a passive role, as she sipped a second drink and smoked one of Viktor's cigars. Perhaps it was her way of studying her new assistant, Sarah thought. But it was Allie who mentioned the prize-winning photographs. Viktor immediately wanted to see them.

'Where are these works of art? Have you brought them with you? Allie, can she go and get them? We must see them at once. An artist and a scientist – what a combination! You have found yourself a jewel, Allie, to grace your dusty plains.'

'I've seen a few of the pictures and they're excellent,' Allie said. 'But if the rest are accessible, I'd like to see them too.'

At their insistence, Sarah retrieved her portfolio and handed it over shyly, nervous of their reaction. Her competition photographs were there, and the pictures she had shot on safari in Samburu. Viktor looked through them in a rare passage of silence, and then passed them to Allie without comment. Sarah's confidence plummeted. She should never have let him talk her into showing them. What he finally said came as a surprise.

'Now, that is an exceptional talent. What do you say, Allie? She has an eye that can capture the spirit of a man, or an animal or a place. If she can photograph your elephants like this, she will make your project world famous. And herself with it.'

'You're right,' Allie said. 'They're high quality. Remarkable. Dan will be delighted to use work like this for our photographic records.'

'Any technician can take a good, sharp picture,' Viktor said. 'But these have soul. She has made the link with her subjects, entered into the core of them. These pictures speak. This portrait, now. This portrait speaks the truth.'

Sarah stared, breathless, at the one he had selected. She had caught Piet unawares, on top of a ridge in Samburu, the evening sun gilding his hair and his face, his eyes looking up into the camera lens with humour and surprise. It was her favourite picture of him.

'This is the face of love,' Viktor said simply. He looked at her with his dark eyes, and she turned away, unsure if he was referring to the subject or the photographer.

'The line of love is here in this picture,' he went on. 'That unique connection. It shines in the air around him. I can see it. Because I am a poet, I can see it.'

Sarah touched the picture briefly, surprised at his perception and sensitivity. He really understood her work and her passion, and it made her confident. She became animated, describing the photographs in terms of the terrain, the light and what she was trying to achieve. Finally, Allie's dry staccato voice halted them both.

'I hate to break up this soul bonding,' she said, amused, 'but we have a long drive ahead of us, and I don't want to be stuck out in the *bundu* at night with a truckload of supplies and a bunch of Shifta bandits on our tail. To say nothing of possible rain.'

Viktor gathered up the photographs, embraced Allie and went down on one knee before Sarah, sighing and kissing her hand again.

'I shall measure the moments until I can see you again,' he declared. 'I shall follow you into the desert, and woo you away from that Afrikaner of yours. He is a mere man of the land, Piet van der Beer, while you and I, ah! You and I are made for the air!'

Sarah snatched her hand away, as a vision of Hannah's clasped hands and shining eyes rose in her memory. Hannah, waiting for her love to return.

'Oh, get away with you, Viktor Szustak!' Allie was laughing. 'Leave the poor girl alone. She doesn't need your gin-soaked flights of fancy!'

She pushed him fondly, and he allowed her to topple him on to the ground where he lay at her feet, his long fingers closing over her ankle as he made a loud, moaning sound. Several people in the restaurant had turned to watch. Sarah was embarrassed, but she found herself laughing in spite of herself.

'Allie, Allie! Always so cruel. Go, then! Go!' Viktor sprang to his feet, calling out farewells, and sauntered away to the bar where they heard him order another drink.

They had not travelled more than ten miles when Sarah understood what he had meant about Allie's driving. She shut her eyes as they lurched round a bend at speed, with the Africans in the back of the swaying vehicle hanging on for dear life. They might have been taking part in the East African Safari Rally, and Sarah wondered if they would make Buffalo Springs alive. Allie shouted a few pithy comments about Viktor over the noise of the engine, but Sarah was too terrified by the see-saw of the road in front of her to take in anything that was said. Dazed by the effects of her sleepless night, the Pimm's and the curry lunch, she dozed fitfully in spite of her alarm. The battered Land Rover jolted through the heat and dust of the afternoon, and she woke only when the rain began to drum on the roof.

When Sarah had visited only two months ago the soil had been baked brown and cracked. But now, at the height of the rainy season, the place had been transformed into a sea of tender green, with wild flowers bursting out in hectic colours everywhere. They were caught in a downpour that lasted for more than an hour, and in some places the road turned into a quagmire. Dry, rocky watercourses had become rushing streams, criss-crossing the route to the Briggses' camp. It made the going even more precarious, as they skidded and lurched and slid along the churned-up track. Several times the two Africans in the back had to climb down and help to get the vehicle out of the mud, pushing and grunting with effort, while Allie swore and revved the engine and delivered orders out of the window. Sarah offered to get down and help, but she was told to sit tight.

'Once I get out of this hole, I have to keep going,' Allie shouted over the straining, spinning sound of engine and axles. 'Can't stop to pick you up. The boys are used to it. They'll jump in as soon as we get under way.'

Sarah was amazed at their agility. One minute they were bent almost double behind the churning wheels, shouting encouragement to one another. Seconds later they were leaping like gazelles over the tailboard, as the Land Rover found a purchase on the ground and surged out of its sticky trap. They landed on a pile of sacks and cartons, laughing and rubbing their hands. Allie applauded their expertise and called out to them over the grinding of gears but the reply from the back of the vehicle was lost. They churned off again, with Allie singing a tuneless song as she hurtled across the muddy landscape towards the next crisis.

They reached the camp at sundown. Thunderous clouds gathered overhead, releasing another deluge as they drove into the compound. Allie blew the horn and pulled up in front of the storehouse. Two Africans ran out of the building and began to unload the supplies, hurrying to get the bulky sacks of grain and flour and *posho* into the stores before the rain soaked them. There were boxes of tinned goods, and several crates of beer and soft drinks. Sarah also noticed a case of Scotch whisky and gin. Viktor wasn't the only one who liked his grog, she thought.

The living quarters were surrounded by deep verandahs that gave additional shade to the rooms, although Sarah anticipated that it would be breathlessly hot for a great deal of the time. There was no glass in any of the windows, but roughly made shutters which hung on the outside walls could be closed to keep out heavy rain or to dim the merciless sun. The kitchen and the housing for the African staff stood behind the main house and the storerooms.

Dan Briggs emerged on to the verandah as they dashed towards him, through the fat drops of rain.

'Come on inside,' he said. 'Good to meet you, Sarah. You're very late. I was beginning to wonder if you were stuck in mud somewhere. We had torrential rain this morning. You're lucky it dried out a little.'

He patted Allie on the shoulder, and held out a long bony hand to Sarah. He was a spare, rangy American with greying hair, a drooping moustache and shrewd but kindly eyes, and she saw that he was a good bit older than his wife.

'We met Viktor in Nanyuki,' Allie said

'Ah! That explains all. Well, come on in.' He turned to Sarah 'You've already done the grand tour, the last time you were here? As you can see, our living room doubles as the office. We usually eat outside when the sky isn't bucketing down. Your sleeping quarters are over there.' He gestured towards a round hut to the left of the main building. 'Not luxurious, and I guess you should check out your bed and your shoes for scorpions, before you leap into either one.'

'I'm used to those,' Sarah said. 'We were on safari up here with Anthony Chapman a few months ago.'

'A great guy, Anthony. But if you were in one of his tented camps, you'll find this is a little spartan by comparison.' Dan fished in the sagging pockets of his shorts and produced a pipe, which he lit up.

'I'm sure I'll be very comfortable, Dr Briggs. I'm not some *safi* memsahib who can't adapt to being in the bush.'

'Call me Dan.' He smiled down at her. 'No formalities here. Now, what about a drink? Allie? What's your poison, young lady?'

The room where the Briggses lived and worked was large, with a beautifully woven thatched roof. It was lit by hissing paraffin lamps that cast a soft light on basic furniture and boxes of books and papers. The rain was drumming in earnest as Dan opened the whisky bottle and poured himself and Allie generous measures, adding a small splash of water from a covered jug.

'Sarah?'

'I think a beer if you have one. After all that mud, and the hot afternoon.'

Dan produced a Tusker from a rickety fridge and poured it into a tankard.

'I hear you were brought up in Kenya, but studied in Ireland,' he said. 'You'll find this place rather different to the halls of academe.'

'What I found hard was being at college in Ireland. This is where I've spent most of my life, and where I want to be.' She looked at him directly. 'I'd like to thank you for giving me this chance. I know I have no experience in the type of research you're doing, but I'll work very hard, and I can learn if you'll be patient with me in the beginning.'

Allie waved her glass at her husband. 'I told you she was interested in photography, remember? And I'd seen a few of her photos. But Viktor made her show us the whole portfolio. They're good. Better than good, actually. He was raving about them, and he has an eye for that kind of thing. If Sarah starts making a proper photographic record of our work, it will be useful when we're making our next pitch for funding. And on your trip to the States.'

'Sounds great.' Dan stood up. 'Now, I guess you're both hungry after that long ride. Let's get some chow.'

He picked up a cow bell from the side table, and shook it vigorously. A thin, wizened little man in khaki shorts and tunic appeared at the door.

'Ahmed, this is Miss Sarah. Ahmed is our cook. Been with us for ten years, since we were down in Tsavo. Part of the family. Dinner straight away, please, Ahmed.'

They moved over to the table, and Allie lit two candles. There was spicy mulligatawny soup, followed by a casserole of francolin, and fresh fruit with tinned cream to finish. Sarah wondered how Ahmed had managed to produce the hot, steaming dishes from the outside kitchen, without it all being doused with water. Over dinner Dan told amusing tales of his student days in New York, and his meeting with Allie at a conference in Edinburgh. He had proposed to her after five days, in front of the lion enclosure at Edinburgh Zoo, and he described the alarm that her acceptance had caused in her solid, upright Scottish family.

'I could have been from Mars,' he said. 'A penniless American with no prospects except for the offer of a few bucks a month to follow elephants around, and a tent in the middle of Africa. Not the kind of guy Allie's folks had in mind at all. But they were generous. They gave us a cheque for a wedding present and that bought us a beat-up old Land Rover. When they thought we had cobbled enough pots and pans together, they flew out to visit us in Tsavo National Park. They used to come come every year, which is more than my folks ever did. My dad died five years ago, and my mother prefers to visit with my sister in Palm Beach, where the beauty parlour isn't more than ten minutes away. Africa is a little rough for her now.'

'Bedtime for all.' Allie stood up after a last cup of coffee. 'I'm bushed. Here's your lamp, Sarah. There's a torch beside your bed for emergencies. If you go out to the loo during the night, make sure to close your door. You don't want to find some curious, uninvited guest sniffing round your bed when you get back. *Chai* at six, and then over here for breakfast. Sleep well.'

Sarah took her lamp, trying to shield it from the downpour as she ran the short distance to her rondavel. The hut seemed to squat low on the ground, beneath the umbrella of an acacia tree. She pushed open the door and heard the rustling of lizards in the thatch as she stepped into what was to be her domain for the foreseeable future. A wood-and-string bed stood against the wall, with a flock mattress, crisp white sheets and two heavy green army blankets, all tucked in beneath a veil of mosquito netting. Geckos scuttled across the ceiling in the lamplight, tutting apparent disapproval at the intrusion. A roughly made chair and a desk with two drawers had been placed by the window, and in the far corner there was a small cupboard that would hold all her other belongings. The floor was made of mud that had been dried and polished, and there was a woven straw mat beside her bed. Above her she could hear the steady drip of the rain, and the rush of the swollen river beyond the compound fence. A few hippos grunted downstream as she unpacked and stowed everything away in the press and the drawers of the desk. Then she undressed and turned back the bed, checking for bugs and creepy-crawlies before climbing gratefully between the sheets. She lay still for a few minutes, listening to the strange sounds of her new home, whispering a prayer for the people she loved in Ireland and at Langani, and hoping, most of all, that Piet would come to visit her soon in this most wonderful of places.

She woke next morning to Mathenge, appearing with the tea tray.

'*Maji moto* outside,' he said.

Sarah heard the sound of hot water being sloshed into the bucket suspended in a small enslosure behind her hut. She drank the hot, sweet tea and ate a biscuit that tasted faintly of paraffin from the camp stores. Then she ran out to stand under the steaming water in the shower hut. The rain had cleared, leaving behind the rich aroma of wet earth. Glistening drops hung from the leaves and made prisms in the sunlight. She could smell the perfume of the African morning, and she heard the liquid whistle of an oriole and the call of hornbills. Allie and Dan were having breakfast when she joined them. They had maps spread on the table beside them and they were planning their route for the day and allocating jobs for the staff. Sarah sat down quietly and listened.

'We're on the lookout for rhino today, while we're tracking our elephants,' Dan explained. 'Ken Smith, the game warden in Garissa, has asked us to log any we come across. He's concerned about the dwindling numbers and he's trying to do a count, because he wants to put an embargo on shooting them. It's going to be difficult to enforce. Hunting licences bring in good money, and on the illegal side rhino horn fetches high prices.'

'Is it true, then, that it's an aphrodisiac?' The moment she had spoken the words Sarah knew how foolish they sounded.

'Only if used as a splint,' said Dan drily.

Allie roared with laughter, and Sarah was furious with herself for asking such a silly question. Embarrassment sent a red tide up her neck and into her cheeks.

'Mark you, though, it *is* sold for that purpose. In powdered form.' Dan came to her rescue. 'It's also prized in the Middle East for dagger handles. But it sure is a tragedy to see the carcasses left to rot, with only the horn removed. Ken is starting a protection programme, so we're doing what we can to help.'

'He's a far-seeing man,' Allie said. 'He's fixed things so that the local council keeps the money for game licences, instead of having to send it to Nairobi. That way, the Samburu can recognise the direct benefits from organised hunting. You'll be working with one of them, here on our team. His name's Erope.'

'The Samburu couldn't see why rich *wazungu* should be allowed to roam around shooting animals with the government's blessing, while they were forbidden their traditional hunting practices,' Dan said. 'Especially when the licence fee went to some government office hundreds of miles away, and the locals never saw a penny.'

'But I thought the whole idea was to stop tribal hunting because there's such a thin line between that and poaching,' Sarah said.

'The plan is to turn nomadic hunters into farmers,' Allie said. 'But it won't work. It's a destruction of their whole culture and way of life. They're resisting it, and they're right.'

'They're a little crazy down there in Nairobi,' Dan said. 'They want to forbid traditional hunting with poisoned arrows and spears. But poachers or bandits are selling rifles to the local tribes, and now we have a much bigger problem. It's a dilemma. Anyway, on a more immediate note, we're going to take a couple of our boys, and drive out to show you the terrain.'

Erope was a tall, well-spoken Samburu who wore the same khaki uniform as the rest of the staff, but he was festooned with beaded earrings and bracelets that sat strangely with his Western dress. The second scout was a wiry Kamba who went by the name of Julius, and wore a large wooden cross on a piece of leather around his neck. They drove out through the gates of the compound and on to the track, with Erope and Julius perched on the tailboard. In the few hours since the rain had stopped the topsoil had dried into a muddy crust. The corrugated surface rattled the wheels and tipped the car at an alarming angle, but Dan did not appear to notice. It seemed that he had learned to drive in the same school as his wife. Sarah clung on to the open window.

'Do you drive?' Allie asked.

'Dad taught me, and I got my licence in Ireland.'

'Good. We'll get you a local one on the strength of that,' Dan said. 'And you need to learn how to handle one of these old bangers in all conditions. We'll begin tomorrow, kid.'

They drove across country for most of the morning, following small trails through the scrub. There were no signposts anywhere, and Sarah wondered aloud how they could find their way in such terrain. She was sure she would have been lost in minutes.

'You learn to look out for certain landmarks,' Allie explained. 'If you can't see the mountains, or some large outcrop of rock, then you watch for a particular tree or oddly shaped bush, or the colour of the earth at a certain spot – it changes hugely from place to place. And there's the line of the river, where the vegetation is different, and the trees are heavier and taller. Plus the position of the sun, of course. As a photographer you're obviously observant, so it should come easily enough. But you'll learn most from Erope and Julius. One or other of them will be with you most of the time. To start with, anyway. They can find their way over any country anywhere.'

'They have an instinctive knowledge that's mighty impressive to see,' said Dan. 'Erope is uncanny. As well as the infallible sense of direction that he's inherited, he notices absolutely everything and records it in some recess of his mind. He's one of the best scouts I've ever come across.'

'*Kifaru*, bwana. A big female, and a calf,' Erope sang out from the back of the vehicle.

Sarah could see nothing in the dense scrub that surrounded them. Dan slowed the Land Rover to a crawling pace, and leaned out of the window. Leading away into a thicket were a series of tracks and he estimated the size and weight of the animals from the depressions in the sandy ground.

'It was raining heavily all night, but these are fresh – the ground has dried out, see? And they'd be much deeper if they'd been made when the soil was soft and muddy. The calf is young. That's an immature foot. The dimensions are small, and the depression much shallower than the mother's. Boy! She's one big rhino, all right. My guess is they're pretty close.'

They backed up a little, to see if they could get a better view. Sarah watched, her heart thudding with anticipation, wondering how Dan would make out if the great prehistoric beast suddenly came charging out of the thicket. Then they heard her. The vegetation cracked and shuddered under her weight as she pushed through the thorny branches to emerge suddenly on the track behind them, with her calf at her heels. She peered towards them and then lowered her head, snorting like an express train.

'Uhuh, time to leave. We're not going to have a friendly encounter.' Dan gunned the engine, and took off down the track at a furious pace.

The rhino hesitated, tossing her huge head up and down, trying to locate them. Then she broke into a purposeful trot, her long horn lowered menacingly, her calf following behind. Sarah lifted her camera, sighting through the lens, marvelling at the speed of such a heavy and apparently ungainly animal. The cow had built up to a full charge, snorting loudly and pursuing them with determination, gaining on the vehicle till she was almost touching the tailboard with the vicious prong of her horn. Sarah braced herself against the frame of the roof hatch, trying to steady the camera as they jolted down the rib-shaking track. Erope was shouting a running commentary for Dan, in case he had to swerve to avoid being rammed. At last, the huge beast began to drop back, her calf already lagging far behind. As they drew away, she gave one last flourish of her heavy, armoured head before she turned and trotted back to rejoin her offspring.

'So what made her chase us?' Sarah said, when she had recovered her breath and her courage. 'Did she think we were a threat to her calf?'

'Maybe,' Dan answered. 'Or maybe she was in a bad temper. They're cussed old critters, and you don't want to wait around to find out what they've decided to do or why. I've seen cars and lorries busted, their radiators skewered and the bodywork pulverised by an angry rhino. That horn, with the weight of the body behind it, packs a lot of punch. Anyway, there's two for the day's count, even though we didn't wait to be introduced!'

They drove on, stopping every so often for the scouts to reconnoitre the terrain. Allie and Dan pointed out trees, birds and animals, and identifying landmarks. They saw two small groups of elephant, but at a distance. Dan described the habits of an average family unit, and Sarah listened, trying to remember a daunting number of facts about the animals and their habitat. She could see from the way they spoke about the elephants that Dan and Allie had a huge love and respect for the subjects of their study. She hoped they would get closer to a herd soon. In the meantime her attention was captured by the passing parade of waterbucks, zebra and giraffes, and a tree full of noisy baboons. The rain was holding off, but heavy clouds had begun to mass on the horizon, and the air was sticky with humidity. Sarah could feel a trickle of sweat making its way down her back, beneath her shirt.

'We need to cool off,' said Allie suddenly. 'Let's go and swim.'

They turned round on the track they had been following, and drove to Buffalo Springs where Dan skidded to a halt. The two scouts sat in the shade of a tree, watching the car. Allie and Dan headed for the edge of the deep pool, stripping off their clothes and leaving them in a pile on the rocks. Then they dived into the cool, green depths. Sarah hung back, embarrassed, wondering what she should do. She had not been naked in front of anyone since her childhood, and she stood with her arms crossed, clutching at her shirt, incapable of shedding even her outer garments in the company of strangers.

'Hurry up and get in. The water's quite clean, you know, and blessedly cold.' Allie flicked wet hair out of her eyes, and dived again as Dan swam over to the pool's edge.

'Never been skinny-dipping before?' he said.

Sarah shook her head, mortified.

'And you a zoology graduate, and a doctor's daughter? Time to break out, kid. Whisk them off, close your eyes, and jump! We won't be looking!'

He swam away and Sarah glanced back at the car. The scouts were apparently asleep under the tree, seemingly uninterested in the crazy *wazungu* frolicking in the pool. In any case, Africans had a sanguine attitude to nudity, she thought. Their women went bare-breasted in most tribes, and often neither men nor women covered themselves. It was no big deal. And it was stiflingly hot. Taking a deep breath, she whipped her shirt over her head, stepped out of her khaki trousers and peeled off her underwear. Then she squeezed her eyes shut and jumped. The shock of the cold water on her skin made her gasp with pleasure as she swam to the other side of the pool, keeping well clear of Allie and Dan. It was strange, this sense of total freedom. Wonderful. She felt braver, and swam towards her companions.

'Attagirl!' Dan blew a jet of water into the air, imitating the noise of a hippo surfacing in the river and making Sarah laugh, dissipating whatever shyness she still felt. After splashing and dousing one another they floated in the water for a while, then climbed out and sat on the rocks to dry themselves off before dressing. Sarah lay on her stomach, still slightly uncomfortable. Allie and Dan seemed totally at ease, but it was all very well for them They were married. She hoped that she would soon become as natural and open as her companions. There was no point in behaving like a prude. She was not in the sheltered environment of a convent school now. Erope and Julius continued to lie motionless in the shade of the tree as she dressed, and for that, at least, Sarah was thankful. Refreshed, they climbed back into the Land Rover and resumed their tour. She wondered if the scouts would have liked to swim too, but no one mentioned it and she let it be. They drove slowly along the side of a *lugga* that had filled to an ooze of slow-moving, muddy water after the heavy rain. To her delight, they came at last upon a herd of elephant, drinking and grazing quietly in the bush.

'Here's one of our groups,' Allie murmured. 'We call this family the Dame Nelly Melbas, in honour of the lead cow. She's a bit of a diva, and she likes the sound of her own voice. You wait till you hear her trumpeting and seeing off those cheeky young bulls. They generally get on with their everyday routine and take no notice of us. They're used to the sound of our vehicle.'

Sarah watched the elephants, enthralled. Before she began to work with her camera she simply sat and looked, awed at their immense size and grace. They approached the Land Rover as they searched for tender young bushes and trees from which they tore off branches. Some were standing so close that she could pick out every pit and line and hair on the wrinkled skin, the light in their small, intelligent eyes, the ridges on their huge flapping ears. There was a remarkable sense of harmony and affection and contentment about them as they moved silently through their domain, the only noise being the crack of twigs and branches as they walked, great feet rising smoothly, coming down on the earth in a small puff of dust. All that power, so contained. She was fascinated at the way they used their trunks, whiffling delicately around a bush or a young sapling, touching the leaves and blowing gently. Within moments they had made their selection, often lifting the entire plant out of the ground by the roots in one neat movement, placing it in their mouths and eating placidly. Some of the older females were down at the edge of the *lugga*, digging with their feet and tusks, making wide holes that gradually filled with water.

'See how they use their trunks, to gather the sand and dirt on the edges, and pile it to one side,' Dan explained. 'And if you look closely, you'll see that one tusk is usually more worn at the tip than the other. That's the one they use as their main digging tool – like humans, they favour either the left or the right side, the same way we use our hands.'

The herd had surrounded the vehicle, and Sarah's pulse quickened. An immature male stood very close to her and she lifted her camera slowly as he sucked water up in his trunk and spewed it over his back to cool himself, spattering her lens. The cows and their calves congregated together, while the young bulls stood at a distance. Occasionally a senior bull would advance, and the youngest members of the herd would receive a gentle touch of his trunk, like an old man putting his hand in blessing on a child's head.

'That's Samson,' Allie whispered. 'He is the big bwana. None of the young bulls dare take him on yet. He's very strong. But until they challenge him, they can't approach the females as he can. It's a very matriarchal society. Cows only consort with the males when they're in season. The rest of the time it's ladies only. Young bulls go about together in groups, and a *mzee* will often be accompanied by two younger askaris, to look after him in his old age. The older females are the leaders, guiding their herd to food and water, defending the young. In fact, they're incredibly protective and affectionate, and loyal to one another. See how they use their trunks to caress, and to tickle, and to console? But they can also use them as highly effective weapons.'

'The more I see of them, the more they astound me,' Dan said. 'Extraordinary creatures! Did you know they even bury their dead sometimes? I don't know any other beast that does that.'

'But they're aggressive, aren't they?' Sarah said. 'You do hear that the African elephant is dangerous. We were charged by a young bull last time I was here. He was definitely not friendly.'

'They're not to be trifled with, that's for sure,' Allie answered. 'But young bulls are often showing off, testing their strength like teenage boys out to demonstrate how brave they are. And don't forget, the elephant up here have been poached to a serious degree, so they are more defensive. Very often, they're provoked. Visitors make a lot of noise, revving up their engines to get a reaction, or getting between one section of a herd and another. That can make the elephant belligerent. And there's always the odd rogue – a bull that's injured or an outcast. But those are isolated incidents.'

'Of course, if you were a local farmer, dependent on an acre or two of maize to feed your family, you wouldn't be kindly disposed to these guys coming to call,' Dan said. 'They can level a whole field in an hour. They've a lot of body weight to supply, and they feed more or less all the time. Then their human neighbours are left destitute, maybe even with their homes demolished. And they had little enough to survive on already. Ask Erope or Julius about raids on their *shambas*.'

'But within the parks they can't do any real damage, can they?' Sarah asked. 'I mean, as long as they're within the game reserve areas?'

'An elephant can do terrible things to trees,' Dan said. 'If there are too many of them in one area they can destroy a whole region, turn the place into a dustbowl. So there are problems of protection, and peaceful co-existence with the local people, and conservation of the habitat. That's what our research is aimed at. We want to indicate some way that man and beast can live together peacefully off the land. But with the human population growing all the time, there's less space for the game. It's not easy.'

They stayed with the herd for several hours, watching and recording their movements. Then the rain began to fall, sprinkling them lightly at first, building up to a torrent that sent them scrambling to wind up the windows and to pull down and fasten the roof hatches. The light faded quickly and the camera could no longer be used, so they drove away.

For Sarah it had been an extraordinary day. It was beyond belief that she could spend her days observing these complex and glorious miracles of creation, in the company of such learned people as Dan and Allie. And she would even be paid for it! The road had turned into a quagmire by the time they saw the lights of the camp blinking at them through the trees. They were mud-spattered and weary as they waited for their shower buckets to be filled, and after dinner Dan and Allie retired immediately. In the rounded space of her hut Sarah sat up and wrote letters by the light of her paraffin lamp. She wanted to capture the magic of this first day in words, to share with her family the excitement that filled her. She wrote to Piet, and to Hannah and Lars, and when she found herself nodding over the page she climbed into bed and was instantly asleep, heedless of the possibility of scorpions or other venomous lodgers.

For the next two weeks, she went out with Allie and Dan each morning, until the land became familiar. Dan put her behind the wheel, and she learned to handle the Land Rover, causing hilarity and alarm at first as she negotiated obstacles in the bush, or tried to extricate herself from the mud, ploughing in and out of *luggas* that might have a trickle or a spate of rushing water flowing through them, depending on the force of the last downpour. She came to admire the eccentric and courageous couple who were her employers and to respect their staff. Soon she felt as though she had been there for ever. Each morning was a different challenge as she tried to absorb and memorise every snippet of information, and to understand its significance. It was not long before she was able to drive over to the game department headquarters, accompanied only by Julius or Erope, to collect the mail and make phone calls for the Briggses. When she had finished their calls, she got through to Langani and Hannah answered.

'I am so, so happy,' Sarah told her. 'I can't begin to tell you how wonderful this is, how lucky I am to be working here. You must come up soon. There's so much I want to show you. How is everyone? Piet?'

Life at Langani seemed normal enough. Piet was out on the farm somewhere, Hannah said, working his backside off as usual. But he had been mighty pleased with the letter Sarah had sent.

'It's a dead giveaway.' Hannah was laughing. 'He's just your average dimwit when it comes to admitting that he's found his one and only. But it's quite clear to me. He never stops talking about you, Sarah. And when someone starts dropping a name into every conversation, then you know for sure that they're hooked.'

Sarah wanted to run outside and shout out her delight to the world, but she decided it might not go down too well. Instead she stood there, smiling into the phone.

'And what about you and Viktor?' she asked. 'I told you I met him. He knows Dan and Allie well. You were right about his charm – he's oozing with it. So what have you to tell?'

Hannah's hesitation sounded a warning, but her words were determinedly optimistic.

'He comes and goes. You know how it is. He has a lot of work on right now, so he can't be around all that much. That's hard for me. But it's worth the waiting, and he makes up for it when he's here.'

'And Lars?'

Hannah's sigh told everything. 'I'm sorry about Lars, I really am. I wish we could be friends, like before. But it's all changed. What I feel for Viktor – it's like being swept along in a flood. And I don't want it to stop. Viktor has changed my life. I can't tell you what he means to me.'

'Well, take care,' Sarah said, trying to hide the concern she felt. There was no point in voicing it over the telephone.

She drove back to the camp, singing. Piet loved her. That's what Hannah had said. He talked about her all the time. And she would be seeing him at Christmas. In the meantime she had a job that was fulfilling beyond any expectations. Life was wonderful.

The more time she spent among the elephants, the closer her bond with them became. Dan had assigned Erope to work with her, and she found him a wise and patient teacher. He taught her to track, to interpret the spoor and the signs of an animal's passing, and to move through the bush unnoticed, keeping downwind of her subjects so that she could get near them without disturbing them. Soon she could identify specific family groups within the herd, and recognise each individual elephant by name. She photographed them and recorded their characteristics in her log, illustrating her observations with sketches and written notes. They knew the Land Rover, and some of them allowed her to approach within a few feet. She found herself sharing her experiences silently with Piet, imagining that he walked with her through the bush, or sat beside her on a boulder above the river or overlooking the swamp where the animals wallowed in the midday heat. She felt very close to him out here. At night, when she had finished with her notes she wrote to him, telling him all she had discovered about her elephants during the long hot hours in the bush. Then she put the letters carefully in the back of her desk drawer.

Sitting out on the rocks with Erope one evening, she marvelled at the glory of their surroundings. The light was mellow as it lit the tops of the doum palms, gradually turning the sky to a pale lavender streaked with red. They had been following a family of elephant led by a splendid old matriarch called Judith. During the course of the day she had taken her group away from the main herd to an area that she considered better grazing. Normally, they would reassemble at sundown, calling out to one another with rumblings and trumpetings of pleasure as the families were reunited. But Judith's small unit had been making slow progress, and Sarah realised that they would not make it to the swamp before nightfall.

'It is time to go back to the car, Sarah,' Erope said. 'There is not enough light now, for your camera to do good work.'

Reluctantly she clambered down from their vantage point and set out towards the place where they had left the Land Rover. By the time they arrived the daylight was gone, and a huge yellow moon hung low in the night sky. Sarah had driven the vehicle deep into a thicket, hoping that maximum shade would save the interior from turning into a furnace. They opened the doors, rolled down the windows and sat in the shadows to drink some tea from the Thermos.

Sarah was about to start the engine when the noise reached them. Shots.

Coming from the direction they had just left. Then they heard the high screaming of an elephant in pain, the enraged trumpeting of its companions, the panicked crashing of animals in full flight. And human voices, shouting. Sarah was transfixed with shock for a few seconds. Then a maelstrom of fury flooded her as she pictured her beloved herd being attacked. She rammed the vehicle into gear and started the engine, a wild notion of pursuing the poachers in her mind. But Erope leaned forward, signalling for silence, his fingers closing over her arm in warning, gripping her wrist, forcing her to turn off the ignition. She glared at him, but he put his finger to his lips and shook his head. She could not dislodge his hand, and she sat, seething with frustration, listening to the sound of slaughter. It was some time before she realised the reason for Erope's insistence. The lorry that the bandits were using came around a bend in the track. As they approached, Sarah saw that there were at least ten men, heavily armed, in the back of the vehicle. Shifta from the Somali border. If they had revealed their presence, she and Erope would now be dead. They watched, unnoticed, as the truck crawled past with several men on watch, rifles at the ready. Sarah could see two pairs of tusks in the back, and panic rose in her as she wondered which of her precious family had been slaughtered. Erope kept a restraining hand on her arm until he was sure the poachers were gone. Then they started the car and drove slowly and cautiously, without lights, down the rough track towards the place where they had left Judith and her little entourage.

They stopped the car at the head of the game trail and made their way down to the place where they had last seen the elephants. The moon was sailing across the sky, remote and unforgiving. When they reached the killing ground, Sarah knelt down and wept. The grand old dame lay on her side, a bullet wound through her forehead, her eyes filmed but still open in reproach, tracks like tears on the sides of her face. There were raw, open and bloody wounds where her tusks had been, already infested with ants and other burrowing creatures. Near her lay Jacintha, a younger female. Her tusks had also been gouged out, and her carcass left to rot.

Sarah reached out to touch the wrinkled skin. Then she heard a noise, the loud snapping of branches coming from behind her. Erope made an urgent sign, and she rose and followed him into thick bush at the edge of the clearing. In the bright beam of the moon's searchlight she watched, spellbound, as the remaining members of the family group materialised like ghosts out of the dense scrub. They gathered around their fallen comrades and tried to raise them up, digging under the bodies with their tusks, pushing with their feet. When it became clear that the two were dead, they stood quietly to one side, mammoth guards of honour, immovable and silent mourners on the field of battle. Sarah and Erope crouched in the thicket, trapped in the cramped space where they had hidden as the elephants approached. The night grew chilly, but they did not stir. This was no time to test the elephants' acceptance of them. If they were discovered, they could be trampled in seconds. The wind would not be in their favour if they attempted an escape. They sat there, cold and stiff, occasionally dozing, watching the silent ritual with awe and sadness. During the long hours of darkness hyenas came, and jackals, attracted by the smell of blood. But the guard of elephants gathered in a solid phalanx and drove the scavengers away. No creature was willing to challenge them. Towards dawn, the two oldest females went into the scrub. They began to pull down branches, and uproot small bushes and trees, carrying them to the place where their dead lay, and spreading them across the bodies like a shroud. Then they began to kick dust and small stones, tufts of grass and sods of earth, building them up over their companions until they were covered. Even the youngest members of the herd joined in the process, and by the time the sun rose the two dead elephants had almost disappeared. In their place were two mounds.

At first light Sarah lifted her camera, painfully conscious of each sound she made, each crackle of twigs and click of the shutter. The elephants turned towards the thicket where she crouched behind her lens, and for a moment she wondered if they would now become angry and dangerous. But they stood their ground quietly, the smallest ones in the centre, protected by the larger cows, all of them facing her as she recorded their vigil. When the first slanting beam of sunlight touched the trees, the survivors turned and melted away in grey silence, into the bush. Sarah and Erope waited for some time before emerging from their hiding place, marvelling at the phenomenon of courage and faithfulness that they had shared. Sarah squatted on the sand, taking pictures of the mounds, wishing she could have photographed all the events of the night. She felt they had known she was there, had allowed her to remain as a witness to their funeral rites. When she was finished with the camera, she left her own reverent offering of acacia blossoms on each of the graves.

Erope's face was grim. In the car she saw his anger in the way he hunched forward and wrapped his jacket around him, muttering words of distress in his own language, pounding his fist on the side of the door. There was no tolerance in him for the senseless butchery and greed they had seen. He was an extraordinary mixture of cultures, and she admired the way that he moved across the boundaries between the two areas of his life, employing the same fluid, unobtrusive tactics that he used when he was tracking an animal.

He had been educated at a mission school, and his research records were neatly written and orderly. When he was not in camp at Buffalo Springs he returned to his *manyatta*, leaving his uniform behind and living, as his people had done for centuries, in a dwelling of mud and wattle, dark and pungent with the smell of goats and cattle dung and wood-smoke. He had worked for a time in Nairobi, before the Briggses found him. But he had no wish to return there, he said. Despite his education and his exposure to the Western way of life, he retained the ancient skills needed to survive in the arid region that was his home. Sarah envied the grace with which he moved through his chosen world, understanding what was required of him in the diverse arenas of research camp and *manyatta*.

Like Dan and Allie, Sarah had graduated from a respected institution of learning. But for all their formal training, none of them could function effectively without the timeless knowledge and understanding that a man like Erope brought to their endeavours. Sarah hoped he knew this, and she wanted to indicate to him that she knew it too. But she could not think of any way to express her feeling adequately, so she only smiled, and reached out to touch him in a gesture of solidarity. She was glad to see the flash of white teeth and the slight nod that was his answer.

'Glad to see you alive and well,' Allie said with relief, when they arrived at the camp. 'We were out looking for you earlier, but we had no idea which direction the herd might have taken yesterday. I thought perhaps you had trouble with the vehicle. Dan was about to mount a search party with the Game Department.'

'You'll have to contact them anyway,' Sarah said. 'There was a Shifta raid.'

They alerted the game warden and returned to wait for him at the site. Sarah watched as he photographed the tyre tracks of the poachers' truck, and gathered up spent cartridge cases and other items of evidence. Sarah shivered. Lack of sleep, and reaction to the night's events was setting in. So much death, so much destruction. Was this the main reality of Africa?

The warden interrupted her thoughts. 'I'd be grateful if you could write up a report for me. With any additional observations your tracker might have.'

Sarah nodded, thinking about what she would have to write, hearing again the screaming of the elephant, seeing the carcasses of the creatures she had come to love, hacked and gouged and left to rot after the carnivores had done with them. She sat on the foot board of the Land Rover, sick and desolate, and began to rock back and forth in misery. After a moment or two, Dan came and crouched down in front of her.

'That's enough now,' he said, his voice firm, but kind. 'You have to pull yourself together, Sarah. There are things to do.'

'They had no chance. I wish she had charged the bastards. Stamped all over them and trampled them to death. I heard her screaming, Dan. I'd have known her voice anywhere. When she was on a rampage and she was trumpeting, she had that special, strident note. It went up at the end, you know? None of the others did that.'

'I know. It's a bugger. You get attached to them. Like your family. Look, you've had a rough night out there. Let's get you back to the camp so you can have a hot shower and get some sleep. And then write your report. The Game Department is going to need all the information you can give them.'

Sarah took a long breath, and tried to steady herself. 'Do you think they'll be caught?' she asked.

'I doubt it,' Dan said wearily. 'They're regulars, these guys. In and out over the border for a quick bit of poaching, or a raid on some *manyatta* where they can steal cattle and make off with the women. Sometimes they'll kill a couple of *moran*. They take the scrotums away with them, you know, as trophies. Then they hightail it back to Somalia. They used to come on foot. Now they have trucks, and I'm pretty sure they have local help too, especially when it comes to trading the rhino horn and ivory. That's big bucks. It may be illegal, but you can be sure there are plenty of people this side of the border mixed up in it – politicians and traders, as well as the ordinary *watu*.'

'But there must be *something* that can be done to stop them?' Sarah could hear the shrill note in her voice.

'It's the same old merry-go-round. We need more patrols, which the Game Department can't afford, and the government is too inefficient or corrupt to organise. And a conservation programme that benefits the local tribes, so they begin to see the value of protecting wildlife instead of slaughtering it.'

Dan's reply was matter-of-fact, and she realised that he was using the discussion to give her time to regain control. She stood up, making a resolution not to fall apart like this again. Dan was looking at her dusty, tear-streaked face and she could see that he was concerned. He helped her into his car.

'I know how you feel about the elephants,' he said, as he got into the driver's seat. 'You want to protect them at all costs. But you have to remember you're a scientist first.' She was about to argue, but he stopped her. 'No, listen to me, kid. Your job is to watch and record. We're here to observe the daily lives of these herds, to understand what they do and why, to see how they react to different situations. We can only ensure their protection if we know what sort of ecosystem they need to survive, and what conditions present the most danger. Disease, drought, poaching. Whatever. But we can't interfere. Otherwise it's not real. We are recording the natural cycle of elephant living in their natural habitat.'

'But what happened last night wasn't *natural.*'

'No, it wasn't, and everything must be done to stop poaching. But mankind has been killing animals since the dawn of time, Sarah. We're dealing with wildlife in the wild, and their predators these days include poachers and bandits. We don't have the resources to create a utopian animal sanctuary, a kind of giant, benevolent zoo, out here. You can't be soft when things like this happen, otherwise it will destroy you.'

She looked ahead, trying not to let her gaze return to the two mounds. Even with their covering, the sickly smell of decay had begun to permeate the clearing as the heat of the day increased. She bit her lip hard, forcing herself to respond calmly to what Dan had said.

'I suppose it was the suddenness of it. The awful savagery and the waste,' she said. 'I do realise what you're getting at. It's necessary to have a certain detachment, like doctors with their patients. But up to now it's been like magic, watching them every day, getting to know them. I was mad with anger, you know. I wanted to take the car and go after those bastards – I suppose Erope told you. It was crazy, of course. We would have ended up dead. Just as well he was thinking for the two of us!'

'He's done the same for me on occasion,' Dan admitted.

'I have a lot of learning to do,' Sarah said. 'I'll take what you say on board, try to be clinical and efficient and not throw a wobbly every time something bad happens. But I don't know if I can ever achieve the detachment you've described. Because I feel so involved. I can't *not* feel that way. And maybe you consider that a hindrance to your research.'

'No. A passion for what you're doing is usually a healthy thing. But you have to be careful that incidents like last night don't cloud your judgment, or tear you apart. Because I'm afraid you're going to see more of them. If you stay.'

'What are you trying to say, exactly, Dan?' She looked at him directly.

'I suppose I'm asking you whether you're strong enough for all this? I wouldn't want to see you destroyed by the random cruelty of this country. I know you love it, that you've been here since you were a kid. But it can be worse than harsh. You have to have a certain iron in the soul to survive. You're a fine young woman, Sarah. We don't want you to give too much and, in doing so, lose yourself.'

She sat for a while, thinking. He was right to challenge her. Was she tough enough to do this kind of work, out in the bush where life would always be dangerous and unpredictable? There was no room here for weakness and self-pity. But she knew that she wanted to stay, to be given the chance.

'I don't know what I'm made of yet,' she said at last, 'but I'd like to stick around and find out. If you're willing to keep me on the right road.'

'Attagirl!' Dan said, smiling at her. 'You'll do great work here. And you'll know you've made a difference.'

Chapter 20

London, November 1965

'You missed your appointment.' Edward sat back in his chair, fingertips pressed together, enquiring, but less than encouraging.

'You sound like a headmaster,' Camilla said, trying to make light of the situation. 'See me in my office after prayers, and all that.'

'As I understand it, you want me to repair your face, otherwise your present career will be finished.' He leaned across the desk, unsmiling. 'Now, I am very serious about this. I'm prepared to use my time and my skill to get you the best possible result. But it seems that you don't feel the same way about what we're trying to do.'

'I'm sorry.'

'Well, things are going to prove more tricky now. It's more than two weeks since I saw you last, and you've come back with a new problem.' He held out a magnifying mirror so that she could see the area for herself. 'The wound was healing well, and it was certainly clean last time I looked. But now the cut has opened, your forehead is swollen and bruised, and you have an infection.'

'I put antiseptic cream on it. And dressings.'

'This is your face. We're not playing at first aid here.'

'I thought it would clear up.'

He ignored her interruption with an impatient gesture. 'I wish you had rung me right away. I could have attended to this before harm was done. It would have made life much easier for both of us.'

'I didn't realise—'

'The damage is in the worst possible place, where the opening curves downwards. You need antibiotics, and I'll have to repair the whole thing. I can fit you in before my main operating list in the morning. If you're sure you'll keep the appointment.'

'I will.'

'May I ask how this happened?'

Camilla shrugged, avoiding his eyes, looking out into the grey street beyond the window. 'I tripped and knocked against something. Then I went down to the country with my mother.'

'How is your mother?' He was sure that there was a significant reason behind her disappearance and now he wondered if Marina might provide a clue.

'The same. Is there another topic of conversation we could try?' She wanted sympathy, a suggestion of the warmth she had seen in him at their last meeting. Instead he was concerned only about Marina. She needed someone to care about how she felt herself.

'I'm sorry. It's just that I thought your mother didn't look well.'

'Marina's dying.' It was the first time she had said the words aloud, made them into a bald fact in her mind. She was ready to vomit her fear and confusion all over his pale carpet and his Persian rugs.

Carradine was visibly shaken. 'Camilla, I have one more patient this afternoon. It's just a quick look at something I did several weeks ago. Can you wait for me? We could have a drink somewhere. Or dinner if you feel like it.'

'I'm all right. I don't need supervision.' She found it difficult to accept his sympathy without wanting to cry.

'Oh, but I think you do,' he responded, smiling slightly. 'Both professionally and otherwise. So unless you have something pressing in your calendar, I'll have my secretary make you a cup of tea and find you the evening paper. And then we'll go somewhere I can keep an eye on you, for an hour or two at least.'

'I've warned you about this before,' she said, trying to recover her veneer of composure. 'You'll be struck off for consorting with a young female patient after hours.'

As she sat in his waiting room her thoughts turned to her mother, and the choices Marina had faced during the early years of her marriage. There was no doubt that she had displayed tenacity in holding her life together. She had been brought up to marry well and take her place in society, and she had done the best she could to protect her husband's career. It was too late now for recriminations, and Camilla accepted that they must both move past the old hurts and live for the present.

'He must have known what he was when he married you,' she had said to Marina on the first evening in Burford. 'But he chose to hide behind you so he could be respectable, keep going up the ladder in the Foreign Office. They don't allow queers there. Not officially, anyway.'

'Don't, Camilla.' Marina's face was pinched with pain.

'Maybe he hoped it would all work out, that he would be able to bury that part of him.' Camilla was determined to follow through, to find a rationale, in spite of her mother's distress. 'But he obviously couldn't. Or he was too selfish to make it happen that way.'

'I was so young,' Marina's hands were restless, fluttering. 'I was twenty when we first met and I loved him instantly. I'm certain he loved me too. When he asked me to marry him everything in my life seemed perfect. We were so happy. And when I knew I was pregnant—'

'I can't talk about this any more,' Camilla interrupted. 'I'd like to spend time with you, Mother, but I don't want to be dragged through all the details, and the guilt and blame and excuses. Whatever happened, however it happened, it's all beyond us now. I can't cope with replays of our messed-up lives. I won't do it, and I don't want to see him. If you can accept those provisos, I'll stay here with you for as long as I can.'

Marina had been appalled by Camilla's cold appraisal of the situation. It was tragic that she should perceive her parents' lives in such a distorted framework. This was what they had done to her, she and George, and there was no one else to blame. There would be no reconciliation between father and daughter. Marina felt a tearing sensation in her heart. She would have to choose between them for the moment, to see them separately. Perhaps she would never see them together again. She thought of this as a punishment for the years of unhappiness she had caused, and she promised herself that she would not fail again in these last months of her life.

They had settled into a companionable routine in the country, sharing short walks, books and television, and the quiet of the small house. There were times when Marina was overcome by fatigue, when she was short of breath, bruised and aching. Then she spent part of her day in bed or sitting beside the fire, constantly cold although there was a woollen rug around her knees and the house was heated to the point of suffocation. She no longer wore any jewellery. Her fingers had become too thin for her rings, and her skin looked almost transparent. Camilla sometimes read to her until she fell asleep. Then she put on a jacket and boots and left the constraints of the house to walk through the fields, with the soft sprinkle of early-winter rain on her face and ice in her heart. She wondered how she would manage if Marina's condition worsened, knowing that she would be obliged to telephone her father and ask him to come down. Guilt hovered over her because she had enforced a ban on George's visits while she was at the cottage, and she never answered the telephone in case she had to speak to him. Each time she thought of him she remembered the horror on his face as he turned to look at her on that day of revelation, and she tried to obliterate from her memory the awful sight of the young man, naked on the bed. But she was not about to canonise her mother. Particularly when Winston Hayford telephoned to talk to Marina.

'What's happened to your admirer from Ghana?' Camilla asked, later in the day.

'I see him sometimes,' Marina said, with a level gaze. 'But I can't go dancing with him any more.'

'Did you have an affair with him?' Now that Camilla had asked the question, she found that she did not really want a straightforward answer.

'He's a very close friend, and I hope he will remain so. He's a good doctor too. I often ask for his advice. And speaking of doctors, Camilla, I wish you'd go and see Edward. I don't like the look of that bruise above your eye, and the area around it seems inflamed. Don't you have an appointment with him any day now?'

'I'll go up soon,' Camilla answered, knowing that her father would come down and replace her.

She had missed her appointment with Edward. It was true that the wound was inflamed where she had hit her head, during her unfortunate encounter with Johnson Kiberu. She looked at it in the bathroom mirror and smeared a thick coat of antiseptic cream along the open wound before re-covering it as best she could. It was time to go back to London.

Back in the city she had found a pile of mail in her flat, including an angry note from Tom Bartlett. He had telephoned countless times, he wrote, and he was damned if he would try again until she contacted him. Camilla could not face a discussion with her agent, but the fact that she had no modelling work created a frightening uncertainty about her working future. Her body felt leaden, and she had no energy. At night her dreams still brought her back to the moment when panga sliced her head, and she recalled the salty-sweet taste of her own blood. The cut was throbbing when she lifted the telephone and rang Edward's rooms to make a new appointment.

'You've been dozing, I see.' He was standing over her, holding her coat out as she opened her eyes. 'We're going to the bar at the Connaught. It's relatively quiet.'

He ordered drinks and frowned slightly when Camilla opened her bag to take out her cigarettes. She lit one anyway, and sipped at her vodka.

'My mother has leukaemia. She says there's nothing they can do.'

'There are new treatments, although they do have unpleasant side effects. But she's a young woman. I would have thought her physician might persuade her to try them.'

'She doesn't want that. And the specialist says it's unlikely that it would make a difference. The cancer is too far advanced.'

'Perhaps she needs more encouragement. What does your father say?'

'I haven't seen him. He's been away. He's busy.' Her manner had shifted in an instant and she stubbed out her cigarette. 'Thank you for the drink. I really have to go, Edward. There are things I need to do at home this evening. And I forgot to ask you if I could have some tranquillisers. I'm still having nightmares, and I'm jumpy all the time.'

'Look, I can see I've broached a difficult subject with regard to Marina's illness. I'm sorry. I thought it might be a relief to talk about it.'

'It is. I hadn't mentioned it to anyone else, and it was beginning to burn a hole in me,' Camilla admitted.

'I know that everything seems to be on a downward spiral just now. But you do need to be careful about tranquillisers, because they can be habit-forming. I'll write you a prescription for a small number, but we'll have to discuss it again before I give you any more. In the meantime, I need you fresh and relaxed for our repair session in the morning. So why don't we have a quick supper, and afterwards I'll deliver you safely back to your flat? Because it would be very unwise to spend your evening smoking and drinking, and worrying about your mother.'

The restaurant Edward chose was crowded, and Camilla was absurdly reassured when the manager recognised her and found them a table in a quiet corner. When they had ordered their food she sat back in her chair.

'Did you see much of my parents on your visits to Kenya?' she asked.

'Yes, I did. We met at a cocktail party in Government House, the first time I went there to do some surgery. After that I saw your mother often. She was involved with a charity that arranged hospital beds for the children I treated.'

'That sounds like her, yes. She was never one to remember that it begins at home.'

He registered her resentment but did not comment on it. 'They were always very kind to me, and hospitable. Your father is an extremely charming, far-sighted man, and a generous host.'

'He's been cheating on her for years, that same, charming George. That wasn't so far-sighted.'

Edward said nothing, waiting.

'Cheating with men. I've just found out.'

'Ah. That must have been a very painful discovery for you,' he said. 'Unfaithful is hard enough, but the other aspect – I can see you would need time to come to terms with that. You've had far too much to contend with lately.'

During their meal she told him the whole story, describing her upbringing and her parents' strange existence together, like a pair of scorpions performing an endless pas de deux. He was moved by her attempt to explain, without sentiment, the isolation of her childhood years, when her love for her father and the friendships she had formed at school were the only constants she knew. She had never attempted to understand her mother or to question the reasons for Marina's unhappiness.

'Daddy was the one person in my life that I always trusted and admired. Unconditional love, I think it's called. He was my hero.' Camilla leaned forward, wanting to emphasise how George had been her beacon in a sea of whirling undercurrents and tides without any discernible pattern. But he, too, had turned out to be false. He was a guilty, hunted man hiding behind the mask of an unhappy marriage.

'I had two friends at school who were the only goalposts that never moved,' Camilla said. 'But when I ran into trouble, I used them as barriers. To fend off reality, to avoid learning hugely painful lessons. And recently I made the worst mistake of all.'

She glanced at him for a reaction, but he was studying the wine in his glass, afraid that too direct a contact between them might inhibit her narrative, erode her confidence in him as a sounding board. He wanted her to learn that she could trust him, and he already knew that he loved her, insane though it might be. He still could not believe the effect she had on him, the foolish, shaky sensation he felt when he was with her. She was young enough to be his daughter, and he had only just met her. But he did not care.

'You seem to have a sort of "tell-all" effect on me.' Her smile lit her eyes so that they shone blue and clear, and he could imagine what she had looked like as a child. 'You're a latter day Edward the Confessor.' She laughed outright. 'Anyway, you might as well know the rest now. To cap it all, I've just made a total fool of myself over a man. I thought he loved me. But I discovered, too late, that I was just a passing fancy. So here I am, rejected, washed up and scarred in every sense. Hanging out in the wind.'

'You're being too hard on yourself,' he said. 'Everyone gets things wrong from time to time, and suffers from hindsight, like heartburn after you've eaten something acid. And we're all guilty of telling ourselves what we want to hear. I keep doing that. I did it this evening, when I told myself you had nothing better to do than have dinner with me.'

'Well, I'm here,' she said, not sure what to make of his odd admission. 'And apparently you didn't have anything better to do either. Thank you for listening. I suppose that's the price you pay for socialising with your patients.'

'Most of my patients don't want to socialise with me, in case anyone we bump into assumes they've had a facelift. Besides, I'm always being accused of being too wrapped up in my work.'

'And is that true?'

'I'm learning,' he said, as he sent for the bill. 'I'll take you back to your flat, young lady. And you're going to promise me that you'll have an early night and be at the London Clinic tomorrow morning at seven.'

'I promise,' she said solemnly. 'It's the least I can do, after offloading that litany of sorrows on you. I'm not usually like this, you know, and I don't want you to feel sorry for me. I'd hate that.'

'That's not what I feel about you at all,' he said.

Camilla rose to her feet and as she turned to leave she heard someone call out her name.

'Camilla, where have you been, for God's sake? You never answer your bloody phone, and I've even written you a letter that you obviously haven't bothered to read. You missed a great job.' It was Tom Bartlett.

'I think you know Edward Carradine,' Camilla said. 'He's going to clear up this mess on my forehead in a few weeks, and then I should look as good as new.'

'Great news. But you won't have to think about your face if you never check in with your agent.'

'I'll go and retrieve our coats.' Edward moved away tactfully.

'Memories are very short in this business, you know.' Tom was really angry. 'Where the hell were you, anyway? I assume you've had access to the odd telephone, wherever you've been lurking.'

'I was in the country. Mother's not well and I was keeping her company.'

'Can you do a session early next week? For Biba? Someone dropped out at the last minute and they're desperate.'

'How flattering,' she said.

'Don't be so uppity,' Tom retorted. 'You disappear and don't even leave a number where I can reach you, and now you're bitching that I've got you a good job. I told them you'd cut your hair, had a fringe. In fact, I told them the whole story. But it's a studio shoot so there'll be no wind, and there are hats in the collection. The forehead won't matter.'

'I'll phone you in the morning, and you can give me the dates and the address for the shoot.' She put out her hand and stroked his arm. 'Thanks, Tom. Thanks a lot.'

When they reached her flat Edward kept the taxi waiting while he escorted her upstairs. To her relief, he did not ask to come in. Afterwards she wondered what had possessed her to confide all her private thoughts. Perhaps it was the fact that he had no preconceptions about her. She sat on the edge of her bed for a few moments before picking up the telephone and calling her mother in Burford. Marina had not changed her sleeping habits. She still stayed up into the small hours and rose late.

'I've been to see your friend Edward,' Camilla said. 'And I have to go back to him early in the morning, so I won't be at home until after ten. Are you all right?'

'Yes. Your father is here, darling. We're coming up to town tomorrow. Would you—?'

'No. I'll phone you tomorrow. Goodnight.'

Camilla lay back against her pillows, but sleep remained stubbornly elusive. She thought of her parents sitting together in the small cottage, facing the miscalculations of their joint past and contemplating the eternal separation of the future. Was her father secretly, guiltily, relieved that it would all be over soon, that he would no longer be trapped in the charade he had created? What could they possibly say to one another now? she wondered. Did he ask Marina if she was feeling well, knowing that the spongy tissue that made up her life's blood was rotting inside her bones? Did she greet him with her light, butterfly touch, ask him how his week had been, enquire after his lover? After a while, Camilla made her way into the bathroom and opened the mirrored cabinet. There were only two tranquillisers left in the small bottle, and Edward had forgotten to write a prescription. She would remind him in the morning.

Outside, the night was cold, banded at the edges by the orange glow of city lights. The sky felt heavy, damp with fog. Unlike the starlight of an African night that had danced through the silhouette of palm fronds and between the lace of acacia branches, to shine on her delight at being alive and in love. She wondered where Anthony was now, and whether he ever thought of her. His postcard had said he might be passing through London. But he had not mentioned her birthday or given any hint that he wanted to see her. Sarah had written, and Hannah too, asking about her face, but leaving out any reference to either Anthony or to Langani and its problems. Camilla was ashamed that she had failed them. But she could not explain what had happened, or drag her father's secret into the open. For a moment she was tempted to telephone the farm to ask how they all were, to find out whether Sarah had settled in to her new job, to explain the sordid discovery that had alienated her from the only people she loved. Then she realised that it was after midnight in Kenya. A phone call would hardly be welcome. It was just as well. She was not sure that she could survive their reaction, the shock that Hannah would try to hide, the pity that would be Sarah's response, and the probable revulsion of men like Piet and Lars. Camilla lay down again and drew the blankets over her, feeling the slide of tears on her face. Some implacable God had taken everything away from her, and she fell asleep asking herself whether she deserved so cruel a reckoning for the wrongs she had done.

Edward worked on her forehead the following morning, and told her she should return in ten days for a check-up.

'Are you going back to Burford?' he said.

'No. Mother's coming up here today.'

'Well, try not to live too much of the high life. Don't go stumbling around in a haze of vodka and fall over anything else.'

She was hurt by his assumption that she had been drunk when she had fallen.

'I'm going to be at a conference in New York all next week,' he said, washing his hands. Washing his hands of her trite, self-inflicted woes, she thought. 'If there's a problem with your face then I want you to call this number at once. It's a colleague's, and he'll take care of any emergency. I'll phone you when I get back. Just to nudge your conscience and keep you in line.'

It was a relief to be working again, and at the end of the first morning Camilla wondered why she had ever complained about the career she had drifted into accidentally. The hot lights and the dust came back to her with a kind of nostalgia that she would never have believed possible. She smiled and pouted, swung her hips in time to the blare of the raucous Stones, and spun around to look over her shoulder at the lens, in the sure knowledge that her allure would shine out of the pictures.

'You're better than you ever were,' said the photographer, James Mann. 'Bloody marvellous. Now put your hands on your hips, stick your fanny out. Smile like you're going to give me the one thing I want. Yeah, that's it. That's good.'

By the end of the week she had several new bookings and her spirits were restored. She was not ruined, even though she would have to wait three or four months for the right time to minimise the scar. There was a possibility that she might be asked to launch a new line of swimwear, and Tom was busy with the negotiations.

'This is a relief,' he said. 'One minute your phone is off the hook and you've vanished without trace. Now you've reappeared as the dream model, always on time, full of ideas for make-up and hair and better ways of doing the shoot. I like this version.'

'I used to think I'd fallen into this job. That it was a poor, second best,' Camilla said. 'But now I realise that it's something I do really well, and if that's my line then I'm going to do it better than anybody else.'

She experimented with a series of hairpieces and wigs that allowed her to change her appearance radically, although she had to keep her forehead covered. She studied her reflection, inventing new ways to emphasise her eyes, her mouth, the planes of her face, so that photographers would recognise her diversity and book her again and again. She no longer chaffed at assignments in draughty studios, or complained about sitting in a van on the edge of a field waiting for the shoot to be set up, or for the sun to come out. In addition to the tote bag full of cosmetics, hair rollers and brushes, and other implements of her trade, she carried a small briefcase full of books. She read avidly between photo sessions, gulping down fiction and history.

When Edward came back to London she had her stitches removed, and soon afterwards she was able to apply a layer of pancake foundation over her scar and wear her hair back off her face. The results were not good enough for close-ups, but they were fine for shots in which she walked and danced and jumped in the middle distance, or posed in soft light like some mythical beauty. Columnists wrote about her in the newspapers, magazines wanted to interview her, wealthy men wanted her to join them in a box at the opera, on their private yachts, in their villas on the Côte d'Azur. The combination of her beauty and her professionalism created another form of pressure. Requests and invitations filled her letter box and poured into Tom's office so that she felt trapped by her own success.

'I can't do any more parties or appearances this month,' she told Tom. 'I'm so exhausted that I can't even sleep. It's like being on some fairground ride that gets faster and faster, and I feel I can't get off unless I fling myself to the ground. You've got to find me some time off. And I need a few days with my mother.'

When Marina was in London they occasionally had lunch or dinner together, or spent an afternoon at a film or a play, if she was feeling well enough and Camilla was free. There was an unspoken agreement between them that George would never be there, and that they would not discuss him. There were times when Camilla missed him with the fierce pain of loss, but whenever she was tempted to phone him she could not imagine what she might say. He would try to explain, to apologise maybe, and she did not want to face this altered man or see his shame at her discovery. She questioned this inability in herself. Many of the people she worked with were openly homosexual. They were often artistic and talented, and they were agreeable dinner dates who shared her appreciation of music and theatre, of beautiful objects and clothes. Best of all, she knew they would not press her for sexual favours at the end of the evening. She was relaxed in their company, enjoying their sometimes exaggerated gestures and the way they flouted their sexuality. But they were not her father.

Edward telephoned twice and asked her to dinner, but she had no time for a quiet evening and she turned him down with some regret. He had been kind, practical and non-judgmental, and she wanted him to know that she appreciated his help. The only time she saw him was at a charity dinner where she was caught in a blaze of flashlights. When she looked for him later in the evening, he was gone. She cut down on late-night parties, limited herself to five cigarettes a day, and drank only champagne and a little wine. Although she smoked marijuana occasionally, she turned down the more potent drugs that were widely on offer.

'Darling, you'll be twenty-one in ten days. It's your big birthday, and because of this tiresome illness we haven't done a thing about it.' Marina finally broached a subject that Camilla had been avoiding. 'We're very late making plans, and I need to know what you'd like to do. Something at Annabel's perhaps?'

'I don't want a social thing with a cast of thousands,' Camilla said. 'And I certainly don't want an all-night spectacle in some restaurant or club, with scores of fashion people. There's no one I count as a close friend among them, except maybe Tom Bartlett. They're good mates, but that's all. Twenty-one. What does it mean, anyway? It's just a number.'

'Suppose we went away somewhere?' Marina suggested. 'We could fly somewhere glorious and stay in the best hotel.'

'Such as?'

'Paris, perhaps. Although it might rain all the time. Or Rome. Rome would be lovely. Anywhere you like.'

'Are you well enough to travel, Mother?'

'Well, I couldn't manage the Kalahari. But I could go somewhere nearby. Dr Ward said he would give me a contact in case we ran into trouble.'

Marina was almost pleading. Camilla saw that this idea had been in her mind for some time, that it might even be her last opportunity to travel anywhere.

'All right. Rome. We haven't been to Italy since I did my course in Florence. Let's try Rome.'

'Camilla, would you consider——?'

'Don't ask me what I think you're going to ask me. Please, Mother. Just don't.'

They flew into the Eternal City on a bright afternoon. A limousine from the hotel met them at the airport and they sat back in the comfort of the car and watched the magnificence of Rome slide past the tinted windows. Domes and columns and monuments stood proud in the light of evening. The hotel was suitably grand, with acres of polished marble and thick carpets that softened every footfall and muffled the sound of slightly forced conversation. Marina was exhausted by the journey, pale and breathless as she walked the last few feet along the corridor to their connecting rooms.

'Siesta time for you,' Camilla said. 'And I'm going to collapse for a while too. Then we'll decide what, if anything, we want to do for supper. But room service is fine with me.'

'Oh, I think we'll do better than that,' Marina said. 'I'm sure we will. You'll see.'

Camilla left the door ajar, and began to unpack. In the bathroom she lifted her fringe and looked at her forehead in the mirror. The red line was clean, but the marks of the stitches were still visible. Now she would have to wait until Edward considered the time was right for surgery. Twenty-one tomorrow. Cards had arrived in the post from Sarah and Hannah, with brief letters that indicated their disappointment in her. Anthony had sent a large bouquet through Interflora, but had given her no clue as to where he was. A packet from Asprey had been delivered to her flat, accompanied by a card from her father, but Camilla had left it unopened. She drew the curtains back and looked out into the swirl of evening traffic, and the life of the city that she could not share as she stood in the hotel room, inured from its noisy reality. But at least she was away from the pressures of her work and her celebrity. What she needed to do was to sleep, and perhaps this brief holiday would allow her that luxury. She was about to run a bath when the telephone in Marina's room rang, and she hurried to answer it, hoping it would not wake her mother.

'Marina? *Cara!* Ah, it's Camilla – wonderful. My dear, it is Claudia Santini. Do you remember, I was a friend of your mother's in Nairobi? And when they were at the Embassy here, after they left Kenya. Then we spent so many good times together. My husband Franco is in the Foreign

Service like your father. We are so sorry George is not here. Now, Marina has telephoned me from London to explain about your birthday, so we will celebrate together, no? I have booked a table in Santa Maria Trastevere for tonight. Very casual and easy so Marina can leave if she gets too tired. Just for family. And tomorrow we will have lunch at our place, in the country.'

Camilla sighed. There was no sidestepping the plan that Marina had concocted. She had been mad to imagine that there would be just the two of them. With a sting of remorse she realised that she did not mind the distraction. If nothing else, it would prevent illness and mortality from casting their shadows over the entire weekend.

'Oh, what the hell,' she said to her image in the mirror. 'Who cares about my birthday anyway?'

The restaurant was hidden in the maze of cobbled streets behind the main piazza. Claudia Santini embraced Marina with tears streaming down her face. Her husband followed suit, making no attempt to hide his emotion. There was a young man at the table, slight and very dark. He stood quietly waiting for the greetings and introductions to take their course.

'Camilla, *cara*. You are as beautiful as your mother.' Claudia put her ample arm around Camilla's shoulders. 'Here is Roberto, our son. Maybe you will remember him from Nairobi?'

They looked at one another, exchanging sympathetic glances that acknowledged their secondary roles in a parental reunion. Camilla sat down beside him, and Franco ordered Prosecco and antipasti for them all.

'I do remember you,' Roberto said, his eyes black and laughing. He was already flirting with her. 'Impossible and snobbish. The boys in my year at St Mary's, we called you the Ice Queen and we all wanted to melt you, conquer you.'

'You all wanted to conquer any girl who would have you,' she said, pleased with the light-hearted atmosphere. 'You boys only had one thing on your minds, all of you. It was the same thing that all the nuns had on their minds. Sex, or abstinence from it.'

'Nothing has changed,' he said, grinning at her. 'I'm glad to see you again, to get another chance. Tell me, where you have been? I know you were in Florence while your parents lived in Rome, but I don't think you came here much.'

Afterwards, what she remembered most about the evening was Marina, shining with some strange quality that rendered her luminous in her frailty. Camilla thought about the unknown quantity that surrounds a pregnant woman as she carries a new life in her body, and she marvelled at the way in which her mother now bore the certainty of death. The uninhibited joy and sadness with which Marina was welcomed proved to be very moving, a surprising vision of a woman loved by her friends. A woman her daughter had hardly known.

'I will come to collect you at the hotel. Tomorrow at noon, if this is good for you,' Claudia said, watching for signs of fatigue in her friend. 'You must not be too tired for the celebration, Marina, *cara*. Let's call a taxi for you.'

'No, I'd like to walk a little,' Marina said. 'It's so mild out, and I love this part of the city.'

They reached the piazza and sat down so that she could rest for a few moments. All around them people were strolling, drinking at small tables set out in the street to take full advantage of the softness in the night air. Lovers kissed and touched, oblivious to everything but their own passion as they strolled with arms entwined. There were stars above and below them, shimmering in the velvet of the night sky and reflected in the trembling water of the floodlit fountain. Camilla thought of Anthony then pushed him out of her mind before taking Roberto's hand.

Marina slept late the following morning, and when the car arrived she was not quite ready.

'Go and join Claudia downstairs,' she said to Camilla. 'It will take me another ten minutes to put myself in order. I'm so slow these days, and it's worse when someone is watching and waiting.'

'It is not a problem,' Claudia said. 'She must take all the time she likes. We will wait in the bar together. What would you like to drink?'

'Espresso please,' Camilla said.

'Many happy returns to you, my dear. I wish you everything that is good in life.'

'Thank you.'

'It is hard for you now. This I know. You should be with people of your own age, celebrating that you are twenty-one and beautiful. At the beginning of everything you want to do. But the sadness of your mother's illness has come at the same moment.'

'Timing has never been my best suit.'

'Still, you have time on your side now, when it is so important.'

'In what way?' Camilla had begun to regret coming down early to be with Claudia. It occurred to her that this was some arrangement cooked up by Marina and her old friend. An opportunity for a sermon, a little pep talk.

'You did not know my daughter,' Claudia said. 'Young and beautiful like you, full of spirit and life, with so many plans. She was always arguing with her father and me, because she did not want to study, to stay at university, to be like her friends. She wanted independence, a freer way of living. She wanted to escape us, like all young people want to leave their parents behind, because we are so old-fashioned, so out of touch with the world. She went to India, two years ago. She just left one day, without telling us, and she went to India. We did not even have a chance to say goodbye.'

'I have several friends in London who did the same thing,' Camilla tried to sound reassuring. 'It's become fashionable to find a guru to follow, to look for a different way of living. But for most people it's a phase they grow out of. That's all.'

'But Gina will not grow out of it. She died in an accident, three weeks after she arrived there. And we will never have a chance now, to say how much we love one another.'

'I'm so sorry. I can't imagine—' No adequate phrase came to Camilla's mind.

'Your mother helped me so much,' Claudia said. 'She knew about daughters who wanted to break free. I do not know what we would have done without her. My Italian friends did not understand really. They had not lived overseas like us, and they were mostly from Roman families where it is all about tradition. I thought some of them even blamed us, in a way, for bringing up our children in other countries. For sending them to foreign schools, where they learned more about other cultures than they did about their own. We had been away so long that old connections were broken. But George and Marina understood, and that is how we became such good friends.'

'You're telling me that I have a chance to say goodbye.'

'It sounds too obvious, perhaps. But yes, that is what I am saying. And in the meantime you can make her happy and comfortable.'

'I've never been much good at that,' Camilla said.

'She is so frail.' Claudia appeared not to have heard. 'There must be some way that she can take more nutrition to help her. She cannot fade away. She must fight. She must fight for him.'

'For who?' Camilla was puzzled.

'For your father. I know why he is not here with her. Of course he is not away travelling, too busy for his daughter's birthday. Your mother did not expect us to believe that. And we understand how it is not true, how she is protecting him.'

'You know?' Camilla was astounded. Perhaps she was the only one who had not known the true state of her parents' relationship.

'We know his heart is breaking, poor George. That it is impossible for him to accept what is happening. But at least he will have the daughter he talked about always, his princess, so beautiful and so clever. At least you will be with him when she is gone. And he must be so proud of you, that you are so successful and famous.'

'I don't imagine he really—'

'You must not think he does not love you enough,' Claudia interrupted, her round face anxious. 'It is only that he cannot be brave. He cannot face the idea of a life without her. They had good years here in Italy. Marina said they were the best of all their years. So it is easy to understand why he would not come back now, knowing that they will never be in Roma together again. I am sure he will celebrate with you in London, when you return.'

Camilla said nothing, a bitterness flooding her mouth. Claudia reached across the table and took her hand.

'He seems so strong, George. But he relies on her for everything, he trusts only Marina to guide him. To keep him steady. I do not know what he will do without her, because she is the strong one. So, you will help him, even though it is difficult, because you are very young and loss has not yet been a part of your life. It is something you will learn. But today, let us be happy like Marina is happy, for all the hopes she can see in you. This is very precious.'

'Sometimes things look different from the outside,' Camilla said, nettled by Claudia's sermonising, so wide of the mark. Her analysis simply confirmed George's ability to deceive, and Marina's willingness to play to perfection the role of the sympathetic diplomat's wife, to draw a veil of illusion over reality. 'Sometimes they are not what they seem and you only find that out when you get close to them.'

'No, my dear. I think it is more often those inside that cannot see, because they are too young or too old, or too close to the picture, and because they have suffered. I think that is what happens more often. I hope you will forgive me for my words, but she is my friend and I love her. Ah – here she comes, and she is beautiful, no?'

The Santini house was on a lake, half an hour from the city centre. The countryside basked in the special gold light that Camilla always thought of as pure Italian. The sky looked startlingly blue through the framework of bare branches that opened out on to the landscape, revealing ancient fields and imposing estates, usually hidden by summer leaves. They swept up a driveway of cypress trees to a house of perfect proportions set in a sweep of formal gardens with a flight of stone steps to the main entrance. Inside, Camilla's heels tapped a rhythm on the marble floors as she followed her mother and Claudia through several large reception rooms that seemed more like museum exhibits than a family home.

'Impossible, this place of Franco's family,' Claudia said, flinging out an arm in a gesture of love and exasperation. 'It is a struggle every day, the preservation of these old walls and the ceilings, and the battle with damp and peeling plaster and window frames and stones. Sometimes I shout at Franco, I tell him to let it all rot so that we can live in a modern apartment in the city, and I can spend my days shopping in the Via Veneto or playing bridge and having coffee with my friends. But then I walk in the garden and I am in love again.'

They stepped out of the faded grandeur and gloomy half-light of the interior, on to an open terrace that overlooked the gardens. The central feature was a fountain, out of which rose the figure of a young man, naked and beautiful, astride a lion whose stony mane had been slowly worn away by centuries of splashing water. Lunch had been set out beneath the umbrella pines on the edge of the lawn and a handful of people were standing in the sunshine, drinking champagne. The late-autumn sun danced on the glitter of glass and china, and on heavy bowls of fruit and flowers that filled the long table. Roberto raised a hand to wave at them and then ran up the steps to lead Marina down into the garden, glancing over his shoulder at Camilla with an expression of undisguised lust. She was laughing as Franco Santini made introductions, and pleased when she saw that several of the guests were her own generation. After a few hesitant sentences her Italian returned, smooth and fluent, and she found herself relaxed among Roberto's friends who responded to her in the way of the Italians she had known in Florence, during her year of art and language studies. Their uninhibited enjoyment and willingness to celebrate with her was infectious, and she felt resilient and uplifted.

Lunch was long and languorous. Marina ate very little, but seemed to have no trouble with the champagne and the wines that were constantly replenished by a white-gloved butler. She was in her element, turning her head in the deliberately artful way that Camilla knew so well, flirting with the men in the party, making witty remarks in her light, breathless voice. She looked as though she had not a care in the world, as if life had treated her with astonishing generosity, heaping on her indiscriminately the gifts of beauty and intelligence and riches of every kind. It was almost six in the evening when the last birthday toasts had been made, and coffee cups and brandy glasses littered the table. Stoles and jackets had been placed around the women's shoulders as the light faded, making a sombre silhouette of the trees, casting long, slanting shadows across the grass. Camilla shivered.

'Now we will leave the old ones,' Roberto said. 'Come with me, and I will show you Rome without the dinosaurs.'

Claudia nodded her encouragement. 'Go with Roberto. I will drive Marina to the hotel, and we will sit together for a while. When she is tired I will help her into bed.'

It was difficult to express appreciation for the hospitality she had received and the thought behind it. Camilla had arrived feeling defensive, anticipating among the guests an awkward sympathy for the girl from London who was to celebrate her twenty-first birthday in the company of strangers. She was aware, too, that the lunch party had been arranged as much for Marina as for herself. Now it seemed right. She put her arms around Claudia.

'Thank you,' she said. 'Thank you for all that you've done, and for the wise words you put into my head.'

She kissed her mother on the cheek, took her coat and her handbag, and followed Roberto to the garage round the side of the house. His car was low and sleek and he drove fast with the windows open. Camilla's hand went involuntarily to her forehead where the fall of her fringe had blown away to reveal the scar. He glanced at her, but made no comment. The city spun towards them in the evening light, traffic tumbling on to the streets from every direction. They left the car parked on a busy street with its front wheels up on a pavement. It was cold now and she was glad to be inside the bar he chose. The music was loud and the place was smoky and vibrating with energy. He found a table in a corner where the vaulted ceiling was lit by guttering candles. She was flattered when several people recognised her from Italian fashion magazines where she had featured several months before. They talked, drank champagne and danced, smoked and talked and danced again. Roberto held her lightly, seducing her in an obvious but charming way that was pure old world in character.

'Tell me about your face,' he said.

'I was on holiday back in Kenya. There was a robbery and I was cut by a panga.'

'It will heal of course, in time. But in your mind, do you still see it? Do you dream about it?'

She was surprised by his question. 'Yes. I was lucky. We were all lucky that night. But I do have nightmares. They'll go away eventually, I suppose, but I'm still frightened if I hear footsteps behind me, and I can see the faces of those men when I close my eyes at night.'

'I have nightmares about my sister and how she died. I think they will never go away, and that scar will never be covered over.'

'Your mother told me, and I'm so sorry,' Camilla said. 'I'm an only child, but I had two very close friends who were like sisters to me. I've lost them, though, and that's much more painful than my bad dreams or my scar.'

She was a little drunk now, and tears were stinging behind her eyes. Roberto leaned forward to kiss her, but the time for flirtation had suddenly passed and she felt a great weariness.

'Roberto,' she said. 'Do you think you could take me back to the Hassler? Being twenty-one has aged me suddenly. Or perhaps it's just that I've drunk at least three bottles of champagne all by myself. I could take a taxi, if you'll order one. I'm sorry, Roberto. Really I am.'

'It's not possible,' he said, laughing at her. 'I am going to take you to a party at a friend's house. You will wake up there, and feel wonderful again. You cannot go to bed now, on your birthday, like an old lady.'

The room of the ancient palazzo was heaving with young people dressed in the extravagant finery of affluent Roman society. Roberto introduced her to their host. She did not catch his full name above the noise of the party, but he was a prince of some kind. All around her there was music and dancing and couples lying on velvet sofas, locked together and kissing, drinking champagne and small shots of liqueurs, smoking marijuana and popping brightly coloured pills from little gold and enamelled boxes.

'I can't stay long, Roberto,' she said. 'I really am wilting now.'

The prince was standing at her elbow. 'Ah, but you have arrived just as we are serving dessert,' he said. 'Drink some champagne, and I will bring you something that will make you forget you were ever tired.' He signalled to a waiter who offered a tray laden with tiny, glistening cubes of sugar, and dropped one into her glass.

Camilla looked at him as he walked away. Then she raised her glass to Roberto and smiled as she drank the cocktail. He beckoned her into the centre of the room and she danced with him, following his slow movements, allowing him to hold her very close, until her fingers began to tingle and she realised she was dizzy. When there was a break in the music she disengaged herself and moved to the window of the palazzo, to breathe in the night air and to look down into an ancient square with a fountain. Roberto followed her, whispering something in her ear that she did not catch. Below her the fountain suddenly leapt high into the air, the jets of water shooting upwards in a series of brilliant colours and shapes, turning into huge, iridescent flying fish. She gasped in surprise and turned back to the room where the walls were moving in and out, exploding with colour and force, heaving with each breath she took. People were gliding past her, indescribably beautiful, so that she wanted to reach out and touch them. The music melted into bright colours that flowed like streamers, and she could taste each note of the saxophone, feel every beat of the drum deep in her stomach.

'Acid?' She looked at Roberto, saw his eyes shining like dark pools, his mouth cherry red and glistening. 'Oh God. I've never done this.'

She began to laugh, holding her arms out to the people who swirled around her, tracing circles of colour in the air with her fingertips. Her heart was beating very fast and she wanted to embrace them all, but she was laughing too much. A surge of joy rushed through her, and she felt as though she could fly, out and away across the piazza into the whirl of sound and colour on the horizon.

'Come, *cara*. Come outside with me.' His head was swaying on his shoulders, and his voice sounded strange and high as he led her through the pulse and spin of the room and down to the square below. She was still laughing as she climbed up on to the edge of the fountain, leaning over to catch the drops of water as they tumbled and leapt and chased one another through the air in a silver arc.

'Come home with me,' Roberto said, pulling her back from the water's edge. 'I have good hashish at home, and we can smoke it and play together. Come.'

She followed him to the car and lowered herself into the seat beside him. But now the buildings around her began to press downwards so that she felt they might fall and crush her, and she was suddenly frightened. There were people on the street with masks covering their faces, but she could see the glint of their eyes and the envy in their stares. Figures appeared out of the luminous fog that wrapped itself around her, and they were grotesque and cruel. When the car stopped at an intersection, she turned to find a man staring in at her through the window. As she gazed at him his face darkened and became black, and she saw that he had a knife in his hand, a panga-type knife with a sharp blade, and that he was raising it into the air as the traffic lights changed and they sped away. She cowered in her seat, whimpering, clinging to Roberto's arm, leaning back. Her eyes were tightly shut, but a series of floating faces pressed through her eyelids, angry and threatening. Roberto was speaking to her, but she could not hear what he was saying above the babble of other voices. As they drove through the city she saw the street lights bend and sway above the car, like giant hooks reaching down to trap her, to scoop her up and hurl her into some far abyss.

When he stopped the car and helped her out, Camilla realised that they were back at the hotel. He put his finger against her lips, and she looked at him in terror.

'Don't talk while we are in the lobby,' he said. 'Just ask for your key, and I'll take you upstairs. Don't worry, Camilla – everyone has bad trips. It won't last. I'll stay with you until it's finished.'

At the reception, the man behind the desk gazed at her with suspicion, his head shrinking to the size of a pea, his voice squeaking as he reached out his hand and took the banknotes that Roberto pushed into his palm. In the bedroom she began to shake with fear as the pictures on the wall expanded and flew towards her. She rocked back and forth on the edge of her bed, pressing her hands over her eyes to rid herself of the demons that had invaded her brain. It was suddenly clear to her that she must escape, and she jumped up and rushed to the window. Her hands were clammy and her fingers fumbled and slipped as she wrestled with the window latch, rattling the handles and banging her fists against the panes of glass until one side swung open and she climbed up and sat with her legs hanging over the sill. She was aware that Roberto was clutching at her arm, talking to her, pleading with her not to jump. Neither of them heard the soft click as the connecting door opened.

'What on earth is—?' Marina scanned the room. 'Oh! Dear God, please help me now. Please, just this once, don't let me down.' She moved across the room, trying to keep her steps measured and calm and smooth. 'Come in now, darling,' she said, her voice low. 'It's terribly cold out there. Come down, Camilla. I'm here to look after you. I'm going to help you into bed, because it's very late, darling. So come to bed. Please.'

No one moved. Camilla sat poised on the window sill, her arms spread out as if for flight, gazing out at the domes and spires and chimneys of the city, heedless of the traffic in the street below or the soft pleading behind her.

'Have you had any of this, whatever it is?' Marina turned to Roberto, her voice iron-hard with hatred. He shook his head and she gripped his arm. 'Get out,' she hissed. 'Get out of here without making a sound, and never contact my daughter again. And understand that neither of us will ever talk about this to anyone, least of all to your unfortunate parents.'

Interminable minutes passed before Camilla reached down and clutched at her mother's outstretched hand. Marina clasped her fingers and talked on, her tone light and soothing, until at last Camilla swung her legs slowly into the bedroom, and allowed herself to be guided into bed.

When she woke at mid-morning she was awash with lassitude. She opened the connecting door and saw that Marina was still asleep. It was too difficult to decide whether to dress and go out for a walk, or simply remain in bed and give in to the heavy, liquid sensation in her limbs. Room service seemed to be a reasonable option, but when Camilla turned to the phone she noticed an elaborately wrapped packet on her bedside table.

There was a note attached to it, and she read it several times before putting it aside.

> *Darling Camilla,*
>
> *Your father gave me this on the day you were born because he loved us both so much, and we were so happy. We want you to have it now, because we still love and cherish you above all else in our lives. We hope that you will wear it and think of us, in the wonderful life you have ahead of you.*
>
> *I love you, my darling, my precious, beautiful daughter, on your twenty-first birthday and every day.*
>
> *M*

Camilla undid the ribbon and peeled off the paper. The flat leather box was dark green in colour and tooled with gold. Her mother's initials were on the lid. Inside, the necklace lay on a bed of velvet. It was a collar of complex and delicate artistry, made of coral beads and pearls with a centrepiece of small enamelled flowers and leaves, joined together by a web of fine gold chains. Camilla recognised it as a Renaissance piece. She had never seen it before, and did not remember her mother ever wearing it. Her fingers trembled as she lifted it out of the case and walked over to the mirror to fasten it round her neck where it lay, glittering, against the pale skin of her throat. Her eyes starred with tears, fracturing the image, and she returned to her bed and slid between the sheets. Within moments she was asleep, her hand resting lightly on the necklace, and a jumble of childhood images cramming her dreams.

Chapter 21

London, December 1965

'I don't understand why you spend so much time with that ghastly, vulgar crowd, Camilla. There are models, and even photographers, who are educated, well-groomed people with some sort of acceptable background. Couldn't you see more of them?' Marina's voice was peevish on the line. 'You looked so glamorous and civilised in the photographs John French took.'

'I can't always look the same, Mother. Clients need a variety of images and styles, to show their clothes.'

'But David Baxter and his set are so scruffy, darling. It's all very well working with them, but in your own time you don't need to be with people who obviously have no idea how to behave. And I can't imagine why you need to buy things like that dreadful astrakhan coat and the cheap trousers you were wearing in the *Daily Mail* photograph. You have so many wonderful things in your wardrobe that are—'

'You can wear whatever you like these days. It's called freedom – like throwing away your corsets and stays at the beginning of the century.' Camilla was smiling. Marina might be ill, but the core of her remained unchanged.

'I saw your name in the paper again this morning,' Marina went on, her voice now shaded with fear. 'Apparently you were in Ad Lib until four in the morning on Saturday. I am told it's full of people taking drugs.'

'I don't take drugs, Mother, except for an occasional joint, which might even be good for me. I learned my lesson in Rome. You know that.'

'I don't think you're careful enough, darling. You have so many undesirable hangers-on. You may be very "in", as they say, but you still have to think of your reputation and your future.'

'No one has what you would call a reputation these days,' Camilla said.

'Everything's changed, Mother. All that rubbish about stiff upper lips and stiff upper classes has gone out the window. Half the country's landed gentry are queuing up to get into Ad Lib and be seen with Baxter. How are you feeling today?'

'Like a hideous old crone with rheumatism. All I need now is a stick and knitted stockings that wrinkle around my knees.' Marina's laugh was thin and high. 'I have an appointment with the medicine man at four.'

Camilla turned over in bed and looked at the clock. It was almost eleven and she had to be in the studio at twelve. She looked like nothing on earth. Felt like hell, after a party last night to show off a new line of jewellery. It had been a long evening.

'I'm leaving for work in half an hour. If I'm finished at the studio in time I'll join you in Harley Street and hear what Dr Ward has to say.'

'No, you don't have to do that.'

'Even so, I'll try and get there.'

'I'm not going to see David Ward this afternoon.' Marina hesitated. 'I'm going for another kind of blood test.'

'Perhaps we could see a film afterwards,' Camilla suggested.

'I don't think so, darling. I'm a little tired and I think the doctor's appointment will be enough of an outing for me. But you might like to come here for supper. It looks like you've covered enough nightclubs for one week. My friends the Willoughbys saw you in Annabel's on Tuesday. You can't stay up all night every night, Camilla. I thought Edward told you to stay away from all that. The smoke alone takes its toll on your face.'

'My face is fine. Apart from the fact that I've got a bright red line gouged across my forehead. I'll see you for dinner.'

Camilla hung up. George was obviously away somewhere. Marina never had them at home together. It was an arrangement that rankled all round, and caused a festering anxiety in Camilla. On occasion her mother had cried, used her illness as a bargaining tool, begged her to reconsider. But each time Camilla thought of George she saw him again in her mind's eye, bending down towards the erect young man on the bed. Then she wanted to spew out the fury she felt, so that the hideous image would never return. She had tried to rationalise her distress, but each time she considered the mix of betrayal, adultery and the added ingredient of her father's homosexuality she buried the idea in the deepest recess of her consciousness. She didn't feel revulsion, or even distaste, for other men who preferred lovers of their own sex, and she had considered herself modern enough in her thinking, to avoid judgment on such arrangements. But she still could not think of her own father in this way. Nor could she bring herself to face him. When Marina wept and pleaded, Camilla turned away, lost in a well of sadness and confusion.

'We must try to talk this through,' Marina had begged. 'Why can't we discuss the whole issue and try to put it to rest? I don't know where or how you first heard about this, and I wish that I'd somehow been able to explain it to you myself. But perhaps I can help you to find a way through it all.'

Camilla shook her head, incapable of telling her mother what she had seen, the graphic awfulness of her discovery, and she did not believe Marina had ever found a way through it all herself. So she said nothing until the subject faded into the background once more, and their relationship returned to calmer waters.

She pushed the telephone aside and swung her legs gingerly out of bed, groaning a little as the full force of the headache hit her. Her eyes ached too, when she looked sideways into the bathroom mirror, and there were shadows beneath them that needed camouflage. She had drunk too much as she sat wedged between two directors of a knitwear company with whom she had signed a contract. Both of them had made heavy-handed attempts to proposition her, and she could not disguise her boredom without a good deal of help from the waiter with the champagne. The line on her forehead was still red and difficult to conceal entirely. She examined the scar in the mirror and frowned. Then she shrugged off her anxiety and dressed quickly, flinging hairbrushes, rollers and make-up, and an apple from the fridge into a large bag. As she left the sitting room she picked up the two novels she was currently reading. They passed the time during the long hours of sitting around, while lights and backdrops were put in place and clothes were discussed and changed and then changed again. This was not a session she wanted to do, but she was still limited in the jobs she could accept. No outside close-ups, in case her hair blew away from her face. No multi-page stories for the better fashion magazines, because she could not change her hairstyle radically enough for the contrast demanded by the best photographers. She had a sense of being damaged goods and it made her nervous.

There was also the problem of her flat. Marina could no longer manage the stairs, and they had to meet in cafés or restaurants, or at her parents' apartment when her father was away on business. But Camilla did not want to sell her home and she was aware that whatever she did, her mother would soon be unable to visit her anywhere. Unless she went through a miraculous remission. This deliberate calculation made her ashamed, and she wondered if other people with a dying relative were heartless enough to think things out in this way.

It was less than two weeks to Christmas, and she knew that within the next few days the whole issue of the holiday period would be raised again. When she thought about it her stomach churned and she had a taste of ashes in her mouth. She had been invited to Morocco to stay with friends from *Tatler*, but she was stalling. Her need to escape was close to desperation and she longed to go away, to be left in peace, to forget for a short while the miseries of her situation. It would be a blessing to give herself up to the exotic offerings of a country she wanted very much to visit. But Marina would be devastated and hysterical if she spent the holiday in Marrakesh, knowing they would never spend another Christmas together. And there was George. It was only a matter of time until the pressure began again, rekindling Camilla's guilt, and the shame she felt over her continuing refusal to contemplate a reconciliation with her father.

She was weary and dispirited when she rang Marina's doorbell some hours later. The housekeeper answered the door and took Camilla aside in the hall. She was a kindly woman in spite of her glum expression and the grey, wispy hair scraped back into a severe knot.

'She hasn't been at all well either yesterday or today, dear,' Mrs Maskell said. 'I offered to take her to her appointment this afternoon, but she wouldn't hear of it. Dr Hayford phoned afterwards to see if she was home safely. He'd had his nurse put her into the taxi, but he said he was worried about how poorly she looked. Your father will be back at the weekend. Perhaps she'll feel better then.' She pursed her lips, highlighting the strange lack of communication between father and daughter, even in such dire circumstances.

'Thanks, Mrs Maskell. The nurse will be here around nine, and I'll stay tonight.'

Marina was in bed. Her face was grey, her skin chalky, and Camilla saw that her fingers and her wrists were swollen and bruised. She took her mother's hand and felt the heaviness of pain and fatigue.

'Sorry I'm so late. The session dragged, and the designer was behaving like a prima donna over some very ordinary clothes.' She sat on the edge of the bed. 'You should have taken Mrs Maskell with you, Mother. You can't go out alone if you're not feeling right. What did the doctor say?'

'There's nothing new,' Marina said. She lay quietly with her eyes closed, and then her mouth trembled and she began to weep. 'My white cell count is very high. All my joints are swollen, my elbows and knees, everywhere, and you can see the awful bruises. It's too much pain, darling. I don't want to end my life like this, lying around like a dead weight, useless and ugly. I'm so hideous I can't bear to look at myself. All I ever had was beauty, and now that's been taken away from me too. I don't want everyone to remember me withered and helpless. Oh God, I can't do this. I just can't do it.'

She began to cry. Great gulping sobs shook her frail body. Camilla found a soft facecloth and sprinkled it with cool water and cologne, smoothing it over Marina's face and arms, trying to calm her. There was no sense in cheery phrases intended to bolster her confidence or to offer false hope. They both knew that the circumstances were bleak and finite, and neither one of them was given to platitudes. When Marina was quiet again, Camilla made her way to the kitchen and heated a little vegetable soup that Mrs Maskell had prepared. The smell of toast made her realise that she had only eaten an apple all day, and she cut two slices of bread and ate them quickly, spread with a thick layer of butter and jam. Then she put her mother's tray together and spent half an hour coaxing her to take a small amount of nourishment.

'You must eat something before you have your medicine, otherwise it will give you a horribly upset tummy and add to your problems. Would you like a hot-water bottle? Some socks on your feet? You seem to be very cold. Mother, are you sure you shouldn't be in the hospital, just until this swelling subsides? What about another blood transfusion?'

Marina shook her head. 'Not yet. I'm seeing David Ward again next week, but I don't want to be in the hospital. Not yet, please. Give me my tablets for the pain and then I'll sleep. That's what I'd really like to do – just sleep.'

'I'm staying the night. Will that be all right?'

There was a question within the question and Marina nodded, resigned.

Camilla helped her into the bathroom, looking at the delicate limbs with their angry, bulbous appearance and the bruised skin. It was an effort for Marina to use even a soft toothbrush, and there were crimson traces from her bleeding, swollen gums when she rinsed her mouth. She was like a rag doll that flopped and dragged as she moved, and Camilla staggered a little as she half carried her to bed, surprised at the dead weight of the slight body. She pulled up the bedclothes and turned out the light.

'Call me if you need to get up. I'll be next door.'

She poured herself a drink and slumped down in front of the television, exhausted and on the verge of tears. It had been a wretched afternoon. She tried all the channels for some mindless entertainment that would take her into a fantasy world, but there was nothing that she wanted to watch. The doorbell rang and she let the nurse in. The flat was quiet and gloomy, and the clock ticked heedlessly away.

'You have to put your life on hold for a while,' Tom had said, in his brusque manner. 'Everything has hit you at once – your injury and your mother's illness. There's not much you can do except wait the bugger out for a while, and then, *caramba*, life will begin again.'

He had meant to be kind and Camilla was surprised by his effort. He was usually dismissive in his approach to everyday trials and woes, and he did not like his models to bring their personal problems to work with them. He had met Marina several times, however, and something within him was genuinely saddened by the idea that this lovely creature had been handed down a death sentence, with no possibility of appeal. Camilla had been grateful, aware of real, human sympathy. But there was no such thing as putting one's life on hold. The days rolled on and not one of them could ever be returned to her, or played out again. Marina was dying, her future had been snatched away from her, and even with her mastery of self-delusion she could not escape this one shocking fact, or deny the swift disintegration of her body.

Camilla stood up and closed the sitting-room curtains to block out the evening rain that beat against the windows. She did not want to go to bed but she had no desire to linger in the deathly quiet sitting room, and she paced the carpet, trying to rid herself of self-pity and anxiety, searching for a focus that would bring her peace of mind. When the telephone rang she picked it up without thinking, only to hear her father's voice.

'Marina? Are you all right, my dear?' George's voice was full of tenderness. 'I'm sorry it's so late, but I've been tied up at some infernal banquet all evening and this is the first chance—'

'She's asleep. You can ring tomorrow morning. Not too early.'

She hung up, shaking, and looked in on Marina whose stillness was a tribute only to the strength of her sleeping tablets. The nurse was in an armchair, and she glanced up from her book and smiled.

'I'm going out for a little while,' Camilla said. 'Back later – I'm staying here tonight.'

She let herself out into the pouring rain, waving her hand as a taxi loomed out of the torrent. There was a party in Chelsea that she had been invited to, and she paid the cab driver and pushed open the front door. Upstairs there was loud music and laughter and people lolled on the staircase, smoking grass and hash, with glasses of champagne and wine and vodka in their hands. On the first-floor landing she stepped across a couple whose limbs were tangled together in a twist of half-removed clothing and bare flesh. Within moments she was in the midst of the crowd, sinking her first drink and holding out her glass for a refill. Several couples were dancing, swinging, wildly spaced, limbs flailing. Others were locked together and moving to some link they had spun only for themselves. Someone grabbed her arm and she found that she was dancing with Tom Bartlett. She flung herself into the mêlée, turning and spinning and bending her legs so that she was soon twisting her body inches from the floor, leaning back to project her pelvis from side to side, her arms spread out like wings as she swayed with sinuous motion. People were calling her name and hooting encouragement as she strove to keep her balance, using every muscle she had, rising with slow grace to an upright position. There was applause as she reclaimed her drink and took a deep drag on a proffered joint.

'You're in high good form, whatever way you'd like to take that.' Tom led her away from the centre of the room and stood looking at her with a cryptic expression. 'How was the afternoon?'

'Bloody awful. Dull clothes, awful old hag fussing over everything. I must have changed those horrible outfits fifty times.'

'I've got something for you that's rather more interesting. It's an advertising thing for a new line of jewellery. Ethnic-looking stuff. They're going to shoot it in Morocco. And the offer of a big magazine interview. Come in tomorrow morning.' He wheeled away, leaving her alone in the midst of the noise and swirl of the room.

She looked around, acknowledging familiar faces, greeting people she did not specially want to see with an enthusiasm she certainly did not feel. The hash was beginning to get to her and she felt calm, benevolent in her attitude towards the surrounding throng as she negotiated her way across the room in search of the bar and somewhere to sit. She sank into an armchair and leaned back against the cushions, surveying the room through half-closed eyes. It was then that she saw him. He was standing close to a window, tanned and very blond, his face alight with intelligence and interest as he listened to what the girl opposite him was trying to say above the din. Camilla stood up abruptly, slightly off balance, spilling her drink. Her only thought was to leave immediately, before he noticed her. She bent to retrieve her handbag, but when she straightened he was standing in front of her.

'Are you leaving?' he asked. 'I'll come with you.'

'Stay away from me,' Camilla said, putting out a hand to stop him. She made her way through the room and clattered down the stairs, snatching her coat and stumbling out into the wet night. There were no taxis in sight and she started to walk towards the King's Road, anger welling as she heard his footsteps behind her.

'Didn't you hear me?' she said. 'Stay away from me. Just go away.'

'I must talk to you,' he said, putting out a hand in an attempt to detain her.

'No. Get right away from me.' She stopped and turned, hissing the words at him. 'The very sight of you is making me ill.'

'And you're making your father ill,' he said. 'Don't you know that he cares about you more than anyone? You're destroying him. I wish he loved me half as much.' He grabbed her arm and shook her. 'For God's sake, don't you understand anything at all except your own superficial life?'

'Don't touch me, or come near me. I want nothing to do with you.' Camilla quickened her pace so that she was running ahead of him along the slick pavement. A taxi passed and she lifted her arm, but in the film of rain the driver did not see her and the cab sped away into a side street.

'Come back, for Christ's sake.' He had caught up with her again. 'Please. We have to talk.'

Camilla stopped. 'No. We don't ever need to talk. And I don't want to see you or hear from you again.'

'Please,' he said. 'You really must listen. You—'

'What are you, anyway?' she yelled at him, her voice full of loathing. 'You're just someone he uses to live out his double life. His bit on the side. I suppose he pays you, too. Stay away from me, and don't come near me ever again. D'you hear me, you little shit?'

He stood stock still for a moment and she saw that he had come out without a coat and that he was soaking, his clothes hanging sodden from his drooping shoulders.

'I know your mother's dying,' he said desperately. 'He wants to spend these last months with the two of you. Because he wants her to end her life loved by both of you. What's the matter with you, that you can't grasp that? Are you so heartless, so bloody righteous and bigoted, that you can't even accept that simple idea? Why won't you give them a few weeks together, instead of forcing them apart? Haven't they got enough grief, without you putting your spanner in the works?'

Camilla saw another taxi at the far end of the street and lifted her arm to flag it down. As she leapt out into the middle of the road she missed her footing on the edge of the pavement and fell heavily, losing her shoe. Her handbag flew into the gutter and she felt a sickening pain in her right foot as she tried to get up and retrieve the purse that held her keys and her taxi fare. He was there ahead of her, picking up her scattered belongings, helping her into the taxi, climbing in beside her. He gave the driver the address and they sat in silence, with the rain thrumming on the roof of the cab. The stuffy heater made Camilla cough. She turned away from him, spluttering and choking, furious that he had dared to mention her parents' home address, remembering her first sight of him in her father's bedroom. When they reached the flat he helped her out and up the steps to the entrance, his fingers on her arm like a steel vice.

'My name's Giles Hannington,' he said. 'I'm sorry I've upset you. Believe me, I am. I know it's hard for you to come to terms with this, and you don't have to see me again. But I hope what I've said will make some impression on you, before it's too late. Goodnight.'

She did not look round as the taxi vanished into the veil of rain. Inside the flat she hobbled to her mother's bedroom. Marina had not moved at all and Camilla sat down for a few minutes beside the bed and took her hand.

The nurse murmured an assurance and said something kindly about catching one's death of cold, with wet hair and shoes. In the bathroom Camilla inspected her ankle as she stripped off her sodden clothes. It was throbbing and swollen and she groaned with frustration, knowing she would have to ring Tom in the morning and tell him she had sprained her foot, anticipating his exasperation. She turned on the taps, pouring half a bottle of perfumed oil into the tub. The flat was very warm, but Camilla found herself shivering as she lay back in the water, willing herself to relax. The image of Giles Hannington would not go away. It was clear that he had his hooks into her father and that he was not about to let go. No doubt he imagined his future would be secure once Marina was dead, and he had George's undivided attention. Maybe he was a blackmailer, already living off his victim's fear of discovery. He was good-looking and well spoken, and Camilla wondered if he was an out-of-work actor or some such thing. Her father must be his meal ticket, probably paying for the hours when he met the boy, to play out his sordid desires. Perhaps Giles Hannington was only one of many such liasions in George's life. Her throat closed and she felt panic rise in her. She stepped out of the bath and hobbled into the kitchen to put on some hot milk. In bed she lay and listened to the unrelenting rain, raging at her father and his lover, resenting her mother's illness and the position it had put her in, and above all despising herself.

'I've done something to my ankle,' she said to Tom Bartlett the next morning.

'Oh, for God's sake, Camilla,' he exploded. 'Can you walk at all? The jewellery thing has been confirmed. Can you get to the magazine interview this afternoon?'

'Yes. It's only a sprain. I'm going to get it strapped up now, and then I'll be reasonably mobile, I think.'

'All right. I'll phone *Good Housekeeping* and let them know.'

'*Good Housekeeping*? That's a laugh.'

'It'll be a laugh when you get the cheque. This is editorial, and they pay far more than the posh mags. If you do the interview they'll offer you the cover. They want a story about your adventures in Africa. Courage in the face of adversity and all that kind of shit. What about your admirer Edward Carradine, by the way? Do you think he'd do an interview, tell them how he plans to remove any sign of the scar on your face, restore you to peerless beauty, etcetera?'

'You know doctors aren't allowed to talk about themselves in magazines. It's considered advertising, and that's against the rules. He'd never do it anyway,' Camilla said, imagining Edward's distaste at the whole idea.

'If that's the case, you'll have to make some suitably inspiring and grateful comments about him. Does he usually dine with his patients in fancy restaurants?'

'Who knows?'

'From the way he was looking at you the other night, I'd say he wasn't just studying your face for professional reasons. The ruined, disfigured model and the plastic surgeon who saves her beauty and comes to love her. "Swinging star deserts nightspots for permanent love nest." Perfect for the magazine in question. Great story.'

'Don't be ridiculous, Tom. He'd heard about my mother, and he invited me out to dinner to cheer me up.'

'You needn't sound so defensive, unless there's a wee grain of truth in what I'm saying. No man can resist the idea of being out and about with a beautiful model. It always amazes me, Camilla, that you can't figure out the most obvious things, even though you seem quite bright. I'll put money on it that he'd like to get into your pants. Like every other man you know.'

'Your mind is a sewer.' She had begun to laugh.

'Yeah. What about lunch, darling? One o'clock, and afterwards I'll come with you to the magazine. The editor's mad about me – putty in my hot little paws. See you later.'

Camilla rang her doctor and took a taxi to Sloane Street where she sat in the waiting room next to young mothers with wailing children, and old people with coughs and arthritis. He moved the swollen foot and she yelped as he began strapping it up.

'It's only a sprain,' he said. 'Don't stand around on it too much or it'll keep swelling. You'll need to do some exercises later. I'll give you the name of a physiotherapist for a few appointments. You should be fine in a month.'

She arrived at the restaurant a few minutes late and toyed with her food as Tom put away a large plate of pasta and half a bottle of wine.

'So what happened to you last night?' he asked. 'I wanted to introduce you to a German photographer who's mad keen to work with you, but you'd vanished. Someone said you'd gone off to another party with Giles Hannington. You won't get far with him – beautiful girls aren't his thing.'

'Do you know him?' She wondered if she might throw up and hastily swallowed some iced water.

'Yes, I know him,' Tom said. 'Comes from a wealthy family in Dorset, or somewhere down there. He's a banker in the City. He's lived in Hong Kong and Italy. Rome too, I think. Does very well for himself and he's a nice guy. Pity he's queer. I'd quite fancy him myself if I was that way inclined. He's clever and amusing, and he's got a flat stuffed with expensive art and a great sound system. I'm surprised you've never been to his parties. He hangs around in the exalted circles your parents move in. So did you go on somewhere with him last night?'

'No.' Camilla let go of another preconception, now in tatters. 'I went to stay the night with Mother. She's not doing very well.'

'Bad luck, old thing. Drink up your coffee and finish the wine. Then we'll go and conquer the world of *Good Housekeeping*. Just the thing for you to appear in, with your great domestic talents. Have you ever worn an apron in your life? For even thirty seconds?'

When they left the magazine offices Camilla made her way to Hyde Park, where Marina was resting on the sofa.

'What on earth happened to your foot?' she asked.

'I slipped on the pavement this morning. It's nothing.'

'Will you stay tonight?' Marina was querulous. 'Your father rang. He won't be in from Geneva until tomorrow afternoon. Mrs Maskell left soup and a cold chicken in the fridge and she's made some sort of pudding.'

'Yes, I'll stay with you. But first I have to go home. I need clothes and there are chores I have to do.'

Camilla was yearning to be in her own space, to be private and calm, to prop up her throbbing foot on her sofa and do nothing at all. She found a taxi and climbed gratefully into the back of it. The streets were decorated with lights that looked festive in the swiftly darkening afternoon. Pavements spilled over with shoppers, jostling and bumping into one another, walking quickly and with happy purpose. Camilla had a list in her handbag but she could not bring herself to hobble through the Christmas crowds, elbowing her way into long queues and waiting at tills. She tried to decide what she would buy for her mother. The bedroom cupboards were already brimming with silk nightgowns and handmade slippers and cashmere shawls. Another gift of expensive lingerie would only serve as a reminder of the imminent time when Marina would be bedridden.

The only people for whom she would have bought gifts with any pleasure were Hannah and Sarah. But she was afraid that an attempt to contact them now would bring rejection, and her brain shrivelled with dismay when she tried to find a way of bridging the distance between them. She wondered if they ever talked about her, or asked themselves what had become of her. Sarah's early letters had gone unanswered, and now neither she nor Hannah wrote at all. Camilla could not remember what she had said in that last telephone conversation. She had been so distressed about her father, and so drunk. On the other hand she could not have written and betrayed him, and she was hurt that her closest friends had never guessed there must be something terribly wrong in her life. In vivid dreams that left her sick with loss, she saw Anthony. But he was always beyond her reach, standing on the far side of a gorge with his back turned to her, or facing her across the leaping flames of a campfire, unheeding as she called out to him or stretched out her hand in a futile effort to bring him closer. Dreams of knives and shouting and the sound of gunfire still dogged her, and she veered between nights of sleep induced by pills, and dark hours filled with terrifying memories which showed no signs of abating.

Halfway up the stairs to her flat she wondered why she had bothered to come home at all. Her ankle screamed objections and she had to stop on each landing and rest, standing on one leg, cursing herself for her stupidity. When she let herself into the quiet sitting room and was finally alone, she tried to block out the memory of her confrontation with Giles Hannington. With her father's boyfriend. In the kitchen she made strong tea and sat down to look through her post. She wrote cheques for two overdue accounts and then made her way into the bedroom to select clothes and accessories for the following day, putting them haphazardly into a tote bag with her books. Sharp currents of pain were running up her leg by the time she had finished, and she sat down with a drink in her hand and turned on the television to watch the news. The telephone interrupted the newscaster as he intoned the day's disasters.

'How are you, Camilla? I tried to contact you yesterday but you must have been out.'

She did not really want to talk to Edward and her answers to his enquiries were almost curt. But he was gently persistent, and she was already familiar with his subtle but determined way of gleaning information. She could not fathom why or how she always ended up answering his questions and it irritated her, made her feel vulnerable.

'I stayed with Mother last night,' she said finally. 'I'm going back there shortly. She's having a bad spell.'

'Do you think she'd mind if I dropped in for a drink? Might it cheer her up, do you think?'

'Why don't you ring and ask her yourself? And if you are going round there, then I needn't rush to get through the evening traffic.'

'I'd like to see you too, Camilla. I was hoping to see you this evening.'

On balance, the idea of Edward's company seemed preferable to a night alone with Marina as she struggled to eat birdlike helpings of food and dozed in front of the television.

'The housekeeper always prepares dinner, so you could stay and have something to eat if you like,' she said. 'It will be pot luck, and Mother may not even stay up for supper. I've twisted my ankle, by the way, so I'm not in good shape.'

'I'll pick you up. In about forty minutes, judging by the traffic outside the window here.'

He had brought champagne and an impressive amount of caviar, and he went straight to the kitchen and made toast points. Marina was delighted. She sipped her drink and flirted with him, and he reminded her of amusing experiences they had shared in Nairobi and London over the years. Her face was flushed and her eyes were bright and feverish, but her mood was cheerful. It had been a good idea to bring Edward. He did not mention George or ask where he was. It was after ten when Marina began to fade and the nurse helped her into bed. Edward showed no signs of leaving.

'I'll just say goodnight to her. If you're not leaving right away, you can toy with this.' Camilla felt obliged to pour him a snifter of brandy.

He nodded his thanks. She was annoyed by his assumption that she would want to stay up and entertain him, but she could think of no way to politely evict him. When she returned he was comfortably ensconced on the sofa, his long legs stretched out in front of him. She had closed Marina's bedroom door and now she put a record on the turntable.

'I'm glad you like French chamber music,' he said. 'I must send you some Ravel trios that are sublime. Maybe you'd like to come to a concert

420

at the Wigmore Hall one day? I go there all the time since it's only five minutes from my rooms. What happened to your ankle? Did you stumble across yet another immovable object?'

'Which question would you like me to answer first?'

'The last one.'

'I tripped in the street last night. It was raining and slippery, and I was waving at a taxi.'

She felt that he did not believe her, and she found herself explaining.

'I couldn't face being here on my own all evening, so I went out for a couple of hours,' she said.

'You're a true night owl, aren't you?' he said. 'When do you sleep? Every time we meet you've been up all night at some party or nightclub. I've been reading about your nocturnal habits in a paper I picked up on a train. I hope you don't have many photo sessions early in the morning.'

She shrugged and helped herself to a brandy before settling herself in an armchair opposite him. He sat up and leaned forward so that he was level with her, looking directly into her eyes. He did not say anything, but there were questions in the air between them. She sighed.

'Actually, I went out because my father phoned. I hung up on him because I was a coward and I didn't know what to say.' She touched her forehead, briefly stroking the line the panga had made. He wondered if touching the scar had become an unconscious habit.

'I couldn't stay here.' She stood up, frowning at him. 'I was afraid he'd phone again. Do you want another brandy?'

'I want to kiss you,' he said.

'What?' she asked stupidly.

He put down his glass and rose to take her into his arms. He kissed her, slowly and with tenderness, and she felt his breath on her cheek and on her eyelids. His lips were firm and very warm. Camilla opened her mouth a little and immediately felt the pressure of his tongue and the taste and smell of the cognac. His kiss became passionate, and for a second she drifted with the sensation before the memory of Anthony catapulted to the forefront of her mind. She was instantly jolted into the present, one hand out in front of her as if to push away both Edward and the very possibility of intimacy. He moved away at once and went to stand by the window, looking down at the haze of car lights splashing through the rain below them.

'I'm sorry,' he said. 'I shouldn't—'

'You don't have anything to be sorry for,' Camilla said. 'I'm just not ready. There are things in my mind that are still raw, and I've done enough harm all round without deceiving you.'

'I hope that my wanting to kiss you wasn't a shock. I'm a great deal older than you and a friend of your parents, so you've probably never thought of me in those terms.' He was not looking at her as he spoke, and she realised how vulnerable he felt, and how easy it would be to make him feel ridiculous.

'This is nothing to do with your age or mine,' she said. 'I've had enough of boys who don't know what they want, beyond a little fun for a week or two. The thing is, I'm still trying to accept that I made a fool of myself with this man in Kenya. I suppose it's just vanity, but it's hard to swallow the fact that I was just a roll in the hay, as he saw it.'

She looked so forlorn that he could barely resist putting his arms around her. He wanted to tell her that he had fallen madly and foolishly in love with her, that it had happened the instant he saw her and that he had no idea what he could do about it. He longed to confess that he spent hours of every day thinking about her, making plans to see her and then retreating from them because he did not want to go too fast and ruin his chances. He would have liked to explain that he was a fool, because he was a mature, successful man who felt like an out-of-control teenager. Instead, he sat down again and tried to look as though he was master of the situation.

'Do you want to tell me about the phone call with your father?' he said.

'There's nothing to tell. I couldn't talk to him, that's all. But then something worse happened. I was afraid he'd ring back and try to speak to me again, so I went out to a party in Chelsea. It was pretty awful.'

'And this morning you were feeling the worse for wear.'

'No. Well, yes, I was. But that wasn't the awful thing. The boyfriend was there.'

Edward frowned, not following her, and it was some moments before her experience became clear to him.

'Well, one of his boyfriends, anyway.' She bit her lip. 'The one I saw here. When I barged in on Daddy that afternoon and discovered what he was. What he is. Last night I recognised this person straight away. His name is Giles Hannington, and he tried to talk to me. I ran away from him and that's how I tripped and hurt my ankle.' She was on the verge of tears.

'Maybe it's time you talked to your father, difficult though it will be,' Edward said. 'At least you would have overcome your worst obstacle. Conquered whatever it is you are afraid of confronting.'

'To say what? "Hello, Daddy, all is forgiven, so why don't you come to tea and bring your boyfriend along, and we can all have a nice little chat with your dying wife"? I feel ill every time I think about it. And it's no better with Mother. All her life she's ignored me, left me to my own devices, found fault with everything I did. And now I'm the one who has to be here and cope with her until death do us part, while marvellous George is away doing God knows what. Isn't that ironic, to say nothing of a little unfair?'

'At this point, what's being asked of you is beyond what most people could endure. But your father can't change, although he must have tried. He is what he is, and no doubt he has paid for that a thousand times over.'

'Oh, you're on his side now,' she said angrily. 'You're telling me that he can't help being queer, and that it was fine for him to marry Mother and hide behind her. Use her to keep his career prospects looking rosy. I suppose I should be wilting with compassion for him. And for her too. They put me through a rotten childhood, but I should now rise above it all.'

'No. I'm only suggesting—'

'Well, I'm not sorry for either one of them and the mess they made of their lives, and my life too. My mother's dying of leukaemia and I'm quite prepared to do whatever I can to make her comfortable. But if she wasn't deathly ill, I wouldn't see her at all if I could help it. And I certainly don't want to see him.'

'You miss him, though. You were very close. Isn't that the truth?'

'No, it's not the bloody truth. We weren't close at all. It was just an illusion. A cruel bit of make-believe, like the rest of his life. That's the real truth, pleasant or not. And I'm not going to be railroaded into some sentimental reunion. Not by him or by my manipulative mother.'

'Then they'll both have to respect your decision on that score,' he said, wanting to help her towards a more peaceful view of her situation, but unwilling to push for fear of damaging his own tenuous links with her. 'You must be careful, though, that you don't hurt yourself any more than you've been hurt already.'

'I'm a survivor,' she said defiantly. 'I've managed this far, and I'll go on managing. You mustn't start talking to me like the family doctor or a friendly uncle. I couldn't take that.'

'What are your plans for the next week or so? If you can forgive my clumsy advances, I'd like to invite you out somewhere. Try to take your mind off all this for an hour or two. What about lunch on Sunday? We could drive out of town and have one of those gargantuan English lunches in some old manor hotel. I'd like to see you succumb to the trifle. How does that sound?'

'You know I can't – that I'm not—?'

'I know. Consider me a true friend and someone you can confide in. The rest isn't important. Lunch on Sunday?' His heart was racing with absurd delight when she nodded. 'Good. I'll pick you up at your flat around twelve.' He kissed her on the cheek. 'Goodnight, Camilla. Be well.'

When the front door closed behind him she went to the window and watched as he got into his car and pulled away into the rain. She was puzzled by the odd turn of events, and surprised that he had kissed her. She was his patient and the daughter of old friends. And, as he himself had pointed out, she was half his age. It all seemed rather cheap. She thought of what Tom Bartlett had said and it occurred to her that she might have misjudged Edward as she had misjudged so many others, that her growing confidence in him had been misplaced. It was a depressing thought and she tried to banish it, but the idea persisted, making her feel flustered and unsure. For the first time she wondered what had happened to his wife. He had only mentioned her once, on the first evening when he had taken her to the cinema and dinner, and she had never enquired about his marriage or his past. Perhaps Marina knew. Camilla shrugged mentally and looked at her watch. It was very late and she was tired. Her father was coming back tomorrow but he wouldn't be here before early evening. At least she would not need to be up at the crack of dawn.

She cleaned her face, brushed her teeth and fell into bed. The novel she had brought with her felt impossibly heavy in her hands and she put it down and turned out the light, hoping for oblivion. But she could not put Giles Hannington out of her mind. His desperation struck at her heart repeatedly. Could he genuinely love her father, as he had claimed? She wondered how many other men made up George's emotional life, and whether he was given to affairs that were simply physical encounters. Homosexual men seemed to be endlessly on the prowl, and the few couples that she knew well had not been together for very long. In the main, Camilla considered them wildly promiscuous. It was difficult to imagine George Broughton-Smith, well bred and urbane, dignified and charming and respected, in the midst of the flagrant queens and preening young men she had come across. When sleep finally overtook her she dreamed that Edward and her mother had eloped on a train, leaving her to explain their disappearance to her father as he stood sobbing on the station platform.

In the morning she felt tired and out of sorts. Marina was still sleeping and Mrs Maskell was fussing in the kitchen when she came looking for some breakfast. Camilla glanced without interest at the newspaper headlines as she drank her coffee, lingering at the table and reluctant to face the day.

'I'm working later today,' she said to Mrs Maskell. 'But my father will be back this evening, so everything should be under control for tonight. He should phone Dr Ward as soon as he gets in – could you tell him please, or leave him a message?'

'Are you doing something glamorous, dear?' Mrs Maskell loved to recount embroidered versions of Camilla's shoots to her friends.

'Today? Oh very fancy, yes. Photos that are going to be used to advertise corn flakes. Can't get much more glamorous than that, can you? Unless you count the pictures for knitting patterns, and all those woolly jumpers I had to struggle in and out of last week. I've still got a skin rash on my back and I feel itchy every time I think of it.' Camilla laughed. 'It's not all it's cracked up to be, the model's life. Don't let your pretty daughter even think about it.'

Tom was waiting for her in his office. It was in Soho, a grubby place with a narrow flight of stairs leading up to it, and he made sure that his meetings with magazine editors were held elsewhere. The lights on the stairwell and in the corridor seldom worked, and Camilla had tripped on the steps several times before learning her way up the uneven, ragged carpet.

'Why don't you move somewhere decent?' she asked him for the hundredth time. 'Or at least get a cleaner and a good secretary. God knows, you earn enough to be more comfortable than this. Look at these disgusting coffee cups – they were in the sink when I was here last week, and no one's washed them since. You're a slob.'

'Thank God I don't want to marry you. You'd be a real nag as a wife,' he said cheerfully. 'There are more cups in the corner cupboard, so make us a coffee, there's a good girl. You've been offered another catalogue job, but the clothes are grim and I think you should turn it down.'

'I can't afford to turn anything down right now,' she said.

'You mustn't take any old offer, or word will get around that you're desperate. You don't need the cash, and you've got the Paris booking for the new year. Here's the paper to sign. It pays rather well, this one.'

'I might be desperate soon. I'll be out of commission altogether in March or April, when I have my scar removed. I won't earn anything for weeks.' She had a horrible fear of being without money, of having to give up her flat, or rent out the guest bedroom to a stranger. There was no question of her living with her parents again, and retaining her independence was the most important issue in her life.

'You've made plenty of money over the last couple of years.'

'Spent it too. On safaris and other foolish things.'

'Don't worry, darling. I'll always take care of you. In any way you choose. You can be sure of that.'

There was something about his tone that was unfamiliar, and she turned from the sink where she was scrubbing the black line from the inside of a coffee cup. He was watching her, his casual expression betrayed by a tic at the corner of his mouth. An awkward silence hung between them, and then he rose to his feet.

'Come on,' he said. 'Let's go and finalise this jewellery whats-it and do the pictures for the magazine, so you don't wind up in a shelter for the homeless next week. You've got bloody great bags under your eyes, by the way. I'd nip into the bathroom if I were you, and put on another layer of something. What with that and the limp, you look a wreck. Lucky you've got me around to protect you.'

Back in her own flat she made herself a cup of tea and lit a cigarette. Edward Carradine and now Tom. Could one or both of them really have some special feeling for her? And if so, why was she unable to respond? She had tried to rid herself of Anthony, telling herself over and over that she had been just another witless girl who had become fodder for the insatiable appetite of the white hunter. He did not care about her, had never cared about her, had not called or written to find out what had happened to her body or to her soul. She wished that she could hate him, despise him for his callous lack of feeling. But she was too honest to fool herself into believing that he did not matter any more. Her foot was throbbing, and she pulled a rug over her legs and propped up her ankle with a cushion. She had been dozing for a good half-hour when the telephone rang.

'My dear, your mother's not well at all.' Mrs Maskell was clearly frightened. 'She has a fever – she's very hot and her breathing sounds strange. Dr Ward is on his way. Your father's plane is held up by fog in Geneva and he telephoned to say he's going to be very late. He doesn't know what time he'll get in. I think you'd better come over, if you can.'

Marina lay in bed, her face clammy. She had a rash on her arms and her back, small red dots that looked inflamed and painful. Her breathing was shallow and laboured, and every time she moved her swollen joints she cried out. Dr Ward examined her briefly and turned to Camilla.

'My dear, she has pneumonia. I'm afraid that's going to be one of the main hazards from now on. I think we should get her into hospital straight away. Is your father here?'

'He's trying to get back from Geneva. Stuck at the airport in fog.'

'Well, I'm sure you'll want to stay with her. This doesn't look so good.'

In the hospital Camilla sat in a stiff, upright chair beside the bed, her fists clenched, her jaw clamped tight to prevent her teeth from chattering. She did not want to deal with this by herself, did not want to be alone with her mother when she died. It was too frightening, too solitary to bear. Marina turned her head and opened her eyes, glittering with fever and pain, her breath short.

'My chest hurts so much. I think it's the end, darling, because it's too hard to keep breathing. And I can't struggle like this. I can't do it. Where is he? Hasn't he come yet?' Her whispered entreaty was pitiful, and she tried to find Camilla's hand and to touch it in an appeal for comfort and even reassurance.

'He's on his way, but his plane's delayed. Just rest, Mother. He'll be here soon. Very soon.'

When the nurses arrived with a trolley Camilla cringed as they tried to transfer Marina without causing her any further distress. But each movement was a separate agony and the brief journey to the X-ray department became a series of unbearable moments as they rumbled along the shining corridors. A potent injection had been administered to deaden the pain that now filled Marina's chest, making each breath a gasping, faltering effort that Camilla thought would be her last.

'I'm afraid she has double pneumonia,' David Ward said, when he re-appeared an hour later. 'And I honestly don't know if she has the strength to deal with the infection. She's terribly weak already. But we're starting her on antibiotics right now. And then we can only wait and see.'

Camilla sat beside the bed, mute with shock and fear, praying that her father would be with her soon, dreading the moment of his arrival, counting the minutes until she might hear his step in the corridor. Hours slid away in an unmeasured haze, and when she glanced down at her watch her eyes were tired and unfocused so that she could not be sure what time it was. The nursing staff came and went, offering her cups of tea and coffee which she held in trembling hands, and a light supper that she refused. Her lips were dry and her head ached. She wanted a stiff drink, a little yellow pill to calm her, anything that would take away the apprehension and anxiety of the sterile room and the lonely vigil. Her mind was seething, as if a swarm of bees had invaded it, buzzing and stinging, constantly in motion. She could not follow any one train of thought or banish the disquiet that had invaded her.

It was impossible to imagine what she might say to her father when he arrived, or what she might do if she was alone when her mother died, waiting for the figure that they had both loved so much. There was no resentment in her heart now. The anger she had felt at both of her parents was gone, to be replaced by a feeling of isolation. She wanted to get up and go outside into the waiting room where she could light a cigarette, but she was afraid to leave Marina in case she might slip away during those few minutes. She could hear the low voices of the nursing staff at their station, and the occasional sound of a door closing on another room where another patient awaited some miracle that might never materialise. There was an unreal quality about the hospital floor that made Camilla herself feel disembodied, drifting helplessly without compass, tiller or sail.

She did not know what time it was when Marina opened her eyes and tried to tell her something, through lips that were dry. She leaned closer to hear the whispered words and the harsh sound of laboured breathing.

'Camilla?'

'I'm here, Mother.'

'Don't let me die before he comes.' Marina tried to raise herself up. 'Please don't let me die now, before he gets here.'

Minutes later Camilla heard footsteps. Her heart began to hammer so that she found it difficult to stand up and be on her feet, on guard, when the door opened. He stood still for a moment, looking at Marina without a word, his eyes filled with tears. Then he opened his arms to Camilla. She ran to him and he folded himself around her as she began to sob like a small child.

'Daddy! Oh God, Daddy! Oh, thank God you're here.'

Chapter 22

Kenya, December 1965

During Sarah's first weeks at Buffalo Springs there were radio calls from Langani, but Piet's voice was distorted, his sentences punctuated by the crackling of static. Each time he signed off, the last 'over and out' made Langani seem very far away. She could not gauge his feelings for her and their relationship felt frustratingly stagnant. Then the letter arrived – a single sheet of paper.

Langani Farm
9 December 1965

Sarah,

I've been hoping to drive up and see you, but it doesn't look possible for the time being. There is so much to do here. All the usual business of the farm, and the last-minute details at the lodge. Finishing is always the hardest part of a building project. Of course, Viktor has been here working, which has made certain things difficult. It's very tense now between Lars and Hannah. Another reason why it's not ideal for me to take off from here.

No more incidents on the farm, although there is still bad blood between David and Simon. Childish, heh? Thank God for Kipchoge who is always sensible. Like me!

I loved your letter. It seems your new job is all you hoped for. Maybe you won't ever want to leave your elephants and come back to Langani. But I hope I can still persuade you, because we're all looking forward to your being here for Christmas.

I'm waiting impatiently for your return, because I have so much I

want to say to you. Things I know you will understand. Things I hope
you will want to hear .
   So I'm counting the days.
   Piet

It was so little to go on, but she treasured it anyway. In camp there were
never enough hours in the day and she sat up late each night, writing up
her notes and watching as the geckos ran across the walls or clung
motionless to a single spot, waiting for a mosquito or some other
unsuspecting insect to land in their target area. She liked their splayed feet
and translucent skin, and the shine of their eyes in the flickering light.
Outside she could hear the chatter and shrieks of the hyraxes as they made
their night-time sorties. One night she was woken by the unmistakable
sound of a lion close to the compound. Dan came to fetch her, and they
climbed into the Land Rover with Erope and Julius, and drove to the gate.
Just outside their thorn fence they saw him. He was old and battle-scarred,
but he had killed a young zebra and dragged it under a tree. He stood his
ground, yellow eyes glowing in the headlights, master of his territory,
roaring out his claim to the kill, his tail swinging slowly as he faced them
down. When he was satisfied that they would approach no closer he
returned to his trophy and began to tear it apart, his muzzle glistening with
blood. After a while he raised his head and called for his mate to share the
spoils. When she returned to bed, Sarah lay awake, listening to the
grunting of the old beast, admiring his unwavering sovreignty over his
territory.

   In the field, Allie and Dan were patient and meticulous. They taught
her to log her observations and findings, and never to jump to hasty
conclusions or attempt any quick analysis. Discussions were stimulating
and informed. Dan's comments were a mixture of determination and
humorous resignation, and his balanced views on Kenya's political
evolution were optimistic but tempered by the reality of experience. Their
staff admired and trusted them, that was clear. After a day of blistering
heat in the bush, they would sit down with Erope and Julius under the
trees in the compound, squatting on their heels and drinking sweet, milky
tea out of tin mugs as they discussed the day's findings.

   'You have to listen to these guys,' Dan told Sarah from the beginning.
'Listen to everything they say, because they understand that every small

sign and sound is important. Their ancestors have been walking through this bush since time began, finding everything they need to know in a footprint or a torn branch, following a star or a flock of birds in the sky. They are your true guides and teachers. I think they carry a collective memory, and their wisdom is much older than anything you and I can ever aspire to.'

Sarah had been in Kenya most of her life, but she had never met Africans like Erope or Julius. Their harmony with their surroundings was an education in itself. Each day brought a new lesson as she observed their methods of gathering information, learned the art of waiting and watching, of melting into the bush without disturbing their subjects.

'All the Africans I knew in my childhood were working as cooks or gardeners, or farm labourers,' she said as she sat with Allie and Dan one night beside the campfire. 'We never considered where they'd come from, or tried to discover much about their wisdom, because we were so sure our ideas were better.'

'They are. When we're in our own neck of the woods,' Allie said. 'Let's not get carried away here. I don't want to be a circumcised third wife, or grind *posho* and herd goats.'

'That's for sure,' Sarah said. 'But when I was in Dublin I began to feel guilty about the way white people treated their staff. Yet I've watched Piet and Hannah dealing with the labour, and their *watu* do seem to be childlike and primitive from our point of view. It's complicated.'

'Not really,' Allie said. 'We arrived here at the turn of the nineteenth century and right away imposed our way of life on the land and the people. We brought schools and medicine and other advantages, but we didn't listen enough, because that was perceived as a sign of weakness. If we whites were to rule, then we had to behave as though we knew everything.'

'The deaf ear isn't peculiar to government, or to Africa,' Dan said. 'It exists on every scale. If you took a redneck Georgia Cracker from some Southern plantation and brought him up to a swish New York restaurant to be a waiter, you wouldn't stand around listening to his views. You'd be hammering all that laid-back Southern shit out of him, and turning him into something else as fast as possible. We all have that urge to change people, make them into our notion of who they should be.'

'Time is the real issue,' Allie said. 'We have to accept Africans as equal players now, which is something we've never thought about until recently. But there's plenty of goodwill in the air, and we can build on that. We're talking generations, though, not just a year or two of transition.'

Sarah sent away her film of the elephants' burial rite, and was encouraged and warmed by the praise she received from the Briggses who were not normally effusive. This time she knew that her pictures were exceptional and that she was right to be proud of them. When she came in from work late one evening, weary and looking forward to a shower and an early night, Allie was waiting for her. There had been a radio call from Hannah, she said. Sarah should contact Langani. Had there been another raid? Sarah wondered with alarm. Another slaughter? Hannah's voice came over the hiss of static. There was a staccato delivery to her words, but she was emphatic when Sarah questioned her. There was nothing to worry about. The call appeared to be purely social. An invitation for the weekend.

'I can't do it,' Sarah said. 'It's only a short time until I come down for Christmas. I can't take any time off now. I'm sorry, Han. Are you sure everything's all right?'

'No worries,' Hannah replied. 'See you soon. Over and out.'

Sarah was working on her notes when the Land Rover drove up on the following afternoon. She was engrossed in her records, and she did not even look up to see who it was until Allie hailed her.

'Sarah! Visitor for you. It's Lars.'

She dropped her file on the desk and ran out, faintly alarmed. She threw her arms around him, genuinely glad to see him. Then she stood back and studied him with some concern. He was unshaven, his clothes were rumpled and sweaty, and he looked tired and strained.

'Lars! It's good to see you.' She paused, waiting for him to say something, but he did not respond. 'Is everything all right? Piet? Hannah? The farm?'

'As far as I know,' he said. His tone was cryptic and he did not meet her eyes. 'I haven't been there since yesterday.'

He did not volunteer any more information, and she wondered what he was holding back. She saw his glance flicker towards Allie who was working on some maps that she had spread out on the table in the mess tent. Something was definitely wrong, and he obviously did not wish to discuss it in Allie's hearing. Sarah thought of Hannah's radio call and hoped the two were not connected.

'Come in out of the sun,' Sarah said. 'It's scorching.'

She led him under the shade of the verandah and pulled out two camp chairs. 'Sit down. Let me get you something – you must be parched. Allie, can I get Lars a beer? Is that what you'd like, Lars? We actually have cold ones. The fridge was acting up for a couple of days, but our *fundi*, Amos, has fixed it. I don't know how we'd survive without him.'

She knew she was gabbling, but his unexpected arrival had flustered her. Lars smiled apologetically at Allie and accepted the beer. They talked of the research work for a few minutes, and then Allie made some tactful excuse and vanished. Lars sat in morose silence, his hands clamped tight around the arms of the chair.

'Lars.' Sarah leaned towards him. 'Tell me. You didn't just decide to leave work and come up here for a beer.'

'No.' His face was grim. 'I've left Langani altogether.'

'What?' She was incredulous.

'I finally packed it in, Sarah.' He took a long swallow from his tankard. 'Hannah hasn't told you?'

'No. No, she was on the radio last night, asking me to go down. But she didn't say why.'

'I took it for as long as I could. I did like you said, Sarah. Waited, looked after things, tried to be patient. Ja.' He nodded his head slowly. 'I waited and I did my best. When that bastard Viktor arrived, with his smooth talk and his mad laughing, I drove into Nanyuki and played tennis. Had a drink at the club. Kept out of the way. But I couldn't stay and watch it any longer. He is a predator and she can't see it. I know he has other women. There is talk of it, even in Nanyuki, but she won't listen. It makes me sick to see him prowling around her, to see how she is mesmerised. Ja, that is the word – mesmerised by him. It makes me seethe.' He blinked hard, as though there was a speck of dirt in his eye, and he was trying to clear his vision. 'I saw him take her to his room. I said to Piet that he must stop it. But he can't, of course. And I tried to tell her what he is, to warn her that he will not stay. I even told her that I loved her.' He looked away, out at the torn trees that ringed the camp, and his smile was thin. 'But what good was that?'

'She's stubborn,' Sarah said. 'But—'

'Stupid! I was stupid to say anything. She was furious. She said it was none of my business, what she did. If I did not like how she behaved, I should leave.' He put his hands behind his head and stared up into the bleached sky, so he would not have to see the pity in Sarah's eyes. 'So I told Piet I couldn't stay. It made me feel very bad, to leave my friend Piet. But I could not go on working under those circumstances. Not after she told me to go.'

'I'm really sorry, Lars.'

'I found them a temporary manager,' he said. 'Bill Barton's son has come back to take over their farm. Help his old man. So their manager, Mike Stead, is looking for a job. He'll work for Piet and perhaps he will stay if they get along well. Or maybe Jan and Lottie will come back now. That would be best. So, here I am. No job and no prospects.'

He drained the last of his beer. Sarah felt for this faithful, generous man. She could not believe that Hannah had been half-witted enough to drive him away, to deprive Piet of the friend and manager he relied on. And what would she do when Viktor tired of her, as Sarah feared that he would? Thoughts swarmed, but could not be expressed.

'Do you have a plan, Lars?' she asked, eventually.

'I'll go back to Norway, I suppose.'

'For good? You can't do that. You belong in Africa.'

'I don't know that any more.' He was noncommittal. 'I will go home for now. I have not had a holiday for more than three years, you know.'

He was right. He had always stayed at Langani while everyone else went on safari, or on courses, or away on business. No one seemed to have considered that he might want it otherwise. A trip to Europe could be good for him. And perhaps while he was away, Hannah would come to her senses. Sarah left him briefly in the mess tent, and went to find Allie who shook her head in disbelief when she heard the story.

'What an idiot that girl is. But she's not the first to fall for that lone wolf. A bit of bad can be devastatingly attractive, and that's the problem. Not fair, is it? Let's try and hold on to poor old Lars for the night. Help him drown his sorrows. Dinner and whisky, and a bit of man-to-man talk with Dan. I'm sure he'll be delighted to oblige.'

Lars seemed grateful for the invitation. His departure from Langani had been precipitate and unplanned. He had thrown his belongings into the Land Rover in a chaotic pile. Books, clothing and all the paraphernalia accumulated over his time at the farm littered the back seat of the car. He was not given to spur-of-the-moment actions, and his present situation was a source of turmoil as well as misery. Sarah sent him off to the guest

435

hut to clean himself up. After dinner, Dan brought out the whisky, and the two men were soon roaring drunk. There was raucous singing and back slapping and reminiscences of happier times. Allie and Sarah exchanged looks and retired to bed. They would pick up the pieces in the morning.

Lars left early the next day. Despite his hangover he was in better spirits, and he promised to keep in touch. He was going to his uncle's farm in Kiambu for a few days, he told Sarah, and then he would fly to Norway. He promised to let her know when he had a long-term plan. She watched him drive away and hoped they would see each other again. Piet must be devastated. Maybe she should call Langani. But then she would have to explain that Lars had come straight to Buffalo Springs. That might put her in an awkward position with Hannah. She groaned and picked up her camera. Better to get out into the bush and start work. She could think out there. She gathered up her notebooks and set off with Erope to find her elephants.

She dropped by Samburu Lodge a few days later, to enjoy an ice-cold beer in the bar. It was a change from the often lukewarm drinks from the leaky paraffin fridge in camp. Standing on the verandah, watching the tourists coming and going, she felt like an old stager, one of the locals, and she was proud of this identity. She placed a call to Langani, but it was Mike Stead, the new manager, who answered. Piet and Hannah were out, he said. He would give them a message, if she cared to leave one. Sarah was disappointed. She would phone another time, she told him. As she made her way out towards her vehicle, Sarah heard her name called out. There was no mistaking the voice.

'It's the Irish scientist! What are you doing all alone? Have they released you from your labours, let you down from your watchtower?' She turned to look up into the knowing eyes of Viktor Szustak. 'You will stay for lunch with me, and tell me all you have discovered.'

'Viktor.' She regarded him with suspicion and distaste. 'Actually, my tower is a little grass-roofed hut with an army of geckos and a noisy group of hyraxes. Thanks for the invitation, but I need to get back right away.'

'Good. I was about to drive over there.'

'So, what brings you to Samburu?' she asked

'I came to see you. Only you. I have a room here,' he said, gesturing behind him. 'Come to bed with me now. We can go to the camp later, after an afternoon of passion!'

436

'How many women have you propositioned today?' she asked mockingly. He was play-acting, she was sure, but she felt strongly that he should not be flirting with her. She was Hannah's friend. In fact, he should not be flirting with anyone.

'There are no women here as alluring as you,' he said. As she opened the door of her vehicle his fingers closed over her hand, massaging her palm. 'But I can wait. I will follow you back to the camp. I have a bottle of Jack Daniel's for Dan. He will be very happy about this, for he cannot get it here.'

They drove out of Samburu Lodge in convoy. In camp everyone seemed pleased at his arrival. He was obviously as popular with the African crew as with his hosts. Dinner was a noisy affair, after Viktor had opened the bottle of Jack Daniel's. Sarah opted out, feeling that she would be safer sticking with wine. They sat up late, talking and laughing, and it was midnight before Sarah rose and took her lamp to go to bed.

'I will walk you to your quarters to protect you from being devoured by wild beasts,' announced Viktor, jumping to his feet. He seemed in perfect command of himself despite the quantity of alcohol he had imbibed. When they reached her hut, he took the lamp from her and put it on the table inside. Then he drew her back to the door.

'Listen,' he said. 'Can you hear the night speaking to you? You must learn to know what the dark is saying, learn the beauty of its secrets.'

Sarah stood beside him, listening, enchanted as he identified the sounds of the bush that she did not yet know. He was tremendously knowledgeable about the calls and rustles around them. But suddenly he turned her round to face him, and she was assailed by the heavy scent of cigar smoke and alcohol from his breath. She knew that he would try to kiss her and she felt a cold fury rise in her. What was Viktor doing here, making passes at her? The man had no integrity. Piet had said he was a womaniser and a drinker. Everyone seemed to know it, except Hannah.

'Goodnight, Viktor,' she said, pushing him away from her. 'I must get some sleep.'

'You will sleep,' he said. 'With dreams and recollections of me, and of what we might give each other.'

'You're talking nonsense,' she said. 'I'll try and make allowances because you've had so much to drink. I presume you're going to the farm on your way back to Nairobi. To be with my friend Hannah.'

He laughed. 'The warrior queen,' he said. 'Alas, I will not be seeing her for a while. My work at Langani is finished, and I have a commission in Tanzania. I am going down there next week. A new hotel I have designed. I'll be there for some time.'

'Does she know that?' Sarah's rage was increasingly difficult to contain.

'Women know everything,' he said. 'They are the source of knowledge. Come now, the night is only beginning and we have so much to discover.'

'I've discovered quite enough for tonight, thank you, Viktor. You'd better go.' She pushed him hard and he staggered backwards in surprise as she slammed the door of her little hut, so that the lizards rushed across the walls, making tsk-tsk-tsk noises of agitation. Outside, she could hear him scratching on the wooden shutters, whispering in theatrical tones.

'Little girl, little girl, let me come in, or I'll huff and I'll puff and I'll blow your house down!'

She stood inside the door, infuriated by his antics. Minutes later she heard him walk away, whistling cheerfully. She sat down at her desk, thinking of Hannah. Discarded, just as Piet had feared. Did she know that Viktor wasn't coming back? How could Sarah tell her? She wondered if she should call Piet on the radio, explain what had happened. She longed for the sound of his voice, even for one moment. But it would be better to write, she thought. And the talking could be done at Christmas.

In the morning, when she reached the breakfast table, Viktor was already gone. Allie said he had set out early for an appointment in Nyeri. She looked at Sarah with amusement as they prepared for their morning expedition. Dan was staying behind today, to write reports for their sponsors. Sarah thought they both looked much the worse for wear after Viktor's bottle of whisky. Today they had arranged to visit a Samburu *manyatta* to discuss traditional hunting practices with the elders. Sarah was going to be permitted to take photographs. They drove off more slowly than usual, and Sarah reached into her canvas sack and produced a couple of aspirin. She proffered her water bottle.

'Thanks.' Allie downed them in one swallow, wiping her mouth with the back of her hand. 'I always promise myself I won't drink that man's whisky, and I always end up with a pile-driver in my head the next day.' She squinted into the sun from behind her dark glasses. 'So, you sent him off with a flea in his ear,' she added. 'It's not often he gets a refusal. Good for you, girl.'

'I wouldn't want to offend a friend of yours,' Sarah said, 'but you know Viktor's been having an affair with Hannah, and yet he was flirting with me all day yesterday. I may be a prude, but I don't like that.'

'Viktor is your quintessential wolf,' Allie said. 'Always on the prowl. The fact that you didn't fall for his advances will probably fuel his interest. He mostly gets his way with women. It's the way he is, and he makes no secret of it. I'm sorry for your poor friend Hannah. That she fell for him.'

'She's besotted with him. I can't understand how she doesn't see him for what he is.'

'For her, he's irresistible, I should think. And he's fantastic in bed. Take it from me.' Allie grinned, at the shock she had generated.

'You and Viktor? Really? But when . . . ?' Sarah subsided in embarrassment and confusion. 'Sorry. No business of mine.'

Allie gave a loud guffaw. 'It's all right. I wouldn't have told you if I was going to get all coy about it,' she said. 'And there's no need to look so surprised. I clean up pretty well when I'm going out on the town.'

'I didn't mean – God, Allie, I'm really crass. I apologise. It was just that I thought you and Dan were so . . .' She trailed off, out of her depth.

'Dan wasn't around at the time, needless to say. He was working like a maniac, and I wanted to go to Nairobi because it was my birthday, but he wouldn't go. I was really cross. We were in Tsavo then, and we hadn't landed the grant we have now. We'd been slaving away without a break for months. Things were a lot less comfortable then, with flimsy tents and precious little to live on. Dan didn't care – he never notices his immediate surroundings. But I wanted, well, I suppose I wanted to be cherished for a few days. To be feminine. To be the most important for him, even if it was only on my birthday. Anyhow, he bloody well wouldn't go anywhere. We had a flaming row, and I drove to Nairobi on my own. I met up with Viktor that night, in the house where I was staying with some friends. I was pretty drunk, and so was he, but we hit it off. We spent the weekend together and it was marvellous! We did things I've never done before or since!'

Allie was chuckling, but there was a note to her usually brusque tone that moved Sarah to sympathy and a deeper understanding of this small, tough-seeming woman.

'On Monday morning, it was time to go back. And of course I went. Back to Dan, who is the one I want to be with always. Viktor's mad and wonderful, and I spent a couple of other nights with him. But then I realised I was playing with fire. In danger of hurting someone who is ten times the human being that Viktor is. He's a great-looking, talented, interesting man. But there's a dark side to him. He's strictly dirty weekend. Enjoy him if you want, have a fling, by all means, but never be fooled into looking for more. He lives on the edge, always, and drinks like a fish. I've heard that he can lose his temper and be pretty bad, although I've never seen that myself. He'll love some girl madly today, convince himself she's the only thing he could ever desire, and then he'll move on tomorrow. It's the way he is.'

'I've already found an extraordinary man,' Sarah said, 'so I can't imagine ever having a fling like that. With Viktor, or anyone else.' She paused, wondering if Allie had told the whole story. Perhaps Viktor had let her down, and she had gone back to Dan because she had no choice. 'But wouldn't you mind? I mean, if he showed up at your camp with someone else?'

'No, I wouldn't mind. Not any more. I like Viktor. We had a good time. That's all it was, and all it was meant to be. It's in the past. Dan never knew a thing about it, and they get on really well. So everybody's happy. But you know, if he was your first, he'd be an experience to remember.'

Sarah blushed. 'Is it so obvious?'

'Not at all. But I'm a trained observer of animal behaviour and it's my business to notice things. Don't look so discomforted – it's very special. Many young women these days are willing to be out rutting with any man that takes their fancy. I think it's a pity, myself.'

'I want to wait till I marry. I want it to be the man I'm going to spend my life with.'

'Aha! And you say you've found him?'

'Yes.' Sarah turned to Allie, needing to confide in someone. 'It's Piet van der Beer, Hannah's brother. He's true, and straight and beautiful inside and out. I've loved him since I was a child.'

'So, what's the hold-up?' Allie asked.

'He was in love with someone else. But I think that's all over now. At least, I truly hope it is. Hannah says he does love me, but he was very hurt the last time. Maybe that's why he seems keen one minute, and aloof the next. He has kissed me, though. But when I'm on my own, I think it's impossible he could feel the same for me as he did for this other girl. So perhaps I'm fooling myself, and it's a leftover childhood dream. All in my head.'

'I think you know better than that,' Allie said.

'When it comes to love, none of us seems to know better,' Sarah said. 'Piet made a mistake. And look at Hannah. She could have had Lars, who's a far better person than Viktor. And I don't know what I can tell her that will make her see sense.'

'Tell her to stick with the good guy,' Allie said instantly. 'The one who'll be there for her when she's going grey, and her skin is getting wrinkled, and covered with brown blotches! Maybe Lars should have made his move earlier. Maybe he was too safe, too solid, when she needed a bit of excitement. But she needs to know that with Viktor you have your fill and you move on. Or go back to the tried and true.'

'I have to find a way of saying that,' Sarah agreed. 'And it won't be easy.'

'And you, my girl, shouldn't spend too many hours wondering whether Piet loves you as much, or the same, or more, than this other lass. Grab what he offers with both hands, and celebrate it! The rest will grow.' She gave Sarah an affectionate nudge. 'I thank God for Dan every day and I love him, warts and all. He's the man for me and I wouldn't want to spend my life with anyone else. But for great sex? Hmmm. And there endeth the sermon.'

She was laughing as they drove on towards the *manyatta*, the sun high over their heads. Sarah looked at her and smiled, glad of the trust and affection growing between them. I have made the right choice, she thought. I was right to come back to Kenya, and I'm right in thinking that Piet is the one for me, no matter how long it takes.

Chapter 23

Kenya, December 1965

As Sarah drove in through the gates of Langani Farm, her hands were clammy. She had tried not to imagine her first moments with Piet, but now she could no longer put her hopes aside. The roof of the farmhouse came into view at the last bend, honeysuckle obscuring the chimney tops, the sweep of lawn and the glowing mosaic of Lottie's garden. The dogs ran out to the car, and Hannah stood waiting on the steps. With Lottie.

'Oh Lottie! Lottie, what a wonderful surprise!' Sarah tried to hug them both at once. 'Hannah never told me you were home!'

'She was sworn to secrecy.' Lottie was holding Sarah at arm's length to have a good look at her.

'Surprise, heh?' Hannah was delighted with the success of her subterfuge.

'Is Jan here too?' Sarah saw the answer in Lottie's face.

'He's still trying to get here for Christmas. For New Year at least,' Hannah's smile was too bright.

The verandah and the sitting room had been decorated with Christmas garlands and hung with lanterns. Everything looked festive and welcoming, and Sarah felt a great rush of love for this homely place that was so precious to her, and for the family whom she had regarded for so long as her own. The dogs were running circles around her, and as she bent down to acknowledge them, she felt two strong arms around her.

'Piet!' It was all she was able to say before he was crushing her ribs, kissing her on the mouth.

'It's good that Ma is home, heh? I nearly gave it away when you called to say what time you'd be here.'

'I would have killed him!' Hannah was laughing.

'We bought champagne for Ma's arrival, but she insisted on holding back till you could join us.' Piet was pouring each one of them a glass. 'But now we're all going to drink to our future. To everyone here who has made the present what it is.'

'And to Pa, who will be with us soon,' Hannah raised her glass towards her mother.

'Will the bwana be coming now?' Mwangi had appeared from the kitchen.

'He is getting ready right now, Mwangi,' Lottie answered.

'Eeeh!' Mwangi made the Kikuyu sound of approval or astonishment. 'It is good. I will tell everyone, so that we will be ready.'

'This is my first Christmas at Langani,' Sarah said. 'In fact, this is the first Christmas I haven't been at home. Wherever that is now.'

'It's wherever your family is. The ones you love best,' Lottie said. 'That's where your home will always be. It doesn't matter where it is geographically. So now your home is here with us, Sarah. We are your family.'

Discussion about the opening of the lodge, and the *ngoma* took up most of the conversation during lunch.

'Piet plans to join the dancers. I think he should be with the Maasai and not the Kikuyu, because he's so tall,' Hannah said. 'He'll look well with the ochre and the cow dung in his hair, and all the beads and feathers, don't you think, Ma? A regular warrior.'

Lottie was smiling, but the lines that now tracked her face told the story of a time that had tested her endurance and left its mark on her. She was watchful and subdued, holding herself a little at a distance from the rest of the gathering. When lunch was over she stepped out on to the verandah and Sarah followed.

'Is everything all right?'

'Of course it is, my dear. I'm a little tired, that's all,' Lottie said.

'It will be so wonderful to see Jan for Christmas,' Sarah said.

'He's changed the date twice,' Lottie said. 'I think he's afraid to come. He's so changed, Sarah, and he cannot see how he can take up where he left off. I don't know if I've done the right thing in coming back.'

'It might be hard to begin with. But when he sees this place that he loves, looking so good . . .' She hesitated, then decided it would be better to be open about what she knew. 'Lottie . . .'

'Yes?'

'Hannah told me. About how it was down there. About why she left. So I know it's been hard for you.'

'When we left, Janni said he was uprooting himself to help his son.' Lottie was facing Sarah, looking directly into her eyes. 'But now I think that he was running away. Quitting the farm for Piet's benefit was only a part of it. Since then, I've tried to forget how beautiful this place is, and I know that Janni has tried too. Perhaps I shouldn't have come back, to see all that we have lost, only to feel that we should leave again. Piet is the young bwana here now. He has earned his place, and he must run the farm as he sees fit.'

'Yes. And Hannah has found her role too,' Sarah said.

'We lost Lars, though. And while Mike Stead is willing, he's not of the same calibre.'

'Where is Mike Stead?' Sarah realised she had not seen the new manager.

'Piet has given him a few days off. He has elderly parents who live at the coast, so he's gone down there for Christmas and New Year,' Lottie said. 'And Hannah is very unhappy, because Viktor has gone.'

'Does she think that Viktor has gone permanently?' Sarah's first reaction was relief that she would not have to be the one to break the news.

'She was angry with me for not coming back after the robbery, when she was so frightened by what had happened to you all.' Lottie's shoulders were hunched and tense. 'She thought I didn't care about what had happened to her. But I couldn't leave Jan at that moment. Now I wonder if I could have prevented this disaster with Viktor, if I'd made her a priority and flown up here.'

'I've run across Viktor a couple of times,' Sarah said. 'I wish I'd run over him, frankly. But I don't think anyone could have prevented what happened between him and Hannah. It's a pity that Lars was a casualty, though.'

They walked out on to the lawn that Lottie had tended with such care for so many years. 'I find myself asking the same question you asked earlier, Sarah,' she said. 'Where is my real home? I said it was where you find the people you love the best. But I don't know if what I feel for Jan is love, and I don't know if he is capable of loving any more. He is dead inside, my dear. He has been dead inside since Camilla's terrible mother, that bitch of a woman—' She spat the words out. 'I have not found my

444

husband since that night, and I am not sure if I will be able to love him when I do. If I do.'

'Oh, Lottie! Jan was a good man, a good father, and you'll find him again. I'll pray that you will.'

'I hope you're right. And I hope that I'm strong enough for whatever comes.'

'Come on in, you two!' Hannah was calling from the verandah. 'No more gossiping.'

'I'm going to read and sleep for a while,' Lottie said. 'I'll see you girls later.'

'OK. Do you want to come and sit in my room, Han?' Sarah asked. 'Or maybe go for a walk somewhere?'

'You're going to ask me about Viktor,' Hannah said at once. 'It's all over, Sarah. Just as everyone said it would be. Let's go to your room and talk.'

She slumped into a chair, her face in her hands. It was so hard to tell the story, but she wanted to say it out loud to Sarah who would not judge her, who would listen to all her stupid mistakes and love her still.

He was everywhere, Lars. His face had been stony when he looked at her, or angry and filled with a pain she did not want to see. No matter where she went on the farm, it seemed impossible to avoid him.

'He's following me around,' she had said to Piet. 'Can't you tell him to leave me alone? Stay out of my way?'

'Following you where?' Piet asked. 'When?'

'He looms up in the office every morning,' Hannah said.

'He's supposed to be in the office in the mornings,' Piet tried to reason with her.

'And he's at the stores. In the dairy. Everywhere.'

'Hannah, you've always worked together, and you'll have to go on doing that. He's my manager, for God's sake, and you shouldn't let go of that vital fact. He has his job to do, and you have yours. So stop talking about Viktor all the time. Use some tact and common sense, Sis, and get on with your work.'

In the office she had tried to concentrate on the week's accounts, but it was a grey morning and her mind refused any attempt at discipline. After an hour she gave up and went outside, calling for the dogs. She was halfway down the drive when she came across Lars, walking out of the stores.

'Where are you going?' he asked her.

'I thought I'd take the dogs for a walk.'

'I will come with you,' he said. 'We need to talk.'

She could think of no reason to refuse his offer. They walked for a while in silence.

'I was wondering whether you are planning to visit Sarah soon,' Lars said.

'No. I'm going to stay here for the time being. I want to stay at home.'

'Waiting for him to return, I suppose,' he said. 'So that he can play with you and hurt you, and drive a wedge between us, and then leave you.'

'For God's sake, Lars, I don't know what's got into you,' she said. 'What I think about Viktor is nothing to do with you. I know you have special feelings for me, but I've told you I'm not ready for that. So don't bring it up again. You're here to run this farm, not to act as some kind of policeman in my private life.'

'Is that how you see me, even now?' He was furious. 'As a hired hand that you can just ignore, because some fancy gigolo turns up from Nairobi and gets you into his bed?'

They came to a halt and were standing face to face on the path. There was an awful silence around them, and even the birds and crickets had ceased to sing so that the air was oppressive and deathly still.

'Don't you dare to talk to me in that way, Lars Olsen,' she shouted at him, all composure gone. Her heart was hammering in her ears and she was scarlet with rage. 'I'm a grown woman and I'll decide what I want to do with my life. If you're going to work here you'll have to respect that.'

'Respect? What respect do you have for me? I tried to take care of you after the raid, and before it too. I tried to smooth over the bad days and the bad dreams. You seem not to remember any of that. I was almost killed that night, but you don't care. You don't care about me at all, Hannah, except as a dogsbody. I should go, that's the truth. But I owe it to Piet to stay and do my job. Not as a hired hand, but because he's my friend. And it's time you thought about him, too.'

'It's my land as much as his,' she said. 'And there are plenty of farm managers around. So if you're going to loom over me like a thunder cloud because I'm in love with someone else, then you really should go. I wish you would. And then we can all get on with our lives.'

As soon as she uttered the words she wanted to take them back, and she looked after him in consternation as he turned and strode away towards the house. Then she whistled for the dogs, who had been sitting out the fracas in the shade of a bush. They trotted out to join her and she continued down the hill, resolving to mend their differences when she returned to the office. She would give him an hour or so to calm down. It was difficult for him, and she had not given enough consideration to his feelings for her. He was jealous and she had not been sympathetic enough. She walked on, and within minutes he had faded out of her mind to be replaced by an image of Viktor bending over her, lifting her up to caress her and make love to her.

When she reached the house the sun had turned the morning air into a shimmering mirage of heat and dust devils. Hannah wished the rains had not finished so early. The land was already parched, stubbled with broken stalks of bleached grass. Grazing was poor and the cattle would soon need costly extra feed. She went straight to the office, but there was no sign of Lars. Nor was he there when she made her way into the dining room for lunch.

'*Pole*, memsahib. I am sorry. *Pole sana.*' Mwangi's face was mournful.

'What are you sorry about?' she asked, puzzled. She was not ready for any more problems. 'It's a bad day, Mwangi. It is a day to avoid any new *shauris*. So maybe this one can wait until tomorrow.'

'We are all sorry that the bwana Lars has gone,' he said. 'He was a good man.'

Hannah stared at him, trying to muster some kind of composure, fighting the dread that had made an assault on her. She wanted to gag. It was impossible to swallow any food.

'Yes. Well, these things are not always for long, Mwangi. So we will go on as we have always gone on, and then we will see.'

Her mouth went dry as she heard Piet's footsteps on the verandah.

'We'll talk in the office.' His expression was tense.

'I didn't know he would leave,' she said defensively, as soon as he shut the door behind them.

'Have you any idea how serious this is?' he asked her, his voice low and cold with rage. 'Lars has stayed on here as a friend, at a salary that would be laughable for anyone else. He's my friend and my adviser and the best manager we could ever have.'

'And I'm not responsible for his jealous tantrums,' she said, her resolutions evaporating in the face of Piet's fury.

'You knew he loved you. OK, so you don't love him. Those things happen every day. But you wiped his nose in the affair you're having with Viktor. You flirted and fawned over him, with Lars sitting right next to you. No consideration. No discretion. No thinking, Hannah. About anyone except yourself. You've done a really stupid thing.'

'Piet, I'm sorry. Could we get him back?'

'He phoned from Nanyuki half an hour ago. He's going to stay with his uncle in Kiambu. Then he's thinking of going back to Norway.'

She began to cry, and after a few moments he came and put his hand on her shoulder.

'We'll work it out somehow,' he said. 'Lars has recommended Mike Stead as a replacement, so I'd better arrrange to see him as soon as I get back from Nairobi. He's looking for a job and he's a good bloke. We may be able to make an arrangement with him. Something that will tide us over until we see how this works out. Will you be all right here on your own tonight, by the way? I'd planned to leave this afternoon, but I can put it off.'

Hannah stared at him. She had forgotten that he was going away.

'It's all right,' she said quickly, anxious to make peace. 'You must keep your appointments in Nairobi, and I don't mind being here for a couple of days. Honestly.'

When he had gone she went to her bedroom, not wanting the servants to see that she was on the verge of tears. There was a letter on her dressing table and she opened it unwillingly, with her hand up to her mouth as she realised the full implication of what had happened.

Dear Hannah,

You were right. Your personal life and your private needs are nothing to do with me. It is unfortunate that I have allowed my feelings for you to cross over the line between employer and manager, and between friendship and love.

In these circumstances I cannot work at Langani. It is not good for either of us, or for the farm. But I would never let you and Piet down. I have found a replacement manager, and I hope he will work out fine. I've told everyone I am leaving because of a family problem in Norway. And that is where I will go.

Hannah, I hope that you will be safe and that you will find happiness.
You are full of courage and beauty and I will never cease to admire and
love all that you are.

Thank you for the good years at Langani Farm.

Your devoted friend,
Lars

Hannah read the letter twice. She sat down in her chair, trembling but determined not to cry. He would come back. She was sure of it. They had had arguments before, and he had always come around. This was what she had feared – that any romantic connection between them would jeopardise the workings of the farm. Now, ironically, it was the lack of any such liaison that had sparked the crisis. She spent some time in the office and then went to find Juma in the dairy.

'What about Bwana Lars?' he asked hopefully. 'Will he be back soon?'

'I hope so, Juma. But he has a *shauri* with his family in Norway, and he has to go there. So we will have to wait and see.'

The afternoon seemed endlessly long. There was no one she could talk to. Except Sarah. But when she got through on the radio only Allie was there. Later, when Sarah said that she could not leave Buffalo Springs, Hannah kept her voice light and said nothing about her troubles. But when the call was over she sat beside the phone and cried, until it suddenly rang again, forcing her to pull herself together. It was Viktor and her heart leapt with the excitement of hearing his voice.

'I want you to come to Nairobi tomorrow,' he said. 'Come down, my warrior queen, and conquer the city. I want to take you to the opening of an exhibition. The artist is a friend – he made your bronze leopard. And then we will dance at the Equator Club and make love all the rest of the time.'

'I can't leave here, Viktor,' she said. Her disappointment tasted bitter in her mouth. 'Piet is going to be away for the next couple of days. I'm needed at Langani. Maybe you could drive up for the weekend.'

'Ah, Hannah. Leave your serious self at the farm and come and play with me. Start out right now. I want to touch you and see that look on your face, and see you opening for me.'

'Viktor, I can't leave.' Her voice was strangled.

'Well, my little jam pot, I am sad. But we will see each other soon.'

He hung up and she saw that her hand was shaking as she put the receiver back on its cradle. Why could Viktor not come up to Langani, if he had any real feelings for her? Even he, a man who had certainly seduced many women in his time, had said that he could not get enough of her, that he could not exist without her for any measurable length of time. But how did Viktor measure time? And surely she was more important to him than an exhibition. She wondered where Lars was right now, and she felt profoundly saddened by the idea that she might never see him again. An hour later she decided to phone Viktor. If she could not see him, at least she could talk to him. The telephone rang for a long time before anyone answered.

'Bwana Szustak is not here,' the voice said. 'He has gone away. I am the houseboy taking a message.'

A dark mood settled over her as she went to sit by the fire in lonely silence. She poured herself a stiff measure of whisky and turned on the radio, but the music made her sad. She fixed another drink and waited for dinner to be served, dreading the solitary meal under Mwangi's sympathetic eye. When he announced that it was ready she stood up, weary and dispirited, and took her glass to the table. She heard the sound of the car as she unfolded her napkin. Her skin crawled as she grabbed the rifle that stood next to the sideboard and rose from her chair. Then she planted her feet firmly and aimed the gun at the door. Seconds later, Viktor's loud laugh filled the room as he rushed in and lifted her off her feet. When he set her down she was still holding the gun, stunned and disbelieving.

'I could have killed you,' she said. 'My God, Viktor, what are you doing here?'

'Come, Hannah – I have brought champagne. Then we will eat.'

She could not think beyond the sight of him. 'I have to find out what's in the kitchen and—'

'I would like to eat quickly,' he said. 'And afterwards I would like to take you to your bedroom, and fuck you until you are exhausted and crying out for mercy. And then my hunger will be satisfied. That is what I would like.'

When she lay beside him later, happy and sated, he propped himself up on his elbow.

'Where is your Viking guard tonight?' he asked. 'I have become accustomed to him, glowering at us, casting his Northern gloom upon our pleasures.'

'He's gone.'

'Gone where? For how long?' Viktor demanded.

'He's gone to Norway,' she said, but her voice was hollow. 'Someone in his family is very sick and he had to go home. No. He didn't.' There was no reason to lie to him. 'He's gone for good. Lars has left the farm.'

'I thought he was a fixture.' Viktor was frowning and his voice was sharp. He got up and moved away from the bed.

'He was jealous,' Hannah said. 'You know that. He made no secret of it. Of the fact that he loved me. It was shock initially, but now I see that it's best this way. Because I don't have to hide what I feel about you any more. What we feel for each other.'

But Viktor was not listening. He had turned on the shower in the bathroom, and was singing loudly. When he returned to the bed he put his arms around her and slept immediately. And in the morning he left early, his hand waving an extravagant salute as he raced away.

Hannah sat up straight and wiped her eyes. She had told Sarah the entire, horrible story now, humiliating though it was.

'Don't say anything kind,' she warned. 'I couldn't cope with that.'

'You were taken in by him, Hannah. It's not much consolation, I know, but it happens all the time. It happened to me in a smaller way. With Mike in Dublin, remember?'

'But you didn't go running after him.'

'I didn't care enough about him,' Sarah said. 'Otherwise, God knows what I might have done.'

'I didn't hear from Viktor after he left that morning.' Hannah's voice was far away, in another time and place, remembering. 'But I wanted to know that he loved me. I wanted to be sure. So I drove down to Nairobi. A couple of days after Piet got back from all his meetings, I said I needed to do some Christmas shopping. It was late when I arrived, but I know where Viktor lives so I just rolled up there, thinking I'd surprise him. And I did,' she said bitterly. 'He was very surprised. And so was the woman in his bed.'

'Han, what a terrible thing. What an awful way to find out.' Sarah finally put her arm around Hannah's shoulders.

'She was black,' Hannah said, her voice still resonating surprise and shock. 'She was a black woman and I stood there screaming at them, until he took me outside. Stood next to me in the driveway, with only a towel wrapped around him, and told me he didn't want to see me any more. That's what he said. I don't remember driving home, but when I got here Piet was wonderful. He was the very best. He never asked me where I'd been, or why I'd come back in the middle of the night and he's never brought it up since. No one knows this except you. Not even Ma.'

'So what now?' Sarah asked.

'It's Christmas,' Hannah replied. 'And as Ma said earlier, we're a group of people who love each other, and best of all you're here to join us. So we should concentrate on that for now. I love you, Sarah, and you're my sister. And you look like you need some sleep. I'll see you later.'

Sarah lay down on the comfortable old bed, thinking about Hannah and Lars and whether anything could be salvaged from the mess. She sighed, and took out a paper that Dan had given her about the mating habits of the jackal. But within moments her eyes closed and she slept, like the trusting child she had once been in this same room. A light knock woke her.

'Come with me to the ridge,' Piet said. 'Bring a sweater or something warm.'

Piet brought a rug and cushions in the car, and they sat looking out over the bright sweep of the land where the wind stirred the vlei grass, feathered and green after the blessing of sudden rain. He put his hand on the back of Sarah's neck and made a soft, clicking sound in the back of his throat that she remembered from her childhood. It was something Kipchoge had taught him, and Piet had often made this special noise as he walked beside her in those innocent years, pointing out birds and plants and animal tracks that he knew and wanted her to share. Sarah sat watching the changing colour of the sky, and the pink that stained the snow peaks of Kirinyaga as the sun began its descent towards the edge of her world. Then Piet spoke.

'I love you,' he said, simply. 'I've always loved you, but I was just too dim-witted to know it. To understand and see it. I want you to forgive me for that, because I do love you, Sarah, more than anything. More than life. And I know that you are the only one for me.'

She turned to look at him, and made a small sound as he put his arms around her and kissed her over and over.

'I love you, love you, love you,' he repeated, stroking her hair, touching her eyelids and cheeks, running his fingers tenderly across her lips. 'I don't remember any time when you weren't a part of me, and I can't see any future when you're not with me. Is that all right with you?'

She nodded and tried to respond with words, but she was dumb with happiness and wonder, so she lay back on the rug and let herself dissolve into the ecstatic joy that came over her as he kissed her, and touched her body for the first time. They lay side by side, breathless with love and discovery, watching the first stars pierce the darkening bowl of the sky.

'I love you, Piet,' she said finally. 'I always have, from the first day you came and jumped into the river beside me. And I always will.'

'We'll love each other and take care of each other for all of our lives, little Sarah, and our world will be a fine place.' He stood up and held out his hand to her. 'Come now, my beautiful woman. It's getting cold up here on our ridge, and I want to take you home to our farm.'

They folded up the rug and cushions, and stopped once more to look down on the beauty of their shared universe.

'This is our own piece of the earth,' he said. 'Everything down there was fashioned out of courage and strong will and hope. I believe it is a place given to us by God, and we will try to look after it and preserve it always, you and I, whatever the cost. I know that you love it like I do, and that you are the one who will always help me.'

'I do,' she said. 'And I will. Always.'

When she looked into the mirror before dinner, Sarah saw that on this night she was truly beautiful, filled with the knowledge of Piet's love and her vision of the future they would build together. Her skin was glowing, her eyes shining, as she entered the sitting room and Piet took her hand.

'I want you all to hear something now,' he said. 'For years I've been a dumb Afrikaner who couldn't see beyond his nose, couldn't think straight about the things that matter. A young dunce, heh? But at last I've woken up. I've found the most important thing any man can find, which is someone I can love and trust with my life. So, Sarah Mackay, I'd like to ask you if you would agree to take care of this poor farmer. I'd like to ask you if you would marry me and make me the happiest man in the world. Could you do that, do you think?'

She could hear the cries and exclamations as she flew into his arms.

'Yes, I'll marry you. Yes. I love you, and I'll always love you.' She turned to face them all then, to accept their congratulations through the blur of tears. 'I love each and every one of you,' she said. 'I'm so happy, and I love you so much that there aren't any other words.'

The door opened as she spoke and Mwangi appeared with Kamau, their dark faces shining with approval as they pressed Piet's hands. He put his arms around them both and hugged them fiercely, and they murmured Kikuyu words of gladness and blessing on the young man they had cared for and watched over since his birth. After a few moments Kipchoge joined them, shy but beaming, holding out an offering of two beaded bracelets he had made for Piet and Sarah, hoping that this day would come about. He slid them carefully over their wrists, and then everybody was clapping as Piet kissed her again. Sarah turned to look for Hannah and caught her in an unguarded moment of sheer desolation that made her lead Piet over to his sister, and draw her into their own joy. They stayed up late into the night, talking and laughing and planning, and finally they gathered around the telephone as Sarah called the operator and gave him the number in Ireland.

'We'll come out in the new year, darling girl,' Raphael promised, when she had spoken to her family. 'Goodnight now, and God bless you both. Hannah and Lottie too. We love you all.'

When they retired to bed Piet and Sarah were left together.

'I want to make love to you right now,' he said. 'To make us really one. But I think you would like to wait, maybe? So I'll do whatever you choose, because it won't be long until you are my wife, for all the rest of our lives.'

'It's old-fashioned and silly, I know,' she replied, unable to think why she would need to wait any longer. Her whole body was shot through with currents of desire and excitement. 'But I think that's what I would prefer.'

'Tomorrow we will make our plans,' he said, touching her blushing cheeks and kissing her. 'We'll decide how soon we can get married and so. It must be very soon. You'll have to think what you're going to do about your job, because I know it means so much to you. And by the way, there'll be no more swimming with your boss with no *brookies* on! Not for my girl.'

It was a night when everyone slept with a sense of peace and sweetness surrounding them, a turning point when the cloud over Langani had lifted at last. Christmas would be a time of joy long overdue. Anthony called from Nairobi and Piet persuaded him to join them at the farm, to celebrate the engagement.

'Great news, girl,' he said to Sarah when he arrived. 'You have a good man and he's a lucky chap. What are you going to do about your elephants?'

'I don't know,' she said. 'I'm helping Dan to write his proposal for more funds to expand our programme, and I'd love to be a part of it. But I haven't even thought about it yet.'

Anthony looked down at the floor, considering before he spoke again. 'Speaking of funds, I ran into George Broughton-Smith a couple of weeks ago. I was with one of my clients at the New Stanley Grill.'

'George, in Nairobi?' Hannah asked. 'What about Camilla? What about her twenty-first birthday last month? Did he say anything about that? I sent her a card, but I haven't heard a thing. As usual.'

'I'm not sure what's going on there,' Anthony said. 'I haven't actually been in touch with Camilla, what with being away on my sales trip and on safari. And I rather feel that George doesn't think much of me because of that.'

'Perhaps not,' said Sarah, fixing him with a piercing gaze.

'I didn't get any reply to the card I wrote,' he said. 'I did send flowers on her birthday, but my plans changed and I ended up in Cincinnati around that date. So I never actually got to London in the end. Well, just one night in transit,' he trailed off lamely. 'Anyway, George didn't have much to say. He's only seen Camilla once since September. He wasn't even with her for her birthday. She went somewhere with Marina, and he definitely did not want to talk about her.'

'That's very strange.' Sarah was frowning, sure now that she had missed some vital clue during her own frustrating telephone conversations with Camilla. 'They've always been so close. What about her face?'

'He didn't seem to know what she was doing about her face, or anything else. And Marina's been ill, apparently. I brought up the subject of money for conservation at Langani, and he told me Camilla had never mentioned it. But now he's aware of the problems, and he's going to contact you and see what funds he can dig up. He was very positive, in fact. There's nothing to be done until the new year. But he'll get to it then.'

'I knew this would happen,' said Hannah sourly. 'She just forgot about us.'

'No. That's not it. There's definitely something wrong here – I know there is,' Sarah said. 'Maybe her injury was worse than we thought. That would take away her work, her money, everything. She might have had to give up her flat. Or maybe it's that George and Marina are getting a divorce. I don't know, but there's something skewed here that we don't understand.'

'Ach, you're always ready to make excuses for her,' Hannah said. 'She's not capable of connecting with anyone. It's a shame, and she probably can't help it, growing up with that terrible woman. But it's time to be realistic about her, Sarah.'

On Christmas Eve, Sarah drove with Lottie to the nearest mission school where there was a midnight Mass. Kneeling in the pews of the small church she knew that she was the most fortunate and happy human being in the world. Around her voices swelled in the starlit chill of the night, rising with the incense, giving old Christmas hymns the high, keening tone and rhythm peculiar to African songs. The congregation was largely made up farm labourers, dressed for the occasion in unaccustomed, ill-fitting jackets and shoes without laces. The women wore thick, hand-knitted sweaters, and the babies were tucked into blankets tied across their backs, their round heads and wondering faces topped by bright woollen hats. Sarah lit candles for her family in Ireland, knowing they would have loved to be here with her. But they had promised to fly out for the wedding. Lottie took her hand as they joined the songs of praise and celebration, mingling with the jubilant chanting of Kikuyu voices. Sarah felt that for the remainder of her life she would sing like this, in harmony with all the races that surrounded her, sharing and contributing with Piet to the brave hopes of their new nation. Later in the service Lottie knelt beside her, bowed in prayer, her face composed but sad. Jan had not come for Christmas, but he had promised to be there in time for the new year. The midnight air was cold and their headlights pierced a band of mist as they drove home to Langani.

Piet was waiting up for them, and they sat by the fire and drank mugs of hot chocolate before Lottie decided to turn in. Then he kissed Sarah and led her to her bedroom. They lay down together and he ran his hands over her, holding her close to him. She heard him groan a little as she unfastened her dress so that he could stroke her, exploring her bare thighs and her stomach, caressing her breasts, leaving her breathless with desire. Her skin was on fire and she felt drunk with the intensity of the sensations that he created in her, unwilling to let him go as he leaned back and away from her, and finally stood up. He stooped once more to kiss her and to whisper his words of love in her ear, and then he closed the door and left her. She lay awake and burning, in a state of confused longing, wondering why she had asked him to wait. They were meant for one another, they would always be together. Why deny their hunger now? But she wanted to thank God for the precious gift of him, her one wish, now miraculously granted. She wanted it all to be right, and besides, it would not be long.

They exchanged Christmas gifts after breakfast. When they had finished unwrapping the presents, Piet took a small box from his pocket and asked Sarah to hold out her hand. The diamond glittered through her happy tears as he slipped it on her finger and kissed her, while everyone crowded around to wish them joy. There were telephone calls to Jan, and to Sarah's family in Ireland. But there was no answer from Camilla's flat, and she was soon forgotten, eclipsed by the dazzling spotlight of Piet and Sarah's happiness. Later in the day Sarah found herself alone, and again she dialled the operator to ask for the London number. But thousands of miles away the phone shrilled in an empty room. Sarah hung up sadly, resolving to write to Camilla before the day's end, to persuade her to return to Langani for the wedding. They had made a promise, and in her heart Sarah knew that their friendship must stand firm and that somehow she would make it so.

Chapter 24

Kenya, December 1965

Immediately after Christmas they began their preparations for the *ngoma*. The event had taken on a new and wider significance, since it would now mark both the opening of the lodge and the engagement between Piet and Sarah. The telephone rang endlessly with congratulations and acceptances. Piet had arranged for an ox to be roasted for the farm workers, and a huge pit had been hollowed out some distance from the labour lines, so that the beast could be cooked whole on a spit. An air of excitement prevailed in the house and in the workshops, and the *watu* sang songs on their way to work, about the *ngoma* and the marriage of the young bwana. Around the huts, the smaller children who tended the goats made spears from sticks and slivers of stone, and fashioned shields from pieces of wood and cardboard. They practised making experimental jumps on their spindly little legs, imitating the leaping warriors they so admired. At the dispensary where Lottie reigned once more, the talk was of nothing else.

Sarah spent hours around the farm with her camera, photographing the farm labourers, the house staff, the cooks and the kitchen *totos*, the women in their huts adorning each other's hair, and making beaded necklaces for the great event. Wherever she looked, she could sense only anticipation and excitement. There were no disaffected men or women here that she could identify, and a sense of peace and contentment descended on her as she began to make plans for her life at Langani. She still had not decided what she was going to do about her job with Dan and Allie. She might have to spend at least part of the coming year at Buffalo Springs. But it was not so far away, and she was confident that she could come home for alternate weekends, or that Piet would be able to join her in camp until something permanent could be worked out. Three days before the great feast, he appeared in the storeroom where Lottie and Sarah were counting sheets and towels against the invasion of guests.

'You can leave most of this with Simon,' he said. 'I'd like us all to go up to the ridge. We could take a few bottles of beer or some wine, and something to munch on. How about it? Hannah says it's a *lekker* idea and Anthony too.'

'I'll stay here,' Lottie said. 'I'll finish off with Simon, because I want to phone Janni in a little while. But you young people go. I'll expect you back for dinner.'

'I feel like an old lion, sitting up here and surveying my territory,' Piet said, leaning back against the boulder. Behind him the red gold of the rock and the tawny bushes that grew out of it were drenched in the evening sun, framing his head like a golden mane. Sarah lifted her camera to capture his beauty as he sat there above his domain. His stance illustrated the ease with which he possessed his space, and the pride that welled in him as he looked out over the place of his life's dreams. He was lost in contemplation, and did not even notice the click and whirr of the shutter.

'They say the Egyptian pharaohs started looking for the right place to build their tombs the minute they ascended the throne,' he said. 'This is the place I'd choose, if I was asked. No man-made structure could rival the beauty of this spot, heh? The way it looks out over the farm and the mountain and the plains. You can see every part of our world from here. Better than a pyramid any day!'

'The Egyptians didn't have the benefit of these natural contours for their memorials,' Anthony said. 'I suppose if you're faced with a flat desert, you want to create something that will rise out of the sand and survive the storms. Dominate the land so people will remember your great works. Tremble with awe . . .'

> 'My name is Ozymandias, king of kings:
> Look on my works, ye Mighty, and despair!'

Piet intoned in a stentorian voice, and Sarah looked at him surprised.

'I didn't know you read Shelley,' she said.

'There's a lot you don't know.' Piet gave her a long look. 'I did learn to read as well as farm. And not only Shelley. There are books in my room

459

that we're going to read together. And some that we'll read to our children. I've started a collection of great records too. I went to concerts in Edinburgh with friends, and I finally learned to understand that Beethoven and Mahler and Mozart might be as satisfying as Elvis.' He drew her in to his side to caress her hair and she shivered with the pleasure of the gesture. At last, to break the silence, she finished the quote.

> 'Nothing beside remains. Round the decay
> Of that colossal wreck, boundless and bare,
> The lone and level sands stretch far away.'

'Just what I was getting at,' Piet said. 'Man-made monuments will crumble and disappear, like the city in the Masefield poem you quoted that day in Gedi, Sarah. But this –' he waved his outstretched arm over the panorama before them – 'this has been here for millions of years and will be here for millions more, unless we destroy the whole planet with our giant, mushroom-shaped clouds. If we want to be remembered for what we have done in our own puny moment of time, then we must make the beauty of this earth the heart of our endeavours. Then our efforts will hold, and we might even deserve to be remembered.'

'And that's our philosophy lesson for this evening.' Hannah finished her beer. 'We'd better be getting back.'

'Let's start down the track.' Anthony took the cool box. 'And these two can follow us. But if they keep us waiting too long, we'll leave them to walk home.'

They disappeared into the trees, leaving Sarah and Piet alone. In the blue dusk she could see his eyes shining with love. He cupped her chin in his hands, and kissed her with a tenderness that made her want to cry. Away in the distance came the first whoop of a hyena, calling to his fellow hunters. A chorus came back to him, closer to the ridge than they had expected. Piet took Sarah's hand, and they were imitating the calls and laughing at the replies as they moved down the rough incline to where they had left the car.

At the house Lottie was on the steps to meet them, her face transformed. 'I spoke to Janni and he really is coming! He has his ticket and he will arrive in Nairobi on the thirtieth. So, he will be here for the *ngoma* to celebrate with us all.'

After dinner, Sarah brought out her photographs to show to Lottie, spreading out the Dublin portraits, and the pictures she had taken on the September safari and during her time at Buffalo Springs. She had captured perfectly the raw landscape and the effortless beauty of the Samburu tribesmen with their herds of goats and cattle. Her lens had preserved the light as it caught the spiky stalks of parched grass and turned them into golden rods, their feathery tops dappled with the passage of passing clouds, or shadowed here and there by the wide umbrella of an acacia thorn or a group of doum palms. There were pictures of the plains, with the ferocious points of whistling thorns in the foreground, and the crazy shapes of termite cities rising into the air. But best of all she had caught people and animals in moments of revelation that made them gasp. The last groups portrayed the mourning elephants as they built their cairn.

'Ach, Sarah!' Piet spoke softly, as though he was afraid the great creatures he was looking at would hear him, and go away. 'I don't believe anyone has ever photographed that extraordinary ceremony before. There has to be someone who will publish these.'

'You'll be famous for pictures like these one day,' Anthony said. 'I guarantee that.'

Piet had picked up the set of photographs taken on their September safari and had begun to go through them slowly. Sarah watched him covertly. It would be revealing to see his reaction to the luminosity that Camilla had, that every camera loved. There were several photographs of her with Anthony, deep in discussion. He was explaining something to her, his hands gesturing, his whole body full of a boyish excitement. Camilla leaned towards him with an expression of such absorption in her eyes that the viewer could feel the jolt of her longing. One hand was stretched out towards him, as if she had wanted to draw the essence of him from the air. They were framed in the tracery of overhead branches, and in the foreground the flames from the campfire danced in the evening light, sending wisps of smoke and sparks into the atmosphere around them. It was clear from the picture that they were unaware of anything but each other. Piet stared down at it for a long time, then he put it down and shook his head slightly.

'What?' Sarah asked, unable to remain silent.

'You see too much through your magic eye,' he said. 'Sometimes it leaves the subject too exposed, too raw. So you can see the lines.'

'What lines?' Sarah was puzzled.

'The invisible lines that bring people together. Body language some call it. The way a head turns or an arm reaches out. Like that.' He pointed to the picture of Anthony and Camilla. 'Or the line between a predator and its prey, as it's hunted down. Like in this cheetah picture here.'

'I'm not sure I'm ready for that kind of exposure,' Anthony was hastily shuffling the pictures. 'But here's a picture of Hannah that shows all her strength and courage, and leaves you knowing that there is a brimming sweetness there too. That she's vulnerable and must be loved and protected.'

Hannah turned away, her expression unreadable. Anthony cleared his throat, realising he had touched a raw nerve. He disappeared into the kitchen to promote more coffee.

'We should all be filmed by a genius from time to time,' Piet said with new understanding. 'It would teach us to face up to many truths about ourselves that we try to avoid. And there's one thing I'm sure of. My girl will have an audience for her photographs, and she will become a big name. Bigger behind the camera than Camilla ever was in front of it.'

'I'd like her to be here for our wedding,' Sarah said.

'You're really hopeless, you know.' Hannah's words carried resignation, but she was smiling. 'You never accept that there's a time to give up.'

'No, she's right, Han. Camilla should be here,' Piet said. 'We'll track her down somehow, over the next few days. Now listen, I'm going to go out to the lodge early tomorrow morning and I'll stay out there for the night. I want to make sure the lights are set properly, inside the buildings and around the pool and the waterhole. And to check that the plumbing is all working. We don't want any hitches when our guests arrive.'

'Do you want any of us to come with you?' Hannah asked.

'No. You have plenty to do here. I'll take Kipchoge and Simon. Ole Sunde, the nightwatchman, is out there already and he can give us a hand.' He grinned at Sarah. 'I'll be back first thing on Saturday morning though, because I can't stay away from my girl longer than that. You should give our friend here a couple of those pictures, you know.' He slapped Anthony on the back as he spoke. 'Take a close look, old chap. They might knock some sense into you. You're even slower than I've been. And keep these women in order tomorrow, heh?'

Sarah dressed quickly the next morning and went outside. It would be good to have breakfast with Piet before he left for the lodge. No one else seemed to be around except the birds, welcoming a new day with raucous enthusiasm. Everything looked so fresh at this time of day, she thought, entranced by the palette of the sunrise and the moon fading, ghostlike, into the high azure of the sky. It was cool, but she knew that it would be scorching later. As she turned towards the dining room she saw Simon, standing very still, observing her. She had not heard him approach.

'Good morning, Simon. You're here early.'

'Good morning, Madam. Bwana Piet told me to be ready at seven, for the lodge.'

'Oh yes. You seem to have settled very well into the work at the lodge,' she said, for the sake of making conversation. 'And I suppose you've made some friends here now.'

'I work hard for Bwana Piet, Madam,' he answered. 'I hope I will be very good in my job. And then he will be pleased. Later I will think about making some friends, but I do not go with these Kikuyu clans here.' He made a disdainful gesture with his hand. 'They are not good people.' A small nerve was jumping in his neck, and he pursed his lips disapprovingly.

'So what do you do with your time when you're not working?' Sarah felt sorry for him. It was difficult enough being a stranger, an orphan with no family to support you within the tribal hierarchy. But to be ostracised by your fellow workers as well must be especially hard, particularly if their rejection had grown out of jealousy.

'I have books, Madam. The father at the mission gave them to me. He told me, "Simon, read and read all the time. It will make your brain good." So I read, and I prepare to make my English better, and my brain. You think it is good?'

'I think your English is extremely good, Simon. Which father gave you the books? Was it the priest who wrote your references?'

'No, Madam. He was an old priest. A *mzee* who gave me lessons when I did not know anything. Always I read what he gave me.'

She was moved by the image he had conjured up of the small boy, abandoned at the mission, ignorant and lonely and probably frightened out of his wits, and the kindly priest who had given him the precious gift of a new world, opening up for him the written word. She could picture him vividly, sitting there, struggling with the strange symbols, and then one day being able to read.

'Simon, wait here a moment.' She had a sudden inspiration.

She ran back to her room and rummaged through her collection of books. She had an anthology of English literature that she had won as a prize in her fourth year at school, and she still carried it with her everywhere. It had excerpts from works of prose and poetry, and there were fine woodcut illustrations and engravings. In the front was a dedication, stating that she had won first prize in English. She thought Simon would like that, and would see that she had given him a book that meant something to her. Below the prize label, she wrote an inscription:

To Simon, I hope this gives you great pleasure, and helps to increase your knowledge. With best wishes, Sarah Mackay.

She also rifled through her portfolio until she came to a photograph of him that she had taken the first day they had ridden out to the lodge, and she inscribed the back of the picture too. There was a Christmas carrier bag on her chest of drawers and she slipped the two gifts into it.

'I hope you will like this book, Simon,' she told him. 'I have treasured it since the day I received it, and there is good writing in it. The best. It will bring you many profitable hours.'

He had opened the bag, and was looking at the book with reverence. He read the label in the flyleaf silently, his lips moving over the words, and then saw what she had added in her own hand. Finally, when he looked up at her with a smile lighting his eyes and all of his face, she realised that she had never seen him smile before.

'You are giving me such an important thing?' he asked. His hands moved over the leather binding, and he fingered the gold embossed edges of the pages. 'Why, Memsahib Sarah, are you doing this?'

'Because I want you to have it and I know you will learn from it, as I did. And because you have worked hard for Bwana Piet. He depends on you now, to help him make the farm and the lodge into a place where all people can work together to make a good life. And it's Christmas, too,' she said.

He nodded and closed the book, and she saw that he had pressed his lips together and that he shut his eyes quickly as if to blink away tears.

'You don't have a family, do you?' Sarah asked. 'I think I can understand how that feels because this year my family is very far away, and I no longer see them. In a way I am alone too, without my family. So I know it is good when someone thinks about you.'

He was clearly battling with his emotions, and she wondered if she had said too much and embarrassed him. He had turned away from her, and was looking at the photograph. When he looked back, his eyes were bright with tears.

'I have never had a present before,' he said. 'Madam Sarah is very kind.'

He stopped suddenly, his eyes darting away from her, and she turned to see Piet striding across the lawn towards her.

'You're up!' he exclaimed, delighted. 'Join me for breakfast?' He kissed her and then put his hand beneath her elbow to lead her back to the house, calling out to Simon over his shoulder. 'Get the gear into the Land Rover, Simon. Kipchoge will give you a hand.' He looked at Sarah. 'What's he doing hanging around the front of the house?'

'I asked him to wait for me on the lawn. I wanted to give him a book. He says he reads a lot.'

'He's a good fellow. But I don't want him getting too familiar and doing things the other staff don't do. He's in enough trouble already because they're jealous of him, and he needs to respect the boundaries. At times he can be too smart for his own good.'

She was disappointed at the criticism in his remark. 'He's having a hard time,' she said. 'He hasn't any real friends, and he's still an outsider through no real fault of his own.'

'Well, I'm going to move him to the lodge for the next week or so. We only have the nightwatchman there at present. He's not a Kikuyu, so there shouldn't be any tension. Simon foolishly got himself into trouble with Kamau and David, and a week out there will give them all a cooling-off period.'

'But it was David who started this *shauri*, egged on by his father. It can't be much fun to be on the wrong side of them,' Sarah said.

'He's not here for fun. He's here to do the job that he came here begging for. And he's a good choice for the lodge, because he has no family, so he won't be complaining that he's away from his wife and *totos* when he's out there.'

'He draws the short straw, just because he's unlucky enough to have no family?' Sarah was frowning.

'He's lucky enough to have a job with good prospects. He drew the right straw for that. He's doing well for himself, as I'm sure he would admit. And now he also has your book.'

He grinned at her, and her slight irritation dissolved instantly. She would have to reassess her opinions, and to guard her tongue as she learned to deal with all the staff who lived with their own traditions and expectations, and a different hierarchical system.

'I didn't mean to interfere,' she said and he reached out and squeezed her fingers.

'I love it when you get fired up about something,' he said. 'Like a lioness, all tawny anger and flashing claws and teeth!'

'Ah, stop. You're teasing me now,' she protested. 'I haven't bitten or scratched anyone that I can recall. Not in the last week or two anyway.'

'But the threat of it, heh? That's what makes it exciting.' He growled at her.

'Oh, go on, Piet. You're just winding me up.' She watched him from over the rim of her coffee cup, her eyes filled with happiness. 'You made some pointed remarks at Anthony last night, by the way.'

'Anthony is a permanent Boy Scout, living a life of daring deeds and adventures. He's had an endless series of girlfriends, but he's never been able to settle down and make a lasting connection with any of them.'

'Maybe he's not ready for that. Maybe he'll get there when the time is right, but it's not yet.'

'I'm not sure he'll ever grow up enough to be ready,' Piet said. 'He never thinks beyond his next trip to the bush where he can sit down with his *watu*, who don't demand anything of him except his protection and their wages. And then there are his clients who are paying him to be there. And paying him to climb into his bed, some of them. It sounds ideal, I suppose, for a Boy Scout. Or Peter Pan.'

'Until he ignores someone with real feelings for him. And then there are tears,' Sarah said.

'That's why he should look at that photograph you took of him with Camilla, and maybe he would begin to understand what she was offering him. What he was too stupid to see before she left. They'd make a good couple, you know. She could charm his clients and help him make his camps a little more classy and comfortable. Add the feminine touch. He's a good fellow, Anthony, but he's hollow somewhere. He doesn't see the importance of other people, especially women who place their trust in him.'

'And would you have been different, Piet, in those circumstances? Would you have taken what she offered, grabbed it with both hands?' She cursed herself for having asked the question. It was madness to risk spoiling their happiness, for the sake of laying Camilla's ghost to rest.

He studied her seriously before he answered. 'She never looked at me like that,' he said. 'The lines were never running in my direction. I had an adolescent crush on her for too long, and I never understood that there's a void in the centre of her. Anthony is like her in that respect. So maybe they're too similar to be good for each other. Maybe no one ever will find out what makes either of them truly happy, or whether they're capable of being happy at all. But on the other hand, they could have given each other the missing part, and that would have been good, heh?'

'Do you believe there's a special person chosen for you, that you are meant to be with, meant to build your life with?' she asked.

He nodded, smiling. 'I surely do.'

'So do I,' she said. 'And I think Anthony was Camilla's soulmate. She saw it, but he didn't. I wish he'd gone to search her out, instead of making a couple of phone calls and sending a postcard. They seemed so wrapped up in each other when we were in Samburu. I thought they were in love. And then he ran scared, I suppose.'

'Yes,' he agreed. 'He should go and look for her. He's afraid of losing his freedom, of making a commitment, but he'd be a better man if he had someone who really cared about him. And freedom isn't all he thinks it is. He's still playing silly buggers, looking in the wrong places, behaving like a rutting male. Man, I'm blessed because I woke up to reality. I found the one woman for me. And it's far, far sweeter and more wonderful than I could have dared to imagine.'

He drew her to her feet and kissed her.

'Am I interrupting something? Simon said to tell you everything is ready.' Anthony was standing in the doorway. Sarah leaned on the back of the chair, and her eyes seemed glazed as she reached out and touched Piet on the arm.

'Do you really have to go now?'

'Yep. But I'll call you on the radio tonight.'

'Couldn't I—?' She was pleading with him

467

'Absence makes the heart grow fonder, they say.' Piet was laughing. 'I'll talk to you tonight. Around five for sure. Maybe earlier, if I'm done with the outside work. I promise.'

He kissed her again and left the dining room, whistling to his favourite dog, a great loping ridgeback that sprang into the back of the Land Rover. Sarah stood in the doorway looking after the car, watching him drive away and finally disappear in a balloon of trailing dust. Now she would begin counting the hours until sundown, when he would speak with her again. In the meantime he might change his mind and ask her to join him out at the lodge. Unable to sustain a sensible conversation with anybody, she went to her room and picked up her camera. Then she set off with the other two dogs to take some pictures.

The day crawled by in a pointless procession of hours, and she was reminded of the times when she would be watching out for her parents' arrival at boarding school. Like that first time, so many years ago, when she had mistaken Lottie for her mother, triggering the whole train of events that had brought her to this day. And now Piet loved her, and she was going to be his wife. He would ring this evening, or perhaps come back early, or ask her to drive out and join him. Meanwhile, the anticipation and frustration of waiting were almost more than she could bear. The sun seemed to take for ever to climb to its zenith, hanging there interminably through the middle of the day, and descending more slowly than usual to sink away below the edge of the world. Once five o'clock came she stayed in and around the house, so that she could reach the phone quickly. But it remained obstinately silent.

Lottie appeared at sunset, carrying a plant in a clay pot. 'Look, Sarah – I took cuttings of these, and they've just begun to flower. I'm going to put them on the verandah just outside your room. Do you remember them?'

Sarah touched the three flowers, white and pale blue and violet, and nodded, smiling. 'Yesterday, Today and Tomorrow. Three different-coloured flowers on one bush. They're the ones that always reminded you of Hannah and Camilla and me. That's what you call them, isn't it? They're beautiful and the scent is heavenly.' She felt a shadow of regret hover over her happiness. 'I wish Camilla was with us, so that we could all be the same again and she could share what we have.'

'She's gone, my dear. For the moment, at any rate. I hope the poor girl will be happy some day, but it will be difficult for her.'

Sarah took the heavy pot and put it on the coffee table, which was bathed in the crimson light of the setting sun. The shrub seemed to be in the heart of a conflagration.

'A burning bush,' Sarah murmured. A cloud overtook the sinking disc on the horizon, leaving the room in near darkness. She shivered involuntarily and looked at her watch. 'Lottie, would you mind if I tried to raise the lodge? Piet said he was going to call at five, but he hasn't. Maybe he's decided to come on back to the farm, in which case there'll be one more for dinner tonight.'

'Of course, my dear.' Lottie was smiling, a knowing, affectionate light in her eyes. 'Go ahead and talk to your lovely boy. I'm going to the kitchen to chat with Kamau about dinner, and you can let me know if he's going to be back tonight after all.'

She left the room and Sarah lifted the telephone, drumming her fingers on the table as she waited for the lodge to respond. There was the sound of crackling, but no answer. Sarah was puzzled. He would surely be back there by now, to turn on the lights. Test them all. She put down the phone and went in search of Hannah, but it was Anthony she came across, reading a tome on birds of prey.

'You know, Piet said he would ring, but he hasn't. I tried the lodge a few minutes ago, but . . .' Now that she was putting it into words, there was really nothing to say and she realised that she sounded foolish.

'Can't wait to hear the beloved voice?' He was grinning at her indulgently. 'He's probably on his way back there now. He was going to check the fencing around the lodge and stores area where the elephant walked through last week. Try him again in about half an hour.'

'You're right. I'll go and see if I can help Hannah.' As she walked down the drive towards the dairy, Hannah rounded the bend in her truck.

'Hey there!' Her greeting was light. 'Do you want to ride back with me to the house?'

'Piet was going to call on the radio at five,' Sarah said. 'I tried him, but there was no answer. There should be someone there, shouldn't there? Simon or Kipchoge, or the watchman?'

There was no basis for the unease that was rising in her and she gripped the door of the jeep, willing herself to gain control, to stop behaving like a teenager. Hannah took her arm, sensing her concern and surprised by it.

'Come on, Sarah, man. He's probably sitting up on his ridge with

Kipchoge, spouting his philosophic insights and pining for you. I have a couple of things to drop off in the office, and then we'll try the radio again. But don't hold your breath, because half the time that connection doesn't work properly.'

Back at the house Sarah went into the sitting room and tried to sit calmly as Mwangi lit the fire and offered her tea. It was twenty minutes before Hannah returned from the office and cranked the telephone. The line crackled, but there was still no reply.

'Shouldn't someone answer now? It's already dark.' Sarah tried to sound reasonable. 'They must have a problem, don't you think?'

Hannah's face was troubled. 'Anthony, I know this sounds dumb and you might think Sarah's overreacting, but sometimes, well, she senses things. The watchman should be there now, no matter what Piet is up to. I taught him myself to answer a radio call.'

'They could have had a breakdown in the Land Rover and need digging out, I suppose,' Anthony said. 'I'll get a couple of your *watu* and drive up there.'

'I'm coming with you,' Sarah said firmly.

'Me too,' Hannah said.

'Anthony, take a gun. Just in case,' Lottie had appeared in the doorway.

Anthony shrugged and opened the gun case to remove a rifle and a revolver. Now that they were going, Sarah was afraid that she had provoked a wild goose chase. Piet would be furious. But she was grateful that Hannah had taken her seriously. Anthony clearly thought she was crazy, befuddled by pangs of love. But she didn't care, as long as they were on their way out there.

The night was clear and the full moon was rising as they churned up the last part of the trail to the lodge. There were no lights on and Anthony pressed the horn in three long blasts expecting one of the staff to come out with a lantern, but there was only silence. He jumped out, gave the two farm boys torches, and signalled for them to follow him round the back of the building. Within a minute he had returned.

'The Land Rover's not here,' he said. 'Looks like something's gone wrong and Piet's not back. But there doesn't seem to be anyone else around either.'

He had his rifle loaded now and Hannah was out of the car, her revolver ready. Sarah trailed behind them, her legs shaking, a rising alarm threatening her ability to remain logical. They walked quickly through the reception area, flashing their torches into corners and around the back of the bar. But there was no sound. The viewing platform was in darkness, and none of the floodlights that lit the waterhole had been turned on. The place was deserted. Sarah could feel her heart hammering against her rib-cage, and her breath was coming in gasps. They searched the lounge and the dining room again, and then the kitchen and the storerooms. Nothing. Anthony made his way to the generator shed to turn on the lights. It was then that they discovered that all the wires and the radio line had been cut.

'Oh God, let me have made a mistake.' Sarah could no longer control her rising panic as she muttered her desperate prayer. 'Let me have made a fool of myself, please, dear God. Let him drive in now, and ask what the hell we're doing here and be angry with me. Let me see him, please. Just let him be safe.'

She ran back to the platform, straining her eyes to see what was below. For a second, she thought she caught a movement, down by the waterhole in deep shadow, and she leaned forward. As she did so, a heavy hand came down on her shoulder from behind. She screamed and whirled round to find herself face to face with Kipchoge. His eyes were wide and rolling and he gripped her shoulder with enormous force. His lips moved and a sound came from them, bubbling out in a rush of dark blood as he toppled to the floor at her feet.

'Kipchoge! Kipchoge! Oh Jesus! Kipchoge, answer me for God's sake! Where is Bwana Piet? Kipchoge, please . . . Oh God, don't die now. Tell me, tell me please what has happened!' Sarah was screaming the words, sobbing as she bent over the body, shaking him as his eyes disappeared into the back of his head, and she knew he was gone.

Anthony was beside her, lifting Kipchoge's head. His eyes were still wide open, and they saw in the torchlight that a series of murderous slashes had ripped through his whole body, almost severing one of his arms that dangled from his shoulder.

'He's dead, Sarah.' Anthony held the sobbing girl close to him, trying to calm her and to turn her head away from the horrible sight. 'I don't know how he survived long enough to get here. Was he able to say anything?'

Sarah shook her head, fear and revulsion rushing over her in waves. Anthony was looking over the ground.

'It must be poachers,' he said. 'But they don't seem to be armed. Only pangas, it looks like. Or they were saving their ammunition for something larger.'

Hannah was on her knees beside Kipchoge, her face like parchment in the moonlight.

'Where has he come from? How did he get here with those injuries? Piet must be nearby, because Kipchoge would never have left him, especially if he was hurt too.' She began to shout at the top of her voice, calling out his name with desperate terror, her voice rising to a shriek. 'Piet? Piet, where are you? Piet, answer me for God's sake! Piet?' She turned to Anthony. 'What about Simon? Maybe Piet and Simon went after the poachers. If there are too many of them, they'll have to hide. Oh God. Oh God, what is happening here, what's happening to us all?'

She had begun to sob hysterically when one of the farm workers appeared beside Anthony.

'Bwana, the Land Rover is behind some trees at the back of the stores. There has been a fight. Ole Sunde, the watchman, is there.'

'Where is he? Is he saying anything?' Anthony helped Hannah up and they ran down the steps and round to the stores. Piet's vehicle was parked deep in the clearing. Beside the open door lay his dog, her body sliced through with powerful blades. In her jaws she was still clenching fragments of cloth and what looked like flesh.

'She did for someone before she was finished,' Anthony said, resting his hand for a second on her big brown head. 'I hope she hurt him bad.'

Close to the staff quarters they found the watchman lying face down on the ground, a dark pool of blood gathering around his head.

'Jesus God Almighty,' Anthony said, turning over the old Maasai to find his eyes glazed in death.

He stood up abruptly and raced towards the stables, Sarah and Hannah running after him. They were empty, but here too they found signs of a struggle and the ground was trampled and bloodstained. Sarah clasped Hannah by the hand, feeling her trembling, hearing her teeth beginning to chatter. In the distance, the hyenas had begun their nocturnal cacophony, and their cackling laughter sounded obscene on the night air. Terror shot through Sarah's veins, making her limbs heavy and her vision blurred as she realised the danger.

'Quick. Quick, Anthony. If the hyenas have scent of the blood and

Piet's hurt . . . Or Simon . . . Oh God, Anthony, hurry.' Hannah had begun to sob.

They ran back to the Anthony's vehicle. Using the torches and the headlights, they began to follow the tracks left by the fugitives, driving carefully across the rough land, frantic to make speed, but afraid to lose the trail in the dark. As they broke free of the trees along the river, they heard the hyena pack in full cry. Sarah's blood ran cold and she clung to Hannah, listening to the sickening howls to the left of the road. Then one of the farm boys called out.

'Bwana! They have gone this way!' It was a narrow trail leading away from the pack, and after a moment Sarah realised where they were heading.

'This is the way to the ridge. Piet must be making for the ridge. Maybe they've found somewhere there that's safe to hide. Oh Jesus. Anthony, can we go any faster?'

'I can't risk it,' he said, hunched grim and tense over the steering wheel. 'The ground is very hard here and we could lose them, if for any reason they turned off the track.'

But as they climbed, Sarah was convinced that she was right. They came to the bottom of the scree, and she leapt from the car.

'Come on. Come on, they can't be that far ahead of us.'

'Sarah, stay back here, behind me,' Anthony ordered. 'Don't go on ahead without a weapon.'

But she was beyond fear as she ran on, branches snapping and whipping across her body, tearing at her skin. Behind her she could hear Anthony and Hannah calling her, but she drowned them out with her muttered prayers.

'Don't let him be the one who's hurt, God. Don't let anything have happened to him. Oh God, please, if You love us, don't take him from me now. Please . . .'

She broke out of the low bushes that surrounded the summit, and stood on the highest point of the ridge, staring around, frantic. Nothing. Then she felt it. A malevolence that chilled her, and she turned. A large male hyena stood in the rocks, staring at her. It was close, crouching low. She could see its massive jaws and the fetid stench of its breath stung her nostrils, making her gag. She stepped back, slowly, wondering if there would be time for Anthony or Hannah to reach her before it sprang. There

473

was no use running from it, over this ground. She stood still, mesmerised by the muscles bunching in the powerful shoulders, muzzle stripped back to show the teeth that could tear her apart. Then she heard a whirring sound and saw the flash that was a spear. The animal spun into the air and hurtled past her, knocking her to the ground as it fell, so that she found herself rolling down and across the rocks towards the dense scrub on the other side of the ridge. As she tumbled, she saw the man for a split second. A Kikuyu warrior was standing on the edge of a gully, his arm still drawn back from hurling his spear, naked except for his leg and arm ornaments, a leather loincloth and a ceremonial feathered headdress and collar. She landed with a sickening thud at the base of the rocks and heard the crunch of bone. There was an excruciating pain in her shoulder that shot down her arm, but in the seconds that followed it was forgotten.

In front of her, the ground had been cleared and a shallow pit dug. Lying in it, spreadeagled, was a man. His body had been slit open from the neck down, the contents of his stomach and his manhood cut away, so that the sweetish smell of blood and organs lingered on the wind. With terrible, rasping sobs, Sarah crawled towards the apparition. His hands, tethered to the ground with wooden stakes and creepers, were outspread as though in supplication. His blood had seeped on to the soil in grisly sacrifice, and was sticky and dull. His face was turned up to the moon, and the light shone on his empty eye sockets. Piet van der Beer was dead.

Sarah could hear herself howling like a desolate animal as she crawled into the pit beside him, trying with her one working arm to untie the thongs that held him to the ground. His blood was all over her as she leaned across him, talking to him incoherently, touching his hair and the ruins of his face and body. She was only vaguely aware of Anthony and the farm men lifting her from the pit, and the sound of Hannah's high-pitched, petrified wailing. She knew they were taking her away from Piet, and she fought to prevent it, flailing out with her arms and legs, screaming her horror. Then she found herself vomiting into the bush, bile and rage and terrible grief that spilled on to the earth to mingle with the blood of her dead love. She staggered towards the path and took hold of Hannah who had fallen into a trance of shock, her lips drawn back into a silent rictus of horror as she stumbled away from the barbarous place where her brother had died.

Chapter 25

Kenya, December 1965

The night moved in a series of fractured images, like camera stills lit by flashes of jarring sound and light. At the farm Lottie was waiting for them, her face ashen. It was Anthony who had to take her into his arms and try to explain to her the unimaginable thing that had happened. He guided Sarah and Hannah into the sitting room and sat them down, beside the fire. There was a confusion of voices, the sound of agonised weeping. Mwangi and Kamau came and went, tears streaming unheeded down their faces. They brought tea and coffee, and small dishes of food that Hannah had loved since childhood, and sandwiches that Lottie had taught them how to make a generation ago. Kamau stood behind Sarah as she sat numb and silent on the sofa, and every few minutes he reached down his hand and placed it on the top of her head in a gesture of shared grief and love. Any slight movement of her arm sent a searing pain through her shoulder, but she scarcely noticed it. Someone was asking questions that she could not comprehend. Hannah sat on the sofa staring into a void, her body rigid. Lottie was holding her daughter, murmuring something over and over. Anthony went to the telephone, and after a period of time, the police appeared and Jeremy Hardy was talking. Then the phone rang again, and Lottie was clinging to the receiver, sobbing into it, Anthony supporting her. Jan. They must be talking to Jan.

The pain in Sarah's shoulder began to penetrate the numbness of her mind and she concentrated on it, willing herself not to think beyond it. Dr Markham arrived from Nanyuki. He tried to coax her gently to her bedroom so that he could examine her, but she refused to move from the place she had chosen beside Hannah. He probed carefully for a few moments. Then he sat down beside her, telling her in his kindly voice that her shoulder was dislocated, that he knew that she did not want to be taken to the hospital right now. He was going to give her a local anaesthetic and try to push it back into place. Later, there was a shriek of pain which she realised came from within herself, and then the doctor was strapping her arm close against her side, and suggesting that she should come to the hospital for an X-ray in the morning. She struggled to sit upright and to respond, but her voice would not work properly and she could only shake her head, indicating that she must stay here with Hannah and Lottie. The doctor turned to search in his bag. His face was crumpled with sadness as he handed Sarah two tablets and held the glass of water for her, lifting it to her mouth as she swallowed.

Then he spoke to Hannah, reaching up to tap her face lightly, trying to get a reaction. It seemed only yesterday that he had brought her into the world, and her brother too. Jan and Lottie had been young then, like himself. They had all been so hopeful, so optimistic about their futures in such a blessedly endowed country. Now Hannah was staring through him, unblinking and outwardly calm. He filled a syringe and gave her an injection, but she did not flinch or appear to notice as the needle pierced her skin. Lottie stroked her hair, weeping soundlessly, her face a portrait of appalling desolation and grief. Sarah looked at them and a chill struck her, making her shake uncontrollably.

Anthony forced a tot of brandy between her lips. She seemed to be outside her own body, hovering somewhere beyond reality, removed from the gathering as Anthony moved about the room, directing everyone quietly, answering the telephone, tending to them all. Sarah observed herself from some great distance, half lying on the sofa, supported by cushions to keep her from moving her arm. Her shoes were muddied, her clothes torn and bloodstained. Piet's blood. *No! Don't go there. Don't say the name. Don't look. Don't look.* A wave of nausea overtook her, and she retched and tried to sit up. Anthony was at her side instantly, holding a small basin in his hand, seemingly able to anticipate each new crisis as it arose. He held her head over the bowl but only a small dribble of bile came up. She had already shed everything on the ridge. *Don't think about the ridge. Don't look. Don't look . . .* Anthony wiped her face and tucked a blanket tight around her. He left the bowl on the floor beside her and returned to Hannah's side. The policeman was talking again. When had he returned? Or even left the room? Sarah tried to concentrate on what he was saying, but the sound was distorted, as if he was speaking through a long tunnel.

'There was someone on the ridge, just a few yards from us,' Anthony was speaking now. 'He threw a spear, took down a bloody great hyena very close to Sarah. The leader of a pack. I caught the movement as the spear went through the air. I saw her falling and then she began to scream and when we got close to her we saw the . . .' He broke off, unable to continue, passing his hand across his eyes.

Jeremy Hardy waited for him to regain his composure. After a few minutes he prompted gently. 'So, you didn't get a look at him? The man on the ridge?'

'No. I went to help Sarah. When I looked up, he was gone.'

Sarah made an effort to speak, trying at first to clear her throat without success. Then her voice broke through, hoarse and choking. 'I saw him. The hyena was closing in on me. He killed it with his spear.'

They were looking at her now, Anthony and Lottie, and Hardy. Hannah remained unmoving, her gaze fixed and staring. Sarah felt her throat constrict as she forced herself to continue.

'He must have been waiting. Waiting for us to come up there. He was dressed like a warrior and he threw his spear at the hyena. Then I fell.' She choked again. The other hideous memory that she had blocked out moved suddenly into the forefront of her mind, and the nausea rose. 'But I saw his face. He was wearing a feathered headdress and I could see his face.' She saw him distinctly once more, etched against the skyline with the cold, bright moonlight shining into his eyes. She looked up at Anthony and Hardy.

'I knew him, you see,' she whispered. 'I knew him. It was Simon.'

'Simon?' Hardy leaned forward. 'My dear, are you absolutely sure? The light could have been deceptive. And there was the danger of the hyena, and then you were falling.'

'No. It was Simon. He had killed—' She could not say the name. 'I know he was the one. He was waiting for us to come.' Her voice broke in horror as she saw herself crouched over the pit, looking down at her love with his lifeblood seeping away into the earth. 'It was Simon,' she repeated. 'But I can't . . . why he would do that?' She began to sob incoherently, her body rocking to and fro, shaking with shock and fear and the terrible pain of loss. 'Oh God, why? Why would You let him do it? Dear God, why have You taken him away?'

'Simon is missing, Jeremy,' said Anthony. 'He went out with Piet this morning and he's the only one not accounted for.'

Hannah spoke for the first time, her words coming in a sibilant whisper. 'I want him dead,' she said, calm and cold at first, but as she repeated the phrase her voice rose into a scream. 'I want him dead. I want him dead . . .'

Lottie put her arms around her daughter and Anthony bent to put his hands on her shoulders, trying to offer strength and the comfort of love. Hannah looked at him, silent again, her eyes glazed, her hands clenched.

'I want him dead.'

Later in the night Sarah opened her eyes, realising that she had been sleeping fitfully. The fire was piled with logs, crackling and hissing, throwing out a great heat, but she was shivering again. Hardy had been gone for a while, but now he was back and talking quietly to Anthony and Lottie about bringing Piet's body down to the house. Hannah flung out her arm, gesturing to them as she tried to rise.

'No! We must not take him away from there,' she said. 'You all heard him, when we were on the ridge yesterday.' She looked at Sarah directly and her face collapsed, punctured by the memory. 'It was only yesterday. Ach, Jesus! Jesus!'

Anthony made her sit back against the cushions and she grabbed at his hands, looking into his eyes, pleading with him in her anguish.

'His blood has already soaked into the earth in the place that is his. Now his body should go with it. He should be a part of the ridge where he died. He said he wanted to be there when he died. You heard him, Anthony.' She was shaking the big man, her words rising to a wail of desperation. 'You were with us when he said it. Don't let anyone move him, Anthony, don't let them take him away to some cold place where he's shut in, away from his world.'

'Hannah, what do you want me to do? Do you want him buried up there? Is that it?'

She stood up. 'We should make a pyre. We should burn him up there and scatter his ashes over the ridge. Now.' She was making a chilling sound like moaning, raw with misery. 'Now. Tonight. To finish the pain. His terrible pain . . .'

She wrapped her arms around her body and began to sway, her eyes

478

shut, her voice murmuring something in Afrikaans. Lottie tried to hold her steady, to make her still. Hardy cleared his throat.

'Hannah, my dear girl, I understand what you are asking, but we can't do that. One, it wouldn't be legal. Two, there's the investigation. We have to bring in the body. And three, there will have to be an inquest. I'm sorry, Hannah, but—'

'No! No, you don't understand at all.' She reached out to clutch his arm. 'What can you want with his body, heh? Do you want to cut it up some more? Destroy what's left of him, with knives and steel instruments in some laboratory? Ach, Jeremy, you've seen how he was killed and there is nothing else you need to know. The only thing we can do now, to give him peace, is to burn him on the ridge where he wanted to be. And then his ashes will float across our land and set him free. Please, Jeremy, don't lock him away in a morgue, in a dark closed-in place where he would hate to be. Please.'

In her acute distress, her breath had begun to come in heaving gasps, and Dr Markham stepped foward to monitor her pulse and to persuade her to sit down again. Then he took Hardy out on the verandah, out of earshot.

'It's not as strange an idea as you might think, old chap. If they take the body away for a post mortem, and to carry out further investigations, it could be weeks before they release it for burial. We all know that. In the meantime, we have the whole family in a state of shock that can be seriously damaging. It's impossible to know the real effects of what these young girls have just witnessed, and to prolong those memories could do irreparable harm. For the sake of the whole family, I urge you to consider it. A cremation on the site where he died could be a merciful thing for them all. It would be a catharsis, some sort of end to an appalling situation. It would give them an opportunity to grieve in the way they think best.'

'It's highly irregular, and there's something deeply primitive about it,' Hardy said, shaking his head. 'God, what a bloody awful thing. Even during the emergency I never saw anything like this, although it has the hallmarks of those bastards and their savagery.'

'Come on, Jeremy,' Dr Markham lowered his voice, to be sure that only the inspector could hear him. 'I would be really concerned for Hannah's mental state if this should drag on, and for Sarah Mackay too. She'd only just got engaged to him. What they saw was beyond any reasonable human capacity to absorb and survive. We don't want another, indirect victim in either of these young women. They're in a pretty bad way already. Look, I'm willing to sign the death certificate and make a statement saying that the body was too mutilated to be removed from the place of death. It's not that far from the truth, anyway. This young man is lying up there on the ridge, pegged out like a sacrificial goat, with his organs cut away, and no eyes in the sockets. If the body is retained, pending a coroner's inquest, that's what the family will be forced to think about, to focus on, every day. Because it wouldn't be finished. I don't think a young, impressionable mind can hold out in circumstances like that. I'm sure you could square it with the authorities.'

'I don't know. I agree with your reasoning, and I've known Hannah and Piet since they were teenagers, admired the whole family for their hard work. But there are regulations.' The policeman rubbed his eyes, exhausted and sickened by the night's events.

'Look here, you may already know who's responsible for this, if what poor Sarah says is true. God knows what his motives were, and it may take you a while to find out. But in the meantime, you should allow the family to cremate Piet, and then you can concentrate on catching this bastard and be finished with it.'

The inspector hesitated, deeply troubled, as Anthony stepped out from the shadows to join them.

'Forgive me, but I've been listening,' he said. 'If I may say so, I agree with Dr Markham. I can prepare the fire. There's a lot of dry brushwood all around the site. If you give us the go-ahead, I'll do it. Now. Tonight. You have all the witnesses you need as to the state he was left in, and I suppose you've already been up there with your cameras, or you'll go at first light. Surely you can release the body to the family in such circumstances?'

Hardy looked at them both, reflecting, and then returned to the sitting room where he spoke directly to Lottie. 'What about you, my dear?' he said to her. 'What is it you want to do for your son? Do you really want to cremate him, up there on the ridge? Is that what you truly want?'

She nodded, her eyes filled with tears as she stroked her daughter's head. 'Yes,' she said in a low voice. 'It's what I want. It's right.'

'But don't you think you should wait for Jan? You've spoken to him already, I gather. When will he be able to get here? I take it you would want him to be here for — well, for any ceremony.'

480

'He couldn't talk to me. I had to ring a friend to go over and stay with him for the night. I asked her to phone in the morning.' She began to cry. 'But he won't be here, Jeremy. I'm afraid he will not come.'

'All right then,' Hardy sighed and bent to touch Lottie's ice-cold hand. 'I'll leave a couple of askaris on the ridge for tonight with your men, to protect the – to protect your son. He was a very fine young man, Piet, and I admired him no end. I always enjoyed his company and I was proud to be his friend.'

'We can't wait long,' Dr Markham urged. 'For obvious reasons. If you are going to allow this, then the sooner it happens the better.'

'I'll have to file a report tonight. And I must go back up there and give instructions to the askaris. If this Simon was hanging around instead of making a run for it, then he could still be a threat. I'll put police guards on the farm, while we hunt him down. No one here is safe until we find him. Can you give me a couple of good trackers for dawn, Anthony, to see if we can catch up with him?'

When Hardy had left, the doctor stayed on at the house, nursing a cup of black coffee, watching Hannah solicitously. She had sunk back into a state that seemed catatonic and she did not seem to register any word or action. Sarah sat up straight, wedged against cushions, her shoulder a pounding, relentless pain.

'You need another painkiller now, Sarah,' he said. 'And then I'd like you to try and lie back a bit into these cushions so that you can sleep. I'd suggest that you might be better in your bed, but I'm sure you'd all prefer to be here together. I can give you a sedative too, you know, like the one I've given Hannah?'

But Sarah shook her head and for the remainder of the night she drifted in and out of a nightmarish doze, jerking into wakefulness with every new sound. Mwangi and Kamau came and went through the long hours, their faces grey with misery as they tried to minister to the family they loved, mourned with them for the young bwana whose future had been entwined with their own. Sarah's body was stiff through fighting her pain and fatigue. Whatever Dr Markham had given Hannah had sent her into a deep sleep, and she lay on the other sofa covered by a blanket, her head resting on her mother's lap. Lottie did not seem to have stirred at all. She stared into the embers of the fire, her eyes dark with tragedy. There was no sign of Anthony. Later, when Sarah woke again to the crackle of a falling log, Lottie's head was bowed as if in defeat, and her eyes had finally closed.

As the dawn broke Anthony returned with Hardy. Sarah tried to sit up, her shoulder ablaze with pain, her mind whirling through the barbarous images of the night. There were questions she wanted to ask, but Anthony touched her lips gently with his finger as he sat down beside her.

'We've wrapped him in cloth,' he said in a low voice, so that he would not wake Lottie and Hannah. His face was grim from the tragic office that he had performed for his friend. 'I took linen sheets from the lodge and wrapped him in them. We've constructed a pyre on the top of the ridge – the *watu* came from all around, and helped me build it. Jeremy will not stand in our way. He's a decent man and an old friend of the family, and he'll do whatever he can to make this what you all want it to be.'

'But why would Simon have done this? Why? Piet gave him every chance. I talked to him about it yesterday, before they left. I gave Simon a book. Oh God.' She could not prevent the onslaught of sobbing and she put her hands over her face to muffle the sound.

'We saw the footprints,' Anthony said. 'Where he was standing when you fell. And the hyena is there, with the spear, which will have fingerprints. But there's no trace of Simon. The *watu* are spooked by it – they say he has taken the spirit of the hyena, and escaped into the bush. By daylight we should be able to make out more, find his tracks. We'll get him, I do promise you that.' He touched her hair, smoothing it from her forehead. 'Are you in a lot of pain?'

'It's all right as long as I don't move too suddenly. Dr Markham thinks I need to go to the hospital for an X-ray. But I don't want to leave here. It's not important right now . . .'

'And Hannah? Has she been asleep since?'

'Yes. I woke a few times, but she hasn't moved. Poor Lottie was awake till about an hour ago. Oh God. Oh God, Anthony!' A wave of desolation swamped her and she began to cry again, no longer heeding the sleeping forms beside her. 'I can't live through this! I wish I'd died up there with him. I wish I'd gone with him in the morning and we could have ended our lives there together. Because I can't go on. We were just beginning and I can't do it alone. I don't want to do it alone, living every moment that he isn't here. Knowing that he'll never be here. I just want to die, Anthony.'

'No,' Anthony said. 'You can't think like that. None of us must think in that way. You must be brave now for him, and to help Hannah and Lottie. We must carry each other through this terrible thing. Promise me you will not say those things again, and never in front of them.'

'But you don't know,' she said piteously. 'You can't know, and I hope you never will. He loved me, Anthony. We loved each other. We were like one person, one life starting out with the same dream.' Sarah shut her eyes. 'He said he'd be in touch around sunset. It was hard to be apart for even a moment in the day, because we'd only just found our way. That's why I was so uneasy. I knew he wouldn't have been late. I should have gone up there right away. When I started to feel something was wrong, I should have trusted my instinct. Gone to the ridge instead of . . .'

'You couldn't have known. None of us could have imagined anything like this. He was with Simon and Kipchoge. No one could have suspected . . .' He stopped and turned to see Hannah, sitting upright on the sofa, watching him. 'Han, you're awake.'

She stared at him in silence, then she said, 'If we had gone earlier, if we had listened to Sarah and gone straight away, we could have saved him, couldn't we?' Her voice rose, and she tore at the blanket and threw it aside. 'Couldn't we?'

Anthony looked at Sarah, a silent plea in his eyes. He took Hannah's wrists and turned her towards him so that she had to look directly into his eyes.

'Listen to me, Hannah,' he said. 'It would have been too late. He was dead when we got there. Piet had been dead for some time. And with his injuries I don't think any doctor could have done anything for him. I don't think he would have wanted . . .' His head dropped and he spoke with terrible sadness. 'Han, my darling, I am so sorry to say those words to you. But if we had reached him, we would only have kept him with us for a short time of pain. Another hour or two at most, and suffering.'

Hannah stared at him, then over at Sarah. Her face was ghost white. 'Is he right?' she asked, her voice strained and hoarse.

Sarah drew a long breath. She had been in the pit. She had felt him, held him, touched his mutilated form. The blood that oozed from his terrible wounds on to the ground had not yet congealed and she had smelled the sweet, sickly odour of it. There were no insects around or in his body. The hyena had just arrived, drawn by the scent of fresh blood. It would not have taken the animal long to find the pit. But there could be no sense or

483

reason for Hannah to torture herself, to spend her life in a series of hopeless, bitter regrets for what might have been. It was plain what Anthony was silently asking, clear that Piet could only have lived through hours of additional torture, blind and mangled and damaged beyond repair.

'Han, we were far too late,' Sarah said in a low voice that was firm. 'There was nothing we could have done, even if we had left here straight away . . .'

Tears welled as she uttered the words. She should have insisted on leaving the farm when she had first felt that disquiet, when he did not call in. She would carry this guilt and remorse within herself for all her years to come. If she had been there in time there might have been some small thing she could have done for him. At least she could have said goodbye, whispered her love into his dying consciousness, eased his unimaginable pain. But Anthony was right. Had he survived, her beloved Piet would have been a crippled wreck, a helpless invalid, his sight gone, his beautiful face and body disfigured, his limbs useless. What life would he have had? She saw again his bloody face and eye sockets, staring into the black cavern of the night. With a stabbing, twisting horror, Sarah wondered how long he had suffered, whether he had been conscious to the end, how much pain he had had to endure. She doubled over, feeling his agony ripping through her, and when she began to vomit into the bowl she felt Hannah's arms around her shoulders. They sat together in silence until their closeness was interrupted by the sound of the phone, loud, insistent. A cold fear settled on Sarah as Anthony picked up the receiver, but she knew that there could be nothing more to hurt them now. They had suffered everything that any human being might be asked to endure.

Anthony had wakened Lottie and he handed her the phone. She listened for a short while and then shook her head. She was still holding the telephone to her ear when she said his name.

'Janni? Janni, I'm coming dear, yes. I'll come as soon as I can. Just wait for me now, wait and I'll be there soon. I don't know, but very soon. I promise you.'

Hannah leapt to her feet and snatched the telephone, her voice rising with misery and anger.

'Pa? No, Pa, no! You can't do this. You can't take her away from me. Not now. You have to come here to help us. You can't leave me here alone.' She listened for a moment and then began to scream down the telephone. 'No. I won't leave here. I won't run away like you did. And I need Ma now. You can't take her away from me, you bastard.'

Lottie took the telephone from her and spoke quietly into it for a few moments. Hannah returned to her chair by the fire, her face blank, and when her mother came to stand beside her she turned her head away and closed her eyes.

Much later Hardy returned to the house to find the sorrow and anguish so overwhelming that he could feel its power settle on him as he came through the door. Anthony took him aside.

'We have to go ahead, Jeremy. There's no chance that Jan will come back here now. Lottie wants to fly down there, leave as soon as she can, to be with him. He's in very bad shape, out of his mind with grief over his son, on the edge of God knows what. She'll probably want to leave tomorrow, to deal with the situation. I want you to tell me I can go out to the ridge now, Jeremy. Let them have their cremation. Finish it today. Right now. Everything is ready.'

The policeman nodded, making no comment, appalled at the chaos and tragedy that washed around him.

'I know there's nothing I can say that will be of any help. There are no words. Lottie, my dear, I'll organise the paperwork later. But we'll go now, up to the ridge, and pay our last respects to Piet. Your son and my friend.'

As they came out on to the verandah, they were greeted by a great assembly of the house staff and all the workers from the farm. Since daybreak they had been gathering on the lawn around the front of the house, heads bowed and silent, standing and waiting all through the night since the news had come in. There were gifts of eggs, woven baskets of fruits and vegetables, fresh bread from open fires, flowers from the slopes of the mountain, beaded necklaces and bracelets, carved platters and gourds and clay pots of food, placed on the ground and up the steps of the verandah. The crowd surged forward, weeping openly, reaching out to touch the hands of Lottie and Hannah and Sarah as they came down into the garden, pressing Anthony's arm as he went ahead to make way for the women. Hannah stood still on the verandah steps, frozen and unseeing as Lottie moved among her people, holding each hand, thanking them for their sympathy, for their gifts, assuring them that Bwana Piet would be honoured by their thoughts, expressing her sadness for the families of

Kipchoge and Ole Sunde who had died with her son. Anthony returned and touched Hannah on the shoulder, speaking softly into her ear.

'Let them share it with you, Hannah. They loved him too, and they need to show you.'

She moved like a sleepwalker and Anthony followed, his hand supporting her back, as though he feared she would topple over in the press of people reaching out to touch them. Sarah walked behind Lottie, feeling the isolation of being a friend, not yet one of the family. Never now to be one of the family. She had almost been Piet's wife. So close. She shut her eyes against the pain and then she heard Mwangi's soft voice.

'Memsahib Sarah, I grieve for you. He was your man. I have seen this and we were all happy for you and for him.'

'Mwangi. Thank you, Mwangi.' She took his gnarled hands and held on to him, drawing strength from his understanding and affection and loyalty as he walked beside her, moving on into the assembly, still clinging to him as she made her way towards the waiting cars. All around them they heard a gentle swell, a humming that began as a soft harmony of voices before the sound rose in volume and rhythm into a swaying hymn of love and loss and remembrance of the young man they had all known. He had carried their security and their hopes with him, and now he was gone and they wanted to share in mourning his departure, to sing him into peace.

Sarah remembered nothing of the drive to the ridge, or even the climb from the end of the track to the summit. A shroud of misery had wrapped itself around her, suffocating her so that she could not even help Hannah up the last steep section of ground. It was all she could do to concentrate on putting one foot in front of the other, oblivious to the pain of her shoulder and the thorn bushes that scratched her legs, catching her trousers in their spikes from time to time so that she had to tear the fabric in order to continue. When they reached the top of the ridge, she was standing once more where they had spent their last evening together, looking out across the plains. Below her the curl of the river remained the same, the lodge still stood on the kopje, and in the blue distance she saw the roof of Langani and the stern, unmoving silhouette of the mountain. She could hear the morning call of birds, the rustle of monkeys gathering berries and seeds in the trees around her, the busy creaking of frogs and cicadas. It all sounded so normal, except for the ragged breathing of Hannah and Lottie, as they stood at the base of Piet's funeral pyre.

Anthony had piled the brushwood very high. Piet's body, wrapped in its linen shroud, had been placed in the centre of the pyre, with further layers of wood above him. The sticks were bound in bundles and laid, crosswise, with a precision that was beautiful. The bush had been cleared back for some distance, to prevent the fire from jumping into the surrounding trees once it had been lit. A series of large drums filled with water had been placed around the edge of the clearing, in case the platform threatened to burn out of control. Four of Hardy's most trusted askaris stood to attention as a guard of honour around the edifice, rifles loaded. Juma, Kamau and Mwangi walked into the cleared space, followed by the remainder of the farm labourers, and everyone stood together before Piet's tower, heads bowed. The morning sun beat down on the quiet scene, turning brassy as it rose in a cloudless sky. Anthony and Sarah held fast to Hannah and Lottie, and each of them reached out to touch the wood. Lottie pressed a bouquet of flowers from her garden into the lattice work. Her voice was low and trembling, but she reached into her own deep resources of love and bravery to say her words.

'Sleep now, my darling son. I will always hold you in my heart, my Piet, as I held you to my breast when you were born. You never wanted to leave this place and now you will rest here for ever. Be at one with this land that you loved, my only son, my first-born, beloved boy . . .'

The tears made runnels down her cheeks, but she was unaware of them as she turned from the pyre, to put her arms around her daughter and Sarah, her daughter-to-be. Hannah stood erect, her head high, staring up at the crest of the tower, her arms rigid at her side. Anthony put his hand on her shoulder in a gesture of comfort, but she flinched and he moved away. High above them Sarah could see a circling vulture, curious, watchful, ready to signal to the rest of the scavengers of the bush. She shuddered. Perhaps they should say prayers now for Piet, ask God to receive him. But her soul was a wasteland, and it seemed to her that God was dead, that it was futile, because her earlier prayers for Piet's safety had gone unheard, that the heavens were empty and her faith had turned to dust. They were going to burn him now, so that he would be gone from her into the ether on a hot wind and she would never see him again. She had not told him clearly enough, often enough, the extent of her love for him. Her loss was like a sword run through her belly. She was afraid that if she cried out now she would scream and scream, until the land was crusted with her grief as the ground beneath Piet had been crusted with his blood. She clamped her lips together, biting down until she could taste her own blood in her mouth.

Jeremy Hardy cleared his throat. 'Do you want to say anything, before we . . . Lottie or Hannah? Or would you, Sarah? Anthony?'

Anthony looked at them, but they remained silent. Lottie shook her head. Hannah did not move.

'Then I will say this for us all,' Anthony spoke out clearly in Swahili, so that all the workers could hear him. 'The man who died here was a great man. He was my fellow worker and my closest and most honourable friend. I have been privileged to know him. Bwana Piet was a man of vision, a man of integrity. He saw his country and his land as a gift to be worked and shared, and made plentiful for us. And he did that to his last breath. We cannot understand the reason for his death.' His voice cracked and there was a pause as he composed himself. 'The waste of it, and the manner of his death are things that have not yet been revealed to us. We do not yet know why this has happened, but we will find the man who committed this terrible act and bring him to justice. Now, we give Piet van der Beer, the beloved son of Bwana Jan and Mama Lottie, the brother of Hannah, the man promised to Sarah, and my own finest friend, back to the earth that he loved from the day he was born on this land. And we wish him peace, after his untimely going.'

He signalled to Juma to come forward with cans of petrol, which they sprinkled over the timber. Then Kamau and Mwangi brought lighted brands and thrust them into the pyre. In a roar of flames the tower ignited, so that the mourners had to step back from the searing heat that formed an orange ball and rose into the African morning. The Kikuyu men began to sing, a deep-throated hum, interspersed with sounds resembling the animals of the wild, and the women's voices rose to join them in a long, ululating wail. A group of Maasai herders stepped forward and placed ceremonial spears and shields into the fire. Hardy gave the signal for his askaris to fire several rounds into the air. Fragmented lines from the psalms that Sarah had recited at school sprang, suddenly, into her mind. She found her voice, and over the crackle and spit of the burning wood, she called out the words, very loud and clear above the sound of the fire.

For my days pass away like smoke,
And my bones burn like a furnace.
My heart is smitten like grass, and withered;
I am like a vulture in the wilderness,
Like an owl in the waste places;
I eat ashes like bread
And mingle tears with my drink,
For thou hast taken me up and thrown me away.
My days are like an evening shadow;
I wither away like grass. . . .
My God, My God, Why have you forsaken us?

They stood together on the ridge till the last embers had died and only the ashes were left. Then Juma signalled his men, and they poured sand and earth on to the remnants of the fire, to quench it. As the last wisps of smoke died, they walked in procession down the track.

Chapter 26

London, December 1965

'I don't want to be here for Christmas. In London, I mean.' Marina looked at her husband, biting her lip, on the brink of tears. 'It's too much, George. I'm so tired. I didn't know I'd be this tired. I was so glad when I was allowed home that I thought I'd be able to do anything. But just having visitors today has made me see that I haven't the strength to talk to people. I don't want to see any more friends. I look so frightful. I could see their faces – the shock and the pity – and I can't face it. Please, George. Let's go down to Burford tomorrow and stay there until the new year.' Her lip quivered and her hands moved across the bedspread, clutching the quilted silk.

Camilla sat down on the end of the bed. 'Mother, we can't just up and disappear into the country. And things have been organised just like Daddy says.'

'You can ring everyone and tell them I'm not well enough for tomorrow. It's only special friends, darling. They'll understand.'

'It's not a question of that,' Camilla said. 'Dr Ward said yesterday that you could come home because there's medical help nearby. That's not something we can arrange in Burford, two days before Christmas.'

Marina sat up and smiled. 'I know, darling. But I've worked it all out. Edward could come with us.' There was a childish triumph in her words and the effect they had on her daughter.

'I'm sure Edward has other plans for Christmas,' Camilla said. 'Besides, there's nowhere for him to stay.'

'There's the Bear,' Marina said.

'We're not going to ask Edward to spend Christmas in some awful room above a pub in Burford. It's an insane idea. Let's just cancel the drinks tomorrow and spend a quiet Christmas here on our own.'

'George, please do this for me.' Marina turned a beautifully tragic face to her husband. 'Please. I don't want our last Christmas to be in this flat. I don't like the city any more. It makes me nervous and panicky, with all the noise and mess and hurry, and the buses and cars hurtling past. I know they're outside and far away really, but they frighten me. I want to be somewhere calm and quiet. Please, George.' Marina had begun to cry.

'I'm going to make some tea,' Camilla said.

She felt a terrible compassion for her mother, but it was mixed with annoyance at Marina's endless ability to manipulate. Even now, with death staring her in the face, hovering beside her as she took each slow, unsteady step, she was capable of controlling their lives and thoughts. Dr Ward had opposed the idea of her being discharged from the hospital. She was still in pain, weak from the pneumonia, responding too slowly to the antibiotics. It was sheer will power, he said, that had kept her alive through the crisis. On the other hand, the most important thing was to make her comfortable, and to keep her spirits up. She had argued with him, forceful and piteous and charming in turns, until he agreed that it might be better for her state of mind if she was at home for Christmas. But now that was not enough, and she wanted to be taken to the country.

George emerged from the bedroom. 'Do you think we could do it?' he said.

'It's not remotely feasible, for God's sake.' Camilla's annoyance surfaced as she saw that he was determined to indulge Marina. 'I'm certainly not going to ring Edward and try to blackmail him into spending Christmas in the boondocks with us.'

'Your mother says he's in love with you,' George said.

'You seem to have conveniently forgotten that I was in love with someone else, very recently. You can't turn love off like a tap, or change lovers as you would change your shirt. Well, I can't anyway.' She saw the shock in his eyes and was grimly pleased to have wounded him. 'Edward is a doctor who's going to fix my face. And he's old enough to be my father, as he pointed out himself.'

'Did he now? So this has already come up?' He was smiling a little, trying to encourage her to confide in him. But her face froze in resentment and he realised with sadness that he could not tease her yet. First he had to regain her love and respect, and he was a long way from that. 'Well, we definitely have to cancel the drinks party. And then we'll see. I said we'd discuss Burford later and she seemed happy with that. She's going to rest for an hour or so, and then get up for dinner.'

Camilla reached for her coat. 'Will you phone around and cancel your chums then? I need to go out for a while. Mrs Maskell has everything ready for dinner tonight.'

He looked at her with sorrow, aware that she had no desire to be alone with him. 'Yes, I'll do that. And I'll see you later. For dinner perhaps?'

She had nowhere to go, and she wandered among the hordes of shoppers as they wrestled with cumbersome packages and searched for last-minute gifts, or prayed for an empty taxi. The shops were crowded and the insistent blinking of Christmas decorations spilled out on to the pavements to create random patches of light on dragging feet. Camilla had no present for her father, nor could she think of anything she wanted to buy for him. But it would be bad for all of them if he were to receive no gift on Christmas morning, so she made her way into an expensive shop and chose a silver hip flask in a calfskin cover, and an Italian leather flight bag that he could use on his endless comings and goings. Or on his overnight stays with his lover. When she returned to the flat she found Marina dressed and sitting on the sofa, a drink in her hand. Her face was waxen, but her eyes were bright as she greeted Camilla.

'Darling, there's a glass of champagne for you. We're celebrating because Daddy's arranged everything beautifully. We're going to Burford tomorrow. Around twelve, because it takes me an age to get myself together these days. Will you help me to pack a few things tonight?'

'I've organised a car and driver to pick us up,' George said. 'If I need to come back to town before the new year, I'll take a train up. But it's unlikely.' He stopped and made an elaborate task of pouring Camilla's champagne. He glanced at Marina, but she had found something of interest in the newspaper, and he was left to flounder on alone. 'Edward will drive down and join us tomorrow evening. He's spoken to Dr Ward and they've worked things out in case of emergencies. He seems to be happy with the whole idea.'

It was Camilla's idea of a nightmare and a farce. She tried to imagine them all in the sitting room in Burford, deliberately and falsely cheerful, playing out a charade for a spoiled, dying woman. Now there was no way that she could get out of being there. She was a pawn again in her parents' sparring match, and there was nothing she could do but accept her role.

'You shouldn't have done this,' she said after dinner, as she packed Marina's clothes. 'I think you should telephone and say you've changed your mind. It's so unfair on Edward.'

'He said he'd be delighted.' Marina was pouting.

'What else could he say, for heaven's sake? Honestly, Mother, you have no limits.'

'If he doesn't want to join us and you think it would be such a trial, then we'll ask Winston Hayford. I know he's free for Christmas and he wouldn't mind being with me.'

'You're sick. Your mind is sick.'

Camilla spun out of the room and flung on her coat, passing her father in the sitting room as he sat staring vacantly at the flickering screen of the television. At Tom's flat the crowded party was in full cry, but he saw her right away and pushed his way towards her, taking her to one side.

'There's someone I want you to meet. His name's Saul Greenberg and he's been in my office half the afternoon. He has a proposal for us.'

'Not tonight, Tom, for heaven's sake. It's Christmas, in case you haven't noticed, and I'm going to the country with Mother tomorrow, on nursing duty. Tonight I just want to have a drink and smoke a little, and get myself psyched up for it all.'

'This is important,' he insisted, handing her a glass filled with ice and vodka.

'I'm Saul Greenberg. I'm in the rag trade.' A large man with a handsome, fleshy face had joined them. 'Has Tom told you about the deal?' He had an open, good-tempered expression and grey hair that had been cut very short, so that he looked as though a forest of toothbrushes was growing out of his head. His suit was well tailored and made from expensive silk, although it was a little tight. He sounded American, but Camilla was not sure.

'No, Tom hasn't told me anything,' Camilla said. 'I don't want to seem rude, but I'm not interested in talking about a business proposal tonight. I'm not here on business. Strictly off duty. In the new year perhaps we—'

He simply ignored her snub. 'I'd like to start a dress label, using your name. Have you do all the pictures for the range, get the clothes into the main American department stores. I have another company, and a partner in the United States that's mad for this deal. I'm from New York

493

originally, but I've been in London for twenty years. It's big bucks for you, with generous modelling fees and a cut of all the sales. The clothes are all ready to go for the spring season, so I need to know right away if you're interested. I need to have everything ready to roll after the holidays. I thought we could meet tomorrow morning and discuss this.'

Tom had placed a hand on her arm, squeezing hard, hurting her and leaving a red mark on her skin.

'It could be an interesting project for you, Camilla,' he said. 'Saul would like us to come to his office and warehouse tomorrow, so that he can take us around. Show us the lines he already does and the quality of the stuff. They're designed for the budget market. Made for this whole idea of buying up-to-date clothes cheaply, and being able to replace them twice as often. We're talking about hundreds of thousands of garments here, and the advertising to go with them.'

'I'm going to the country in the morning,' she said. 'I'll be there until after the new year.'

'You could go down in the afternoon. Straight after lunch.' Tom was glaring at her.

'Sure you could,' said Greenberg affably. 'I have a car and driver that can take you anywhere. But I'd like a couple of hours in the morning, to talk this over with you guys. I'm flying to New York tomorrow night.'

'I'm sorry,' Camilla said. 'After Christmas, maybe.'

She turned her back on them both and drifted away to join a small group standing in a fog of sweet-smelling smoke. As she accepted the joint and pulled on it, she heard Tom's angry voice in her ear.

'Are you crazy? This man can make you huge amounts of money. I know his lines and they sell. All you have to do is put your name on the bloody label and you get a cut of every dress that every little shop girl buys, to look like you. Not only here but in the States as well. Plus there's the shoot that he'd like to do in New York. You're not thinking straight. In fact, you're not thinking at all. Of what this can do for you.'

'Of what it can do for you, you mean.'

'Don't be bloody stupid, darling. You haven't many bookings right now, and when you disappear to have your face fixed in March you won't have any at all for a few weeks, at the very least. I'm sick of trying to sell you to reluctant photographers and magazines. You need to get back on track, Camilla. I'm fed up making up excuses when you don't answer your phone, and I can't confirm whether you're available or not. This guy doesn't seem to care about any of that. In fact, it suits him that his dresses and the advertising pictures will come out when you probably can't take on any other work. Gives him an exclusive, he says. And I, too, have to make a living, in case you had forgotten. Of course I'll take a percentage for setting up the deal and handling the arrangements. I'm your agent after all. But you'll make a fortune, for Christ's sake. So get down off your fucking pedestal, and be nice to the man.'

She stared at him for a moment through a swirl of smoke. 'I didn't want to travel down with the parents tomorrow anyway,' she said, suddenly contrite. There weren't many people willing to look out for her. Maybe not any. 'What time in the morning?'

'Eleven o'clock in Golden Square. Here's his card with the address. I'll see you there.'

Camilla finished her drink and left the party. When she put her key in the door of the flat she was glad to find that the lights were out in the sitting room and her father had gone to bed. After her initial relief at seeing him in the hospital she had carefully avoided any occasion when he might be inclined to try and explain himself. For his part, he had realised that he must proceed with extreme caution, to salvage something from the catastrophe of their previous encounter. As yet there was no real communication between them, beyond the crucial priority of Marina. Camilla poured herself a vodka and reached for the telephone.

'I hope it's not too late to phone you,' she said.

'It's not even midnight, so it's certainly not late for you,' Edward said. 'I suppose you're calling about tomorrow. Marina told me you'd be furious, but believe me I'm pleased to be getting away. I'm not fond of Christmas. Normally I lock myself in the flat and watch television. It's not an ideal time of the year for a solitary old bachelor.'

'You won't be quite so pleased when you see the Bear Inn in Burford, with its fake beams and commercial traveller's carpeting,' Camilla said. 'And God knows what the plumbing is like.'

He laughed, relieved that she had accepted the idea of his presence with none of the awkwardness or resentment he had anticipated.

'What time are you leaving tomorrow?' she asked. 'Could you give me a lift down? I've got a last-minute appointment in the morning, so I won't be going with the parents, although I could take a train.'

'I can't leave until after four. I'd love to drive you down, but I must warn you that the traffic will be bad. You might be stuck in gridlock with me for days. Everyone will be escaping for Christmas.' His heart had started to churn and jump in his chest, making him feel foolish. Making him smile. 'Where shall I collect you?'

'From their flat,' she said. 'Around five would be fine. Thanks. Night.'

It took an hour to work out a deal with Saul Greenberg, and three hours to have lunch with him afterwards. His shrewd business sense and dark humour appealed to Camilla, and she understood the enormously profitable step she was taking. Her income would double if the clothes that bore her name were successful. She would be the focus of an advertising campaign on both sides of the Atlantic, and her photograph would be on magazines covers and billboards. After the new year there would be a fashion shoot in New York. Tom was barely able to contain his jubilation as they raised their glasses to toast the new partnership.

But it was plain that Greenberg's interest was not confined to their business dealings. He questioned Camilla about her family background, her African childhood and her life in London. At first she was irritated by his attempts to see into her private life, but he was engaging and he had no pretensions so she found it difficult to remain aloof or to resent his interest. Tom sat in silence for most of the meal, listening to things she had never talked about during the time they had worked together, wondering how the man had managed to extract so much personal information from Camilla in so short a time. They parted in Berkeley Square, Camilla refusing an offer of a chauffeured limousine to take her home, or even to Burford.

'I like him,' she said to Edward as they crawled through the evening traffic, everyone fleeing London. 'He's very clever, apparently, but with a reputation for being honest. Straightforward, at any rate. And if this thing is successful, I have another dimension to my life. I'm not dependent just on my face and my body. So we've agreed that his lawyer can draw up a contract for us to sign. We'll go to New York in mid-January to shoot the clothes. Tom will come too as my manager. It should be fun.'

Camilla was elated, her face glowing with excitement and the challenge of the new enterprise. It was something she had never thought of, and now she was impatient for Christmas and New Year to be over so that she could get started on this new venture. There was a chance now to learn business skills that she had never considered necessary before, and she had mentioned her interest in designing clothes as well as wearing them. Greenberg was enthusiastic on all fronts.

'And we'll be able to take care of your scar in the spring,' Edward said.

'Yes. I'm so limited in what I can do, looking like this. I could get it done in New York, I suppose. We'll see how it all fits in.'

He was shocked at her casual announcement. He wanted desperately to heal her with his own hands, to make her perfect again, so that she would be grateful to him, see how much he cared for her. 'We can set a date, you know. In March sometime.' But she did not answer, and when he looked across at her, he saw that she had fallen asleep.

By the time they reached Burford, Marina was resting, exhausted by the journey. But when Camilla went upstairs to see her, she was forced to admit that the whole exercise has been a good idea. Her mother's face was relaxed, displaying a contentment that was new.

'I sleep so well down here,' she said. 'Is Edward all right? Have you been to the Bear?'

'No. We came straight here. Daddy will go down there with him, after dinner. They'll have a nightcap together.'

'He's a charming man,' Marina said. 'Do you think you and Edward—?'

'No, Mother. I don't think about that at all.' She wondered why no one could understand her sense of loss, her longing for Anthony, the misery and humiliation of his rejection. 'Things are looking good for me in my work. I had a stroke of luck this morning, thanks to Tom. I met this man who manufactures clothes and he wants to name an entire collection after me. I'll be going to New York in the new year for the photos, and to set up all the advertising. He thinks we can get good coverage on television and in the big magazines.'

'I hope you're clever enough to understand his way of doing things,' Marina said. 'It will be quite different from anything you've experienced, especially if you're going to New York. They're all so brash over there. So mad about money and more money. You need to be careful, Camilla.'

'Apparently he has a good reputation. After New York I can have my scar removed. Maybe I'll even do it there.'

'Edward would be hurt by that, Camilla. I can see that he's in love with you.'

'Mother, can't you try and understand that I don't want to get involved with *anyone*? Not now or any time soon.'

For a moment Marina lay with her eyes shut and Camilla wondered if she had fallen asleep. Then she reached out and took Camilla by the hand. 'He wasn't good enough for you. He wasn't right. Lovely for a little romance on holiday, but he has no depth. An empty young man. Your father said he'd seen him in Nairobi on this last trip. He told me about the girl. You must put Africa behind you now, darling. It's time to forget all the sadness and danger and violence.'

'Daddy saw Anthony?'

'Didn't he tell you?' Marina closed her eyes again. 'Well, I don't suppose he thought it very important. Camilla?'

'Yes?'

'You won't be away for long periods at a time, will you?'

'No, Mother. I'll be close by.'

All through dinner Camilla was distracted, her mind returning constantly to George's meeting with Anthony. She could not think of any way to bring the conversation round to the subject without giving away her anxiety, and she did not want to display her vulnerability in front of Edward. When the two men left for the Bear Inn, she reluctantly decided to wait up for her father so that she could question him. He returned within the hour and was plainly happy to see her still up.

'Nightcap?' he asked. 'I had a drink with Edward but another small whisky would be just the thing. It's bitter out there. I have some twelve-year-old Glenfiddich in the cupboard.' He poured the drinks and stood with his back to the fire.

'Mother says you saw Anthony Chapman in Nairobi?'

'Look, my dear, I understand that didn't work out and I'm sorry. I hope you didn't care for him too much.' George was decidedly uncomfortable. 'But I did run into him, yes.'

'And?'

'He had a girl with him. An American. They seemed to be, well, they were obviously . . . Oh God, the fellow's a complete cad. She was all over him and I suppose it's hard to fob that kind of woman off, but I wasn't impressed. I really didn't want to tell you about this, Camilla, and I can see that you're upset. I'm sorry, darling, you don't deserve this.' He swirled his drink in the bottom of his glass, avoiding the pain in her eyes.

'He told me he didn't want anything long-term. I made an idiot of myself, if you want to know the truth,' she said bitterly, tears sliding down her face. 'I'm only upset because of being tired, and because of Mother. And I still can't believe I fell for the big white hunter thing. But I'll get over it.'

'What about Sarah and Hannah?'

'I haven't been in touch.'

'Why not?' he said. 'I thought you'd had such a wonderful time in Kenya. Until that terrible incident. When I saw you in Nairobi, after your time at the coast, you were all so happy to be together again.'

'I'm going to bed,' she said. 'But there's something I'd like to talk to you about tomorrow. Something you might be able to do for me. For them, really. Goodnight.'

There was no opportunity to discuss Langani on Christmas Eve. Camilla found herself fully occupied, shopping with Edward, caught up in the humdrum activity of making lists, and searching the village for the ingredients of a Christmas dinner.

'The first thing I need is a cookbook,' Camilla said. 'I've never roasted a turkey in my life, and you may have to flee to the Bear or some other local hot spot.'

In the evening they assembled in the sitting room for caviar and champagne and foie gras, which Edward had brought from London. Marina was dressed and Camilla had helped with her hair and her make-up. She was almost ghostly, ethereal in her beauty, as she leaned lightly against George and looked up at him with an expression that was rapturous. He placed his arm around her thin shoulders to draw her closer to him and then he bent to kiss the top of her head. Watching them, Camilla saw that he was quietly weeping. She accepted then that he did indeed love Marina, and she admitted to herself that she had never before seen her mother truly happy. But the realisation was cruel, and she found herself unable to deal with the irony of it all. She went into the kitchen where Edward was putting the finishing touches to dinner. He had turned out to have a passion for cooking, and during the early evening he had whipped together a meal that would be light enough for Marina to enjoy, but festive all the same. Camilla had set the table with candles and decorations they had found in the village, and her father had made a careful selection of wine, while Marina arranged flowers in her favourite

499

bowl. They had never worked together to create a simple, family occasion that was full of love and harmony, and the effort carried a poignancy that affected them all. They knew that their time together would be brief, and there would not be another Christmas to share.

There was a sprinkling of snow on the ground when Camilla awoke on Christmas morning. She felt light-hearted and full of energy as she drank some coffee and made herself toast. Then, on the spur of the moment she left the house, walking briskly through the village to the small church on the green. The notice said there would be a service at ten o'clock and she was half an hour early. It was cold and she pushed the heavy door ajar and sat down in a pew close to the back, finding unaccustomed security and nostalgia in the smell of incense, the candles and flowers, and the traditional Christmas crib. A few local church members came and went, preparing for the service, smiling a season's greeting but making no attempt to intrude on her. After a few moments she knelt down and prayed for the first time since her days in the convent chapel, begging for the strength to care for Marina in her last days, asking for the courage to build a new relationship with her father and to try to understand his suffering. Later today she would talk to him about Langani. And then she would telephone the farm to let them know she had not forgotten, that she loved them still with all her heart and would always love them. When the service was over and the carols had been sung she made her way to the Bear Inn and rang Edward's room.

'It's glorious outside, with the sun and the snowfall. Would you like to escape from here and go for a walk?'

'I'll come down right away.'

She rang the cottage to tell her father where she was, and then set out with Edward. They walked slowly, rejoicing in the fine weather and the crunch of glittering snow beneath their feet. Robins hopped in the hedges and smoke curled from neat cottages, where the shine of Christmas lights could be seen through a veil of newly washed curtains.

'Don't you have any family at all?' Camilla asked.

'I was an only child. Like you. My father's been dead for years and my mother died eighteen months ago. They were great people.'

'I'm so sorry.' She hesitated, unwilling to pry. 'But you were married once. I think you said that the first time we had dinner together, didn't you?'

'Yes. That's what I said.' He did not offer any further information, and she saw that he had thrust his hands deep into his pockets, and there was a muscle twitching along his jawline. For a time they walked in silence and then he stopped abruptly and turned to her. 'My ex-wife is an American. We married very young. She hated my job. Well, not my job but the amount of time I spent on it. She said I was obsessed with work. We quarrelled about it all the time, and about the fact that she wanted children right away and I wanted to establish myself first. Things we should have talked about before we tied the knot, I suppose.'

'You told me something wise about hindsight once,' Camilla reminded him.

'She had an affair. With an American she met in London. And then she was pregnant. So she asked me for a divorce and she left with him for Boston.'

Edward turned away and resumed walking, his face grey and sad. Camilla walked beside him, searching for a way to bring up a new subject.

'She had a massive stroke when the child was born,' Edward continued his narrative. 'She's a vegetable. He has the child. She's in a home, and her parents take care of her. Keep her alive in the hopes that a miracle will one day restore her. They're hugely wealthy and they don't want to see me ever again because they feel I was to blame, that if I hadn't neglected her, she would still be living and vibrant and happy, and surrounded by perfect children.'

Camilla put her hand out and took his arm. 'I'm terribly sorry,' she said, shocked by his sad story. 'And I'd like to tell you that I'm grateful for all your kindness. I mean towards me, and Marina too. Now, let's go and make merry. Because we all deserve it, and I think we're actually meant to be here, helping each other along. Come on, Edward, you're dragging your feet. By the time we've cooked that bird it will be about five, and I'll be starving. Chewing the carpet. And you know how little Marina would like that.'

Marina had brought a small tree from London. It was festooned with decorations and lit with star-shaped lights with a heap of parcels under-neath. Gifts and embraces were exchanged, and Camilla was thankful she had found the time to buy Edward a book before she left London. He had come with presents for them all, thoughtfully chosen and beautifully wrapped. Camilla opened her package to find a bangle, oval in shape and made from several woven strands of gold. It was an extravagant gift and she caught her father's eye and Marina's knowing smile as he slipped it on to her arm.

'Thank you,' she said. 'It's much more than you should have—' She looked down at the bracelet, wordless and confused, unprepared for his hands turning her face up to him so that he could kiss her. She stepped back quickly, trying to make light of the incident, aware of her parents' approving glances. It was Edward who saved her further embarrassment.

'Into the kitchen with you. I need an assistant. Marina, I suggest you lie down for an hour or two. Doctor's orders.'

'I'll get some wood from the shed and keep the fire banked up,' George said, a shade too hearty.

As the sky darkened in the afternoon Edward left to freshen up at the Bear, and Camilla sat down with her father, pouring him a cup of tea.

'I want to tell you about Langani Farm, and what's been happening there,' she said. 'Piet's built this wonderful lodge, you've probably heard about in Nairobi. It's going to open very soon.'

George had already discussed the question of Langani with Anthony. But he did not want to bring that name into the present conversation, so he listened without comment as Camilla detailed the incidents and troubles surrounding the farm and the lodge.

'Piet can't finance the farm and the lodge, and protect the wildlife area he's set up, plus organise rangers or guards, all single-handed. It's very expensive. So I wondered if your organisation could help. If you do that kind of thing.'

'It's possible,' he said. 'I'll be leaving for Nairobi around the middle of January. Maybe I can work out the basis of a grant before then, although it would take a few weeks before any money actually started to flow. Langani as a conservation area looks like a worthwhile project. Our organisation likes the idea of ranchers and farmers doing this kind of thing. I'll give it priority as soon as I get back to the office.'

His words brought a kind of absolution for Camilla, a reprieve from her failings, a flicker of hope that would enable her to repair her broken connection with the people she loved most. The remainder of their Christmas celebration passed quickly. Edward left for London two days later. He wanted her to join him on New Year's Eve when there would be a small dinner party at his flat, but Camilla was noncommittal. Marina had fared remarkably well, but it was time to return to London and the close supervision of her doctor.

'I've done so well,' she said. 'And now I feel strong enough to enjoy the Santinis' visit. They're coming from Rome for a few days. We could have a quiet dinner with them on New Year's Eve. You'd like that, George, wouldn't you? And Camilla's been wonderful, but she'll soon be getting cabin fever.'

The chauffeur dropped Camilla at her own flat on the following afternoon and she telephoned Tom.

'Saul is back tomorrow from New York,' he said. 'I've set up a meeting with him on Monday. And in the meantime my lawyer has a few comments about the contract, but nothing major. It looks good, doll.'

Camilla sat on the sofa, happy to be in her own space, optimistic about the new project, and comfortable with her parents, perhaps for the first time in her life. Marina's illness had brought them all a kind of peace that had sloughed off their troubled past, and she was grateful for that. She thought about telephoning Langani, but decided against it. Her father would let her know within a week whether a grant was possible. It would be better to wait for a decision. She was pleased with the prospect of an evening to herself, and she lifted down a storage box from above her wardrobe, and took out her Samburu beaded collars and bracelets. In a drawer she found an Italian suede waistcoat, and she sat at the dining-room table and began to unpick the seams. It was almost three in the morning when she finished her work and she held it up for her own critical inspection. It was good. She had studied the traditional bands of colour and design, before dismantling the African jewellery. Then she had painstakingly sewn the beads and small metal trinkets on to the soft leather, stitching decorative borders around the neck and hem, and along the seam lines. The waistcoat smelled a little ripe, and she smiled, thinking of the fastidious buyer in Bond Street who would be presented with her creation tomorrow.

A loud knocking woke her in the morning and she surfaced slowly, pulling on her dressing gown as she opened the door. Her father was standing outside, his expression anguished. She drew him into the sitting room, fearful that Marina had experienced a setback, or worse. He slumped into a chair and put his head in his hands, trying to compose himself. Then he looked up at her.

'Camilla, I have some terrible news and I don't know how to say it, so I'll tell it to you straight. Piet van der Beer has been murdered. At the farm. It was in the newspapers this morning, and I didn't want you to see it like that. Oh my dear, I'm so sorry. I'm so very sorry.'

She looked at him, mute, her brain sluggish as she tried to absorb what he was saying. He put his arm around her, but she resisted him and moved away to sit in an armchair as he told her what the newspapers had reported. The crime harkened back to the days of the emergency, the *Daily Telegraph* said, when European farmers had feared for their lives and members of the Mau Mau were sworn to kill anyone, black or white, who was not of their persuasion. It had the appearance of a ritual killing, a barbaric act that had not been seen for many years in the former colony, and it underlined the precarious circumstances in which the remaining white farmers lived. Better policing and security measures were needed, the paper said. Although of Afrikaans origins Piet van der Beer was a British citizen. His death would be investigated thoroughly, perhaps by Scotland Yard as well as by the Kenya police. For a long time Camilla stared fixedly ahead, shutting out of her imagination the savagery that had taken Piet's life from them all.

'What about the others?' she said, drying her tears.

'No one else was harmed. It says that his fiancée was the one to find him.'

'Are you sure? Are you absolutely certain that's what it says?' When he nodded, she stood up unsteadily. 'Oh God. Oh God, it must be Sarah. They were engaged, and she never told me. I never even knew. Oh God, it's too hard to bear, to believe. And now—' She shuddered, and her voice deserted her.

'My dear, would you like to telephone? Now, while I'm here?'

'It's my fault,' she said in a low voice. 'They asked me to get help and I never did anything about it. If I'd spoken to you months ago, when I first came back, this would never have happened. You'd have been able to do something for them, to get them money that would have made them safe. And now he's dead, killed by some poacher on his land, because I didn't help them in time. Oh God.' She began to sob, loud, rasping sounds that gripped her body and shook her frame as she hung on to the window ledge for support.

'Camilla – this isn't your fault. You can't think you're in any way responsible. That's insane, my dear. I think you should speak to Hannah or Sarah. So that you can get through this together, so that you can get through this together. What do you say, darling? Shall I ring for you?'

'No, oh no,' she said, collapsing into a chair and wringing her hands, inconsolable, consumed by the force of her grief. 'I can't talk to them. I can't. I can't ring that number because I know he'll never answer the phone again. None of us will ever hear his voice again. And they'll never forgive me. Never.'

George opened the cupboard and found a bottle of brandy. He poured a stiff measure and handed it to her, but she ignored the proffered glass. She sat with hunched shoulders, rocking back and forth, her arms wrapped round her body. After a time she became very still and finally she turned back to her father, her gaze dull and despairing.

'Show me the paper,' she said.

He handed it to her, and waited while she read the article. When she had finished she stood up.

'Tell me,' she said, 'is this about what Jan van der Beer did?'

'Camilla – I can't divulge—'

'Tell me, damn you!' she screamed at him. 'Tell me what Mother knew. Tell me the truth, because otherwise I can't live with myself.'

George sat down heavily. 'Jan killed a man,' he said. 'During the Mau Mau years when he was in the Aberdares, tracking the gangs in the forest.'

'It was a war,' she said. 'British soldiers were brought in. They killed people. African policemen killed people.'

'This was a particularly brutal killing,' George said. 'The man was tortured. Jan would have been tried for murder but for the amnesty. There was a blacklist circulating just before Independence, and his name was on it.'

'So Piet's death – was it about revenge?'

'It has the marks of it, although I can't be certain. And if it was revenge, then there is nothing that you or any one of us could have done to prevent it.'

She paced the room for a time, before coming to stand in front of him. 'Hannah will need to know why this happened,' she said. 'I have to tell her. And it will help the police, give a direction, a reason.'

'No. I don't think you should tell Hannah anything. She's just lost her brother. Would you tell her now that her father was a murderer? That he might be responsible for the barbaric death of his own son? Neither Jan nor Lottie ever told their children about what happened. That much was clear on that unfortunate evening in Mombasa. What good could it do, to tell Hannah now?'

'It could bring justice, find who did this thing.' Camilla was crying again.

'And destroy what remains of the poor girl's family. Are you going to do that to her? Those files are closed. I don't believe there's any point in their being opened again.'

'You should go now, Daddy. I want to lie down. I need to be on my own for a while. No, don't – I can't talk about this any more. Not now.'

He left her reluctantly and she spent the rest of the morning in a dark place from which she felt there was no return. She was drowning in a lake of sorrow and loss, buffeted by waves of remorse. Her body was weighed down with a terrible weariness, but after an hour she dressed and tried to think of something she might do, or somewhere she might go to ease her pain. Nothing came to mind. As she was putting on her coat the telephone rang.

'Camilla, your father just tracked me down and told me the news. What can I do?'

Edward's voice was the only normal sound in this terrible morning and she tried to match his measured calm. But when she began to speak the words would not come, and she could only sob down the telephone. After a moment she hung up and flung herself down on her bed, holding her stomach where the pain had become a physical thing. She did not know how much time had passed when she heard the knocking. Slowly she made her way across the sitting room, wiping her hand roughly across her tear-stained, swollen face. She was not surprised to see him.

'I've come to take you to Charles Street,' he said, without preamble. 'I'll give you a sedative to help you through the day, and my housekeeper is there, in case you need anything. I'll be home around six. Then we'll talk. Or whatever you would like. But you shouldn't be alone.'

His flat was spacious and restrained, like his consulting rooms. He installed her in the guest bedroom and handed her two tablets and a glass of water. She lay down on the bed, empty and exhausted, and he wrapped the covers around her. Within moments she was asleep. When he returned just before six she was sitting up in the drawing room, staring into some private inferno of leaping, flaring pain. He took her hands and kissed the palms gently, and she put her arms up around his neck and leaned into him, no longer able to cry or even to think.

'There's no one,' she said dully. 'No one I can love. No one who can trust me or love me or rely on me. This is what I have done to them all, and to myself.'

He hesitated for a moment and then stood up, taking her by the hand. She did not object when he led her into the bedroom and set her down on his bed. He lay down beside her, stroking her hair and her face, kissing her gently on the forehead where the scar still formed an ugly line. She reached for him and buried her face against him, giving no sign of resistance when he began to kiss her more fervently, following his lead as passion took over from sympathy. Slowly, he took her clothes off and she lifted herself up and pulled him into her body. As he placed his hands beneath her, he heard her murmuring to herself, over and over.

'I want you back, I want you back. Oh please, please come back. Come. Come in me, now.'

He knew that her words were not for him, but he did not care. She was his now and he lay awake beside her, to watch over her as she slept.

Chapter 27

Kenya, January 1966

Anthony dialled the operator, holding Sarah's hand as she was connected to her parents in Sligo. Their shocked voices and loving condolences did nothing to lessen her grief. They listened in disbelieving silence to the bare outline of the story, unable fully to comprehend what had happened to Piet. Raphael felt chiefly gratitude. His daughter had been spared. She was alive, unharmed, and her safety was the only thing that was truly important to him. It was not until afterwards that he thought about the torment of the van der Beers. For Sarah, the act of telling reduced her to broken, incoherent sentences. Several times she gave the receiver to Anthony, and attempted to regain control of her voice before beginning again. She tried to explain how it was unthinkable that Hannah should be left alone now. Only their shared loss could help them to find the courage to go on. Raphael and Betty could not mask their worry. There had been no arrest, and whatever had inspired Piet's killing could be repeated. Langani was not safe. They feared for their daughter's life. But Sarah was adamant, pleading for them to accept her decision, and they were powerless to make her change her mind. When Tim came on the line, pressing her to return to Ireland, she said goodbye and returned to the nightmare in which she was trapped.

The telephone rang incessantly. Neighbours and friends began to arrive and the house filled up with people. There were things to be done, food and drinks to be organised. It was dusk when Lottie decided that she would leave for Nairobi and fly south the next day, to face her husband and give him what support she could. Hannah sat in wordless misery, refusing to acknowledge her mother's silent appeal for understanding, unable to accept her father's greater need.

When the last sympathisers were gone, Lottie went to her bedroom to pack and Sarah followed, wanting to do something to mitigate her pain. There were no words she could say, but she stayed to offer the touch of her hand, the taking and folding of a garment to put into the suitcase — small acts of service that might demonstrate her love. Lottie tried to smile as she closed her bag.

'I've begged Hannah to come with me, but she doesn't even seem to hear me,' she said. 'Although it may be better this way, because I don't know how I will deal with Janni's sorrow. I'm afraid of what this will do to him.' She sat down suddenly on the bed. 'My God, it's so futile. It's all so futile and senseless. What did we struggle for, through all those years? What were we building that my son should have died for it, while I have to live on? For what, Sarah?'

'I don't know, Lottie. I can't think how we will go on, or live through days that begin and end without him. I don't know how I can get through tonight or watch the sun rise tomorrow. But Hannah and Jan need you, and maybe you can find a purpose in that.'

'Hannah has locked herself away,' Lottie said. 'She's angry with me for leaving her, for choosing Janni over her. I suppose it's a part of coping with death, to be angry. But I have to go and I don't think I can ever come back, while she has chosen to stay. We are on two sides of a divide that neither of us can cross. Perhaps it will heal in time, but for now I am asking you to take care of her, for as long as you are here. I love my daughter more than I can ever make her understand. But there is too much pain in this place. I don't believe I could ever find peace at Langani again. Not ever.'

She rose, and walked with Sarah to the sitting room, where Hannah was staring into the fire, a glass of brandy untouched on the table beside her.

'Come with me, Hannah,' Lottie whispered, holding her one last time. 'Come away from here, my dear. For a little while, until we decide what to do with the farm.'

Hannah answered without hesitation, unsmiling and distant. 'I've already decided, Ma. I will not leave Langani. I have to carry on for Piet. So that they cannot destroy what we have built here. They will not drive me off our land.'

She turned away and Lottie clung to Sarah briefly before walking out to the waiting car and driver. She did not look back. Mwangi and Kamau wept as she took her leave of them. Then the beam of the headlights swept the walls and finally the sound of the engine faded into the night. In the sitting room Hannah slumped on the sofa. Her head was in her hands and a high, keening noise came from her lips.

'Help me get her to her bedroom, Sarah,' Anthony said.

He sat at Hannah's bedside, saying words that she did not hear, stroking her hand until she was quiet. Sarah stood in the doorway, watching. There was comfort for Hannah in his presence. But all Sarah had ever needed or wanted lay in ashes up on the ridge. She was utterly alone. She turned and fled the room. Outside on the lawn she saw the askari on duty, wrapped in his heavy coat, his rifle at his side, his breath misting in the cold air. Like a sleepwalker waking from a dream, she found herself in Piet's bedroom, surrounded by his belongings, his school photographs, the books he had loved and planned to read with her. She took his shirt from the back of a chair and put it on over her clothes. Then she lay down on his bed and buried her face in his pillow, to breathe in the last scent of him.

Two days after the cremation there was a memorial service in Nanyuki, and after that Hannah moved through each interminable day as though she inhabited a separate world. She could not answer the telephone or face the questions and concern of old friends. She spent her time in the dairy, or driving around the farm, finding and taking on unimportant tasks that normally she would have delegated. Although Mike Stead was helping out, he had been offered a permanent and better-paid job and he had told her that he could only remain at Langani for two months. There had been no word from Lars, no sign that he had heard the terrible news of Piet's death. He had seemingly lost all contact with Kenya, or he had chosen to bury Hannah's rejection of him and to put his time at Langani behind him.

Both Hannah and Sarah threw themselves into an excess of activity during the daylight hours, hoping that by nightfall they would be bone-weary and ready for oblivion. Sarah went to the dispensary each day, desperate for something to occupy her. The little room was full of people, their ailments forgotten in the face of the tragedy that had overtaken them all. They had come to offer their condolences. She accepted their sympathetic murmurings, and with each one her suffering grew. Every waking moment threatened a memory that might derail her faltering progress, cracking the thin veneer of control. Fear cast long shadows across the days and nights. Even familiar sounds created anxiety. Everyday words and phrases took on sinister innuendoes, as Hannah discussed the wheat crop or the cattle with farm workers they had always trusted in the past. The nights were the worst. Sleep was dangerous, a time when nightmares crashed through their fragile guard, drawing them down into a vortex of abject grief and fear.

Anthony found a colleague to take out his next safari, and stayed on at the farm. He tried to anticipate their needs, and to avoid intruding. It was a side of him that Sarah had never seen before and she tried to show her appreciation. Hannah seemed unaware of him. She was aloof from everyone, her expression flinty, her words clipped. She ate little and seemed not to taste the food put in front of her. Mwangi watched over her like a parent, shuffling about and muttering to himself in sympathy when she failed to answer a query, or did not respond to some domestic matter he had raised. He took over the daily running of the house, turning to Sarah on the rare occasions when he needed guidance. It was a relief for her to be doing something useful. She was aware that Mwangi and Kamau were fully capable of dealing with most of the tasks they set her, and she was touched by their wish to make her feel needed. Love and compassion shone in their faces as they moved about the house, their presence familiar and comforting. During that first week, Sarah came into the dining room one morning to find Mwangi weeping over the table. She saw that he had unthinkingly set a place for Piet and he was now removing it, his body bowed over the chair that had once belonged to Jan and then to the young man he had known since infancy. She moved forward and they put their arms around one another, drawing comfort from the sadness they shared.

Meals became a series of short sentences and yawing silences, as they skirted around potential minefields in their conversation. Anthony would say something light and amusing, and there would be a moment of respite before a word or a gesture brought the cruel stab of remembrance. Then Hannah would become still, her eyes clouded over. Sarah looked inwards, tracing patterns with her fork on the tablecloth, concentrating fiercely on the position of her glass and plate on the table, asking whether they should have coffee at the table or in the sitting room, while Anthony cast about for a new subject. They were like a group of dancers in some elaborate but unfinished sequence, circling one another, moving forward, standing away, touching hands briefly, but unable to achieve lasting contact.

Lottie telephoned and made excuses when Hannah asked to speak to her father. Janni was not well, she said. She was trying to prevent him from drinking heavily, but it had become a near-impossible task. She pleaded with Hannah to come south, so that they could share the burden of their loss.

'Meet me in Johannesburg, Hannah,' Lottie begged. 'You don't need to come back here. You and I, and Pa, we could all stay with your uncle Sergio for a while. He wants us to go down there together.'

But Hannah would not leave Langani, even for a short time. Neighbours and friends called in to see if there was anything they could do for her. Hannah was polite, remote in her rejection of any offer of help, and after a while the visits dwindled to phone calls. No one could break through the barrier that she had erected. It would take time, they told themselves. Better to leave her to the privacy of mourning. When she was ready to accept their love and assistance she would call, and they would be there for her.

Sarah could not go to the lodge. Each time she thought about the place her mind veered away, suppressing the dreadful darkness that had formed in the centre of her consciousness. Only Anthony had the courage to go there. He had arranged for the removal and burial of Kipchoge and Ole Sunde, after the police were finished with the site. It was Anthony who persuaded Hannah to attend their funerals. She stood stiffly at the graveside, trapped in the straitjacket of her own grief, clutching Sarah by the hand as the simple coffins were lowered into the earth and Anthony made the speeches of praise and gratitude expected and required. But as the last shovels of rich soil were levelled on to the fresh graves, Hannah reached out to the bereaved families, embracing the women and presenting them with gifts of food and money. They pressed her hands and murmured in their soft voices, while the children caught at her skirt and looked up at her in wide-eyed silence, recognising her terrible sadness. The lodge was closed up until Hannah could decide what to do about it. But all of Langani's dwindling savings lay in the abandoned structure, and already weeds and cobwebs had begun to encroach on the place that had represented Piet's dream.

The police had no information that might throw light on a motive for the killings, or lead to Simon's whereabouts. The young Kikuyu seemed to have vanished into the surrounding forest. Police and trackers had followed his trail into the near-impenetrable bush at the base of the ridge, and there all traces had disappeared. He had been clever, Hardy said, in the way that he had used the terrain to cover his passing, moving across the land without leaving any mark. The policeman's frustration was evident. He had questioned the workforce at Langani and on surrounding farms, but they could not, or would not, give him any leads. Simon had kept to himself, and had never talked to anyone about his background. Enquiries at the mission in Nyeri had resulted in few details. When the police tried to track down the man who had brought Simon to the mission as a small child, they found that the name he had given was false. There were many children who had no knowledge of the people who had brought them to the orphanage. The boy had been a model student, quiet and hard-working, anxious to learn and to advance himself. The priests who had taught him were mystified. Simon Githiri was an enigma.

'We don't know that he's finished, Jeremy,' Anthony said. 'He could be waiting, planning more atrocities. Hannah's terrified that he'll come back. She doesn't say it aloud, but it's in her mind all the time, and in Sarah's too. As long as he's free, they'll have no peace of mind or security.'

'That's why I've left a police patrol here. I thought all these incidents were part of a vendetta aimed specifically at Langani, but now I'm not so sure. He may be planning to attack other white farmers. And he must have had outside help, which is a major worry. That first raid was carried out by an organised group. The poaching too, although they may not be the same people. Either way, Simon didn't plan those events by himself. But when you look at the senseless slaughter of the cattle back in September, and the way—' He stopped, as Hannah came into the room.

She fixed him with an intense look and finished what he had been going to say. 'When you think about the way he hacked my brother to pieces? Is that what you were going to say, Jeremy? You think it was a ritual, a sacrifice of some kind, don't you?'

'He could be insane,' Hardy said, but it was clear that he did not give much credence to this theory.

'Simon isn't mad,' Hannah said. 'I'm sure what he did was considered and planned with cold logic. Even to getting the job here initially. I wonder, now, if he came here just for this. To kill.'

'We haven't found any family called Githiri that is related to him. But even if there is someone who knows who he is, they're not going to admit it now. There was one old priest who taught him and took a special interest in him,' Hardy offered. 'But he's in hospital in Nairobi. On his last legs, poor man. Apparently he's very frail and forgetful, and no one at the mission in Nyeri seemed to think he would have anything to add.'

'But somewhere there's one little scrap of information that will give us a direction,' Hannah said, her face taut. 'There has to be.'

'We'll hear something eventually that's linked to our enquiry.' Jeremy put an arm around her. 'I know it sounds pretty weak, Hannah, but believe me that's how it usually happens. Often the killer leaves a clue, because he wants to be recognised for what he's done. And that's what makes the difference.'

Hannah sank on to the sofa as though her knees had given way. 'I don't think anything can make a difference. But I want Simon caught. I want him dead, for what he did to Piet and for what he has done to us all. Whenever I close my eyes I see the ridge on that night, and I don't know if I'll ever be able to sleep again.'

'Jeremy will find him,' Sarah said. 'We have to hold on, Han, and try to stay as strong as we can be, for another little while.'

'Ach, I'm so beat.' Hannah leaned back, slow tears escaping from her closed eyelids. 'So tired. I don't know what to do . . . What can I ever do? Because I was the one who brought him in here. I took him into our home and destroyed us all.'

'You can't think like that,' Anthony said. 'It wasn't just you, Hannah. Everyone was taken in by him. It wasn't your fault.'

'Yes, it was,' she said doggedly. 'If I hadn't sent Lars away. If Piet . . .' She could not go on after the mention of his name.

'We will find Simon.' Sarah knelt in front of her, looking into her eyes. 'We'll never stop looking, never give up, till we get him. Isn't that right, Jeremy?'

The policeman's expression was grim. 'I have the maximum number of men working on this,' he said. 'Good, experienced fellows. I've got people out in the reserve and in the townships, asking questions. Sooner or later we'll turn something up.' He stood up and took his hat. Then he reached down and planted a clumsy kiss on Hannah's cheek. 'I'll be in touch. Goodnight.'

In the silence that followed his departure Sarah cleared her throat. 'I rang Dan and Allie this afternoon,' she said. 'To ask if I could defer going back to the camp for a while. If you'd like me to stay?'

Hannah nodded. She had retreated into her other world again, and Sarah was increasingly worried about what would happen when Anthony left, and she herself had to go back to Buffalo Springs. Sometimes she could barely contain her need to be among her elephants, away from the oppressive atmosphere of this house. Everywhere she turned at Langani he was there, in the forefront of her memory, in the familiar objects and surroundings that had been the fabric of his life, and the life together that they had planned. A pair of boots, a book, his sweater hanging on a rail in the stables, his rain jacket on the peg inside the door of the office. She felt intensely close to him, could almost imagine that he would come striding into a room, pushing his bush hat back off his head. In the murmur of voices she would find herself nursing an insane expectation that she would soon hear his voice, calling out a greeting or a question, making one of his jokes. She might find him standing in a doorway, throwing back his head to laugh. Reality, when it swooped down on her, was insupportable. For a few precious seconds she would imagine his presence and her spirits would soar. Then the dead weight of sorrow and disbelief crashed down on her once more, leaving her choking on the pain.

Her grief was merciless, haunting her thoughts by day and her dreams at night. She could not speak about Piet, say his name or think about him, fearing that she would suffocate in her desolation, that she might never regain control. She found herself unable to cry. Normal people would cry, surely? Allow themselves some form of release. But for herself, and for Hannah, there was only a kind of paralysis. A silent waiting for something to change. For the time being Hannah needed her, and Sarah felt she had to stay. But she could not afford to give up her job, and increasingly she craved the silence of the bush, and a day when she could sit quietly and observe the timeless routine of the elephants and the world they inhabited. The Briggses had assured her that there was no pressure to return to work before she was ready, but it would be unfair to ask for too much time away. Things became more difficult after Anthony left, and their parting had not been the way she had wanted it.

'I've said goodbye to Hannah,' he had said, on the morning of his departure. 'You're both welcome to use my place in Nairobi any time you like, whether I'm there or not. It might be good for you to spend a couple of days in the bad old city.'

'Thanks,' Sarah said. 'Thanks for everything, Anthony.'

'I'll probably see George Broughton-Smith within the next week or two,' he cut in, wanting to avoid speeches of gratitude and tearful farewells. 'So I'll bring up this question of money for Langani with him. Hannah needs it now more than ever.'

'Yes. If you do see him, could you find out about Camilla? I feel we've all let her down, me especially. I should have phoned, but I haven't had the strength. I'm working myself up to it. Or maybe you could try and track her down. You were very special to her, you know.'

Anthony's fingers were drumming on the door of his vehicle, and his expression was less than encouraging. He had been evasive about Camilla, and he was plainly uncomfortable.

'Listen,' he said, pushing back his hat and scratching his head, 'Camilla is one of the most ravishing creatures on the planet. But she's way out of my league, really. As she's always pointed out herself, I'm just a bush baby. I spend most of my time out in the *bundu,* and I wouldn't change that part of my life for anything. She thrives in the big city – a place I can't cope with at all. We had a blast, but then it was time to go our separate ways.'

'You told her that, did you?'

'Yes. Of course I did. I'm not a candidate for married quarters and *totos* and all that. I did try to get in touch with her in November. But it was like you said, she didn't answer the phone or reply to the card I sent. So I decided to bow out gracefully. It was easier than long goodbyes and so on . . .'

'Easier for whom? It's easier for the one who wants nothing to do with love or commitment, sure.' She glared at him. 'A ravishing creature? Different lifestyles? That's the biggest load of shit I ever heard! You knew she was in love with you, and you shouldn't have taken advantage of that.'

'Hey! Steady on there. I never led her to believe it was anything more than a special moment that fizzed between us. It was great fun for both of us.'

'Oh, really? And when did you tell her that? On the last day of her holiday, when you'd taken all you wanted from her. Then she could be discarded like a shirt you'd got tired of, so you could go out and get yourself a new one. Is that it?'

'Sarah, look, I know things are pretty difficult for you just now, and—'

'So tell me, where's respect for other people's feelings in your scheme of things? Don't you ever stop to wonder if you might be hurting someone, sucking them dry and spitting them out like that? Don't you believe in love at all? Love that transcends all obstacles, makes all things possible? You bloody well knew that was the way she felt about you. But you didn't give a tinker's curse about that, did you Anthony? You amused yourself while it suited you, and then you moved on. *Lots of fun and no harm done*, like the song goes. But there was harm done, dammit. Terrible harm. Only she was probably too proud and too hurt to tell you, and you were too selfish and shallow to see it.'

'I'm not ready for commitment,' he repeated. 'For the one and only thing.'

'In that case you shouldn't have led her on. Even you must have known that it was different for her, that she loved you. That's not something to be squandered, or treated lightly.' Sarah was unable to check the flow of fury or the tears that had begun to well. 'It's the most precious thing that anyone can ever have or give. And you should at least have recognised it as something to be grateful for. You're the definitive cad, Anthony.'

'Sarah, you're overwrought. It's no wonder, with everything that's happened. You're not being—'

'Here, I've got something for you,' she said, producing the photograph she had taken of Camilla and Anthony at the campfire in Samburu. 'It was Piet who said I should give it to you, remember? What she offered you was not some cheap commodity. It was a gift beyond value that you don't deserve to find again. So take this to remind you.' She shoved the picture into his hands. 'From him and from me.'

He stared after her, his mouth slightly open, as she fled into the garden. Then he climbed into his vehicle and started the engine. He did not see her in the trail of dust behind him, running after his car, waving and shouting.

'Anthony! Anthony, stop! Please wait – I'm sorry. I'm really sorry.'

She stood in the driveway, arms hanging limply, wondering how she could have submitted him to such a diatribe after all he had done over the past ten days. She was still chiding herself hours later when she went to bed. As she turned out the light Simon's face filled her memory. She recalled his sudden smile as he accepted the book she had given him, saw the pleasure in his eyes, the same eyes that had glittered as he turned towards her on the moonlit ridge and aimed his spear at the hyena. The sounds of the night pressed in on her, the furtive rustlings and creakings of the house that she had once loved and now feared. She sat up and lit the paraffin lantern, her nerves jangling as she saw the shadows loom in the hissing light. The cold night air and her own loneliness struck her with a force that made her suck in her breath.

She wanted Piet, needed to hear his voice, see his face, feel his arms wound tight around her. She went to stand by the window with her eyes closed, reliving him, imagining, his arms tight around her ribcage, lifting her face into the empty darkness to receive his kiss. Then she was back on the ridge with the hideous sight of him spreadeagled on the ground, with his leaking eye sockets, and her nostrils were filled with the fetid odour of the hyena as it prepared to spring. She cried out and clapped her hand over her mouth, afraid that she would be heard. For a few moments she stood shivering in the middle of the room. Then she took the lamp and stepped out on to the verandah, nodding to the nightwatchman as she made her way to the sitting room and lifted the telephone. She dialled the operator and waited for a connection, leaning against the wall, willing an answer.

'Hello?' The voice was sleepy but there was no mistaking the rolling accent. Deirdre. Not the one she had hoped for. Her own voice broke as she tried to speak.

'Deirdre, it's Sarah. I need to speak to Mum or Dad. Or Tim, if they're not around. Anybody.' Oh God, she prayed in her head, please let one of them come and talk to me. Help me, please. Help me now.

'They're all in bed, Sarah. It's one o'clock in the morning.'

Oh God, stop talking about the bloody time and get someone. 'It's three here.'

'Three! Are you all right, Sarah? You don't sound so good.'

'Just get someone. Please.'

'Hold on.'

Sarah hung on, one hand pressed against the wall for support, the other clutching the phone, twisting the cable that connected her with consolation, no matter how distant.

'Sarah? What is it, kiddo?' It was Tim's voice, familiar and comforting. 'What's the matter?'

'Tim?' She wept with the relief of it. 'Tim, I keep getting these nightmares, only I'm wide awake. And I can't deal with them. I can't bear this any more. I'm afraid. If I could end it all right now, that's what I'd do.

I know that sounds terrible, but it's how I feel. I can't go on. Help me, Tim, please. Talk to me and help me.'

His words flowed over her, calming and full of endearments as he sought to console her. He did not try and persuade her to come home, but concentrated on restoring her balance, on drawing her back from the edge of the abyss on which she was standing. Later, there were loving words from Raphael and Betty, and gradually the conversation moved into quiet exchanges of news. When finally she hung up she was dry-eyed and worn out, and frozen with cold. She could not remember their exact words, only that they had brought her back from disintegration so that she thought she could face another day, and maybe another and another. One at a time. It wasn't life, but it was survival. She could survive, and that would have to be enough for now.

The days took on a rhythm in which Sarah immersed herself. Mike Stead was kind in his efforts to help and protect Hannah, and he worked hard to keep the farm running smoothly. But he did not have the same eye for detail, the same burning interest that Lars had brought to his work at Langani. Sarah came into the office one afternoon to find Hannah sitting beside her manager, with a sheaf of invoices in her hand.

'I didn't want to bother you with all this right now,' he was saying, 'but our balance is running down, and we need to think about improving the cash flow. Otherwise we'll have the bank yapping at our ankles again. So I'm wondering whether you're thinking of opening the lodge? I was up there a couple of days ago, and there's already some deterioration. Natural materials like that disintegrate rapidly, if they're not maintained.'

'The lodge isn't going to open. I can't go there.' Hannah's voice was shrill.

'That's up to you, of course,' Mike said with sympathy. 'But you'll have to address this other problem soon. We'll talk again when you've had a chance to think about it. I'll see you later, down at the dairy, I expect.'

When he had left, Hannah sat with the stack of bills in her hand, staring at them, her eyes glazed. Sarah drew up a chair and sat down.

'How bad is it, Han?'

'I haven't balanced last month's accounts, so I'm not sure.' Hannah rubbed tired eyes. 'And I don't know where I'm going to find a manager when Mike leaves at the end of next month. I don't know anything much any more.'

Sarah though of Mike's words. He was not one to overstate any issue, and she could understand how Piet's buildings would soon begin to sink beneath the grasp and pull of creeper, the stone split asunder by invading roots, the beams eaten through by the determined inroads of insects and weather. She had a graphic vision of it, in ruins, peering out of the smothering jungle. Like the ruins of Gedi. She shuddered. But it was hard to see how the lodge could open without a professional manager. Hannah was already juggling many of the tasks that Piet and Lars had dealt with between them, and now she would have to replace Mike as well. At the same time, it had been Piet's dream. It was his monument too, and Sarah could not bear to see his achievement disappear without a trace.

'He could be right, Han,' she said. 'The lodge represents a huge amount of money, and it's lying there empty.' She saw Hannah's mouth twitch, but she felt she must continue. 'Don't you think Piet would want the lodge to be used? He put all he had into it. It was to be for you and me too, and for the wildlife. Remember what he was saying, on that last day when . . .' She fell silent.

Hannah's back was turned and she was looking out into the garden. She made no comment. Sarah composed herself and with difficulty began again.

'If you don't want to run it as a safari lodge, then maybe it could become some sort of training centre. You could have courses on wildlife and birds. On the plants and trees and rivers and so on. Or teach people like David who want to work in hotels. And women could learn how to turn out better handicrafts. As Camilla was suggesting when we were in Samburu, remember? Maybe you could invite famous ornithologists and game wardens to come and give lectures, in return for a small fee and a week's stay at the lodge. You could set up a foundation in Piet's name, and get outside funding for it. It would make the lodge into a living memorial to him. What do you think?'

Hannah spun round. Her eyes were flat, her mouth turned down at the corners. 'Do you really think I should make the lodge into a charity for training the very people that killed him? A reward for his murder?' Her bitterness permeated the small room. 'Piet died up there. He was hacked to pieces. And they did it. His so-called brothers and sisters. They poached the game, they slaughtered our cattle, robbed our house and killed my brother. And now you want me to turn what he built into something for them. Are you crazy? Have you completely lost your mind, Sarah Mackay?'

'Not everyone is evil, Hannah. Your own *watu* aren't responsible for what happened. They had nothing to do with it. In fact, you could start with them.'

'How do any of us know who was involved, or whether any of them helped Simon. Brought him here, even?' Hannah raged. 'You're so easily fooled, Sarah. An idealist, like he was. But I don't trust a single one of these kaffirs any more, and none of them will gain from his death. Not one. So we don't ever need to talk about this again.'

She left the office, slamming the door behind her. Sarah was appalled, crushed by her antagonism. God, how stupid she had been! She should not have brought this up so soon. And perhaps Hannah was right. They could not be sure that no one from Langani had been involved. Simon must have had help. She leaned against the desk, drained. Would this terrible cycle ever end, or would everyone at Langani be forced to live with suspicion and hatred until the whole enterprise collapsed back into the African soil? As she left the office one of the dogs thrust his cold nose comfortingly into her hand and wagged his tail, coaxing a smile from her.

She went to sit on the verandah outside her bedroom, and Mwangi brought her a tray of tea. The dogs lay on either side of her chair, feigning sleep, the twitching of their furry eyebrows betraying their interest in the biscuit she was eating. Only Piet's dog was missing. Piet was missing. He would never call out to her again, full of dreams and optimism and plans for the future. Their future. She began to cry, her body shaking as she tried not to let her emptiness unravel her precarious self-control. The dogs looked up, whining softly, licking at her hand. Stroking their smooth heads and speaking to them helped to dilute her anguish. After a time she straightened in the chair and looked out over the horizon. With a chill she realised that she could just make out the line of the ridge. She would have to go there, one day. And to the lodge. It was something she would have to face, if the nightmares were to stop. Part of the process of coming to terms. But not yet. She could not do it yet. Just to look at the outline of the land made her feel ill, and brought everything back to haunt her again.

She was relieved when Hannah asked her to go riding next morning. They walked down to the stables in a strained silence. Sarah took the reins of the chestnut gelding from the syce and concentrated on tightening the girth, trying not to think of Kipchoge's cheerful cackle as he had saddled up the horses. Hannah wheeled her mount around and they trotted out of the yard. It was the first time they had ridden together without Piet. It was Hannah who set the pace when they reached open ground, galloping out across the short grass. When they drew up in the shade of a wild fig tree and dismounted, she took a Thermos and enamel mugs out of her saddle-bag and poured coffee.

'I want to apologise for yesterday,' she said. 'What I said was horrible. I know you were trying to help me, and I couldn't go on without you. I've tried to think about him, about what I have to do, but I can't manage it. I don't know what else I can say, except that I'm very sorry.'

She looked up, and Sarah could see the unshed tears in her eyes, and her mouth set hard to maintain control. She was gripping her horse's mane, and the animal tossed its head uneasily.

'You're going to have to let someone help you, Han,' Sarah said. 'You have to begin living again. Not in the same way, because none of us will ever be the same. But you must make a start.'

'I'm trapped!' It was a cry of desperation. 'I'm in this dark place, and I can't escape from it. It's always there, swallowing me down. I thought I could run the farm, but it's too much for me on my own and I don't know what I'm going to do.'

She was looking away towards the ridge and Sarah shivered, sharing the torment of visions that did not fade. She reached out her hand but Hannah flinched and moved away.

'Have you ever thought of asking Lars to come back?'

'No!' Hannah looked appalled. She broke off a twig from a bush, and stabbed viciously at the ground with it. 'I could never ask Lars to come back. Never.'

'Because you still have feelings for Viktor?' Sarah asked.

'Hell no!' Hannah rammed the stick into the ground, and it broke in two with a sharp crack. 'To tell the truth, I don't think I ever had deep feelings for him.' She shook her head. 'He came at a time when everything around me was so hard. With the robbery, and so. I needed an escape from the misery and loneliness, and from being scared. And along came Viktor.' Her expression was sad. 'It was my pride that he injured more than anything else. A roll in the hay with a willing farm girl. That's all he wanted, and if I'm truthful it's what I wanted too. He was fantastic in bed, but he never made any promises.' She poked at the ground again with her stick. 'I was the one who dressed it up to make it feel like a great romance. But it was all in my head.' She gazed down at her hands, twisting her fingers together. 'Look,' she said abruptly, 'there's something I have to tell you, Sarah. I haven't said it before, because I didn't know how to.'

She sat on a boulder and stared at the ground for a few moments, frowning. Sarah waited for her to go on, but Hannah drew a stalk of grass from its sheath and chewed on the end of it as she marshalled her thoughts. When she began to speak, the words came like sporadic bursts of gunfire.

'When I drove down to Viktor's place in Nairobi on that night – the night I found him with the black woman – I had something in mind. Something I needed to say to him.' She put her head in her hands, unable to continue.

'What?' Sarah prompted. 'What, Han?'

'That I'd missed my – that I thought I was pregnant.' Hannah's voice was barely audible.

'A baby? You're going to have a baby?' Sarah was dumbfounded. 'When? How many weeks? What did he say?'

'I didn't tell him. When I saw the way he looked at me, I knew I meant nothing to him whatsoever. So I never said the words.' Her smile was lopsided and sad. 'He would have told me to get rid of it. I thought of it, but I was scared and I just couldn't do it. The baby's about two months on, and I don't know how I'm going to manage. I never told Piet either. I wish I'd told him, but he'll never know now, because he's dead.' Hannah wrung her hands and began to cry, a wailing sound, like a lost child. 'I don't know what to do. I didn't say anything to Ma either, because I thought she'd go crazy. Tell me I'd been careless and stupid. And I was. Maybe I should have an abortion, Sarah. It's not too late. Because I'm on my own, now. There's no one to take care of me, let alone a baby.'

'You can't have an abortion.' Sarah was horrified. 'This is your child, Han. Yes, Viktor is the father and he's a bowsie, but you thought he loved you and it's your child. Everybody is going to love this baby, Han, because it's your son or daughter. You'd never forgive yourself if you had an abortion. And besides, I want to be the godmother and spoil it rotten.'

'Ach, Sarah, I know why you're saying that about an abortion. But I don't believe most of that stuff the nuns told us. I'm not a Catholic like you. I'm an Afrikaans farm girl who's going to have a baby without a father. Without a husband. It's different.'

'No, it's not,' Sarah said 'This is a new life, a new person to love. And Lottie won't be angry or scornful, any more than I am. She'll be glad because your child will chase away all the sadness. You'll be the best mother ever, Hannah. I know you will.'

'No. I don't think I can do it.' Hannah brushed away new tears with the back of her hand. 'You make everything sound so simple, when it's not. You'll soon be gone, back to Buffalo Springs. And I'll be stuck at Langani, on my own, trying to run the farm and everything. I can't look after a baby as well. It's too complicated. And Mike Stead is going soon, because I can't pay him enough. I'm trying to find someone else, but it's hard.'

'Someone like Lars,' Sarah tried again.

'I ruined everything with Lars. I lost the best possible farm manager, and I destroyed our friendship,' Hannah said. 'We'd have made a good team if I'd kept my head. But it's too late now. We haven't even heard from him since he left. He doesn't want to think about Langani ever again. That much is clear.'

'I don't know, Han. You could try and talk him into coming back,' Sarah said. 'I think he would—'

'And what would I say?' Hannah interrupted, with some bitterness. '"Would you like to come back and run my farm, Lars? I'm having a baby, you see, by a man who made an idiot out of me. In fact, it's the very same man you warned me about when I told you to leave. But I'm sure you won't mind helping out now that I've got myself into this mess." Is that what I should say, heh?'

'You might need a teeny bit more tact and a large slice of humble pie.' Sarah was smiling. 'Not your strongest attribute.'

'Lars isn't a saint, Sarah. He was working here and he was in love with me, and I had an affair right under his big, straight Norwegian nose. And then I threw him out. He has his pride, you know.'

'He might surprise you,' Sarah insisted.

'He wouldn't want to work for me, knowing that I'm going to have Viktor's child.' Hannah drew a circle on the dusty earth. 'I don't see why he would want to have anything to do with me. Or the farm. And who could blame him?'

'You can't be sure of that,' Sarah said stubbornly.

'Sarah, this is one of your fantasies,' Hannah said. 'I don't believe we could ever be friends again, or work together. I can't talk to Lars. I don't even know where he is.'

'Then we'll find another way to make this work,' Sarah said. She could see that the subject of Lars was too fraught. 'We can get through anything together. Like we always promised. I love you, Han,' Sarah said.

While Hannah was making her afternoon visit to the dairy, Sarah went to the office and sat at the desk. It was littered with papers and bills and lists of tasks, few of which had been crossed out as completed. She found the telephone directory and turned the pages hastily. There was only one Olsen listed in Kiambu, and she closed the door before dialling. When she had spoken to Lars's uncle she dialled again, this time asking the operator for a number in Norway. The conversation was a struggle. Lars's mother was not fluent in English, and it took some time before Sarah understood that he had left for Denmark the day after Christmas, in order to visit his sister who lived there. Sarah put down the telephone, fearful now that Hannah would come back to the house and discover her plan. She dialled again, and gritted her teeth as the overseas operator commented that he had never placed calls to any of these countries before. He was inclined to chat. Sarah drummed her fingers. Finally Lars's voice came on the line.

'It's Sarah,' she said. 'I have something terrible to tell you.'

He listened and then she heard the tears in his voice as he talked about his friend, asked for Hannah, began to cry openly.

'How are things with you, Lars?' Sarah asked finally.

'This country seems so small now, after being away. And far too cold.' He attempted a laugh. 'I'm thinking of Australia.'

'Would you consider returning to Langani?' Sarah asked him. 'Hannah needs someone.'

'It could not be me,' he said. 'She made that clear.'

'Things have changed.'

'Does she want to see me?'

'She's afraid,' Sarah paused, closed her eyes and took the plunge. 'She's pregnant, Lars.' She felt his shock, heard the harsh intake of breath and the scrape of a chair as he sat down heavily. 'Lars?'

'She is having the child of that man?'

'Yes.'

'So where is he?' he asked.

'It's over. It was over before she realised she was pregnant. And she's not going to tell him.'

'So. She has thought of me. But you have to tell her no.'

'She doesn't even know I'm ringing you.' Sarah was desperate, dismayed at his bitterness. 'I can understand your reaction, Lars, I really can. But I'd like you to think about it.'

'I am not that good a man, Sarah. I hope things will turn out OK for her, but I cannot help her in this. It is asking too much.'

They spoke for a few more minutes, but he was adamant. He could not come back to Langani.

Three days later he called from Nanyuki. 'Could you drive over here and meet me?' he said to Sarah, in his slow voice. 'I don't want to work at Langani, but maybe we can talk.'

'Hannah, would you come in to Nanyuki with me this afternoon?' Sarah tried to make her voice casual and failed.

'What for?' Hannah looked up from her accounts ledger, her face pinched, shadows under her eyes. 'I don't like going to Nanyuki now. I don't want to meet people. Listen to all those sad speeches and see how awkward they feel when they see me. You go, if you have to.'

'I don't want to go by myself. Please, Han.'

They drove into town and parked at the Silverbeck. Sarah remembered the first time she had been there, on her way to Buffalo Springs when life was so glorious and full of promise. She turned off the ignition and faced Hannah.

'Lars is here,' she said. 'And you are going to ask him to come back to Langani, and you are going to tell him the whole truth.'

Shock and anger were Hannah's first reactions, but after several minutes she opened her door without a word and went into the hotel, her face set like granite. She was finding it difficult to breathe. Her mouth had gone dry and she could not swallow. Where had he come from? Had Sarah brought him back, and if so what did he know? What could she say to him? She stopped and turned back towards the entrance. Sarah was watching her from the car, mouthing words at her. *Tell him.* Hannah turned again and found him standing beside her. They sat down at a small table in the lounge that overlooked the garden.

'I miss him,' he said. 'I can't believe he's gone. For you, I can't imagine how it must be. Or for Sarah. Oh, Hannah . . .'

She did not want to cry. She did not want to feel the burning guilt that always came when she thought of Lars. If she had not sent him away – her mind refused to complete what might have been. She swallowed with difficulty.

'You look well,' she said, realising what a lame, pointless remark that was, and following it with another. 'I wasn't expecting to see you.'

'How are things at the farm?' he said.

Hannah glanced around in panic. She could see Sarah, still in the car, making no move to join them. 'Everything is ticking over,' she said. 'It's fine. No. It isn't fine, actually. I need to ask you – I was thinking – well, there's something I should tell you.'

She was floundering. Lars studied his glass of beer with intense scrutiny and did not look up. Hannah straightened and set her chin in the attitude of defiance that made her look so like her father. 'Look, Lars,' she said, 'there's something I need to say.'

Sarah could see them in the distance, sitting stiffly on opposite sides of the table. She began to pray silently. *'Don't let her mess this up. Don't let him refuse her. Please God, let one good thing come out of all this. Please! Don't let him walk away.'*

Twenty minutes passed before Hannah came out to the car, her face pale, her eyes red.

'Han? Are you all right?' Sarah's heart plummeted.

'I told him all of it, as you said. I asked him, even so, to take over the farm. I told him I needed him, said I was sorry for everything that had happened. And he said he would come on a trial basis. For a few months. To see if it can possibly work. He wants to live in the cottage where Mike is now. Not in the house like before. But he will come back. He says we should join him for tea.'

On the night that Lars returned to Langani, Sarah slept for the first time. In the morning she knew that she could now return to Buffalo Springs. She could watch her elephants move across the arid beauty of the northern landscape, following the tracks through the thorny scrub, in a deliberate procession towards the blue of distant mountains. Here at the farm there would be no peace until Simon was found and brought to justice, and she could not hasten the process. She looked up at the glass-blue sky, digging into her dwindling reserves of courage before she could undertake what she had decided to do.

'I'll be out for most of the day,' she said to Mwangi. 'Tell Memsahib Hannah that I'll see her this evening.'

Her hands were shaky as she started the car and made her way down the driveway from the house. The track had not been used in a while and occasional rain had created a jigsaw of cracks on its surface and crumbled the edges, so that the wheels spat sand and pebbles as the car whined its way up the hill. Branches scraped at the doors, and the screech of thorns on the paintwork set her teeth on edge. At the top of the trail she parked the car and set off on foot, panting a little from the steep climb and the heedless omnipotence of the sun. At the top of the ridge she came to a halt, wiping the sweat from her forehead, looking out across cloud-dappled plains.

She sat on the rock where she had leaned against Piet, and surveyed the world he had loved. All around her was a harmony of birdsong and grasshoppers. There was still a dark area where the pyre had been, and she felt that with each intake of breath she was absorbing him as he floated above the ridge, eternally present but lost to her for ever. Now that she was here with him, she did not know what to say or do. Perhaps there was no need to search for words, because he would know that she had come to say goodbye. Her sense of him would never change now. They would not see their children grow up on the land that should have been their home and their heritage, and they would never be old together, blind to one another's wrinkles and forgetfulness and encroaching frailty.

After a while she lay down in the sun and closed her eyes. She did not anticipate any danger from the wildlife, although it was possible that she was being observed by a pair of dik-dik or a bushbuck, from within the camouflage of the surrounding bush. They would not harm her, and predators would be sleeping in this heat. Piet would protect her. She was sure of that. For a second she heard the sound of his voice in the wind, saw his face in the play of sunlight and cloud. Then there was nothing. When she opened her eyes again and looked at her watch she was surprised. She had been sleeping, and more than two hours had passed. There was a stiff breeze and the sky was grey and spattered with dark clouds that raced past her, making the trees look as if they would topple on to her as she lay on her rock. She rose to her feet and smoothed out her clothes. Then she went to the spot where they had burned him.

'I'm going now,' she said, her voice soft with love and sorrow. 'I have to leave you for a while, although I'm not ready. But I think it's the only thing I can do. It's the right thing. Please look after Hannah and bring her peace. I know that you will be with me wherever I go, and that I don't have to say goodbye. I will never say goodbye.'

Her tears had begun now, and she bent down to scoop up a handful of the scorched earth and put it in her pocket. Then she stumbled away from the ridge, slipping on the steep path, clutching at dry, thorny branches to prevent herself from falling. When she reached the car she felt the first drops of rain. The clouds had bunched together, and a flicker of pink lightning sliced the sky. There was a growl of thunder as she drove down the escarpment, the vehicle lurching on the rough terrain, sliding perilously close to the edge of the cliff from which the track had been carved. The trees loomed dark and gaunt in the torrent of water that rattled the windscreen. Within a few minutes she was skidding across the road, driving as fast she dared to avoid being sucked down into the mud. Once she had to climb out into the downpour and push some brushwood under her tyres, holding her breath as they spun and slid before gaining purchase. When she finally reached the house she was drenched and spattered with mud.

'Sarah! Where have you been? I was about to start out looking for you!' Lars took her by the arm. 'I thought you might be bogged down somewhere. We're in for a stormy evening, that's certain. There's been a phone call for you. Hannah will tell you. Hurry up and get into some dry clothes.'

'A phone call?'

'Later, or you'll catch cold.'

When she had showered and put on trousers and a sweater she returned to the sitting room. Hannah was standing by the fire, but she did not respond to Sarah's smile.

'I was frantic when the rain started,' she said. 'I didn't know where you'd gone, and I was afraid you'd be stuck somewhere for the night.'

'I thought I'd drive around and look for some game. Take a few pictures,' Sarah said. 'Who phoned for me?'

'It was George Broughton-Smith,' Hannah's face was forbidding. 'I told him you weren't here. He wanted to come and see you. See us both. But I told him no. I don't want him here, not now or any time. So if you want to see him, it will have to be somewhere else.'

'Did he say anything about Camilla?'

'I didn't stay on the line long enough to find out. He'd heard about what happened here. It was in the papers in England, so she must know too. But she never wrote or even picked up the telephone.'

'Did he leave a number?'

'No.' Hannah was looking into the fire, her fists clenched at her sides.

'Hannah?' Sarah paused for a moment, waiting for a reply. But there was none. 'Han, I went up to the ridge today. I went to see Piet.' Her throat closed and tears pricked her eyes as she said his name. Hannah spun round to gaze at her with eyes that were unnaturally bright, but she said nothing. 'I think it's time for me to go now, Han. Back to work. And you need some time and space for yourself. Lars is here and he will help you, and I won't be far away. I'll come whenever you need me, or you can come up to the camp. Any time.'

Silence. Hannah folded her arms in front of her, as if for protection. Her eyes darted towards the door as Lars came to join them. She looked at him intently, almost as though she had never seen him before.

'Sarah is going away,' she said. Her expression was unreadable.

'Lars, I thought originally that maybe I'd go next week sometime. But unless you have something in particular for me to do here, I'd prefer to leave tomorrow.' She caught his look of surprise. 'I'll come back soon. For a weekend or something.'

'Good,' Hannah squared her shoulders. It was clear that she was making an effort. 'I will come up there one day. When it's over. But for now I must stay here and wait. How are you going to get there?'

'Dan or Allie could collect me in Nanyuki. One of them is coming down tomorrow, to pick up some supplies.'

'Good.' Hannah said again. 'You can take my car and leave it at the Silverbeck. Lars and I will drive in together and pick it up from there. You should bring vegetables from Langani, and eggs and honey and jam to feed you up in that desert, heh? In the morning I'll help you to get ready.'

It was mid-morning when Sarah left the farm. She stood with Hannah in the driveway, engaged in meaningless small talk, delaying the moment of parting. When finally they embraced, Hannah withdrew quickly from

530

the contact and walked away. It was impossible to gauge her feelings, but Sarah felt a sense of release as she left the farm where the see-saw of Hannah's emotions mirrored her own. It was too painful to watch.

'I'll take care of her,' Lars promised, as he closed the door of the car. 'I think she is beginning to come round. I hope so, because we are soon going to be forced into making some big decisions, and I can't make them without her.'

'Such as the lodge?'

'There's so much of the farm capital tied up in it, and we're going to have a serious cash-flow problem unless we open it. Or do something else, like leasing it.'

'That's a horrible thought.'

'I know. I've tried to bring it up with her, but it's too soon.' He smiled and squeezed her hand. 'Don't worry, I will find a solution. Go back to work now. That is the best thing you can do for yourself, and for Hannah too. Life will be better here when you come home the next time.'

She could see him in the driving mirror, standing there on Lottie's lawn, until she rounded the bend in the driveway and left the farm behind.

Chapter 28

Rhodesia, February 1966

Jan van der Beer came to a halt in the scant shade of an overhanging rock. He was out of breath, exhausted by the pitiless heat. He mopped his face and neck, and shrugged away the trickles of sweat that ran down his back under his shirt. There was a brackish taste to the water he was drinking but he gulped it down, wiping the last drops from his unshaven chin with the back of his hand. Then he searched in his bush jacket and took out the whisky flask, turning his back to his companions as he swallowed greedily. The patrol had been moving at a rapid rate since dawn, but the temperature and blinding glare of midday had finally forced them to stop. The trail they were following had temporarily disappeared on the rock-strewn ridge, and the trackers were casting about in the scrub, searching for signs of recent human passage. Jan watched them in silence, cursing under his breath, resentful of the fact that he was out with his cousin once more, chasing through the bush after the gang that had attacked the Maartens' farm. They had murdered the elderly couple, and torched the house and the farm buildings before slipping into the scrubland that stretched to the border with Zambia. The houseboy had raised the alarm, running through the darkness to the next homestead. It was four in the morning when the telephone rang in Jan's bungalow.

'There's more trouble,' Kobus said. 'Old Maartens and his wife are dead. I'm putting a patrol together. We'll leave in an hour to get the bastards.'

They had set out before dawn, taking advantage of the cool temperature, and moving slowly at first so that the trackers would not miss anything significant in the poor light. Now it was midday and the heat was intolerable. There was no doubt in Jan's mind that the killers were insurgents from one of the black political parties banned by the prime minister. Since the sweeping election victory of Ian Smith's Rhodesian Front Party, most black opposition leaders had been jailed. The exceptions were those who had fled across the border into Zambia where they had set up guerrilla groups, operating frequent armed raids into their home country.

'Man, this is a temporary thing,' Kobus van der Beer had said, when Jan first expressed doubts about the government's harsh policies. 'Smith understands these munts that organise the raiding parties. They're out to scare us whites away, but he knows their limitations. He's not going to give every black man a vote and sell the country down the river. We know what we're doing down here, and we won't give in like they did in Kenya. Hand over our farms to the kaffirs.'

'They gave them enough land to keep them happy,' Jan said. 'It was a political thing that might work in time.'

'It'll never work,' Kobus had replied angrily. 'These kaffirs only want to sit on their arses and grow enough for a few days' food supply, or buy more cattle they can't feed. And they're not going to do it on any land of mine. I'm forming a patrol with my neighbours. We'll catch the bastards when they come in here to strike at our farms. Show them what they're up against. You're my overseer, part of my family, Jan. And for as long as you're here I'm expecting you to put plenty of muscle into this.'

'You didn't come down here to fight someone else's war,' Lottie objected, when Jan was summoned for the latest patrol. 'Kobus can say what he likes, but you know very well this is only the beginning of trouble here.'

'I have to go out with him. To protect his land and to stop people like us being murdered in the night.'

'We've lost our son, Janni, because of a war over land,' Lottie could not keep her voice under control and she clung to his arm and shook him, forcing him to look at her. 'Don't try to escape from what I'm saying. You and I both know what Piet's death was about. Haven't you learned anything? Or are you determined to go out there and kill yourself too?'

'I've learned that Piet's dreams could never have lasted, because these kaffirs don't care about partnership and peace. They want us all off the land we own, or dead.'

'We don't own this land, Janni. If you want to fight, then go back and help Hannah to protect our farm. Because we have nothing to gain here except your destruction. And mine too. In this country there is no hope because there is no compromise. These rebels have money and weapons given to them by other African states and by communist countries. Some of them are being sent to Russia and China to be trained. This is ugly, Janni. We should go home to Kenya, where you were born. We've made a terrible mistake.'

But he could not go there. He could not return to the place where he had crawled up into the cold forests and lived like an animal, where he had lain at night alert to the telltale crack of bamboo, or the startled movement of an animal that told of fugitives in flight – men he must hunt down and kill. He would never forget the sight of his brother's savagely mutilated body, with the flies buzzing and humming in a black halo around the half-severed head. He could still see the men in their animal skins, squatting around the fire, eating and laughing in the early light. Laughing as he descended into madness. He could not return to Langani where the ghost of his son would stalk his every step, and his daughter would look at him with silent hatred. He reached for the whisky and drank straight from the bottle, listening to the sound of his wife's sobbing from behind the bedroom door. Then he went out to join his cousin.

Kobus van der Beer enjoyed the vigilante-style patrol he had set up with his neighbours, and their forays were becoming more frequent. The man gloated over the number of rebels he had hunted down, and the harsh punishments meted out. Jan had been strict with his labour at Langani, swift in disposing of any worker who cheated on him or did not obey the rules. But he had always been fair, providing food rations, money for education, sound advice and medical care for his staff. His cousin dealt with wrongdoers as though they were animals, throwing them off his land, shouting at them and tossing their belongings out of their huts to lie broken and scattered in the dust. Jan had seen him beating men that he found asleep in the tobacco fields. And since the farm attacks had begun, Kobus was in his element. His patrol would set out heavily armed and ready to go 'kaffir hunting', as he called it. The man derived a vicious pleasure in shooting down his quarry. Jan's early objections had resulted in barely veiled threats about losing his job. And since Piet's death, he no longer cared.

'Man, you're needed here,' Kobus said. 'These *terrs* are no different from the one who killed your son.'

Kobus was barking instructions to the group now, to make ready and be off again. Jan spat in the dust and pulled his hat down over his forehead as his cousin approached. He took a last draught from his water bottle and followed it with another shot of whisky, knowing full well it was crazy to drink in the middle of the day. The combination of the heat and liquor would sap his energy and increase his thirst. But the alcohol deadened his misery. It was the only way he could force himself to go on. When all this political unrest died down he would take himself in hand, he vowed. Until then, liquor was the fuel that kept his legs pumping and his life from falling apart. The tracker signalled that he had found the quarry's new direction, and the patrol went forward at a trot, through the scrub and thorn, rifles at the ready.

It was another hour before they caught up with their prey. The guerrillas had realised that they could not outrun their pursuers, and they had set an ambush among the rocks. When the shooting started, the patrol scattered, diving for cover into the thick bush. Jan was in the lead, shouting orders, racing towards the area where the gang was hiding, dodging and weaving through the rocks, firing off rounds as he went. Faced with this onslaught, the defenders turned to run. It was all over in a few minutes. Kobus walked around the bodies, counting his trophies. They were a ragged bunch, five men of disparate ages, dressed in threadbare camouflage uniforms. Only two of them wore ill-fitting shoes. The others were barefoot. Their guns were old, and they had little ammunition.

'You took a chance out there, man. But it was good,' Kobus said to Jan, as he bent down to strip the corpses of their weapons.

Jan shrugged, took another swig from his flask and lit a cigarette. 'Not many of these people are well enough trained to stand their ground, if you go straight for them,' he said. 'They chose a spot where they thought they'd surprise us, and pick us off. They're never prepared for us to go on the attack. They have no plan of action beyond the first few minutes.'

'And if they had decided to stand fast?'

'We'd have been shot. But we were getting shot at anyway.'

Kobus grunted and turned over another body with his foot. This one couldn't be more than fifteen, Jan thought. For a second he saw the eyes flicker. The boy had been lying very still, feigning death. Jan deliberately turned away, but his cousin had seen the movement too. He lifted his rifle and put the barrel to the boy's forehead. For a second the youngster's eyes opened wide with terror and mute appeal. Then Jan saw a scarlet cloud of blood and bone and brain tissue, spattered over the dusty ground. Kobus laughed, wiping the gun on his khaki trousers.

'Christ, man, he was just a kid!' Jan protested, sickened at the casual dispatch.

'One less to grow up a terrorist, heh? Stinking *tsotsis!.*' Kobus turned away and walked over to join his companions. They broke out rations and began to eat, sitting alongside the dead, unmoved by their presence and the sight of vultures circling overhead. Jan felt the old nightmares descending on him, and he took out his flask and drained it. They left the bodies where they lay. A warning to others, Kobus said. It was a long trek home, and darkness had fallen when Jan stumbled into the house. Lottie was sitting at the dining table, the remains of her half-finished dinner before her.

'What happened?' she said.

'Another successful operation,' he muttered, going straight past her to the sideboard and pouring himself a drink.

Lottie stood up abruptly. 'Your dinner is probably ruined. But I don't suppose you'll notice that.'

He turned to look at her with bleary eyes. 'It's not my choice, you know, to spend hours out there in the bush, tracking down munts. They killed old Maartens and his wife. Someone has to stop them.'

'Not you. It doesn't have to be you.' Lottie's eyes were blazing. 'I've been here alone all day, not knowing whether you would be alive or dead in the back of the truck. One of these gangs could have turned up here and attacked me while you were away on your crusade. Does that matter at all, or do I not deserve your protection? And now you come in here, drunk and—' Jan pushed past her but she stood her ground. 'No, you let me finish. You stink like a polecat, and you're full of whisky. I can smell it on your breath and I can see your hands shaking. Look at you, Janni! You're not so young any more. There are plenty of younger men on the farms around here who can do this. It's not your fight. I'm sorry about Maartens and his wife, of course I am. But you don't owe them anything, and nothing you do will bring them back. Kobus is using you. He treats you like cannon fodder, so that he and his son will live to fight another day. And you seem all too willing to go out and kill yourself.'

'Lottie—'

'It's too much, Janni.' Her eyes filled with tears. 'I can't do this any more. We came down here for the sake of Piet. To give him a chance on the farm. But he's dead, Janni. Dead. And Hannah is struggling to carry on alone. We have no life here either. I'm working every hour for half of nothing, and you're gone all day, and when you do come home, you're drunk.'

'Do you think I don't hate what's going on here?' Jan was swaying on his feet. 'But I have no choice. I need this job. If I don't go on the patrols Kobus will sack me, and then we'll have nothing at all. Nothing.'

'There has to be somewhere else you can work, if you won't go home.' Lottie's voice was weary. 'What Kobus is making you do will destroy you, Janni. Last time it was for our farm, for our family. And there was a terrible price for that. But this is not your battle. Ian Smith is a madman who is going to plunge this country into war. We should leave before it's too late.'

Jan took a step towards his wife and tried to pull her close to him, but she turned away from him in disgust.

'Go and have a bath,' she said coldly. 'I can't take the smell of death on you. Or the stink of booze. It's in your clothes, on your body, in your eyes. Go and clean up while I try and do something with your dinner.'

She took the casserole out of the oven, tossed the potatoes in gravy and warmed a plate for him. When he returned he looked sullen, and he did not speak as he sat down at the table.

'Janni, please listen to what I keep saying.'

He pushed his plate aside. 'It's not all bad here,' he said.

'It's hopeless,' Lottie said. 'Ian Smith has isolated himself from everyone except South Africa. No other nation is going to back Rhodesia as long as he refuses to consider a future where black people have a say. The police and the army can't keep out the people who've been exiled and are now coming back here to fight. The Russians and Chinese and the Cubans will help them to make trouble. And the natives think these parties in exile will remove Smith one day, and give them all the land that the white people own now. It's only a matter of time before we are living in a full-scale war.'

'It will change, if we can hold out for a while.'

'You're just fooling yourself if you think any good can come of the way things are going here,' Lottie said. 'Kobus and people like him will be dispossessed some day, maybe even massacred. And so will we, if we stay and support him. You're spending your time defending what cannot be defended. And for what? For a man you despise, and for his land, and for a country that has nothing to do with us!'

Jan stood up, shaking his head, and went to pour himself another whisky. Lottie sat back on her heels and rubbed her hand across her eyes. When she spoke again her voice was low and desperate.

'You don't need another drink, Janni. Please. Stop this now. If you love me, don't do this.'

He held the tumbler to his lips in defiance, and downed the liquid in one long swallow. Then he slammed the glass down on the table and left the room. Lottie rose to her feet, cleared the kitchen table and put Jan's uneaten dinner in the bin. He was asleep and snoring when she reached the bedroom and she stood looking down at the lines of strain on his face, the broken veins on his nose, the bloated features and the bubble of spittle that had formed at the edge of his open mouth. She had come to detest the stale smell of alcohol on his breath as he lay beside her. And his dreams were troubled. It was like the months after the Mau Mau and the enquiry, when he had locked himself into a spiral of despair and she had feared for his sanity. He was a good man at heart, she told herself as she lay awake beside him. He had been a loving husband and father. But now he was no better than a slave. Kobus enjoyed watching his cousin's gradual decline, and Lottie had seen that it gave the brutish man a sense of power. In addition, he had made several passes at her, and he watched her with a cunning, predatory look that made her flesh crawl. She was close to despair as she thought of her murdered son, and of what might become of her husband.

But there was no way out of this terrible place without money. Her meagre savings had gone with Hannah when she fled, and they would not have been enough in any case. Jan earned a pittance and he had no hope of putting money aside to take them home to Kenya, even if he stopped drinking. She heard him grinding his teeth, muttering in his sleep, and she said a prayer that she would find a way to take him out of this place and give him back his dignity and sense of purpose. Lottie pulled on her old dressing gown and went into the kitchen to make tea and to think things over again. She had one ally on whom she could always rely. Perhaps he would lend her some money – enough to take Jan and herself back to

Kenya. Tomorrow she would telephone her brother in Johannesburg. She returned to the bedroom and fell asleep instantly, oblivious for once to Jan's alcohol-fuelled snoring.

She rang Sergio the following morning and found it hard to speak to him without crying. He immediately offered his support.

'Bring him down here, Carlotta. It would be good for him and you need some love and comfort. Even for a week. And once he is here, maybe we can find something for him to do. If he is adamant about not going back to Langani, he could find work in Natal on a sugar estate, or on one of the farms in the Cape Province. Just get him here, and we'll work out a solution.'

'He won't come if he thinks I engineered it.' Her throat tightened, and she tried to keep the desolation out of her voice.

'Don't cry, *cara*. I'll send you tickets. I'll write to you both, say I miss you, that it's been too long. We will sort out this man of yours once you arrive.'

Heartened, she went out to deliver the sewing she had finished to an Englishwoman with a flower-filled garden and a farmhouse that made Lottie want to cry out in her loss and pain. She said nothing to Janni about her call to Johannesburg, but she waited impatiently for the letter and the air tickets to arrive. Jan was very fond of her brother. If he would listen to anyone, it would be to Sergio. And she realised how much she wanted to see Sergio herself, to be cared for by someone loving and strong. Since Piet's death she had suppressed her grief, wept during the day or in night hours when Jan could not see or hear her. She had tried to stay strong for him, but she could not do it for much longer.

Johannesburg was not a city she particularly liked, although she had spent her childhood there. But it offered an escape from the hopelessness of her present surroundings. The tickets arrived five days later. She ripped open the envelope, and read her brother's letter with gratitude. The prospect of the holiday lifted Lottie's spirits. She made a special effort with the midday meal, searching out a clean tablecloth and putting a vase of fresh flowers on the table. But when Jan arrived, his cousin was with him, big and loud and following her with lascivious eyes.

'Lottie, my dear.' He rested a hand on her shoulder for too long before letting it slide down her back. And across her hips. 'Looking good, you are. Yes.'

She moved out of his reach. Perhaps it was good that he was here. If she asked for time off now, they could fix a day for their departure right away.

'Hello, Kobus. I'm glad you came over. I've just had a letter from my brother in Johannesburg. He wants Janni and me to go down there for a few days. I think we need to get away. It's been hard since . . . since what happened at home.'

Kobus frowned. 'A holiday? Well, maybe near the end of the year or so. Right now is out of the question. Jan has too much work on the farm. We'll talk about it in November. In the meantime, I'd like a whisky. Pour me one, Lottie, will you?'

Lottie did not answer, but handed Sergio's letter to her husband. 'We should try to go down there,' she said in a low voice. 'We wouldn't be away for long.' She turned back to Kobus. 'If Jan could go for a week or ten days, that would be enough.'

'I'll think it over,' he said. 'But I don't usually give holidays at short notice, you know. Even to my family.'

'God knows, he deserves a break.' Lottie could not suppress the temper rising in her. 'He's grieving for his son, and he hasn't had any time off for two years. He's out there working night and day, between the farm and your vigilante ventures. He's entitled to a few days' leave.'

Jan slopped large measures of whisky into two glasses, and handed one to his cousin. Lottie could tell by his eyes that this was not his first of the day. He had taken to hiding bottles in cupboards and under the furniture, and even out in the tobacco fields, she suspected.

'Entitled, heh? That's not a word I know.' Kobus was smiling, but his eyes were cold and angry. 'And there are security issues. We are going out on one of my ventures, as you call them, this afternoon. I don't know how long we'll be away this time. It's a big one. We have information that we have to act on right away.' He swallowed the whisky, and put the glass on the table. 'I'll be back for you in an hour, Jan. Be ready.'

Lottie followed him to the door. 'Wait a minute,' she said. 'Where are you taking him this time? How long will he be gone? He's not fit for this, Kobus. There must be other people you can use. You said yourself, there's so much work on the farm. Why don't you leave him to take care of that?'

'I need all the men for this one, Lottie. Unless you make it worth my while to leave him behind, heh?' She flinched and stepped back. 'Right.

Then he will be going with us in an hour. Everyone must do his job here, otherwise there will be no job.'

Jan was in the bedroom, pushing a few clothes into a canvas knapsack. He did not speak, but walked past her into the dining room where he opened the gun cabinet and took out a rifle, two pistols and boxes of ammunition. As she watched him, all the misery of the past two years welled up, and her voice cracked with her pleading.

'Jan, please. You must persuade Kobus that we need a break. I can't go on, Janni. I have to get away from here. And Sergio is expecting us, because I spoke to him last week. He says he could find you work down south, if you really don't want to go home to Langani. And a counsellor to help you with your drinking. Let's leave here, Janni, go and stay with Sergio for a while. Talk about what we can do.'

'You spoke to Sergio about me? You were discussing me, your husband, behind my back? And now he has sent tickets because he thinks of me as a charity case.' He hurled the knapsack across the room at her, and it hit her on the shin before landing on the floor at her feet.

She was shocked by his violence.

'So what did you tell him, then? That your husband is all washed up, a drunk who can't hold down his job, or take care of his wife?'

'Janni, he's my brother. He loves me and he cares about you. About both of us. I told him that I could not go on, day after day, thinking of Piet and all that has happened. I told him that you are suffering, and that you're drinking too much. You need help.'

'You told him that? You've told him all our private business?' He was shouting now. 'And what do you suppose your fine brother will find for me to do in Joburg? I'm a farmer, for Christ's sake. Would he like me to wash dishes in his restaurant, or peel his carrots? Heh?' Jan's face was livid, the veins standing out on his forehead and his neck, his eyes bulging with rage. 'And that way, you can go back to your life as a city lady. Well, I won't take his bloody charity, and I don't need his pity. You hear?'

Lottie gazed at him, appalled. This was not her Janni. This was the whisky talking. She put out her hand to touch his face, but he pushed her violently away.

'I'm doing the job I came down here to do, managing my cousin's tobacco farm. He looks to me for advice about these bloody kaffir terrorists coming in over the border. Because I know how they operate, how they think, how to catch them. It's one thing I can do well, and I will do it to stop them killing any more of our people. There's a big raid planned over the next few days. Kobus's boys caught a *terr* last night, a scout, and they got it out of him. So we'll be waiting for them when they cross the border.'

Lottie walked to the window and looked out on the scorched grass, and the broken fence that ringed their small compound. She could hear the dry rustle of tobacco leaves as the hot wind caught and shook them and made them whisper to each other in the sun. She thought of the scout, and wondered about the methods by which Kobus's boys had forced him to tell what he knew. It made her shiver to think of her husband as a party to any of this. She tried one last appeal.

'Of course you're good at what you do, Janni. But there's no peace of mind or pride to be had from lying in wait for other men and planning to kill them, no matter what colour their skin is. You can't go on killing, whatever the provocation. Because this way it will never end, this madness of blood for blood. Come away with me, I beg you. Just for a week. Then you'll see what is right. You know I love you. I admire you. But the man I care about is being buried alive in this horrible place. Let us leave here, leave all this hatred and anger behind us. Come Janni, please.'

She put her hand on his arm, and for a second it seemed he would agree. Then he turned on her, gripped her with both hands, and flung her against the wall. She fell like a rag doll as he picked up his knapsack and stormed out into the white-hot light to wait for the truck. Lottie pulled herself up, dazed and sickened, and made her way to the door where she stood looking at him. He must have heard the creak as she opened the fly screen, but he did not turn round.

'Go then,' she said, sobbing. 'But I will not be here when you come back. If you drive away in that truck, with your pig of a cousin, then I will go alone. And I don't know if I will return.'

He did not answer. She went inside and sat down on a chair, and soon she heard the noise of the old Bedford, gears clashing as it roared up to the front of the house. There was shouting, and she heard the tailgate being slammed into place, and finally the sound of the engine revving and grinding away down the hill. For a time she sat still, empty, with no sense of grief, or loss, or anger. Only numbness. Then she went to the phone and rang her brother.

*

As the truck roared down the dirt track away from the house, Jan stared out from beneath the tarpaulin, his eyes narrowed and straining. Waiting for Lottie to appear. She would run out now, before they turned on to the main road. She would wave, shout out how sorry she was for betraying him. The Bedford turned the corner and he watched for a last glimpse of her, but she did not appear. Anger settled in his heart. She had not spoken to him with respect. A man was entitled to respect, especially from his own family. That was what Kobus said, and he was right. No woman should be tolerated giving lip to her husband. She had always been outspoken, Lottie. And she had discussed their problems with her brother, an act that was disloyal beyond tolerating. He wondered if she would carry out her threat and leave for Johannesburg without him. No. She would never go away and leave him alone in this place. Not now. He stared back at the diminishing house, willing her to appear in the porch for just one second before his home disappeared from view. But the screen door remained shut.

Kobus pulled up outside a storage shed on the edge of his property. His oldest son, Faanie, jumped down from the back of the truck, and rolled open the door of the building. Two white men emerged, and after a few words Faanie followed them inside. The rest of the patrol stayed in the back of the pickup, smoking, and drinking from beer bottles. Jan took the whisky from his canvas bag. Conversation was desultory as they waited. Then Faanie and the other men emerged from the shed, dragging something that looked like a sack. They came round to the back of the truck and threw their burden inside, heaving it over the lip of the tailboard so that it landed with a dull thud on the floor. There was a sound, and only then did Jan realise that it was a body. The black man was a heaving mass of welts and raw flesh on which flies were already feasting. His face had been beaten to a pulp. Jan felt a jolt of shock, and bile rose in his throat as he looked at the mangled creature. This must be the guerrilla scout that Kobus and his boys had been interrogating. They had certainly taken their victim to the limit of endurance. He wondered how accurate the man's information would turn out to be, extracted under such circumstances. A dark vision hovered on the periphery of Jan's conscience and he felt the old horror in the pit of his stomach. No one else paid any attention to the broken body, or to the desperate sound of shallow panting. They continued to smoke and drink and to discuss the potential of the tobacco crop and the state of the country, as though they were sitting around the bar in the local sports club. Jan stared down at the man on the floor. When Faanie and his two companions had climbed into the Bedford, they moved off again.

'We're heading for a spot close to the border,' Faanie shouted, above the rattling noise of the vehicle. 'This munt says there's a camp there, and the leader has around thirty of these bastards waiting to carry out a major raid soon. We're going to lay a trap and get every bloody one of them. Jan, Pa's relying on you to plan the whole thing and take charge.'

Kobus had already discussed the strategy of the ambush with his cousin. If Jan had had a row with his wife in the meantime it was all to the good. He'd be looking for a little action to restore his self-esteem. Otherwise he'd be useless, both on patrol and on the farm. As the truck lurched, Jan felt waves of nausea sweep over him each time he looked down. The man had rolled over on to his back and was staring directly at him. Pain and fear had pulled his mouth into a crooked grimace, making him look as though he was attempting a grotesque, ingratiating smile. Why does he keep looking at me? Jan asked himself. Does he think I am the weak one who would let him go? He deserves everything he gets. Stinking *tsotsi*. He dug in his pockets for a cigarette and lit it with trembling fingers, hating himself for his shaking hands and for the pity that he could not suppress. In the back of his mind, a nightmare sound was playing, a high-pitched screaming that went on and on, burning into his brain, although he knew it was not real. The men on either side of him had dozed off, and he opened his water bottle surreptitiously and leaned forward as if to adjust his shoe laces. He poured some drops of liquid into the captive's torn, bloodied mouth. The eyes blinked once, then again. A silent signal of gratitude for the small act of mercy. Jan straightened up and drank from his flask of whisky, leaning back against the tarpaulin and the frame of the truck. He closed his eyes, feeling the irritation of grit and sand that had already begun to settle on his skin and in his hair. It would be better if he could sleep. Then he would not have to look at the prisoner. For a long time he remained resolutely blind to his surroundings, until he felt a dull pain in his eyelids from keeping them so tightly shut. His consciousness began to drift.

He was back in the shadowed place with the flickering firelight, listening to the unremitting screams. He wanted to run, but his legs had become too heavy. He wanted to look, but he did not dare. Somewhere beyond his line of vision was the thing that he feared most of all to see. He understood this was a dream that he had known before, but the knowledge did not diminish his dread of it, or his frantic effort to wake up and move away. He struggled as the apparition hemmed him in, as a hand stretched out of the shadows to take him in a vice-like grip, and to turn his head towards what he did not want to see . . .

'Hey, Jan! Settle down, man!'

'Huh?' Jan opened his eyes, to find that Faanie had grasped his shoulders and was laughing loudly.

'You were flailing about, shaking your head as if a bulldog had got hold of it. Or a bloody *terr*, maybe. Ach, that's it! You were dreaming about what you'll do when we catch these kaffirs. I tell you, it seems to me you'll be bloody dangerous!'

The whole patrol group was looking curiously at him now. Jan wiped away the rivulets of sweat that fear had caused to run down his face.

'Must be something my wife put in the dinner,' he said, and was relieved at the sound of laughter, and for Faanie's heavy arm that reached out to slap him on the back. He took another slug of whisky and accepted a cigarette as the truck shuddered on through the blaze and dust of the afternoon. They travelled for most of the night, rattling through the bush, taking it in turns to drive, stopping only to refuel and to eat. When the Bedford pulled up at their base camp, Kobus jumped down from the cab.

'From here on we're on foot,' he said. 'This is where the fun starts, heh? We'll rest up for a couple of hours now, and then we have a long walk to where this munt said he'd be meeting his friends.'

The men dropped out of the back of the truck and put up a canvas shelter. Most of them were soon asleep, lying on rolled-out mats or wedged against low bushes and trees. As the sun rose they cooked breakfast on a small primus stove and assembled their gear, glad to be on the move, eager to start the operation. Faanie hauled down their shattered captive, dragged him over the rocky ground and tied him to a tree. There was no need to restrain the quivering ruin of humanity – he would never be able to go anywhere again. Jan could hear the rasping of the man's breath, and a pink fluid was bubbling from his twisted mouth. He was finished. They should put him out of his misery. What else could he tell them, in that state? Jan turned away as Kobus made a game of extracting some last item of information from the wreckage of the scout. The rest of the patrol moved closer to join in the charade. Jan deliberately walked away. He tried to concentrate on the noises of the wilderness around him, the rustle of small animals, the bird calls, the hum of insects and the hot wind sighing in the thorn bushes. Then he heard Kobus call out to him, and he went back to the group and opened his map to show them the route he had chosen through the bush. The captive lay still, his eyes half open and flickering, his limbs twitching although he was barely conscious.

'We'll move out in groups of three,' Jan said. 'I'll lead. There's plenty of cover between here and the spot for the ambush, about a mile from here. Once in place, nobody moves, right? No cigarettes from now on, no talk, no frigging around. Get it? Some of these *terrs* are good trackers, and if they get a sniff of us they'll be gone in a flash.'

'Softly-softly will do it,' Kobus said. 'I want every last one of them. A couple of live ones could be useful for information. But the best *tsotsi* is a dead *tsotsi*. So keep quiet till they walk into the trap, and then finish the bastards off.'

It was a long, hot walk and an interminable wait during the suffocating heat of the afternoon. The sweating, recumbent men crouched in the cover of rocks and scrub waiting with rifles cocked, listening for telltale signs of movement in the surrounding bush. Jan kept his whisky flask in an outer pocket, taking frequent advantage of the comfort it offered. He had pushed a second bottle into his knapsack where he could reach it easily when he needed it. It could not be much longer before their quarry appeared and he could dispose of them. And go home. He did not care to remember how often he had done this years ago, lying in wait for Mau Mau fighters to come creeping through the Aberdare forest. He closed the shutter on his recollections. It would all be over soon and then he would go home and try to patch things up with Lottie. They had tried to bury the grief of losing their son, and his name was unmentionable between them. But Jan thought that it was now time for them to share their pain and to comfort one another. His head ached with the heat and the alcohol, and his vision blurred for a moment.

The sun dipped behind the trees, robbing the surrounding rocks of their heat. The evening dragged on, and Jan began to think the captured scout had given them false information. Mosquitoes whined in his ears, and a host of invisible insects crawled under his shirt and up his nose, stinging and biting as he lay in wait. Jan drained his whisky flask, took the second bottle out of his knapsack and put it into his pocket so that it was accessible. The insurgents did not appear until after midnight. They crept out from the rocks and the heavy bush, about twenty of them, carrying guns and an assortment of knives. When Jan gave the signal for the firing to start, the guerrillas were completely surrounded with no hope of defending themselves. Some fled in the direction of the border, but they were chased and shot down. Others attempted to move forward and were caught in a devastating crossfire. A small group managed to break away, and Jan shouted out his plan.

'They're heading in the direction of the truck. We should be able to drive them right down there.'

He set off at speed, shooting as he ran. One man went down and Jan put an extra bullet into his chest, hardly breaking his stride. Kobus and his son were running closest to him, whooping with triumph as another of the insurgents fell, limbs twitching for a second before he lay still in the dust. Faanie doubled his pace, passing his father and Jan. He was the first to reach the clearing where the pickup had been hidden beneath a camouflage of branches. One of the remaining terrorists appeared on the edge of the bush, and caught sight of the informer fastened to the mopani tree. With a wail of grief and fury he ran towards the sagging form, but Faanie fired and the force of the shot tossed the man into the air before he fell at the feet of the man who had betrayed them. Jan signalled to his cousin.

'There are more, just inside the treeline.'

Kobus nodded and began to scramble away, keeping low, Faanie right behind him. Jan was left standing close to the tree where the scout struggled feebly. His face was spattered with dried blood and his eyes rolled in agony. Jan stood watching him, and then took out the whisky, drinking deeply, feeling the heat of it in his throat, the buzz in his head. The man was trying to speak, spitting the words through his broken teeth and bloody lips.

'My brother.' He moaned and tried again, jerking his head in the direction of the body on the ground. 'My brother.'

In a sudden rush of pity, Jan took his knife and cut the rope. What the hell, the man was clearly dying. The scout toppled forward and began to crawl towards the body lying in the dirt. It was pitch dark now, but Jan caught a movement to his left and fired. A figure staggered into the open, screaming in pain, blood blooming on his ragged shirt. Faanie was behind him and he pushed his rifle into the man's back, so that he fell to his knees.

'I'll finish him off.' Faanie raised his rifle, grinning.

As his fingers tightened on the trigger there was a whistling noise, a thud, a faint rushing, squelching sound as he fell with the knife lodged in his throat his blood pumping in a dark stream down his chest and on to the ground. Jan stared at him in horror. Where had the weapon come from? Looking around he saw the scout he had freed. He had reached out and taken his brother's knife, half raised himself from the ground, and with one last, extraordinary effort he had hurled the weapon at his torturer.

'My fault. Christ, it was my fault,' Jan muttered.

He was responsible for Faanie's death. Kobus had lost his son, just as he and Lottie had lost Piet. If he had not cut the kaffir loose it would not have happened. Jan felt for the whisky bottle and stood there in the fading light, his head tipped back, his throat open, gulping, swallowing, choking, and swallowing again until he had drunk half of it. His head was spinning as he tried to focus on Faanie's body, to stoop down and pull out the knife. He could hear shots in the distance and the sound of running feet, and he spun round with his gun in his hand. His head was fogged, and all around him the trees had begun to whirl and dance and bend towards him in a great black circle, their branches stretching out to claw him, to tear at his clothing as he fell, hitting his skull on the stone that had tripped him. He felt himself floating in a strange silence, and then the clearing was full of people and he heard Kobus shouting, listened to his howls of desolation rising into the dome of the night as he knelt beside his dead son. For a moment Jan wanted to explain that he was responsible. But he was too tired to speak. He could still see Faanie's eyes, malevolent and cruel as he aimed his rifle, followed by an almost comic expression of surprise and terror as his life's blood drained away into the heedless African soil. Somewhere on the edge of his consciousness the informer lay, staring. Knowing. Then blackness.

When he awoke Jan was lying in a narrow hospital bed. Lottie was sitting in a chair beside him. She had fallen asleep, her head lolling forward, her hands clasped in her lap. Jan could see her fingers twitching. He made a sound and her eyes opened at once.

'Water.' He was surprised at the effort it took to form the word.

Lottie rose to her feet and ran to the door. 'Nurse! Nurse Sweeney! He's conscious! He's come round!'

'Water,' he said again.

'I'll give you just a little, through this straw,' Lottie said. 'But only a tiny amount, because too much could make you sick. Come now, Janni. I'll raise your head, and you take one sip.'

The water trickled into his mouth and Lottie dabbed a little on to his dry lips. 'Janni?' But he had slipped away from her again and she turned to Nurse Sweeney, her eyes questioning.

'Don't worry, dear. He's going to make progress from now on. He's back in the land of the living, and he can speak. The rest is just a matter of time. I'll find Dr Jackson and let him know.'

Lottie nodded and sat down again. She had been constantly at his side, watching as Jan fought for his life. He was still a terrible colour, his skin mottled, his breath laboured. It was blood poisoning, the doctor had explained. His head wound had become infected, and the sepsis had raced through his system. By rights he should be dead. He had arrived in terrible condition after hours in the truck, drifting in and out of consciousness, raving and screaming and weeping, until they had sedated him. Then he had sunk into a coma, and it had taken days before Kobus tracked down Lottie in Johannesburg. She had returned at once to take up her vigil, waiting for a sign of change, turning over in her mind the pain of her decision and the uncertainty of her future. A future without Mario.

Her first evening in Johannesburg had changed her thinking, her sense of right and wrong, tumbled her world and all that she had held dear for so many years. Sergio had encouraged her to cry, to tell him about the tragedy of her son and her problems in Rhodesia, to pour out all her sorrow and to empty herself of pent-up emotion. Then he insisted that she should rest for a couple of hours, before coming to his restaurant for a late dinner.

'Look at me. My eyes are puffed up and my nose is scarlet, and all my clothes creased,' Lottie said. 'I can't go out tonight.'

It was Elena who persuaded her to get ready, putting ice on her eyes,

549

helping her with her make-up and her hair, calling the housegirl to press her clothes. Then she handed her sister-in-law a stiff drink.

'You look fine,' she said. 'You'll enjoy this evening. We have friends joining us, but we're only eight.'

Lottie knew all but one of the guests. Elena had seated her beside a tall man, his face deeply lined, his eyes dark. She had the impression of an intense, sombre personality, and a reserve that made her wish she had been placed next to someone more light-hearted. His name was Mario, she discovered. And when he smiled unexpectedly she was reminded of sunrise above the darkened ridge she could see from her bedroom window at Langani. At first she found it daunting to make dinner conversation, after such a long absence from social gatherings such as these. There had been no parties in the wretched bungalow on Kobus's farm, and she felt that she would have nothing interesting to say. But she found the conversation stimulating as the guests compared Kenya and Rhodesia, debating the precarious conditions that Ian Smith's politics had generated and their own system of apartheid. No one mentioned the murder of her son, and Lottie was grateful not to be a subject of pity. When she spoke of Jan's being obliged to go out on security patrols and described her fears for his safety, her grief and anger threatened to return. She saw that Mario was listening with intense sympathy.

'It is hard to face the possibility of injury or death for someone you love,' he said. 'This is the most difficult thing.'

She looked at him more carefully and saw a sadness in him that mirrored her own, and she knew that for some reason he understood. After dinner they returned to Sergio's house to gather round the piano. Lottie's voice was a rich mezzo-soprano, and she found that Mario had a broad repertoire of Italian love songs and arias that he delivered in a fine baritone. And then there was Mozart. For Lottie it was as though everyone else in the room had faded away as she sang Zerlina's duet with Mario as her Don Giovanni. When it was finished he took her hand and kissed her fingers, and she was shocked by the sensation of his lips on her skin.

'*Bellissima*,' he said. 'A beautiful woman singing sublime music. There is nothing better.'

Lottie smiled at him, conscious for the first time in years of being admired for herself. She was filled with the pleasure of the music, and the sound of laughter and Italian voices. And the sensation of Mario still holding her fingers. She glanced around to see Sergio watching her closely, and snatched away her hand in confusion. As she prepared for bed, she was shocked to find herself wondering what it would be like if Mario kissed her, and she told herself that she was a crazy, middle-aged woman fantasising about a handsome stranger. But for one evening she had been able to rise above the quagmire of anguish and drudgery and loneliness that her life had become. She had been allowed a Cinderella moment as a carefree individual with no responsibilities, no tragic memories, no fears. It was a natural reaction. She had found Mario a wildly attractive contrast to the melancholy alcoholic that her husband had become and she did not need to feel ashamed. In a week or two she would be back in the bleak, dry rustlings of the tobacco fields and all would be the same once more. Lottie wondered if he had a wife, and if so where she had been tonight. She slept late next morning, something she had not done for years. Elena and Sergio had left for the restaurant when she got up. The maid knocked on her bedroom door as she was contemplating a morning's relaxation in the garden.

'A gentleman is on the phone for you, Madam,' she said.

Lottie's heart sank. It would be Jan, back from wherever he had gone with Kobus and furious that she had gone to Johannesburg, leaving only a terse note and his air ticket lying on the kitchen table. He was the only one who knew she was here. She braced herself to speak to him.

'Carlotta? This is Mario.'

Her breath was coming very fast. She felt foolishly self-conscious. 'Mario? I'm afraid Sergio and Elena aren't here. They went early to the restaurant.'

'I know. I spoke to them already. I was trying to organise lunch for all of us, but they are too busy. So I thought you might like to join me. Unless you have something else arranged?'

'No. No – that is, yes. Well, I don't know. I was going to the restaurant around lunchtime, to see if I could help. But I might only be in the way and—' She felt ridiculous.

'Then why don't we find a pleasant place for lunch?'

He drove her to a small hotel with a flower-filled terrace where they sat outside in the sunshine, drinking wine. She told him about Langani and the unbearable loss of her son, and Hannah's frightening determination to stay on. There were tears starring her eyes, and his expression was one of such sadness that she felt it was beyond normal compassion.

'Do you have a family, Mario?' She tried to smile at him and saw his face change in an instant, his eyes becoming dark.

He did not answer her, but concentrated for a moment on pouring wine into their glasses. 'You do not know my story, then?' he said.

Lottie shook her head, regretting that she had brought up what was evidently a harrowing choice of subject.

'I was married, yes. I had a wife and a daughter. At that time I owned a restaurant in Cape Town. My girl was just starting college, and Angela was taking her to meet the tutor at the university. It was an open day, for parents of the new students. I could not go with them. There was a big wedding and the restaurant was very busy. It was important, or so I thought. And then the police were at my door, telling me they were dead.'

Lottie made a small exclamation and leaned forward to put her hand over his.

'In those few minutes, my future died too, crushed like the car they were travelling in. He was drunk, the lorry driver. There was nothing Angela could have done to avoid him. The only mercy was that they were both killed instantly. No suffering. But one does not know what their thoughts were in those last seconds. I kept imagining them, seeing that juggernaut filling the windscreen, knowing they could not escape. I had to identify them. She was unrecognisable, Angela. Her face was . . .' He stopped. 'But Paola – her injuries were internal. She still looked so perfect, a beautiful girl at the beginning of her adult life.' He was gazing into the past. 'They called out to me as they were leaving the restaurant that morning. I was checking the menus, and I can't remember what I said. My last words to them, and I still do not remember what they were.'

'Mario,' Lottie whispered, 'I know how this is. I know.'

'I have never told anyone that. About my last words to them. But I have said it to you, perhaps because you know about pain and endurance. And you are a beautiful woman, Carlotta. In every way.' He looked at her. 'I feel that I have known you a long time. So, tell me, do you want to talk about Jan?'

She found herself pouring out all the wretchedness of her life in Rhodesia, trying to describe with honesty what she felt about her husband as he sank into a morass of despair, grieving alone, with no thought for her or for their future.

'Let us give ourselves some days of laughter while we are here,' he said, when she had finished. 'We will try to put our sadness behind us just for a while. What do you say?'

'I think it's the best idea I've heard in a very long time,' Lottie said.

They spent the remainder of the day sharing the details of their lives, holding up memories and incidents for the other to discover. He told her about his restaurant in Cape Town, how successful it had been and how he could not bear to walk into the place after his family had gone. He had known, even in the first numbing moments of his loss, that he must leave it and go away if he was to remain sane. For a time he had drifted, returning to his family in Tuscany. But last year he had come across an ancient building in the countryside close to Siena, and he had bought and restored it. Now it was gaining a reputation for hospitality and fine cooking.

'It is a way of passing the time,' he said, shrugging. 'Maybe one day I will turn the rest of it into a small hotel. For now, it is a way to get through my life, and that is all I need to think about.'

The days passed swiftly, and she spent them mostly with Mario, not caring what anyone else thought, grasping the allure of this wonderful man who understood her needs, and tried to anticipate her every wish. Sergio was anxious, she knew. But he did not press her to discuss the situation, and it was clear that Elena was not critical of the affair. Lottie had never dreamed that she could be unfaithful to her husband, but when Mario kissed her and began to caress her she drew him into her with a passion that was thrilling, and she could not look beyond the moments of their lovemaking, or think of what might happen in the future. It was as if she had been transported to another existence and she hardly knew herself. A surge of initial guilt was swept away in the relief and joy of being a desirable woman once more.

Five days later they were lying in Mario's hotel bed, sated and half sleeping, when the telephone rang. It was like the force of a hurricane, ripping apart the fragile structure of her happiness.

'Carlotta.' It was Sergio, and his voice was grave. 'There's been a phone call from Rhodesia. Jan's cousin, Kobus.'

She sat very still, the sheet draped across her breasts, the receiver clutched in her hand.

'There was an ambush. Jan has been injured. They took him to the hospital in Bulawayo several days ago, but they did not know where to find you.'

'How bad is it?' She found herself whispering for no reason. Mario was sitting up, his hand in the small of her back, supporting her, watching her with concern.

'He had a head wound that became infected. Turned into blood poisoning. He's very ill. I don't know what you want to do. But if you feel you should go, I can book you on a flight tomorrow morning.'

She was numb as Mario helped her up, finding her clothes, buttoning her dress, like a parent with a sick child.

'It may not be so bad,' he said. 'From what you have told me, he is a strong man.'

'Yes.' She looked at him, ill from the pain of leaving.

'Carlotta, I know he needs you now. But we have found something . . .'

The tearing sensation of parting was excruciating, and the guilt of having left Jan, of not wanting to go back to him, was as bad. She swallowed a sob and clung to Mario.

'I don't want to go back. I'm so frightened I'll never escape from there. But even if we never meet again—'

'We will meet again, *cara*. What we have found is only a beginning. I believe we are meant to be together. We will write to each other, and you will promise that you will not give up or forget?'

She promised, but the cold wash of reality was already sluicing away her joy. She reached up to Mario and kissed him one last time.

'Let me drive you,' he said.

'No. I'll take a taxi to Sergio's. I could not say goodbye again. In front of others. Now is the best time.'

They stood together for a few moments, embracing, whispering to one another, memorising every line of face, curve of flesh, nuance of voice. Then she phoned the reception desk for a taxi.

In the white, antiseptic ward in Bulawayo she drew up the chair and sat down again beside her husband, trying to banish the memories of passion and completeness she had felt with Mario. What had she been thinking of, anyway? There could never have been a happy ending to this holiday romance. He would return to Italy and file her away in his mind as an enjoyable interlude, something that had soothed his grief, filled the void of his own loss for a short time. She had gone into the affair willingly, without considering the inevitable outcome, and now she must put it aside and tend to her husband. It was over.

She lifted Jan's hand, and said aloud, 'I'm here, Janni, if you want another sip of water. I'm right here.'

He turned his head and his fingers closed over hers. Like shackles. She tried to smile as he opened his eyes.

Chapter 29

Kenya, February 1966

When she arrived at Buffalo Springs, Sarah was light-headed with relief. The heavy presence that had dogged her for so long seemed to evaporate in the afternoon heat, leaving her free to make adjustments. There was no pressure on her to tread carefully, to watch every word she said, or to try and conceal her thoughts. Dan had met her at Nanyuki, sympathy recognisable on his thin face and in the firm grasp of his hand as he greeted her.

'I won't ask any questions,' he said. 'I know they're too painful to answer. But I want you to understand that there's nothing Allie and I wouldn't do to help you through. You only have to say the word.'

Sarah nodded, her mouth clamped shut to prevent the sob that rose in her throat as she got into the Land Rover beside him. Allie was waiting for them in camp, and there were tears in her eyes as she hugged Sarah without a word. Dan placed an arm around her shoulders and led her to an armchair before making her a stiff drink. Neither one of them spoke, allowing Sarah to compose herself and to signal the direction that their conversation might take. She was grateful for their silence and glad to be in their company.

'Do you want to talk about it?' Allie asked her. 'Or shall we leave that for another time?'

'Another time. Can't manage it today. But thanks. Tell me what's been happening here,' Sarah said, when she could trust her voice again.

They kept the conversation focused on the next phase of their work, and the discussions Dan had had recently with their sponsors in Nairobi. Sarah took out her portfolio and they studied the recent photographs of their elephants, suggesting pictures to submit with the annual report that was near to completion. Dan was about to make a formal presentation to the board of the African Wildlife Federation who had been their sponsors for the past three years. Funding for the following year would largely depend on the impact of this next presentation.

'We've had a nibble from *National Geographic*.' Allie's pride shone in her eyes. 'They're going to send someone up to have a look at our project later in the year. That would be great for all of us. We'd benefit from the extra money of course, and a feature in the magazine would bring Dan the wider recognition he deserves. Maybe they'd want to use your photographs, Sarah. That would be something.'

She spent the afternoon reading Dan and Allie's latest records, and preparing her notebooks and cameras for the following day. Allie had arranged that she and Sarah would spend the next few weeks watching a new group, getting to know the elephants by their individual marks and habits. After dinner, when she returned to her rondavel, she opened her suitcase and began to stow her clothes and books on their customary shelves. As she was putting her pencils and notebooks into the drawer of her desk, her fingers touched a bulky shape. When she took it out, her limbs turned to lead. Folded carefully into the packet were all the letters she had written to Piet during her first weeks at Buffalo Springs. A continuous conversation with him, documenting in prose and in sketches all the miraculous discoveries of her first experiences at Buffalo Springs. There were descriptions of animals and the people, drawings of flowers and trees and birds, words that revealed her thoughts, her most fervent hopes and her overpowering love for him. She had not sent them to him, because she had not known whether he truly loved her. And they were too personal a testimony to offer as a friend. When he asked her to marry him she had decided to put them all together into an album, with a collection of her best photographs, and to give them to him on their wedding day. She sat down at her desk and read each line slowly, dwelling on the way she had always felt that he was beside her in those early days. She remained in her chair, holding the shreds of her dreams in her hands, until the sun rose and offered her another day.

A week after her return, a safari car drew up outside the fence of the compound, and George Broughton-Smith got out. It was amazing, Sarah thought, how he could arrive in a cloud of dust and emerge as fresh and well groomed as ever. Just like Camilla. He looked tanned and fit and his linen shirt was rolled up at the sleeves.

'I'm sorry to arrive without warning,' he said. 'I've been in Samburu, looking around and talking to the warden about their problems. I knew you were here, Sarah, and I very much wanted to see you. I'm so very sorry about what happened at Langani. I know you had just become engaged to that terrific young man. There's nothing I can say that would be adequate. I'm just so sorry.'

'I've only been back at work for a few days,' she said, knowing that she would begin to scream out loud if one more person mentioned how sorry they were. What use was their sorrow now that Piet was gone for ever? But his offering of consolation was genuine and she saw that he had been appalled by the tragedy that had overtaken her.

'I admire your bravery.' George saw her face begin to crumple and moved on to a safer subject. 'Look, my dear, I'm staying at Samburu Lodge tonight, and I wonder if we could have dinner together. You could stay the night over there and be back here first thing in the morning.'

Sarah did not respond immediately. She was not sure that she wanted to talk to him.

'I'd like to discuss something important with you,' he said, and there was something in his tone that made her accept his invitation.

He was waiting for her in the bar, but she was already regretting that she had come at all. There was nothing she wanted to say to him. It was too late now, for Piet and for Langani and everything they had hoped to build together. His face was tense, as if he was about to impart some vital secret.

'I want to tell you about Camilla,' he said, when they had ordered dinner.

'I know she doesn't want anything to do with me. Or with Kenya. I wrote to her after Piet's . . . after he . . .' Sarah blinked away the sting of tears and tried to continue in a steady voice. 'I never heard from her, though. I suppose it's because of what happened to her at Langani. It must have been a terrible ordeal, the cut on her face, worrying about how it would affect her.'

'Sarah, I have to tell you that it's my fault she hasn't been in touch with you.' He saw her surprise. 'We had a rather bad falling-out, I'm afraid. Soon after she came back from Kenya. It was a problem largely of my making – no, it was all of my making, in fact. And then I didn't see her or talk to her for almost three months. So she felt badly, because she never had an opportunity to discuss Langani with me, or to tell me about Piet's problems. But it wasn't her fault at all. It was because I was not available for her. And then Marina became ill.'

'I didn't know any of that.' Sarah began to feel some regret. 'I phoned Burford looking for Camilla, you know. I asked Marina to pass her a message. But perhaps she never did.'

'Marina has leukaemia,' he said. 'She's extraordinarily brave. Camilla has been spending a great deal of time with her. That's why she didn't fly out here when she heard about Piet's death. It was a terrible choice for her to make, but Marina was very weak and we thought . . . well, she has rallied since then, but it won't be for long.'

'And Camilla's face?'

'There is a scar, but she's going to have an operation to remove it. The timing depends on Marina's illness.'

'I'm so sorry,' Sarah said, using the word she had wanted to banish only hours ago.

'We've had some difficult months. Especially for Camilla, what with her injury and her mother's illness and the love affair.'

'Does she talk about Anthony?'

George shook his head. 'I saw him in Nairobi. With the newest thing in his life. A brunette who can't be more than seventeen. For all his admirable passion about conservation and wildlife, his attitude towards humanity leaves a great deal to be desired. He hurt her very badly.'

'We've all hurt her,' Sarah said. She felt she must be honest. 'I knew there had to be something wrong, but I stupidly went along with Hannah's theory that she wanted to blot us out of her mind after the robbery. And I was so taken up with my own happiness, the fact that Piet and I were going to get married, and . . .' She could not go on.

George put his hand over hers, grieving for her and the tragedy that had snatched all the joy out of her young life. And out of his daughter's life too. 'I think Camilla has someone who loves her,' he said. 'The doctor who is looking after her face, actually. And now Hannah has the funds for Langani, so that may change things for her too.'

'Your organisation has given funds to Langani?' Sarah tried to hide her bewilderment. 'She didn't say anything.'

'Perhaps it's hard for her to discuss it,' he suggested. 'I can understand why she would feel that it's all too late. She didn't want to talk to me at all.

Anyway, I have managed to arrange a grant for Langani from my foundation, and it will help her to continue. If that's what she wants to do.'

'That's wonderful for her.' Sarah's head was spinning. She had spoken to Hannah on the radio two days ago, and no mention had been made of the grant. 'I'd like to contact Camilla,' she said. 'Where will I find her?'

'You could try the flat in Hyde Park Gate. We spend most of our time with Marina these days. She was in Burford until recently, but she's too weak to stay there now. I'll give you the address and telephone number.'

Sarah said goodbye to him after dinner, because she intended to leave at dawn so as not to miss any of her day's work. Sleep did not come until the early hours, and she lay under her mosquito net in the unaccustomed space of a double bed and thought about Camilla. What must she be feeling now, with her mother so close to death? And what could have caused such a serious rift with her father? She adored him, had always sought his love and approval. There was something odd about the story. Sarah frowned in the darkness. If she had only followed her instincts. But tomorrow evening, when she got back to camp, she would write.

She left Samburu Lodge early and drove fast. Allie was waiting for her, but she did not ask about George Broughton-Smith or the reason behind his visit. Later, when they found a shady tree where they could eat their packed lunch, Sarah told her what he had said.

'I'm glad to see Wildlife Federation money going to Langani,' Allie remarked. 'It's a great chance to show this country, and the world at large, what can be done if private ranchers give some of their land and their time to conservation. Will Hannah open up the lodge now, do you think?'

'I don't know. She can't cope with the idea at the moment. I suggested that she might use it as a training centre. Set up a fund in Piet's name, to carry on his work. But it was a mistake. Tactless and much too early. She was very angry with me.'

'Anger is the weapon people use to beat off grief. But it causes problems if it's allowed to fester too long.'

'I know,' Sarah said. 'I hope Lars can help her through it, now that he's back.'

When they returned to the compound in the evening, Viktor's car was parked outside. Sarah's heart sank.

'Well, well,' Allie commented drily. 'You're getting your fair share of visitors this week.'

'You can keep this one,' Sarah said. 'I need time to myself. I don't need visitors right now, and especially not Viktor.'

He was surprisingly sensitive, offering condolences and then keeping the topics of conversation to elephants, politics and architecture. But Sarah found it hard to master the anger that simmered in her when she thought of the way he had discarded Hannah like an old pair of socks. She sat quietly through the dinner, making little contribution to the discussions. It was Dan who mentioned her night at Samburu.

'Did they have any leopards there last night?' he asked. 'I'm not sure I approve of this idea of hanging bait up in a tree and encouraging them to come to one spot all the time. It's not natural, and God knows what the long-term effects may be.'

'You were at Samburu Lodge overnight?' Viktor was surprised.

'She was dining with the money man,' Dan said, grinning at her. 'George Broughton-Smith was here. I hear his outfit is going to donate some money for rhino protection in the area.'

'He's a good man,' Allie said. 'Sound. Doesn't get carried away with wild schemes or get bullied by politicians. How much time does he spend in Nairobi these days?'

'I do not move in those circles,' Viktor said. 'He is still friendly with the diplomatic crowd, but I think he spends his leisure time engaged in other pursuits that are not of interest to me.'

'What pursuits?' Sarah said, puzzled.

'You are too young and innocent to discuss this subject,' Viktor said, with a knowing look, and his wicked laugh. He lit a cigar. 'We will not talk about such things at dinner. They make me nervous.'

Sarah refused coffee and excused herself. She was weary and she wanted to look over her notes for the day, and think about what she would say to Camilla. If she could find the energy to write to her tonight, perhaps Viktor would take it to Nairobi and post it. She sat down at her table, turned up the paraffin lantern and took up her pen, just as there was a knock on the door.

'Viktor.' She was less than pleased to see him. 'I'm trying to write an important letter. Now that I think of it, perhaps you'd post it for me in Nairobi tomorrow?'

'You have barely spoken a word to me this evening,' he said. 'And I have travelled across stony deserts and dangerous country filled with man-eating beasts in order to find you.'

'Viktor,' she said, placing her hand firmly on his chest and pushing him away, 'I'm sure you're trying to cheer me, but actually it doesn't help.' She stopped, her mouth twisted in pain. 'Please understand that it's all I can do to open my eyes every morning, and try to carry on like a normal human being. I can't deal with anything else.'

'Of course. I understand this,' he said. 'But there are many forms of consolation, and—'

'No, Viktor. It could never be like that. For heaven's sake, leave me be. Go to bed. In the morning I'll give you my letter to Camilla to post. That's all I want from you.'

'Ah, the daughter.' His smile was not pleasant. 'Strange how they try to hide it, these men. But it always comes out in the end.'

'What comes out?' she asked. There was a mild fluttering in her stomach.

'He is like many of these very grand, high-born Englishmen.' He was waving his hand in a little upward gesture, the meaning unmistakable. 'From their school days they learn to like little boys.'

'No, that can't be right. Nairobi is full of ugly rumours and vicious gossip.'

'You are so innocent, Sarah. For a scientist who is trained to observe animal behaviour, you are quite blind. You can give me the letter in the morning. But in the meantime—'

He reached for her again, insistent now, pulling her close. His arms tightened around her and as he bent towards her he was murmuring something about carrying her away from her grief into a place where she could forget her sorrow for a while. Sarah was boiling with rage. She was in mourning for her beloved Piet. How could this disgusting man think that a casual sexual encounter could ease such a cataclysmic loss? And what kind of man would abandon one woman in the blink of an eye, and then have the gall to try and seduce her best friend? She made an attempt to free herself, but his hold was too strong. For a second, she went limp against him, and he smiled down into her eyes, certain that she would surrender. Then she brought her knee up hard into his groin, and her own smile was one of triumph as he buckled with a groan and collapsed on to the ground, his breath coming in gasps of pain and surprise. As he staggered to his feet, Sarah raised her foot and shoved him unceremoniously through the door, slamming it after him. Her small hut shook with the force of it and she sat on the bed, aghast at the violence of her reaction. But she was not sorry. He deserved it. After a few moments, she heard him stumble away.

In the silence that followed his departure, she thought about George Broughton-Smith, unable to accept the idea that Viktor had put in her mind. It could not be true. George was a normal husband, a loving father. He had been married for over twenty years to the same woman. It was not a happy marriage, but surely this was not the reason for the animosity between himself and Marina? And if it was, did Camilla know about it, or had someone told her? George had said that he had fallen out with his daughter. With dread, Sarah read the letter she had started. What could she say to Camilla now? Was there no end to the ruinous events and revelations that had overtaken them all? She undressed and got into bed, but sleep eluded her. After a while she went to her desk and opened her file. She lit her lamp once again and read her day's notes. Animal relationships were definitely easier. When she had finished revising her work she took up the letter she had started to Camilla and tore it into shreds. There would have to be another time.

There was no sign of Viktor when she came to breakfast and she was glad. For the rest of the week she worked with Allie, listening to her advice, learning something with every passing hour, impatient to be out studying her own group of elephants. She said nothing about Viktor's visit to her hut, or the reason for his precipitate departure, but somehow, she thought Allie knew.

'I'd like you to pick up a package and collect the mail today,' Dan said to her one morning. 'You can spend some time using your social skills in the Game Department at Isiolo, so you don't forget them as Allie and I have done.'

When she collected the parcel and a bundle of letters her spirits lifted. There were two for her, from her mother and from Tim. She resisted the temptation to open them at once. It would be better to read them in camp and savour them there. Allie had left a note pinned to the door of the rondavel. *Grateful if you could type up Dan's notes. Left them on the tray in the Mess Tent. Good luck with his chicken scrawl. See you later. A.* Sarah poured a cup of tea out of a Thermos and sat down to digest the family news. The first page of her mother's letter was in bold print. Tim and Deirdre had decided to get married. They were planning a quiet wedding immediately after Easter. Sarah must come home, if only for a week or two. Raphael could send the money for her airfare. It would be wise to take a little time off, to step back from the trauma of the last weeks. They longed to see her, to hold her close, to help ease the pain that she lived with, day and night. The practice and the house were coming on well, and she would not believe how great the garden looked already, and the stables. Tim's letter, in his illegible shorthand, was typically brief. It was unthinkable that he should get married with his little sister half a world away. Maybe he was crazy, he said, but Deirdre loved and needed him, and he was taking the big jump. And he wanted, above all, Sarah to be there.

She knew immediately that she would not go. Could not leave here. She did not even want to return to Langani for the time being. It was only in the harsh, uncompromising beauty of this remote place that she might eventually find some kind of reconciliation and peace. It was only here that she could learn to remember Piet, without dying inside each time she thought of him. Here she could try to come to terms with her loss, and regain her vision of him, whole and vital and happy. The other would destroy her. She did not want to be influenced by outside ideas as to how she should live now that he was gone. If she left the camp she would be subjected to a version of herself as seen through other people's eyes – the object of compassion and pity. She would be smothered. Here she had a goal, something she could do that would make a difference, something that he would have been proud of. Sarah folded the letters carefully and placed them in the drawer of her desk. Then she made her way to the small office and sat down to decipher Dan's notes. It was Lars's radio call that brought her back to Langani. Jeremy Hardy had been to see them, he said. He described the policeman's startling news.

'There's been no arrest,' Hardy had said. 'But there's something that I have to tell you.' He paced the room, his hands behind his back. 'We had a report this morning, from one of the patrols in the area of dense woodland just beyond your eastern boundary. There's a clearing in the forest where they found an abandoned, makeshift hut. More of a shelter, really. The type of things these illegal hunters use.' He paused and turned to face Hannah. 'On the ground was a pile of bones. Human remains.'

Lars heard Hannah's gasping breath, and he put a hand on her shoulder. She sat very still, her gaze directed towards the ridge.

'I went down there straight away,' Hardy said. 'I wanted to look for myself. There were the ashes of a fire, and a number of bones lying around the clearing. And we saw some Kikuyu ceremonial items littered about. Cowrie shells, a few strips of leather from arm or leg decorations, some copper wire and a panga. Most important, though, we found a feathered headdress caught in the bushes a few hundred yards away. Like the one Sarah described. It looks as though the wearer had stopped in the clearing to prepare some food. We believe the man who died was cooking a meal, because we also found the bones of a small antelope.'

'He's dead then.' Hannah's voice was flat and hard.

'I can't say that for certain,' Hardy said. 'But we haven't been notified that anyone is missing in this area, and the location fits the route he might have taken that night. It's logical to assume that he worked his way down from the ridge, going over the rocks and then skirting the edge of the plains until he came to a section of the forest that would make a good hiding place.'

'How – how did he die?' Hannah could barely find her voice to ask the question.

'Looks like hyenas. There seems to have been a pack of them. He must have put up a good fight, because the ground around the site was pretty churned up. There's evidence that he killed a couple of the pack before the rest got him. My theory is that he had been running since he left here, and he was exhausted. He probably killed a young buck for meat, and got careless while he was skinning it to put on the fire. The hyena pack could have been following his scent – he must have been covered in blood himself.'

He saw Hannah place her hand over her mouth, biting down on her knuckles.

'I'm sorry I can't give you anything more definite,' Hardy went on, 'but the trackers who found the bones say that the kill could have been made around the time of Piet's death. From the condition of the bones themselves, and the surrounding ground. It fits, my dear, although we may never be able to say it with complete certainty. But I am as sure as I can be that the remains are Simon Githiri's. A grim ending, but he got his just deserts. We have removed all the bones for forensic examination, but there's not a lot else we'll be able to learn from them, I'm afraid.'

Hannah looked up at him, her face ashen. 'Then it's over?' Her voice was hardly more than a whisper. She put her hand up to touch Lars's fingers, as though she needed physical support, no matter how slight.

'I hope I can say it's over, yes,' Hardy met her gaze. 'But if these are Simon's remains, then we will never know the reasons for what he did here. It may be that Langani was the first of other properties that he planned to attack. There are a number of young hotheads who feel they've been cheated. By the white men who took their land, and then by their own politicians who promised them everything after Independence, and delivered nothing.'

'I wanted him to die,' Hannah said, her eyes bleak. 'But I wanted him to have to face what he had done, to explain, and then be made to pay for it.'

'At least he died a terrible death,' Lars said, 'a punishing death. And even if we do not have all the answers, Hannah, it is enough to know that he is gone and he cannot hurt you any more. It is finished, and you can start a new life.'

'Can I?' Hannah was holding on to his hand, and he could feel the tremors running through her body.

'You have to,' he said, simply. 'You have to leave it behind you now, and concentrate on bringing a new peace and new life to Langani.'

'There's one thing that might clarify this,' Hardy said. 'Sarah saw Simon on the ridge that night. She saw his headdress and decorations. I'd like her to look at the items we found, and see if they match what she remembers.'

'I'll get her on the radio,' Lars said. 'Let you know when she can come down. Meantime, thanks, Jeremy, for coming to tell us yourself, and for everything you've done since this case began.'

Hannah stood up, and gave Hardy a small smile. 'Lars is right,' she said. 'We owe you a great deal. Thank you, Jeremy.' She stood on the steps, watching the jeep drive away.

'We should call Lottie and Jan.' Lars came out and stood beside her. 'And I will contact Sarah now.'

*

'On the following day Sarah met him at the Nanyuki police station.' The headdress lay on the table in Hardy's office, with the remains of the leather loincloth and the bands that had encircled Simon's arms and legs. She had expected to feel something when she saw them, a kind of release, a feeling of finality. There was no doubt in her mind that they were his. But she felt only a heaviness in her heart that made her want to weep again.

'That's the headdress,' she said. 'And the other things he was wearing.'

'Then I think we can now say that Simon is dead,' Hardy said. 'And be thankful for it.'

Hannah was waiting at Langani. They held one another tight, and then went to sit in the garden under the flame tree.

'There's something that's been on my mind these last weeks,' Hannah said. 'I'd like to open the lodge, Lars. Have it the way Piet wanted. You and Sarah told me that before, but I wasn't ready. Now I think we should make it happen. If I'm going to have a child then I'll need every part of Langani to be viable.'

'It's a good decision, Hannah,' Lars said.

'Would you come up there with me? Drive us there?' Hannah's voice was shaky, but her expression was stern, defiant. 'I'd like to go there with you both.'

The lodge was eerily quiet. It seemed that even the wind had died away as they stepped inside. Lars had maintained the buildings so that they were clean, and free of the devouring bush that surrounded them. Hannah felt a catch in her throat as she saw the shrubs she had planted, leafing out with greedy energy around the bedroom doors. Two crowned cranes were standing at the waterhole, looking down at their own reflected beauty. Sarah and Hannah stood there, hand in hand, barely able to keep their emotions in check.

'I'll start next week,' Hannah said. 'I'll come with David and we will put the furniture back in place and clean it all. And I'll interview possible staff. I've been thinking that some of the wives on the farm could learn to take care of the rooms, and to help in the kitchen too. And now I want to go to his special place. To tell him what has happened. That it is finished and we will go on, just as he wanted.'

They stood on the ridge looking down over Piet's last resting place.

'Hannah, I have an idea,' Sarah tried to keep her voice light, and to banish the sense of desolation that still rushed through her when she thought of him. 'It was the elephants that made me think of it – when I watched them cover their dead ones so lovingly, with the stones and branches. I don't think Piet would have wanted a carved memorial. But a cairn, built from the rocks that belong here naturally. That could be right. We could put them where the pyre was, and plant a tree in the centre. Something that would give shade. A place where birds could nest. He'd always have company then.'

'An acacia,' Lars said. 'That would do well up here, and we could see it from the house.'

Hannah said nothing, and Sarah was apprehensive. Perhaps she had been too precipitate, offering this proposal without waiting for the right moment. Another stupid mistake.

'I think an *Acacia tortilis* would be perfect,' Hannah's face was soft. 'It will grow very tall, it has that wonderful flat-topped crown like a big umbrella, and when it flowers it's quite beautiful. He'd love it. It's a beautiful plan.'

She bent down and picked up two smooth, white stones. 'These would be perfect for Piet's cairn,' she said. 'Let's look for some more like them.'

In a short time they had developed a steady rhythm, selecting stones and pebbles for their shape or colour, setting them down one by one on the blackened earth. It became a meditation, a communion with Piet in his death, a ritual burying of the violence that had reduced his life to ashes. Now those same ashes rested beneath a gentle weight of bleached, sun-warmed stones. At last, hot and sweating from exertion, they stood back to survey the result of their efforts.

'It looks good,' Hannah said. 'I know Piet is happy with this.' She wiped her face with a handkerchief. 'I need a cold drink. Let's take the Thermos and go up to the top of the ridge.'

They sat with their backs against the rock that Piet had always favoured, side by side, searching for peace as the sun began to spread its evening band of colour across the horizon, and the god of Kirinyaga watched them from his icy summit at the edge of the plains.

'I saw George Broughton-Smith,' Sarah said over dinner.

'He's given us a grant,' Hannah said. 'For a while I couldn't accept it. I didn't even tell Lars until a week ago. But it will help us, and if I think about it rationally I should be grateful.'

Sarah waited for a moment, considering whether she should continue with what she wanted to say in Lars's presence. Then she explained what she had been told about Marina, and finally she told them what she had heard about George, although she did not disclose the source.

There was disbelief in Lars's expression, but Hannah showed no sign of surprise.

'If it's true and she didn't know, then that would have been hard on her,' she said. 'And now we have to write to her, both of us, or phone. Maybe we can do it together while you're here, Sarah. We must ask her to come, when she can. To come back so that we can be together again.'

Late in the evening they booked calls to both London and Burford, but there was no reply, and they concluded that Marina must be in hospital, or that things were better and Camilla had gone out somewhere with her mother.

In the morning Lars drove them both into Nanyuki, where Hannah had an appointment with Dr Markham.

'How are things going at the farm?' Sarah asked, as they sat in the waiting room.

'Fine,' Hannah said. 'Better than I'd expected. Lars seems cheerful. He's installed in the cottage where Mike Stead lived, and he's working too hard. I don't see him all that much, except to discuss the farm. He keeps his distance.' Her tone was sad when she said the last words, but then she brightened. 'I'm so grateful he's here.'

She looked well, Sarah thought. Pregnancy suited her. Her skin was almost luminous, and her golden hair gleamed in the sunlight. She wore a loose shirt over baggy jeans that hid the slight expansion of her waist. Sarah realised with a shock that the shirt was one of Piet's. Hannah saw her glance.

'I didn't have any maternity clothes,' she said with a shrug. 'And most of my normal clothes are an inch or two too tight now. I thought we might look in Patel's *duka* after this, and see if there's anything I can buy in bigger sizes. So what do you think, heh?' She patted her stomach, laughing. 'Soon I'll start to bulge, and I won't be able to hide it any more. But it doesn't matter. Nothing matters as long as the baby is OK.'

She was talking fast, seemingly happy and confident, but Sarah realised that she was nervous. She was meeting neighbours and friends who would soon know that she was pregnant. It would be hard to deal with the inevitable gossip. The door to Dr Markham's consulting room opened and he beckoned Hannah inside. Lars came back from the bank and the petrol station, and sat down with Sarah to wait.

'He says I'm disgustingly healthy,' Hannah announced. 'I have to come back in a month. Let's go to the *duka*.'

Mr Patel's shop was piled with general stock, and smelled of burlap sacking and dried meat and paraffin. In one corner, behind the wooden counter, were Cellophane-wrapped packages of garments stacked in piles. Sarah and Hannah examined the possibilities without enthusiasm. Lars was ordering supplies for the farm at the other end of the shop, avoiding any involvement in Hannah's purchases. With suppressed giggles they selected two voluminous blouses, and Hannah chose material to make additional clothes. As they took their parcels and headed for the door, Hannah swore under her breath.

'Bloody hell! I did not want to run into her, of all people.' She dived towards the back of the shop as a large woman came in, but it was too late. Hettie Kruger was bearing down on them, her small eyes observant and full of malice.

'Hannah, my dear. How nice to see you out and about. You look very well, considering.'

'Considering what, Hettie?' Hannah's chin went up.

The large woman gave her a condescending smile. 'Considering all your troubles, my dear. I heard your mother had left. That must be hard for you, all alone in your condition. It's good that we have Dr Markham still here with us, but you'd think Lottie would have wanted to stay and help. But then, with things as they are . . .'

Lars had loomed up, out of the depths of the shop. He came to stand beside Hannah, putting his arm around her shoulders and fixing Mrs Kruger with a cool stare.

'Good to see you, Hettie. I hope you're keeping well?'

She gave him a cloying smile, eyes gleaming in her puffy face, reminding Sarah of a hippo lying in the shallows, poised to attack the unwary.

'I'm well, thank you, Lars. I heard you'd returned. It must be difficult at Langani, with all that has happened. It's very good of you to keep working in the circumstances. Will you be staying on?'

'What circumstances would those be, Hettie?'

Hettie Kruger's eyes travelled slowly over Hannah's figure. 'There are no secrets in our little community,' she said. 'But we're happy to make allowances for mistakes. And we're here to help anyone who has been left high and dry.'

Hannah flushed scarlet and opened her mouth to speak, but Lars squeezed her shoulder hard. He glared down at Mrs Kruger for a moment, and then seemed to make up his mind. His face cleared, as though he had suddenly understood something that had been puzzling him.

'Ah! You're referring to our happy event, is that it? Hannah and I are delighted. We've just been for her check-up, and you'll be pleased to know everything is fine. Of course, we had thought of having the wedding earlier. Only we couldn't do that. We needed a little time, after all the sadness. But we have decided we should go ahead now and get married. We'll have a ceremony that will bring back the joy in our lives. Won't it, Hannah?'

Hannah was staring up at Lars, dumbfounded. His fingers dug into her shoulder as he prompted her again.

'We haven't decided on the exact date, but it will be very soon, won't it, Han? Very soon now.'

Hannah looked at Hettie Kruger's hard, disbelieving face, and then back up at Lars who was smiling at her with enormous tenderness and some humour. She turned her gaze back to Hettie, and found her voice.

'Yes. Yes, Lars and I are getting married very soon,' she said feebly. 'And we are so happy. Really very happy.'

As Hettie Kruger sailed out of the door, bristling with the news, Lars turned Hannah round to face him. He took her into his arms and kissed her mouth, and then kissed her again.

'Yes, we are. Very, very happy,' he repeated.

Chapter 30

London, February 1966

Camilla was bone-tired. She had survived a punishing week of shoots, a magazine interview, two television appearances and a charity dinner. Her one wish was to escape to a place where no one could possibly recognise her. The sky was dull and overcast. As darkness came in the early evening she longed for sunlight and the smell of hot African dust, for the scarlet blaze of a Maasai herdsman driving his cattle across a yellow plain. Above all, she wanted to be with Sarah and Hannah, so that she could share their grief. But she was trapped in London, unable to be away for more than a few days, shuttling between assignments and visits to her mother.

She spent many of her evenings in Edward's flat, although it was often late at night before he came home. He had cut down on some of his commitments over the past two months, but there were still many days when he was consulting long after normal hours, or lecturing, or at the hospital where a complex emergency had been brought in. Camilla had mixed feelings about his all-consuming dedication to his work. There were times when she arrived at his flat drained after a long day's shoot, or emotionally threadbare at the end of an afternoon with Marina. Then she longed for company, for a companionable dinner with light conversation and laughter, or a spontaneous outing to the cinema. But on some evenings she was glad Edward was occupied, so that she did not have to think of anything other than a long, hot bath and an hour or two beside the fire with a book and the distraction of television.

'I love you, Camilla,' he said to her frequently. 'Come and live with me. We spend most of our time together. I can look after you better, see you more, if we live in the same house.'

But she refused, unable to explain either to him or to herself the reluctance she felt about giving up her flat and her independence. It was the only place where she could still relax, climbing the stairs and turning the key in the door to slough off the artifice of her public image. She did not want to live with Edward, any more than she wanted to fulfil her mother's hopes of having her at home permanently, rather than dropping in on a daily basis. She had promised Marina they would have supper together this evening, but in the meantime she had a date for lunch with her father. He had been in Kenya for ten days and he was anxious to see her.

At his club in Pall Mall she was amused by the elderly porter's admiring appraisal of her short skirt and patent leather boots. He escorted her to the bar where George was waiting. Their conversation jumped from London's theatre and galleries to the forests of India, where he had lately been to study the conservation of tigers and their habitat. Discussion of Marina's health was postponed. They would both be seeing her later in the day.

'I've had letters from both Sarah and Hannah,' Camilla said. 'I don't know how they are able to function at all.'

'I didn't see Hannah,' he answered. 'But she should receive the first instalment this month, of the grant I arranged for Langani. And she has Lars to help her. Sarah was very brave outwardly, but it's a thin shell. She's an exceptional young woman.'

'I should have gone when Piet died, but—'

'You couldn't have gone, my dear,' George said. 'You had to be here for your mother.'

'Don't, Daddy. You don't have to make excuses. The truth is that I didn't go because I was afraid. I hadn't seen them or been in touch since September, and I was ashamed. But I will go when I can. As soon as—' She did not need to finish the sentence.

'I have another piece of news,' George said. 'I'm moving my base of operations. Not now, of course. Not immediately, but later in the year.'

'Where to?' Camilla was surprised.

'To Nairobi, oddly enough. I'll be working closely with the Ministry of Tourism, and supervising the projects to which we've given funding. Keep a tight rein on where the money goes.'

'Haven't you been doing that anyway?' Camilla asked. 'From here, with visits to Kenya?'

'Yes, I have. But we've got four or five new East African proposals in the pipeline, and now someone has to be on the ground there full-time.' He paused for a few moments. 'I offered to take it on, actually. I started up most of these projects, and I'd like to see them through myself.'

'I can't believe you're going back to live in Nairobi,' Camilla said. 'It seems very strange.'

'I'm enthusiastic about it,' he said. 'I hope to see more of your young friends once I'm there. Help them along in any way I can. So what do you think?'

'Well, if you can spend time out in the parks and game reserves, rather than sitting at a desk . . . It's odd, the way life zigzags in unexpected directions. You're off to the wilds of Africa, and I'm still in the big city, locked into the eye of a camera. Moth to the flame.'

He wondered whether he should mention that he had seen Anthony Chapman again, and that they would work together in the future as members of a conservation board. But he decided against it. That was probably the real reason she did not want to go back. Memories of Kenya made her sad.

'How's Edward?' he said.

'Busy.'

'Would you ever think of marrying him, Camilla?'

'I wouldn't think of marrying anyone,' she said crisply. 'I'm much too busy. Too much going on. When it can be fitted in, there's an Italian company that wants to do some photographs in the Bahamas and New York. I'll be in Paris next week for a couple of days, and again in a month, if things are still the same with Mother. And I've found someone really professional to start doing beading and embroidery for me. I took my African designs for jackets and handbags to a place in Bond Street, but before they made up their minds Saul Greenberg bought them. He wants to do a limited, exclusive line for a boutique in New York. Suede clothes and handbags, banded and embroidered with Kenya beads and trinkets and feathers. I want to supervise the first collection myself, so I'm getting everything made in London. Because I can't go to New York just now.'

'Don't push yourself too hard,' George said. 'You spend a great deal of time with your mother, and that takes its toll though you may not realise it. It might be sensible to slow down with your other obligations.'

'You have no choice but to be constantly in the spotlight in my line of work, Daddy,' she said. 'Otherwise you're forgotten. There's always someone new and different and better on the way up and I need to shore up my bank account before I'm cast aside in favour of some skinny teenager. Designing clothes is my plan for doing that.'

'You know what they say about all work and no play,' George said. 'It's more than simply good for you to take a breather now and again.'

Camilla inspected her father more closely. His hair was thinning and his face seemed to have lengthened, grown older. There were undisguisable lines of sadness at the edge of his mouth. But he was still handsome and his grey eyes keen. He was wearing a suit she remembered him buying in Rome. His cuff links flashed as he reached to take his knife and fork and she saw that they were a pair Marina had given him for his birthday years ago.

'You've lost some weight,' she said. 'It's all these soup and toast suppers with Mother. You look as though you could do with a few more square meals. Like this wonderfully stodgy stuff they serve here. And maybe you'd better lighten up yourself.'

'I come here to see my chums. And for the wine list.' George was smiling. 'But never for the food. Are you going to see your mother now?'

'I'll be there for dinner. Such as it is.'

'I haven't mentioned this Nairobi thing to her.'

'Of course you haven't,' she said. 'There's no point in bringing up anything that's not immediate.'

He hugged her tightly on the steps of the club. When she looked back at him, out of the taxi window, he seemed somehow diminished, walking along Pall Mall, his body bent into the cold afternoon wind. Camilla wondered about his private life, but she quickly decided that she did not really want to know.

At home she made herself tea and began to read a novel, but it was difficult to concentrate. She felt restless, displaced and apart from everything. Her father was going back to Kenya where he would be seeing the people she loved most. The man she loved who did not love her. Outside the window a weak sun faded, leaving the light smoke-grey and mean. Camilla thought of the wild brooding spaces and colours of Kenya, of the breathless afternoons when even the weaver birds had fallen silent in the stifling heat. English rain tapped on the window as she conjured up the heady African nights, the way she had lain beneath Anthony and opened herself to receive him. They had listened to the sounds of the bush.

She had clung to him in their canvas bed when she heard a lion roar in the distance, and they had laughed at the snorting and splashing of hippos in the river below their tent. Was love always this painful she wondered. And then she thought of Sarah, and her own sense of loss seemed to shrink in her mind. The telephone interrupted her train of thought and she was grateful.

'Camilla? Don't put the phone down. Please.'

'Who is this?' Camilla asked. There was something familiar about the voice, but she could not place it.

'It's Giles Hannington.'

'I'm on my way out,' she lied.

'Please listen to me,' he said. 'I need to talk to you.'

'I don't think so,' she said. 'I'm late already, so I'm hanging up now. And I'd be grateful if you wouldn't phone me again.'

'You had lunch with your father today. I want to talk to you about him.'

'Just stay away from me,' she said, and hung up.

But he telephoned again. And again. 'We do need to talk,' he said, when she picked up the receiver for the third time, angry and brusque. 'Just for a few minutes. I know how much he means to you. This is important. If you'll see me this once, I'll give you my word that I will never bother you again.'

'Where are you?'

'Just around the corner, in the Brompton Road.'

'You can come up here,' Camilla said, against her better judgment.

She gave him the address and poured herself a vodka over ice, gulping it down in one swallow. When the bell rang she opened the door and motioned him inside, and then she sat down on the sofa and indicated an armchair. He chose to remain standing, his back to the window, hands thrust into his pockets.

'George is very depressed,' he said without preamble. 'You must have noticed the change in him. He doesn't eat, drinks a little too much. He's spending all his time brooding, grieving in advance, blaming himself for your mother's illness. He's convinced it was partly brought on by the unhappiness he caused her. He's almost dying with her. He won't go anywhere, see anyone.'

'I suppose you mean that he won't see you,' Camilla said coldly.

'I mean exactly what I say,' Giles said with impatience. 'Your father is in a bad way. He has spent most of his life trying to be what everyone else wanted him to be. Laws and rules and hypocrisy forced him into that, made him ashamed of what he is. And now he's decided to leave London and go to Africa, because he's afraid of what you might think if he stays here. With me. But the truth is that you don't think about him at all.'

'Don't you dare talk to me about my feelings for my father, or about what I think,' she said, anger burning in her throat.

'Oh for God's sake, listen to me. You have a life. Everyone wants to know you, be seen with you. You don't have enough hours in the day for your admirers and sycophants, and you certainly don't put any of them aside for him. He needs someone to help him through this. Someone who genuinely cares about him. He deserves to be loved and accepted for who he is.'

'And who is he, in your expert opinion?'

'He's an outstanding human being. Full of integrity and dignity. He's the finest person I will ever meet. But he's cooped up, constrained by your prejudices. You're angry because he's queer. But I've seen you in clubs, eating and drinking and dancing with men who have their boyfriends in tow. You're not so picky then, it seems, but you have another set of rules for your father. He's devastated by your disdain. So I'm asking you to give him a chance, give him a hand, some encouragement to get on with his life.'

'We're talking about his life with you, I suppose?' she said. 'Is that what you want? That I should tell my father that it's OK by me if he's shacked up with some pretty boy who fancies him of a Thursday afternoon?'

'You're sick,' Giles said with disgust. 'I was wrong to come here. But for the record, yes, I would like him to be with me. I'd be the happiest human being alive if I could look after him for the rest of my life. But it's futile trying to explain any of this to you. Goodnight.' He strode to the door and let himself out before Camilla had time to get up from the sofa.

She finished her drink. In the bedroom she opened the drawer of her dressing table and took out a photograph of her parents. They gazed back at her, smiling, their arms around each other. Such a perfect couple. So charming and witty and sophisticated, everyone said, and so well matched. Had they really loved one another in some odd, twisted form? What was it that had kept them together through the years? As she asked herself this question, Camilla realised that she herself had no experience of unconditional love. With a sigh of frustration she put back the picture. It was no use fretting about the past. She picked up her coat and umbrella and set off to visit her mother.

Dinner was slow and the talk sporadic as Marina struggled to eat tiny portions of food. She watched television for a while, wrapped in a rug on the sofa, her fingers curled around George's hand, her head on his shoulder. When the nurse arrived and put her to bed, Camilla left her father alone in front of the television. He looked up as she went into the hall, and raised a hand in sad farewell. She headed for the liveliest nightclub she knew. Edward was at an official dinner of some kind, and she did not want to be alone. There was an impatient mob outside the entrance, but the doorman spotted her and swept her past the queue, into the throbbing, booming mêlée of people like herself, who were bent on oblivion. Tom Bartlett waved from a table on the edge of the dance floor.

'We're celebrating,' he said as she joined him at his table. 'The contract has been tied up for the cosmetics deal. Perfumes first, and then their new line of potions for the face. So let's hope Edward goes to work on you soon.'

'I can't do that while Mother's still here,' she said. 'You know that.'

'Don't worry,' he said. 'The Frogs are prepared to wait. This new line of expensive rubbish isn't ready yet anyway.' He ordered champagne and sat back with a broad smile of satisfaction on his face. 'I think we should fix up a dinner party for them, the Frogs, I mean. Not a huge mob, better something intimate. Let's pick about twenty people who've been involved in your career from the beginning. We could take a private room at Annabel's. Civilised and exclusive.'

Camilla looked at him, considering. His plan had triggered an idea. 'Maybe,' she said. 'I'll let you know tomorrow.'

She telephoned her father in the morning and was glad to find that he had no immediate travel plans. Then she rang Tom.

'Get caterers,' she said. 'We're going to have this thing at my flat.'

'It's rather small,' he said doubtfully.

'We'll have it at Edward's place, then. He won't mind. He has a dragon of a housekeeper who'll supervise everything. And don't worry about the invitations. I'll send them out myself. It will save you wondering if that ghastly girl in your office has dribbled coffee on the cards. More important, it will save me worrying about it.'

Edward was happily surprised. 'Of course you can have it here,' he said. 'But I thought you didn't like to mix our professional and private lives.'

'What private lives are those?' she asked. 'Neither of us has time for a private life.'

He looked at her and then sat down in an armchair and took her on to his lap. 'I'm so sorry, darling,' he said, his voice cracking. 'I'm so terribly sorry.'

She was taken aback by his reaction. 'It's all right, Edward. It's only that I wanted to—'

'No. It's not all right at all,' he said. 'I love you, Camilla. I adore you, and I'm not spending half enough time with you. But I'm going to put that right from this moment.'

She smiled at him and he kissed her and ran his hands under her shirt, closing his eyes, reminding himself of the miracle she was in his life. When he made love to her he was conscious of a heightened tenderness within him. Afterwards he held her very close and stroked her until she fell asleep.

On the evening of the party Camilla dressed with great care and knew that she was very beautiful. Edward stood beside her, his fingers touching her fleetingly and often. There were already five or six people there when her father arrived. She handed him a glass of champagne, made introductions, and then left him with Edward and stationed herself near to the door. Giles Hannington arrived a little late. She brought him from the hall into the sitting room, watching as George turned round, unable to mask his confusion. Camilla smiled across the room at him and then busied herself with her other guests, keeping a discreet eye on Giles. He accepted a drink and moved over to talk to Tom who was looking at her hard, his eyebrows raised in enquiry. But she had done what she thought best, and it felt right. She was a little light-headed and her stomach was fluttering as she placed her father halfway down the dinner table, and seated her French client on her right and Giles on her left. Edward looked the young man over, and wondered why Camilla had given him priority seating. Perhaps he was a new model. He was good-looking, although not very tall. As the evening progressed and the wines softened his edgy manner, Giles proved to be an agreeable and entertaining guest, and she was impressed by his knowledge of art and music, and his love of theatre where he was well connected. George watched his daughter, puzzled as to her motives, but after dinner she drew him aside and kissed his cheek.

'I didn't know how to tell you that whatever you do, it's all right with me,' she said. 'I love you, Daddy, and I want you to be happy.'

She saw that he had tears in his eyes and she turned quickly away, only to meet another of Tom's curious gazes. When all the guests had gone he threw himself down on the sofa next to Edward.

'That went well,' he said. 'Very sporting of you, Edward, to let us do this here. Camilla's new clients loved being invited to your home. It's not usual for French business people to be entertained in a private house.'

'Yes. It was a good evening and I'll be ready to collapse when I've finished this coffee. I'm operating early tomorrow morning.'

'I hadn't realised Giles Hannington was a friend of yours, Camilla,' Tom said. 'I was surprised to find him here.'

'He's my father's lover,' she replied, amused to hear him choke on his brandy. Edward was smiling.

'You never cease to amaze me, Camilla,' Tom said. 'You're the coolest customer I've ever come across. Too cool. No matter what happens to you, there's never any lasting effect. I'm thinking of the disaster with your face, the robbery, your mother's illness, the friend who was killed in Africa, and this thing with your father. Doesn't anything ever get to you?'

She looked at him sadly, knowing for certain that he had no understanding of her at all. 'I only worry about things over which I have some control,' she said, flicking a hand dismissively. 'There's no point in wasting time on the rest.'

'That was a very kind and courageous thing to do,' Edward said later, sliding his arm around her and bringing her closer.

Camilla lay beside him with all her energy drained away, as though it had evaporated with her guests. She wondered where her father was now and veered away from the answer. This evening's gesture was enough. Time would take care of the consequences. She turned over and pressed her body against Edward's lanky frame, moulding herself into the secure form of love that he offered. Then she slept.

She awoke to another wintry day, with a percussion of rain and bare branches beating a light tattoo against the window pane. Edward had already gone, and Camilla put on jeans and a sweater and went to find the makings of breakfast. She drank her coffee slowly, her mind deliberately and carefully vacant. The morning papers had been delivered earlier, and Edward had left them on the table for her. The story was on page four and took up very little space, but the headline leapt out at her: *Kenya Police Discover Remains Linked with Murder of British Farmer.*

The article stated that remains thought to be those of the murderer, Simon Githiri, had been found in a forest near the home of the white farmer he had killed in December of the previous year. The bones indicated that the Kikuyu had been attacked and eaten by wild animals during his attempt to escape. Piet van der Beer had been savagely hacked to pieces on his property, Langani Farm, and left to die. The murder was reminiscent of the barbarous killings that took place after oathing ceremonies during the Mau Mau emergency. The deceased had been a close friend of international model, Camilla Broughton-Smith. She herself had been injured on the property during a holiday in the autumn of last year.

Memories pounded her brain and with them came the suppressed fear, surging back into her body as she relived the night of the raid, the bursting in of the men with their knives, the warm sensation of blood running down her forehead. She thought of Hannah, grieving for her brother, unaware that his death was probably an act of revenge for something her father had been involved in years ago. George had been right. What use to disclose Jan's past now? Piet was dead and it was enough of an effort for Hannah to learn how to live without him, to go on surviving in the shadow of his horrible death. She should not have to accept the additional burden of her father's sins. And there was Sarah, whose love and future husband had been torn from her, at the very moment when their happiness had blazed out for all the world to rejoice in. She lifted the telephone. There was a long wait and then disappointment.

'The number in Kenya is busy, I'm afraid, miss. Would you like to ring back later?'

Camilla decided to wait for half an hour before trying again. She sat down in an armchair and lit another cigarette. The jangle of the telephone made her jump and she lifted it quickly, wanting to dispel the ominous atmosphere that had enveloped the morning.

'I saw the piece in the paper,' Edward said. 'You must be terribly upset.'

'I'm fine.' She knew that she sounded shaky. 'No, actually I'm not fine. It's a shock, and I can't imagine what they must be going through. How this has brought it all back again.'

'Do you want to meet me at my rooms this evening? We'll go somewhere quiet for dinner.'

'Yes. I'd like that. I'll be there about six. I'll see Marina earlier.'

She was wholly unprepared for the flash of bulbs and the shouts of reporters, all pushing forward as she stepped out of the taxi in front of her parents' flat.

'Do you have anything to say about Piet van der Beer's murder?'

'Was Simon Githiri a servant in the house when you were there?'

'Is it true that Piet van der Beer's eyes were gouged out?'

'Can you give us any details about the killing? Was this Githiri involved in the robbery where you were injured?'

'Is the Mau Mau movement still active in Kenya? Was Simon Githiri a member of the organisation?'

'Is it true that Piet van der Beer was your lover?'

Camilla fled into the building and the sanctuary of Marina's bedroom.

'What on earth is all that noise?' Marina said. 'I can't make out what they're doing down there, but I wish they'd go away.'

Camilla tried to blink away tears of anger and frustration as she explained the grisly development to her mother.

'I don't know how they found me here,' she said angrily. 'I can't leave. They're like vultures picking at a carcass. I was going to do some shopping and then meet Edward later, and now I can't go anywhere. They've ruined my whole day.'

'Darling, the porter will let you out through the service entrance. Don't worry. But I'm so sorry. It must have brought back all those terrible memories.'

Camilla sat on the side of the bed. 'Mother, what did you see in the file that night? About Jan van der Beer?'

'Oh, Camilla.' Marina's eyes filled with tears. 'I should never have brought up that matter, and I've felt terrible about it ever since. I was jealous, because you loved them all so much more than you ever loved me. But all that is past, and I don't want to think about it any more, darling. Let's only think of the good things now.' She brushed her eyes with her fingers and a sob rose in her throat, setting off a hacking cough that left her exhausted and unable to speak.

'It's all right, Mother. And it's true. It doesn't matter any more,' Camilla said. 'Would you like me to read something to you?'

Later in the afternoon Camilla looked out of the window again. The reporters were still there. She sighed and picked up the telephone to explain her quandary to Edward.

'They were outside my rooms earlier,' he said. 'My staff are accustomed to seeing them off, when some celebrity needs to come here for a consultation without being seen. Why don't I come round there in an hour or so? We'll have supper with George and Marina, and then go home. It's not what we'd planned, but I'll be with you at least.'

She was grateful, and even more so when he insisted that she take a shoot in Rome for three days.

'I'll go and see Marina while you're away,' he promised. 'Have dinner with George. I think you should go, darling. Take a breather.'

She was in Rome when the call came.

'Your mother's in the hospital,' George said. 'I think you should come back, Camilla. It won't be long. She's very weak but peaceful, and she's not in pain.'

Marina lay very quiet in the hospital bed, her husband sitting beside her. She had insisted that the nurse bring her a mirror and her make-up.

'Put some of this foundation on. I'm too pale. And lipstick too.' She looked at the results as George held up the hand mirror. Then she smiled.

'Camilla's coming home,' she said faintly. 'I want to be pretty. I want her to remember me as being pretty.'

They were her last words. Her eyes blinked for a moment as the mascara was applied and her hair was brushed. She made a gasping sound in her throat and lifted a thin hand in alarm. And then she was gone.

George looked round as his daughter came into the room some minutes later. She knew at once that it was too late. He came towards her and held out his arms, and she hugged him fiercely as he sobbed out his remorse and his sorrow. Then they rang the bell for the nurse, putting into motion the mechanical things that would have to be done before Marina was laid to rest.

The invitation came on the day of the funeral. Camilla saw the Kenya stamp immediately. She opened the envelope and read the words with pleasure. Lars and Hannah. She was smiling as she tucked the notice into her black handbag. Throughout the service she was aware of its presence, its power.

She stood close to George at the reception afterwards, receiving words of consolation from friends and strangers, listening but not hearing, thinking of the card in its envelope waiting for a response.

'I think we can leave, darling,' Edward said. 'Almost everyone has gone, and George has a few close friends around him. Let's go home.'

'I'd like to go to my flat,' she said to him, pleading with her eyes not to try and persuade her otherwise.

Inside the door she took off her hat and kicked off her high-heeled shoes. 'I'd like to go away for a while,' she said.

'I think you should. You need the break,' Edward agreed, handing her a drink. 'And then we'll take care of your scar. Remove it once and for all, so that no one will ever know it was there. I'll take time off afterwards, and we'll go somewhere quiet for you to recover. It's only the first few days that are at all sore. The rest is patience. An ideal time to take a very private holiday.'

'No. I don't want to think about my scar. It's not important.'

'Not immediately. But we'll need to talk about it when you're rested and recovered from all this.' He felt the grateful pressure of her fingers. 'Would you like me to stay with you?' he asked.

She shook her head. He kissed her and smoothed her hair, and left her alone. She saw him emerge into the square below and hail a taxi. Camilla sighed. He was kind and strong and successful, and he offered her love and security. He would never let her down or humiliate her.

When she got through to Langani it was Hannah who answered. She wanted Camilla to be there. And Sarah had come down from Buffalo Springs. She was here at the farm. Hannah would put her on the line.

'Will you come for the wedding?' Sarah asked.

'I don't know,' Camilla said. 'I've turned down a number of jobs lately because Mother was so ill. But she's gone. Three days ago. I don't know what I feel exactly. And now I have to go ahead with the surgery on my face. But there's one thing I would like to do that will make me a part of the celebration. I want you to send me Hannah's measurements. I want to make her wedding dress.'

'Camilla, she's going to have a baby. Around the end of August or early September.'

'What? But—'

'I'll write and tell you. Han will write too. She's so happy. And this will bring a new beginning for all of us here.'

'I read about Simon.'

'Yes. The police are sure that they were his remains. But I wish we had heard him say himself why he did this . . . to Piet, who had taken him in, given him work and a future.'

There was nothing Camilla could say. Hannah was going to be married, she was going to have a child. It was time to move on, to take the happiness she had found and to let go of the past and its shadows.

'I thought I'd feel something,' Sarah said. 'Because he killed Piet, the other part of my soul. And somehow I thought I would have known, when Simon died.'

'You were so distraught,' Camilla said. 'It was just after Piet. There was no room for anything in your mind other than his death.'

'You're right, I know,' Sarah said. 'And now is the time to make a new start. Not in order to forget, but in order to go on. And we will all use Hannah's marriage and the baby as our guiding light.'

The measurements arrived in a telegram the next day and Camilla went to work immediately, putting aside the clothes for her new collection to concentrate on Hannah's wedding dress. For three weeks she searched for the right material, for the trim and the beads and the feathers she wanted to use. She supervised the cutting of the dress, watched as the beading was painstakingly sewn into place according to her design, insisted that the sleeves were undone and restitched to her satisfaction. When it was finished at last she folded it herself, placing it in its box, ready to be sent to Nairobi. Her throat constricted when she looked down at it, lying in a bed of tissue paper. She wanted to be there to share their joy, and to start afresh. She had thought of taking a break, of postponing or even cancelling some of her photo shoots. She telephoned her father.

'I was thinking of going on holiday, Daddy. In about ten days.'

'I heartily approve,' he said. 'Where will you go?'

'I'd like to ask if you'd come with me, Daddy. I'll tell you where in a minute. We could go away together, take some time and enjoy one another's company. As we did in Italy years ago.'

There was a long silence. The phone crackled and she could feel his unease creeping towards her along the line.

'Actually, darling, I'm going away myself. Next week. I'm afraid I've already arranged it. I felt I needed to . . .'

He was going somewhere with Giles. She was sure of it and she wanted him to be happy, but now that the time had come she could not be glad.

'Wait, Camilla, I can put it off. Really.'

'Where will you be going?'

'To Morocco. But I can go another time.' He was beginning to sound guilty. Desperate.

'With Giles?' She had to know.

'Yes.' She heard him swallow hard.

'That's fine, Daddy. Ring me when you get back. I know you'll have a lovely time. Bye.'

Over dinner with Edward she broached the subject of going to Kenya. His eyes grew wary.

'It's not wise to go so soon after surgery,' he said. 'The flight is too long, and it's a place where you could easily pick up an infection. Ideally, we need to go somewhere that you're not going to be in the blazing sun. I thought we could go to Switzerland. Take a chalet at Klosters or Gstaad.'

'I don't want to do my face right now.'

'But the French contract is coming up, and it will take several weeks before you can be photographed.'

'I don't care. I want to go to Kenya. My friend Hannah is getting married. I want to be there with her, and with Sarah.'

He wiped the corners of his mouth with his white napkin, preparing his words, remaining measured as always. 'Camilla, your last visit to Kenya brought you nothing but unhappiness and appalling danger. And you may run into situations that are best left buried in your memory. In the past. I don't think you should go there at all. Not now, at any rate. Why don't you send a wedding present of a visit to London, for Hannah and her husband. They could stay here with us, and—'

'You're not really thinking of Hannah. You're thinking about Anthony Chapman.'

'He hurt you very badly.'

'You don't have any faith in me,' she said.

He rose from the table. 'I'd rather you didn't go. And I'd already pencilled in your surgery for the end of next week. You should think it over. Didn't you say something about going away with George?'

'He's taking his boyfriend to Morocco,' she said. 'And I don't think they want me along.'

When he left for his consulting rooms in the morning she feigned sleep. Then she dressed, took a taxi back to her own flat and sat in front of the mirror. Beneath the camouflage of her fringe the red line had faded. She had been able to cover it successfully for shots of clothes and accessories. But the French contract required close-up pictures of her face. She could not afford to delay much longer. She rang Tom.

'You can't go away,' he said, exasperated. 'We're all set to do your new beaded collection with Saul. He's wild about it, and he's going to be hopping mad if you dodge the interviews and the television and the promotion in the States.'

'I'll be back in time.'

'But we have a meeting with him next Monday. What do I say about that?'

'Tell him I've got mumps, and I might be infectious.'

'Tell him yourself,' Tom said.

'Oh, come off it, Tom. I haven't missed a day's shooting or a conference in months, even while Mother was so ill. I'm never late, and I don't scream at the photographer when he's taken five hundred pictures where ten would do. I don't throw tantrums or say I've got a headache or my period, and then flounce off the set. You can get me off the hook this one time.'

'Where are you going?'

'Away.'

'Is this something I should know about? Should I be alarmed? Are you and Edward—?'

She laughed and rang off. And then the reality struck her with force. What had she been thinking of? Tom was right. She had responsibilities here in London, in Paris, in the States. And Edward, too, was right. She had tried to pretend that Anthony did not matter. But now she was not sure if she could see him. She had battled for months to get him out of her mind, to recover from the humiliation and the havoc and the pain he had caused her. He would certainly be at the wedding. And he would not have changed. She sat on the bed, her childish excitement evaporating as she thought things through. If George had agreed to come with her she would have felt safer, more confident. But he had turned his back already on what remained of his long and unhappy family life. There was only Edward left for her to rely on, and he did not want her to go. It was better all round that Hannah and Lars should come to London later – they would love that. She glanced up at the top of the wardrobe where she kept her suitcases, and shrugged. Her life was here in London and there was no sense in opening old wounds, going back to torment herself with dreams that could never be.

Chapter 31

Sarah was there when the box arrived at Langani. She watched Hannah open up the folds of tissue paper, and stared down at the contents before lifting them out. The floor-length dress was a rich, cream-coloured silk cut on the bias. The hem and seams were bordered with satin ribbon and sewn with glass beads and pearls. But it was the jacket that took her breath away. It was short and made of the softest suede, banded with tiny white feathers, African beads and seed pearls. The mandarin collar and the cuffs had a similar trim, and there was a silk tassel at the neck, strung with silver and glass beads and finished with the same feathers. With it came a suede cap embroidered in the same style, with a collection of white feathers and a short tulle veil attached to the back. Camilla had written in her card that the agave silk and the suede came from Morocco, and all the trimmings had originated on the African continent. She had designed the dress and the jacket herself. They were her contribution to Hannah's celebrations, and came with her love.

'It's the most beautiful thing I ever saw, Han.' Sarah stroked the folded gown. 'Try it on.'

'I thought you were organising my dress,' Hannah said. 'You took my measurements.'

'I sent them to Camilla. She wanted to do this for you.'

Hannah reread the card. She had hoped that they would be together, the three of them, on her wedding day. But Camilla had said she could not come. Pressures of work, commitments she couldn't get out of. It was wonderful news, she said, the best, and she would be thinking of them, wishing them joy, but she would not be there.

'I don't think I could wear this,' Hannah said, holding up the dress and jacket against herself. 'Look at me. I'm a pregnant Afrikaans farm girl.

This is like – this is Paris catwalk. It's too elegant for me. And think what it must have cost?'

'Put it on, you fool.' Sarah's look was stern. 'It's her wedding present. She's created it for you and it's something that's all about Africa, not London or Paris. You're going to be the most beautiful bride ever seen. Lars will be mesmerised! And think of that wagon, Hettie Kruger! She'll be sick as a parrot when she sees you in this.'

Hannah had to laugh. And when the dress was fastened and she had slipped on the jacket, she barely recognised herself in the mirror. Her eyes filled with tears of gratitude.

'I'd like her to have been here. I understand about the dress, but the best gift would have been for her to come. It's amazing what she's suggested. That Lars and I go to London. She's always been like that – too generous. Still, I can't believe she's so busy that she couldn't fly out for a week or so.'

'There has to be a particular reason,' Sarah said. 'And I have a theory.'

'What theory?'

'Perhaps she's afraid to see Anthony.' Sarah saw the open disbelief in Hannah's expression. 'I know. She's famous and beautiful and her plastic surgeon is in love with her, so George says. But maybe those things are not that important to her. She may still be in love with Anthony. Or she might be frightened to come back after what happened here.'

Hannah put the card back into the box. 'If that's the case she should be able to tell us.'

'She probably will eventually.'

'I just wish she could see me, looking like this.' Hannah turned in wonder. 'She's made me into a Cinderella.'

'Well, I'm your official photographer, so I'll make sure she does. But you looked pretty good in your jeans, by the way. You should have lots of babies. It suits you.'

They stood gazing at their reflections, smiling at one another, and Sarah could almost see the shadow of Camilla, watching from the corner of the room. Would they ever again, the three of them together, be able to share their hopes and dreams? She reached out and tugged at Hannah's long plait. 'Come on,' she said briskly. 'We have to decide what you're going to do with this. You can't wear it in a pigtail.'

But to Sarah's surprise, Hannah moved away and sat down in a chair. Tears slid down her cheeks and she bowed her head.

'Han?'

'Ma always used to plait my hair, when I was little,' Hannah said, her voice choked. 'We used to have fights about it, before I went to school in the morning, when I wanted it loose and all messed up around my face. And now I'd like her here, more than anything, to braid my hair on my wedding day. And Pa too. I wish they could be here.'

'They will be here, Hannah, in their hearts. You'll feel them here with you.'

'But I've lost them,' Hannah cried. 'I've lost them all, my mother and my father and my wonderful brother. I loved them so much, and some days I think I can't go on, no matter what.'

'You will go on, Hannah. With Lars, you'll be able to start again. There are wonderful times ahead. Jan and Lottie are not lost to you, Han. They'll weather things just as you have, and somewhere down the road you'll see them again, even if it's not on your wedding day.'

'You're right, I know,' Hannah dried her eyes. 'So come on then, and tell me what to do with my pigtail.'

They spent the next morning arranging the wedding presents on a table in the sitting room.

'You never sing any more,' Hannah said, out of the blue.

'I do, in the shower,' Sarah replied, inspecting an antique silver jug and putting it in a prominent place.

'Would you sing something at the wedding?' Hannah asked. 'At school I always wanted a voice like yours, and it's been so long since I heard you.'

Sarah stared at her in astonishment. 'What do you want me to sing?' she asked.

'I don't know. You used to make up things. Do you think you could do that? For Lars and me?'

'You're mad, Hannah, but yes, I'll try.'

The house was full of flowers and laughter and excitement. Anthony had been chosen as best man. Lottie's brother, Sergio, and his family arrived from South Africa, and Lars's parents came from Norway. Friends from farms all over the country gathered, and put up tents in the field beyond the garden. On the day of the wedding, the sun blazed out of a cloudless sky, and Kirinyaga stood out clear in the azure morning, its snow peaks glistening. Mwangi said the mountain was giving Hannah its blessing. At five o'clock in the evening, the house staff and farm workers and their families formed a guard of honour around the verandah, as Sergio led Hannah down the steps and into the garden where Lars stood waiting. Beneath a garlanded arch on the lawn was the table that Hannah had chosen as an altar. It had come to the farm on the family's first ox-wagon, and it was covered with a white linen cloth embroidered by her great-grandmother as part of her own trousseau. The dominee of the Dutch Reform Church rose to begin the ceremony. It was a bittersweet occasion, with the joy of Hannah's marriage overshadowed by the memory of Piet, young and vital and golden, and lost to them all. In the hours leading up to the ceremony, Sarah had been assailed by the same terrible grief she had experienced at the time of his death. There were moments of pure agony when she followed Hannah through the con-gregation and saw Lars's craggy features, soft with love as he took the hand of his bride. It was Anthony who steadied her, placing his arm lightly around her waist as she swallowed the beginnings of a sob.

The dominee was speaking his first words of welcome when a move-ment caught Sarah's eye. She made a small exclamation and tugged at Anthony's sleeve. Hannah heard the sound and turned, following Sarah's gaze. Camilla was standing at the end of the aisle, hesitating, looking for a place where she could slip unnoticed into the gathering. There was a low murmur of surprise as Hannah whispered to Lars and left his side. She took Sarah by the hand and they moved down through the congregation to embrace Camilla, and to lead her back to join them at the altar. Sarah had dreaded the moment when Hannah and Lars would make the vows that she had once hoped to exchange with Piet in this very place. But as they said the words, promising to love and cherish one another all the days of their lives, she was filled with a boundless happiness for them, and her own loss dissolved in the tenderness of their expressions and the beacon of Hannah's smile. She stepped forward to sing.

Sarah had wrestled with the song for days, but on the eve of the wedding, words and music had come together, and now her clear soprano soared into the evening air, carrying all her love and her hopes for her dearest friends. She had been afraid she would break down, overcome by the emotion of this wedding and all that had gone before it. But as the last note died it was the gathering of friends who stood transfixed, with tears welling in their eyes. Then the sound changed to a gradual crescendo of chanting, as the farm workers offered their own jubilant music. The dominee pronounced the blessing, and everyone crowded around the bride and groom, but Hannah pushed her way through the throng, searching out Sarah and Camilla, laughing and crying with joy as they hugged her until she thought she might never have breath again.

As the wedding supper drew to a close, the sound of drumming filled the air, and all the guests walked down to an area that had been cleared for a bonfire. Every worker on the farm had assembled, dressed in their tribal costumes. The women gathered around Hannah and Lars, dancing and ululating and clapping their hands, while the men chanted and leapt and somersaulted, their goatskin cloaks and scarlet *shukas*, ornaments and headdresses glowing in the firelight. Lars had arranged for a roasted ox and beer, and as evening slid into night the entire community of Langani joined hands and danced together in a vast circle of celebration. It was almost dawn when the bridal couple left for the Mount Kenya Safari Club where they would spend the weekend. Then they would fly to the coast, where their destination remained a well-guarded secret. As Hannah ran down the steps to the car she was looking for Sarah and Camilla.

'Thank you. Thank you, my dearest, most wonderful friends. Sarah, some of today has been so hard for you, but one day I know you'll have the same joy I have now. Camilla, I wanted so much for you to see me in my beautiful dress. There are times when love is so close that you don't even have to go around the corner. I know that now. And I love you both.'

Then she was standing at the door of the car, laughing, her arm curving in an arch, her wedding bouquet soaring into the air behind her. Camilla heard the roar of anticipation, but as she raised her hand she saw Sarah reaching upwards, and she dropped back and faded into the cheering crowd. The car slid away down the drive, tin cans and balloons trailing noisily in the dust. Sarah stood watching them disappear, her hands gripping Hannah's flowers, hardly aware of the press of people around her.

'What about that?' Anthony was smiling down at her.

'Perfect.' She looked up at the sky. It would be getting light soon. All at once, she wanted to be away from the party. 'I think I might go for a drive,' she said. 'I've had enough drinking and dancing. I need to clear my head.'

'You're going up to the ridge.'

Sarah glanced at him in surprise. 'Yes. I did think of it.'

'Can I drive you?'

She was about to refuse, but he cut in. 'I won't get in your way, but I would like to visit Piet's grave. What you did with the cairn and the tree – it's beautiful. Just what he'd have liked.'

'I'm going to find Camilla,' she said. 'Then we'll leave.'

They drove out into the sunrise, savouring the teeming life around them. A flock of vulturine guinea fowl were having an early-morning dust bath in the middle of the track. The birds rushed ahead of the Land Rover, deep blue heads and black-and-white spotted plumage glistening in the growing light. Herds of game moved out across the open plain to graze. When they reached the track at the base of the ridge, they saw the car.

'She came to say goodbye.' Sarah's eyes were full of tears.

They started up the path, helping each other over the rough ground, pausing to take in deep breaths and to touch one another lightly for comfort. At the top, Lars and Hannah were standing together, their arms wound around each other. They showed no surprise and they did not speak, but simply smiled their welcome. Anthony and Camilla walked to the edge of the boulders, to give Sarah some moments to herself.

'It's magnificent up here,' Anthony said, his voice thick with emotion. 'It's a place of true peace. I can feel him with us, watching us.'

Camilla made no comment, but when he took her hand she moved closer to him and leaned against him, listening to the sounds of Africa all around her, filled with the wrenching sadness of Piet's death, conscious of the tendril of excitement and fear that crept into her as Anthony put his arm around her shoulders.

Sarah stood at the grave with Hannah's wedding bouquet in her hand. Her eyes blurred as she looked down at the white stones and heard the whistle of birds in the acacia tree.

'This is for you, Piet,' she said, her voice low but steady. 'It's to tell you that I love you today and every day. And to let you know that Lars is strong and Hannah is happy, and that they are here beside you on their wedding day. Camilla is with us too, and we will always look out for one another as we promised when you were with us. We're trying to build our lives again now. But we'll never forget, and we will love you as long as we live.'

She bent forward and laid the flowers on the cairn. When she looked up it was to see a young male impala, his head crowned with lyre-shaped horns, high and proud. He stood motionless and perfect in his beauty, watching her from the edge of the trees, his coat shining, burnished and coppery in the morning light. They gazed at each other for a timeless moment, and then he turned and bounded away across the rocks to vanish into the bush.

Glossary

Afrikaner:	person of Boer origin, from South Africa
askari:	policeman or guard
ayah:	child's nurse
banda:	bungalow or small cottage
bhang:	marijuana
biltong:	strips of dried meat
boma:	a fenced-in enclosure for dwellings and livestock
braai:	an outdoor meal or barbecue
brookies:	knickers
bundu:	bushland
bushbaby:	a nocturnal animal, one of the smallest primates
bwana:	title of respect to a white man, or boss
chai:	tea
daktari:	doctor
djinn:	a demon or genie that may act as a guardian
domkop:	idiot, or fool
dorp:	dump, backwater
duka:	a shop
fundi:	handyman, carpenter, expert
harambee:	everyone pull together
hodi:	hello, anyone home?
jambo:	greetings, hello

kaffir:	derogatory term for a black man
kali:	fierce, cross, sharp
kanga:	brightly coloured cloth, worn by women
kanzu:	a long white robe used as a uniform by domestic staff
kaross:	a cured animal skin made into a rug or cover
kifaru:	rhino
kipande:	an identification card
Kirinyaga:	Kikuyu god, believed to live on Mount Kirinyaga or Mount Kenya
kopje:	a rocky outcrop
lekker:	wonderful, fantastic
lugga:	a dried-out river bed
mahindi or mealie:	a corn cob
maji:	water
manyatta:	traditional dwelling of Maasai and Samburu tribes
Mau Mau:	violent uprising by the Kikuyu tribe, initially against white settlers
memsahib:	title of respect towards a white woman
moran:	a Maasai or Samburu warrior
moto:	hot
mpishi:	cook
munt:	derogatory term for an African
murram:	red-coloured earth
mzee:	a title of respect towards an old person
the Mzee:	title given to Jomo Kenyatta, who became president of Kenya
ndio:	yes
ndofu:	elephant
ngoma:	celebration dance
ngombe:	cow
nguvu:	vigour or gumption
nyati:	buffalo

panga:	large flat-bladed knife, like a machete
pole:	slowly, or sorry
pole sana:	very slowly, or very sorry
pombe:	illicit home-brewed alcohol
posho:	ground maize meal, used as a staple food
purdah:	the segregation and veiling of women
rafiki:	a friend
safi:	clean, smart, nice
salaams:	greetings – as in hello
shamba:	smallholding, a garden
shauri:	a problem or argument or matter of disagreement
shenzi:	shoddy and run down
Shifta:	Somali bandits
shuka:	traditional red blanket worn by Maasai and Samburu warriors
siafu:	aggressive type of red ants which march in columns
sisal:	fibrous plant from which rope is made
swala twiga:	gerenuk
syce:	a groom, who takes care of horses
taka taka:	rubbish
terrs:	Rhodesian slang for 'terrorists'
toroka:	get on with it, hurry
toto:	child (short for *mtoto*)
tsotsis:	terrorist insurgents in Rhodesia
Uhuru:	freedom, the political term for Independence
veldt:	grassy plain
wananchi:	the people
watu:	men, labourers
wazee:	old people, elders
wazungu:	white people
yaapie:	term for a person of Afrikaans origin